DARK SECRETS

Book One

-Book One of Dark Secrets-

Model: Jessica Truscott FayStock
Editor 2018 Edition: John Edmunds

www.angelamhudson.com

ISBN/SKU: 9780648328025
ISBN Complete: 9780648328025

OTHER TITLES IN THIS SERIES

(SHOULD BE READ IN ORDER)

Dark Secrets

The Heart's Ashes

Mark of Betrayal

Lies in Blood

Echoes & Silence: Part One

Echoes & Silence: Part Two

Bound by Secrets

ALSO BY THIS AUTHOR

Bound Series Book 1

Bound Series Book 2

In Another life 1

In Another life 2

In Another life 3

In My Blood

The Legend of the Raven Wolf

~ 1 ~

We all face battles. We all take roads that test us for the sole purpose of making us stronger. This is not unique to my story. But I am my own worst enemy, and so everything I've suffered, everything that led me here, I brought upon myself.

I've made so many wrong choices.

Hurt everyone I love.

But worst of all, it took me so long to realize what a needy brat I was, that now, as my short life comes to an end, I'm afraid it's too late. Afraid no one will really care how I changed.

Not even David.

My name is Ara, and my horrific ending began in high school, when I first met a vampire, who looked like a human.

Part One

THE VAMPIRE,

AND HIS

DARK SECRETS

1

"Tell me your darkest secrets, and I'll challenge them with mine."

Across the road from Dad's house—*my* house now, I guess—I stood staring up at the brown-bricked school, considering the mundane scene beyond the doors with a bit of disappointment. Coming from another country, I'd expected something entirely different. But it was nothing like American high schools on TV. Everything was plainly colored, and all the kids looked normal; no glamorous groups of girls walking down the hall, flicking their hair, while the unpopular kids made a path for them. No one was dancing or singing and, thankfully, no Slushy showers. There were lockers, though, but they weren't big enough to be stuffed inside.

A few boys ran past me and up the cement steps in a tight, sweaty group, oblivious to my neon "New Kid" sign. Which gave me hope that maybe I could just blend in and go unnoticed today.

"Wishing you'd taken my advice now?" said a familiar voice from behind.

I turned, narrowing a cold eye at my half brother. "I don't take fashion tips from dorks."

"At least *I* won't stand out like a sore thumb," he noted, spreading his arms to indicate his plain blue shirt and jeans. "Girls don't wear dresses to school here, Amara. Especially not bright yellow ones."

"It's pastel," I advised him. "And don't call me Amara. No one calls me that."

"Sorry." His shoulders dropped. "You're right. Butt-face suits you so much better."

"Oh, yeah?" I said as he darted past, taking two steps at a time with his long, lanky stride. "Well… it suits you better more!"

"Nice try," he called, slamming the glass door on my shame.

I slapped my brow, infuriated with my lack of skill in the art of sibling rivalry.

"He's right about the dress," said Sam's equally annoying friend, coming up from behind me. "It's a bit… feminine."

"Well, maybe it'll take the focus off my scars," I muttered, angling my chin down to make them less obvious. It didn't work. They were heinous, ugly little dots all over my chin and one side of my neck, expected to fade, eventually. But they hadn't given me enough time. Hardly a few months had passed since… it happened. It all still felt like fire in my soul—the voices in my head screaming in a raging battle against my conscience, trying to convince me that the guilt, the pain, the sadness of it all would just hurt a little bit less if I accidentally stepped out in front of a speeding car. It's not like I wanted to be dead, I just needed the pain to stop for a while. And it was so much worse having to carry physical scars as well. I'd tried to arrange my hair to hide them, but then a part of me said not to, because they were a reminder of what selfish, childish behavior can lead to; they were a mark, a stain, a punishment for the simple crime of being me.

But I wouldn't let myself feel pity, because every ache, every horrible thing that happened today, would only be a small step toward atonement.

"In the interests of being honest," he said, wincing apologetically, "people *are* gonna notice the scars. Not much you can do about that."

"Thanks," I mumbled, because I did appreciate the honesty. It was refreshing after spending the last few months in a new household, where everyone tiptoed around my grief.

"No problem," he said, turning on his heel and heading up the stairs as easily as Sam had. I wished I could do that—just walk in there like it was an everyday occurrence. I knew it would be, one day, but today... the first step just felt like too big a hurdle to overcome. I wasn't ready for school, and I wasn't ready to face the nastiness that came so naturally to people my age.

Almost as soon as I'd braved my first step, I stopped dead, noticing a pair of heavy black boots facing me beyond the glass. My eyes moved over the denim jeans above them to a black shirt, the sleeves rolled up over the elbows of a guy with tan, silky skin. I couldn't see his head behind the door handles, but if I had to guess, just from his body language, I'd say he was about to greet himself a new kid.

I dumped my bag on the step and grabbed my cardigan to feel more secure, hoping maybe it'd take the focus off the scars. If I was going to meet a guy in my first five minutes, I refused to fall all over myself with nerves brought on by my gruesomeness.

With my eyes closed, praying he'd just disappear, I climbed the steps and pushed the door open, waking with a gasp when a hand grabbed my arm.

"New?" said a girl with a very bright smile, her blonde ponytail swinging behind her.

I looked to where the boy had been standing and, thankfully, my prayers were answered. "Is it that obvious?"

"Only as obvious as your dress. I'm Emily Pierce." She grinned, shaking my hand. "Cheer Captain, and your clearly much-needed self-appointed tour guide."

Self-appointed tour guide? I considered this bouncy girl for a second, forming an opinion of her that probably wasn't fair. But, as far as I was concerned, it really should be illegal to wear skirts that short to school, and perfect skin, mixed with a confident disposition, should be banned as well. It just wasn't fair to us normal girls.

The door swung closed behind me then, pushing me into the school with a whack on the butt. "I uh—" I moved out of the way for another group of people coming in. "I have a map, so I don't really need a tour guide." Barbie. That's what I wanted to say: Tour Guide Barbie.

"Okay, but good luck finding anything around here. Kids strip the labels off the doors and switch them around for just this sort of occasion." She turned away. "If you want to end up in the wrong room—"

"Okay." I caught up. "Fine. Where's room one?"

"It's this way." She started walking. "So, do you have a name?"

My fingers tightened around my backpack. "Um, yeah. Amara… actually, Ara-Rose."

"Yikes." She looked back at me. "Bit of a mouthful, Amara-actually-Ara-Rose."

"Ha-ha," I muttered sarcastically.

"Do you go by just *Ara*? The whole *Rose* thing'll get dropped around here anyway, you know, 'cause it kinda sounds a little… antique."

I smiled pleasantly, remembering that being normal meant fitting in; slapping a girl you just met led to detention. "I guess just Ara's fine," I said, but it really wasn't.

"So, what brings you to our school?" the girl asked.

Death. Tragedy. Throwing myself at my best friend and then being brutally rejected. "My feet."

She looked at me and, seeing I was joking, actually laughed. And I suddenly liked her so much more. "Seriously. Did you just move here, or were you, like, expelled from another school?"

I wondered if I looked like the sort of kid who'd get expelled. "Sea change." I shrugged.

"Eccentric mom?"

My brow crinkled. "What do you mean?"

"Most of the new kids come here because their moms decided to be a painter or marry a man they met on a dating site. Eccentric moms."

"Oh." I attempted a friendly laugh. "No. Just a sea change."

"Well, our gain," she said, linking arms with me as if we were friends. "You don't really say much, do you?"

"Uh…"

"Because, you know, we started back last week. If you wanted to be a wallflower, you really should have started with all the other new kids."

"I…" I looped my thumb around my backpack strap again, feeling awkward being this close to a stranger. "I wasn't quite ready to start last week."

"Then, I hope you like attention."

I did, in ways. But it was the *questions* I wanted to avoid, or… actually, answers.

"Wait!" She stopped, eyes wide. "Room one. First period. Show me your schedule!"

Catching her overexcited vibe, a little concerned that maybe I had something wrong, I put my bag down and dug into it for the twice-folded bit of paper. "Why? What's wrong?"

"I bet you have English first period." She snatched my schedule, looked it over, then grinned widely. "You do. I hate you."

"Nice to meet you too." I laughed, throwing my bag over my shoulder as I stood up.

"You just don't get it yet." She started walking again, handing me the schedule as I followed. "Your luck just changed."

"How so?"

"You have *David Knight* in your class."

I stuffed my schedule in the open pocket of my bag, choosing to ignore her complete lack of composure. "School heartthrob?"

"You guessed it. I mean, he's a bit of a jerk, really… to most girls, but he's got the kind of face that gets him off almost any hook."

My lip curled. I bit it. This girl had *issues*. "I'm not a huge fan of jerks, you know—not even the cute ones."

"Mm-mm." She shook her head, lips pressed to shape her sound. "He won't be a jerk to you. You haven't done anything to annoy him yet."

"Lucky me."

"Yeah, and he totally goes for that lost lamb thing you've got going." She motioned to me—all of me.

"Um, yeah, well my biggest concern for senior year is not what some jerk thinks of me. No matter how cute he is."

"That's because you haven't seen him yet."

I rolled my eyes. As if I'd ever be that pathetic.

"Yep." She considered me again. "He is just going to snatch you up."

"Should I be worried?" I wasn't partial to being snatched.

"No way. They'd deny it, but any girl in the school would give their right arm to be *snatched* by David."

Or maybe just you would, I thought.

"Okay." She stopped again. I wanted to keep walking—right past the glass doors, out to the front parking lot and into the cupboard under the stairs back at Dad's house. "Here's your class. You're late, which means everyone will stare and whisper about you, but you look like you can handle it."

"I probably can," I lied.

"That's the spirit." She curled a fist in front of the door and rapped lightly, sending my nerves into a frenzy. Don't get me wrong, I could handle nerves, and butterflies in my stomach were just yesterday's breakfast, but these felt more like bats. Big, black, hairy bats.

The door opened a little, and a shiny head with hairy ear tufts popped out. "Emily. What can I do for you?"

"This is Ara. She's new." Emily presented me.

"Ah, yes. We were wondering when you might be joining us." Because of his warm eyes and his grey-brown moustache curving atop a grin, I felt sort of *welcome*. "Are you just going by Ara then, Amara?"

I nodded, wishing I'd used my words instead. Like a big girl.

"Well, Ara, I hope you're a much quieter student than *this* lot." He jerked his thumb to the noisy class. I tried to look past him to get a handle on the room, so as not to trip on anyone when I walked in, but he was in the way.

"I don't think you need to worry about that, Mr. Benson. She's hardly said two words."

The teacher looked back at me and straightened up a little, making my heart race as if I'd just run a block, which seemed like a viable option right now, just… in the other direction. "Are you nervous, Ara?"

I nodded slowly. "I've never been to a new school before."

"I know. But… I tell you what…" He touched his chin, then turned and signaled into the class. "I think I have a solution."

"Yes, Mr. B." A boy stepped up before I expected him to, and a short breath escaped my lips, making my heart skip a beat that it would never recover. I'd seen my fair share of gorgeous guys, but this one topped the list, and he wasn't even my 'type'. I really hoped this wasn't Mr. B's idea of a 'solution' to my anxiety.

As the boy settled into his lean on the doorframe, his dark-brown hair fell into his eyes. He swept it back with one hand, and any hope of composure withered away with the hold of that smile—how his dark-pink lips sat closed and turned up sharply in the corners. His emerald green gaze fixed mine in place, as if he was completely unfazed by my shameless ogling.

"Ara? This is David," Mr. Benson said, eyeing the proverbial drool on my lip.

Time came rushing back like a smack across the face. I snapped my gob shut and wiped my chin, glad there wasn't actually drool there. I already figured that boy was David. My reaction completely mirrored the stupidity I despised in Emily two minutes ago. I'd seen hot guys before, but there was something… odd, and… for lack of a better or less lame word, sort of alluring about this one. It was like I just had zero control over the sudden fluctuation of hormones in my body, which immediately set off several alarms.

David's smile changed then, drawing my gaze to his perfect teeth, while the dimples beside his mouth dipped sharply. "Hello, Ara."

I lifted my hand to wave. No words came out, though. Pathetic.

"David?" Mr. Benson prompted.

David stole his gaze away, head turning before his eyes left mine, and as he shoved his hands into his pockets, his shoulders lifting a little, I got the sense that he was maybe a bit of a shy guy.

I felt like a pervert then, and a bit nasty, because I'd made assumptions about him in the nanoseconds after we met, and a lot of them regarded him as nothing more than a dangerous slab of hunky meat, ripe for ogling. If he were a woman and I were a man, he'd have slapped me.

"Ara's a little worried about coming to a new class," Mr. Benson explained. "Would you take her to the library and fill her in on last week's lessons, please?"

A sudden wash of relief brought my body back to life. I wouldn't have to go into that class of staring strangers after all! I wanted to hug Mr. Benson for being so considerate.

"Of course." David smiled at me again, the sound of his voice running through me like milk for my soul—liquid with maturity, yet deep and heavy and simultaneously weightless.

"Excellent." Mr. Benson went to walk away but stopped. "And keep your charms to yourself, young man."

"I'll do my best, sir," David said, looking right at me with those smiling green eyes.

And that was it. My cheeks exploded with heat, sending it to my ears. I looked down at my feet, biting a spreading grin.

"Okay. Well, Ara, you take care, and I'll see you in class tomorrow." Mr. Benson patted my shoulder.

"Thank you," I said, looking him directly in the eye this time.

"You are more than welcome." He turned to face the boy. "David, you can get your stuff."

For a split second, as David and Mr. Benson walked away, I braved a glance into the room of dread, seeing only a desk and a whiteboard. It all looked normal enough. I'd imagined fiery pits and wailing souls. Guess I was wrong.

Emily squeaked, waving two handfuls of spirit-fingers. "Oh my God. You're *so* lucky."

"*Lucky*? I have to spend forty minutes alone with that guy." I pointed into the class.

"Trust me, Ara. You're going to *love* David."

That's what worried me: that I'd like him, but all he'd see in me is my scars. "He's not that cute," I said, but the lie showed in my tone, shouting to the world that I was as pathetic as Emily.

She patted my shoulder. "It's okay to like him, you know. We're only human."

Yes. But I was a very flawed one in more than just the physical ways. Despite that, I had to ask, "Does he have a girlfriend?"

Emily leaned closer. "He—"

"Sure thing, Mr. Benson." David's smooth voice filled the hallway a second before he stepped out of the classroom, carrying his bag and a stack of books.

Emily straightened up, poorly masking her conspicuous smile.

"Everything all right, Emily?" he asked, clearly catching on that we'd been talking about him.

"Mm-hm."

He looked at me then, and studied my face with slightly narrowed eyes. I felt myself shrink; felt my scars burn and become more obvious. But he wasn't even looking at them.

"You ready, new girl?"

I managed to nod. Somehow, staying with Mr. Benson seemed less unnerving.

"Don't worry." Emily touched my arm. "David will take good care of you."

"You're late for class, Emily," he said in a dull and sort of authoritative tone.

"Okay, well. Have fun, Ara. And… I'll see you at lunch?" she asked, her eyes round, hopeful.

Terrific, I'd just made a new friend without even trying. Which would be great if I hadn't decided to avoid doing just that. "Um… yeah, I'll see you at lunch."

She skipped off, but stopped to fan her chin, mouthing what looked like "He's so hot", right as David turned to catch her. Quickly pressing her hands behind her back, Emily disappeared around the corner, leaving David and I completely alone.

My heart pumped blood the wrong way around my body, and the beat bounced off every wall in the school—a suspenseful soundtrack to a gripping scene. I forced myself to look up from my shoes so I wouldn't seem like an immature twat. And though I sat for hours last night scripting topics for just this sort of occasion, when I met David's gaze, all I could find was a white cloud of wordless stupor. I was without ammunition, alone in the wilderness with a lion.

"The library is this way." He started walking.

I stayed put, safe and snug against the wall where I couldn't trip on my own nerves. He didn't even notice I stayed behind, just walked ahead without me. Or maybe he did notice but chose to ignore it, figuring I'd eventually move. And yet, staying behind gave me a great vantage point. I could see the definition down his back through that black shirt; could see the marvelous contours of his arms and how his torso seemed to taper inward at the waist from his shoulders, despite his otherwise slender form. I'd seen that kind of physique on guys in the football teams back home. Which made me wonder if David was on the team. If so, he disguised that stereotypical arrogance really well under the facade of a kind, well-mannered guy.

"Are you coming?" he asked, walking backward.

"Um, yeah. Sorry." I pushed away from the wall and started after him, grinning to myself when he turned away. I always knew the world was unnaturally cruel, and today, I learned it could also be cruel in an unbelievably giving way.

DAVID DIDN'T UTTER A WORD AS WE WALKED THE HALLS. I DIDN'T know if I should—or could—say something to break the silence, which made it mutate into the uncomfortable sort. And to make matters worse, his self-satisfied grin made me feel almost like he could hear every deranged, lustful thought I was having.

I rocked my jaw, searching deep inside for that level-headed girl in me who didn't get pummeled by a cute face. She was dead though. David stomped her out with one sweep of his careless hair, and a flash of that gorgeous grin.

"What were you reading in your last school—for English class?" he asked in a buttery voice, like, if I could swallow it in one gulp, it wouldn't even touch the sides of my throat.

"The standard stuff," I murmured. "I wasn't in any advanced classes or anything."

He nodded. "Do you read much?"

"Not anymore."

He looked down at his feet.

I felt bad for that answer. It was probably a little vague, maybe even rude. It's just that… I wanted him to keep talking, but… not ask any questions.

"Why not?" he asked.

"Why not what?"

He cleared his throat, that private grin slipping into place. "Why don't you read *anymore*?"

"Um, no reason. What do you like to read?"

David seemed a little thrown off by the question. "Uh… Dracula, anything by Stephen King, Pride and Prejudice. I actually read quite a bit. Though, not so much *anymore*, myself."

"Why not?" I asked, curious about his reasons. Also curious as to why a guy his age would admit to reading Pride and Prejudice of his own free will.

"Well, let's just say"—he leaned against the wall near a brown door —"I have better things to do with my time at the moment."

"Er, yeah, me too," I said quickly.

He laughed and stood from his lean, patting the door. "So, this is the library."

"Really?" It sat inconspicuously in the long wall of the first floor corridor, rather oddly-placed for such an important room. If David wasn't with me, I might've passed it.

"Don't let looks deceive you. It's actually quite well stocked," he said, opening the door.

We stepped inside and ceiling-high shelves of books greeted us with the rich smell of old pages. A group of study desks marked the center of the brightly lit space, while computers lined the back wall. It seemed the school made up in supplies for what it lacked in style.

"They fit a lot into a small room, don't they?"

"Yes," my unfairly gorgeous guide said simply, standing motionless beside me. "Would you like a seat?"

I wanted to ask if he meant I could take one home with me to keep, but was afraid the corniness might show me up for the dweeb I really was. So I started off with a determined stride and, using my ankle, kicked a chair out at the circle of study desks. The lone student beside me didn't bother to look up as I dumped my bag down. Or he most likely didn't hear me approach, since the music coming from his earphones could be heard in London.

"Are we allowed to have music in here?" I asked, looking up to meet David's stare.

He made no effort to look away, smiling before saying, "Yes."

My pulse quickened at that gorgeous grin. He just looked so pleased with himself for something, or like he was in on some joke that I wasn't getting.

"We weren't allowed at my old school." I looked back at the kid for a second. "Private school."

"Figured as much."

"Is it that obvious?"

"No. I'm just good at summing people up."

"Hm, me too."

"Then we should get along great." He dropped the grin and placed a heavy rectangle book on the table in front of me, tapping it twice. "This one's for you."

I grimaced at the book. The pages were thin and the cover was hard, which could only mean *boring*.

"You know," David said, dumping his bag as he sat down, "you're awfully quiet. I expected you to say more by now."

"We're in a library," I whispered.

He laughed once, motioning around the room. "No one cares if you talk."

He was right. The room was pretty much empty—of people. There was no reception desk, and no grey-haired woman with large-rimmed glasses shushing us when we breathed. "Cool."

"Yeah." David sat back. "It's pretty cool."

I looked away from him, finally calm enough to act human, and opened the giant book. "What page?"

"You know"—he inclined toward me, his voice low in a husky whisper—"it's your first day, so we can either fill you in on Mr. Benson's lessons, or..." He paused, looking at the student near us.

"I already prefer the *or*," I said, leaning on my hand, and the second that creepy sentence left my lips, I wanted to die.

David leaned back in his chair again, crossing his hands behind his head, the smooth musk of his deodorant stronger now, making me inhale a little deeper. "You know, I think I'm beginning to like you already, Ara-Rose."

I wanted to beam at his words, but as much as I liked David, I needed a boy to distract me like I needed a hole in the head. "It's just Ara, by the way," I said, kind of wondering why he called me that, considering Mr. B introduced me as "Ara".

"Okay, *Ara*." He looked me over with one slightly narrowed eye, folding his arms. "What's your next class?"

"Uh, hold on a sec." I pulled out the schedule and map then passed them to David, who read the page, wearing an impish grin. "What?"

"We have quite a few classes together."

"Oh. Okay."

"Including music." He cleared his throat into his fist.

"Is that... bad?" All the blood ran from my face as he handed the schedule back.

He shook his head. "I mean, not all bad. We have Mr. Grant, but I'm in your class."

"Is he nice?" I kind of expected a two-headed monster, judging from the smirk on David's face.

"It's okay, I'll be there with you."

I folded my bottom lip between my teeth.

"He doesn't stay in the room long," David added. "Mr. Grant. He comes in, tells us what to do, and leaves."

"And then what?"

"We usually just have a jam session."

"Wicked." I shut the textbook in front of me, finding my cool again. "So... what instrument do you play?" I could sum up a lot about a person by the kind of music they liked and by the instrument they chose to express that love with.

David drummed his fingers on the desk, his smiling eyes small with thought. "Well, I actually play all instruments. But this year, I'm focusing on the guitar."

Damn. Well, that blew my prejudice out the window. "Guitar, eh? I would've figured you for a bass guy."

"Bass? And… what exactly would *that* say about me?"

"Cool? Confident?" A soft breath left my lips before I added, "Sexy?" And though, on the outside, I shrugged as I said it, every ounce of cool I'd mustered stopped moving and groaned, slapping its head. That was such a loser thing to say!

David stared at me for a second, his lip twitching as if stuck on a word.

"I'm sorry. That was *so* creepy." I covered my brow.

"No, it wasn't at all. It was just…" He stared forward, frowning. "Unexpected."

I looked down at my book, unsure what to say.

"You just seem so shy and quiet now. I never expected you to say something so… honest."

"I'm not really shy." I traced the edge of the book. "I'm just quiet because I'm new. But you won't be able to shut me up in a few weeks." I laughed, but stifled it quickly. As if that would be reassuring. And I was off again with the assumptions. Who said this guy would even talk to me after today? He was only here because the teacher forced him to bring me up to speed. I kind of felt sorry for him now.

He suppressed a smile, nodding softly. "Well, I look forward to seeing your more talkative side."

"It's okay," I assured him. "You're under no obligations to befriend me, you know, just because the teacher told you to babysit me."

"Who says I feel obligated?" he said. "Perhaps I have a mind of my own."

Was he serious? I was so clearly infatuated with this guy, and yet he wasn't jumping at the easy-out I just gave him! At this point, it wasn't just my own sanity I was questioning.

When David laughed suddenly, I glared at him with curious eyes.

"What?" I asked, hoping my facial expressions hadn't given away my strange internal monologue. "What are you laughing at?"

"Nothing."

"Normally, people don't laugh at nothing."

"Maybe I'm not normal."

"Hm." I nodded to myself, and since there was no rock to hide under in here, I covered the awkward tension with a very normal question that I was rather proud of. "So, are the people here nice?"

David nodded, taking a deep breath as if to dispel his own nervous tension. "Yeah, mostly. You shouldn't have a problem, though. Seems you've struck up a friendship with Emily Pierce?"

"Is that good?" I hoped it was. Emily seemed nice, but I'd hate to have ended up friends with the school bully.

"Um, yes." He cleared his throat, looking away. "It's good. Emily has… a special gift for making people like her."

"So *you* like her?"

"She's just easy to be around. I think you two will be good friends."

Did that mean *I* was easy to be around? And there it was again: the crazy in me looking for hidden meanings in words that weren't there.

"I'm sure you'll be fine here, Ara. You've already made two friends today, and school has only just begun."

That was nice of him, I thought. It felt so weird that only half an hour ago I was terrified to even step off the driveway, and now I was here, alone with David, and he just called himself my friend—completely tarnishing all my first impressions about this once seemingly nightmarish brown building.

"Well, thanks." I shrugged passively, hiding my smile. It was a strange sensation, but for the first time in over two months, I just smiled because I wanted to.

2

"Dave, too cool for the team jacket this year?" a bold voice called as we walked through the corridor. "Didn't get your name on the list."

David jolted forward a little with the affectionate slap on his shoulder. "I'm skippin' out this year, man."

The guy stopped, spreading his arms out wide in confusion. "Dude. Why?"

"Tell ya later."

"Okay, later, bro." He nodded and kept walking, giving some brotherhood click of his fingers that David copied.

"Are you on the football team?" I asked.

"Not anymore," he said in short, cutting off eye contact as we weaved through the oncoming traffic.

I took his lack of elaboration as a giant 'None of your business'. So, with my nose tilted slightly to the roof to take in the dim lighting and rich burgundy color of the walls, I walked in silence for a while, ducking and dodging the odd stare here and there. "Why is this area so different to the rest of the school?"

"They hold concerts open to the public in that room at the end."

He pointed past the trophy cases to a set of heavy-looking double doors. "Guess they wanted to give the illusion of grandeur."

"And parade the victories of their student body?" I nodded to the over-stuffed trophy cases as we passed them.

"Yeah. Mr. Grant's a bit of an exhibitionist. We tour around and enter just about every contest there is."

"Sounds like my kind of music teacher."

"Oh, yeah," he said, pushing on the heavy door with his shoulder as he glanced back at me. "He's real loveable."

I laughed.

"So, we always have music class in the auditorium. Good acoustics. And more space, but a bit dark," he said, leading me in to the giant open room. "It's much brighter in here when the House Lights are on."

"Are you kidding? This room is great even in the dark." My eyes followed the long columns of steeply inclined seats, stopping on the red velvet curtains framing the large stage. It reminded me instantly of ballet—with the smell of latex, chipboard and wool carpet—while the sound of feet on the floorboards over a hollow stage took me home again. In the aisle before the front row, students had dragged tables and chairs into a disorderly cluster, where they all sat tuning their instruments or laughing and talking.

In the seconds it took to size up the group, my eyes swept past them and stopped on a long-forgotten acquaintance of mine. "A piano?"

"Very observant," David said, and I rolled my eyes at him. He laughed. "Come on, I'll introduce you to her."

"Her?"

"Yep," he said simply, and as he let go of the auditorium door it thudded loudly behind us, making everyone look up. The shambolic wailing of their instruments stopped abruptly, leaving a dense silence as we started down the aisle. "It's okay." He leaned closer to whisper. "They're not necessarily staring at you, Ara, more the fact that you're walking with *me*."

"Why? What does that matter?"

"You're a girl."

"I know, but..."

"Guess I just don't really ever talk to girls. Willingly."

"Oh." I folded my arms around myself. "Why?"

He grinned and slipped a guiding hand through the strap of my backpack, resting it just under my shoulder blade. "I uh… I don't like any of them."

"Oh." I tried to laugh off the nerves, but nothing came out. All I could focus on was his touch against my cotton dress, so close to my skin.

As we neared the stage, some of the kids stood up, but their eager smiles sent my shoulders to my ears.

David nodded his greeting, keeping his hand safely on my back. "This is Ara."

I took a deep, shaky breath and waved, but the forced smile probably made me look more like a troll than a friendly newcomer.

"Ah, a fellow muso." A vertical palm appeared at my midsection, ready to shake my hand. I looked up from his thin wrist to his sandy-blond hair, then back down to his broad, honest grin, warmly inviting friendship.

"Um, hi."

"Nice to meet you. I'm Ryan." He shook my hand then inclined his head to a small dark-haired girl in the corner, quietly tuning her violin. "And that's Alana."

"Hello." I smiled at her, but my troll face clearly scared her back into the shadows after a quick nod my way.

Ryan laughed, leaning closer. "She's shy."

"No kidding."

"Anyway, that there is Fiona, and that's Jess, Jay, Dan…" He rattled off names as I nodded and smiled at the faces, forgetting their names instantly. They should've been called Bob—all of them—it'd make things so much easier.

"So?" Ryan asked. "What's your poison?"

I stared at him, trying to figure out what the hell he meant.

"He means *what do you play*?" David added, barely masking his amusement.

"Oh. Um. Piano?" I said, but it sounded more like a question for some reason.

"Nice." Ryan nodded, then pointed to the old brown upright. "Well, that's Big Bertha. She's old and large and always in the way—but she's in tune."

"Big Bertha?" I scratched my head, looking at David.

"We have a name for everything around here," David said.

Before I could laugh, a loud clap resonated around the auditorium. Everyone stopped and looked to the silhouette at the entrance. "I hear we have a new student today."

"Right here, sir," Ryan said, and I was pretty sure I just shrunk about two inches.

"Excellent." His booming voice reached my ears with the presumption that he was a big, tall man, but as he stalked toward us he became amusingly short and round. I tightened my lips, trapping the laughter when I caught sight of his blond ponytail, tugging heavily on the few straining hairs that clung for dear life around the edges of his bald spot. *Stylish.* But, short as he was, he was a centimeter taller than me, just enough to be threatening as he burrowed into my soul with an accusing glare. "Miss Thompson, I presume?"

Self-amusement turned to fear and dried my throat. I looked at Bertha, considering hiding behind her. "Yes, sir."

"And what will you be playing for us today, Miss Thompson?"

"Uh. Playing?"

"We expect a performance from *all* our students on the first day." He grinned, cupping his hands as he looked around the class. And at that point, the second head I'd earlier assumed he'd have showed itself.

Everyone in the class waited for me to respond, or maybe to run away crying. Clearly, this was the reason for David's smirk in the library. I felt like saying, "FYI, David, you being here with me does *not* make this spotlight on my awkwardness okay. Not even a little bit!" But I bit my tongue instead, my eyes narrowing when David tipped his head in a slight nod. It was so obvious. He knew Mr. Grant was going to do this. Why didn't he warn me? Then I could have made some lame excuse to run back home for the day.

Mr. Grant stood back from his disconcerting lean, offering the piano stool. "If you please, Miss Thompson. Or do you require *sheet* music?"

Groaning, I shuffled out of the straps of my backpack and went to dump it on the ground.

"I'll take this for you." David grabbed it and placed it by his feet.

"Uh, thanks," I said, then walked over to Bertha. The weight of two options dragged me to slump a little heavier on the stool: burst into tears and run away, or play a song?

"If you can only play Chopsticks, Miss Thompson, that will be fine," Mr. Grant snickered, and I just wanted to pull his ponytail. Jerk. But there was no way I'd let this know-it-all music professor make me cry in front of all these kids. I was sure he'd reduced many a student to tears in the past, and it was time somebody taught *him* a lesson. If there was one thing I hated in this world more than anything, it was people using their talents or skills or, worse, *knowledge,* to make other people feel small. And that's exactly what Mr. Grant was doing to me. And it worked.

Everyone watched. I hesitated only a breath more, then lifted the cover and touched the very tip of one finger to the high C, too afraid to press down.

"Ara?" David rested his elbows on the top of the piano and smiled at me. I did not smile back. "You'll be okay. Just play."

My lip quivered a little, tears burning in my eyes. That little bit of control I had over my life was just about to slip away.

Mr. Grant, standing uncomfortably close, watched me reposition my stool so I could reach the foot pedals, then he held out a stack of papers. "Your sheet music."

"I'll be fine without that, thanks, Mr. Grant," I stated calmly and politely. Really, I wanted to take them from his puny little hands and clonk him over the head. Instead, I traced the columns of black and white keys for a second, drawing a tight breath through my teeth. I wasn't familiar with the weight of these keys or the force it would take to draw a sound from them. This piano was old, and after two months without so much as hearing a piano, I wasn't sure I could even play anymore. This could end badly.

"Today, Miss Thompson," said the intolerant imp.

David gave me a reassuring nod, leaning a little closer to watch my fingers as they found their way home.

I looked around the room and grinned. "Has anyone here heard of the band *Muse*?"

Under the cheers of the class, David nodded and sat back against the table behind him, while everyone else pulled their chairs into a neat circle around me. Even Alana moved from her desolation in the corner, and stood beside Ryan with her violin still in hand.

"Go get 'em, Ara." Ryan waved an encouraging fist.

"Thanks," I muttered, strangely feeling a little better now.

The world disappeared for a second then. I inhaled and felt the cool of the keys under my fingertips—heavy and solid. Breathe.

The first notes of the song filled the air, and a familiar flood of excitement rushed through my heart then flowed down my hands. The keys were heavier than the ones back home, but it only took two chords to get used to it.

"This is called *United States of Eurasia,* followed by *Collateral Damage*," I said.

A few people laughed loudly and cheered.

As I panned over the notes, feeling the long-forgotten muscles in my hands stretch, I cleared my throat and sung the words. David looked down into his lap, keeping a smile hidden as he nodded in time with the music.

On the second verse, a violin came in out of nowhere. I looked over my shoulder and smiled at Alana, who had her eyes closed. But her accompaniment gave me a new kind of confidence, and my voice flowed, unwavering into the echo of the auditorium. It just felt so damn good to release the air from my lungs this way again, as if this was my first breath in two months.

Everyone else in the room became a part of the performance then, keeping the beat with their hands and feet as I played. It was like a journey; a story with a beginning, middle, and end. And right where I'd have done so if it were me, the violin cut out, leaving an eerie stillness as I drew the song to an end—the high notes sorrowful, laden with a distant kind of pain that reminded me of home, of my best friend.

With my eyes closed but open to the memories of my old school and the softly weighted keys of the baby grand piano in the music room there, my fingers played for me, allowing me to drift away to the days when life was simple. Alone, in that place, I felt the last note leave, and only silence remained, hovering like a breath held.

I opened my eyes to David's beautiful face.

Beside him, Ryan stood suddenly and started clapping like a seal at a marine park.

"Way to go, New Kid," one of the girls said.

"Thanks." I smiled sheepishly, steering my eyes away from David's soul-penetrating gaze.

"Well"—Mr. Grant peered down his sharp nose—"I can see I have nothing much to teach *you*, Miss Thompson."

"That's okay, Mr. Grant," Ryan said. "Dan still hasn't gotten past open chords."

A boy ditched a pencil at Ryan.

"Right." Mr. Grant turned on his heel and walked back up the aisle. "Carry on, people. We will be working on our performance pieces for the Halloween concert."

My eyes stayed on the keys until the heavy door to the auditorium closed behind the two-headed beast. What was that guy's problem?

"Did he expect me to fail?" I asked, looking around the group.

"He does it to everyone new." Ryan patted my shoulder.

"Well, thanks for the heads-up, David." I frowned at him.

"I figured you could handle it." He looked at Ryan and they both laughed.

There was no way he could've known that, unless he'd read my student file, which I *highly* doubted. I folded my arms. "So what gave you that impression—that I could handle it?"

David stopped laughing and folded his arms, too, looking a little smug. "Your fingers, actually."

Slowly, I pulled them out from the fold and studied them. My nails used to be perfectly rounded atop the long, thin digits, but looked a little worn these days from being munched on so often. But he was right.

"The hands of a pianist," he added.

Very observant, Mr. Know-It-All. "Fine. I'll pay that one. But next time, a little warning, thanks."

"Sure. Well, in that case, maybe you should ditch History class," he said, holding back a smile. "That guy gives really boring lectures."

"Thanks, I'll keep it in mind." I rolled my eyes, not really meaning to smile as well. It was hard to be annoyed at David. He was just so sweet, and I had to hand it to him: I could handle it. I *did* handle it. I was grateful to Mrs. Baker now for the three hours every Tuesday and Thursday, where she would painstakingly force me to play piano until my fingers seized up and turned bone-white. Mrs. Baker was one thing I would *not* miss about my old life.

"Seriously," David whispered in my ear as the hovering crowd dissipated and went back to their projects. "There was a reason I didn't tell you about Mr. Grant."

"I'm listening," I said, shuffling over so he could sit beside me.

"I was afraid you'd run home."

I would have. "I'm not that weak," I said. "But I could've at least prepared myself."

"I'm sure." He smiled to himself, his upper arm brushing mine as he laid his long fingers to the keys. "Heart and Soul?"

"Huh?" I looked up at him.

"Heart and Soul. You wanna play it?"

"That's a bit… *simple*, don't you think?"

"Oh, I'm sorry, Mozart," he said with a breathy laugh. "Would you prefer a more complicated duet?"

"Can you handle it?" I asked teasingly.

"Young lady, I can handle anything *you* can dish out."

"*That*, I strongly doubt."

After David escorted me all the way to third-period Math class—even though he wasn't in my class—I watched him walk away and then fell inside myself at the back of the room. There were no kids in Math from Music class and, for the most part, no one bothered to strike up a conversation. So I sat quietly and thought about David until the teacher said, "Five minutes left to finish those questions and hand them in. If you're done already, you can leave."

A few students jumped up, placed their work on Miss Chester's desk and left the room. I pushed my unfinished paper aside and reached into my bag for my map—to hopefully locate the nearest bathroom. But as I pulled my schedule and pencil case out, and looked into the empty space beneath my purse and keys, a wave of panic washed over me.

I checked the ground, the desk, even in my pencil case. Nope. Definitely gone. But I was sure I had that map in the library.

The familiar heat of panic flushed through my arms, rising into my cheeks as I dropped my face against my hand. When the bell screeched, I stood, packing my stuff into my bag with the speed of an old arthritic lady. As the last of the chattering dregs shuffled from the room, I herded out behind them, dumping my paper on the teacher's desk before stepping into the corridor. The hot, damp air trickled over the balustrade from the courtyard below, wetting my lungs as I breathed it in.

Of all the doors nestled into the brown bricks around the square lot, not one of them looked like a bathroom. And of all the kids hanging over the guardrail, tossing things to their friends on the ground floor, not one of them looked like the kind of kid I could ask for directions without them later responding to a 'Have you met the new girl?' with a 'Yeah, she asked me where she could pee!'.

I swung my bag over my shoulder, and as I looked up, my gaze met with a pair of amazing green eyes, shining out like glass marbles as the sun hit them. "Hi!"

"Hello, Ara." David flashed his mischievous grin. "Need a guide?"

God, yes. "Well, I wouldn't if *someone* hadn't taken my map," I said accusingly, then smiled back as I stood beside him.

"Sorry. But those things are impossible to read, anyway." He looked down at me. "You'd have gotten lost without me to show you the way."

"Is that so?" My playful tone drew a smile to his lips again.

"Yes."

"You seem pretty sure of yourself."

He nodded once.

"So, are you saying I'm incapable of finding my own way?" I said.

"No. Only that life's easier when you have someone to guide you."

"Life?"

"Er, yeah, I meant… in the context of getting from A to B." He rubbed a hand across his mouth. "That was kind of awkward, wasn't it?"

"Uh, yeah." I let the laughter out with a breath. He had foot-in-mouth-disease almost as bad as me. "You know, Emily warned me about you."

"She did?" He turned and looked forward as we started walking, his natural cool spreading calm out over my awkwardness.

I hugged my book tightly to my chest. "Yeah, she said you had a tendency to snatch up lost lambs."

"Did she tell you why she thought that?" He stopped and took my math book from me, tucking it under his arm beside his books.

I watched it for a second. "Not really. I came to my own conclusions, though."

"And what might they be?"

"Well, it's not the lost lamb thing you're into. It's fresh meat."

"Fresh meat?" He laughed nervously, looking away.

"Yeah. You know? A new toy—something different to play with than all the old ones."

David stayed quiet for a moment. "You don't think of me like that, do you? That I am only talking to you because I want something more interesting to play with?"

I shook my head. "I did. But, I actually think you might be a very genuinely nice guy." I tried not to let the surprise seep out in my tone but it did anyway. "I mean, I've *never* had a guy carry my books."

We both looked at the books.

"I'm not sure I've ever carried a girl's books. Not at this school, anyway."

"Oh, you didn't grow up here?"

He swallowed. "No."

"Are you new, too?"

He turned and started walking. "No."

Hm. King of Elaboration. I'd noticed this a few times today, so far, but it didn't seem like he was trying to be vague. Just… more like he wasn't good with conversation. So I decided to push for more details. "Have you… been here long?"

"No."

"Longer than a year—less than a year?"

"About two years. Almost."

"And, um… so, you don't really talk to many of the girls?"

"No."

"Because you don't really like them?"

"Correct."

"Why?" I asked as we came to a stop. "Why don't you like them?"

David scratched his ear. "Why do you ask so many questions?"

"Because you evade so many answers."

His lip tugged on one corner into an almost-smile. "Yes, I suppose I do."

"So…" I twirled my hair nervously around my finger, vaguely noticing a few girls giggle as they rushed in through the door beside us. "Are you going to tell me why you don't like the girls here?"

"Guess I just feel, sometimes, like I'm a hundred years older than them."

I smiled at the way he smiled. "So you're too mature for them?"

"You could say that." He stepped into me, showing no respect for my territorial bubble. The length of his entire body hovered barely a centimeter away from mine, forcing my gaze to roll upward just to meet his lovely green eyes.

Deliciously tense, I tried to deflect. "And… do you stand this close to everyone, or am I just special?"

"I don't know," he said, narrowing his eyes in thought. "I haven't decided yet."

My mouth opened, but I wasn't sure what to say, because I had no idea what that meant, if anything. Only a soft breath came from the very back of my throat, stopping on the sweet scent of his vibrant, chocolaty cologne.

David nodded to the door beside us. "Did you need to go?"

Go? I forced myself to look right.

"The bathroom," he added.

"Ur, yes, I kinda did." Oh, God, awkward meter off the scale.

"I'll mind your bag."

"Okay, I'll just be a sec." I passed it to David then pushed the door open to a nose-burning bleach smell, mingling with other rancid scents in the heat of the only non-air-conditioned room in this school. And as the door shut quietly behind me, a voice rose above the putrid smell with familiar content.

"The girl in the yellow dress?" it said.

I stopped dead, remaining in the concealment of the dividing wall.

"Yeah, the new girl," another replied.

I cringed. This was that moment where you decide to either walk in there and act like you didn't hear, or stop and hide, hoping they wouldn't discover you. I should've read up on this in the *How to be a New Student without Looking Like an Idiot* guide.

"What did you think of her?" she continued.

"Well, she's pretty, I guess."

"You *think* so?"

"Yeah, I mean, did you see how blue her eyes are? Like, so wasted on her face, right?"

Ouch.

"Yeah, totally. You want some?" the other girl said.

"What scent is it?"

"Sunlight Breeze."

"Yeah." A long hiss of a spray can sounded before the sharp, choking fumes of deodorant filled the tiny bathroom. I covered my mouth, silently coughing into my hand.

"And did you hear? She's already got her *claws* into David Knight?"

My heart jumped. *Claws*?

"Yep. Typical. He doesn't like her, I heard. He's just interested in her because she's wearing a dress and it's, like, easy access."

My eyes all but jumped out of my head, but as soon as the echo of her voice retreated, I felt my heart break a little. David *was* being overly nice to me. I'd met new guys before. Cute guys, ugly guys, nice guys, and jerks. Never a guy like David. Which did have me wondering all day if he was put up to this—if he was being nice because someone dared him to.

"That must be it, I mean, come on," she said. "He's *way* out of her league."

"Yeah, I don't know what she thinks he wants with her. Did you see her outside just now?"

"Yes, oh my God!" The other laughed. "She has so never had a boyfriend before."

"Probably still a virgin."

I swallowed, shrinking.

"Mm. I give it a week before he loses interest."

"A week? That's generous. Maria said the girl has, like, scars on her face."

My breath froze halfway through a gasp, the walls closing in around me.

"True? No way? That's so gross. I wonder if he's noticed them."

"How can he not? Apparently they're—" A face appeared right in front of mine, and everyone took a breath.

While I stood frozen in humiliated stillness, a blonde girl just looked me over, focusing on my scars, then threw her hair back and opened the door, dragging a dark-haired girl behind her. I hid myself in the corner as bright light from the corridor filled the room, disappearing with their sudden high-pitched cackles.

Layers of my soul slowly peeled away like an unfurling blossom, petal by petal. I blinked the tears free, unable to move or think or breathe, focusing only on the impression of my nails digging into my palms.

They were right. David was probably showing interest in me as a joke or a bet he made with a friend. I was stupid to think he hadn't noticed my scars.

I touched my jaw, my fingertips shaking, and as my desperate urge to go to the bathroom faded, a longing to go home came in its place, stepping aside for the rolling in my stomach. I clapped a hand across my gut and ran for the toilet.

Even as I rinsed my face and washed my mouth out, the

voice of that girl played in my head: *"Out of her league… A week before he loses interest… scars."*

Somehow, the idea that David would be grossed out by me had taken over my fear of being new, and I wasn't sure what had gotten in to me even thinking that his sudden and exclusive attention could be genuine.

In the mirror, my face looked pale and washed out, which made the scars look red and menacing, worse than they did this morning. I leaned closer and poked about my chin, moving my skin to get a good look at the tiny little dots covering the right side of my jaw from under my chin to the top of my collar bone, like a fine sprinkling of nuts on a sundae. The weird thing was, I hardly ever noticed them anymore. It was like my mind subconsciously blacked them out. But I knew they were there, and I knew everyone else could see them. Including David. I just felt so stupid now.

The real world sucked so much more than my mom said it would.

I splashed another handful of water over my face and grabbed a few sheets of paper towel, pausing when the door opened but no one came in.

"Ara?"

I froze. "Uh, yeah?"

"Are you… are you okay?"

I laughed. He probably thought I fell in. "Um. I'll be out in a sec."

"That's not what I asked," he said, his tone a little flat. "Answer me, or I'm coming in. Are you okay?"

"I… I'm good." But I wasn't, and the mirror too clearly reflected the sadness in my eyes. The mask I'd become so good at holding in place hadn't slipped, but cracked completely, and the self-pity I'd battled so hard against suddenly won the war. I took a deep breath and looked my reflection square in the eye. "Every ache is a step toward redemption," I told myself. I still didn't believe it, though. Nothing could undo what had been done and I knew, eventually, Karma would come to claim my life in repayment. But not today.

I straightened my shoulders. I just wanted a little more time believing David might like me—even if it was just a bet or a game. If I could just believe it for today, I would never ask for anything else. Ever again.

As I stepped into the corridor, I drew a deep breath and looked sadly at the boy leaning over the railing. Midday shadows highlighted the contours of his shoulder blades and showed the bones along his spine. If I knew him better, if we were close, I'd slowly trace my finger down his back, feeling how solid and real he was under my touch. Except, right now, I wanted nothing more than to run over and tell him everything those girls just said in the hopes he might correct me —tell me that it was insane and that they were wrong. Only problem was that, if they were right, he wouldn't care if my feelings were hurt; he'd probably just cringe at my hysterics, and dust me off like a cobweb.

He turned around and smiled at me with those kind, warm eyes, and I almost cried, blinking rapidly until, as the tears receded, David's arm landed around my shoulder. "Are you okay?"

"Mm-hm." I nodded.

He stood taller, his jaw going stiff as he looked at the two girls from the bathroom, now whispering to each other by an open locker in the corner. "You're not okay. I can tell."

"Perils of being new." I flashed a grin.

"Or perils of gossip," he said, checking over his shoulder before looking back at me. "Do you mind if I teach those girls a lesson?"

"Why would you want to do that?"

"Just go with it, okay?" he whispered in my ear, so close that his breath tickled my cheek. "Are they watching?"

I cast my eyes to them. They stared on with arched brows, lips curled in disgust. "Yeah. They're watching."

"You ready?"

"Ready for what?"

"This." He gently wrapped his fingers around my arms and walked me backward, past our bags and the stack of books, until my spine pressed against the cold wall.

"What are you doing, David?"

"Giving them something to talk about." He propped his forearm on the wall, bending at the knees as his face came in line with mine.

My eyes stayed on him, locked to his every move, trying to predict his next. But even though he moved his hand slowly to my face, I still jumped internally when his thumb unexpectedly touched my cheek, gently sliding down then across my bottom lip. I could taste something sweet on his touch, and I wanted so badly to make a joke, wanted to run or hide, or close my eyes and breathe him in. In fact, I thought I was holding my breath, but as his lips hovered in front of mine, the warmth he exhaled went into my lungs. But he didn't kiss me. He just smiled into me, speaking with his eyes. I knew what he was doing, and he knew, if he had any sense at all, what this closeness was doing to me.

I swallowed, my mouth watering, but the good feeling slinked away as the two girls walked off in a huff, flipping their hair. I looked up at David, who smiled in a way that made me feel like I belonged here. "Why did you do that?"

"Do what?" He leaned a little closer.

I stopped him with a hand to his firm, cool chest. "You… you made them think we were kissing."

"Yes."

"But, don't you get it? They'll spread this around to everyone—tell the whole school you were kissing *me*!" I swallowed the lump in my throat.

"Precisely."

"But—" Against everything inside me, I pressed my hand more firmly to his chest and shoved him away, then rolled out from the wall and flung myself across the corridor. It was true what they said: this was a bet. Why else would he have done that?

"What does it matter if they tell everyone?" He slowly turned around, holding his arms out wide.

I looked into the sunny courtyard below, leaning my elbows over the cold metal bar. "Do you really want people thinking you like *me*?"

"Ara." He appeared beside me, our arms touching. "What would be so wrong about liking you?"

I shook my head, refusing to point out the obvious.

"You're a very sweet girl. And you don't deserve to be the victim of other people's cruelty. I would rather they told the whole school I was kissing you in the corridor than to have them talk about you like *that*." He pointed back to the bathroom.

"You heard that?" Everything suspended in slow motion around me. "How did—"

"Bathrooms echo, Ara."

It felt like a hot-air balloon had just been let off in my face. I bit my quivering lip tightly. "I can't believe you heard that."

"Don't worry about it." David gently grabbed my wrist and started walking, dragging me along behind him. "They're not nice people. I'm just sorry that, of all the girls you had to run into in there, it was *those* two."

"Well, thank you"—I stopped and pulled my arm from his grip—"for standing up for me. No one's ever done that before."

"Really?" He looked amazed, or maybe mortified.

"I never needed it." I reached down and picked up my bag as an excuse to avoid eye contact. "Thick skin and quick wit were kind-of a requirement at an all-girls' school. But… I guess I just lost my nerve."

"You shouldn't *have* to stand up for yourself, Ara. People should mind their tongues." David softened a bit then, quickly bending to grab our books off the floor by his feet. "And for the record, mon amie, despite what those girls just said"—he took a step closer—"you are not a dare or a bet, and I happen to think you are *very* pretty."

Yep, that did it. Cheeks hot; heart tumbling down the stairwell; lust-meter at fifty. "So, you… you speak French?"

"Seulement quand je parle avec mon cœur." David started walking, but I caught a glimpse of a smile as he turned, shouldering his bag.

"What does that mean?" I asked.

"Google it."

A second passed before I forced myself to run after him. "I will, you know."

He just stared ahead, his dimpled smile keeping my eyes as we walked in silence.

3

"How do *you* know where my next class is?" I asked David, walking quickly to keep up with him.

"I read your schedule, remember?"

"Yeah, for two seconds. I can't even remember what classes I actually signed up for."

David said nothing, just smiled—a kind of secret smile—as we headed back up the stairs past a waving carrot-top girl.

"Um, hi," I muttered, returning the wave.

"That's Ellie." David leaned in. "She's in our music class."

"Oh, okay." I looked back down the stairwell at her just as she glanced up to gush over David. "She likes you."

"No, she doesn't. She's just… I don't know." He shrugged once. "I think they all suffer from the same disease around here."

"Disease?"

"Wanting what they can't have. It takes over their minds." He tapped his head.

"Oh, so you think you're too good for them?" I challenged playfully.

He fanned the collar of his shirt, humor lighting the smugness on his face. "I don't *think* I am. I *know* I am."

I laughed. "So… you've really never dated *any* of the girls—ever?"

"No. And I don't plan to."

"Oh," I said, falling suddenly through the earth. Guess that ruled me out, too.

David's head whipped up as he came to an abrupt halt. "Oh. I… uh. I really didn't mean it like that. I—"

"I need my books now." I pointed to them, masking my disappointment.

He gently drew them from the stack and placed them in my waiting hand.

"Thanks."

We stood looking at each other for a moment, the sound of the teacher's voice echoing out from my History class beside us.

"So, this is your class," David said.

"I figured." I smiled softly, but my heart was completely broken.

"Right." He nodded to himself. "Guess the voice was a giveaway."

I frowned at him. The teacher's voice was the giveaway, but I wasn't sure how he could know that unless he knew who the teacher was to me. I turned away quickly to avoid that conversation. "Well, thanks for walking me."

"Hey, Ara." He grabbed my arm. I looked up from his hand to his lovely green eyes. He let go. "When I said I don't plan to date, I wasn't talking about y—"

"It's okay, David, you don't owe me an explanation." I tried to grin. "I only just met you, right? And I hadn't placed myself in that category anyway."

David's jaw set stiff, his eyes fixing on the ground.

"So, I'll see ya later?" I said, slowly backing in through the doorway.

"Ah-ha!" the teacher said. "Ladies and gentlemen, we *finally* have a new student."

I turned away from David, leaving our conversation before he could respond, feeling better seeing a familiar face in the room. "Hi, Dad," I whispered so no one else would hear, stealing a quick glance at the now empty corridor.

"Attention, please." Dad's voice rose above the chatter. Everyone hushed. "This is Ara-Rose. I'm sure some of you have already met her—"

"Actually..." I cringed. "It's just Ara."

He looked sideways at me. "Okay, this is *just Ara*."

"Nice to meet you, *Just Ara*," someone called from the back of the room, and a low hum of laughter erupted over the entire class.

"Settle down, Maverick," Dad said sternly.

"Good one, Dad," I said sarcastically under my breath.

"Uh, Emily?" He ignored that, aiming his voice to a girl in the front row of the raised auditorium-style seating.

Without hesitation, the same girl I met this morning, with her swinging ponytail, bounded over like an excited puppy. "Yes, Mr. Thompson?"

"You've met Ara?" Dad aimed his thumb at me.

"Yes, sir." She added a little too much 'cutesy' to that eyelash batting, and my mouth fell open. She totally had a crush on my dad.

"Right. I want you to help"—he looked at me as he passed some papers to Emily—"Just Ara?"

"*Ara's* fine," I said. Hint, hint.

"Help Ara get up-to-date with our lessons, please?"

"Sure thing, Mr. Thompson." Emily grabbed my hand and dragged me to sit next to her—right in the front row; right where Dad would be able to see my every move.

"Um, do you always sit here?" I asked, plonking down.

"Yup. I can see the teacher better." She watched Dad walk across the room and push the antique gramophone that was normally in our attic out of the way.

"Why would that be a good thing?"

"Are you kidding me?" She motioned her open palm to my dad. "Look at him."

Uh-oh. "Um, Emily—"

"Isn't he cute?" she continued. "Don't you think he looks just like Harrison Ford, but, like, Indiana-Jones-Harrison-Ford?"

I glanced at my dad, my nose crinkling as I took more notice of his greying light-brown hair and the creases he'd get around his kind eyes when he smiled. I guess he did sort of look like Indiana Jones.

"Emily," I whispered again.

"Yeah." She sighed, dreamily gazing up at him.

There was no easy way around it. I had to tell her before she embarrassed herself further. "He's… my dad."

She spun around so quickly that I jumped. "You are kidding me. Oh my God, Ara. Why didn't you tell me?"

"I'm so sorry. I just… I didn't realize you were—"

"We are *so* having a sleepover at your house." She practically jumped in her seat. "I've had a crush on Mr. Thompson for, like"—she flipped her head to one side—"two years."

My tongue pushed into the side of my cheek. I really did not expect that. I thought she might be a little humiliated at the least, but I guess it was better this way. "Two years, huh?"

"Yup. It's why I take History."

"That's… disturbing."

"Not really." She shrugged, gnawing the tip of her pen. "You could look at it as though your dad is inspiring my education."

I wondered if *he'd* feel the same way. Instead of rolling my eyes at her, I turned my head back to watch Dad writing the words 'Religious History' on the board.

"Oh, come now, it'll be fun and you know it," he announced to the groaning room, then turned back to write on the board again.

Emily leaned in. "He's right," she whispered. "He always makes boring topics fun."

"I know." I smiled to myself. "He even used to do all the voices of characters when he'd read to me."

"He does that in class"—Emily laughed—"when he reads direct from text books. Sometimes he puts on different accents, like, perfectly."

As I went to laugh, my eyes darted quickly from my dad to a boy beside me, who jolted forward in his seat, a scrunched-up piece of paper bouncing off his head. He spun around, presenting his middle finger to the boys up the back, while my dad remained oblivious, glancing from a textbook to the whiteboard.

"What a loser," one of the boys said.

I turned away and leaned closer to Emily. "Do they know that by making that L sign on their own heads, they're technically making *themselves* look like losers?"

She rolled her eyes. "They are losers."

I let out a small laugh.

In the seat across from me, the boy scrunched up a sheet of paper under the concealment of his desk, keeping his eyes on my dad the whole time. I looked back at the jerks, who watched the kid with an amused kind of interest, until they broke formation suddenly, launching to their feet as he sent a paper cannon into enemy territory.

"Oh, crap." Emily covered her head with her notepad, smiling. "He just started a war."

I went to duck too, but Dad started in with something about Greek gods, forcing a cease-fire. The jerks sat down, and the boy knocked the ammo into his open backpack.

"Looks like they'll live to fight another day," I said.

"No," Emily whispered under my dad's lecture. "It'll just be a cafeteria continuation."

"Great. Food fight?"

She shrugged. "Probably."

"Will David be in that?"

It was a simple enough question, but my newfound affections rested too thickly in the undertone. She turned to me quickly, and before she could say *Oh, my God, you like him*, I said, "So, does my dad know you have a crush on him?"

"No way." She leaned back, her eyes wide. "I would be so humiliated."

I scratched my temple, wondering how admitting it to his daughter was any less humiliating.

"So, how was the library with *David*?" She kind-of sung his name.

I froze, wondering which parts of my amazing morning I should leave out. "It was okay. He seems nice." I nodded casually, but Emily's smile grew.

"You like him."

I cleared my throat, repositioning my chair. “I think he’s… a nice… kid.”

She scoffed in the back of her throat. And I knew from the look on her face exactly what she was about to say. “You *so* do like him.”

I wore the face of denial, but the cheesy grin in my eyes must have changed the wording on my neon sign to ‘Oh my God. I totally do.’

“I knew it.” She pointed at me. “I knew it.”

I grabbed her finger and pushed it down. “I do not like him.”

“Oh, I’ve seen that look before. You have *Knight Fever*.”

“Knight what?”

“It’s what we call it when all the girls *swoon* over David.”

“I’m not swooning.” I turned my face away.

“He’s charming, isn’t he?” She leaned on her hand, her thoughts a million miles away. “It’ll kill you, you know? Knight Fever. Have you heard the *I don’t date* speech yet?”

I drew a tight breath.

“Oh no. You have. Oh, I thought…” Her head moved slowly from side to side. “Well, now I’m sure he’s gay. I mean, I was sure you had to be his type. We girls have pretty much got it down to a science.”

“Got what down to a science?”

“David’s type: the girls he will and most definitely will not… let’s just say *scope*, since it’s not like he shows an interest, per se.”

“What’s scoping?”

“Perving, you know… checking out.” She shrugged.

Oh. “He scopes?”

“He’s a hot-blooded male, Ara. Of course he does. Just, very subtly.” Her tone dropped its certainty. “Like, he never actually looks, but he’s nicer to some than others. So we’ve grouped together a sort of profiling on him.”

“Okay, that’s just creepy,” I said, turning away.

“It’s not”—she paused when my dad glared at us—“it’s not like that. It’s just a bit of gossip. We don’t have, like, a file on him or anything.”

“So, you thought *I* was his type?”

“Well, I was sure, but… I guess not.” She shrugged, staring forward.

And that was it: a shrug. That's all I was? I really liked this guy, and I'd just been graded down with a *shrug*?

I drummed my fingers on the desk, trying really hard to focus on the legends of Zeus, but my stomach grumbled, making a fuss about my missed mid-morning snack—since high schools over here didn't do recess. I mean, what kind of cruel institution was this?

Eventually, my hunger-induced mood got the better of me. I spun back to Emily. "He walked me to every class. He was so nice, and really sweet," I said, then told her about the bathroom gossip and the theatrical kiss.

Her eyes rounded into her brow. "Are you serious?"

"Yes. So what's the deal?"

"He has. Never. Done. That before," she exclaimed.

"Okay? So, am I a bet, or a dare?"

"What do you mean?"

"Did someone tell him to befriend me? Am I gonna get a bucket of blood tipped on my head at the school dance, or something?"

Emily laughed. "If it were any other guy, I'd say that's probably the case. But David doesn't really get in on things like that."

"Are you sure?"

"Yeah." She nodded, eyes darkening. "I won't go into detail, but… he's the guy that usually puts a stop to that sort of thing. Well… ever since he and I first became friends, anyway."

"Then why did he give me the 'no dating' speech? I mean, he's kind of given me the impression all morning that he actually likes me."

She slowly looked away. "I can *not* figure that boy out."

The bell rang loudly then, cutting my dad off and startling me. I swallowed the last of my next sentence, offering Emily a smile. David was right. She *was* easy to be around. At first, I thought she was a bit stuck-up, but that was clearly just a nasty first impression.

We stood up then and I jammed my books into my bag, frowning at the elbow in my rib. "What?"

Emily nodded across the room. "Look."

At the end of my gaze, David came into focus, hands wedged in his pockets, shoulder on the doorframe, and a very sexy grin across his lips.

"Hi," I mouthed, looking down at my bag before he could see my cheeks change color.

"Mm-mm." Emily shook her head, hugging her books.

"What's mm-mm?"

"Hm, he likes you, Ara—he's just trying not to *show* you."

"You think?" I looked back at David, now talking to my dad.

"Come on, girl. Even Mr. Thompson noticed the way he was staring at you."

"Oh no." I hid behind my hand. "It's the touch-my-daughter-and-you-die speech." I wanted to melt—hide under my desk or slink away.

Emily hummed again, smiling. "They're both so gorgeous."

"No, Emily," I said flatly. "Only *one* of them is gorgeous."

"I agree," she said. "Your dad is so much better."

We both laughed, but mine ended in a sigh. "I hope Dad doesn't give David the creeps. I only just met the poor guy."

"Nah, he's just making the lines clear. Can you blame him?"

"Yes. He's breaking all the rules I set out before I came here."

"You gave your dad rules?"

I nodded.

"Okay?" Dad said, clapping David warmly on the shoulder.

"I had no intentions of that, Mr. Thompson," David said, looking him right in the eye.

I watched on in horror. "Oh God, just hide me now."

Emily laughed. "Let's just hope you don't receive the tail-end of that lecture."

"Exactly what I was just thinking." She must've known my dad pretty well. It felt kind of strange then to know I shared him with so many other kids. I always knew that, but never experienced it firsthand before.

Dad sat back at his desk, and I chose the opportune moment, as he reached for something on the floor, to slink quietly past, sinking my neck into my shoulders.

Emily, however, shamelessly stopped in front of the desk just to tell Dad how great his lecture was today. Never mind that she wasn't even listening. I really quite liked Emily.

"Hi, David," I said.

He just smiled and took my bag as we walked into the corridor.

"Look, I'm so sorry about my dad. What was he saying to you?"

He laughed once. "You know, it's okay, Ara. If I was your father and I saw some punk kid look at you the way I'm sure I was, I wouldn't have used words."

We stopped walking, and I groaned, slamming my back against a row of lockers as I tried to rub the ache of mortification from my temples.

"Of course," David continued after a short breath, "if I'd known he was your dad, I might've thought twice about—"

"Hanging out with me?" I dropped my hands to my sides. "I'm sorry. I should've told you." And so, I lost my first friend. I was in no way offended, though. I knew going to the same school my dad taught at would have its pitfalls. I'd accepted that.

"No." He stepped closer to me, shaking his head. "No, Ara, I would have thought twice about staring at you that way in *front* of him." His words softened on the end.

"Oh. Okay. Well, uh… I'm sorry I didn't mention it earlier."

"Well, a *heads-up* would've been nice," he said.

"Touché." I smiled, surprised he remembered me saying that in music class.

"So?" We both said, and then laughed.

"You go."

"No, ladies first." He bowed his head.

"Um, about before—"

"Okay, wait." His hand came up like a stop sign. "What I said before about dating? It was a mistake. I'm so used to having to give that speech that it just came out on auto. But I didn't mean it for *you.* I was just illustrating how I don't… I mean… I'm just not that kinda guy." David's fists clenched beside his jeans. "What I meant earlier was that I'd never date any of *them.* I didn't mean that to include yo—I mean, what I'm trying to say is…" He looked directly into my eyes, and all the students in the hall seemed to disappear. "You're not just any girl, Ara, I"—he swallowed—"I've known you only half a day and already I… *like* you."

My lungs went tight, like a softball just got lodged in my chest. I looked around, waiting for a group of kids to jump out from behind the lockers and laugh at me, screaming *"April Fools"*. Despite it not being April.

David laughed to himself then. "I'm sorry. That was very forward of me. You don't even know me yet, and I—"

"Um, David?" I stopped him. Oh my God. I had no idea what to say. I mean, for all I knew, I had merely *imagined* him saying that, and at any minute, I'd wake up, still in Dad's class with Emily beside me and a piece of paper stuck to the drool on my chin. I wanted David to like me, but I wasn't sure I wanted him to admit it yet.

I hugged my arms across my waist. "This is all a little bit weird."

"I'm sorry." He ran his thumb across his upper lip, clearing his throat. "I get it."

"No, you don't get it." I chased after him as he turned away.

"No. Really." His smile radiated sincerity. "I really do. You don't have to explain."

"But—"

"We're late." He walked a little faster then, but slowed and turned back to face me, aiming his thumb toward the stairs. "It's uh…. it's this way."

I walked after him, smacking my own brow. I wished I could scream it out—tell him exactly what I was thinking. But I was never good with words. I always fumbled and tripped on them, and my 'I like you too' might easily come out as 'You like me? Great, now I can show you how good my initials look beside your surname'. Creepy.

David stopped walking. "Did you just say something?"

"I uh—no." I hope not. "Was I thinking out loud again?"

"Uh, I don't know. Did you mean to say that?"

"Say what?"

"You two!" A door burst open beside us, and an evil-villain-type-scary woman, who probably kidnaped Dalmatians, popped her angry face out. "Why aren't you in class?"

"Sorry, Miss Hawkins, we were just going," David said slowly.

"Well, make it quick, please, the bell *has* rung." She slammed the door, leaving David and me alone again.

The awkwardness of my accidentally vocalized thoughts separated us with an invisible line. I hoped I didn't only let the word 'creepy' out. On its own, that could be totally misconstrued. Then again, talking about our paired initials would be much worse.

"Lunch?" David said, shattering the tension.

"Lunch?"

"Yeah. Can I..." He stuffed his hands in his pockets, looking up from his shoes. "Can I walk you to lunch after class?"

I smiled a simple smile. "Sure."

THE WORDS 'COWARD', 'MORONICALLY DERANGED' AND 'STUPID, stupid, stupid!' stared at me from the page where an equation was supposed to be solved. But if I couldn't find the formula for curing regret, how was chemistry going to be any easier?

I dropped my face against my hands, slamming my elbows on either side of my book, the entire conversation with David playing in my mind like a regret marathon on repeat. How could I have just stood there with my giant gob open and let nothing out? I should've told him. I should've said, "Thanks, David. I like you, too." What is wrong with me?

"Everything all right, Ara?" Miss Swanson asked.

I sat up straight and grabbed my pen. "Um, yeah. All good."

Satisfied, the teacher turned back to the board and, one by one, the students followed suit, leaving me alone again with my scribbles. After a while, I turned them all into doodles, each word transforming into a snake or overlapping circles and other various works of notepad art, all twining together to form two words: Knight Fever. I had it bad —bad enough to be drawing love hearts.

I scratched them out quickly when I realized, practically ripping the page with my pen. It was way too early to use *that* word. This was in no way love at first sight. It was just my deep-seated need to feel accepted manifesting itself into emotions that weren't real. I nodded, satisfied with my psychological assessment. That would've made Vicki proud.

Except, I didn't want it to be right. It felt good to like a boy. It felt good to be that distracted. But I couldn't let that feeling divert me from the plan to put my head down, get through this year and hopefully, somewhere in the mix of all my moving on, I might actually move on—without dragging anyone down with me.

When the lunch bell rang, I stayed in my chair, sharing my pendulum thoughts with the Bunsen burner. He didn't talk back, thankfully, but I wished he would. If it was even a *he*. "Sorry," I said, "If you're a girl, you have a lovely figure."

"I assure you, I'm a boy," it said in a velvety voice. And my cheeks went really hot when I realized it wasn't the Bunsen burner that spoke.

All I could do was laugh, staring forward with a rock of tension making my head want to sink down. "I'm… just gonna go hide under the desk."

David cleared his throat into his fist. "Don't do that. It's okay, I talk to inanimate objects all the time."

"You do?" I said as he sat beside me.

He nodded. "Is something on your mind, new girl?"

"A lot of things are, but only one of them is bothering me right now."

He clasped his hands together on the table in front of him. "I'm all ears."

I tried to think of something funny to say, but couldn't. "I'm sorry about before."

"Before what? Before the beginning of the world, before the coming of Christ?"

"Ha-ha." I slapped his forearm, noting the silkiness of his skin just below his sleeve. "No, about before, when I choked up."

He laughed. "Oh, don't worry about that, pretty girl. I have a tendency to…"—he smiled—"over-share."

"Not really. All you said is you like me." I dipped my shoulder a little, feeling funny about saying that out loud. "And I just choked because no one's ever said that to me before."

"Well, it wasn't a confession of love. *Like* can mean many things."

"I know." I just wished it were a confession of love. "And I guess… in that sense, I actually like you, too."

He grinned, making a thin line of his lips. “Good. Then, friends?”

“Yeah, friends.”

David frowned then, looking down as my belly added its two cents. “Hungry?” he said.

I wrapped my hands over the rumbling. “Uh, yeah, just a little.”

4

Though the rest of the school was unbelievably free of clichés, given that I'd expected a High-School-Musical type scene when I first arrived here, the cafeteria was not. The buffet style cabinets, the old ladies in hairnets, and even the giant hall with long lines of plastic picnic tables, looked just like something out of a movie. Nothing like the old window-in-a-wall we had at my old school, where you could buy pies and sandwiches and that's pretty much it.

"This is so much cooler than back home," I said, sliding my tray down a few seats to sit at the center of the empty table. The warm weather had attracted most of the students outside today, so we had free pick of the room.

David slid in next to me. "*Cooler* would be if they hired enough kitchen staff to accommodate the great number of students."

"I thought they did just fine."

"Today, yes," he said. "But it usually takes until the end of lunch period to be served, and half of us end up eating in class."

"Oh, why was today so quick then?" I looked back at the now-empty buffet—all the kids seated, eating, aside from a few dregs gathering by the drink machine or buying sweets.

"They had help today."

"Volunteers?"

"Of a sort." David covered his smile with a fist. "Half the football team is serving detention in the kitchen."

"Really? Why?"

"Something about throwing balls of paper." He picked up a corn chip and held it near his mouth. "You planning to eat?"

"Oh, um, yeah." I straightened my tray and leaned my elbows on the table. "So, what's the deal here anyway, like, social hierarchy? I'm guessing they're at the top." I pointed to the group of well-built guys in the corner of the room.

"The guys having the fruit war?" He smiled as a piece of banana hit the glass window then slid down into a pile of pulp on the floor. "That's the other half of the football team, and yeah"—he nodded, looking away from them—"they're pretty much the top of the food chain. Fourth on the list would be these guys." He waved at one of the girls at the table in front of us. "Music class. They pretty much hang out together. The lowest ranking would be the boys behind you."

"Let me guess." I smirked, looking at their paper-wrapped sandwiches and milk cartons beside the chessboard. "They're the geeks."

David laughed. "You must be psychic."

"Well, the whole scene is self-explanatory, but the 'Chess Club' jacket was a dead giveaway."

"Yes, I suppose it is. Do you play?"

"Play?"

"Chess."

"Oh, yeah. I do. Should I be sitting with them?"

"No." He chuckled. "Unless you want to wear fruit juice home every day."

I shrugged. "Strawberry would look rather fetching on me, I think."

"Your hair smells like strawberries," he said, and I wondered quietly how he could smell that.

"So where do *you* fit in?" I asked.

David looked to the side. "Well—"

"Hey, guys." Emily perched herself on the seat across from David.

"Emily." He nodded his greeting.

"Hi," I said, then shoveled a mouthful of lasagna into my gob—an offering for the empty hole in my belly where a green ogre dwelled.

"Hey, do you guys mind if Ryan and Alana sit with us?" she asked. "They've got new-girl fever."

"No," I scoffed, "why would I mind?"

David lifted one shoulder. "Fine with me."

After Emily signaled them over, she leaned forward and a bright grin lit up her caramel eyes. "So, what d'ya think—a new love blossoming, or what?"

New love? My head burned as if a warm towel had just been wrapped around it.

"I think you might be right, Emily," David said, a sassy smile twinkling in the corners of his eyes. And as I was about to grab both cheeks and scream like a girl at a boy-band concert, he redirected his gaze to the pair walking toward us, standing as close to each other as possible. "But I don't think either of them has figured it out yet," he finished.

Emily sighed, gazing dreamily at Alana and Ryan, while I caught my breath.

"Hey, all." Ryan bumped knuckles with David, then sat down next to Emily, sliding Alana's tray closer to his.

"Hi, guys." I smiled, still feeling silly.

"Hey, Ara, so cool what you did to Mr. Grant today." Ryan pointed gun-fingers at me. "I'm sure it'll go down in high school history: The Newbie Bites Back. Part One." Beneath his docile tones, he made himself sound like the voice-over for a movie trailer.

"I wasn't biting back," I said with my mouth a little full, "not really. I was just… politely not taking any crap."

"So noble." Ryan nodded, lost in awe. Alana sat quietly beside him, not making any effort to stand out.

"So, Ara?" Emily said. "We just finished French class, are you taking French this semester?"

"Nope. Foreign languages just don't click up here." I tapped my head. "My friend tried to teach me some French once. It was bad. I sounded like I was spitting insults at someone who made me hungry."

Ryan and David chuckled to themselves.

"That's a pity." Emily propped her cheek against her hand. "I was kinda hoping we'd have someone to take the spotlight off us for a while."

"Spotlight?"

"Yeah. Our teacher, Ms. Sears"—Ryan pointed his chip at me—"total cow."

"You mean grenouille?" Emily said.

"Uh, Em?" David frowned. "You know that doesn't mean cow, right?"

Her cheeks flushed pink. "Uh—"

"Well, what's being a cow got to do with a spotlight?" I asked. Unless she was a Broadway cow.

"Oh, nothing." Emily sighed. "I just thought she might play nice in front of a new kid for a while."

"She's not nice?"

"Sometimes, but she's just so finicky. Everything has to be done a certain way. If you don't follow her rules to the T, she goes all PMS on you," Emily added, then looked at Ryan.

"Yeah. She's so stuck-up, Ara, like you wouldn't believe. She came from some private school in the city, and she just doesn't understand our ways." Ryan waved his hands about in the air, making 'scary fingers'.

Alana shook her head and smiled into her salad.

So I guess they don't like private school people around here. "Well, *I* come from a private school. I'm not stuck-up, am I?" I asked.

"*You* come from a private school? No way." Ryan leaned back in his seat, making a cross with his index fingers.

"Yes way." I sipped my milk to wash down my lunch. "It's nothing like this place. A different world."

"So where did you go to school?" Alana finally spoke up.

"Really far away."

"How far?" Ryan asked.

"Very far."

"Yeah, you have a bit of an accent there. What is that? British?" Emily leaned in slightly, as did Ryan and Alana, and the eager curiosity in their eyes made me want to smile—until I looked at David. I wasn't sure if he didn't care, or didn't want to know, but he sat still, with his fingers clasped just in front of his simple smile, as if he wasn't interested in the slightest.

"Okay. Promise you won't laugh." I pointed at each one of them in turn.

Ryan crossed his heart. Emily crossed her fingers, laughing already.

"I'm from Australia." Almost closing my eyes, I awaited the onslaught of giggling and pigeonholing, but they just gawked at me.

"No way, you're all the way from Oz? You're totally like Dorothy," Ryan said.

"Yeah, and that makes David Toto." Emily laughed.

"Yeah, um, Dorothy was from Kansas," I said. "If anything, I'd be the Cowardly Lion."

"No, the Tin Man. Didn't that Aussie guy play the Tin Man in that play?" Emily looked up at the ceiling as though her answer would be there.

"No way—Tin Man? Ara has too much heart," Alana added. "You saw her play the piano."

I tilted my head and sighed mockingly. "Aw, thanks."

When Alana ditched a piece of lettuce at me, David's hand shot out and caught it—right in front of my face. My mouth dropped and everyone else burst out laughing. "Nice catch, David."

"He used to play baseball," Emily said.

"Really?" I turned to look at him.

"It was"—he stood up and reached across the table to drop the lettuce on Alana's plate—"a long time ago."

"So, all the way from Australia, hey? You don't *sound* Australian," Emily teased.

"Actually, I do. Just not so much anymore." I smiled softly. "I've spent the last month or so working on my accent, but you can hear it when I get upset."

David shifted awkwardly in his chair.

"Are you ashamed of it?" Alana asked.

"No." I shook my head. "I just didn't wanna draw any extra attention to myself."

"So, is it different over there to, like, how school is here?" Emily held a forkful of carrot just in front of her mouth, waiting.

"Yeah. In ways. I mean, we have our school year from January to December, and we break for summer as well, except it's over Christmas."

"Christmas in summer?" Ryan stared into the distance. "Weird. But cool."

"Actually, it's not cool," I said. "It's really bloody hot."

Emily and Ryan stared at me blankly.

Alana stifled a soft giggle. "Summer is hot, Ryan?" She nudged his arm. "Not cool."

I looked at David, who shook his head. Emily and Ryan did the same, half smiling.

"Okay, that goes in the vault as the worst joke of the week." Ryan pointed at me again with his ketchup-covered chip.

I feigned insult.

"But you did sound very Australian when you said *bloody*," Emily added.

David chuckled beside me.

"Yeah, say it again?" Ryan leaned forward, turning his ear toward me, making a funnel of his hand.

"She's not a circus freak, Ryan." Emily pushed his hand down.

"Thanks," I mouthed, and with my belly full, all my pre-rehearsed questions came flooding back. "So, where do you guys normally sit?"

"Well," Emily chimed in, "David sits with the giant, incredibly gorgeous guys throwing food at each other." She grinned at David. "More like gorillas, really. And I sit with that group out there by the tree." She pointed to the windows covering the back wall of the cafeteria. Outside in the sunshine, a large group of cliché-ridden boys and girls gathered under a big oak tree, laughing and throwing water.

David leaned closer and whispered, "Second in command."

I wondered where that placed me if I hung out with one from each group.

Emily's voice trailed back in suddenly with my attention span. "Ryan hangs out on the basketball courts, mostly." She looked at Ryan for confirmation; he shrugged with a small nod. "And Alana hangs with those guys." She pointed to the music class kids.

"Cool." I nodded. "Well, thanks for keeping me company today, you guys. I would've felt like a total loser sitting by myself."

"That would never happen." Emily tilted her head to the side. "Someone would've come and talked to you. If they could get past David, that is." She threw him a mock-annoyed stare.

David grinned and leaned back in his chair, resting his hands behind his head, making his cologne obvious again. "Can you blame me? I kinda like fresh meat."

I jokingly inched away from him as if he might eat me, and a sudden whoosh of air brushed past my hair, impacting something that screeched loudly.

Silence washed over the room.

We all turned to the kid behind us, who sat straight again, rubbing his head.

"What gives?" His friend stood up, aiming his voice at the gorillas.

"What up, losers? Mommy forget to pack your helmet?"

Apple pulp covered the boy's hair and Chess Club jacket, while the remainder of the offending fruit rolled around on the ground just near his feet. "That's it," he said, and with his fists tight by his side, he jumped up and grabbed the apple.

"Just leave it, Dominic. It's not worth it," one of his friends said.

"No. I'm sick of this." His knuckles turned white around the apple.

No one in the room seemed to have moved. I think they were bracing for an all-out war. But someone should have done *something*. If even one person stood up for that boy, just once, maybe those jerks would leave him alone.

I pushed my chair out, and as I took a step toward him, Emily squeaked, "David? Don't!"

My eyes flicked from Dominic's suddenly empty hand to the other side of the cafeteria, where apple juice rained in a shower over the ducking gorillas, a million tiny pieces of pulp sticking to the wall behind them.

A cool silence lingered. David's arm came back down to his side, his shoulder still leaned into a throw I hadn't even seen him take.

The whole room erupted then. Every person, sitting or standing, started clapping and cheering. Even the gorilla that threw the apple raised his thumb.

David took a few pats on the back and shook a few hands, and when he looked at me again, his eyes oddly round with anger, I closed my gaping mouth and walked up to the damaged kid.

"Hey, are you okay?" I asked.

"Yeah, I'm fine," he moaned and sat back down, rubbing his head. "Those guys are just assholes."

"Yeah. They had no right to do that. I'm so sorry. If I hadn't moved, it would've hit me."

"Guess it's good you moved then." He gave me a smirk, his whole face still red.

"Nah, I can handle embarrassment pretty well."

"Lucky you."

I smiled softly at him. "Are you sure you're okay?"

He nodded, and shifted his black knight to another square on the chessboard. "I'm used to it."

"Yeah, but you owe David for saving your ass like that, Dom," one of the other guys piped up, still laughing.

"Saving it?" I said.

"David's friends with those jerks, so he can get away with it, but if Dom had thrown that apple, those guys would make his life hell!"

"And they don't now?" I asked.

He glanced back at David before quickly looking away, and the fear in his eyes tipped a bucket of realization over me. "David doesn't normally stand up for people, does he?"

The boy just moved his next chess piece, ignoring me.

"We'd rather not say." His friend put his head down too. "Can you just leave us alone now before you get us in more trouble?"

"Sure," I said, backing away, feeling heavy with the idea that maybe I was wrong about David. Maybe he wasn't all that great.

David dropped his head as I turned around, tension making a stiff line across his shoulders. I sat down beside him again and waited, but he didn't look at me. "So you're a bully—like those fruit-throwing jerks?"

"Really, Ara," Emily said. "He sits with them, but he's not like them at all. Anymore."

Anymore? I searched his face for a second, but he kept his gaze on the table between his wrists, darkened by what I read to be shame, as if maybe he knew how strongly I felt about this sort of thing.

"Those kids behind us clearly disagree," I said.

Emily took a breath to speak, but David cut in. "Look, I *was* a jackass, Ara. When I first came to the school, I used to do stuff like that all the time."

"But not anymore?" I blinked, studying the side of his face.

"It takes a long time for people to forget," Emily said. "And—"

"I had hoped it might be some time before you learned of this. You know what they say—about first impressions." David looked at me with those big green eyes, and all I could think was how unfair it is that guys have thicker, darker lashes than girls.

"I doubt Ara's first impression of you is that you're a jackass, David," Ryan said.

My eyes went from him to David again, humor-laced confusion making them smaller. David Knight, school heartthrob and easily the most gorgeous personality I'd ever come across, had *nothing* to worry about. I was the one doing the worrying. "Why the hell would you be worried about *my* first impression of *you*?"

David exhaled slowly through his nose.

I wanted to laugh. "Look, even if you were a bully once, what you did for that kid *today* was really nice. Jackasses don't generally do things like that."

"And neither do fragile, very breakable young girls." He grew taller in his seat, his tone sharp. "Do you have any idea what those guys would have done to you if you'd thrown that apple at them?"

I inhaled a huff of insult. "I can take care of myself, thank you," I scolded. "How'd you even know I was gonna throw it back at them?"

"I could tell—from the way you charged forward, guns blazing."

"Really, Ara. You should avoid revenge throws when it comes to fruit at this school," Emily warned.

"Yeah," Ryan added. "We've had kids hospitalized with lemons in places they don't belong."

I cringed, hiding my disgust. "Well, I went to an all-girls' school. I know how to hold my own."

"Sure. Until you hit the wrong person in the head, and they come after you," Ryan said.

I doubted they'd come after a teacher's daughter. "I'd be okay. I've done self-defense training."

"Seriously?" Emily sat taller.

"Yeah, kind of. My friend's a cop, so he taught me how to fight off rapists and stuff."

"Cool. You should teach us some moves." Emily motioned to herself and Alana.

"Won't matter, Ara," Ryan said. "If they know you've done self-defense, they'll make a point of showing you how weak you really are. And you're like"—he presented me with a flat palm—"tiny. They'd pin you in two-point-one nanoseconds and they have no qualms about hitting girls."

David glowered at Ryan then looked back at me, turning his whole body to face mine. "Look, the fact is, they don't care who you are or who you hang out with. If they get it in for you, you might as well leave the school."

"Then I'd just leave."

"Precisely why it was better for all if I turned it into a game."

"Well, I don't need someone making those decisions for me. If I want to get myself in trouble, that's my prerogative." I folded my arms, sounding too Aussie on the last word.

After a second, David breathed out through his nose, his shoulders sinking. "You're right. I'm sorry I stepped in; it was not my intention to offend you. I just didn't want..." His jaw went tight as his eyes narrowed, tracing every inch of my face like I was the most irritating person in the world, which made me angry.

"It's an apple bomb," I said. "Get over it."

"It's not the apple bomb I have a problem with." He sat back a little, gaining distance. "It's you and your altruistic need to get yourself marked as a target."

Altruistic? Me? Boy, he so did not know me. I cleared my throat, half aware of all the eyes at our table bearing down on David and me.

"Why would that irritate you so much? You don't even know me. I'm not your problem."

My words only made him rub his brow. He took a long breath, turning the tension around the table into dense air. "Ara. You just don't get it."

"Don't get it? Don't get *what*?" I wanted to stand up so I could yell. "That you had no right to play white knight and step in when I was going to help someone. I am not a little girl. I can take care of myself."

He opened his mouth then closed it quickly. "You know what, fine. Go ahead. Throw a damn apple at them, and see what they do to you."

"Fine." I stood up and grabbed the apple off Alana's plate.

"Whoa!" David had his hand on my wrist before I even drew it back by my side. "I was bluffing, Ara."

A smirk formed laughter in the back of my throat, my shoulders shaking with the sound. "And I was calling your bluff." I pointed at him, letting him take the apple. "You should see the look on your face."

Emily and Ryan laughed, but Alana just looked ultimately worried. David, however, drew a breath to support a probably very massive tongue-lashing.

"So, Ara?" Emily interjected. "You moved over here from Oz. Why?"

My posture drooped. Not likely noticeable, but enough to make me feel smaller. David sat down again, and I followed with a little too much weight in the slump.

"I… uh." As I scanned the room, wishing the gorillas would throw a banana or something, David reached across to grab the salt from my tray and somehow managed to knock my milk carton flat. Everyone jumped back just as chocolate rivers spread across the plastic table, trickling onto the floor right where our feet had been.

"Ara, I'm sorry. That was an accident." He pushed our trays out of the mess, shaking his head. "I'll get a sponge."

After he walked away, I looked at Emily, and we both broke into laughter.

David didn't know it, but he just saved me from having to explain my tragic life. I owed him. Big time.

When the bell rang, I stacked my tray on the trolley and smacked straight into David's chest as I turned around. "Crap. You scared me!"

"Sorry." He smiled and placed his tray on mine, staying awkwardly close to me. I took half a step back so I could look up at him without straining my neck. "Are you okay, Ara?"

I crossed my arms over my chest and hunched my shoulders a little. "Why would you ask that?"

He glanced around the almost empty lunchroom before speaking. "I've seen you avoid the topic of your family and your home twice today."

"And?"

He closed the gap I made between us. "And I just want you to know that I am an excellent listener."

"I—" I couldn't speak with his body so close, distracting me. His lips nearly brushed my hair as I nodded, and the heat of his warm, sweet breath—with an underlying cool, like he'd just had a mint—trickled over the bridge of my nose. I took another step back from him, afraid I might accidentally stand on my toes and kiss him. "I… um. It's nothing. I'm fine. I just—" really should've made up some elaborate lie before I came to this school, is all.

"Okay." David exhaled, standing taller. "Like I said, I'll be here when you want to talk. I can see there's something bothering you. I don't have to know you to notice that."

"Well. That's… a little bit concerning." I laughed it off, but I was worried others might notice. "Look, when I need a friend, I promise you'll be the first person I come to."

He looked into my eyes for a long moment. I wondered what he could see there. I'd been told my emotions displayed themselves on my face, but for my sake, I really hoped not.

"Come on." He ushered with a nod. "Let's get you to class."

The shrill peal of a whistle summoned football practice to start behind me, and the dull thud of a boot on the ball made my skin itch to be off the field. But I wasn't ready to go home, so I perched myself on a tree stump at the edge of the road and looked at the white house on the corner. It was like a different world over there. The maple trees lined the paths on both sides of the street, and behind them sat quaint little houses—whimsical yet mysterious—like something from a fairy tale. They were pretty much all the same as my dad's, just different colors; some grey, some olive green, but mostly white. The kind of houses that, on the fourth of July, had flags hanging from the porches and kids running from the long, grass-lined driveways, waving sparklers around. Most houses had low wooden fences around their backyards—to keep their dogs in—but ours was a hedge fence because my stepmother had an aversion to Man's Best Friend. Instead, we had an overfed cat, whose one value was keeping my feet warm in winter. I could see his tail sticking out from behind the gutter over the porch, the same place he was sitting last time he fell from the roof. Stupid cat.

"Hey, Ara."

I looked up, squinting in the sun. "Hi?"

"Do you live around here, or are you lost?" asked a lanky boy with sandy hair.

"Uh, yeah. I live just over there." I pointed across the road.

"The house with the blue door?"

"Yeah."

"Hm." He nodded, thoughtful. "That's pretty cool. Ours is brown."

I chuckled. I knew he was just trying to be friendly and make conversation. I didn't think he really cared about the color of the door. "Yeah, blue is supposed to bring good luck."

His lips tightened. "Didn't know that."

"Yeah." I nodded. "Well, red's actually good luck. But, I didn't have the heart to tell my mom. She's old. She gets confused," I joked.

"You should just paint it red then, and tell her it's blue. She probably won't even notice." He smiled down at me and extended his hand. "I'm Spencer, by the way."

"Hi." I shook it.

"Well, since you're not lost and don't need saving, I better go. Later." He flipped his chin before walking across the road, disappearing into the shade of dancing maple leaves.

Dad was right. I nodded to myself. The kids here weren't so bad.

"You can go in," someone muttered sarcastically from behind.

"Hey, Sam."

"Hey. What ya starin' at?"

"Cat's up on the roof again."

He chuckled. "So go get him down."

"No way. I already fell off that roof. Not planning to do it again."

"Ha! Yeah, I remember that. What were you, like, seven?"

"Six, actually." I looked at the second story of the house. "And you shouldn't laugh. It was a big fall. I could've been killed."

"Mom thought you were, remember?"

"No."

"Don't you remember her running down the stairs behind Dad? '*She's dead! Oh, my God, Greg, she's dead*'. Vivid memory." He tapped his temple. I chuckled. He imitated a very good version of Vicki's panicky voice. "That was my first traumatic experience, y'know? And I owe it all to you."

"Well. You're welcome." I rolled my eyes.

"Isn't that why Dad bricked up your balcony door—and put a desk there?"

"Yes. But probably also 'cause it's harder to sneak out a window than a door."

Sam smiled, and somewhere, as the day had gone on, despite what I felt for him this morning, I kind of felt a pang of a connection then —seeing my dad's eyes in his.

"Do you smell that?" he asked.

"Yeah, Vicki's making casserole." I inhaled the scent of gravy and Italian herb.

Sam took off running. "I'll race you."

"Hey. No fair. You got a head start!" I darted after him, catching up as we both jumped the creaky bottom step of the porch then burst through the front door.

"Sam? Ara-Rose, is that you?" Vicki called from the kitchen.

"Who else would it be?" Sam muttered to me as we dumped our schoolbags on the staircase.

"Come in here and have a snack before homework please," she called.

As I walked into the dining area, Italian herb blended warmly with garlic and onion, sparking a flashback of cold winters and roast dinners. But the oak dining table by the window—littered with Vicki's scrapbooking mess—and the island counter sitting center to a dark wood kitchen held too much class above the little beach house I grew up in, obliterating any sense of 'coming home' after a long day.

"Did you shut the front door? You're letting all the cool air out," Vicki yapped from her position at the counter.

Sam waltzed past, grabbing an apple from the fruit bowl. "Sorry. I got homework to do. Ara-Rose can shut it."

"What, like I *don't* have homework?"

He shrugged, biting his apple, and wandered into the forbidden formal rooms through an archway on the other side of the kitchen.

"You're such a pain, Sam."

"Be nice, Ara-Rose," Vicki warned.

I groaned and headed back to the entranceway, shut the front door, then stomped into the kitchen again.

"Tough day?" Vicki asked.

"No. Why?"

"You just seem moodier than your usual self."

"Moody? I'm never moody." I grabbed an apple and plonked into a dining chair facing the window. Outside, football practice was in full swing across the road, with shirtless guys running back and forth over the grass. I kind of wished David was on the team this year so I could sit on the tree stump and watch him train. Then again, Vicki would probably be sitting right here in the chair watching me watch him. I knew she'd been sitting in it just before we came in, probably watching me talk to that Spencer kid, because the seat was still warm.

"So?" Vicki prompted. "How was school?"

That question hit my ears like bad news, because it so clearly wasn't just a light-hearted attempt at decent conversation. It was a probe. She wanted me to tell her she was right—that school wasn't as bad as I thought—and busying herself washing coriander couldn't disguise that meddlesome undertone. She should've known better. After all, it was her profession. Okay, so she hadn't worked as a psychiatrist since she married my dad, but she still practiced—on me.

"School was fine," I muttered absently, fingering through the mess of photos and cardboard frames.

"Did you make any friends?"

"No one makes friends on the first day, Vicki."

"Oh. I'm sorry to hear that."

She wasn't sorry. She didn't really care.

"Did you see any cute guys?" Her tone became light, inclusive.

With a short sigh, I bit into my apple, licking the sweet juice as it spilled onto my lip.

"Ara-Rose?" she prompted.

"What?"

"I asked you a question."

I sat back, closing my eyes slowly. I really didn't want another mom. I didn't want to have these cozy after-school conversations about boys and friends with anyone but my real mom. But Vicki wasn't going to let this go. She was hell-bent on 'assessing' me this afternoon, when all I wanted was to sink inside myself and brew over my troubles. But if I didn't attempt to play along, she'd tell my dad I was exhibiting asocial behavior again.

"Ara-Rose?" she said, standing right beside me.

"Cute guys? Uh… yes." I grinned widely, keeping my face down. "A guy that's so cute he makes Stefan look like a dweeb."

"Who's Stefan?"

I groaned. "Never mind. He's cute, he's fictional, that's all that matters."

"Do you… like him?"

"Who, Stefan?"

"No, this boy you saw today."

"Like him?"

"Yeah, do you like him?" she repeated. "As more than a friend?"

Yes, I do. "No. I just met him. But he's cute."

She exhaled, her shoulders sinking. The movement was small, but so obvious to me. I was accustomed to the casual displays of indifference she used in order to psychologically assess or relate to me. She counted on the fact that I was a docile teen with no clue what went on around me. Clearly, she'd never been a teenager. I knew all the tricks, and I never gave anything away about my psychological well-being, or lack thereof. I wouldn't give her the satisfaction. I knew that falling for a guy on the first meeting was a very clear indication that I was *not* okay, and I knew it spelled trouble to come. But he made me feel happy, and I was not going to let her 'rationalize' that away.

She walked away again, and I shifted the photos until the dark wood of the table bared itself from under them. Not one of those photos was of me. I had spent every summer and at least six winters here since I was a child, but the absence of my face in these scrapbooks was just another indicator that I really was just a walk-in—a temporary fixture made permanent by circumstance. I was like a painting you hung on the wrong wall using your last nail.

"Did you sit with anyone at lunch?" Vicki asked.

I spun around again and watched her fussing about near the stove. "Yes."

"Well, that's good. I knew you wouldn't end up sitting alone, even though you were *so sure* you would." She laughed lightly.

"Guess you were right."

She ignored my disingenuous tone, tipping the chopping block over the pot and breaking the cloud of steam with the veggies. "So, do you like any of your teachers?"

"No." But my friend likes your husband.

"What about Dad? You're in his class, right?"

"Yeah, but he gives boring lectures." I assume. Not that I was listening.

"Well, don't tell him that. You'll hurt his feelings."

Almost as if his past self heard me, his smiling face stood out among the pile of photos. He was so much younger in this picture. His hair was darker and the crinkles around his eyes weren't as deep.

Vicki was younger, too. Her hair was still the same straight blonde, but the smile lines hadn't yet formed on her thin white face. They were abysmal now, running down from her nose to the outside corners of her mouth like a V… for Vicki.

"What did you think of the cafeteria food?" Vicki asked, tasting her casserole.

I spun my apple core between my fingers and watched her rinse the spoon off under the faucet. "It was okay. Pricey, though."

"Shall I give you some extra money tomorrow—did you have enough today?" She looked up with round eyes of concern.

"Actually, I didn't use my own money."

"Well, how—"

"Someone offered to spot me." Well, forced me to let them.

"Oh, that was nice. Who was it?"

"A guy named David Knight."

"Hm. David… David," she muttered his name under her breath, her brow wrinkles deepening. "Nope. Never heard of him."

I shrugged.

"Well," she said, "sounds like you've made an impression, Ara-Rose. I told you people would like you. You're a very lovely girl."

I dropped the snotty teen facade and sat back against my chair. It was hard to be hostile when she was being genuinely nice. For once. "Um thanks. I mean, that's great and all, but I don't think being a *lovely girl* is an asset in high school these days, Vicki. Also, I'm just gonna go by Ara now."

"Oh really? But you always loved your name. What does your dad think of that?"

"Well, it's *my* name."

"But you were given the name Rose for a reason, dear. I know it would break your fathe—"

"Mike always called me just Ara, Vicki. It doesn't bother me, so it shouldn't bother my dad."

"Okay." She nodded and turned back to the stove. "If you're sure."

But I wasn't sure. I didn't want to drop the Rose. I didn't want to go to a new school, make new friends—pretend to be something I just wasn't sure I could be anymore. And being called 'Ara' was a constant and painful reminder of the friend back home that I'd never see again.

"I'll be in my room," I said, shoving my chair out and tossing my apple into the bin. "I have a lot of homework to do."

"Okay, *Ara*," Vicki called after me with a hint of detest behind my new name.

Why did she have to make it worse? She could just be nice about it —supportive, even. I mean, in what twisted version of this life was I supposed to seek my dad's permission to omit my middle name?

"Is Mom still cooking?" Sam asked, coming in through the arch that led to the den.

"Yes, why?"

He grinned and dropped his books in his schoolbag, then dumped it back on the stair. "I'm gonna watch TV. Don't tell, okay?"

"She'll hear it."

He held up his wireless headphones.

"Whatever," I said, then grabbed my bag and stomped up the stairs. I pushed my door open, and the tension of the day trickled away a little as the afternoon sun reached through the crystals hanging over my window and splashed dancing prisms across my lemon walls.

Back home, I'd lie on my bed in the afternoon sun, talking to my best friend Mike on the phone and watching the prancing spectrums perform their final act for the day. But here, my window faced east, giving me only morning sun. Dad somehow knew how much that daily routine meant to me, so he bought *Plane Mirrors* that we'd positioned carefully outside, so they'd catch the light of the retiring sun and cast it onto my crystals. It was just a little piece of magic from a lost life that he wanted me to hold onto.

"Homework. Now," I heard Vicki say from downstairs.

"But, Mom," Sam whined.

"Now."

I smiled to myself and shut my door, kicking my shoes to random corners as I flopped backward on my bed and let out a long sigh.

It was over. The torturous first day was over.

"See?" I called across to the girl in the mirror. "It wasn't that bad."

"Muuuum!" Sam yelled from the hallway. "Ara-Rose is talking to herself again."

"Shut up, Sam!" I threw a pillow at the back of my door.

"Time to call the men in white coats," he yelled.

"That's enough, Samuel," Vicki said loudly.

Sam's boisterous cackle faded down the hall, but he'd left a great cloud of infuriation behind him. I huffed out loud. Talking to myself did not make me crazy. Hearing myself answer back did, but… let's not go there.

I smiled then, thinking about my day; thinking about how David said he liked me, and how I read into that so poorly I couldn't even speak after. I think he took it pretty well, though. He didn't make me feel like a total loser. Well, until Society and Environment class, when he corrected the teacher on the Emancipation Proclamation. It wasn't even on topic, but it took one simple comment from a kid up the back, and our discussion on North America turned into a full-blown slavery debate. David, rather heatedly, put everyone in their place. I stayed quiet through the whole thing, but his mere presence made me want to pick up a book and read it. I think he had that effect on everyone—even the teacher.

"Ara?" Vicki knocked on my door.

I jumped up and sat at my desk, quickly grabbing my books from my bag. "Yeah?"

"Dad called—asked if you need some help with homework," she said through the door.

"Um. No, thanks," I said.

"Okay. Well, just give him a call if you do," she added. "He's supervising detention today."

"Got it," I said. I waited another few seconds, and when she added nothing else, spun around to face the window. The day outside was so bright and the afternoon breeze had settled among the leaves of my oak tree, rocking the rope swing in a soothing wave as if to say, "Come to us, Ara-Rose." And I wanted to. I really did, which made homework feel like a rock of pressure on my neck.

I looked at the pink phone on my desk and slowly pulled my nail from between my teeth, grabbing the handset quickly to dial Dad's mobile.

"Ara?"

"Hi, Dad."

"Hey, how was school today, honey?"

"Um, great. So, I was just… I'm a bit stressed, Dad—with homework. Can I…"

"Why don't you leave it for today?" he said, and I grinned. "Maybe just do a bit of reading, and I'll talk to your teachers for you. Sound good?"

I breathed a sigh of relief, which was maybe a little forced. "Thanks, Dad. That'd really help."

"Okay. That's good then. Hey, since you're finally using that phone I got you, why don't you call your pal in Australia? I know he's—"

"Dad. No."

"Ara, he's been calling every day."

"Yeah, but he's stopped now, right? You said he hasn't called for a week."

He went quiet for a moment. "That's not necessarily a good thing, honey."

I sighed heavily, resting my head on my hand. It wouldn't be easy to talk to my best friend again. I wasn't even sure I had the right to after evading his calls so often. And then there was the shame…

"Ara-Rose, he cares about you. He's just worried—just wanted to make sure you're doing okay."

"I know, Dad."

"Then why not give him a call? Maybe after that you can sit back and read a book for a while?"

"I just… what if he hangs up on me, because I ignored him for so long?"

Dad laughed. "Just call him."

I jammed my thumbnail between my teeth again. "Okay. Maybe I'll think about it."

"That's great. Now, go rest up, and don't stress over homework, okay? I promised you we'd ease you back into this slowly, so that's what we'll do."

"Thank you, Dad."

"Anytime, honey. Bye."

"Bye." I hung up and, before placing the handset down again, flipped it over and stared at the numbers. I'd dialed Mike's number so many times I could do it with my toes if I wanted, but it took me a minute, as I stared at the phone, to remember the first digit. And in that moment, a pocket of fear crept in, asking me what I was going to talk to him about. I mean, what would I say? *"Hi, Mike. I haven't called to see if you're coping, but I just wanted to let you know that I'm not. That I feel tired and sad all the time. That I went to school today, and fell in love with a boy at first sight, and I'm pretty sure I might be going insane, because that's just not normal. But I thought I'd just tell you that, because you have no reason to care how I feel anymore after I've ignored you the way I have. And I was hoping maybe you'd be jealous of me liking another guy, but that's just never going to happen, is it? And I don't know how I can face you, knowing now that you never loved me the way I thought I loved you."*

With a sigh, I looked at the phone again.

"Go on," it teased.

I pinned the number in, my hand shaking, and it only rang twice before the husky voice on the other end made my heart jump, reminding me of everything I loved about him. "Hello?"

"Hey, Mike."

"Ara?"

"Yeah. It's me."

"Hey, kid. How you doin'?" His voice pitched high on the end, making a pathway from my ears to my soul and guiding me all the way back home.

"Um—" I scratched the wood grain on my desk. "I'm good."

"How'd your first day go?"

"How did you know I was starting school today?"

"I spoke to your dad on Saturday."

"Oh."

"So…?" he said. "How was it?"

"Um, well, it was good, actually."

"Really?" He exhaled. "That's great. I've been worried 'bout ya all night. I haven't even slept."

"Oh crud, the time difference thing." I slapped my forehead. "I'm sorry, Mike. Should I go?"

"No. No, of course not." I heard a ruffling sound on his end and imagined him sitting up in bed, his black cotton sheets looking blue in the moonlight under him. "So, did you make any friends yet?"

"I did." I grinned, then Mike got the run down on all the happenings of the day: Emily, Alana, how cool Ryan was—a tiny bit about David—and a massively overdramatized recap on music class with Mr. Grant.

"No joke? What an ass." Mike laughed. "I wish I'd been there. I would've played Chopsticks and deliberately done a bad job of it."

"I know you would. I was thinking about that while I was playing." I chuckled.

"You were thinking about me?"

I nodded, even though he couldn't see it. "I really missed you today."

A heavy silence lingered for a moment. "I… I'm actually really glad to hear that."

"Really?"

"Yeah," he said quietly. "I just. Ara, about that night…"

"Can we not talk about the past?" I said quickly. "Can we just talk about… normal stuff, please?"

After seventeen years of knowing Mike, I could tell from his tone that he didn't want to brush things under a rug, but for the sake of my mental health he said, "Sure thing."

"So…" Right, normal stuff. I could think of something normal to talk about, right? Um... "What've you been up to the last few months?"

He exhaled heavily, probably running a hand through his sandy hair. "Well, you know how I applied to Tactical last year?"

"Yeah?" I said, getting excited at the excitement in his voice.

"I've got one more interview to go, and I'm pretty much in."

"You're kidding me? Mike, that's so awesome. I can't believe you've finally done it."

"Well, don't jinx it. I haven't made it yet."

"Yeah right. You're, like, super fit and super smart. You were in when you were born, and you know it."

"Yeah. I know. Hey, listen, I was thinking... once I make it in, I've got a few weeks before training begins. Can I come see you?"

"Are you kidding?" I stood up, practically squealing. "Of course you can. I'd love that. There's so much I wanna show you, and I really want to talk to you about this guy, and—" I paused, trying to reel my words back in.

"What guy?" Mike's tone changed with interest. I pictured his face, the way the corners of his lips would turn up under his rough sandy-brown stubble and make my heart do flips. But all that had changed now. He didn't want me to love him like that, so maybe moving on with someone else would ease some of the longing I still felt.

"I really need your advice actually." I slumped back down in my chair.

"Sure, I'm good for it. What's the deal?"

"Well, his name's David."

"The one who showed you around today?"

Does he not miss anything? I barely even mentioned David. "Yeah, except I left everything out. He didn't just show me around, Mike. He, like, I don't know, he stayed with me *all* day and didn't really make a secret of the fact that he likes me. And... I kinda *really* like him."

"Well... that's great, right?"

"No."

"What's the problem then?"

"After one day?" I looked out at the corner of the school's front parking lot, just visible from my window. "Does that make me creepy?"

"How long did it take you to fall completely in love with Leopold?" he asked, referring to my favorite movie.

"That's different."

"How?"

"Because Leopold's not real. David is, and I'm not some character in a love story."

"Ara?" Mike groaned. "You've always been like this."

"What?" I asked, defensive.

"You like a guy, flirt with him, befriend him, but whenever"—he cleared his throat—"*whenever* they like you, show the tiniest bit of interest, you run the other way. I don't know, it's like you're afraid they're gonna wake up one day and realize you're not that pretty or something."

I pressed my lips together, closing my eyes. "You know me better than I thought."

"I know I do, Ara. I'm your best bud. Now stop worrying, and just let yourself like this David guy, if that's what he wants, too. I mean, you said he likes you back, right?" He sounded so mature, so unlike my Mike—my fun-loving, carefree Mike.

"Yeah, but—"

"But what? You're afraid that liking someone you just met means you're abnormal?"

"Well, yeah. Kind of." I shrugged, scraping at the wood grain.

"It's not creepy or weird if you both feel the same way. And, do you think *he's* creepy for liking you?"

I might if he liked me the way I like him. "No."

"So, then, you're not creepy—you're a teenager. You're supposed to fall head-over-heels with every guy who has a cute smile." He laughed.

"I guess you're kinda right." What harm could it do falling for a guy I just met?

"I *know* I am," he said. "So just don't sweat it, kiddo. I mean, don't go marrying the guy or confessing your love for him tomorrow, but don't worry if you're a bit hot for him, either. It's not gonna hurt anyone at this stage. And you could use the distraction."

I shook my head, smiling. "How do you always know what to say to make my head clearer?"

"You do the same to me when I'm having a girl crisis."

"Yeah, how are things on that front?"

He groaned loudly. "Well, the last time a girl kissed me, she ran away from me after. So, I think I'm pretty well done with chicks for now."

I sighed and leaned on my hand, wishing I could be the last girl he'd ever kiss. But the Friend Zone had been firmly established, and I needed to stay on my side of the line. "I should go, Mike. I asked Dad to get me out of homework, and now I feel kinda bad."

"Why?"

"I told him I was too stressed, but I actually just couldn't be bothered doing it."

Mike laughed. "Good to see you're still the same Ara."

I smirked, not sure if that was an insult or an observation.

"Okay," he said in a tone that began the end of the conversation. "Well, keep ya chin up. I'll come see you in a few weeks, okay?"

"Yeah, that'll be great."

"Talk to you later."

"Bye." I hung up the phone, and the room felt suddenly empty, like I'd just caught the first vortex back to my cold new reality.

"ARA?" DAD SOUNDED PANICKED.

I flung my door open and the concern on his face dropped instantly.

"What were you doing, honey? I've called you six times."

"Sorry, Dad. I was reading the compulsory books for English class. I had my earphones in."

"Oh." He seemed surprised. "Any good books?"

"Eh." I nodded, rolling my shoulder forward.

"Well, I spoke to your teachers and—"

"Um, about that, Dad," I said as we walked down the stairs. "I think I'll be okay. I can handle a little homework."

He smiled widely and pulled my chair out at the dining table for me. "Good girl. I'm very glad to hear that."

As I sat down, I glanced at Sam who, for the first time since I moved here, didn't smile at me. He pushed his vegetables around his plate with his fork, hiding under his baseball cap. Poor Sam. I felt bad that he'd suddenly inherited a permanent sister after fourteen years being an only child. And I guess maybe that's why he picked on me so much, but something else seemed to be bothering him tonight.

"Samuel." Dad's stern voice made us both look up as he sat down. "Cap, son."

Sam sighed to himself, slipping his baseball cap off and dropping it to the floor without protest.

Weird.

"So, Ara met a boy today," Vicki said, serving a pile of peas onto Dad's plate.

Dad winked at me.

"He knows," I said, my cheeks burning. "He already interrogated him."

"I did not interrogate him. What ever gave you that impression?"

"I saw you talking to him—in class."

"Oh." Dad scratched his brow. "Yes, that. Well, I might've *lightly* threatened his safety. A little."

Vicki sat back down beside Dad. "You didn't? Greg, how's the poor girl supposed to make a life for herself here if you scare off all the kids that look at her sideways?"

"That was more than a sideways glance, Vicki." Dad chuckled, sprinkling salt all over his dinner. "I used to be a boy myself, remember."

She shook her head and snatched the salt. He reached for it again, and without so much as looking at him, Vicki moved it away.

"It's okay, Vi-er-Mom," I said teasingly. "His grilling didn't work anyway. David still walked *everywhere* with me."

"David? As in… David *Knight*?" Sam almost rocketed forward.

"Yeah. So?"

"David's a nice kid," Dad said in an almost warning tone.

"He's a bully!" Sam demanded.

Dad's lips turned down with thought. "I don't know about that. We teachers have never heard sultanas about him."

"Sultanas?" My forehead twitched. "Dad, is that some kind of weird teacher-lingo?"

"Actually. It is."

"Sultanas are bad gossip on the grapevine," Sam informed.

"And grapes are good gossip," Dad finished.

"So, where do sour grapes come in?" I said.

Four long lines formed across the top of Dad's brow. "You know what? We don't have one for sour grapes. I'll bring that one up in the lunchroom tomorrow." He nodded, spooning casserole into his mouth.

"So, no sultanas about David then? That's good," Vicki said, eyeing me. "Must be rare?"

"It is, actually. We teachers scamper about the halls, unnoticed, so we get some good gossip, and believe me"—Dad winked at Sam—"I hear it *all.*"

Sam shuffled in his seat. Dad looked away, chuckling to himself.

"Okay. What have you done, Samuel?" Vicki asked, sounding kind of bored.

"Nothing." Sam looked her right in the eye.

She focused intently on him for a moment, then laid her napkin slowly beside her plate. "You might as well tell me, Sam. I will find out one way or the other."

Sam liquefied.

"Spill it. Now."

"I got a lunch-time detention today."

"Why?" Vicki asked.

He stayed quiet.

"Sam!" Vicki reached across and took the salt from Dad again, her eyes never leaving Sam's face. "Either you tell me, or I come into the school for an appointment with the principal."

Sam stewed in his own nerves, looking at Dad, who laughed into his plate. "I got caught sneaking into the girls' locker room," he muttered to his chest.

Unable to hold back any longer, Dad burst into a loud, burly laugh, covering his mouth to keep his dinner in. I looked at Vicki, unsure if I should laugh or not, but a smile crept across my lips.

"Greg, I can't believe you weren't going to tell me!"

"I just"—Dad caught his breath, still laughing, the infectious sound spreading over the whole table—"I couldn't."

And then *I* laughed, making Vicki laugh, too.

"What on earth were you going in there for?" she asked.

"It wasn't like you think." Sam's cheeks went bright red.

"Oh, sure. No. A fourteen-year-old boy goes into the girls' locker room to buy a sandwich," Dad joked.

Sam's jaw clenched. I felt a little sorry for him. He obviously didn't want to talk about it. They should be able to see that. And they were probably just making light of the situation, but I felt a sudden urge to protect—something I'd never felt for Sam before.

"So, Dad?" I said. "You know my friend from Australia—Mike? He said he might come over in a few weeks. Can he stay here?"

"Here? You want a boy to stay *here*, under the same roof as you?" Vicki jumped in.

"He's not a boy," I corrected. "He's a man."

"A man? Oh, well that makes it okay then," she said, poorly attempting sarcasm. "How old is Mike now, anyway?"

"He's twenty," I said, and looked at Sam, who mouthed *thank you* before returning to his casserole.

"Twenty? Ara, you're not even eighteen yet. It's against the law."

"Vicki?" I screeched. "Mike and I have *never* been like that with each other. God, we used to take baths together."

"Not to mention, Mom," Sam said, "legal age of consent is sixteen. I checked."

"Now, why on earth would a boy your age be looking up that kind of information?" she asked, horrified.

Sam just smirked.

"Look." Vicki closed her eyes for a second. "I'm sorry, Ara-Rose. I'm just not used to having a daughter. I"—she exhaled—"I just don't want anything bad to happen to you."

"Well, I appreciate that, Mom," I said with a mouthful of carrot. "But you don't have to worry about Mike. There's this, like, invisible barrier around him that repulses me from loving him that way." Or, more like repulses *him* from loving *me* that way, but I would never admit that aloud.

She nodded. "Well, all right. But when does he want to come?"

"As soon as he gets his acceptance into Tactical—in a few weeks," I beamed.

"What, the SWAT unit?" Dad asked.

"Yeah, that's not what they call it over there, though."

"Is he gonna be a sniper?" Sam asked, sitting taller.

"Um, no." I frowned at him. "But, anyway, he's got one interview left, then he gets a few weeks off before training begins."

"Well, that's great, Ara." Dad reached across and patted my hand, as if this was *my* victory. "It's what he always wanted, isn't it?"

I nodded, swallowing my mouthful. "Yep, he's doing well for himself."

"Shame you don't like him then," Vicki added.

"Nah, he lives in Australia, anyway." I shrugged. "Could be a bit tricky."

"At least you couldn't get pregnant," Dad said with a completely straight face.

I stopped chewing, and Sam coughed a carrot out onto his plate, but Dad just sat there eating and sipping his wine as if nothing had been said.

"Moving on then?" Vicki suggested, raising her glass.

5

Bright yellow sunlight beamed off my mirror and into my eyes, blinding me. I rolled over and faced the wall, snuggling back into the warmth to seek out a few more minutes in the bliss of this cloud-soft bed.

As I fell asleep last night in my own world of fantasies, I came to know David so much better than I did yesterday. Perhaps maybe even well enough to invite him over after school today. Except, that would mean introducing him to Vicki… and cleaning my room. Hm, perhaps not. But I felt grounded today for the first time in so long, and actually ready to have friends again. Maybe because this was the first morning I'd woken without crying since I got here. I'd almost forgotten what that felt like. And I knew it was because of school—because I met David, Emily, Ryan, and Alana yesterday. When I thought about getting out of bed, getting dressed and going to school, I actually felt a bubble of excitement in the place where I used to feel dread.

After finally getting out of bed, I threw on my light denim shorts and a pink tank top, then wandered out of my walk-in robe. The floor rug—woven entirely out of dirty laundry—stared back at me, its evil laughter making demands for the release of my shoes.

"Where are they?" I muttered to myself, lifting a sweater and some jeans then tossing them beside the empty laundry basket.

"You nearly ready for school, Ara?" Vicki asked, opening my door without knocking.

"Yeah. I just can't find my shoes."

"Well, I'm not surprised." She laughed.

"It's not my fault." I stood up, dusting my hands off. "My wardrobe got a stomach flu and threw up all over my room."

"Why don't you go down and have breakfast? I'll find them for you—maybe even tidy up a little."

I smiled at her, about to accept, when I spotted one shoe under my bed. "Ooh, there it is."

She walked in and started picking up clothes, as I sat on my bed and slipped my shoe on. "Here."

"Oh, thanks. Where was it?" I asked, taking it from her.

"Near your dresser. How it got so far away from the other one, I don't know."

I shrugged and, seeing my favorite sweater in the pile of clothes over Vicki's arm, stood up and tugged it out. "I never wash this."

"Why?" she asked, horrified.

"I just… it was Mike's." I hugged it to my chest.

"Fine." She took it from me and laid it over my chair. "Now go down and eat, please. You'll be late for school."

"Okay." I grabbed my schoolbag and, after scoffing down a bowl of oatmeal, practically ran to the front door.

"A little eager today, Ara?" Dad said, dropping a quick kiss to my cheek as I passed him.

All I could do was grin.

"Want a ride to school?"

"Dad? Why don't *you* try walking for once?"

"I have to go 'round the front. Easier to drive."

"Wow, that's so lazy. Walking's better for you."

"I've got better things to do with my time."

"Oh, really? Like what? Work on that heart attack you're trying to have?" I nodded toward his travel mug, which we both knew was full of coffee with way too much cream and sugar.

He saluted me with the mug, taking another sip as he walked away. "Have fun at school, honey."

"Bye," I said, closing the front door behind me, but my conceited smirk went flat when I heard a low growl coming from the end of the porch. Skittles, with his fluffy grey tail thrashing about, sat curled up like a porcupine, hissing and snarling at something. I followed his evil-kitty stare to a boy standing across the road. Just standing there—a guitar case by his feet, eyes on his phone, the sleeves of his black shirt rolled up to just below his elbows. And my heart dropped into my feet.

David.

"Psst. Shut up, Skitz." I stomped on the floorboards.

The cat startled to silence, but his tail kept thrashing.

I wondered if David was maybe waiting for *me*—if he even knew I lived here. Then again, everyone knew which house was Mr. Thompson's, so it was a safe bet I lived here, too.

As I leaped off the porch steps and onto the grass, the frogs in my belly jumped up to my chest, making my heart pound. I didn't know what to say to him, or if he'd even remember me. But that was silly. Why wouldn't he remember me?

All around me, the summer sun warmed the ground, making the grass look almost yellow. I closed my eyes for a second and took a deep breath, tasting the flavor of fresh dew blowing in on the breeze. When I opened them, David looked up and met my smile with a grin, and I practically floated across the road. He looked really sexy in that shirt. It wasn't black, like I first thought, but dark grey, and way too much for my hormones to handle. I almost didn't care if I freaked him out with my ogling. It was his own fault for looking so sexy.

"Hi, David," I said cheerfully—maybe too cheerful.

"Hello, Ara." He took my backpack and tossed it over his free shoulder. "You look pretty."

I bit my lip, practically melting into a puddle. "Um, thanks."

He laughed. "Okay, now you just look pink."

Both hands slowly rose to cover my cheeks. "Well, don't say nice things to me then."

"Okay. But that doesn't leave me a whole lot to say."

I smiled up at him, forgetting every thought when the morning sun beamed down across his hair, highlighting the golden tones and making every strand obvious. I just wanted to run my fingers through it. "I like your hair," I said, instantly snapping to the realization that I just said it out loud.

"Thank you." He grinned mischievously, sweeping his hand through it. "I uh… I grew it myself."

I laughed. "Sorry—forgot to put my brain-to-mouth filter on this morning."

"That's okay. I like you that way." He dropped his hand into his pocket, and my eyes strayed from his hair to his jaw, then down to the top button of his shirt, sitting slightly open to reveal the golden skin beneath. "Ara?"

"Hm?"

"Stop biting your nails." He gently pushed my fingers away from my mouth.

"Oh." I stuffed both hands tightly into my pockets. "Didn't realize I was."

After a soft smile, he started walking. "I know. You do that a lot."

"I know." I grinned sheepishly, then pointed to his guitar case. "What kind of guitar is it?"

"Oh, uh—" He looked down at the case as if he needed reminding. "It's a Maton. Twelve string."

"Nice." I nodded, yawning.

"Did you sleep last night?"

"Actually, I did. For the first time in *months*." I smiled, but dropped it instantly, realizing my response could be bait for more questions. Please don't bite, I thought.

"You don't normally sleep?" he bit.

"Uh. Well. I, um. Yeah, of course I do. I just meant that…" Wow, I'd really put my foot in that one. "I stayed up late talking with a friend last night."

"But you said you slept."

"I did. After." I looked at my feet, wishing he'd just drop it.

"Who's your friend?"

"Huh?"

"Who were you taking to last night?"

"Oh, a guy I grew up with—in Australia."

"*A guy*?"

"Yes. *A guy*."

"And he's… a friend?"

"Yeah."

"Was he a school friend?"

"Not really. I mean, he was a few years ahead of me in primary school, then I went to an all girls' high school so, you know, we played at school as kids, but not once we grew up."

"What did you do then?"

I laughed. "Then? He practically lived at my house, or me at his."

David nodded, his eyes straying slowly forward. "And you miss him? That's why you stayed up talking?"

"I—" I closed my fist around my thumb, resisting the urge to munch it. "I don't really know."

"You don't know if you miss him?" he confirmed.

I felt his eyes on me; felt him searching inside me, sending my shoulders around my ears.

"How many years ahead?" he asked, changing the subject out of nowhere.

"What? Who?"

"This guy." He smiled. "You said he was a few years ahead in school. How much older is he than you?"

"A little over three years," I said, growing taller without the tension shrinking me.

"So… he's twenty?" David asked.

"Yup. Twenty one in May next year."

David nodded. "And what about you? When's your birthday?"

"What, you can't guess that by studying some random feature of mine?" I said sarcastically. "Like my piano hands?"

"I *could* find out for myself, if I wanted to. But I'd rather ask you."

"Well, when you put it that way… March seventeen."

His eyes narrowed slightly. "Pisces, huh?"

"Yup."

He chuckled, shaking his head. "That explains a *lot*."

"Hey! What do you mean by that?"

"Nothing," he said. "It's just funny how much that fits you."

"Says he who's known me for a day."

He smirked.

"Hey-you-two." Emily waved before we reached the top of the stairs.

"Hi, Emily." I waved back, noticing that, aside from her top being blue, we'd pretty much dressed the same.

"Good morning, Emily." David nodded in his cool, charismatic way.

"Ready to start another day?" she said.

"Alwa—"

"Em. David," Ryan called, running out from the school. "It's Nathan, guys," he added, stopping in front of us.

"Who's Nathan?" I looked at David.

"Oh, right. Sorry, Ara, you wouldn't know about this," Ryan said, "but he's our star quarterback. He got sick last week. Hasn't been able to get out of bed."

"Oh, that's awful. What's wrong with him?" I asked.

"Well, at first they said it was a really bad flu or something, but my mom just spoke to his mom in the pharmacy." Ryan looked at David. "He's had to go to the hospital, man. They couldn't keep him at home any longer."

"What? No!" Emily covered her mouth. "Will he be okay?"

"They're not sure. He's on machines and stuff to keep him alive, but you know Mrs. Rossi? She was crying 'cause she doesn't have insurance—said she can't get Nathe the care he needs without mortgaging her house."

Emily's eyes watered, her whole world coming down around her. "What are they gonna do?"

"Are you all good friends with Nathan?" I asked.

"Everyone is. He's just one of those guys, y'know?" Ryan told me.

"Well, why don't we do a fundraiser?" I shrugged. "We could put on a concert and charge people to come—give the money to Nathan's mom."

As if a light bulb had been switched on, they all looked up at me with a shimmering glint in their eyes. "Oh my God, Ara." Emily grabbed my forearm and bounced on her toes. "That's such a good idea."

"Yeah, good one, Ara." Ryan grinned.

"We should get moving on this right away," Emily said. "I'll talk to Mrs. Hawkins about it… er, if you don't mind me taking over your idea, Ara."

"Oh. Yeah, Em, this is better your project than mine."

"Great." She beamed, rocking back on her heels. "Well, I'll get things moving, and maybe have everyone meet in the auditorium at lunch if they want in?"

I nodded, shrugging.

"Okay." She went to walk away, then stopped. "Way to go, newbie."

"Yeah. You rock," Ryan said before skipping off to inform Alana, as she came out from the school.

And David and I were finally alone again. Or maybe just I was. He seemed distracted, wearing a kind of fake smile I thought belonged only to me: the tight-lipped one that covered a set of gritting teeth.

"David?"

He bent down to pick up his guitar case, his arched brows prompting my question as he stood up again.

"Are you okay?" I asked.

The edgy concern lifted from his face instantly. "Yeah, sure. I'm fine."

WHILE MISS CHESTER PRATTLED ON UP THE FRONT OF CLASS, I drew pictures of eyes all over my notepad: sad eyes, smiling eyes, secretive eyes, but all of them *David's* eyes. Not that they really looked anything like his. I doubted even a camera could capture the true beauty of his face if my memory could do it no justice.

I tapped my pencil on the page, trying to see through the solid classroom door, hoping David was waiting for me out there. The clock on the wall sat at three minutes to lunch, but the corridors were already bustling with students, and I was in the only class whose teacher didn't give early marks.

Then, almost as if it obeyed my command, the bell wailed loudly and the class broke into noisy shuffles, fleeing the room. I tucked my books under my arm and pushed my chair in, looking up to the sound of my name.

"Yes, Miss Chester?"

"Can I talk to you, please?"

"Um, sure." I glanced quickly at the corridor again—to freedom, to David leaning on the locker with his hands in his pockets, looking down at his shoes. "Did I do something wrong?"

"No, I was just wondering how you're doing?" she said softly, busying her eyes on some papers.

"Doing? Uh… I'm… fine."

"Just so you know"—she looked up at me, her pale lips forming a smile—"I'm a good friend of your dad's. If you need to talk, at *any* time, I'm always available. Okay?"

I smiled politely, hugging my books a little tighter. "Um, thanks."

"Okay, and, Ara?" she said as I turned away.

"Yes."

"Try to pay more attention in my class."

"Okay. Sorry."

"See you tomorrow."

"Yep," I said, feeling stupid after. *Yep?* Who says 'yep' to their teacher?

"Everything all right?" David stood from his lean as I came out of class.

"Yeah. Fine. Why?" I let him take my books.

"What did Miss Chester want?"

"Sheee… just wanted to see how I was going."

"Going with what?"

"Uh, homework?" I cringed at the obviousness of my lie.

David smiled warmly, keeping his eyes on the path ahead. "So you're not paying attention in class, huh?"

Damn it. He heard. "Um, no. Not really." I looked down at my feet as we walked, half noticing the walls go from white to burgundy.

"Why not?"

"Why not what?"

"Why aren't you concentrating?"

"I... I guess... I'm tired?" And there was that questioning tone again.

"I thought you said you slept last night."

Damn it! I did, didn't I? "Um..."

"You can talk to me, Ara." David gently grabbed my arm, stopping us by the auditorium door. "You don't have to make up a lie."

"Lie? About what?"

"I heard what she said." He waited, looking right into me as if I'd just spill the beans in the middle of the school corridor. "She wasn't just asking how you were coping with a new school, was she?"

"I uh—"

"Hey-you-two." Emily popped up out of nowhere. "Ready to start our first official meeting for the benefit concert?"

"Yup." I stepped away quickly to stand beside Em. "Ready."

"Great. Did you get lunch, yet? Cafeteria lines are out the door today." She nodded toward her tray of food. "Mr. Grant said we can eat lunch in the auditorium if we're rehearsing."

"Really?" I said. "That's great."

"Yeah, I know, hey. So, I'll go reserve a table near the stage. See you in a minute?"

"Why don't you go ahead, Ara," David said, passing my books and his bag. "I'll brave the cafeteria lines."

My fingers tightened around his backpack, finally touching something that belonged to him. "O...kay."

He tried to smile, but his clearly agitated gaze kept drifting toward Emily. "Anytime."

As he turned away, I squatted down and reached into my bag. "David! Money."

"Keep it."

"No way." I stood up. "Take it."

"Ara." He held his palm against my outstretched hand, glaring down at me.

"David." I glared back.

"Come on." Emily grabbed my arm and dragged me gently away. "One thing you'll learn pretty fast is not to refuse David when he wants to spend money on you."

I turned my head slowly to look at her. "How do *you* know that?"

"David and I have been friends for a while." She watched him walk around the corner. "We used to be closer, but..."

"But?" I probed.

"Nothing. We're just not anymore. People grow apart."

With a heavy sigh, I grabbed our bags and books, and headed into the auditorium behind Emily. "I can't let him buy me lunch all the time. When's it going to stop?"

She giggled, walking ahead of me. "You really don't know him, do you?"

SINKING INTO MY QUILT, I DRIFTED IN THAT BLISSFUL MOMENT between sleep and wake, where dreams mingle with reality, slowly and magically merging until everything in the now disappears. Here in this halfway world, I could be with David in any form imaginable: friend, girlfriend, lover. And the real world couldn't judge me.

But a cold screech of reality rang through my room so loudly and suddenly that I sat bolt upright in my bed. "Argh. Shut up," I said to the phone, flopping back down with my pillow over my face.

To my surprise, it actually did, and I once again drifted off to fantasyland, finding myself beside a tree with warm beams of light wrapping around me again, but no David. I could sense that something was off. I wasn't so asleep that I didn't know a dream when I was in one, but I never expected to hear my mother's voice.

"Ara-Rose?"

I turned slightly, seeing only my reflection in the glass of the phone booth behind me, disappearing with each flicker of a fluorescent light outside the corner store. "Mom?"

"Ara-Rose, where are you?"

The weight of the payphone in my hand became apparent then. I squeezed it. "I had a fight with Mike."

"With Mike? What were you doing at *Mike's*? I thought you went to Kate's."

"I lied to you, Mom," I said, but the line went dead and the night icy cold.

"Mom." I hung up the phone a few times, pressing all the numbers, but the receiver was empty. No static, no noise.

Behind me, the lights in Ronnie's store went out suddenly and the wind stopped. I pressed a hand slowly to the glass, and when another shot up to meet it, I screamed, jumping back.

"Ara!" A deep voice snapped my mind back to the waking world like an elastic band on a wrist, and my eyes flung open.

"Dad?"

"Ara, your phone's been ringing every few minutes for the last twenty. Will you *please* answer it?"

I rolled over, rubbing the haze from my eyes. "The phone?"

"Yes," Dad said, and closed my door, leaving me in darkness.

I jumped up, grabbed the phone, tripping over the clothes and shoes on my floor, and landed in my desk chair. "Hello?"

"Hey baby, did I wake you?"

"Mike?"

"Yeah, how you doin'?" he asked, then took a quick breath. "Oh, the time thing. Sorry, Ara. I'll go."

"No, wait. I…" I put the phone to my other ear. "I was dreaming about her, Mike."

He was silent for a moment. "Your mom?"

"Yeah." My voice crackled. "I keep thinking she's gonna come pick me up and I'll go back home again, and—"

"Aw, Ara, please don't cry, it… you'll break my heart, baby." He completely lost his voice then. "You don't know how much it kills me that I can't be there with you right now."

I smiled softly, sniffling. Even though he wouldn't love me like I needed him to, having his friendship meant everything to me still. "I'm sorry I didn't take your calls the last few months, Mike."

"I know. And you know me, Ar. I'm always here for ya, no matter what. Okay? You can never do anything so wrong that I'll stop being your friend."

I wiped the mess of warm tears from my cheeks. "I just… it's been so hard without you. It's one thing coping with losing mom, but the one person who always got me through bad things isn't even around anymore."

"I know. But I will be soon. I promise." He sighed then. "Have you talked to your dad yet—about what you told me on the phone the day you left? Have you told anyone?"

My head rocked from side to side.

"Ara, I can't hear you when you shake your head." He chuckled.

My sudden burst of laughter forced static down the phone line. "You always know how to make me laugh."

"Look, you need to talk to someone." His voice took on a serious note. "It's not healthy for you to keep all of this inside, baby girl. You said you made friends. Why don't you have a sleepover and do one of those big deep-and-meaningful things?"

I shook my head. "I don't know them well enough, Mike. I'm just not ready to share that part of my life with anyone."

"Well, what about that David dude, I bet he'd listen?"

"He might. But I don't want him to hate me if I tell him the truth."

"Why would he hate you?"

"Because he'll think I'm selfish, and—"

"Ara, grow up. You need to talk to someone about this. Now, I don't care who. Your dad, Vicki, Sam even, but—"

"I've got you to talk to."

"I'm not there, Ara."

"But like you said, you will be soon. And my dad said you can stay here."

"Yeah? Tell him thanks. And stop changing the subject."

"I'm not. Look, I'll talk to someone, okay. I do know you're right. I just—"

"You're just gonna bottle it up until you're in a straightjacket."

I bit my tongue.

"I'm gonna call you the second my interview's booked, Ara, and we're gonna pencil in a day for me to arrive. Then, if you haven't told

David or Emily or someone what happened, I'm gonna do it for you," he said. "Got it?"

"Okay, Zorro." I laughed. "When do you think they'll do your interview?"

"Two weeks or so."

"Cool. So, Mike, why did you call?" I asked, realizing that *he* woke *me*.

"I was just thinking 'bout ya, that's all. The ice cream man came past, playing that stupid jingle. Made me remember the time he ran over your foot when you chased him for your change."

My left toes twitched. That stupid truck cost me six weeks off ballet and a permanently demented pinkie toe. "Well, I'm glad it brings you happiness to remember me in pain."

"Aw, I really miss ya, kid." He breathed the words out. "I'll let you get back to sleep."

"Okay."

"Night, Ara."

"Night."

6

"David! You waited?"

"Of course I did." He laughed, watching me cross the road, still pulling my shoes on. "Stayed in the shower too long, did we?"

"No, I uh"—I placed my bag in his outstretched hand, a little puffed—"my diary was begging me to write in it. I was compelled to obey."

"Compelled?"

"Yeah, you know how it goes with these things," I joked. "If you don't do as the voices tell you, they just get louder."

David stopped walking. "You hear voices?"

"What?" I frowned. "No. It was a joke."

"A joke?"

"Yeah. You do know what a joke is, don't you?"

"Of course I do. Just—"

"Just, when it comes from me, it isn't funny." I nodded.

"Not about hearing voices."

"Why?"

"Because you phase out all the time. If you're hearing voices as well, it might mean there's something wrong."

"Oh." I dragged the word out, nodding my head, then shrugged. "Makes sense, I suppose."

"Did you eat breakfast?" he asked accusingly.

"Yes, *Dad*," I responded in the same tone.

"Sorry." David laughed, shaking his head. "I've just noticed that you get a little... *tempestuous* when you haven't eaten enough."

"Tempestuous?"

He nodded.

Hm. "It isn't my fault, you know. I have an ogre living in my belly. He makes me do bad things."

"So you phase out, hear voices, and blame your tempered outbursts on a fictional creature living in"—he looked down at my stomach—"your belly?"

"Precisely. The boy catches on quick."

"Well"—he shook his head—"one thing I can say about you, Miss Ara, is never a moment passes where I am not entertained."

"Is that... a good thing?"

He chuckled once. "Yes. It's a good thing, mon amie."

Mon amie. I repeated the words to myself, unable to hide my grin. "Why do you speak French?"

"Why?" he asked, surprised.

"Yeah. I mean, what made you want to learn French and then randomly use it?"

He looked ahead, both of us slowing simultaneously as we neared the big brown building. "I uh... I grew up in a community that was inhabited mostly by the French."

"Oh. Cool. Where did you grow up?"

"Not too far from here."

"And... they all spoke French?"

"Yes."

I frowned. I couldn't think of anywhere in New England that was grossly dominated by those speaking mainly French. But, Mr. I-Don't-Elaborate had, indeed, elaborated. I wasn't going to push for more. Not yet, anyway.

I exhaled, looking up the stairs ahead of us, wishing it were Friday. "Do we have to go to school today?"

"Yes," he said kindly.

"Well, I think we need an evasive action plan for Her Royal Dictator-ness at rehearsals today."

David tossed his head back, laughing. "She was pretty moody yesterday, wasn't she?"

"Yeah. I mean, I know it's just 'cause she's trying to get things done. And I guess, if it weren't for Em, this benefit concert really wouldn't be happening, but…"

"Hm, yes, but if she wanted to get things done, then casting the football team in a comedy skit was a terrible idea."

"Yeah, but it breaks the monotony of all the musical numbers."

"Yes. How many do we have now?"

"Ten, I think."

He nodded, slowing his steps to match mine. "Good line-up, too."

"Yeah. But Emily should be letting us practice our songs at lunch; not forcing us to spend the whole period separated like kindergarten kids, painting ticket signs."

"Well, if we hadn't joined the pencil-throwing fight, she wouldn't have separated us." He smirked.

"She shouldn't have anyway. We're not children, we're practically adults."

"Then we should act as such," he said with a nod.

"Fine." I folded my arms. "No mucking about today then."

"I don't know about that." He tilted his head almost bashfully toward one shoulder. "I kinda liked *mucking about* with you yesterday."

I couldn't help it, I laughed, remembering it. "Yeah, me too."

"Then, we shall endeavor to be discrete today."

"Discrete chasing, giggling and poking each other?"

He chuckled. "Yes, except now that I know where your ticklish spot is, I don't need to chase you. I can just poke you whenever I please."

"Not in English class, though. You know how ticklish I am."

His smile grew, his eyes small with thoughts I wanted him to share. "Yes, and your infectiously sweet giggle is at my disposal."

I tensed, noticing his eyes on my lower ribcage. "You wouldn't."

He clicked his tongue and winked at me. "You can *try* to stop me."

I hugged my ribs and bit my lip, grinning. "Maybe I don't want to."

EMILY LEANED FORWARD ON HER DESK, EAGERLY ENGAGED IN Dad's lecture. I hoped she was getting an A for all the extra listening she was doing. Then again, her interest wasn't companionless today, since most of the class seemed to be paying attention.

"Now, who here believes in God?" Dad asked, holding his hand in the air. Stunned silence replied. "It's not a trick question, people. Hands up if you believe there exists something bigger than yourself."

No one moved. Well, until Emily's hand shot up into the sky.

"Oh my God. You suck-up." I elbowed her, but put mine up, too —to save getting in trouble from Dad later. A few other people followed, while the rest of the class just laughed and pointed at us.

"Okay. Now, hands up who believes a man in the sky makes the thunder."

Everyone in the class laughed. My dad, with his own hand up, nodded then started writing on the board: "Myths and legends: Religious History." He read the words out, tapping each one, then popped the lid on his marker with a thud from his open palm. "Who can tell me what that means?"

Emily put her hand up again.

"Emily?" Dad pointed the marker at her.

"It means, like you mentioned last week, that nearly everything we know about religion is based purely on some story or, like, Chinese whisper that's been passed down from one generation to the next. Not too many cold, hard facts."

"Right." Dad wrote *What is real?* on the board. "Now, I'm not saying there's no God of Thunder, but what I am saying is that, like young Emily just said, nearly every story you've ever been told has been written by someone else. We don't know the facts for ourselves. But there is a fact behind every story. Since it's my job to inspire freethinking, not encourage atheism"—he wrote something else on the whiteboard: *Assignment: Facts from Myths*—"For the next few weeks, you'll be researching the origin of a myth or legend. It doesn't have to be religious, but if you sift through any myth and go deep enough, you'll usually find some religious connection, like most things in life. So, find a myth, research the legends around it, and make a report based on *your* opinion whether or not there could be some truth behind it and what it originally had to do with religious beliefs." He looked around at all the students. "Because, let's face it, if Jesus could walk on water, then why do we think Santa Claus is so improbable?"

The class broke into laughter.

"Mr. Thompson?" a girl asked. "Does that mean you're suggesting Jesus didn't walk on water?"

"No." My dad leaned against his desk, crossing his arms. "It means I don't see why there can't also be a Santa Claus."

The class roared with laughter again. But I didn't, because I knew he was being serious.

"Maybe he wasn't lying when he told me Santa is real," I whispered to Emily.

She started laughing. "I can *so* picture your dad saying that."

"I'll bet you can." I grimaced.

"So, find the myth and decide the truth from your *own* perspective. That's all everybody. Have a good day," he called out over the bell.

Emily and I walked out of class shoulder to shoulder, still laughing at Dad's unusual lecture. "And if he actually caught a burglar in your house on Christmas Eve, he'd think it was just Santa."

"Oh my God. I could so see that happening."

"Yeah, then, in the morning he'd be like, Gee, Sam"—she lowered her voice to sound like my dad—"I'm terribly sorry, but when Santa came last night he *filled* his sack with your presents instead. And… er… and he took the china and the silverware and the jewelry."

I folded over in a fit of teary giggles. "Oh my God, Emily. That's so spot on. I mean, his belief was unyield…" My sentence ended in a snort as my cheek smashed into a warm, firm chest. The boy stumbled back an inch, looping his arms around my shoulders.

"There now," he said. "I knew you'd fall for me eventually."

"David." I looked up into his sparkling eyes, melting within the circle of his arms. "I'm so sorry. I wasn't watching where I was going."

"Don't sweat it, pretty girl. I got ya." He flashed me the most insanely gorgeous grin, making no effort to move away.

"Not on school grounds please, you two!" Dad called.

I jumped back from David's arms, avoiding eye contact with my dad. "Sorry, Mr. Thompson."

"Keep it PG." He pointed at David, then took a blind shot with a scrap of paper, tossing it into the wastebasket beside his desk.

Emily's eyelids fluttered as he walked away again. "He's so cool."

"Ew." I winced.

David laughed at her, dropping his lingering arm back down to his side. I wanted him to ignore my dad and just pull me close again—steal me from this place so we could lay together, my head in his lap, talking for hours about nothing. But, unfortunately, he was no mind reader, and I would never muster up the courage to say that. So, staying at school and pretending not to want him was my only option.

"So, I hear Mr. Thompson gave an unusual lecture today?" David asked Emily.

"Oh my God, yes." She sunk into her knees, moving her hands around as she recounted the lesson. A few other kids joined in, adding their own theories on what my dad was aiming to teach us, and I just stood there watching David—watching the way he interacted with the others. When he noticed, he sent a soft smile my way, the crescent-shaped dimple above his lip showing; the one that only showed with that certain kind of smile. And that certain kind of smile made me think about the moment I fell into his arms back there. Except, this time, I owned the moment, because it was all in my head, so I imagined he'd sweep me off my feet and prop me against the wall, drawing my legs up and all the way around his hips. My lips would finally be on his, and his hands would sneak up my skirt, forcing a sharp intake of breath in me when he pulled my underwear across and…

"Earth to Ara?" Emily waved a hand through the cloud of my fantasy.

I snapped back to the reality of a noisy corridor. "Huh?"

"Welcome back," she said.

Ice rained through me. "Did I phase out again?"

David cleared his throat, growing seemingly taller as he slowly rolled his shoulders back.

"Uh, yeah. Just a bit," Emily said.

"David?" I looked right into his emerald eyes, seeing them turn almost black.

"I uh… I have to go." He wiped a hand across his mouth, holding dead still for a breath, then he stalked off into the crowd.

"What happened?" I asked Emily. "Where's he going?"

She just stared at me blankly. "What were you thinking about just then?"

The ice rain melted as my bones turned to lava. "Uh. Nothing PG, that's for sure."

She cackled. "Yeah, I guessed that much."

My shoulders dropped. "Was it that obvious?"

She smirked. "Have you ever looked at your face when you do that —when you disappear like that?"

I shook my head.

"It's funny. You just… your eyes drift off to the ceiling, and your lips just sit apart like you're waiting for someone to kiss them." She tried to hold back her laughter, but it shook her whole body. "Except, this time, you were looking right at David, chewing your lip, kind of blushing at the same time. I think"—she pointed to my chin—"I think you need to wipe the drool off."

"Stop that." I brushed her hand away. "God, I can't believe I let my imagination run away with me like that."

"Why not? I do it all the time."

"Because, unlike normal people, my face gives away my every thought, and I just happened to be in front of the star of my fantasy."

She hugged her books, looking down the corridor after David. "Maybe next time just do it with a book in your hand so people think you're reading something juicy."

"Good idea," I said, groaning. "Do you think David's upset with me?"

"Upset?"

"Yeah. I mean, he wants to be friends, right? So if I like him more than he likes me, that ruins it for both of us."

"Are you kidding?" Emily laughed, pointing to where he'd disappeared. "Ara, that's not David upset."

"So, that's… offended?"

"No way, not unless he's gay. And judging from how his fists just clenched up and his whole body went all rigid, I would guess he is *definitely* not gay."

"So why did he run away?"

She started walking. "He does that. I think he really likes you. And if he got the vibe I got coming off you, then he walked away because you made him feel something."

"What do you mean by that?" I hoped she wasn't being rude, implying I made him… you know, feel *something*.

"I mean, David doesn't really do emotions. The few times I've ever seen him close to feeling anything, he takes off."

"Why?"

She just shrugged again. She seemed to pass everything off with that move.

"Well," I said, "I'm just glad he can't read minds, or he might never come back."

Sam caught up and babbled about his day while I nodded and smiled and drifted in and out of consciousness, my mind on my own day—on the fact that David never came back to school after I practically jumped him in the corridor. But I fell back to attention with the hot sun bearing down, the smell of topsoil and wet grass all around me, when I heard the word *David*. "Huh?"

"Yeah, you and David Knight. My friend Steve said he heard from Trav that you slapped David in the hallway at school today."

"What?" I practically yelped, my steps coming to a halt.

"Yeah, they say he left school in a real hurry—tires screeching and all."

I rolled my eyes. "That's a grape turning into a sultana, Sam."

He stared at me, blinking.

"I mean, it's gossip. David left school today because he was sick." Sickened by my desire to fornicate with him.

"Oh yeah? Well, I saw you two on the stairs this morning. He was standing real close to you. Rumor has it you guys are an item."

"Nope. Nothing going on there."

"Nothing going on… *yet*?" He grinned.

I chuckled quietly. "It's not like that, Sam. We're just friends."

"Do you like him?"

I smirked. If I so much as hinted on the truth, the whole school would know by first period tomorrow. "No. I really don't. I mean, he's cute and we have a lot of fun together, but he's not really my type."

"Does he know that?"

"Yeah. And what's it to anyone else, anyway? How does what two seniors get up to become news to Freshies?"

Sam just laughed lightly. "Very little goes on in that school, Ara. Star football player quits the team this year then starts talking to a girl after notoriously dismissing every advance so far. People are wondering if you've got a golden vagi—"

"Whoa!" I held my hands up. "What a horrid thing to say."

He rolled his eyes. "So there's nothing going on with you and lover-boy?"

"God, no," I said, flooding with fury.

"Liar."

"Sam, look at me." I motioned to my scarred face. "I'm damaged, on the inside and out. I'm never going to be *anyone's* girlfriend."

He went quiet until we reached the driveway. "Hey, Ara?"

"Yes?"

"When we get in, can you peel me one of those apple snakes I saw you do the other day?"

"You *saw* that?"

He nodded.

"Uh, yeah, sure. I'll even teach you how to do them."

"Really?"

"Yep."

"Thanks, short-stuff." He wrapped his arm over my shoulder as we jumped the creaky bottom step and ran to the top of the porch.

WITH HOMEWORK PUSHED DOWN ON MY LIST OF PRIORITIES FOR today, and with a playlist of 'David' songs an hour long, I kicked off my shoes and went outside to my rope swing to try and forget everything. Including David.

Yellow leaves rained to the ground, falling from the old tree as the weight of each sway drew a low creak from its branches, reminding me I was growing up and that, soon, this swing would be a thing of my past.

My light-blue dress wavered around my knees in the gentle breeze, sweet with the diluted fragrance of frangipanis. I felt better just breathing again. But from here, I could see the school parking lot, which only brought back the memory of my embarrassing eat-the-cute-guy-in-the-corridor display, making me hold that newfound breath.

When my head dizzied from the movement, I sunk my toes into the slightly moist soil and grabbed my guitar. The stranger I saw in my mirror every morning glared back from its glossy surface. I ran my fingers over her face then gently along the strings, making a dull, tuneless song as I thought back to when I first saw this guitar. It had been on display in the music store window, and I fell in love with it immediately. How was it so uncomplicated to love an inanimate object, yet when it came to a boy, a girl would fall all over herself to hide her true feelings?

Well, unless she was me. Then the truth would come out in embarrassing displays… in corridors… at school.

I dropped my head into my hand, replaying that whole phasing out thing for the hundredth time.

But what was the point? Really? I mean, it wasn't like I could take it back by reliving it. So I squared my shoulders and twisted the pegs on the neck of the guitar, then strummed a soft A-minor; the first chord my mom played on this when she bought it for me. And a song formed from there, taking me through my David playlist until I realized my stupid brain was thinking about him again.

"Drat!" I stopped dead in the middle of a verse.

"Please, don't stop on my account."

"David?" I spun slightly to look back at him. "Where did you come from?"

"Seriously? Do I have to give you the birds and bees talk?" His fingers circled the ropes of the swing just above my head.

"Funny," I said sarcastically, but in truth, I actually did think it was funny.

"I uh… I went back to get my books from my locker and saw you sitting here," he said. "I hope it's okay I dropped by."

"It's more than okay," I said, lifting my feet as he gently pushed the swing.

"Hey, uh—" He cleared his throat. "I'm sorry I left like that at school today."

"David, don't *you* apologize. I was the one who—"

"Ara, you did nothing wrong."

I planted my feet, stopping the motion of the swing, then laid my guitar on the grass. "What do you mean? Emily tells me I practically licked you."

"Licked me?" David laughed, settling onto the ground right in front of my legs, his knees up, arms flopped loosely over them.

"Yeah, the whole… phasing out thing."

"Oh, that." He dusted his hand off on his jeans, leaning back on it after. "Sorry, I never even noticed that. I mean, I knew you phased out, but it was actually your strawberry shampoo that reminded me I had something to do."

"My shampoo?" I raised a brow.

"Yeah." He grinned, his white teeth showing.

"O…kay."

"So, what *were* you thinking? In the hallway?" His eyes searched mine for a moment, an incredibly suggestive grin warming them.

I looked away, feeling almost naked. "Just that…" I like you! I like you and want you to like me so bad it kills me! It. *Kills*. Me! "Just that it'd been a long time since I was in anybody's arms."

"Why's that?"

I shrugged. "Guess I just don't really like to be touched anymore."

"Why not *anymore*?"

I rubbed my chin, kind of wiping off my scars.

"Don't do that," he said, rising onto his knees.

"Don't do what?"

He pulled my hand down from my face. "You can't rub them away."

I studied the grass under my bare feet.

"Ara, look at me," he asked softly, tilting my chin to lift my gaze. "Why do you hide your face so often?"

"Because it's hideous."

His eyes lit up, shimmering like a green marble held up to the sun. "Hideous?"

"Okay, maybe not hideous. But—" I couldn't bring myself to ask how he could possibly even look at my scars.

"Can I say something?" he asked.

I nodded, keeping my eyes on his.

He reached out and brushed his fingertips so slowly over my face that all the fine hairs down my spine stood up. "These scars you despise so much, Ara, they're not what you think they are."

I held on as long as I could, but I just couldn't let him touch them anymore. I gently pulled his hand away and turned my face.

He sat back down on the ground. "I know you think everyone can see them, but that's not true. It's only up close that I've ever noticed, and I have not once ever thought you were hideous, Ara. Not ever."

I rubbed my jaw into my shoulder, seeing a flash of memory—of waking with tiny cuts and slivers of glass in my face. "I don't see how you can say that."

"That's because you don't know how beautiful you are."

I smiled at my feet, afraid to look up, afraid to see sarcasm in his eyes. And as if it came out of nowhere, a hand slowly appeared under my gaze, moving cautiously toward mine. It stopped just above my fingertips, as hesitant as a tough question, making sure it was okay to be there. I tensed from my ankles to my knees, feeling my heartbeat surround everything in my world. It all could've turned to ash under my feet—the ground, the swing, the day, the future—and I would've remained oblivious to it, because even the suggestion of touching him, of holding his hand, closed off everything else that could possibly matter.

"May I?" he asked.

I tried to say yes, but only a squeak came past my lips.

David's cheeks lifted with a soft grin. He turned his hand, sliding his fingertips under mine, and then pulled me down gently to the grass in front of him.

"You might wanna take a breath, Ara," he said with a laugh.

I took a deep one and, though daylight remained, all around me night enclosed my world—tunneling my vision to the only thing in the universe worth looking at. I smoothed my thumb over his, feeling myself lean closer, our eyes locked so intensely that if we were any nearer the colors would've blended.

"Are you okay?" he asked quietly, holding my hand with a kind of gentility that made me feel precious.

But I wasn't okay. Not anymore. I was lost, fallen completely into some feeling I wasn't ready for. Somehow, our fingers fit so perfectly together, like they were created only for this purpose. I was the lock and he was the only key. How would I possibly be okay, ever again?

"No. I'm not okay," I said softly.

"Let me tell you something." David edged a little closer. "And I say this as your *friend*, Ara."

I braced myself.

He brushed my ponytail over my shoulder, the softness of his touch sending a shiver down my neck. "Your scars make no difference to the way I see you. I know you're afraid that you aren't good enough for me, but how could I ever look past those eyes long enough to see scars?"

I half-smiled, rolling my face downward. "Why are you always so nice to me?"

His fingers tightened on mine. Behind me, the swing stirred gently in the breeze, and the golden glow of sunset surrounded the sky in a blanket of soft pink-and-purple clouds, making his eyes dark and shadowed. "Because I like you."

"*Why* do you like me?"

"Because you're funny, cute, sweet, smart—"

I scoffed at that one.

He smiled. "Believe it or not, you're actually quite witty and, from what I can tell after this short period of time, I have a lot more in common with you than any other girl I've ever spoken to."

"Not hard since you never talk to girls."

He shook his head, smiling as he ran his fingers down my ponytail again. "I feel a connection to you, Ara—one I've not felt before."

"Connection?"

"I"—he smiled, looking past me for a second—"I think we roll on the same wavelength, if you know what I mean."

"Yeah." I nodded, feeling enlightened by the prospect. He'd put the feeling so perfectly into words. "I think I know exactly what you mean."

"You wanna know something else, pretty girl?"

"Only if I'm going to like what you have to say."

His serious eyes warmed, a wide smile showing his teeth again. "I kinda like holding your hand."

On that note, I had to agree completely.

7

The rain had left a chill that made my toes cold under the strappy shoes. I hugged my arms across my chest, making myself small as I passed a group of obviously drunk boys.

"Hey." One of them broke from the cluster.

"Oh, hey." I waved, relieved it was only Mark from school.

"What you doin' out this late, Ara-Rose?" he said, but kind of kept walking past me.

"Just headed home."

"You want a ride?" He motioned behind him to his group of drunken mates.

"Nah. I'm gonna call my mom."

"Okay." He nodded and turned back, jumping into the huddle as I headed for the corner store, where the only payphone still in existence resided. The flickering light beamed down on me inside the booth, making my skin almost blue. I picked up the receiver with two fingers and held it just beside my face, not touching my cheek, then dialed reverse charges. It picked up in two rings.

"Mom?"

"Ara-Rose?" she sounded groggy and confused.

"Yeah, it's me. Um—" My lip quivered. "Can you come get me?"

"Why?"

"I'm at a payphone." I burst into tears. "Can you please just come get me?"

"What happened? Why are you crying?" Her voice became clear with panic as she threw a dozen questions at me.

"I had a fight with Mike."

"Mike? What were you doing at Mike's? I thought you were at Kate's."

"I was, Mom. Okay. I don't wanna talk about it. Can you just come get me?"

"Ara-Rose. It's the middle of the night. I just got Harry down again, and he's—"

"Mom!" I yelled down the line, holding the grotty phone in a tighter grip. "It's three in the morning. I'm cold and tired and—"

"Ara, just…" She let out a breath. "Hang up, okay. I'll call Mike. He can come—"

"No, Mom. Don't. Please don't. I don't wanna see him ever again."

"Why, honey, what happened?"

"Nothing," I practically screamed, my tears coming out in streams. "Just come get me."

"Harry's sick, Ara." She went quiet, as though waiting for me to see reason. "He shouldn't go out at this time of night. You know I care about you and, quite frankly, I'm terrified of the fact that I don't know where you are. I'm guessing you're on a payphone, aren't you?"

"Mm-hm." I sniffled, wiping my cheeks.

"Honey, you're seventeen now. You're too old for this. Just stop being a baby and go back to Mike's. I'll come get you first thing in the morning."

"No!" I held the phone right in front of my lips to make my voice as clear as the goddamn day. "I am never going back there, Mom. Never. If you don't come get me, I'll hitchhike home."

"Please, honey, just—"

"Fine. I'm hanging up," I said. "I see a car." I didn't see a car. "I'm sticking my thumb out, Mom. I'm doing it."

"All right. Okay. I'll come get you. Just… just stay there, okay?"

"Okay."

"Where are you?"

"The corner store."

"Ronnie's?" she screeched. "Ara, that's three blocks away. You can walk that."

"I'm scared, Mom. And I'm… I'm wearing heels."

It clicked then. I knew it did. I knew she knew the only reason I'd be wearing heels when I was supposed to be at a sleepover would be if I weren't at a sleepover.

"Just stay there, Ara-Rose. And by God, child, you are in a world of trouble when we get home." She hung up.

I held the phone for another few seconds, resting my head on the glass, feeling the swirl of alcohol mix in my system with fear, making me want to puke. But when I opened my eyes again, daylight flooded my world.

It took a second for my eyes to adjust—to see the dresser mirror on the other side of the room, the yellow walls, the white door and the new morning greeting me—and I could still feel her; still feel her voice in my ears.

I smoothed the covers out on top of me and let the proverbial rock on my chest keep me in place, on my back, unable to breathe.

Downstairs, Dad's burly laughter rose above the clatter of Vicki making breakfast, arguing about something with Sam.

But I was okay.

Slowly, the air came back into my lungs and, breath by breath, the rock lifted, leaving me picturing only one thing: David.

I jumped out of bed and headed straight for the shower, eager to start the brand new day.

Sam burst back through the front door after being gone only thirty seconds. "Ara, David's waiting for you across the road."

My spoon hit the side of my bowl, splashing milk onto the placemat as I leaped from my chair to peer out the window. David's head whipped up, his eyes meeting mine for a split second when I pulled the curtain back, as if he could actually see me.

I grabbed my bag, dumping my bowl in the sink, and ran out the door. In the case of David versus Breakfast, the judge and jury were in; we all knew the verdict.

Outside, the morning sun cast a spotlight on his perfection. I wanted to stop walking and just stand there gawking at him for a while. But he looked sort of different today than he did yesterday. His mysterious green eyes held the same smile in the corners it usually did, but the depth of focus in them, combined with thinly pressed lips, made him look almost uneasy.

"Hi, David."

He took my backpack and threw it over his shoulder, then started walking without saying a word.

My eyebrow moved down in confusion. "David?"

"Mm?" he said, but his eyes didn't answer like they usually did.

"Is… everything okay?"

"Uh, yeah." He dropped his fingers from the bridge of his nose and looked up, remembering suddenly that I was alive. "Sorry. I have a lot on my mind."

"No kidding." I stared forward, wishing I had pockets to shove my hands in so I wouldn't chew my nails. "Anything I can help with?"

"No."

"Maybe I can at least listen? You know, lend an ear."

"If discussing this problem would solve it, then I would. But it won't, so there's little point."

So he'd taken a leaf out of my book: swallow the problems and just hope they'd go away on their own.

After sitting with David in my backyard last night under the setting sun, just two friends holding hands, I'd almost considered telling him what brought me to live here. So many times I even opened my mouth, and after speaking to Mike, I guess I had resolved to 'let David in'. But this sudden distance, like someone had flicked the 'reality' switch, made me think all that magic I felt with him was an influx of hormones and, today, the world was back to its usual cold self.

I stole a glance at David. He was walking beside me in physical form but with his mind and spirit so far away that his eyes had completely fixed on one spot—narrowed with deep concentration. I wondered if he was trying to start a fire with mind bullets.

"So... did you... did you get up to anything interesting last night?" I said in a feeble attempt to make conversation.

"Interesting?" he asked, kind of confused.

"I just... never mind." I looked away. And he didn't mind. Didn't even bother to engage in small talk.

At the top of the stairs, Emily and Alana chatted casually, as if they'd been close their whole lives, despite their friendship being only as old as theirs to mine. They didn't really match as friends. Alana was so plain and almost gothic; she was smart and read books by indie authors, whereas Emily was so colorful; she always looked fresh and happy, or maybe overexcited. I figured she must drink coffee every morning—*lots* of coffee. Mind you, that never worked for me. But despite originating from different ends of the galaxy, they seemed to fit on exactly the same page. Kind of like I thought David and I did. Except, now I wasn't so sure. This thing between us was fragile. I could feel it. I wanted to tell myself I was being silly—that his coldness was just an 'off day' for him—but I didn't know him well enough to really believe that yet.

"Hi, guys." I waved enthusiastically as we reached the top step.

"Hey." Emily smiled.

"No cheer practice this morning, Em?"

"Not for me. Had a meeting with the school board."

"Oh, okay," I said. "What for?"

"Benefit concert."

"Cool. So, where's Ryan?"

"Right here." He popped out from behind the glass doors, wearing a wide grin.

"Hey."

"Hey." He gave me a quick hug, then cupped hands with David, who'd managed to wake up enough to appear social all of a sudden.

"So, new girl. You made it through your first week, and—" Ryan scratched the back of his neck and looked at Emily.

"Well, we were thinking," Emily jumped in. "Would you like to come to Betty's Cafe tonight to celebrate?"

"Is that the little fifties-style cafe?" I asked.

Emily nodded. "Yeah, the one with the pink-and-blue neon sign."

"It belongs to Emily's aunt." Ryan hooked his thumb in Emily's direction.

"Aunt… *Betty*?" I raised one brow in question.

"How'd you guess?" Emily laughed, waving a dismissive hand in the air after.

"Well—" I looked at David, wondering if he'd go. He placed his guitar case on the ground and rested his hands in his back pockets, then ever so subtly winked at me. It was like looking at a different David, as if the one that'd greeted me just a few minutes ago was his evil twin. "Uh, sure, you know what?" I looked back at Emily. "That sounds really great." The distraction would be a welcome relief from… my life.

"Okay, it's settled then." Emily bounced on the balls of her feet. "So, we'll carpool?" She looked at Ryan and Alana, then especially at David.

"Um." I froze, trying to think of a way to tell them I avoided riding in cars with teenagers. I didn't want to insult their driving ability or have them make the standard enquiry about why I was so afraid of cars.

"Actually." David took a small step forward. "I uh… I was going to ask Ara out tonight." He looked directly at me then. "So, perhaps *I* could be your escort?"

My brow folded into a frown. He was going to ask me out? What kind of out? Friends? More than friends? Friends who liked to hold each other's hands then ignore each other in the morning?

"Oh, a date. Really?" Emily said. "I'm sorry, I didn't realize you two had—"

"We're just friends," David said in a very businesslike tone.

"So you don't mind sharing her for the night, man?" Ryan asked.

"Not at all."

"Yeah, and um," I chimed in, looking sideways at him, "really, hanging out with you guys'll be great."

"Okay. So you bring Ara, and I'll go with Ryan and Alana." Emily linked her arm through Alana's.

Ryan sighed enviously at Emily, subconsciously imitating the Leaning Tower of Pisa. It was so obvious he liked Alana. I wondered why he hadn't just got with the program and asked her out. I mean, it was obvious the feelings were mutual.

The routine catch-up at the top of the stairs continued then without my cerebral focus. They were all smiling and talking, but I couldn't really hear them. My thoughts were off with my troubles somewhere in clueless land. David wasn't really present, either. He was smiling and talking, but kept looking at me with those narrowed eyes —studying me—probably unaware he was even staring. And all my brain could do was worry that he felt he'd made a mistake talking with me that way last night.

What else could it possibly be?

DAVID LAUGHED AS HE CAUGHT A SCRUNCHED-UP BIT OF PAPER, then hurled it up the back of the room, where its journey ended on the brow of a gorilla. I slinked down lower in my chair to avoid getting a headache from unfinished English homework. It was bad enough that Mr. B, with his 'strict designated seating plan', placed me right up front next to David. Not that I minded the David part, I was just kinda worried I might do something to embarrass myself, like drool all over his notebook or start playing footsies with him under the table.

"Morning, class." Mr. Benson walked in, oblivious to the origami air raid going on behind him.

David turned quickly in his seat, playing the good student.

"Faker," I scoffed.

He opened his mouth to speak, then dropped his words with a smile as his hand shot up behind his head. Everyone behind us broke into claps and cheers. "Nice catch, man," one of the gorillas called.

"Settle down, class." Mr. Benson eyed the room for a second before turning back to write on the board.

Totally and utterly confused, I frowned at David. "What was that all about?"

He smiled broadly and opened his palm to reveal a ball of paper.

"Did you just catch that behind your head? Without looking?"

He dumped the cannon onto his desk and leaned closer. "Of course not. I just made it look that way."

"Liar."

"Okay." His face cracked into a grin. "Maybe I did."

My head rocked in amazement. "Well, you're a good catch. *Er.* I mean catch*er*."

He looked to the front of the class and crossed his arms over his chest, laughing to himself. He smelled so fresh today, like he'd just stepped out of the shower still steaming and hot, then sprayed deodorant all over his naked skin. I left my lips slightly parted as I smiled, because the sweet scent of his cologne brushed pleasantly over my tongue every time he leaned in or spoke.

"I need everyone to take out their notepads and jot some things down for…" Mr. Benson started, but I lost focus as David leaned down and unzipped his bag. With his body angled that way—one side lengthened, his arm slightly up as he stretched forward—that fresh smell dominated our private little space. I drew a really deep breath then opened my eyes slowly, meeting then with his direct gaze.

"You okay?" He held back a chuckle, placing two pens and two notepads on his desk.

"Uh. Yeah."

"Were you thinking about ice-cream?"

"Ice-cream?"

"Yeah." He bit his lip, looking at mine. "You looked like one of those girls on a seductive ice-cream commercial."

I flashed him a grin, and he sat back, breathing out his laughter.

"Okay." Mr. Benson folded his arms, leaning on the front of his desk. "Today, we'll be having a class discussion about…"

Toes in the sand, standing on a beach at sunset, kissing, making everyone who passes jealous…

"Ara?" Mr. Benson said. "Perhaps you can answer that question for us?"

"Uh—" I sat up a little. Crap!

David nudged me and held out three fingers under the desk.

"Um… three?" I said.

"That's correct." Mr. B turned back to the board. "There were three characters in..."

"Thanks," I whispered.

"Don't mention it." David folded his arms again and kicked his legs out straight in front of him, crossing his ankles. He was wearing those heavy black boots again. I'd seen him in those nearly every day, except yesterday when we sat on the grass by my swing, talking for hours—our fingers entwined; his cold, like mine, yet warmer than mine. It felt so good, but for such a short time, because as soon as the sun went down, he left. I offered him to stay for dinner, but he said he already had plans. Talk about disappointment. Now, I wanted to touch his fingers again to make sure they really felt the way I remembered.

When David's head turned to watch the pacing teacher move around the class, I stared down at his hand just to gauge the distance. Maybe I could accidentally brush past or...

"You could at least *try* to concentrate." He leaned his head a little closer as he spoke, keeping his eyes forward, his arms folded.

But how could I concentrate, when every time he breathed, I could feel it and hear it? All I wanted was to rest my head against his chest and listen to his heart.

"Ara, stop that," he whispered gruffly.

"Stop what?"

"You... you know that look you get when you're thinking... *things*?"

"Mm, what about it?"

His lips parted, his eyes sparkling with a grin. "Well, you're... thinking."

"Maybe you shouldn't sit next to me then," I whispered back playfully.

"I shall ask Mr. Benson to move my seat if you wish," he muttered.

"No, David, I—"

"Eyes forward please, Miss Thompson," Mr. Benson said.

The eyes of every student in the class made my spine go stiff. Damn this tongue.

When Mr. Benson looked away, I tore a strip of paper from my notepad, coughing over the sound it made.

David smiled, watching my not-so-crafty display of rebellion. "What are you doing?" he whispered.

"Shh." I nodded toward the teacher.

"Show me," he said, leaning over.

"No peeking." I hid it with my elbow.

He sat back in his chair, chuckling quietly.

Sorry, I wrote. *When I said that, I just meant that you make me lose my concentration. I want to be next to you. I just wish we weren't at school.*

There, that should do it. Somehow, it was so much easier to say what I wanted to say when I didn't actually have to say it. "Here."

David placed a fingertip on the top corner of the note and slid it across the desk.

"I want you all to write this down," Mr. Benson said, scribbling on the board.

When I dared to glance back to see what David thought of my note, he slipped it into his pocket, smiling my favorite smile—the one that lit up the corners of his eyes before showing in his lips—but he didn't say anything.

"Point one." Mr. Benson wrote numbers one to ten on the board, and kept talking about something I cared nothing for right now.

David, with his left hand, started taking notes without reading them off the board, yet still managed to write them down word-for-word, while I watched in amazement. How did I not notice he was left-handed? His guitar wasn't left-handed.

"Here." He slid a page across to me.

"Thanks. But, don't you need these?"

He smiled down at another page in front of him: the same notes.

"Oh." I toyed with the edge of the paper nervously, still wondering if he even read my note.

"Ara?" David whispered, his head nearly touching mine.

"Mm-hm?"

"Can I hold your hand?"

"In class?"

"Yes. In class."

The idea took my breath. I couldn't even nod. I felt his cool touch just above my elbow before he slid his fingers slowly down the length of my arm, making little bumps lift the fine hairs as they followed the curve to the back of my hand. I flipped my palm over and our fingers laced.

"You okay?" he asked.

I nodded, squeezing his hand tightly, wishing he'd never let go.

We sat with our hands concealed under the desk for the rest of class. But every now and then, David ran his thumb over mine and smiled at me. And every time he did that, my heart skipped into my throat like the rush you get on a roller coaster.

I grinned like the Cheshire cat, silently praying the teacher wouldn't notice the reason for my happiness, and as I sat there feeling closer to this boy than I had to anyone in my life ever before, I drew a conclusion again that I thought I'd discarded completely: I was falling in love. Even though I didn't believe in love at first sight, my heart didn't care. It didn't change how I felt. I could only hope, as I watched David trying to conceal his own smile, that he'd one day feel for me the way I did about him.

DAD PACED THE FLOOR, HANDS BEHIND HIS BACK, DRONING ON about some faerie myth, while Emily and I quietly gossiped our way through the hour, as usual. She scribbled another fact about the guy sitting behind us on a page and passed it to me.

"You already told me that," I said, sliding the paper back to her.

"Oh, sorry." She smiled bashfully. "Did I tell you he lives near you?"

I half-glanced over my shoulder at him. He was plain and kind of quiet, like Alana, but with sandy hair. His only redeeming quality was his dazzling hazel, almost green-grey eyes. "I met him once—on my first day," I said.

"Really?"

I nodded.

"Well, what did he say to you? Was he nice? Did he—"

"Em?" I put my hand up between us. She had somehow managed

to excite herself so much she'd almost drifted onto my lap. "Why don't you just talk to him?"

Emily ducked her head and stole a glance back at him. "I can't."

"Why?"

"What if he doesn't like me?"

In my mind, I flicked my hand out and whacked her across the back of the head. In the real world, I just rolled my eyes at her. Ever since she first took real notice of him at rehearsals yesterday, all she'd done was talk about what this person told her about him, or what that person said he did in Math class. But I had to agree with her when she said that, ever since she first decided he was perfect, she'd seen the world move in slow motion. See, *that* I understood.

"So, are you and David going out now?" she asked.

"Yeah, we're going out tonight, remember?"

"No, dummy." She slapped my arm. "I mean, has he asked you to be his girlfriend?"

"Do guys do that?"

Her expression said it all. "Yes, Ara. Guys ask girls out."

"Oh. Well, no. He didn't. He um… he said he liked holding my hand."

"Hm. PG."

I laughed and sat facing the front again.

"Maybe he's just being a gentleman." She leaned a little closer, keeping her eyes on Dad as if we were paying attention to him. "I mean, that would be very like him, Ara. He might be waiting for you to make the first move?"

I sat up in my chair. "Yeah, he does have that freaky old-world charm thing. Maybe he's ultra-traditional."

"It would make sense," she offered.

I chuckled once. "Maybe I should offer him my intentions in writing."

"Nah, I don't think—"

"Em?" I elbowed her. "That was a joke."

"Oh." She frowned. "Ara, you tell the worst jokes."

"Yeah, I must get it from my dad." I grinned as the whole class broke into laughter at one of his inadvertently humorous comments.

"No." Emily sighed, leaning on her hand and dreamily gazing at Dad. "He's funny. You must've inherited your terrible joke problem from your mom."

My heart stopped for a beat. "Yeah. I guess I did." And it was true. But not from the mom they all thought I grew up with.

I got my terrible joke problem from the mother I just buried.

It was kind of our little game, almost an art form: lame 'Dad' jokes for a girl without a dad around. I just didn't realize until now that I was still playing it.

My chin trembled involuntarily then as I saw myself like a fresh memory, standing by a graveside, wondering how I would walk away —say goodbye to someone I'd loved my whole life.

Dad looked up suddenly, and started talking with a slight stutter as he realized that I was struggling to hold back my tears.

"Sorry, class"—he sauntered casually over to his desk and lifted a piece of paper—"just remembered I need to send a note up to the office."

"Ooh, I'll go Mr. T," one of the girls said, holding her hand high in the air.

"Actually—" He scanned the room. "Edmond!" All eyes turned to look up the back, following Dad's unusual tone. Edmond dropped his phone and sat up straight, pulling his headphones out of his ears. Dad handed me the note and whispered, "Go."

I went, my feet carrying me swiftly to my quick exit as the lecture on why we don't play with phones in class absconded into the empty corridor, ending as the door slammed shut behind me.

I couldn't breathe. I dropped the fake note to the floor and felt for the wall as the hot tears blinded me. But for every one I swiped away, another took its place, and I fought to quiet my sobs, but the pain just went too deep.

"Stupid jokes." I kicked the base of the wall. This was why I swore I'd never let my guard down, why I swore I wouldn't try to make friends here. As soon as they found out, they'd all crowd around me in the lunchroom, using my pain to fill the boring hour. I'd seen it happen before when a girl lost her mom at my old school. I couldn't let that happen to me.

As the tears slowed and the receding anger turned my body cold, I rolled my face upward to look at the classroom door, wishing my dad would come out to see if I was okay, if I needed a hug, because, for the first time since I lost her, that was all I really wanted. Just a hug. Just to feel like someone could hold me down—stop me from floating away.

I dropped my forehead against the wall and hugged myself, not really sure I could do this anymore.

"Ara?" Long, cool fingers slowly gripped my arms from behind. "What happened? What's wrong?" His words were barely a whisper, but I recognized his voice right away. And he was the *last* person I wanted to see.

"I'm okay, David. I just..." I wiped my face, keeping my head down. "I guess being new just got to me."

"This is not nerves or fear, Ara. This is grief." His fingers tightened on my arms, his gently melodic tone forcing a new rise of heartache inside my chest. "Talk to me."

"I can't." I sobbed, wrapping my fingers over my entire face.

"It's okay." He tried to turn my shaking body, but I held fast, afraid to let him see. "It's really okay."

"No, it's not. Why does everyone always say that?" I asked, almost incomprehensibly. "I'm so *sick* of hearing that."

"Ara. Please. *Please*. I'm worried about you." His hand came forward, cupping my shoulder as he spun me gently into his chest and wrapped me up in his arms. "Please, don't cry."

"I'm trying not to," I said, shielding my face in the darkness against his shirt. And he smelled so good, so real, and he was so warm. He smelled like something safe, like a person who could hold on to me if I fell. And I wanted to hold on. I wanted to wrap my arms around his waist and just hold on. But right now what I *needed* was to be small, closed-in. Held on *to*.

"Okay." He rubbed my back and took a step, keeping me close to his chest as we walked. "Come on."

I hiccupped in an embarrassingly high-pitched tone. "Where're we going?"

He looked down and smiled at me. "We're going somewhere we can be alone—talk."

And like that, in one sentence, David hit every chord I ever wanted to hear. My heart squeezed tighter then twisted into a large, pulsing knot—a good knot—slightly weighted by dread. I wanted to be alone with him. Talk. But not about this.

Still, I went with him willingly, because even if I didn't talk, I at least needed some fresh air.

As we hurried into the front parking lot, I glanced over my shoulder every few seconds, watching for teachers. David stayed calm though, walking with the grace of a king. We stopped by the passenger door of a shiny black car with a soft-top roof, and David pulled his keys from his back pocket.

"Is this your car?" I asked.

"No, I'm stealing it." He jammed the key in the lock and twisted it, then laughed at me. "Yes, it's my car, Ara."

"How old is it?"

"Uh—" He looked at the car, then at me. "It's a little old."

"Classic old?"

"Kinda. It was my uncle's." He held the door open for me. "Hop in."

As David shut the door, the exasperating heat closed me in right away, and the tan leather seat burned the backs of my thighs under my skirt. I lifted one leg, then the other, and wiped the sweat from under my knees, placing fabric between skin.

"You okay?" David asked, releasing the tight pressure of heat for a moment as he opened his door.

I nodded, slinking down lower. "I've never ditched school before."

"This isn't ditching," he said. "Your dad will understand."

I nodded. "I guess so."

He smiled across at me and shook his head, sliding forward to reach into his back pocket.

"What are you doing?" I asked.

"Easing your conscience." He pinned a number into his phone and pressed it to his ear, taking my hand. "Miss Apple?"

I heard her voice muffled on the other end.

"Yes, I have Ara Thompson with me. Can you let her father know she's fine, and I'm taking her for a walk to clear her head?"

I slowly inched up in the chair, inconspicuously wiping a few dots of sweat from my upper lip.

"Yes, I'll bring her home later. Give him my number if he wishes to check on her. Okay. Bye." He hung up the phone and dumped it in the center console, then started the engine.

"Thank you," I said.

"You're very welcome."

I sat back then and rubbed under my eyes where the tears had dried in the heat, making my skin stiff. Even my nose felt dry and swollen.

We sat at the exit sign for a second until the traffic passed, then David took off down the street, going slightly over the speed limit. "How long have you had your driver's permit?"

"A while." He looked at my forehead and frowned.

I wiped the sweat away with the back of my hand. "It's hot today."

"Oh, sorry, Ara. I don't really feel the heat as much as most people. Here." He turned on the air-conditioner. The blinding heat eased after the first blast of hot air passed and the chilly wind blew against my face. "Is that better?"

With my nose pressed to the vent, I nodded. "Yeah, thanks."

"If you get hot or cold, Ara, you really need to tell me. It's just not something I think about."

"Why?" I sat back in my seat and angled the vent to blast along my hairline.

He grinned. "I'm insensitive."

"Yeah, you're so neglectful of others' feelings, David," I joked.

"I know. Sometimes I lose sleep over it." He laughed.

"Mm, I don't know how you live with yourself."

"Takes practice," he said, but there was an undertone of suggestion that seemed aimed at me, like maybe he meant that it takes practice to *live with yourself*.

"What are you saying?"

"Regret. It takes time to live with it." He reached across and took my hand again. "You called your mom Vicki the other day."

I felt numb then, not just from the crying but the stupidity. "Did I?"

"Yes. And if I am good at only one thing, Ara, it's deductive reasoning. I think I've known for a while now that your mom died. I just don't know why you pretend she hasn't."

I rolled my face slowly toward my chest. "Because I didn't want people to ask how she died. And I didn't want them to feel sorry for me."

"People only feel sorry for you when there's a good reason, Ara. Your mom's gone. People just want to help."

"I know." But I didn't want their help. Every ache was a step toward redemption.

"Redemption?' David said.

I looked up at him quickly. "Did I say that out loud?"

"Uh—" He looked at the road again, his face grey. "Yes. Didn't you mean to?"

I couldn't believe my own carelessness. "No."

"What did you mean by that—about redemption?"

"Just that… when you do something wrong, sometimes you can make up for it."

"By doing what?"

I blinked a few times, and the dried tears made my skin crack a little. "Suffering."

The car slowed for a second, and then as David sat taller, his fingers tighter on the wheel, it went back up to speed.

When I flipped the visor mirror down, I gasped at the mess David had been looking at for the last five minutes. My life was over. I wiped the smudges of black mascara from under my eyes, using the remaining tears around my lashes to smooth it away without too much of a problem. But I couldn't wipe away the blotchy patches of red under my skin that turned my nose bright pink, forming a giant rouge smudge across my face.

"I look like a clown." My voice quivered.

"You look"—David turned my face with his fingertips —"adorable."

Right. Adorable. I folded my arms across my chest, aimed my gaze out the window, and focused on my breathing. The passing houses and tree-lined streets were all the same around here: pretty, with that old-style Halloween kind of feel. It felt like it should be autumn and everything sort of orange and brown, with the slight hint of cinnamon in the air. But the summer had this magic little place trapped in its grasp, making everything yellow and gold, and a little wilted.

The trees thickened as we turned onto a narrow road with dirt strips on both sides, and my squinting eyes relaxed as the sun's glare disappeared over the canopy.

"David, where're we going?"

"Somewhere quiet, where no one can hear us."

I laughed. "That sounded kinda creepy."

He laughed too. "Sorry. I realized that just as I said it."

I sat taller to take a good look at the deserted forest road. "Why should we be where no one can hear us?"

"Because you need to talk. And you won't talk if you think someone might hear you."

I looked away, pinching the base of my thumb with my fingertips. He was right. I did need to talk, but I didn't want to talk to him. He had this delusion that I was some nice, sweet girl. He didn't know the real me—the one that I was fighting not to be anymore.

"Let me guess,"—he smiled, watching the road carefully and taking the curves with a kind of precision that put my dad's driving to shame—"you don't wanna talk to me about it. Am I right?"

"I'm sorry." I looked out the window. "It was nice of you to bring me out here, but I don't—"

"I'm not going to let you go until you talk to me."

"And what are you going to do? Torture a confession out of me?"

He tilted his head a little, keeping his eyes on the road. "It wouldn't be the first time."

"Well, it won't work. I have my reasons for not wanting to talk, David."

"And they mean nothing to me. You're talking. Period."

"You can't make me." I folded my arms and stared ahead, biting my teeth together.

The car slowed noticeably, gravel crunching under the tires as we pulled onto the side of the road. "Ara?"

I shook my head, refusing to let those emerald eyes persuade me.

"Ara?" David said again.

Begrudgingly, I twisted my neck to look at him.

"I'm sorry," he said, turning his whole body to face me. "Sweetheart, you're taking things a little too seriously. I meant no harm. Really. And the more I think about it"—he rolled back in his seat and faced the front, a cheeky grin stretching the corners of his mouth —"the more I think I might just have to kidnap you until you *do* talk to me."

A small smile crept onto my lips. I pressed them together firmly to keep it hidden.

"Ara, please don't be so moody. It's okay to smile."

I sighed. The ogre was obviously dominating my mood right now. I should've eaten more at lunch. "I know you have the best of intentions here, David. But this is really nothing to do with you."

"I can help you," he said after a second. "I want to help you. All the bad things, Ara, all the pain you feel"—he reached for my hand; I let him take it—"I can make it all hurt less. But you have to let me in."

"I can't," I said in a breaking whisper, turning away.

"Come."

"Where?" I looked back at him.

He opened his door, allowing the clammy air to mingle with the pleasant, artificial cool. "Somewhere better."

"I hope you don't think I'm getting out in the hea—"

"Let's go." David appeared on my right, opening my door.

"How did you get there so fast?"

"Come on." He grabbed my hand, leaning in to unbuckle me. "I wanna show you something."

8

After a long and wordless trek through crunchy leaves and tall trees, we walked toward a newly decaying cedar tree, lying sidelong across the slope of the trail, making a wooden partition between us and the sudden openness of whatever was beyond. The muddy clay smell that guided us in disappeared under a damp, kind of mossy scent, spiked with the lemony fragrance of tree sap. I breathed it in with the intention of never forgetting it. This place had an amazing feel to it, and I hoped I could remember the way here, because as soon as I got my license, I'd be visiting again.

David stepped up quickly and took my hand, guiding me around the tree. "Welcome to my secret hiding place."

Maple leaves stole my gaze upward before casting it out widely to the unspoiled body of water down a sloped bank. A grand pathway of clover blanketed the trail toward the edge of the lake, and tiny hovering bugs danced above the star-shaped foliage, making the desolate spot look busy. Even under the open sky, it still felt cool and shadowed, and kind of private here. A place not so very different from the mountain-surrounded picnic spots my dad used to take me to, but with an element of magic to it, like somehow I could believe we were the only two souls left in the world.

"David, this is beautiful." I searched the vacant place beside me where David was a second ago, finding him leaning on a rock right by the water's edge. "How did you find this place?"

"It's not something you'd find on a hike." He unhitched himself from the black rock and walked behind it, then squatted down. "No one comes out to this trail anymore."

"Anymore?"

He stood up and presented a pillow-sized black bag with a smile. "This land is owned by my family. We closed the hiking trails to outsiders about a hundred years ago."

"You say that like you were a part of the decision."

"Well"—he reached into the plastic bag and pulled out a picnic rug—"it's up to each generation to decide. I chose to keep the land private, like my uncle before me."

"Why?"

"I like knowing I can come here to think. That when I do, I'll be completely alone."

"Alone is right." I looked around again. A few meters out in the middle of the lake, a family of trees gathered on a small island, surrounded by a moat of algae, and the only other signs of conscious life here were a couple of ugly brown ducks. "It's very… private here."

"It originated as hunting land." He tucked his hands into his pockets, squinting as he observed the landscape.

"What did you hunt?"

"Hunt?"

"Yeah. You *just* said it was hunting land."

His jaw rocked. "I did, didn't I?"

I nodded.

"It was…" He laughed to himself. "Foxes."

"Foxes?"

"Yeah."

"And… what about now? Do you still hunt here?"

"Only if the foxes stray onto the land—disregarding the warnings around the border."

"What!" I laughed. "Last I checked, foxes couldn't read."

"Well, then they die," he stated, then sat down on the plaid picnic rug, his back against the rock. "Don't be shy." He patted the spot next to him. "I won't bite."

I folded my arms, remembering suddenly why he brought me out here.

"Come on, Ara. You know you wanna talk to me." The arrogant smile on his lips filtered out through his voice. "You also know I'm not going to let you go until you do."

"You can't keep me here."

"I can. And I will, and no amount of kicking and screaming is going to help you. I'm not sure if you've noticed, ma petite, but I'm a lot bigger than you."

"What does *ma petite* mean?"

He smiled to himself, looking down at his outstretched legs. "Roughly? Little girl."

I huffed. "I am not a little girl!"

"Good. Then stop acting like one. Sit down."

I wanted to sit there so badly, but letting him in to my world meant opening it, and I wasn't sure I even could anymore. The thing about pain is that, once you lock it away, it hurts more to bring out again.

David shrugged, and then rested his hands behind his head, keeping his smiling eyes on me. "I've got *all* day."

Slowly, with his conceited stare melting my icy exterior, my frown dropped, my arms following until, with a low sigh, I wandered over and sat down about a meter across from him. And he waited, saying nothing. I was happy to let time just pass around us; happy to be this nice, sweet girl he thought I was for just a little longer. But I knew it would come to an end. It had to eventually. He had to know the truth about me.

"I'm sorry, David."

"Why would you need to be sorry?"

"I think I might've given you the wrong impression about myself." I lowered my gaze. I didn't want to see his face as I said this—the way any compassion would dissolve from his eyes, and the smile that seemed to be reserved only for me would vanish under newfound repulsion. "Actually, I *deliberately* gave you the wrong impression."

"So, you're not a schoolgirl with a broken heart?"

"Is that all you see in me?"

He shook his head when I looked at him. "You know what I see in you."

I nodded. "And that's exactly what I wanted you to see—wanted everyone to see. But I'm not nice. I'm not sweet, and I'm not this golden child that organizes benefits and listens to people talk about their day. I—" I laughed coarsely to myself. "Half of the time, I really don't care what Emily thinks about the latest books she's reading and, most of the time, I cut her off—talk about things *I* want to talk about."

David laughed. "And your honesty is one of the other things I like about you."

I shook my head. "But it's not honesty. It's horrible. I mean, it's not like I don't care about people, but I… I never really put them first."

He exhaled. "And you think that makes you a bad person?"

I shrugged. "Maybe just selfish."

"Okay, so maybe you're selfish. I still like you."

I couldn't help but smile at that, but dropped it quickly. "What if… what if my selfishness went so deep it cost someone their life?"

He rose to his knees and shuffled closer. "Then you have to take a risk. Right now. You have to put faith in our friendship, and just know that when you tell me what you're going to tell me, I'm here. For *you.* Not for anyone else. I don't care about Emily or her trivial conversations either, Ara." He grabbed my hand. "Right now, I'm here with you, my little friend, and you're going to tell me what's breaking your heart."

I stole my hand back, swallowing the tight lump in my throat.

"Ara," he said softly, cupping the side of my face. "Don't hold back your tears."

"I have to. If I let them go, I'm not sure they'll ever stop."

He clicked his tongue. "Can I tell you something? A legend I once heard."

I nodded, resting my hands in my lap.

"They say that the tears one cries for loss are the Tears of the

Broken, or the Devil's Liquid, because, for each one you shed alone, you sacrifice a piece of your soul."

I sniffled, looking up at him.

"And they also say that for each tear *shared*, you give a piece of yourself for someone else to safeguard until you're ready to notice the sun again."

Hot tears doubled my vision. I blinked them out. "And you want to be that someone?"

He stared at me, his round eyes unmoving. "Ara, I *am* that someone."

Only a short sniffle passed before it all fell to pieces—all of that heartache and guilt just so ready to finally come out. "She shouldn't have been there." I covered my face as inaudible gusts of explanation dribbled through my lips.

"Your mom?"

I nodded into my hands. "It's my fault she's dead."

"Why?"

"It was the middle of the night." I swallowed. "I called her to come get me. I could've walked home, but..." I wedged my thumbnail between my teeth, holding my breath as I tried not to cry. I had no right to cry. "It was so stupid. I'm seventeen. I'm not a child. But I was angry and... really hurt. I just wanted my mom. I just wanted to go home."

"So you asked her to come get you?"

"*Made* her."

"And that one act makes this your fault?"

"Yes."

"Why?"

I looked over at the ducks splashing about without a care in the world. I wanted to be them: brown and ugly, but free. "Don't you get it? If I hadn't called her, she'd still be here."

He sat back, his feet flat to the ground on either side of my legs, our faces almost touching. "Put all that aside for a moment, and tell me about the accident."

"Why?" I screwed my nose up.

"Because you haven't spoken to anyone, and you need to—it's a part of the healing process."

I wasn't sure I wanted to recall the details I'd tried so hard to block out.

"Okay, if you're not ready for that, start by telling me how you feel. Right now."

"What do you mean?"

"Tell me what your emotions are in *this* moment."

"Why?"

"Call it a distraction technique. It'll help you calm down, make you more coherent."

With my eyes closed, I searched inside for the words to describe that tight, hollowed-out feeling. I knew that every word I'd said so far came out a mess, but focusing on that immediate sensation in my body actually did help to calm me. "I just feel so, so empty and so full of this incredibly strong… I don't know. I guess… regret."

"Regret for calling her or for what you've suffered?"

"For Harry." My voice completely broke on the end, drowned out by a new wave of pain.

"Who's Harry?"

"My baby brother."

"He was in the accident?"

I nodded, trembling all over. "He'd been sick for a week or so, and I made Mom get him up—take him out in the rain to come get me. But it was like…" I thought back to that gummy smile he flashed me as I hopped in the car, but it was like he'd faded somehow and I couldn't really see it anymore. "He didn't know. He couldn't understand that I was selfish for bringing them out there, and he just smiled at me like I was his *whole world*."

"And how do you feel to look back on that memory?" he asked, sounding way too much like a therapist.

I closed my hands around my face. "Dark. Hollow. I can hardly see his face now. It's just so dark. And a part of me still feels scared, like I'm gonna get in trouble from my mom when I get home, you know —for all the bad decisions I made that night. But, for that one moment, when I got in the car and she smiled at me, I felt like I'd made one right choice. Just one. And then…" I couldn't say it. I just couldn't bring myself to say the words out loud. It wasn't until right then that I realized I'd never had to. My dad broke the news to everyone, while I stood numb and silent.

"Keep talking," David said with the insistent tone of an adult.

"All I remember was feeling this incredible jolt as we pulled away from the stop sign. Mom's hand grabbed mine for a second, but… everything moved—like the most violent hard turns on roller coaster. My arms, my head, everything just…" I searched for the words. "I felt pain, but it was the rush—the speed of things I really remember. I saw the front windscreen turn red; heard my mom's scream get cut off suddenly, but that's it. I shut my eyes, praying for it to end, and when I opened them again, we'd stopped. The crying had stopped. The noise, everything.

"I didn't even know I was upside-down until I tried to undo my seatbelt. But it was stuck, and all the blood was making my head tight until I couldn't breathe."

"Breathe now," David said, placing his palm firmly against my ribs.

I took a long breath and it shook my whole body as it left my lungs again.

"That's it." He kissed my head. "Just breathe."

I let myself cry for a moment, just trying to focus on breathing, and when the wave of pain subsided, I looked up at David's incredible green eyes. "I haven't really thought much about the accident. I forgot a lot of things, you know—things I'm remembering now."

"Like what?"

"The silence." My eyes narrowed into the memory. "After we stopped rolling, it was like the world stood staring on, completely hushed for a moment, maybe waiting for our souls to leave the earth."

"And Harry? Was he conscious then?"

"No." My lips turned down tightly, quivering. "And I didn't want to hear him cry. I didn't want him to be hurt—lost somewhere I couldn't get to him. I was glad he was quiet. But I didn't know what that meant…" My words flaked away as the thoughts that rushed through my head, when I looked into the backseat and saw nothing, came flooding back.

"Where was he?" David asked.

"He was… gone."

He sighed, his hand coming up on my shoulder as he pulled me in, cradling my face against his chest.

"His blue beanie—the one Mom knitted when we found out he was a boy—it was laying on the roof among the glass. It came right off his head. It… I wanted to grab it, but I was afraid."

"Of what?"

"I don't really know. Maybe that I'd see blood or… maybe worse."

David held me tighter.

"I didn't know what to do. No one came. I thought people would come running, but no one came. So I… I just screamed. I knew it wouldn't help, but I couldn't stop it. And"—I looked up into David's eyes—"I never knew before, but it doesn't matter how loud you scream. There is no such thing as the worst things can get. There is no rock bottom. There is only a deep, endless pit of hell that you can fall through. You always imagine, like the movies, that you scream and someone comes, and they save you and they stop you from screaming. But… I stopped because my throat went dry. I screamed so long, and I only stopped because my body couldn't scream anymore." Tears lensed my eyes again. "Where's the humanity in that?"

"There is none, sweetheart," he said, drawing me into him again.

I closed my eyes and pictured the eerie dimness of the streetlights outside the car window, how, in the cold, the glow seemed to settle on the footpath like fog; the endless silence broken only by the hollow ticking of an indicator lamp—distant and lonely in the dead of night.

"If it had happened on another road," I said, "maybe where there were houses, we would've… someone would've come sooner. But the drive home was down this freeway. If I'd walked, I could've cut through. I could've—"

"Shh." He stroked my hair. "Don't go there, Ara. Just don't let yourself go there. What's done is done and—"

"I didn't mean for any of this. I didn't mean for them to die."

"Of course you didn't, sweetheart." He wrapped me in his arms, turning me slightly so my shoulder rested against his chest. "Of course you didn't."

"But even still, it was my fault, and I know I shouldn't think like that, I really do. But I feel like a murderer. I—" I looked back on the memory of the empty backseat and the feeling of everything being gone. It was like lying flat on a steel bed, having someone hit your soul with a rubber mallet, sending it in black splatters everywhere. I had no control. I didn't know where Harry was and couldn't get free to make him okay.

"He was just a baby, David. What if he was awake? What if he was cold and wondering why we'd left him there? What if he wanted to go home?" I burst into tears. "I just wanna take him home."

"I wish I could make you better. God knows, I do. But I know so much better than anyone what that feels like—to lose something precious—and that there's nothing I can even say."

I nodded. "I just… how can he be gone? I was there. I was squeezing my mom's hand when he was born. I *named* him, David. How could all that be gone?"

"Sometimes, my love, life just doesn't make sense."

"It's cruel. It's like…" I thought about it for a moment. "It's like creating something; like crafting it and painting it then, in one stupid move, dropping it to the ground."

He rubbed gentle circles over my back. "I know, but I also know that by talking to me, you're taking the first step toward healing."

"I don't know about that, David. I just feel like I've made it all worse now. Like I've been lashed with something big and hard, and I can't make that go away." I touched my chest where it always hurt. "I tried to tell myself it wasn't my fault. I tried to make amends, pray for forgiveness, but it doesn't matter what I do. This pain, it doesn't go. I feel choked-up and so *damn* sad all the time."

"That's the guilt making the pain worse. But, Ara… this wasn't your fault."

My face crumpled. I truly wished I believed that. "I've been through every one of Vicki's books, trying to find a way to make sense of the guilt. I know all the facts. But science doesn't measure grief,

David. It can't, and it can't make sense of it. In my heart,"—I touched the base of my ribs—"way down here, I think, maybe in my soul. I can't put the guilt away. And it's changed me. I'm bitter and snarky and moody..."

"Time, Ara." David laughed softly, holding me close again. "Time is all that can heal."

"But I get so angry. Sometimes I really think I'm okay, and... sometimes the anger is so much stronger than the grief."

"What are you angry about—just that you called her?"

I shook my head. "So many things. I think the powerlessness, you know, the feeling like I had no control..." I bit my teeth together, folding forward as the feelings I'd pushed down rose up in me again, making everything tight in my core. "They took me away. They came, and they leaned into that car, and all they said was *this one's alive*. Then they took me away. They wouldn't let me go; wouldn't let me find Harry. I was fine. I wasn't hurt. Just glass and cuts, but I was fine. If I could've... if they just let me look. I might've found him."

"Did..." He paused, hesitant. "You say that like they *never* found him."

"They did." I nodded. "They found his seat on the side of the road. Harry wasn't in it."

"What happened to him?"

"They wouldn't tell me. But I heard a nurse say the cop was having counseling—the one that found him."

He clicked his tongue and squeezed me tighter. "You shouldn't have had to hear that."

"I know. And it made me so mad. I mean, I was over sixteen. Legally old enough to make my own medical decisions. Legally old enough to be told what was going on. But they stuck me in that bed, drugged up on who-knows-what and left alone until my dad arrived. From America! They let *him* tell me my mom was dead. They let *him* tell me I'd been horrifically scarred. And he didn't even say it. It was the way he looked at me, David. He hadn't seen me in nearly a year, and the first time he laid eyes on me was when my face had been ripped apart. What do you think I saw in him that morning?"

David's throat shifted. "I know. But you're safe now."

"I don't want to be safe. I feel like I owe a debt."

He tilted my face upward with both hands. "A debt?"

"I'm not stupid. I *know* it was an accident. But I feel like they're coming for me. Like I gave my family to them, and now they want *me*."

"Who wants you?"

"I don't know. The Other Side. Death. Karma, maybe. I don't know."

David's teeth slid slowly over each other as his jaw came forward and his eyes flicked to the place of deep thoughts. "Do you… do you ever think of taking those matters into your own hands?"

"Mm-hm. Like, maybe I could trade places. You know—offer myself in exchange. If I could go back, maybe I could—"

"Ara, my love, there is no going back." His hands tightened on my face. "We make mistakes, we have regrets but, sweetheart—" He opened and closed his mouth a few times, his eyes searching my face for any words he could say to make it all okay. "It was selfish of you to make her come out in the middle of the night, and it if it weren't for that, she would never have been there when that truck tire blew out. But that doesn't mean it wasn't her time to go. You can't control everything, Ara, and what matters is that, if you were to go back, you'd do it differently."

"How is that possibly any good to me—to know that?"

"Because you learned something. And if that's all you can take from this, then it's better than walking away with only grief."

I shook my head. "Don't give me that rubbish, David. They spoon-fed me that crap in the hospital until I nearly *choked* on it. There is no lesson to be learned. There is no goddamn bright side. There are two facts here: they are dead, and if I hadn't called Mom, they wouldn't be."

I could tell David was frustrated. I could tell he wanted to shake me. *I* wanted to shake me. I didn't want to feel this way, and couldn't expect anyone else to understand, which is precisely why I hadn't said it to anyone.

"Why are you shaking your head?" I asked him.

"I just… I'm angry. Not at you, but at everything. What… who's been talking to you about this, who have you had to comfort you?"

I brushed my hair from my face. "My dad."

"Does he know you blame yourself?"

I swallowed, unable to see my shoes through the blur of tears. "No."

"Then what kind of closure have you had?" David sounded almost as angry as me.

"Only the funeral," I offered. "They called that closure. But a storm hit, and it rained so hard I couldn't even see their coffins. And most people left."

"Did you leave?"

I nodded. "At first I refused. I knelt in the mud with my hand on Harry's coffin as if maybe I could hold onto him—stop them from putting him in that hole. I didn't want that to be it for him." I looked at David and nodded, getting control of my voice. "It just seemed so unfair."

"It is unfair."

I nodded, sniffing up my tears. "My dad sat down next to me, got covered in mud too, and I know he meant well, but he just made matters worse. He took my hand and moved it down a little, told me it was over Harry's heart—that he had his teddy and his little blanket in there to keep him warm and that, tucked up right beside his face, was a picture of me and Mom."

"That must have brought you some comfort."

"No."

"Why?"

"He didn't know Harry. He never even met him! What right did he have to make that decision? He should have asked *me*." I wiped my nose on the back of my wrist. "He put a *teddy* in there with Harry. What teddy? Harry would've wanted his monkey. He wouldn't want some *stupid* teddy. But it was too late. It was sealed up—locked up. I couldn't change it. I couldn't change any of it."

David rested his chin on my head, shaking his. "Ara, I just… I just wish I'd known you then. Or maybe if I'd met you when you first got here. I… I knew you were sad, I knew you were grieving, but this…" He kissed my hair. "I didn't know it went this deep."

"No one does. And I won't tell them. And neither will you." It came out as a demand, but deep down it was a question. He held all the cards right now. If he told my dad that I called my mom that night, I'm not sure Dad would ever forgive me.

David's soothing touch wordlessly tried to wash away the pain of my scars. He just sat there shaking his head, making line after line over my jaw. "When did this happen? You arrived here a month ago, but your scars… they're healed too much to have such little time pass."

"It was June."

"But you didn't arrive here until—"

"I refused to come out in public until my wounds healed a bit. My dad and I stayed at a motel in Australia until then."

"A motel? Didn't you have any family to stay with?"

"Only Mike—my best friend. But I didn't want to see him, and we couldn't go back to the house. Dad said it would be too painful."

"It would've been. But you still should have gone back once before leaving."

"I did. I made him take me back there before we got on the plane, but…"

He waited, and when I refused to elaborate, he said, "But?"

As I craned my neck to look at David, the feel of his breath on my nose and lips calmed me with the reality of his existence. He hadn't run away yet. I told him I was to blame for my mother's death, and he hadn't run away. Why?

"Talk to me, Ara. You said 'but'."

I pictured the cold wind of that grey day, the way the rain made waterfalls over the windscreen as we pulled up outside my house. The lights were all out and the remainder of the daylight fought against thunderclouds for right of existence in my world. I took each shaky step up to the porch with a kind of stillness that had my dad lingering closely behind me.

"It hadn't really hit me that they were gone," I said. "Not until I pushed the door open and looked down the hall. And… for a second I waited, truly believing I'd see Harry crawl up to me at full speed, with his little train in his hand.

"Everything looked the same and it *smelled* like home, but it was empty and so quiet, like they weren't there anymore. I couldn't *feel* them there anymore." I tapped my chest with an open palm, trying to push the pain back in. "The dishes were still in the sink, and the clock on the wall was still ticking—that much stayed the same. It felt strange how, even though we weren't there, time just kept moving without us." I blinked a few times, still seeing that ticking hand. "It should've stopped, but it didn't. And it hit me so hard. I just broke apart and cried in the doorway.

"Dad didn't know what to do. He ran next door to get Mrs. Baker. She made me get up. She told me I had to be strong now; that childhood passes with tragedy, and the sooner I came to accept that, the easier my life would be."

David groaned, folding my face into his chest. "What did your dad say to that?"

"Nothing. He just led me to my room and shut the door."

I closed my eyes and saw the dark shadows in the hallway near my room, how the absence of that warm summer sun meant the death of everything I loved.

"I packed a few things, and… as I was leaving, I went to Harry's room to get Pappy, his monkey toy. If Harry couldn't have it, maybe I could. But Dad blocked the door and he wouldn't let me go in there." I broke into tears so deep the words came out in hiccups.

"Why?"

"He said it would hurt more. He said I needed to make Harry a memory—something that didn't feel real anymore."

"He was just doing what he thought was best, Ara." David choked back tears.

"I know." I nodded. "But he was wrong. They all think they know what I need, but they don't."

"What *do* you need, sweetheart?" he asked. "Tell me, and I'll make it happen."

"I need to go back, David—to that night. I need to put down that *goddamn* phone, and if I can't do that, I just need to die."

"Ara." David grabbed both my cheeks, thrusting my face up until I looked into his eyes. "What do you think your mother would feel to hear you say that?"

"That's just it." I pushed his hands away. "She wouldn't feel anything, because she's dead and it's my fault. No matter what you try to say, it's my fault."

"It was no one's fault. Get it through your head." He grabbed me more firmly, not letting me break away this time. "You wanna blame someone? Blame the truck driver, blame the tire shop who fitted used tires, but don't blame yourself, because it won't bring them back."

My brow creased tightly in the middle. I grabbed his hand slowly. "Wait, I never said there was a truck." In fact, I never said it was a car accident. But he knew that before I even told him.

David stiffened, staring ahead, his mouth hanging like he was about to say something.

"David?" I sat back so I could look right into his eyes. "Tell me how you knew about the truck? Did my dad tell you?"

"Not everything." He wiped his thumb over a line of tears on my cheek. "But he told me why you were here."

"When?" I yelled. "Why?"

"Ara, calm down, it's okay." He went to pull me closer, but I pushed away as hard as I could.

"You're traitors—both of you." I jumped to my feet to get as much distance from him as possible.

"Sweetheart, don't be upset."

"No. All this time." I looked away in disbelief. "You knew, and you made me talk about it. Why?"

"Because I knew it wasn't just their death bothering you. I knew it went deeper." He stood up too. "Turns out I was right."

"So…" My eyes went wide, realization sinking in like nausea. "So you were digging for information—for my dad?"

"Ara, no—"

"What would possibly make you want to do that, David?"

"Ara, it wasn't like that." He edged closer, both hands out.

"When did he tell you? How long have you known?"

"Please, just—"

"When!" My scream echoed off the rocks and came back to haunt me with its severity.

"When you first came here." He walked slowly toward me, as if I were a mental patient he was going to grab at first opportunity. "He caught me during football practice, watching you on the swing, and—"

"You were *watching* me?" An eerie sensation travelled over my neck and spine, like a hand just touched my shoulder in a room that was *supposed* to be empty.

"Not like you think."

I backed away, one step at a time, in unison with his. "You're a creep."

David stopped walking, lowering his arms as his green eyes flooded with pain. "I know how this sounds, Ara-Rose. But it wasn't like that. I swear. Just. Listen to me."

I laughed, though it wasn't out of amusement. "All this time you've known about me. Even when we talked in the library?"

He nodded.

"Well"—I shook my head—"I guess it makes sense now why you were so..." Friendly? Eager? Was that it? What was it with him? Did he enjoy the company of messed-up young girls? Perhaps it was a complex of his: Knight Syndrome. I felt like such an idiot.

I turned and marched off to vent my anger away from anyone that could get hurt. I just felt violated; another choice taken away from me by people who thought they knew best. When were they going to realize that it made matters worse?

"Ara?"

"Just leave me alone. Don't follow me!"

I didn't look back. I didn't want to know if he followed or if he turned and went back home. As far as I was concerned, this was a friendship-ending offense. If I *never* saw him again, that would even be too soon.

My feet guided me down an alternative path to the one

we came in on. Billowing grass grew up between old tire tracks, and I followed them, hoping they'd lead me into town. But my trek of rage drove me forward too quickly, submerging me deep into the woods before I realized I was going the wrong way.

I stopped dead where the trail faded to thick shrubs, closing in up ahead by tangled trees and thorn-laced vines. The once-background sound of birds singing and leaves rustling in the wind was now unnervingly loud, making me feel very small and ultimately on my own, in a wild place.

On exhausted legs, I wandered over and slumped heavily onto a nearby log, hugging myself as I looked up at the treetops and then down around the bases, trying to see through them to the distance. I wasn't sure what to be worried about out here. Back home, I knew there could be kangaroos around, but also knew they very rarely attacked. Here, there could be any manner of man-eating creature, or worse, people.

I checked my phone. No service, and it was getting late. Dad would worry soon. And David was probably already worried—not just about where I was but also that I'd never speak to him again. I knew deep inside that he never meant any harm. I was embarrassed that he knew about me all this time, and I guess I felt like he'd pretended to be my friend so he could get into my head for Vicki and Dad. But if I really thought about it, David wasn't that kind of guy. He wouldn't be here unless he wanted to.

I flicked a ladybug off my shoe and stood up, dumping my phone in the pocket of my dress. Maybe he was waiting for me back by the lake. Maybe it wasn't too late to apologize. I steeled myself for a round of groveling, but after only one step back up the hill, crashed right into the warm embrace of strong arms.

"Ara!"

"David?"

He wrapped me up almost restrictively, his fingertips pressing against my ribs. "Don't *ever* run off like that again. I couldn't find you. I was worried sick."

"I'm sorry," I whispered into his chest.

"No. You. Have. *Nothing* to be sorry for."

"But I—"

"No." He shook his head against the top of mine. "I won't let you say that word anymore. Not for anything."

I tugged a little to make him loosen his grip, looking up at him with new eyes. "Why didn't you just tell me you knew about my mom?"

He smiled, breathing out through his nose. "Would you have wanted me to know? Would you still have been my friend?" It was a rhetorical question; we both knew the answer.

"So, what am I to you now? I mean, why would you still be friends with me now that you know all of this? Am I some damsel project, or something? Do you think you can save me?"

David shook his head. "Ara. It was never about that."

"Okay. So if my dad hasn't sent you in as his informant, then what do you want with me?"

"Informant?" He looked down at me. "Is that what you thought?"

"It makes sense. From the first moment we met, you acted like we knew each other—like we were already friends. I just… I wondered why you were so interested, when, you know, I'm no supermodel. I don't really have anything to offer you."

"You have more than you think, Ara." He exhaled, rocking his jaw. "Okay, at the risk of sounding creepy, I'm going to tell you why I was so… *overeager* when you first came to school."

"You weren't really stalking me, were you?"

"Ha! No, I wasn't. But I had seen you several times."

"When?"

"The first time was about a month ago—guess it was the day you arrived. I was on the football field doing laps for practice, and I passed your house, saw this sweet little thing in a yellow dress just standing there, looking up at the blue sky. And I stopped running."

I pictured it for a second: David on the field, me by the car, watching Dad get the suitcases from the trunk. Vicki stood on the porch steps, trying not to cry, and so badly, I knew, wanting to run out and hug me. But she didn't. And I was glad for that, because I'd have pushed her away back then.

"My first thought was how unusual it was to see a girl in a dress like that," he said. "And you looked so pretty, so innocent. But when I looked a bit closer, I realized that you looked sad. And something in me felt tight." He touched just below his ribs, rubbing firmly. "I hadn't really felt that before."

I smiled.

"I just wanted to make you okay," he said. "And I hoped I'd get a chance to meet you. I knew that was Mr. Thompson's house, so I figured you were his daughter."

"So you asked him about me?"

He smiled, his lips spreading wide over his teeth. "Uh, no. I didn't have the guts. I uh—I actually set it up. I guess I set *him* up to *have* to tell me about you."

"How?"

"He was running football practice one afternoon, and you were out in the backyard. I asked your dad if that girl on the swing at his house was related to him. And he told me you were his daughter. And I told him you were beautiful."

"Suck-up."

He laughed. "I waited so long for you to come to school, Ara. When you finally did, and I finally saw you up close, I'm sorry"—he shook his head, grinning—"but I actually couldn't believe how beautiful you were, and I…"

"You?"

"This will sound *really* creepy, and I'm sorry, but… I think, maybe… I instantly fell in love with you."

My heart stopped beating, slipping through each of my internal organs until it hit my feet.

David laughed lightly, tucking my hair behind my ear. "You're going to be okay, you know. We'll get through this. Together."

"Together?"

"Yeah."

I snuggled into his chest, wrapping my arms all the way around him. "I like the way that sounds."

"Me too," he said, and in his arms I stood with my eyes closed, feeling my own heart beat, while each breath I took unlinked my soul from the binds of my shadowed past. I never wanted to go back to before. I wanted this embrace to last forever—to stay here in his arms, where all of my troubles didn't seem so absolute and the world didn't seem so cruel. There was something about the way he held me that made me feel safe; made me realize, as wholly as I knew myself, that the empty feeling I'd suffered so long could only have been cured by this moment—by David, who came into my life as just a boy, and turned out to be a knight.

9

David closed the front door, and we both looked up the dark staircase to the sound of a piano.

"That's weird," I said. "We don't even have a piano."

He smiled. "I'll wait here."

"By yourself?"

His smile softened. "Something tells me you might need a minute."

"Why?" I frowned.

"Ara?" Dad called down from his room. "Is that you?"

"Uh, yeah. I just came back to get changed."

"Come in here first, please."

I looked at David, who took a step back, offering the stairway. "I'll be right here," he said.

Each step I took felt like my last. I was sure Dad had a massive lecture waiting behind his bedroom door on why we don't sneak out of school with strange boys, but as I pushed his door open and saw him sitting on the end of his bed, my heart felt heavy. "Dad?"

He turned his face from the cradle of his hands. "Come in. Close the door."

"Where's Vicki and Sam?"

"Family pizza night."

"Oh yeah. Sorry." I stopped. "I forgot about pizza night."

"It's fine, honey." He patted the bed.

I sat down next to him. "Why didn't you go with them, Dad?"

He gave me a look that suggested the obvious. "My daughter ran away from school today—crying. I wanted to be here when you got home."

"I'm sorry about that." I twiddled my thumbs.

"Ara-Rose, you don't need to be sorry." He rubbed my back. "I'm just glad someone was there for you."

"Yeah." I tried not to, but couldn't help smiling. "David kind of forced a deep-and-meaningful confession out of me."

Dad laughed. "So you told him about why you came to live here?"

No, you did, I thought, wishing he'd just stop playing dumb. "Yeah. We're… he's helping me through it."

Dad sighed massively and wrapped his arm all the way around my shoulders, pulling me into him for a bear-tight hug. "I'm so relieved to hear that. And you're all going out to Betty's tonight, right?"

I nodded. "If that's… is it still okay?"

"Of course it is, honey." He pressed a big sloppy Dad kiss on my brow. "More than okay. I'll even give you a later curfew. How's that sound?"

"Really? What time?"

"Eleven sound fair?"

"Yes!" I hugged him, wrapping my skinny arms all the way around his neck. "Thank you, Dad."

"Just happy to make you happy." He rubbed my back, and as I pulled away, sitting beside him again, my butt landed on the remote, starting up the film he'd been watching. I went to apologize, but my eyes strayed from his smile to the TV set, stopping on the tiny dancer gracefully billowing across the screen.

"I'm sorry, honey." Dad grabbed the remote and went to turn it off.

"Wait." I placed my hand over his. "I want to see."

He lowered the remote as I rose to my feet, walking slowly over to watch the only piece of my mother I had left.

"Did she ever tell you about this concert?" Dad asked.

I shook my head.

"It was the year before she quit ballet."

"Before she had me?"

"Yes." He stood beside me. "It was Swan Lake."

"I know." I smiled, watching my mother dance. "I did this one last year for our ballet recital."

His arm wrapped my shoulders. "I remember. You were such a beautiful dancer."

"I think I inherited that from Mom."

"Yes." He looked at the screen. "Among other things."

I looked up at his watering eyes. "You miss her, too?"

He pressed stop on the remote, and the screen went black. "I always will."

A moment of silence passed between us. "I'm sorry, Dad."

"What for?"

"I… I'm just sorry—about everything."

He looked down at me, his eyes narrowing tightly on the inner corners. "You know, honey, if there's something you need to tell me—"

"I know." I hugged him softly, squeezing once before backing up. "I do know that."

"Okay." His concerned smile dropped for the warm one I always loved. "Well, you go on now and have a good night. Promise?"

I nodded. "Yeah. I promise."

As I closed his door, the gentle hum of piano followed me out into the hall again.

"Are you okay, Ara?" David called from downstairs.

"Uh, yeah," I called back. "Just gotta throw on some jeans. Won't be long."

I slipped into the cleanest-smelling pair of jeans I could find on my floor and grabbed the blue zip-up sweater from my dresser, then scrunched my hair up a few times and grabbed my purse as I tripped out the door.

"You won't be needing this." David took my purse, appearing out of nowhere, and tossed it back into my room. I heard it hit my bed with a dull, leather-sounding thud.

"Why won't I need that? Don't they sell food there? I'm starving."

He shook his head, unamused. "You know I won't let you pay for your own food."

"Why? Is my money dirty?" I followed him down the stairs, my careless feet thumping loudly behind his barely audible footfalls.

"No." He opened the front door. "But when a guy takes a girl on a date, he should pay. It's the way I was raised."

"Well…" I sauntered past him. He closed the front door behind us. "It's weird."

"Don't pretend you object to me treating you as a lady."

"Maybe I do."

Despite that, he still opened the car door for me. "Why do girls always do that?"

"Do what?"

"Spill that equal rights nonsense—argue that we're taking their independence by opening a door for them. That's just not the case."

"Well, what is the case?" I sat down on the front seat, leaving my feet on the driveway.

"Simply that we're demonstrating good breeding; showing the girl we're worthy and capable of taking care of her. That we're polite, considerate, nurturing."

I folded my arms. "Women don't need nurturing—or to be taken care of. We can fend for ourselves. We're equal to men, you know?"

"Ara." He stared down at me, the skin under his eyes tight. "I'm not disregarding equality by being a gentleman; I'm exercising chivalry."

"That's out-dated though, isn't it?" I challenged with a grin.

"Never," he said in a high tone. "Why should courtesy be out-dated—or offensive? Is it not polite to offer a pregnant woman your seat on a bus?"

"Yes, but that's different."

"Why?"

"Because she's pregnant."

"Then, if you want equal rights for all, it would only be polite for me to also offer this to a woman who is not pregnant. Or to the man playing Angry Birds on his iPhone."

"This is getting off topic." I swung my legs into the car. "The point is—" Argh! What was my point? …Oh yeah. "The point is that I should be able to pay for my own food if I want."

"And you can, but not when you come out with me. I have rights, too."

"So… I'm taking away *your* rights by buying my own food?"

"Absolutely."

"What a load of rubbish."

"Think of it like this: some girls believe exerting independence by denying a man his own rights to be respectful demonstrates strength. But women are incredibly strong. We already know this. So, unfortunately, by labeling chivalry to be insolent, she is merely robbing the next generation of civility—ensuring the extinction of well-mannered men. It's my right and duty to preserve the tradition."

"Not all women consider it good manners when a guy forces her to accept a free lunch." I tightened the fold of my arms.

"Oh, really?" He looked down at me with one brow arched. "Yet, if I neglected to wrap my jacket over your shoulders on a cold evening, I'd be regarded as a jerk."

"I—"

"I'm a gentleman, Ara. Get used to it." He closed the door on my retort and appeared suddenly in the seat next to me.

"How do you move so quick?"

"I don't. You just phase out all the time."

DAVID PULLED INTO AN ANGLED SPACE OUTSIDE THE BUZZING corner cafe and shut the engine off. "Welcome to the best burger joint in town."

Beyond the flashing pink-and-blue signs on the windows, the generation gap seemed to be left behind. Kids sat on chrome-rimmed stools by the milk-bar, singing Elvis songs loud enough to hear from here, while others gathered around the white billiard tables on the lower level. Even the staff, in their flaring poodle skirts and sneakers, seemed to have jumped right off the Grease film set.

"David?"

"Yeah."

As I looked back at him, he smiled softly, comfortably, as if he'd not taken his eyes off me the whole time. "I'm sorry about the whole independence thing. I think it's really sweet that you're a gentleman."

He nodded, taking my hand delicately. "I know."

"You do?"

"Yes. I can see right through your *girl power* act, young lady."

"Oh, really." I leaned back in the chair, my eyes employing a defiant glare. "And what exactly do you see, Mr. Know-It-All?"

"I see…" He leaned forward, luring me into his private little world. "I see a young girl who just wants to be loved by a man worthy of her."

Several retorts came to mind, none of them sassy and creative, like I wished. I went with "Aw, how romantic," squeezing my fists tightly to stop from launching myself into his arms.

"Come. Let's get some food." He turned slowly and hopped out, closing the door quietly behind him, then appeared by my door way too fast, offering his hand.

As my fingers touched his, blood rushed up with a quick skip of my heart, and I drew my hand back. "Wow, you are really cold tonight."

"Yeah. I know." He looked at his hand, rubbing his thumb over his fingertips. "They get cold when I drive."

"Mine get cold when I do homework."

"Maybe you should avoid it then."

"Maybe I like cold hands," I said, walking beside him, and when he smiled down at me, I caught sight of his fangs.

"Why are you looking at me like that?" he asked.

"I was just thinking." I braved rejection and reached for his hand again; he let me take it. "With those pointy canines and cold hands, you could pass as a vampire."

His sudden boisterous laughter made me smile. "Better watch out then. We are on a *dinner* date after all."

"Hm," I said. "Guess I better order garlic then, or maybe a steak."

"A steak?"

"Yeah, you know…?" I prompted, stabbing my heart with an invisible stick. "As in… a stake?"

David shook his head, but a warm smile sparkled in his eyes as he opened the cafe door and the nineteen-fifties-time-warp enveloped us.

"I would guess, by the look on your face, that you like it," he said.

"It's great. Crowded, though."

"When you taste the food, you'll see why."

My stomach groaned.

"Ah, I see the very mention of sustenance has awakened the ogre." David grinned at my belly.

"Stop laughing," I said, covering it.

"Make me."

"I can, you know." I looked up at him. "I'm tougher than I look."

He pinched my bony wrist between two fingers and held it up. "Yeah. So much muscle."

"Shut up." I laughed, punching him softly in the arm.

"Ouch." He rubbed it. "That really hurt."

"Really?"

"No." He smirked, offering a seat nearby. "I was just trying to be nice."

I slid into the booth, shaking my head, and David shuffled in beside me, coming closer each time I moved over to give him more space. It wasn't until my shoulder and arm pressed against the cold glass window that I realized it wasn't more space he wanted, but less between us.

I looked into my lap, smiling to myself. "Have you seen the others yet?"

"By the pool table." He tilted his head in their direction without taking his eyes off me.

"Hm. Didn't even see them when we walked in." I leaned around him and watched Emily and Alana giggling flirtatiously at Ryan. "Are they checking out his butt every time he takes a shot?"

David nodded, smiling.

"Do you think we should go say hello?" I asked.

"No, they'll come over when they finish. For now"—he shrugged—"I kinda like this."

So did I. In fact, I kinda hoped they didn't notice us at all.

The corner of David's mouth twitched, breaking his face into a grin.

"What?" I asked. "Why are you smiling?"

"No reason."

I turned my face away, feeling heat rise up in my cheeks. Sometimes it felt like he knew exactly what I was thinking.

"Why do you do that?" He cupped my chin, turning my head.

"Do what?"

"You turn your face away when you blush," he said delicately. "I wish you wouldn't."

"It's embarrassing."

"It's sweet."

"Well," I said, trying to break the awkwardness of his stare. "You know, you have an irritating quirk yourself."

"I do?" he said.

"Yes."

"And what might that be?"

"That!" I pointed to that smile—the one evident only by the two dimples above the corners of his lips; the one he did as his gaze drifted downward. "It's like you… I don't know, it's like you have a secret or a joke, and it's a good one, but you don't want to share it."

"Oh." He nodded, hiding the smallest hint of humor. "I guess I do maybe do that—a lot."

I nodded.

"You're very observant, Ara-Rose."

"So, what is it? Why do you do it?"

"I just spend too much time in my own head, that's all."

"Like I do?"

"Yeah, except… it gets pretty boring up here, so I find ways to amuse myself." The bright smile dropped instantly, and his lost words hung in the air as I folded my arms and stole his smile for my own.

"So, am I boring you?" I joked.

"I didn't mean it like that."

"Hey-you-two." Emily bounced up beside the table.

"Hey, Em."

"Check it out." She inclined her head to one side in a quick movement, hinting with her eyes.

"Oh my God, you guys," I beamed, seeing the joined hands of Alana and Ryan. "When did this happen?"

"Well." Ryan swept his fingers through his hair. "I kinda got the hard word put on me."

Alana raised her eyebrows in Emily's direction to indicate that she had something do with it.

Emily shrugged. "You weren't there to talk with me about David this afternoon, so I had to find *something* to do."

David looked sideways at me, his radiant smile gleaming. "You talk about me?"

I blinked a few extra times, feeling pretty sheepish, but chose to ignore him. "Well, that's really cool, guys. I'm glad you finally got together."

"Yeah." Ryan shrugged. "I'm pretty happy about it."

They slid into the seat opposite us, while Emily slid in beside David, leaving a less than reasonable gap. I all but got my ruler out and measured it to the last millimeter.

"What can I get you guys?" a waitress said, popping up out of nowhere, pulling a pen from her ponytail.

David handed me the menu. I placed it back down, shaking my head. As the others rattled off their orders, he leaned in and whispered against my ear, "What's wrong? Why aren't you reading the menu?"

"I don't need it," I said enthusiastically, logging the cool, minty scent of his breath in my memory. I looked at the waitress then as a tray of burgers and fries passed her head. "I'll have that, thanks."

She turned around and then smiled when she looked back. "Okay, Betty Burger, fries and shake?" She wrote it down and looked at David.

"Same." He smiled.

"Okay, that'll just be a moment." She skated off.

David stared at me. "That's a lot of food. Can you really eat all that?"

Evidence that he didn't know me very well at all. "I think we should have a challenge."

"I'm always up for that," Ryan said.

"Cool. It's a *who can eat the most* challenge." I said.

Emily shook her head. "Ew, no, sorry. Count me out. I'm on a diet."

My eyes bulged. "A diet?"

"Yeah. I mean, no, not like that." She waved her hands around. "It's just a healthy eating thing—to stay fit. I'm on top of the pyramid. If I weigh too much, someone could get hurt."

"Okay then. Alana?"

"Sorry. Count me out, too. I have a really small stomach. I'll probably lose on the first fry."

Ryan grinned wildly. "Count me in, sister." He shook my hand, then we both looked at David.

"I don't know," he said. "I can eat a *lot*. I could probably eat *you* and not think twice about it." He leaned forward and rested his elbows on the table, tilting his shoulders closer to me. "Do you think you're up for that kind of a challenge, little girl?"

"Bring it on," I said, and as I went to shake his hand, a jolt of static shot through us, making me yelp. "Ow. I hate that."

"Sorry." David touched the sleeve of his thin black sweater. "I'm wearing wool."

"Wool?" I exclaimed with a certain amount of accusation in my tone. "How do you even know that's wool? You're a guy!"

He leaned on his hand, resting his knuckles just beside his smile. "A guy who knows what wool feels like."

"Sometimes I think you know too much for your age, David Knight."

"Well, I come from a wealthy family." He distracted himself, swapping the salt label with the sugar one. "Grooming and Deportment were lessons of great significance during my upbringing."

"Grooming and what?" Emily asked.

"Etiquette classes," I informed, leaning around David to look at her. "I had to do them in school when I was ten."

"Oh." She sat back, staring ahead thoughtfully. "Hm, that makes sense on *so* many levels."

Yup, I thought so too. Being raised like an English Lord explained why he was so charming and charismatic and… otherworldly.

When we finished dinner, David and Ryan carried a heated discussion about the best guitar brands, while I lost myself to thought, sliding my finger over the condensation on my milkshake glass. The waitress took our plates and left the bill, which David snaffled quickly, opening his leather wallet. "I'll get this one, guys."

"Are you sure, man?" Ryan offered a fifty.

"Yeah. Hundred per cent." David nodded, laying the cash out with a rather large tip to accompany.

"Well, thanks," Ryan said. "I'll get the next one."

David nodded, leaning forward to stuff his wallet in his back pocket.

"Ara." Emily shoved David back in his seat so she could look at me. "You're not human, are you? How do you eat so much?"

I patted my belly. "I like my stomach to be full."

"No kidding," she said.

"Well, I think it's good to see a girl eating," Ryan said. "Don't you, Dave?"

"Yeah." He looked at me with soft eyes, then threaded his fingers through mine under the table. "I don't have to be one of those guys that's gotta convince his girlfriend to eat. Huh! She'll probably eat mine t—" He stopped mid-sentence.

Everyone at the table stared at him, including me.

"*Girlfriend*?" Emily said. "So it's official?"

David sat incredibly still, barely breathing, and certainly not speaking. He looked so nervous that I felt bad for him so, even though we hadn't actually talked about making it official, I squeezed his hand and nodded to say I agreed.

"Yes," he said smoothly, turning slightly to look at Emily. "It's official."

"Hey, that's really awesome, man. Congrats." Ryan reached out and they shook hands, bumping knuckles after.

"I knew it." Emily practically squealed. "I just knew she'd be your type, David."

"I don't think I have a *type*, Emily," he said, and wrapped his arm around me. "But Ara's pretty much everything I ever wanted in a girl."

Everyone made a cheering-yet-that's-totally-lame noise at David's mushy statement, but my whole body flooded with warmth, making me feel dizzy.

"Way to make me look bad, man," Ryan said, laughing once. "If I even *tried* to say something like that, I'd be accused of reading poetry from the Lame Book of Things Guys Shouldn't Say."

We all laughed, and David pulled me closer until my head rested between his jaw and shoulder, our thighs touching, the warmth from under his arm making the sharp, spicy smell of his cologne so much stronger.

"Guess that just leaves me now," Emily said, leaning on her hand.

"Well, if you're not with Spencer soon, maybe you should meet my best friend," I suggested. "He's coming to visit in a few weeks."

"Is he from Australia?" she asked.

"Mm-hm." I put my drink down on the table. "And he's really cute."

"Cute, is he?" David raised one brow.

"Actually, yes. He is."

"What does he look like?" Emily leaned further around, forcing David to sit back a little.

"Hey, why don't you come have a sleepover at mine next Saturday, and I'll show you some pics?" I offered.

"Yeah? I'd actually really like that."

"Cool. Alana, you wanna come, too?" I asked, allowing myself to feel the excitement of a normal teenager for a moment.

She looked at Ryan and smiled, shrinking into herself a little more. "Um, yeah, if Emily doesn't mind?"

"Mind? Of course you should come. Hey, I'll bring a movie, yeah?"

"Yeah, and I'll get a pizza," I added.

"Better make that two pizzas," Ryan said. "Otherwise the girls'll go hungry."

"Funny." I rolled my eyes.

"I'll bring the popcorn," Alana said shyly.

"Great. It's settled then." And I was actually excited. Mike would be, too, when I told him I was being normal. In a way, I was kind of glad my dad so cruelly forced me back to school this week and that Mike threatened me into talking to someone, because my horrible past was no longer a burden I solely owned. But best of all, David liked me enough to want me as his girlfriend. In fact… *love*. Love is what he'd said earlier.

I looked sideways at David flouncing his hand around in the air as he explained the size of the pizza he ate last night. He didn't know it yet, and I wasn't ready to tell him, but I loved him, too. Not in the way he loved me—like the way you love your guitar or your best friend—but *real* love. The kind of love you hold for someone you want to marry one day.

THE PHONE RANG TWICE. I WAITED IMPATIENTLY, TAPPING MY fingers on the desk.

"Hey, Ara."

"Hey, Mike. What you doin'?" I asked, hearing a strange static kind of sound.

"He's playing a round online. With me," another voice said very clearly into the receiver.

"Oh, hey, Matt." I laughed, wincing. Lucky I didn't just blurt out my news the second Mike picked up.

"How's it going, Ara, what you been up to?" Matt asked, half distracted.

"Well, actually. A lot. That's why I called," I said in an eager, soprano voice.

"Hang on," Mike said. "I'll just de-link the phone line from the headsets." I heard a noise, like someone tapping a fingertip on the lid of an empty tin, and a bleep followed, making the slight static in the phone line recede to a clear, quiet hum. "Okay, I'm alone now. How you doin', kid?"

"Well, actually, I've been waiting up all night for you to get home so I could call you. I've got good news."

"I'm listening."

I paused for dramatic effect. "I'm having a sleepover next weekend with Em and Alana."

"Really?" he dragged the word out.

"No, I was kidding."

"Well, that's great. Are you gonna talk to the girls about what happened?"

I shook my head, watching my reflection in the window. "Nope. Don't need to."

"Why?"

"Already talked to someone."

"Who?" he asked. "Was it your dad?"

"No, it was David."

"Yeah? The guy you like?"

"Yep."

"Well, come on, fill me in then?" His voice glided in that husky smoothness that could only be Mike's. It felt odd to me then, as old feelings surfaced, how I could be falling in love with David but still feel just as strongly for Mike.

"Well, it turns out he already knew." I sighed, rubbing my forehead. "He spoke to my dad before he even met me."

"Well, that's cool. And he still made friends with you?"

"Yes," I said in a flat tone. "I know, I know, you told me it'd be fine."

"Did you tell him about… you know, the other part of it—your inner guilt?"

I hesitated. "Yes."

"And he still likes you?" he asked, unperturbed.

"Actually, that's why I'm calling. We made our relationship *official* tonight," I beamed.

I heard the familiar sound of him dropping his controller. "You did what?"

"What? Oh, no—different kind of *official*, Mike." I laughed, waving my hands about.

He exhaled. "So, official *how* then?"

"As in he said the word *girlfriend*." I couldn't help but grin.

"Well, that's really cool. I'm glad there's someone lookin' out for ya."

"You could make even half an effort to sound happy for me, Mike."

"I am happy for you. I just—"

"You're still my bestie, you know."

"I know, but I'm not there, Ara. And I'm worried. I know you too well, and I know that tone. You're pretty serious about this guy, aren't you?"

"Maybe." I grinned, glad he couldn't see it.

"You gotta be careful. Grief can magnify emotions. What you're feeling, it may just be—"

"Don't say it, okay?" I said, holding the phone away from my ear in case he did. "I don't need you telling me what to feel."

He just sighed heavily. "Okay. Fine."

"Thank you." I sat quiet for a second, considering just hanging up. This feeling was fragile. I didn't want anyone to ruin it with common sense because, in truth, I needed to feel love for David. It was a whole lot better than feeling grief and guilt, or the shame in my unreciprocated love for Mike. "Hey, guess what?"

"What?"

"There's a girl I want you to meet when you come over."

"Ara, don't play matchmaker. I'm coming to see *you*, not go on dates."

"She's blonde. And cute," I offered, my voice rising in question. "She's the one I'm having over next weekend for a sleepover. I'm gonna show her some pictures of you."

"Well"—his voice dragged—"I do like blondes, but not dumb ones."

"Oh, no, don't worry, she's definitely not stupid. But don't get ahead of yourself, Romeo. She might not even like you. You're not that good looking."

"Are you kidding? I'm a hunk." He laughed.

I smiled. "Yeah, I'd pay that. But it takes more than just good looks to get the girl."

"Well, how 'bout my charming personality and witty sense of humor?"

"Might work."

"Worked on you."

"Not funny, Mike."

"Sorry. I take it back. I didn't mean it like that."

"Whatever. Anyway. You don't need to worry about me now, okay. I'm doing well. I'm still not fine. But I'm okay. Today."

"I'm glad, kid. You could use a bit of okay. But"—a long, stretching groan sounded down the phone line; I pictured him rolling his spine and straightening his arms behind his head—"I'll be there soon, and then my mere presence will make you *all* better."

"Don't flatter yourself."

He laughed for a second before it trickled away. "But seriously, Ara? Please don't set me up with this friend of yours. I'm in a difficult place right now with matters of the heart. I'd rather not drag anyone else into that. Okay?"

"Sure thing," I lied. I knew he'd change his mind when he saw her.

THE FRESH SCENT OF CUT GRASS NEXT DOOR MIXED WITH THE lemony fragrance of Vicki's bathroom cleaner, and the sound of the vacuum down the hall reminded me it was Saturday. As I opened my eyes to a bright day, my covers unruffled by sleep, I wondered how today could seem so perfectly sunny when yesterday, despite the weather being the same, my whole life had felt grey and stormy.

With a hint of a skip in my step, I leaped out of bed and stood right in front of my open window, drawing a breath of the fresh morning air. It wasn't even nine o'clock yet, but I wanted nothing more than to be up and a part of the day.

When my crappy old phone bleeped, I dove onto my bed and opened my messages: *Can I come see you today? It's David, by the way.*

An invisible paintbrush swerved across my lips, bringing them up on both corners. I texted back: *Are you kidding? Of course you can.*

Didn't want to seem overeager.

Be there in five, he texted back.

My eyes widened, taking in my ultra-messy room. I scooped the clothes off my floor in one big pile and threw them in the laundry basket, then shook my quilt over my bed and sprayed deodorant all around, waving a hand through the scented cloud to rid the stench of depression from within the walls.

"Vicki?" I called, grabbing my doorframe to lean out into the hall.

"Yes, dear?"

"I've got a friend coming over. Is that okay?"

"Of course." I heard the vacuum cleaner start up again, relieved she didn't ask if it was a *boy* friend or a *girl* friend. I wasn't ready to tell her I had a *boyfriend* yet.

I shut my bedroom door to get changed, but as I lifted my shirt, a high-pitched yowling echoed in the street below.

"Stupid cat." I laughed, pulling my top back on as I spotted the fat grey body swinging from the oak tree, flailing around in an attempt to free its paw from a branch. In three big steps I was out my door, almost smacking into dad as he passed.

"Hey, princess," Dad said. "Where're you running off to in such a hurry?"

"Vicki's dumb cat's got itself stuck in the tree."

"Ara to the rescue, huh?"

"Again."

I passed through the forbidden formal room, pushed the back door open and leaped off the porch, landing on the dewy grass. But instead of climbing up a tree, I stopped dead at the sight of every sunrise that ever brought day standing in my backyard, holding a very sorry-looking grey fluffball.

"David?"

"He's fine," he said, tucking Skittles' lashing tail into the hold as we met under the tree.

"Oh, my knight in shining armor. You saved my baby." I took the cat from him, then squeezed the tip of its paw to inspect the claws.

"He's fine—just a little embarrassed, I think," David assured me.

"He should be," I said, cradling Skittles to my face. He was still growling in the back of his throat, not at all amused to be held like a baby. "Silly kitty."

When I released my hold, the cat charged away at full speed, bolting over the hedge fence and into the front yard.

David brought my attention back to him with a soft touch along my arm. "How did you sleep last night?"

"Lying down," I said, and David laughed. "No, in all seriousness, I actually did *sleep*. And I had normal dreams."

"Then my work here is done." He took a step away as if he planned to leave, turning back after a moment. "Kidding."

"Funny." I slapped his chest, noting a small indent at the center, where his muscles dipped. I just wanted to keep my hand there against his plain white shirt, or maybe lift it off and… never mind.

David gave a short, breathy laugh then, and placed his hands on my hipbones. "So, how are you feeling today? After everything we talked about yesterday."

"I'm really good. I mean, I still hurt inside, but—" I shrugged.

"It will get easier." David ducked his head a little so our eyes met in perfect alignment, the dark regrowth of his beard showing around his chin and upper lip. "You will always think about them, but I can promise you that missing them will get easier."

"How do you know so much about this stuff?"

"I've suffered a lot of loss in my life." He nodded smoothly and looked away. "But I find more people to love, and make my life about them."

As our eyes met again, his warmed with a soft, simple smile.

"If you'd told me that a week ago, I might not've believed you," I said.

"But you do today?"

I nodded, resting both hands flat on the front of his chest, my elbows touching his ribs. I needed to stand on my toes a little to feel like he could hear me talk without me having to yell, but that only made my lips come up to his chin. Not close enough to lean forward and steal a kiss.

"I'm glad my dad told you, David—about my mom. I think I've

decided I'm not going to yell at him. I mean, he was just doing what he thought was best for me, right?"

"He didn't really mean to tell me, Ara. That wasn't his intention. I lead him into it."

My smile twisted up with a frown, and I shook my head. "So why did he give you the touch-my-daughter-and-you-die speech?"

David cleared his throat. "He never gave me that speech."

"But, in History class, he… you said he—"

He shook his head once, a suppressed grin creeping up into his eyes. "I lied."

I dropped my arms to my sides. "I told my dad off, you know, for giving you that speech! And worse, he played along. How could you two just conspire against me like that? And what the hell were you two talking about then?"

David laughed aloud, tilting his head back so his canines showed. "I'm sorry. I shouldn't laugh. But you're just so funny when you get on a heated rant. I love it when you do that." He pointed to my hands, wedged firmly on my hips.

I dropped them. "So what *was* my dad saying that day?"

"He asked me to keep an eye on you, since I already knew why you were here, and since you had apparently taken a liking to me." He combed a fingertip though my hair and swept it back behind my ear. "And I told him I had absolutely no intention of letting you out of my sight."

Hmph! "Well, it's nice to know he approves of you. But how'd he know I liked you?"

"Something about sultanas and grapes?" David's dark brows pulled together.

I laughed, thinking of Dad's weird teacher lingo. And then, so many other things suddenly seemed to fit together, like a three-dimensional puzzle that I had once assumed was only two. "So, when you said you didn't know he was my dad that day after History class?"

David's smile slipped away. "He asked me to keep it quiet that I even knew your name."

I nodded slowly. "I wondered how you knew it was *Ara-Rose*—in the library—because no one here knew that until after History class. You sneaky little thing."

He reached down and took my fingertips in his delicate grasp. "I'm sorry I deceived you. I meant no ill intent."

"It's in the past, David."

"So, you're not still mad at me?"

"I'm incapable of being mad at you. Well, for long anyway." I smiled, drawing my shoulder up to my ear. "I'm glad you talked to my dad. If you hadn't, we'd never have met, and I would've wished every day that we did."

"Not possible. You're not the kind of girl I could ever just pass in the street, Ara. I would've seen you eventually, and it would only have been a matter of time until I made myself a part of your life after that." He cupped his hand over the side of my neck. "Tragic past or none, we would've ended up friends."

"Ara-Rose!" a high-pitched and rather cross voice called from behind. Vicki stood on the back porch, her hand on her hip, still clutching a dishcloth. "Get some clothes on, please."

"Oh my God!" I covered my chest with my forearms. "Why didn't you tell me I was still in my pajamas?"

David grinned, looking at my tiny pink shorts and white tank top. "Relax. You look adorable."

"Adorable?" I said, making myself smaller. "I'm not even wearing a bra."

He took my hand and we walked toward the house. "Yes, I noticed that."

"WHAT'S THIS ONE?" DAVID CALLED OUT.

"What's what one?" I called back from my wardrobe.

"The playlist titled *Mike*?"

"Hey! Are you snooping through my playlists?"

"Of course."

My eyes narrowed.

"Dare I ask why you have a playlist named for a guy?"

"Oh, it's just all the music that makes me think of him. You know, the fun we had, that kind of thing." I shrugged and shimmied out of my bed shorts.

"Should I be worried? There's no *David* list."

"Not yet." I smiled to myself, glad I didn't save the David list under his name.

"Hm, this *Night Fantasy* one looks awfully suspicious." I could actually hear the mischief in his tone, giving him away for his presumptions. Presumptions that were right—if he assumed that list were for him.

"Hey, don't look at that list." I pulled my dress over my head quickly.

"There are a lot of sad songs on here, Ara. I hope this isn't *my* playlist."

"What if it is?" I said, stepping back out into my room.

My gorgeous boyfriend docked the iPod and a *'David'* song came on. "Because it gives me the impression that you think I don't like you."

"Then maybe, after yesterday, I need to make a new list."

"Yes. I would say so." He turned to face me, and his expression changed, an invisible force bringing him toward me like a leaf on a breeze. "Ara, that color is beautiful on you. It really brings out the pinks in your skin."

"Emerald green," I muttered, flattening the front of it as he touched my cheek. "It's one of my new favorite colors."

"One of? What's your favorite then?"

"Yellow."

"Any reason for that?"

"It's a happy color. The color of the sun," I explained, looking into him. "I just refuse to think everything in life has to be all dark and gloomy all the time. So I like yellow. What about you? What's your favorite color?"

He stared at me for a moment, smiling as he looked down at my mouth, then back into my eyes, catching them in a breathless hold. "Sapphire."

"Why sapphire?"

"Because ever since I met you, I've once again started to notice the magic in the world." He gently moved his cold fingers from my cheekbone to the nape of my neck. "You might say that sapphire represents a brighter horizon—a life I never imagined."

"Being in love?"

"Being in love with *you.*" His fingers moved into my hair. "And now, every time I see this color, it makes my heart skip. It makes me think of everything that might be possible, that never was before."

I kind of laughed. That was a very deep confession, and it made me nervous, so I brushed off the displacement with an "Aw, I feel special now."

He laughed too. "Sorry. Does it bother you for me to speak my heart?"

"Not really. I just… people don't really talk like you do,"—like they're from another time—"sometimes I feel like you're just saying what I want to hear."

He held out his pinkie. "I promise I speak only truth."

I linked mine over his. "Then I promise to always try to believe you. But I can't promise not to giggle."

"Well"—he winked at me—"we both know how I feel about that giggle."

A loud rumbling sound mocked the suggestive undertone in his voice.

David looked down at my belly. "You haven't eaten yet, have you?"

I shook my head.

"Come on, we need to feed you before the beast presents itself."

"You know me too well already."

Skittles hissed and leaped out my window, sending my homework scattering when we entered the room.

"What did you do to that cat, David?" I asked, watching the cat scamper across the roof outside and leap onto the ground. "He hates you."

David grinned, closing the door. "Are you suggesting I threw him up that tree to get your attention earlier?"

I laughed. "It wouldn't surprise m—"

"Ara." Vicki opened my door. "This stays open."

My arms fell loosely by my sides. "Seriously?"

She gave me 'the glare' then walked away.

"Looks like the cat's not the only one who doesn't trust me," David joked, smiling.

"Argh." I stomped over to my desk and pressed play on my iPod. "Why does she have to treat me like a child?"

"She's not," he said, tossing my stuffed dog aside as he landed on my pillow. "She's treating you like a teenager who's alone in her room with a boy."

I smiled and turned the music up loud enough to give us some privacy. "Well, she needs to get used to you being around. After all, you are going to come meet me *here* every morning now so you can make me one of those glorious coffees, aren't you?"

He chuckled, opening his arm so my body could slide along next to his. "You liked that, did you?"

"Mm-hm."

"Well"—he kissed my head as I snuggled into him—"I'll think about it."

"Good." But I kinda knew he wouldn't. I think Vicki made him feel really unwelcome.

"I'm not bothered by your stepmother, if that's what you're thinking."

I rolled up a bit to look at him. "I was. I thought maybe she'd offended you, you know, sitting with us at breakfast and all."

"Not even a little bit." He pressed my head until I rested it back on his white T-shirt. "I've dealt with a lot worse than Vicki."

"Well, you're pre-approved by my dad, right? So she has to accept you."

"She does, sweetheart. Just give her time."

I nodded, and we laid that way for a while then, music filling the silence while a summer breeze swept through the window, circling my room with the fragrance of fresh-cut grass and the sharp, spicy scent of

David's cologne. It was so easy to be with David. He asked me a lot about Australia, and we sat for about half an hour comparing the differences in words from the two countries, like jam versus jelly and sweater versus jumper. He originally thought *jumper* was another word for a kangaroo or a really depressed guy standing on a rooftop.

"And the food here is different too, as in the portions. I've never been so happy in all my life." I patted my belly. "The ogre's started raising his demands. I'm gonna get fat soon."

David kissed my hand. "You would still be beautiful, even if you were too big to touch your toes."

That made me smile. "That's the sweetest thing any guy has ever said to me. In a really strange way."

He went quiet for a second, shaking his head. "I don't think you get it, Ara."

"Get what?" I rolled onto my belly, resting my elbows against his chest. "Get what, David?"

With his lips pressed together, he smiled, studying my face carefully. "Never mind. So, what's your favorite genre of film?"

"So we're playing the withholding game again, where you refuse to tell me what you're thinking?"

"I'm not withholding anything," he said in a teasing tone, which just meant he was. Clearly.

I deliberately slumped myself a little too heavily onto my back against his chest again. "Fine then. Favorite genre of film? I guess it used to be action. The nineteen-eighties kind. But now…"

"Now?" David led, when my silence lasted too long.

"Now, I like comedies. You know, it's like"—I huffed through my nose—"I'm always so unhappy. If I can find something that makes me laugh and forget about my life for a while, that's what I like to do. So, comedies." My shoulders lifted once in a semi-shrug.

"What kind of comedies? Stand-up, action—?"

"Romantic." I smoothed my fingertips over David's ribs. "What about you?"

"Horror," he stated, cupping my hand and stopping it from lifting his shirt.

"Really? Why? They're so… icky."

"Not for me. I love a good scary horror. I have this thing for blood. Can't get enough of it."

Well, I never assumed *that* one. Sweet David liked gore? It just didn't fit. I rolled onto my belly again to study his face. "Really?"

He just smiled and placed his hand under my shoulder blade, making me feel so grounded and so real with the weight of his touch. What was it about him that could come across as so harmless, when all I'd heard were stories about his bullying antics, and now he was telling me he liked horror?

"It doesn't suit you," I said.

"What?"

"Gore, horror. All that stuff. I can't picture you watching things like that."

He just laughed. "Guess we won't be having many movie nights then, since we have such different tastes."

"Oh, no way, we so will. You'll just have to watch chick flicks."

His smile widened. "I look forward to it. Of course, I *would* like to watch a horror with you"—he motioned to my hand on his chest—"if it meant you'd snuggle into me to feel safe."

I rested my cheek on his shirt again. "We can do that without the horror."

"What about books? Can you read books with horror?"

"Yeah. I like some Stephen King stuff," I said.

"Have you ever read anything by Anne Rice?"

"Yeah. I got swept up in the vampire craze. Basically any books or movies about fangs, and I was there." I nodded. "You?"

"Yes. Even *I* fell victim to vampire pop culture."

I laughed aloud. "Yeah but, personally, I prefer animal-eating vamps. Killing people is just..." I rubbed imaginary goosebumps off my arms. "It just doesn't appeal to me."

"At all?"

"Nope."

"What if you met a vampire who was nice, like me, but killed people? Would you still like him?"

I shook my head. "I know there're girls who would. But I guess, after seeing death firsthand—how it affects the people left behind—I'm not sure now."

He went ultimately quiet and still. I think he even stopped breathing.

I propped my head up again and his stunned stare drew a smirk to my lips. "You okay?"

"Aspirations," he said suddenly, the stare washing away to a smile. "What do you want to be when you grow up?"

I sighed, knowing for certain that his liquid eyes were hiding some deeper thought he wouldn't share. "Um, I always wanted to be a teacher, like my dad. But now I think I kind of want to be a musician—write my own songs."

"I think that would be perfect for you."

"Yeah, me too." I rolled onto my back and took his hand again. "I'd like to be famous one day. Maybe as a pianist."

"You'd need to get a piano first."

"Oh God, trust me, I know. I've been begging Dad for one since I was four."

"Why hasn't he bought one for you?"

"He wants me to be a teacher. Better income."

"Not if you were to make it famous."

I shrugged. "Guess he's seen Hollywood dreams go sour too many times."

"But it's not just big dreams with you, Ara. You're very talented." He laughed out the last two words. "I don't think you'd ever be happy teaching."

I felt warm then. "It amazes me how well you know me."

He linked his fingers gently through mine. "You know, I wanted to be in a rock band once."

"Really?"

"Yeah. It was a long time ago."

"Why didn't you?"

"Went in another direction."

"What direction?"

He did that pause thing he was becoming famous for. I assumed he was weighing up all the different answers he *could* give against the ones he *would* give to keep me out of his world. "I'm not so sure about that now. Might say I'm at a crossroads."

And that answer, believe it or not, let me into his world more than if he'd said Law or something like that. I smiled. "What direction do you want to take? I mean, what options are there?"

"That's just it. I don't know."

"How can you find out?"

"I can ask."

"Who?"

He sighed. "My uncle, I suppose."

"And what would the question be?" I probed.

His fingers tightened on mine. "If I knew, I'd ask it."

I chuckled. "Is it that you don't want to tell me, or that you genuinely don't know?"

"It's more that I *can't* tell you."

"Why?"

"Because I have secrets."

"I like secrets," I said.

"What if they're dark secrets?"

"What kinds of dark secrets?"

"Bad ones."

I really thought about that for a second—about the fear I had that he'd hate me when he learned my dark secrets. But I never imagined he'd have some—that there might be reasons *I* could hate *him*. "Then don't tell me just yet."

"When should I tell you?"

"One day."

"What if I didn't have much time? What if I had to tell you soon?"

That rubber mallet of destruction came at my soul again. I felt it getting closer. "What's your favorite sport?"

David didn't answer for a few breaths, maybe a little thrown off by my change in direction. "Hockey. You?"

"I like dancing, but as for actual sports, I was never interested. It was a taboo subject in my house—much to Mike's disgust."

David cleared his throat, crossing his ankles over where they dangled off the end of my bed. "So, he really did spend a lot of time there."

"Yep. Every day. He was a permanent fixture—just another piece of furniture. His mom and my mom were really close."

"You and Mike were, too?"

"Yeah. We were. I mean, we are, but we're just so far apart right now."

"Do you think things will be the same as before when he comes to see you?"

"I hope so. He's always been a constant thing in my life. It's been really hard without him." I crossed my hands under my head, losing myself to thought for a second before a smile expanded my lips. "He's kind of like a favorite pillow: you know, you can cry into it, it keeps you warm and comfy, and it's always there."

"But you don't sleep with it?" He tried to make it sound like a joke, but I knew he was also really curious. Everyone was.

"No, David. It's not that kind of pillow," I said slowly, then added, "It's a couch pillow. Mike's just a couch pillow. But this one"—I rolled over and traced circles over his chest. He tensed, his hand ready to move mine if I strayed into forbidden territory—"this is my new favorite pillow."

He let me touch him for three whole seconds before he finally moved my hand, pressing his lips to it once. "I'm sorry. I wish the circumstances that brought you to me had been different. But I am very glad you came here."

"Me too."

"And I'm sure, when you see Mike in a few weeks, you'll fall back into step with each other right away."

"Yeah, probably." I shrugged, but then curiosity itched a new question into my throat. "So what about *your* family? Do you have any brothers or sisters?"

"I have a brother. A twin."

"No way." I sat up next to David's hips, crossing my legs under me. This was way too interesting for a lie-down conversation. "Are you identical?"

"We look the same, but we're very different."

"Well, I gathered that. Why doesn't he go to school with us?"

"He chose a different path—stayed with my uncle in New York."

"So, who do you live with then? Are your parents still together?"

"My mother passed away when I was a baby, and my father followed not long after. So I live alone."

"Oh, David." I covered my mouth with both hands. "I'm so sorry."

"It was a long time ago."

"So, you grew up with your uncle?"

"Well, I was raised by my aunt, and when she passed away, my uncle took my brother and me into his care."

"Wow, you weren't kidding when you said you'd suffered a lot of grief. I feel bad, like I'm making a big deal out of my problems, but you—"

"Don't say that." He pushed himself up on his elbow and took my hand. "You have every right to make a big deal, Ara. You *just* lost your mother. My grief, my loss, it all happened a very long time ago."

"Can't be that long ago. You're only a teenager." I frowned, smiling at the way he brushed off his own grief—just like me.

He looked down at our hands. "I'm older than I look. The things I've been through in life have *made* me older, given me wisdom beyond my years." He lay back, adding through a breathy smile, "Sometimes, I feel like I'm over a hundred years old."

"Sometimes you sound it, too."

"I know."

"So, do you see your uncle much, I mean, since you moved away?"

"Every other week or so. I'll be seeing him tomorrow."

"What for?"

"We're members of a council. We have a few things to discuss."

"What kind of council?"

He cleared his throat. "A… charity organization."

"Oh. What charity?"

He grinned. "Blood donation."

"Then, I must confess." I showed him my arm. "I've never donated."

He laughed out loud. "Something we shall have to remedy."

"No way. No one sticks needles in me."

"I could rent a vampire for the day. He could suck it out of you."

I rolled my eyes. "So what about your brother? Do you see him much?"

"Jason?" David's cheek flinched. "Not so much. We've kind of grown apart."

"Why?"

"He uh"—he eyed Vicki as she passed my bedroom door, pretending not to look in on us—"he and I had a falling out a while back. Things are… neutral now."

"Neutral?"

"Mm," he muttered and sat up. "I'm just waiting for him to find out about you."

"Is that a bad thing?"

"No," he said in short. "At least, I don't think so."

"I don't like that answer."

Vicki passed my room *again,* and David pulled my hand, making me sit beside him. "How 'bout we get out of here for the day—go to the lake?"

A smile spread across my lips. "Sounds great."

"Do you have a picnic basket?"

"Yeah, I think so," I said, standing up beside him.

"Go get it." He leaned in and pecked my cheek. "I'll run to the store and get some supplies."

10

The woodsy smell of David's car made me smile, and though the upholstery was sticky and uncomfortable under my legs in the summer heat, it seemed to retain the aged scent of experience—a bit like riding in the car with my grandpa, which made it emotionally comforting.

Heavy weekend traffic made the trip out to the lake take longer today, so in my boredom I decided to sort through the CDs in David's glove compartment. Most of the bands were plucked straight from my dad's era, but a tickle of elation perked me up at the sight of some familiar cover-art.

"I've actually heard of these guys." I held up the disk. "I know a few of their songs."

David smiled. "I have that album on my phone. I'll bring it with us when we get to the lake—play it to you."

"Okay. Do… do you like them? I mean, I know you have a CD but, like, what's your favorite one of their songs?"

His chest puffed out with a deep breath as he looked at the CD. "Off that album: Overcome."

I nodded, scanning the song titles for one I actually knew. "Why that one?"

"I like the piano."

"Hm."

"We have more in common musically than just that one album, Ara," he said, clearly having sensed my gloom.

"I hope so."

"You'll see. Don't worry. It's as important to me as it is to you."

"Okay." I put the CD back. "What's your favorite song at the moment?"

"Hard to say." He drew a tight breath through his teeth. "I go through phases. I uh—*right now*, I'm actually really enjoying Moonlight Sonata."

"I like that one, too." I smiled, sitting back. "Maybe you can play it for me at school on Monday."

"Ara." He placed his hand firmly on my leg. "I would *love* to."

"Great." I loved watching him play. It was almost as if he never even had to think about where his fingers were going. I wasn't sure I'd ever heard him hit a bum note, and just the thought of watching him play again made me happy. "Hey, can I tell you something?"

"Sure." He tore his eyes away from the road and they locked to mine for a second.

"David!" I sprung upright in my seat. "Watch the road!"

"It's okay, Ara. You are more than safe in the car with me." He reached across and pried my fingers from their grip on the leather seat. "My uncle forced me to take one of those stunt-driving courses once. I know how to handle myself on the road."

"That doesn't mean you're incapable of having an accident," I scolded. "Besides, it's not just *your* driving I'm worried about."

"Would it make you feel better if I told you I've never had an accident?"

"No." I stole my hand back.

"Okay. I'll keep that in mind," he said with a breathy laugh, shaking his head. "No more eye contact when driving. Deal?"

"Deal."

"Now, what were you about to say before?"

I wasn't sure if I should say it now, since the moment had passed.

"Just say it," he demanded playfully.

My uncertainty lingered in the air.

"Ara, say it."

"I'm happy, is all." I shrugged and looked away. "I'm happy that we love each other, even if people say there's no such thing as love at first sight."

We both stared forward for a while, silent. Dead silent. I kind of wished I hadn't said it. One thing I'd learned about life was that happiness is subject to ignorance; as soon as you acknowledged it, it'd disappear—like everything else you care about.

David smiled, reveling in his own private joke again. "It really bothers you, doesn't it?" he said.

"What?"

"Being in love with me."

"I'm just at odds with how I feel and what common sense says, you know, what I *should* feel."

David's easy smile made me feel silly for having doubts then. "You can't make rules for your heart, Ara. And… if you berate yourself for what you feel, you'll eventually convince yourself not to feel that anymore. So"—he studied my face for a quick second then turned his eyes back to the road—"please just let yourself love me. I love *you*, and I don't want to lose your heart to some silly laws made up by man."

"But people just won't understand it."

"Then don't try to make them. If they've ever loved before, then they'll understand and, if not, just let it go. They'll get it one day."

I took a long, slow breath. Those were very wise words for a teenager. "You're right, you know—about being aged beyond your years."

He laughed. "Do you think you can still love me, even if I'm an old man deep down inside?"

"Maybe. How old are you, anyway? Emily said you're older than us."

"Emily should mind her business."

I smirked. "Feisty, aren't we?"

"No. I just despise gossip."

"Well, we wouldn't need to gossip if you ever told me anything about yourself."

He exhaled. "I'll be nineteen in November."

"So you're repeating twelfth grade?"

"Yes."

"Why?"

"I uh—" He scratched the back of his head, resting his elbow on the door after, his fist in front of his lips. "I went through a rough patch a few years ago and… I kind of let my grades slip."

"What happened?"

"That was when I left my uncle to come here."

"And… why did you leave your uncle?"

"I lost someone." He swallowed, putting both hands on the steering wheel again. "I've been hiding from the world, in a way, I guess, ever since."

"I'm really sorry, David." I wished I could kiss all his pain away. But grief just didn't work like that. "So, is that it? Is that one of your dark secrets?"

"No."

"Will you tell me something else about you, something I don't know?"

"Not today."

"Why?"

David's head rocked from side to side, fluid with annoyance. "You are a willful creature, Ara-Rose. I swear you will be the death of me."

"I will if you don't start opening up."

"I'd open up if you could handle the truth about me," he said.

"The truth?" I laughed. "Am I seeing a lie?"

"What if I said yes?"

"Well, which part is the lie?" I looked him up and down. "Were you born a woman and you're only pretending to be a guy? Or maybe you're really a fifty-year-old man in a mask, who likes teenagers—"

He laughed, shaking his head.

"—or maybe… I don't know. I can't think of any more."

"Good, because you're way off the mark."

I folded my arms and watched the trees outside, blurring in hues of green and brown as we passed them.

The drive to the lake was relatively short, but the scenery changed so much, from closely gathered houses to a long stretch of highway and, finally, a tunnel of trees around a hard-packed dirt road. As the tires crunched on the gravelly shoulder, my blue guitar, which hadn't shifted the whole drive, clunked noisily—the vibrations drawing gentle hums of odd notes from the strings. I glanced over my shoulder to check on it, and as I turned back to face the front, David's gaze quickly shifted from me to the road.

"What?" I asked.

"You're not mad at me, are you—because I keep myself a secret?" he asked cautiously.

"No." I offered him a sweet smile. "I mean, I want to know more about you, but… if that also means learning about your dark secrets… if they're so interconnected that one can't be spoken of without addressing the other, then…" I left it at that, and David nodded knowingly.

He shut the engine off, the sudden quiet making my ears ring, and then reached across to cup my knee. "Will you ever be ready to hear it?"

"When I'm okay," I said earnestly, touching my heart. "I just need to heal first, before I face the fact that you're anything other than what I've built you up to be in my mind."

His eyes moved up from my hand to my face, and though his mouth opened to speak, he said nothing. Just nodded and opened the car door.

When we came out to the clearing by the lake, the familiar lemony spice of wet bark and the heavy clay scent of decomposing leaves awakened my senses. With the autumn hovering on the horizon, the leafy trees surrounding the lake began to turn a hundred different colors. An illustration of mottled pinks, yellows and reds emanated off the lake's reflection, while dust motes settled on the water around the moss, like snow. Across the lake at the center of the tranquil masterpiece, several flocks of colorful birds disappeared into the dense greenery of the island, taking my awe of this magical place and doubling it.

"Come on." David took my hand and turned me to face the small patch of grass flattened by the picnic rug, the basket centered, where his iPhone set the scene with some soft music. "Let's sit down."

"How did you set that up so fast?"

"What do you mean?" he asked, suddenly appearing on the rug, his hands behind his head and the cheekiest grin warming his eyes. "That wasn't fast."

"So I'm just phasing out then?" I said, narrowing my eyes at him. "Because I'm sure only two seconds passed."

He laughed loudly. "See, I've become so accustomed to your trips outside your own head now that I use that time to freak you out."

I wandered over and sat down in front of him, noticing then that his skin looked a bit pale and his eyes were sunken. I would have asked him if he'd slept last night, but the song on his phone had the most heartbreaking melody, and I had to ask, "What's this song?"

"'Overcome'." David looked down at his hands. "The one I said I'd play to you."

The words danced around in my head, lilting softly over the wistful tide of the piano like a breeze made of despair. David stared into the tree line, his mind a million miles away, and I watched his angel-like face for just long enough to see how out of my league he really was. His features were almost symmetrical, even down to the width of his mouth on both sides and the sharp, heart-shaped curve of his upper lip. There was this undeniable allure about him, something… maybe an energy that just drew me in, making me want to close my eyes and fall against him. It was too late for me. I'd never be able to go back. Never be able to live without him. 'Overcome' was very suitable for how I felt about this boy.

David looked up from his reverie and frowned at my face.

I wiped away my pout, forcing a look of composure, though inside, my heart was breaking. I wondered how I could possibly ever be good enough for him.

"Do you know why they say *love is blind*?" he asked out of the blue.

"Um..." Okay, that was a strange question. "Because... you can't see straight when you're in love?"

He shook his head. "It's because you don't need to see to fall in love. It's purely chemical. You can fall in love with someone before you've spoken one word to them, and they don't have to be perfect, Ara; just perfect for you."

"What if you're not from the same species, can you be perfect for each other then?"

He sat up a little. "What do you mean?"

"I mean..." I toyed with the hem of my dress. "You're... perfect, and I'm..."

He sat back, exhaling through his smile. "That's what you meant."

"What did you think I meant?"

"Nothing." He reached across and took my hand. "Ara. I don't know where you get this silly idea that we're not right for each other, but—"

"I never said that."

"Okay, sorry, you said you're not good enough for me."

I looked down at my pale white fingers wrapped around his golden skin, seeing the obvious.

"I've never loved anyone like this before. Ever. What do you think that means for me, Ara?"

I shrugged, not meeting his eyes, though I could feel them on me.

"I don't love," he insisted. "Not like this. So the fact that you have changed me, altered the way I view my own reality, means there is something more between us than just the kind of love that's forged from one person's measure against another's."

"I guess," I said, not meeting his eye.

"In short, sweetheart, you are more than good enough for me—from personality to spirit, and all the way to superficial and unimportant qualities." He laughed. "I mean, you're the single most *beautiful* thing I've ever laid eyes on and, believe me, Ara-Rose, I have seen a *lot* of girls."

One shoulder came up to my jaw to hide my scars. Once, I would have believed him when he said that. I knew I wasn't literally the most beautiful girl in the world, but I was in his eyes, and that's what mattered. Only, now… it just didn't feel okay to believe it—not when I had scars that everyone else, if they were being honest, would say made me ugly. "I guess I just don't see what you see."

"Then I'm happy to keep saying it until you do." He touched the backs of his fingers to my cheek. "Just relax into this, okay? We're together. I'm not going anywhere. Not ever."

"Promise?"

He looked at me for a long moment, his eyes awash with several responses. "Yes. But only if you promise to look in the mirror every day and tell yourself you're beautiful."

"Okay." I smirked at his corniness. "I will."

"Good. Hungry?" He jumped up with a movement as light and fluid as a man on the moon.

"Um, yeah. I am, actually." I hadn't even noticed it, but my stomach felt like a hollow pit. It might've even growled at one point, but I'd been too lost in David's flawless face to notice. I could've starved to death and probably wouldn't have cared.

"Here." He handed me a small bunch of grapes and sat across from me, grabbing my guitar.

I picked at the plump round fruit while David plucked the strings, the squared tips of his fingers finding the notes so effortlessly, as if he knew every one like his own flesh. "Do you realize," I said with my mouth full, "that I've never actually heard you play guitar?"

"Yes." He smiled, keeping his head down, twisting the pegs atop the neck. After a strum and a nod of satisfaction, he started playing.

My eyes tried to close again as the sound touched my heart, but I forced myself to open them and watch the phenomenon that was David's every note. In comparison to him, my musical ability was substandard, clumsy even. I hated that.

"You make me feel like an amateur."

"Well, I've been playing for a *very* long time." He laughed out a chest full of tension, and then he shuffled over and picked a grape off the bunch, chewing thoughtfully. "I wanna play you a song."

"Okay." I dumped the grapes back in the basket, readjusting my seat. "Do I know it?"

"You might. It's by Muse but it's an older one." He propped his left leg up, resting his strumming arm on the guitar. "It's called 'Unintended'."

I picked through my music brain, but didn't recognize the melody at all as he started playing.

With each chord change, my mind began to wander deeper into itself, the wind-chime notes carrying me to another place—a dream-like world where emotions were displayed in melody. This one, with its harmony balancing on the edge of sadness, would be the song of a night sky that fell in love with the sun—forever forbidden to be together—watching over a world that would end if one didn't exist.

David looked at me as he sung, the notes starting low and rolling up through the scale, his lips curved into that sexy smile. He tried to hold it back, but it crept onto his face anyway.

I closed my eyes, letting David's perfect voice surround my thoughts, making me want to cry, to be a part of him. And though I couldn't see anything but the golden light turning my eyelids red underneath, I could feel the color of the lake around me; an image carved out in melody.

As the song came to an end, the last notes hovering in my subconscious for a moment, I wiped a fingertip under my eye.

"Ara, you're crying." Sudden warmth spread through my cheek, the bright red glow behind my eyelids becoming shadowed as David's sun-kissed fingers touched my face.

"I know. I'm such a dork."

"Was my playing really that bad?"

"I wish it was." I laughed. "But, it's just that music is something that comes from a really deep place in me. I feel things, feel *everything* so deeply, and that song..."—I leaned back and looked into his focused eyes, noticing that his pupils were so large they'd swallowed most of the green—"it was so beautiful that it hurt."

"It reminds me of you—of us."

"Why?"

"Don't you get it?" The sudden shine to his smile penetrated my watery barrier, making my heart forget how to beat. "Forever doesn't have to be a curse for me. Not anymore. Not now that I have you."

Motionless, with the only connection to the real world being the burning sun above, my mind fought for reason—offering him forever with one look but denying it with common sense. "If only we could actually live forever."

"What if we could? What if you could have an eternity with me?" His thumbs pressed into my cheeks more firmly. "Would you take it?"

I nodded. "If eternity were real, I think I'd give my *soul* to spend it with you."

"Ara?" He shook my face, as if he were trying to snap me out of something. "Open your eyes. Look at me and say that."

The sun brought momentary blindness with its bright glare as I looked at David. "I didn't know they were closed."

"Ara, focus. Look at me." He studied me carefully, his brow tight in the middle.

"What did you want me to say?" I asked.

Nearby, bees buzzed with a gentle hum and a few birds chattered noisily in the treetops above us, and David's round eyes stared, glassy and distant, his lips sitting parted—no words coming out.

"David?"

"Nothing." He lowered his hands and shifted away from me, weighted like the dead.

A cool breath lifted my chest in a long, slow gasp then, and a strange pull of energy—or maybe warmth—withdrew from the physical space between us, like hot ribbons had bound us and then snapped and tore away.

A spell had been broken.

The breath rushed back out of my lungs too quickly, tightening my throat. I touched my fingertips to the racing pulse between my collarbones. "I feel dizzy."

"It's okay." He rolled my cheek onto his lap, brushing my hair from my face.

"What just happened? Why do I feel so sick?"

"Come on." David patted my back and lifted me to sit. "You need to eat. You get dizzy when you're hungry."

"True." But this was different, I was sure of it. It felt more like my soul had been connected to his for a split second. I felt so drawn to him, like I could've stayed there forever, died in his arms and have been grateful for that one, close moment. Now it was gone—that warmth, the breathtaking intensity of our bodies so close to each other —I wanted it back. I felt like it *belonged* to me.

David shuffled over and leaned his back against the rock while I swallowed every agonizing bite of the food he handed me, forcing it down with orange juice because my mouth refused to make saliva. In fact, my body refused to do anything normal—including breathe.

"Did you feel that?" I looked up from under my lashes, pinching the edges of a sandwich. "Before—when we were close?"

"Feel what?"

"That… the energy between us?"

He shook his head once, pursing his lips. "Nope."

My mouth popped open. "You big, fat liar!"

"I'm not lying."

"Yes"—I got to my knees—"you are."

"Look, even *if* I noticed the way you… reacted, that does *not* mean I felt it." He sighed heavily and threw his sandwich into the basket, then sat back against the rock, folding his arms.

"Well, what was that? What was I feeling?"

"Love?"

I dropped the sandwich to the rug. "David!"

"I don't know, Ara. What am I, a scientist?"

I looked over at the picnic basket. "Did you drug those grapes?"

David laughed. "Why would I do—"

"Then what *was* that?" I cut in. "I know you know something about it. I saw how you looked at me." I pointed at him. He shook his head, smiling down at his folded arms. "You felt it, too. I know you did. Now tell me what it was."

"I'm not going to fight with you," he said calmly.

"I'm not fighting."

"Then drop it."

"No. It didn't feel natural, David. I felt a… a *gravitational pull* toward you, like my soul just split in two and then was suddenly"—I scrunched an imaginary piece of paper between my palms—"forced back together."

"Gravitational pull?" One brow arched mockingly.

"Why do you do that?"

"What?"

"Make me feel silly; make me think I feel things you don't."

After rubbing his forehead viciously, he swept a hand through his hair and looked away. "Can we drop this, please?"

I focused on the ant-covered bread in front of me, blinking back tears.

"Ara." His voice commanded I look at him. I shook my head. "Ara, please. Look at me."

"Why?"

"Please?"

Reluctantly, I rolled my face upward.

His golden smile warmed. "Oh, sweetheart. Why are you crying?"

"Because I feel stupid." I nodded to the place on the rug where we'd been sitting during the moment. "If you didn't feel it too… what does that mean?"

"What that was has nothing to do with how I—" His teeth clenched in obvious frustration. "You are one of the most stubborn damn girls I've ever met. Do you know that?"

I bit my lip.

David appeared in front of me, tilting my chin upward. "But it's also one of the most charming things about you. No more tears, okay?" He tugged my hand until I came to sit beside him against the rock, and I nestled the crown of my head under his chin, placing my hand over the cotton shirt that barely contained the coolness of his skin underneath, wondering if, no… *sure* he was getting colder.

"Ara?"

"Mm-hm."

His strong arms squeezed me closer. "We'll talk about things another time, all right?"

I nodded, but I didn't agree.

"Hey?" David leaned around to look at me, and when I refused to respond to his smile, he jammed his fingertips into my ribs, making me squeal.

"Stop it!" I laughed, jerking downward to get away.

He shuffled after me on his knees, continuing his assault through boyish laughter. "Make me."

"I can't. You're too strong." I squealed again, cackling loudly. "Stop it or I'll wet myself, I swear!"

"Go for it. It'd be hilarious."

"Argh!" I sat up, and when he finally stopped tickling, reached over and slapped his arm playfully. "Jerk."

"Ouch." He rubbed his chest.

"What are you doing?" I laughed. "I hit you in the arm."

"Yeah, but it hurt here."

Aw. "Then, where would it hurt if I damaged your heart?" I asked in a light, joking tone.

His eyes darkened, the smile withdrawing like a shadow. "The soul."

I cleared my throat and looked away from his eyes for a new conversation piece. "So what's out on that island? Anything interesting?"

"I could show you, if you like."

"Okay. But won't we get wet?"

David looked down at the tops of my thighs, just covered by the rim of my green dress, and smiled. "*You* won't."

"Well, maybe we'll leave it for today. There's always tomorrow, right?" I rolled onto my knees and sat with my face right in front of David's, the tips of our noses just off touching. We both took a long, shaky gulp of air, and the sweet scent of his breath touched my tongue, making my mouth water as it realized we could kiss right now—if we wanted to.

He slowly lifted his hand, taking hold of me and steering my face toward his. But he stopped and held me there, my lips tingling just in front of his, and softly ran his thumb over them.

"David?" I said, wishing so badly that he'd just do it.

He closed his eyes tightly. "Please don't."

"Don't what?"

He didn't answer. He just sat there, taking shallow breaths. I focused on his mouth, moving slowly forward to steal one.

"It's getting late," he said, and a cold rush separated us.

I turned around to watch him walking off, running a hand through his hair.

"You know, you're right." He stopped about ten paces away. "We can go out to the island another day. I think I remember something about a History assignment being due?" His voice rose in question.

The breath I'd been holding made a huge lump in my throat. "It can wait."

"No." He shook his head, coming over to pack up the picnic basket. "It can't."

"Argh." I flopped onto my back with a huff, secretly checking my breath to see if that's why he sprung up so suddenly while, in the corner of my mind, my silly fantasy continued: David and I, all hands and lips, floating along the rest of the day in each other's arms. But reality shut the door on that world, opening another to the mountain of impending homework I faced instead.

With a sigh, I stood up and folded the picnic rug. "Here, you wanna stash this back in your rock crevice?"

He stepped away from me, shaking his head. "This is your secret place now too, Ara. I'll show you where to hide it."

I hugged the blanket and smiled.

11

Everything had been set out properly. My pencils were neatly lined up beside a notepad, my laptop centered, and I even had a glass of water for hydration. But after surfing the Net for two hours, the only thing I'd accomplished was a mental list of reasons David wouldn't kiss me and a few uneducated theories about what in the world of scientific reasoning that gravitational pull was.

After a while, with nothing but unrealistic explanations dancing around in my head, I lifted the feather quilt on my bed and slid my feet under it, rolling onto my side as I drew it up over my shoulders. Maybe if I could fall asleep until Vicki called me for dinner, I wouldn't have to think about David.

I flicked the lamp out and snuggled down away from the sticky summer air, breathing the fruity scent of my sheets. That was the hardest thing about moving: how different things smelled, like the towels and my shirts as I pulled them over my head. Vicki's clean laundry had a vibrant peachy smell, whereas my mom's was a powdery scent. A bit like Mike's, since our moms always bought the same laundry detergent. But peach was kind of comforting to me now. It meant I was in bed, away from the world, away from my troubles.

I lay perfectly still for a bit, listening for the crickets' closing act, but the air was so thick and dense with heat that even the bugs had taken the back road to anywhere but here.

When I opened my eyes again, Mike smiled down at me from the photo I'd tacked on my wall beside my bed. I yanked it downward and touched my fingers to his bright, cheeky smile. In so many ways, every guy I met, every smile that made my heart flutter, had been measured up against Mike's. It was always the first thing I noticed about a guy, always the deal-breaker.

I kissed the photo and pressed my thumb to it against the wall. "Miss you, Mike."

A freaky sensation stilled my bones then when my phone rang. I jumped out of bed and grabbed it, knowing already who it was. "Hey."

"Hey, kid, did I wake you?"

"Nah. I was just daydreaming. What're you doing up?" I looked at my clock. "Isn't it before six in the morning over there?"

"Yeah, I was in bed, but I was just layin' here thinkin' 'bout ya." I could hear the grin behind his tone.

"Me? Why?" I sat at my desk.

"Interview's booked now for next Monday. Thought I might start planning my trip."

"When do you think you'll be coming?"

He took a long breath. "I was thinking I should fly out that night?"

"Really?" I squeaked. "That's fine with me. I'd be happy if you came now." I flipped open my laptop, clicked on my calendar, then opened iTunes.

"You miss me that much, huh?" He sounded surprised.

"Mike, I've never had to live without you before. You're like my security blanket. I miss hanging out, you know, just being… normal."

"Great. I'm a blankie." He laughed. "What about David? He still in the picture?" His light tone concealed a spearhead—something only I would notice.

"In the picture?" I practically snorted. "He told me he *loves* me! How much more in the picture can you get?"

"After a week?"

"Yes. Well, it's not a week for him. He's had around a month to think about it. But, you know, it's funny 'cause I kinda fell in love with him too, like, the day I saw him." It was hard to admit that, especially to Mike. I knew he couldn't comprehend love, and I never wanted to hear the word *infatuation*. But that's what he'd peg this as, and there was nothing I could do about it.

"So what's the problem then?" He sighed, sounding bored. "You said that like it was a bad thing."

"No, it's the opposite actually. But he has me really confused."

"Why?"

"He pulled away when I went to kiss him."

Mike laughed. I could almost see him tilting his head forward, scratching his brow. "How long have you been official?"

"Well, how long were you and *Bec* official before you guys did more than just kiss?"

"That's different. I'm an adult and you're a kid. Did you ever think that *that* might be his problem—you being under eighteen?" Mike concluded. "How old is this guy, anyway?"

"He's a little older." I brushed over that one. "And yes, I did consider the fact that we're not technically adults." Well I wasn't, but David was. "But we are at the legal age of consent *here*, and he's a hot-blooded male, and there have been opportunities. I just don't get it. A kiss can't hurt, right?"

"Unless you're a hot-blooded male, Ara," he said dryly. "A kiss can make you want a lot more, and maybe he just has"—he paused for a second—"self-knowledge. He might think he won't wanna stop if you were to ask him to go further. And maybe he's afraid if he did have the willpower to stop of his own volition, it might hurt your feelings." His voice dropped on the end.

"That *could* have something to do with it. But it makes me feel—" I knew the word, but didn't want to admit it.

"Undesirable?"

"Yes," I muttered.

He laughed—a loud, full bellow.

The tightness in my stomach spread to my teeth. "Mike. Stop laughing at me, you know I hate that!"

He stopped instantly. "I'm sorry, Ara, it's just that… I've always thought you were cute. I'm not stupid, I have eyes, and I promise that you are *not* undesirable."

"Mike, you can't say that. You're my friend." My friend that rejected my apparently cute-self.

"Yes, I'm your friend, which means I *can* say that."

I typed *pick up Mike* on Tuesday in my desktop calendar then went back to iTunes.

"What're you doing?" he asked, sensing my absence, I guess.

"Downloading a song." I clicked on *search*.

"A legal download, I hope," he muttered in his stern 'cop' voice.

"Yes," I hissed, rolling my eyes.

"What song?"

"It's by this band called Live. You know them, right?"

"Yeah," Mike scoffed. "Why would *you* be listening to them, though? It's a little before your time, isn't it?"

"Mike, I'm three years your junior. If it's before my time, it's before yours."

'Overcome' started downloading, so I looked up the song David said reminds him of me—the one by Muse. I just had to hear it again. My playlist of David was getting very long.

"So, what Live song then?" Mike asked after a moment.

"Oh, um, 'Overcome'."

"Where'd you hear that one?"

"David likes it. He played it today on his iPhone. Why?"

"You know me, baby. I judge how you're feeling by your playlist. Don't you think that song's a little…?"

"What, depressing?"

"Maybe," he said reluctantly.

"Mike. Are you worried that I'm suici—"

"No. Ara. Please don't think that. I just… you normally listen to such happy music. I just thought—"

"Really, I'm fine." Just tired of people thinking I'm depressed. "I know Vicki and Dad think I'm suicidal and, to be honest, if you don't all leave me alone I might have to do something rash just to get some peace in a padded cell. So, shut it! Okay? I'm fine."

For a moment, I thought he'd hung up, until he said, "I'm sorry."

"Good. 'Cause I'm okay. I have David. I have a shit load of grief, too, but he makes all of that easier to carry. Look"—I exhaled and softened my tone—"I love you, Mike. I know you're just worried. But it's really an insult to my character that everyone keeps watching me in case I take my own life. I live with a former psychiatrist, for God's sake." It was supposed to be an attempt at reason, but unfortunately for Mike, he'd just become victim to two months' worth of saved-up ranting. "Mike? You still there?"

"You're not a little girl anymore, Ara," he concluded softly. "What's happened these last few months has… well, it's *changed* you. A lot. You've really had to grow up and I'm sorry for that." I rested my hand over my bellybutton to quiet the flutters his words formed there. "But I'm also really proud of you. I just need to see you again—make sure you're still my girl."

"I'll always be your girl, Mike. You're my *best* friend."

"But you have David now. You won't be needing me for much longer."

"Don't say things like that, Mike."

"Why? You know it's true. But it's okay," he assured himself. "It'll just be an adjustment, that's all—not having you all to myself whenever I wanna talk to you."

"It was the same for me when you were dating Lyndall. It's just the way things are. But I'm sure we'll always be friends."

"Yeah, I'm sure we will." After a second, he laughed softly. "I'm really looking forward to seeing you. I can't wait to pick you up and squeeze you until you can't breathe."

"Ha! No way. I'll totally squeeze you harder."

"Sure, those skinny spider arms'll do so much damage."

"Shut up, Hercules!" I chuckled the words out.

"Miss you." Mike sighed, his laughter ceasing.

"Me too."

THE LAST OF THE MINIVAN PARADE SPED PAST MY DAD'S HOUSE AS I reached the edge of the driveway, and the glowing heat of the sun warmed my skin while the sight of David warmed my whole day. He didn't see me come out, and I thought about sneaking up on him, but once I cleared the windbreak of the house, the morning breeze blew in from the east, sweeping strands of my hair pleasantly along my shoulders like tickly feathers. I closed my eyes and lost myself in the sensation.

"Ara! Stop!"

My eyes shot open as the windshear of a speeding car nearly sucked me onto the road, but a hand yanked me from the edge and I spun away, my wrist barely missing its side mirror.

"Jeeze, Ara!" Sam dropped my arm. "What the hell were you thinking?"

I swallowed hard and blinked. One more step and I would've been under that car. "Sorry, Sam. It wasn't there when I started crossing."

We watched the beaten-up old bomb scream around the corner, smoke billowing out from its exhaust.

A smile spread over my shock. "You just saved my life."

"David. How come you didn't see that?" He looked over my shoulder just as warm hands clasped my waist. David spun me into him, ignoring Sam. "Man, you were looking right at her."

"Are you okay?" David asked in a soft whisper, cupping my cheek.

"Mm-hm." I nodded.

"I—" He shook his head and looked at Sam. "I was looking this way, but I was… I just didn't see it."

I touched my collarbone where it felt like my heart was trying to break through the skin.

"Well, I gotta get to school," Sam said, nodding toward the building as the last bell rang. "You need me to hold your hand across the road, sis?"

"Funny." I rolled my eyes.

"Take care, Ara. Okay?" Sam started walking backward. "Dad only just got you back. It'll kill him if you… do something stupid."

My mouth fell open. "It was an accident," I called out, standing on my toes to make my voice seem bigger.

He shrugged and kept walking.

"I'm sorry, Ara." David's eyes narrowed when I looked back at him.

"I really *should* have seen that."

"It's not your fault. I was totally in my own world." I laughed, but David just shook his head, saying something to me in French with an angry or maybe frightened tone.

"Huh?"

"Come on, let's just get you to class."

"David?" I said, following him as he walked. "Is something wrong?"

He stopped with rounded shoulders, his chest rising and falling as though it was hard to breathe. Everything around me faded to insignificance then. I knew something was wrong. Really wrong. He didn't move, didn't speak, just stood motionless, wordless and unresponsive.

Tiny bubbles of despair flitted around my stomach, making me feel like everyone in the schoolyard was watching us. But the field was empty; we were late, and I suddenly didn't care.

"Are you upset with me about the… the feeling I had yesterday?"

"No," he said in a deep, quiet voice.

"Then does this have something to do with the reason you don't want to kiss me?"

"Is that what you think? That I don't *want* to kiss you?" He stalked away again. "Honestly, Ara, I don't know where you come up with these things."

"You pulled away from me! What am I supposed to think?"

David just shook his head, walking on.

"So if it's not that, then tell me what's wrong. What am I *supposed* to think when you act like this?" I stepped out onto the road. "David, please."

He stopped but didn't turn around, rolling his chin to his chest with a long, heavy sigh. "I spoke to my uncle last night."

"Okay, and?"

"And…" He turned to face me again. "When he comes to visit today, he has requested I return with him."

"Return where?"

"New York."

"Why? For how long?"

David's eyes closed slowly. "For good."

"What?" I sprung forward. "You're *leaving*?"

After a hard sigh, David looked defeated, like this was the worst day of his life. "Ara, leaving was never optional for me."

"But… you said… you told me you weren't going anywhere. Ever!"

"I know. It was silly for me to say that. I got caught up in you, in *this*, and I made promises I knew even then that I probably couldn't keep."

"C—" My mouth hung open, stuck around the incredulity of that statement. "Caught up? You don't just get *caught up*, then make fake promises."

"It wasn't fake. When I made that promise, my every intention was to try to keep it."

"*Try to keep it*?" I yelled, throwing my hands up when he didn't respond. "Well, what's changed? Why can't you keep it now?"

"You might say reality came back to pay me a visit."

I stared at him. "What kind of answer is that?"

"I'm sorry. I've done everything the wrong way here. I just wasn't prepared to come here and fall in love, and now that I have, I need to rethink my entire life."

"But… can't you rethink your life with me in it?"

"It's not viable."

"*Viable?*" I took a wide step back from him. "So, that's it? No negotiations. You're just leaving me?"

"It wasn't supposed to be for another few months."

"Months? You said *never*."

"I know. I'm sorry."

"When were you going to tell me that your promise was a lie?"

He swallowed, guilty as sin.

My eyes narrowed at him as it sunk in, making me dizzy. "You weren't, were you? You were just going to leave?"

"I…"

I died then. Everything that he had made okay within me suddenly broke, like a glass heart hitting a boulder. "Am I a game to you?"

"No, Ara—"

"Get off me!" I rolled my shoulder, pulling my arm away from his touch. "God, how could you do this to me? No, how could *I* have been so stupid to get so invested in this?"

"It wasn't supposed to be like this. I wasn't supposed to love you this way."

"But you do. Doesn't that… I mean, *can't* that change how things have to be?"

He turned slowly and looked at me, his eyes shimmering so green in the morning light, so liquid with troubles that I wanted to look away before they made me forgive him. "I wish it did."

"So, that's it. You're going? Leaving—today?"

He nodded.

I bit my lip to stop it trembling, then walked right past him with my arms folded, my spine as straight as a board.

"Ara?"

I couldn't speak, couldn't even think. I just had to go to school, go to class, just move.

"Ara?" He grabbed my arms and pulled me back gently. "Where are you going?"

"Class. I…" I spoke to his chest. "I can't do this."

"Do what? Say goodbye?"

"No." I laughed at him, the sound filled with derision. "Argue with you about it."

"Then let's not argue." His voice softened. "I only have until—"

"You still don't get it, do you?"

"What?"

"You *can't* leave."

"I…" He seemed shocked, as if he'd just expected me to accept this. "Ara, I *have* to."

"No." I shook my head, folding my arms tighter. "I'll die. If you go, I won't be able to go on. You're the glue. You're everything that's holding me together. I won't be okay without you."

He dropped his arms to his sides. "Don't say that."

"Would you rather I lied? Would you rather I said *great, let's have a freakin' farewell party*? What did you honestly expect by telling me this?"

His gaze sunk to the ground. "I'm not sure. I… I hadn't actually planned to tell you. It just came out."

I wiped my face with my hand and walked away again. "I'll see you in class."

"I wish I'd told you the truth," he called after me. "I should have told you I'd be leaving, Ara."

"No shit."

David caught up and stood in front of me, blocking my path. "I'm sorry for that."

"But you *didn't* tell me. And you wait until now, when I finally let myself need you, finally let myself feel okay again, to tell me you're going to take all that away."

"No. That will stay with you now. Don't you see? You have Em, you have your dad, Mike—"

"As if that matters, David! They're not you!"

He rocked back on his heels like he'd been physically hit with my words. "I'm sorry."

"Sorry?" I nodded, the lump in my throat threatening to rip me open. And it all broke apart then. I dug the heels of my palms into my eyes, shaking, as everything I saw for the future died. I felt as if I were standing alone in the pouring rain, and even the smell of the hot grass couldn't bring me back to earth, couldn't make me believe this was not some nightmare.

"You will get through this," he said dismissively.

"Is that what you really believe?"

He exhaled, chest sinking. "It's not my heart's desire to leave you. If you only knew how much you mean to me, you'd know how the very idea of not being here with you is *killing* me. I've lost sleep over this, Ara. It wasn't supposed to be like this," he said, his voice losing that deep, strong tone.

"Nothing's ever what we want it to be."

"No, it's not. And I betrayed you—betrayed your heart by allowing you to love me, when I knew this would end."

"Did you think you could control this?" I dug my finger into my chest. "Did you think you could stop me falling in love with you, like it's some accident?"

"I could've left before you fell for me."

"So, before my first day; before English class; before you took me to the lake and made me open up to you in a way I never thought I could with anyone?"

He pinched the bridge of his nose. "This is a mess."

I rolled my shoulders back and looked around the field. "Will he let you finish out the day, at least?"

David shook his head. "He'll arrive just after lunch. I need to be there to meet with him."

I looked at his shoulder, realising he didn't even have his schoolbag. "Just go then."

"What?"

"Don't drag this out," I said, splitting open at the seams. I had to cover my face then to hide the ugliness of my world falling apart.

"Ara, don't cry like that. You'll make yourself sick again."

"I can't help it. Do you think I'm doing it deliberately?"

"Come here." He reached for me.

"No!" I shoved his chest as hard as I could. "I said go. I don't want to see you anymore. I don't want to even look at you."

"Ara, stop it."

"No. You hurt me. You made me love you. You made me want to be happy with you!" I drew a deep, shuddering breath as he moved in and wrapped me up in his arms, tucking my hands into my chest so I couldn't fight him.

"Shh. It's okay," he said into my hair. "It's okay."

"I thought it was for always. I pictured a future," I sobbed inaudibly.

"I know," he hummed in that deep, milky voice. "I did too."

"Then what happened? Why are you just letting this go?"

"This isn't what I want. I was stupid. I thought I'd be the exception but… Ara? I'm not. I can't change this."

"But… don't you know what will happen to me when you're gone?" I said, knowing I wouldn't survive, seeing it all play out. I stood a chance, once, before I met him. But this wasn't a before and after kind of love. It was a do or die.

He grew taller inch by inch. "Don't think that way. You're a strong, capable girl."

"You know I'm not—not right now." I shook my head. "That's just what you tell yourself so you don't have to feel guilty, knowing what will happen to me if you leave."

"It's what I *have* to tell myself," he yelled, his gaze fixing mine. I let him look at me, look in to me, seeing everything crack and bleed. After a moment, he gently pushed past me and walked toward my dad's house, jerking around a few steps away. "Goddamn it, Ara."

I crossed my hands over my stomach to keep the contents in, drawing a few deep breaths, watching him do the same.

The bell tolled behind us and students broke through the school doors, their noise filling the field. First period.

David quickly marched toward me with a determined look in his eye, grabbing my arm again before he was at my side. He pulled me close, glaring down at me. "What would you have me do?"

I shoved his hand off my arm. "Stay."

"And what if those secrets of mine, those secrets you're too innocent to handle, were stopping that from ever being possible long-term? Would you be ready to hear them then, even if it meant I would still need to leave in a few months?"

I stepped forward, lifting my chin to feel taller. "Yes."

He was taken aback for a moment, but then his eyes narrowed, seeing through me. "Liar."

"I just..." I twitched a little. "I don't want you to be something bad, David."

"Because you're not sure if you could love me?"

"I've never been in love like this before. I just don't know what it can withstand." I touched my chest. "And I think I'm just too fragile to lose you—whether that's to hatred or to you leaving me."

He exhaled slowly, and I knew it weaselled its way in there—the idea that he couldn't leave until I was okay. "I can talk to my uncle. Maybe I can convince him to let me stay at least for my original designated allowance."

"But not for always?"

David looked around as the students branched out in several directions, intruding on our little battle over the end of the world. "There *are* other options. Some I, until now, haven't been willing to explore, but staying forever is not one of them."

"Well, what is?"

"None of them, really, Ara." He groaned, scratching his brow fiercely. "None of them are right—not for you."

"Why?"

"Because I love you. Because I want better for you. And because all your dreams, Ara, everything you want in life could be destroyed if we stay together."

That seemed like a pretty out-there thing to say, but I could see he meant it, which worried me. Deeply. "Why?"

"That, my love, is as far as this explanation goes without formal approval."

My eyes narrowed as I stepped into him, peering right into his soul. "Who the hell are you?"

"I will explain this to you, depending on what my uncle says. Just… I need to go now, but don't hate me, okay. Let me talk to him, and I'll return for you later."

"When?"

"After lunch," he said, and walked away without waiting for a response.

"Hey, Ara," Emily beamed, racing up to where I stood. She smiled widely, looking at me then at David as he wandered away. "Missed you in rollcall today."

"Em?" I rolled my head to the side. "Don't pretend there's nothing going on. That just makes it worse."

"Sorry." Her shoulders dropped. "Are you okay? Did you have a fight?"

I watched David getting smaller and smaller as he briskly walked toward the front parking lot. "I gotta get to class."

"Okay. Um, Ara?"

I stopped, turning stiffly back to face her.

"I'm sorry. I know you're upset, but if you need to, like, talk or something—" She pulled one shoulder up and touched her cheek to it.

"Thanks, Em." But I'd opened that door to someone already. I would never open it again after this.

12

As we walked to class, Emily babbled mindlessly about the benefit concert and our difficult mythology paper—which hadn't sounded so difficult when Dad assigned it—and I slipped into the safety of my proverbial eggshell-carrycase: happy on the outside, while my guts felt like fricassee. David's pendulum behaviour had finally sent me nuts; my every thought centred on reasons he might be leaving, and I kept coming back to believing I just wasn't enough for him after all.

At lunch, we set the date for the benefit concert and finished making ticket signs with the help of the art students. Then, Emily went as far as to ask that the performers meet after school for further rehearsals. And we actually agreed. Everything for the concert was falling into place while, for me, everything was falling apart.

"Em?" I said, lowering my voice so Dad wouldn't growl at me for talking in class.

"Mm?" She kept her eyes on him.

"Hypothetical question."

"Oh, I love this game."

I smiled. "If you loved someone more than anything, what would be the only thing that could make you leave them?"

"Hm." She watched the projection screen as Dad changed the image, and I caught one or two words of his lecture about some religious topic—something to do with vampire myth. "Death, I suppose. I'd only leave if they could either die or get really hurt by my being with them."

I nodded to myself. "What if you were a criminal and you didn't want them to know?"

She shook her head, leaning on her hand. "Nah, I'd tell them. If they loved me, they wouldn't care."

"What if your horrible truth was that you went from place to place, making people love you, then leaving them—for the fun of it?"

"Then it wouldn't be real love, so it wouldn't count."

My heart wriggled down into my diaphragm.

"Can I ask *you* a hypothetical question?" Emily said, lowering her voice when Dad gave us a warning glare.

"Sure." I tried not to switch off. Too many times, she'd said things and I had to pretend I'd been paying attention. But I just felt like crying—a feeling so deep I had to sit straight and take a few shallow breaths. I knew only too well that if David thought he would be hurting me by staying, then he would absolutely leave and not come back. And I loved him for that as much as I hated him for it.

"Ara?" Emily elbowed me. "What do you think?"

Oh crud. Not again. "Um—"

"Ara and Emily!" Dad said, saving the day.

"Sorry, sir." Emily winced.

"Ask me again later," I said, leaning closer.

She nodded and we tuned in to Dad's lecture.

"So," he continued, "when God created Adam, he also created who?" He pointed his pen to the back of the room.

"Eve."

"In some versions of the story, yes. But it's also told that God first created a woman named Lilith. Now, she has many names in different cultures: Lilith, Kali, Satrina. She's also known as The Snake, The Screeching Owl—" I phased out when I smelled something very similar to David's orange-chocolate cologne, looking around as if he might be in the room.

"So, unlike her sister Eve, Lilith was not created from a piece of Adam. She was created as his equal. However, Adam would not treat her as such. He tried to force her to submit to him as he pleased, and in a stand for her own rights, Lilith left the Garden of Eden."

"Sweet, world's first feminist," one of the football jocks snickered.

"I have to admit," I whispered to Em, "this *is* getting kind of interesting."

"Very sharp, Mr. Grady." Dad paced the floor, gesturing with his hands as he spoke. "At a loss now, God decided to create another woman for Adam. But this time she would be bound to Adam by the flesh." Dad stopped and looked around. "Who knows how he did that?"

"She was created from one of Adam's ribs or something, right?" the kid next to me said.

"That's right. And because she was bound to him, she couldn't…?" Dad pointed around the room, stopping on Emily.

"She couldn't just leave?"

"Exactly. Lilith, on the other hand, believed Eve was made to be naïve—that God had not given her the knowledge of herself. Some say Lilith acted as the snake that conned Eve into tasting the Forbidden Fruit, also known as the—?"

"Fruit of Knowledge." Emily grinned, dropping her raised hand.

"That's right. Ten points to the students paying attention down the front here." Dad grinned and scribbled only five lines on the top right corner of the board. "And deduct five, for my daughter, who hasn't heard a word we've been saying."

The whole class erupted into a murmur of giggles. I sunk down in my seat, staring daggers at my father.

"Now, as the story continues, Lilith, who was created in God's likeness, lived outside the Garden of Eden. If we jump forward in the story a little"—he looked at his watch—"you'll remember from our studies in religion last year that those in God's likeness have the same power as the Almighty, which included immortality.

"You'll find that, in many cases throughout history, Lilith was said to be the Goddess of Seduction and believed to have power over men. In fact," Dad said, raising his index finger, "in many cases, when men were unfaithful, they proclaimed it to have been an act of seduction by the Goddess, and not an act of sin. Sounds like the easy way out, if you ask me." He dramatically loosened his tie.

The class laughed, but not me. I was still mad at him for singling me out.

"Wasn't she also said to be a demon, which ate small children?" a student asked.

"Yes, Grace." Dad raised a brow. "That's exactly right. There are many myths surrounding Lilith. If anyone here knows the story of Cain and Abel, you'll know that Cain murdered his own brother and was punished by God—banished and cursed for eternity with a thirst for blood. Then, he fell in love with the Goddess Lilith." Dad smiled at the class. "Can anyone see where I'm going with this?" He looked around; no one answered.

I shrugged when he looked at me. How would I know?

"Okay, well, it's told that Lilith and Cain had a child—an immortal, who inherited his father's thirst for blood. The world's first myth about…?" He waited, his brow arched, cheeks high.

"Vampires," said a voice from the doorway.

Quiet murmurs spread over the class, as everyone turned to look at the boy leaning on the doorframe, with his hands in his pockets.

"Very good, David, and you're not even one of my students. And so," Dad said as he walked over and took a note from David's hand, "you can see that even legends of the most vile of creatures may have some religious origin."

David looked at me and smiled. It was not returned.

"Ara?" Dad called, still reading the note.

I sat up a little and stared at David, my mind filling with questions. "Yes?"

"Go with David, please?"

All eyes in the class fell on me. I stood up slowly, jammed my books and pens into my bag then shrugged at Emily as I sauntered past, slipping out the classroom door with David behind me.

"What did you say to my dad?"

He started walking. "I told him I needed to rehearse with you for the benefit concert."

"And he bought it?" I asked, the surprise in my voice a little too obvious.

David just laughed.

"Did you talk to your uncle?"

"Yes."

"And?"

"And…" His shoulders dropped. "I have permission to talk to you about my life, Ara, and I still have to leave, but…"

"But what?"

"But, after much grovelling and bribing, he's granted me, provisionally, the original amount of time I had left."

"How long?"

I watched his tongue move between his lips for a second before he pressed them together. "You can count on me being gone by winter."

Dread made my arms heavy—took all control from my body—making me angry. "Then there's no need for us to see each other anymore."

"Oh no you don't." He grabbed my wrist. "You're coming with me, whether you like it or not."

"Where?"

"Somewhere else."

"Why?"

He maintained his tight grip. "If I have to leave in a few months, I won't waste this time we have left. There are some things I want to do with you, Ara-Rose, and I won't let the fear that I might hurt you stop me from loving you the way I've needed to for so long."

"*Hurt* me?" The bridge of my nose crinkled. "Why would you hurt me?"

"Just"—he pulled me along by the arm—"come on. We need to go before we get caught ditching."

"No." I twisted my wrist around in his grip and yanked it out through the break in his thumb and forefinger, standing fast. "Not until you tell me where we're going."

"You stubborn little thing," he said quickly, taking one long stride in my direction, then he arched his body downward as he swept me off the floor and into his arms.

"Whoa." I pinned my dress under my legs, nudging his chest with my elbow. "Put me down. This is kidnapping."

"No, it's not," he stated with a smile, keeping his eyes on the path ahead. "It's a rescue."

"Rescue?" I scoffed. "I don't need to be rescued."

He stopped walking and looked down at me. I shrank into his arms a little. "You need rescuing, my stubborn little princess, just as much as I do."

"But I'm not a princess, and I'm not in a tower."

"You will be if you don't come quietly."

I huffed indignantly. He just looked forward and smiled to himself.

ALL THE WAY THROUGH THE FOREST, I PRETTY MUCH WALKED with my teeth clenched. When we came to the rock where we usually sat, David shook his head and continued on a path we'd never walked down before.

"*Where* are we going?" I whined, dropping my arms to my sides. "I'm tired and it's hot. I don't wanna walk anymore."

He continued ahead in his wordless state, tall and sleek, never looking back.

Argh! I felt like throwing a rock at his head.

David spun around then, his eyes alight with a humored glint. "Forget to have lunch, did we?"

"None of your business."

"Actually, it is, because *I'm* the one that has to put up with your moods."

"I'm not moody." But I knew that was a lie.

"You'll want to take those off."

I looked down at my shoes. "No. Not until you tell me where we're going."

"Fine, leave them on." He shrugged, then reached behind him and lifted his shirt, tugging it past the sharply cut V of muscles diving just below the waistline of his jeans. I looked back down at my feet before it came off completely.

"It's okay, Ara," David said, a hint of laughter in his tone. "You don't have to look away."

"I wasn't looking away."

"No, of course you weren't." He came to stand in front of me, the band of his Calvin Klein's showing just under the rise of his dark jeans, his tan skin calling my eye to every inch of him. And I could look, if I wanted to.

He held my hand firmly, like he was asking me to, and when I finally braved a glance, a body I'd only ever seen on TV gobbled up my wits, destroying me in the end with that cheeky grin he was wearing.

"Something wrong, Ara?"

"I'm not blushing 'cause I think you're hot." I reached down and slipped off my shoes then dumped them by a rock. "You don't affect me, David Knight."

"I know. You're too sensible to be knocked off your feet by a guy without a shirt." He grinned, reaching his hand out. I stared at it. "Come on."

Reluctantly, I walked the five-pace gap and touched his fingertips. "I don't see why you need to take your shirt off. It's not that hot."

"Didn't want it to get wet."

"Wet?"

He nodded and led me to the cold, crisp water of the lake. "Do you see where we're going now?"

I followed the direction of his nod. "The island?"

"Yes. There's a sandbar that extends all the way across. It's only as deep as"—he considered my height for a second—"probably your upper thigh."

My breath caught in my throat as the cold water reached my knees, and my fingers involuntarily tightened around David's. "How did you find this sandbar?" I asked. It was only wide enough for David and me to walk on side-by-side, disappearing into the depth of the lake after that.

"Well," he chuckled as he spoke, "let's just say I kinda stumbled over it one day. It's the only way out to the island unless you swim —or fly."

"Is the water deep outside the sandbar?"

He nodded once.

Above us, thin fingers of clouds patched over the sun, and a cool breeze dragged the shivers in my body to the surface. David's jeans were soaked, the water seeping all the way up to his pockets, but not anywhere on those golden ribs or arms did I see so much as a raised hair.

"How come you're not cold?" I demanded.

He looked down at me, then let go of my hand and wrapped his arm over my shoulder. "You are?"

I nodded.

"It's okay, I can think of a few ways to get warm."

I bit my lip to stop from grinning, already feeling warmer.

Under the crystal-clear water, I saw David's feet for the first time, and smiled. It's kinda funny how seeing someone's feet can make them seem less mysterious; how it can make it easier to imagine them beside yours in a bed or in the kitchen while you make breakfast. But seeing his feet would only make it harder for me to cope when the winter came.

"Are you afraid?" he asked, taking my hand again.

"A little," I said.

"Please, don't be. I won't let anything happen to you," he said softly.

"That's not what I'm afraid of." I laughed.

"Then, what is it?"

"I'm just afraid of what it's going to feel like when you're gone."

He sighed, and a hint of a smile angled the corners of his mouth. "Well, it's not goodbye, Ara. Not yet."

I moved my shoulder in a shrug, feeling detached and outside reality.

"Can we just pretend… just for today, that I'm not leaving in a few months?"

"I don't know."

"Can you try?"

Exhaling the crushing fear and sorrow, I nodded, trying to shove it all down for one blissful afternoon.

"Are you gonna let that get wet?" He motioned to the edges of my dress, slightly touching the water. "I won't look if you want to lift it up a little."

"I'll be fine," I said, regretting it as soon as the water soaked in.

Ahead of us, a thick moss blanket smothered the base of the island. We waded through, parting it with our fingers like cheese on a pizza until the steep, muddy slopes of the banks halted us with warding trees, leaning out like diagonal spears. David curled his palm around a branch and hoisted himself onto it. I waited in the water, imagining all the slimy things that might be lurking under the sludgy stuff.

"Don't worry." David reached down from his perch, grinning. "The worst thing out here is me."

"Well, in that case"—I took his hand—"maybe I should be worrying about my *heart* instead of my toes."

"You just let me worry about your heart, mon amour." He yanked me from the lake in one fluid movement, swinging me onto the sloped shore. The soil sunk and shifted into a small mound between my toes. I scrunched them together, looking up at the knitted crown of yellow and green leaves. I felt so pleasantly closed in, with low-lying shrubs and ferns at my feet, and flowering vines covering nearly every other surface from floor to canopy.

"It's amazing under here."

"I know." David tucked his bunched-up shirt into the waistband of his jeans.

"I feel like I'm in my own little Hobbit hole."

"Yes. It's very hidden. No one can see us, not even if they were flying over."

"Hm. Comforting."

He laughed. "Come on, I'll take you to my favorite spot."

As we walked, my toes tangled in the carpet of loose-leafed clover. I lifted my feet a little higher with each step and placed them flat over the creepers, stabilizing myself with my hand on the mossy tree trunks. It all smelled so grassy, in a hot and moist kind of way.

"Just watch out for these little terrors; they'll give you a nasty scratch." David reached forward to shift the silvery arm of a fern from our path.

"Speak from experience, do we?" I said playfully.

"Yes." He held it in place, dropping it softly back against the hip of the tree after I passed. "My brother and I used to play here as children."

I could actually picture that, too: little David with a companion of exact lookalike, popping up above the bushes, pretending to shoot each other. "I bet you were a cute little boy."

"Stunning," he said, then pointed ahead. "Look up there."

My eyes followed the vertical columns of maples to a deliciously colorful display of twisting climbers, shrouded with palm-sized purple-and-white flowers. "Wow. They look like purple cherry blossoms."

"Want one?"

"Oh, no. It's okay. They're too high u—"

"I can handle it." David grinned, then ran to the base of a tree trunk, took a small leap, wedging his foot against the bark, and plucked a flower from a vine six or seven feet off the ground. "For you," he said, landing back beside me as if he were weightless.

"Thank you." I sniffed its sour, grassy fragrance. And it was only as I tucked my hair back, placing the flower behind my ear, that I really noticed the vibrant songs of possibly thousands of different birds and small animals chiming through the treetops like a symphony. "It's kinda noisy here, isn't it?"

"It's a kind of noise I can handle."

"And what, my talking isn't?

He looked sideways at me. I turned my face to the front and kept walking, well, shuffling, through the thick undergrowth.

"Would you like me to carry you, Ara?"

"I'm fine." I straightened the flower behind my ear. "But how much further do we have to walk?"

"Just to right… over… there." He pointed to a small circle of long grass, center to a ring of tightly-packed trees, with a single beam of sunlight making the busy movements of tiny insects look like sparkles. "Come on."

"Do you come here often?"

"Not so much anymore."

"Why?"

"I used to come here to reflect on the miseries of my life." He kicked a few stones away from the grass and plonked down on his side. "Last few weeks, I haven't needed to."

I sat down too, hugging my knees to keep the tickly grass off the backs of my thighs. "This would be a great spot to bring a book." I could imagine that warm beam of sunlight overhead lighting the pages for me just enough that I wouldn't need to squint. It made me wish I'd brought one with me, but it was great just sitting here, with David.

"I have a chest buried here where I keep books for when I visit unexpectedly."

"Really?"

"Yeah. But right now, it's great just sitting here." He sat up and lopped his arms over his knees, giving a timid shrug. "With you."

"I was just thinking that." I looked away from his ultra-cheeky grin. "Sometimes I feel like you steal my thoughts."

"How do you know I don't?"

I shook my head, smiling. "That's just the thing, I'm starting to wonder if—"

"Wait!" He held up his index finger, angling his head as if to listen for something. "I have a surprise for you."

"A surprise?"

"Come on." David hoisted me off the ground by my hand. His skin warmed the side of my face and the backs of my forearms as he guided them around his bare waist. Little bumps rose over my cheeks and across my shoulders, making me shiver, but not from cold. I'd never felt them from touch. I never even knew that was possi—

"Shh," David said.

"I didn't say anything."

"Shh," he repeated, and opened his eyes for a second, winking at me before closing them again.

I exhaled a laugh, burying my face against the small hollow at the center of his chest. A sheet of sweat broke out along my neck and upper lip in the heat between us, as the rapid climb in temperature made the air damp and almost hard to breathe.

"Wow, it just got really hot," I said, looking up to the soft pattering sound of rain. But there was no rain.

"Stay calm, okay."

"Why do I need to stay calm?"

He didn't answer. He just held me close, his eyes shut tight, his beautiful dark-pink lips twitching with concentration. The pattering sound around us became louder then, drowned out for a second by a flock of birds bursting through the canopy above us, coloring the sky in reds and greens. When silence fell over the island again as the birds disappeared, I saw something move from the corner of my eye. I yanked my arm back when a feathery touch brushed my skin.

"It's okay," David said in a low voice. "You're safe here."

"I know," I said. "I just thought I felt a spider on my arm."

"Not a spider." He gently kissed the top of my head, tangling his fingers in my hair. "Look up."

It took a second for my eyes to adjust, but as the blurry cloud of yellow and pale blue resolved itself into the fluttering of hundreds of tiny wings, my mouth dropped. "Oh, my God." I watched in amazement, the butterflies filling the space around us like pastel snow. "How is this possible?"

"Anything is possible." David smiled.

I smiled back and reached out as the glowing sun filtered down through the leaves, lighting the winged creatures in a soft, misty glow. They flitted across my skin with tiny silk kisses, forming a circle around us like we were in some magical orb of nature. But the gem-like green of David's eyes held more beauty among the pale colors, as if he was backlit by the brightest star in the sky.

As his head turned, unlocking the hold of his gaze, he nodded to the tip of my finger, held way up into the magic. I laughed, staying ultra-still so as not to scare the blue-and-black butterfly there. It fluttered its wings once then before flying away.

"David, this is so beautiful."

He cupped my face, pressing the tip of his nose to mine. "I know."

The humidity made it so hard to breathe, and the closeness of David's lips to mine made the air thick with tension, scented sweetly with his breath blowing over my tongue every time I inhaled. And I couldn't do it anymore. I couldn't be this close and not kiss him.

As if he read my mind, his lips skimmed across the surface of mine, so softly, so hesitantly, coming to rest just in front of my mouth as he breathed for the both of us.

The world stopped. Every sound, every brush of air disappeared until only he and I existed.

His fingers tightened on the small of my back for just a moment, my dress lifting a little with his grip, then he swept me onto my toes so our faces aligned and kissed me deeply, drawing a breath so full it stole mine. I felt the wet soil and grass beneath my toes, the sweat trickling down my back, soaking into my dress, felt everything as if this one moment brought me to life, lit everything in stark contrast—making it real; me real, him real, making the world, somehow, into a place I never knew existed.

He broke away for a single moment to slip both hands along the sides of my face, hungrily catching my bottom lip against his and drawing it in, breaking only to release and drink it in again.

I had to open my eyes—to savor this moment forever—but while the kiss felt like a reality so stark it couldn't possibly become just a memory, when I looked up and the golden beams of sunlight shone through the cloud of butterflies, it felt more like a dream.

David gently drew my face away from his, smoothing his thumb over the moisture of his kiss. "Are you happy here?" he whispered.

"Why do you ask?"

"Because I need this, Ara. I just need to see you happy before I lose you."

"Even if I am happy, you'll be gone soon. And then I won't be happy anymore."

"You *will* forget about me one day," he said in his soft, deep voice. "I promise you that."

I shook my head. "I'll never forget you. I'll love you for the rest of my life."

One corner of his mouth quirked upward. "That, my love, is the length of this entire line that lies between us."

"What do you mean?"

"You'll love me for the rest of your days, but I"—he wrapped his fingers around my wrist, drawing my hand down until it rested over his heart—"I will love *you* until the end of time."

We stood together then in our timeless embrace and watched the miracle of life swarm around us for a while. But all it did to feel him so close was make me fall so much deeper in love with him. So much that I wasn't sure I *could* live after he went away.

13

My fork scraped the plate where the absence of a potato mound left the china bare. Even though I'd managed to create something worthy of special mention in Art Weekly Magazine, I couldn't lift the heavy weight I'd carried to the dinner table with me. I was losing David. He'd be gone by winter and there was nothing I could do about it. Not even a magical first kiss could save our *happy ever after*.

Our dreamy afternoon was followed by an intensely silent drive home, with me trying so hard not to burst into a sniveling mess. And when I walked through the front door and readied myself to run upstairs and sob my heart out, Vicki called on me to help with dinner, forcing me to swallow my grief like a hard wedge of cheese. It was just about ready to catapult out of me at the smallest trigger.

"Ara?"

I looked up from my plate. "Hm?"

"How was practice this afternoon?" Dad asked.

"Practice?"

"With David."

"Oh right—the reason I left class," I said, fumbling over my own words. “Um. Good. I’m gonna perform a piece of music from a movie.”

“You mean *going to* not *gonna*,” Dad said sternly.

I shrugged.

“And you have your friends coming over this weekend, don’t you? Emily and Alana?” Vicki asked, taking the salt from Dad.

I nodded.

“How’s your mythology paper coming along?” Dad asked.

“Good.” But it wasn’t good. I hadn’t even started it.

They all sat silently then, the feel of their stares burning into my face until Sam started laughing.

Dad looked at him with a raised brow. “Something funny, son?”

“Ara’s in love,” he teased.

I sat up straight. “I am not.”

“Yes, you are. You wanna marry *David*.” He laughed, poking his fingers in the air at me.

Dad looked at Vicki and a smile crept up under her lips. “I think you’re right, Samuel. I’ve seen *that* look before,” she said.

I waited for my father to jump in and stand up for his only daughter, but he broke into laughter too. Traitor.

“I’m sorry, honey.” He wiped the napkin across his mouth. “But I think your brother may be right.”

“I wondered why you were suddenly so eager to go to school,” Vicki added.

“Well, I guess we’d better have young David over for dinner—discuss the dowry,” Dad joked.

“Dad?” I moaned, hiding my face in my hands.

“So, he’s taking you to the Fall Masquerade then?” Dad asked.

I looked up. “The what?”

“Oh, that’s right.” Vicki heaped a spoonful of potato salad onto her plate. “Ara’s never been to a masquerade, has she?”

Dad’s eyes lit up. “No, she hasn’t. Well, this’ll be exciting then.”

“Wait, what’s the Fall Masquerade?” I asked, confused.

“Every year during fall, the town holds a masquerade for seniors, like a school ball, but for the whole town,” Sam said. “You have to wear a mask and a giant dress—totally lame.”

"And you know what that means?" Vicki squeaked. "We get to go *shopping*."

"Well, David hasn't asked me yet." And likely wouldn't be here. "When is it?"

"They'll put posters up soon. It's usually held in early autumn," Dad added.

I smiled, thinking about the last ball I went to, which wasn't really a ball at all. It was an end of year dance and my 'date' was my best friend, whom my mom actually had to *pay* to take me, because he thought that wearing a penguin suit was an indication that you wanted to mate with an arctic bird. And since he didn't want to mate with me, he'd told my mom, it was going to cost her. Mike and I had fun though, but the *dance* was no masquerade.

Then, almost as if Dad read my mind, he asked, "When's Mike coming?"

"Oh, um… his interview is next Monday, so he'll be here on the Tuesday some time."

"How does *David* feel about that?" Vicki asked in a provocative, feather-ruffling tone.

My shoulders dropped. "David? Why would *he* care about my best friend coming to stay?"

Vicki's expression suggested the obvious. She didn't even have to speak.

My lip curled. "David doesn't see it like that. He knows Mike's my friend."

"Well, we'll just see, won't we?" She rolled her head to the side. "Ara, sometimes a girl as young as you can misinterpret things, see them as more innocent than they really are. Mike's a fully-grown man"—she placed the salad back on the table—"maybe he feels differently about you than you do about him."

I looked at Dad. He knew the deal with Mike and me, so why wasn't he correcting her? I mean, he didn't know that I'd confessed my feelings for Mike and been *rejected* but he knew our past; knew we could never be anything more than friends.

"Ara," Dad started in that preachy tone, and I buried my face in my hands, shutting out his voice. At this point, with the grief of losing

David, the lump in my throat building all afternoon, and the memories of what happened between Mike and me the night my mom died, I just couldn't handle their accusations. Mike would never love me, never see me as anything but his little *baby girl.* They had no idea what they were talking about!

I threw my napkin down and stood up. "Mike and I are friends. That's all it's ever been!"

"Ara, sit back down. Vicki knows that," Dad said.

"No, Dad! I'm tired of it. People always ask—just because Mike's a boy and I'm a girl. Don't you guys get it?" I said, my voice high. "Don't you understand what *David* means to me?"

"Honey, you barely know him," Dad reminded me.

"Yeah, and one smile was enough to make me fall in love with him," I retorted. "But seventeen years didn't work for Mike? So what's gonna change now?"

"She's got a point." Sam shrugged.

I looked at Dad and he looked at Vicki. "Ara, you're so young," she said. "This thing with David… it's just an infatuation. You can't know what love is yet."

"How can you say that?" I leaned forward slightly. "You don't know what I feel. None of you do."

"Honey, you can't feel that kind of love at your age."

"How would *you* know? I'm sorry, are you the all-experienced love gurus because you've both had a failed marriage?" I waved my hands around at the word *gurus,* and then dropped them onto my hips.

"Yes, because we know that it can sometimes look like love when it's not."

"So, just because I'm under eighteen means I don't know how to feel?"

"We're just saying that love is complicated," Dad said and held his hand up to Vicki, silencing her. "It takes a long time to figure it—"

"Don't tell me I don't know my own heart. 'Cause I can tell you I do, Dad, and it hurts." My voice broke under the strain. "It hurts all the time. It hurts for Mom and Harry. And I loved them. And I love you"—the tears burst past the strain—"so you can't tell me I don't know what love is because I think, of all the people in this room, I'm the most qualified to say what *my* heart is capable of."

Dad's jaw fell open and Vicki looked at her salad. Sam hovered between standing and sitting.

"Well, Ara"—Vicki placed her fork on her plate and folded her fingers in front of her chin—"do you feel better now you've effectively displayed your maturity in front of your fourteen-year-old brother?"

My arms fell to my sides. I just couldn't believe it. I'd had enough —just about all a girl could take. They all watched, waiting for me to respond. But I had no response. Of *course* I didn't feel better. What a stupid question to ask. And this is why I hated her so much. This is why, no matter how nice she tried to be, I would never love her like a mother.

"How do you *think* I feel, Vicki?" My chair fell over and hit the wall as I pushed it out with the backs of my legs and ran from the room.

"Let her go," Dad said calmly as I ran up the stairs, holding my forearm across the ache in my gut. I couldn't stop it. It all wanted to come out: all the fear, the heartbreak, the grief. I knew too well what I felt for David; knew no one could understand it; knew it was crazy. And I knew, if losing everyone I loved so far hadn't killed me, saying goodbye to David would.

I slammed my bedroom door unintentionally hard, sending vibrations through the house and making my open window rattle. I couldn't breathe—couldn't even find a good enough reason to breathe. I wanted to go home. Just wanted to go back and make it all okay again. But I couldn't, and I was so tired of losing people, so tired of hurting to the point where crying just seemed pointless. It never helped. Tears or none, nothing ever changed.

With a wailing breath, I slid down the door and sat on the ground, hugging my knees to my chest. Outside, the sunlight turned orange and the soft yellow glow that filled my room earlier slipped away with an empty blackness. My nose went cold and my cheeks numb and, after a while, an eerie rumble of thunder growled, a flash of white scorching the sky for a split second.

I stayed motionless in my nightmare life, listening to the quiet patter of rainfall that crept into my world under the cover of night, afraid to move, afraid to cry anymore in case the brooding storm should find me here.

After a while, the familiar sound of doors being locked into place and lights flicked off around the house filled the wordless evening with noise. My parents' footsteps thudded up the stairs and, while the lighter ones continued down the hall, the heavy ones stopped by my door. I sunk my face into crossed arms, holding my breath, praying my dad wouldn't come in. I'd be embarrassed to be found sitting here on the floor. I'd then be forced to explain my emotions, my pain. And there was no explaining it. I was hurt and sad and, after knowing this boy for such a short time, I probably didn't really have a right to be so upset over him leaving. I knew that. I wasn't totally crazy. But my heart was. And my heart just wouldn't stop bleeding inside.

"I'm sure she's sleeping," Vicki whispered.

"I know. I just…"

"I know," Vicki said softly.

The footsteps faded to the other end of the house, and silence swept over the night once more as Dad's bedroom door closed. My real mom would've told him to check on me—to open the door anyway and make sure I was all right. She would've followed him in, warming the sudden unwelcome chill in here, and she would've told me not to be silly. Told me to get up off the floor and get into bed; that when I woke in the morning, everything would seem clear again. And a part of me knew that, but not having her here to say it made the pain, made missing her, so much worse.

As I lifted my head and considered climbing into bed, a low rumble rolled across the roof like a hundred horses running past on hard ground, the noise electrifying the skies with silver forks. It was almost as if the storm had lain dormant, building, waiting for my family to go to bed. I covered my head again, whimpering into my knees. I had nowhere to hide. No one to cuddle up safely beside. I was too old to climb into bed with Dad and Vicki now, and too far away from the phone on the other side of the room, in front of my *open* window, to call Mike.

I counted the seconds between the thunder, sliding my hands up the wood of the door to edge stiffly to my feet. It struck hard and loud, making me squeal, and as soon as it grew silent again I ran, wedged my fingers onto the top of the window frame and slammed it shut, drawing the curtains together before the next strike of lightning. It hit as I turned away, and I tripped all over myself to get away from the window, falling onto the stool in front of my dresser.

Sitting on it, with my head in my hands, I took some slow, deep breaths.

With the curtains closed, the darkness of my room swallowed up my reflection, mirroring back only the outline of my head, shoulders and, as the lightning flashed again, the image of my mother smiling down at the tiny baby in her arms. I lifted the photo frame and kissed them both, then wiped away the smudge my lips left on the glass. This was my favorite photo. My only photo. And I so clearly remembered the day I took it: Harry, who was about two months old, had just been bathed, and my mom—I ran my fingers over her face—wrapped him safely in a towel. Then, when she looked down at him again, I took the shot, capturing the exact moment she saw her baby's first real smile. This was how I wanted to remember them. But, at night, when I closed my eyes, it was the last seconds I ever saw them that flashed into my dreams, making the smiles and the sunlight fade from nearly every memory.

Cold now and exhausted from all the crying, I dropped my head between my hands and let the warm, salty tears fall over my nose and drip away. "I'm so sorry, Mom," I whispered to nothing. "I'm so *so* sorry."

My crystals lashed against the window frame as the gloomy sky shoved its way into my morning, blowing papers around in the remains of the tsunami that hit my desk last night. I sat up on my elbows and looked down at the quilt, covering my still-fully dressed self, then over at the shoes placed neatly by my bedroom door as if I'd entered a dojo.

Great, I thought, flopping back and pulling the blankets over my head. So I've finally gone insane enough to put things away neatly while sleepwalking myself into bed.

"Ara-Rose. Time to get up." Vicki banged on my door, making me jump.

"I'm up," I called, throwing my covers back. I wandered over and shut my window on the stormy day, drawing the curtains across, then slumped in my desk chair with a loud groan. All my homework was ruined—every little bit. I tried to separate the dry pages from the wet ones, but dropped them all with a huff of defeat. It was no use. I'd have to start all over again. But I just didn't feel like being a part of the world right now. Everything in my life that was once worth living for was gone, or thousands of miles on the other side of the world. After months of trying so hard to keep it together, to be normal and move on, I'd finally had enough. I couldn't think of one good reason to get dressed.

From under my pile of class literature, I slid out my diary and opened it. Last night's rain missed most of my books, thankfully, but the corner of my diary got a bit wet—well, soggy was a better word.

It cracked as I opened it and turned to a blank page. The fading smell of home lingered in its binding, slowly being washed away by ageing and the sticky, inky smell of a blue pen.

So many thoughts had been written down in here from times when everything was okay—and not so okay. I fanned the edges with my thumb, considering a flip back through memory lane, but thought better. Before I knew grief, my problems were so mediocre, so unimportant. I don't think I could stand to hear myself drone on about my hopeless thoughts on boys or friends who wouldn't talk to me after a fight. Back then, I was so narrow-minded, so naïve and ignorant to the world. I think it'd just make me want to throw up, or slap myself.

I grabbed a pen from my drawer and leaned over the diary, expelling every twisted, deranged and ludicrous thought in my head. The one word that stood out though, as I read back over it, was *Dad*. Somewhere inside me, I still wondered if David was some hired help my dad called on to make me okay, and now that I was okay, David had to give some lame-ass excuse to leave. Bad thing was, I wouldn't put it past my dad to do that. And even if that wasn't the case, it didn't matter. I felt awful last night. I had never cried so much, and I never ever wanted to again. David had his nature-documentary timeline, and that was fine. But I didn't have to put up with it. If he really had to leave in the winter, then he could go, but I wouldn't let him destroy my heart on the way out.

I snapped my diary shut and stood up. I had to end it now. It had to be my decision. I just needed some goddamn control over *something* in my life.

With a new sense of purpose, I jammed my iPod into the dock and blasted my Girl Power playlist. If I was going to take a new approach to life, then I'd need a montage—and a sexy outfit.

I sang along, making a huge mess as I pulled nearly everything out of the neat little crevices in my wardrobe, then tossed my jeans, red tank top, and the only heeled shoes I owned into the bathroom. Then, in true montage style, shut the bathroom door and emerged again as the new, sexy, I-don't-take-no-crap me—complete with red lip-gloss. I stopped by my dresser to dash on some mascara, and the soulless face of my past stared back at me. "Don't pout," I said to her. "We're breaking up with him, and that's that!"

THE NEW ME WALKED FIERCELY TOWARD THE ROADSIDE, HER head down, eyes away from what she knew was waiting there. Then, as the montage music ended with an abrupt and sudden silence inside my head, I looked up at him and my resolve wavered.

He sat there on a tree stump, bag on the ground by his feet, head in his hands, looking utterly overwhelmed by the weight of the world.

But despite how that made me feel, the new me in the heeled shoes stood taller, gave a not-so-gentle reminder of why we were doing this, and charged onward. *No more David Knight.*

He stood up as I crossed the street, his eyes practically bulging from his head. "Ara? My God, you look amazing!"

I shrugged away from his touch, nearly falling backward as the heels of my pretty black shoes sunk into the turf.

"Ara..." David warned, inching toward me as if I were standing on a cliff. "Don't. I know what you're about to say. *Please* don't."

"I'm sorry, David, it's better this way." The words felt like shards of glass in my throat. "Look, yesterday was great and all, but we both know where this is going. I don't see the point in dragging it out."

"Dragging it out?" His shoulders came forward with his words. "We love each other, Ara. Spending the next few months together is not, by *any* means, dragging things out."

"It is to me. *You're* the one leaving. You don't have to care, you don't have to suffer like I do."

"Is that what you think?" He stepped into me. I stepped back, raising my hands. "Ara, you know nothing about what I will suffer for leaving you."

"You're right. I don't. Because you never tell me anything."

"I speak to you of my heart all the time, Ara, so don't try to deny that you know how I feel—"

"But you don't speak to me about your life. Until you suddenly spring up with the news that you're leaving—that you were always going to leave!"

"I *couldn't* tell you that, because it would open doors to conversations that you, by *your own admission*, are too fragile to handle right now!"

"I told you yesterday that I was ready—"

"That was a lie, and you know it."

"I... well..." I shuffled my feet, folding then unfolding my arms. "Maybe I'm ready to hear about it now."

Looking a little bewildered, he rubbed his head. He clearly didn't expect that. Didn't expect me to mean it.

"So?" I said, finally deciding my arms should be folded. "Spill it."

"There are so many things, Ara. I wouldn't know where to begin."

"How 'bout the reason you're leaving? That seems like a pretty good starting point."

"I—" The words hung just on the edge of his lips.

"Just spit it out!"

"I'm not sure *I'm* ready to tell you," he confessed. "Free to do so, with no excuses to hide behind, I just don't think I can say it."

"Then we're done." I turned away.

"I'm afraid of what you'll think of me," he called, so I stopped walking. "I'm afraid because, despite what you think about yourself, I know how kind and loving and warm you are. But you're also very judgmental, Ara."

"And you think I can't handle the truth?"

He smiled tenderly. "I *know* you can't."

I looked away, exhaling.

"Look, we have a few months left. I just want you like this—this sweet, beautiful girl who loves me; who looks at me like I'm good. I couldn't bear it if you hated me, Ara. I can't bear this." He motioned to the distance between us. "Please don't break up with me."

"I have to, David."

"No, you don't."

"I'll fall more in love with you." I forced back tears. "If I keep doing this, it'll only make me break down when you're gone, and I won't get back up this time. I've got *nothing* left in me."

"Please don't say things like that," he said breathily, as though everything I just said turned his lungs to steel. "All I ever wanted was for you to be okay again."

"Yeah, well"—I looked right into him, making sure my words hit the deepest part of his heart—"now you're the one hurting me."

He bent slightly and pressed his hands to his knees.

"Good bye, David." I turned away. "And please don't talk to me if we pass each other in the hall."

"Do you really mean that?" His voice travelled across the distance effortlessly, carrying the entire weight of his confusion. "Ara, please tell me you don't mean it."

"But I do," I said in a weary voice. "If you're going to leave, at least let me be angry at you. I *need* to be angry so it won't hurt so much."

"Ara, you have to trust me; you have to believe that I will only ever do what's best for you. Me leaving, keeping you free from my world, it's what's best. You can't see that now, but if you were to know the truth, you'd see it then, and I know that for a fact. I know I don't need to put you through that."

I bit my teeth together in my mouth.

"Please just give me you; just give me this girl I love, just for a few more months. I'm begging you."

"I'm just not strong enough to keep loving you, knowing I have to let you go. I'm sorry."

"So you have the strength to walk away, but not to stay and fight?" His hands went into his pockets.

"*Fight* for what? For a guy who loves me enough to leave me for my own good?"

"You have no idea how right you are." He laughed to himself, shaking his head.

I stood for a long time, watching him watching me. And I just had to ask. I knew it couldn't be true, but I had to hear him say it. "Is this just you letting me down gently?" I searched his face for evidence. "You promised my dad you'd make me okay again, and now that—"

"Do you really believe that? Do you *really* think I would do that?"

"You're a nice guy, David. But this"—I presented my difficult self—"this is a lot for anyone to take."

"Ara?" He reached for me again.

I pulled away. "Just answer the question."

"No. What you just said… it's not true. I never made any deal with your dad. I love you."

"But it doesn't matter in the end, does it?" I said dryly. "You're leaving, whether you love me or not. Whether you explain why, or don't. Our story still has the same ending."

"Ara. What can I do?" He stepped closer, his hands ready to grab me. "Please just… just tell me how to fix this."

"You can't."

As I turned away, his hand shot out and he spun me into his chest by my arm. "I'm not going to let you go that easily."

"Well, you don't have a choice." I pushed his hands off me. "Just like I don't."

"Choice, huh? So, you want a choice?" he called. I kept walking. "Fine! I can tell you why I can't stay. I can give you a choice, but you won't like your options."

I stopped walking again. "Would one of those be an option to stay together?"

"Yes."

"Then—"

"But not like you want, Ara. It won't be like this—"

"But at least whatever I decide would be on my own shoulders. It would be in *my* control."

"And what then?" His brows pulled in tightly, the pain in his eyes making them darker. "What if you hate me after? I will die inside if you hate me."

"Either way, *someone* gets hurt."

"You're right." He nodded once, as if that only just occurred to him. "It never mattered to me before the way it does now—not with anyone I've ever loved. But I would die a thousand deaths to save you from the pain of a paper cut, Ara, and if telling you the truth does nothing but give you a fire to hate me with—to make it easier for you to let me go—then I will tell you. But I can't do it here. Not now."

"When?"

"Maybe closer to the time I have to leave—"

"Right." I scoffed, shaking my head. "So you get your last few months with me loving you, and then you sneak off, as you planned all along?"

"No. I get my last few months with you loving me before you *hate me for what I am*!" he yelled. "If telling you would change the path ahead of us, I would do it now. Right here, at risk of anyone overhearing. But this information will serve only to keep you from taking your own life *when* I leave, Ara, because you'll be thanking God that I'm gone."

"Do you really think I'll feel that way? You know what your secrets are. You know me, know how I'll react. Do you truly believe I won't accept you for everything that you are?"

"I honestly don't know… anything, anymore. I don't know what to say, what to do here, Ara." He held both hands out by his sides, shrugging softly. "You won't be with me unless I tell you, and yet you need me to stay, because you're not okay without me. But you'll hate me if I tell you. So, please, Ara, just tell me what I should do?"

"I don't know." I hugged myself.

"I've never been in a relationship like this before," he said, hands going in to his pockets, "where I actually care what happens. And it feels like I'm on fire right now, mon amour. I'm so confused that the easiest thing to do… the right thing, just seems to be to walk away."

Exhausted, so over being sad and having holes in my life, I sighed. "I don't think I care anymore. Just go, if that's what you think is best."

He rolled back on his heels, his eyes focusing on some black pit of nothingness, and despite the invisible strings tying my heart to his—trying to make me move toward him—I forced myself to turn away, leaving everything behind.

It only took me ten paces before the cooling wind eased the rage within my heart, though, and I realized I didn't mean it. Not really. It wouldn't be easy to learn things about David that would make me hate him, but at the end of the day, I would rather hate him than see him walk away without us giving this a fighting chance.

I turned back to smile and tell him that, but he was already gone. There was no sign of him. Anywhere. Not even at the furthest part of the field.

"Ara!" Ryan called, running toward me at full speed.

I quickly swiped the tears away, forcing a smile. "Hi."

"Hi." He stopped running and looked at my cheeks. "You okay?"

I nodded, sniffling. "What's up? You look… have *you* been crying?"

He put his hands on his hips, panting. "Yeah."

"What happened?"

"Nathan Rossi." He caught his breath. "He passed away early this morning."

"Oh no!" I covered my mouth.

"I gotta find David. You seen him?"

"Does he know?"

Ryan shrugged. "Don't know. That's just it, he was closer to Nathan than any of us. We're worried 'cause no one's seen him today."

"I have," I said, with a deep feeling of regret coating my open wounds.

"Did he say anything?"

"I never gave him the chance."

He nodded to himself, his hands still on his hips. "Did you have a fight?"

"Mm-hm."

"Okay, come on." The stench of his sweat wafted up when he put his arm around me. "I'll take you to the office—get you a tardy slip."

"Thanks, Ryan."

Emily sat with her hands wedged under her knees, her legs swinging over the edge of the stage, trying to talk through the pain. I wandered down the aisle silently, hugging my sheet music, trying not to disturb her speech.

"If he was here right now, he'd probably clap us on the shoulder and tell us to get up—that the show must go on." She sniffed, wiping her face softly with a tissue. "I know it's been a hard day, and"—she motioned around the room—"most of us have gone home. But Nathan's gone, and… I know this whole thing started out as a way to help his mom with the hospital bills, but now she's got a funeral bill on top… of… that." Ryan leaped up and sat on the stage, wrapping his arm over her shoulder. "So, having said that, rehearsals will continue and so will the show, as a memorial concert."

"But we're not doing it this week, right?" someone in the front row asked.

Emily shook her head. "We don't have to. Any votes on when we should hold it?"

"Yeah," a boy said. "Weekend after next. The funeral's this Thursday, so…"

Emily looked around the rest of the group. "Everyone agree with that?"

People shrugged or nodded. Emily looked at me, and I smiled, bringing one shoulder up to my ear.

"Okay, so two weekends from now. And we'll need to draw up new ticket sale signs—if you guys can take care of that?" She nodded toward the art students, who nodded back. "Okay. Thanks for coming, everybody. Now"—she stood up—"let's get this show on the road."

The small group dispersed, murmuring among themselves, while Ryan walked Emily offstage and talked to her quietly at the base for a second. She nodded, wiped her face, then hugged him tightly and walked away.

"Hey, Em," I said, deliberately avoiding *how are you* or *I'm sorry.*

"Hey, Ara. Where's David?"

"Didn't Ryan tell you?" We slid into the end seats on the front row.

"Mm. No. What happened?"

"He uh… he left school for the day."

"Really?" She slid down in her seat, folding her fingertips over her eyes. "I feel like such an idiot for crying at school. I wish I'd left too."

"Aw, Em, don't. Hell, even I've cried at school before."

"Really?" She sat up a little.

"Mm-hm." I hugged my music sheets.

"Well, why? Was someone mean to you?"

I shrugged.

"Who?"

"Remember the theatrical kiss thing—with David, the toilets, my first day?"

"Oh, yeah. Summer and that short girl she hangs around?"

"Yeah." I laughed.

"Summer was telling us the whole story, you know, that afternoon." Emily leaned back in her chair. "No one believed her, though —about David kissing you. I wouldn't have if you hadn't told me about it in History class."

"Why? Is it so hard to believe David would kiss *me*?"

She laughed once. "That wasn't what we didn't believe. It was how Summer said he was doing it to stand up for you. David doesn't stand up for anybody," she added with a hint of spite.

"He stood up for the Apple King at lunch that day."

"Yeah, it seems you've unearthed a new David." She looked down at her hands, flipping her silver padlock bracelet. "So he went home, huh?"

I shrugged. "Do you think he'll come back?"

"He does this, you know?" She smiled sympathetically. "If things get too… emotional, he takes off for a few days. But he'll be at the funeral on Thursday. I'm sure you can speak to him then."

"But what if it wasn't because of Nathan that he left? What if it was for some other reason? Would he still come back for the funeral?"

"What other reason would he have?" she asked, smiling at Spencer as he walked past. He didn't smile back.

"What's the deal with Spence?" I asked. "Was he close to Nathan?"

"No. You saw that, huh? The quick-look-away thing he does."

"Yeah. Does he do that a lot?"

"Every time *I* look at him."

"And you think it's 'cause he doesn't like you?" I tried not to laugh.

"It must be. Why would he do it if he liked me?"

"Because, Emily"—I shoved my notes on the chair and stood up —"he's a guy. They're more afraid of you than you are of them."

"Ara!" she squeaked. "What are you doing?"

I ignored her, walking over to Ryan, Alana and Spencer. My brilliant idea of setting Emily up with Mike was about to go out the window…

"Hey, guys."

"Hey, Ara." Alana leaned a little closer. "I was thinking… about the sleepover this weekend?"

"Yeah."

"Um, could we… maybe move it to next weekend?" She nodded at Emily sitting low in her chair, staring at her feet. "Might be a bit much."

"Yeah. That's cool. Next week'll be fine."

"So, Ara?" Ryan asked. "Are you coming to the wake at Betty's on Thursday night?"

"I um, I didn't know about it. Why is Mrs. Rossi doing it there?"

"She's not," Ryan said, placing his arm around Alana. "It's just a bunch of us kids farewelling Nathan in our own way. Betty's was his favorite burger joint—we figure it's appropriate."

"Oh, okay. Well, that sounds cool. I guess I'll try, but I may have to go to Mrs. Rossi's with my dad, you know, pay my respects as a family."

"I get it. Totally cool. If we see you there, we see you there," Ryan said.

"Hey, so you two are going together, right?" I asked Alana and Ryan.

"Yup."

"So why don't you take Emily, Spence? I know she needs a ride," I lied, hoping he wouldn't pick up on the fact that I couldn't know that since I didn't even know about the wake before now.

Spencer smiled over at Emily and quickly averted his eyes before she looked up.

Hopefully, this was one match that'd work out well.

14

"Dad, you look nice." My voice trailed up as I set eyes upon my suit-wearing father.

"Thank you, Ara." He nodded solemnly.

It hurt to hear his voice sounding so flat and sad. "You okay, Dad?"

"I'm fine, honey."

I stopped him as he started walking away. "Is this dress okay for a funeral?"

His lips twisted tightly as he studied my mournful black attire: a soft cotton dress with a burgundy belt around the waist. "Ara, are you sure you're ready for this?"

I frowned up at him. "For a funeral?"

"Yes. It's just that… you don't have to be there, honey." His eyes held an obvious memory of the last funeral I attended. "Are you sure you can cope with this?"

"No, Dad. I'm not sure. I'm actually not sure about *anything* anymore. But I *want* to go—for Emily and… David." His name stuck in my throat.

Dad nodded, but didn't speak.

The clock on the wall at the base of the stairs chimed eight. The funeral wasn't until nine o'clock, but Mrs. Rossi asked my dad and his family to attend a church service beforehand.

"Had breakfast?" Dad asked, heading down the stairs.

"Yeah," I lied. I knew I should sit at the table and eat with him—maybe even have a coffee to help ease the chill in my skin from my early morning run—but he was better than anyone at seeing through my mask; I wasn't okay. I wasn't ready to see a coffin or see people crying. But I had to see David one last time before he was gone from my life forever. I had to say I was sorry for breaking up with him on the day he lost a friend.

I sat at the base of the stairs, hugging the post, listening to the calm of the house—the way the smell of toast could make everything seem kind of okay—and my hunger pangs grew, twisting my gut into knots. I thought about getting up to eat but, instead, sat watching my father with a careful eye. I wondered where his thoughts were, where his heart was, as his gaze fell on the road outside, his chin rested on his hands. He said so little about what he felt or how he was coping that, watching him, seeing him look so sad and distracted, came as a bit of a shock.

"All set to go, are we?" Vicki asked, coming down the stairs.

"Yeah."

"Did you eat?"

I nodded, resting my head against the post after.

"Vicki." Dad smiled at her adoringly as he came in from the kitchen. "You look lovely."

"Thank you, Greg." She straightened the front of her skirt. "I'm just sorry for the occasion."

Dad nodded, and the sadness stole the smile from his blue eyes.

Vicki did look nice in black, but it seemed like such an unfriendly color, almost cruel really to say goodbye to someone in. If my last memory were of my funeral, I'd want to see everyone dressed in colors to *celebrate* my life instead of mourn it.

"Sam, you ready?" Vicki called.

"One minute, Mom."

"Hurry up. We'll be in the car."

"Okay."

Dad grabbed the keys and Vicki shouldered her purse, and as she pulled the front door open my breath stopped short of my lips. The cool morning air blew across my knees, and the sun reflected brightly off the damp black road outside, blinding me. But my eyes did not betray the perfection standing before them.

"David?" Dad said cheerfully. "You're right on time."

Right on time?

David stood in the doorway with one hand in the pocket of his tailored black suit as he shook my dad's with the other. "Good to see you again, Mr. Thompson; Mrs. Thompson." He nodded politely at Dad, then Vicki, and turned his head to look directly at me. I was shrinking. I could feel it. I wanted to close my mouth, wipe the dumb-founded stare off my face, but I really loved David too much to hide the elation in my soul.

"Good morning, Ara," he said in that smooth, weightless voice.

"Um… hi," I said, and my eyes fell to the floor.

"Uh, Ara?" Dad broke the lengthy silence that followed. "Since you kids are having your own wake at Betty's, I thought you might like to ride in with David?"

"You mean you *assumed*?"

"Ara?" Vicki gasped.

"No, she's right, Vicki," Dad said softly. "I'm sorry, honey. I did think it would be okay."

I folded my arms, biting my teeth together. It wasn't supposed to be like this; I was supposed to see him from afar—supposed to prepare myself for talking to him; to apologize and then leave it at that—and now Dad had just singlehandedly destroyed all the resolve I had to be sensible and mature and just let David leave my life, like a sane person would.

"I'll just see you there then." David looked at me once, then turned stiffly away.

"I didn't say I wouldn't go. I said you should have checked with me first."

David stopped.

"Okay, Ara." Dad patted my arm. "I'll remember that for next time."

I took off, skulking along behind David, piercing his soul with eyes like daggers when he opened the car door for me. "I can get the door myself."

"I'm sorry." He took a step back. "I know you can. I was..."

I pushed past him and slumped into the passenger seat, shutting the door on whatever he was going to say. "And you can shut up too," I barked at the ogre in my belly.

Alone in the car, while Dad talked to David by the mailbox, the woodsy lemon smell of his seats stirred the memory of our picnic by the lake, making my stomach growl again. I looked over at Dad, his hand on David's shoulder, with Vicki jumping in to touch his arm. It was nice of them to just leave me sitting here in the muggy heat, waiting—with only my beastly ogre to keep me company.

David glanced over at me, just for a second, and then shook my dad's hand, jerking his head in my direction. I saw Dad's mouth move, breaking into a grin, and I knew they were laughing at my mood—they always did.

David slid into the car, closing the door on a roll of thunder. "You okay?"

I cleared my throat and looked out the window. "I'm fine."

"You haven't eaten. *Clearly*."

"I'm fine," I muttered.

"You know, you could've said no." He started the engine. "I didn't force you to come in my car."

"You could've said no, too."

"Your dad asked me. What was I supposed to say?"

"Hmph." I refolded my arms for good measure as we reversed down the drive.

By the time the church came into focus on the distant horizon, the silence in the car had evolved into a big fat cloud of tension. I just wanted to hurry up and get there so my mouth couldn't accidentally start an argument with him again about his dark secrets, but David was driving much more carefully and a hell of a lot slower than usual. I wasn't sure how much longer I could keep quiet.

When the car *finally* pulled up in a parking space, my door swung open and David offered his hand before I even saw him pull the key from the ignition.

"God! Don't do that!"

"What?" He looked ultimately confused.

"You keep popping up, like, way too fast."

"Ara, I didn't this time. I swear. You must have blacked out, sweetheart—"

"Don't call me that!" Ignoring his offer of assistance, I grabbed the doorframe and hoisted my dizzy self from the car, taking inconspicuously deep breaths to steady the ringing in my ears.

"Are you okay?" His hand hovered near my waist. "You're really pale."

"I'm fine," I said, scowling at him.

"You're not fine." He stood taller. "Would you like me to take you home?"

For a moment, my gaze lingered between the church and freedom, but Emily caught my eye and waved softly. I waved back and shut the car door. "No. Then everyone will wonder why the new girl suddenly disappeared from a funeral—questions would follow."

David laughed a little, wiping the amusement from his face quickly when he looked at mine. "I'm sorry. Um… shall we go in?"

"Lead the way," I offered, and walked slowly behind him, in no rush to be stuck in that dreary red-bricked building.

"Mr. Knight." The priest by the door shook David's hand. "Lovely to see you again."

"You too, Father." David turned to a short, portly woman in a black tunic then, and kissed both her cheeks, offering condolences in another language. Italian, I think.

"Thank you for coming, David." She reached up and stroked his face. "My Nathan would be so proud to see you all here."

"He was a good boy." David squeezed her hand.

She smiled, her pudgy face tight with sorrow. "And who do we have here?"

"This"—David stepped back and placed his arm around my waist, pulling me closer—"is Ara Thompson."

Her eyes went from David to me, widening. "My dear child. How sweet of you to come."

I smiled softly, because there wasn't much I could say.

"You're so much like your mother," she said, taking my hand in her moist, plump grip. "And is your father far behind?"

I gave a quick glance into the parking lot. "He'll be here any minute."

She nodded, patting my hand. "Well, I'll see you both after the ceremony."

"You will." David kissed her cheek again and stepped across the threshold of the church, smiling as he made the sign of the cross over his body.

I dipped my fingers in the holy water by the door and did the same. "This isn't the time to smile, David."

He dropped his private, glittering grin. "Sorry. I was… remembering something."

"What?"

"Private joke."

"Same old story," I scoffed, turning away a little too quickly. The walls grew taller around me then, seeming to reach miles up into the sky, gathering a deathly chill from the outer atmosphere and sending it down here to make my stomach churn.

I closed my eyes for a second and shut everything out: the muffled sobs and whispers, the dreary organ music and the sound of paper rustling on the wooden backs of chairs.

"You should have let me take you home, Ara." David grabbed my arm and gently steered me to the edge of the pew, sliding in and pushing me further up to allow room for more people. I wrapped my fingers around the back of the seat in front of me, taking slow, deep breaths until the bile pinching my tongue eased off.

"Mint?" he offered.

I grabbed one from the tiny tin and popped it in my mouth, refusing to look at him.

"You're welcome," he said smugly and stuffed them back in his pocket.

Then the priest began, as did the incessant kneeling and standing. After communion, I knelt beside David and opened one eye to watch him. He seemed intent on his prayer; his eyes closed tight, lips moving fast—speaking in tongues. Okay, so not in tongues, but something that sounded remarkably like Latin. He never mentioned religion before. I didn't even know he was Catholic and did not know he spoke Latin. But why not? He spoke Italian. And French. But then, Mike spoke French, too, but that was different because his mom was French, so he grew up with it.

"Focus, Ara," David whispered quietly.

I turned my head, closed my eyes, and continued the Hail Mary I'd started, just as everyone around us shuffled in their places and began to sit back in the pews.

David reached across and helped me up gently by my arm.

I glared at him, jerking away. "I can get myself up, thank you."

"Sorry." He swallowed, rubbing the left side of his chest as he looked to the front. When his hand dropped back into his lap, I studied the fine lines in his knuckles, the squared tips of his nails and the curl of his fingers, imagining mine wound through them.

Until he folded his arms, readjusting his seat.

The eulogies given by Nathan's family and friends seemed to go on forever. Thankfully, from all the way up the back, I couldn't see Nathan in that open box unless I angled my face the right way. Mom and Harry had closed caskets. I don't think I'd have coped with seeing their faces so still, so devoid of life. Just seeing Harry's tiny coffin beside Mom's was enough to haunt me forever. It seemed strange how, no matter how big you thought someone was in life, when you lay them down with six sides wrapping them tightly, they just look so small. It wasn't right to see a coffin that small.

David moved his hand onto mine and squeezed firmly. "Just don't think about it, Ara."

I turned my head to look at him, but he kept his eyes forward, as if he hadn't said anything.

"Nathan was and will always be a well-respected and much loved friend." I tuned in to the voice of Emily, reading from a stack of palm cards up the front. "He was there to give advice or a quick word of encouragement to anyone—be they a friend, a Chess Club kid, or even someone he didn't know.

"Nathan was the guy we all expected to see graduate with honors, make the national football league, marry the prom queen." Emily smiled shyly then, looking down. "Death is sad in any case, but when it comes so suddenly and takes the life of someone who had so much to offer the world, it truly is tragic." She stepped down and placed the cards inside the casket. "We'll all miss you, Nathe. Rest in peace."

David's hand tightened on mine, and a single cool drop of water fell between our palms. I looked up and saw him nodding, breathing out slowly through parted lips.

"David?"

He sniffed and shook his head, wiping a line of moisture from his chin. "Just don't."

"Okay," I said, squeezing his hand.

THE GREY SKY OPENED UP AS WE STEPPED OUTSIDE THE CHURCH, and the cool breeze eased the trapping tension of my very empty stomach. Small droplets of rain began to sprinkle over the black hearse while David and a group of boys from the football team carried the pine box and slid it into the back.

They walked by the hearse after that, leading the procession line through the church gates and into the cemetery. Each headstone we passed displayed names, dates, flowers, some even pictures of those who lay beneath—every little detail showing the life they once belonged to. I closed my eyes and let the darkness narrow me in, the sobs of huddled mourners around me guiding my blind footsteps until a hand grabbed my arm.

My eyes flashed open to David's face.

"Don't walk with your eyes closed," he said, "it's dangerous."

I nodded, tucking my cold, shaking hands into my elbows, and David walked away, back to his place beside the black car. When a loud grumble rolled across the darkening sky, everyone looked up—squinting against the white sun until a cloud shadowed its glare. Icy patters of rain came down again, and little black umbrellas popped up all around me. I folded over ever so slightly, remembering how the uninvited rain ruined my last chance to farewell my family; how it blinded me, made me so cold and so wet I had to fight with myself to stay. I hoped it wouldn't do the same to Nathan's family.

"Are you okay, dear?" a haggard old lady asked, reaching for me.

I nodded, about to take a step away when a long arm scooped my waist and pulled me under the shelter of a black canopy. "She's fine. She's with me."

"Okay." The old lady smiled at David.

"Aren't you supposed to be up front?" I asked, craning my neck to look up at him.

He winked at me, a smile warming his face. "I thought you might need some shelter."

I pushed his arm from around my waist. "You need to go back to where you're supposed to be."

"Right, um. I'm sorry." He placed the umbrella in my hand, squeezing my fingers around the handle before stepping back into the rain.

"Wait, David—" I reached out as I realized he took that the wrong way, but he strolled away too quickly, disappearing into the mist as the congregation dispersed suddenly, forming a semicircle around a hole in the ground.

I scanned the crowd for my dad or Vicki, finding them beside the priest.

The rain came down harder then, making my ears feel blocked with the noise. Droplets of cold water splashed up onto my shoes and wet my toes, while we stood around and waited for the boys to position the pine box above the ground.

The priest readied himself, straightening the cloth over his shoulders while an altar boy tipped and swayed, standing on his toes to keep an umbrella over the man.

"Friends and family," he started, and the rain stopped abruptly, all eyes moving to the heavens for a moment as umbrellas closed like flowers at dusk. I leaned the one David gave me against a nearby headstone and folded my arms over my chest to keep out the cold.

As the priest began again, Dad wrapped his arm around Mrs. Rossi and cast a quick glance at me. I smiled reassuringly. On the outside, I knew I looked strong, but the pressure of all the grieving people was starting to penetrate my emotional wall, and when I looked at Nathan's mother—crying her heart out for her only child—the memory of Harry came flooding back to the surface with vengeance. I fought to suppress the grief, but it was just no good. All I saw was myself in place of Mrs. Rossi. I remembered how much it hurt. I knew what she felt, knew I couldn't help her because nothing anyone said would ever make the pain go away.

"As we lay this child to rest," the priest said, "may the angels greet him in Heaven. Father, for you are the All Mighty…"

But what if there was no Heaven? What if Harry's spirit was lost out there where he died—alone, crying for us? He was too small to be alone. Too small to be gone. He shouldn't have been there. He should've been safe in his bed.

I wiped my face, smudging the rain into the tears.

"Ara?"

My mind snapped back to reality, to the people sobbing hysterically beside me, and David's arm around me. "I'm okay," I said, letting my gaze drift back to Nathan's box.

As it slowly lowered closer and closer to the ground, I thought about the empty space—the horrible moment which brings everything into reality the minute you leave the funeral and walk into that empty house. Before they're gone, before you bury them in the cold, loveless ground, everything seems surreal, like they're just on a shopping trip or somewhere in the house where you can't hear them. But when their flesh touches the earth and settles in its final destination for all eternity, it takes with it the cloud, the safety of the cage that hides you from believing they're never coming back. When Nathan's mom got home she'd fall apart. She'd cry until there were no tears left and it would still do her no good. Nathan would never come back.

Harry was never coming back.

David's grip tightened on my shoulders.

All the things they'd miss out on circled around me, turning my hands to ice. It was too much to bear. Nathan would never graduate; Mom would never see me get married, or hold her first grandbaby; Harry would never go to school, never paint his first picture, never learn to walk. He never even got to have a birthday party.

The oxygen around me felt overused. The blood in my head pulsed, and as the shivers ran from my hands, up my arms and into my chest, I heard a quiet gasp, and everything went black…

…GRAINS OF SAND FELL THROUGH A NARROW PASSAGE IN A GLASS jar and hit the base with a soft pattering sound. The ground swayed gently beneath me, and the frosty rushing of my whole world felt calm now, closed in by the warmth of the summer sun. It was just David and me watching the rain fall onto the leaves above us, staying perfectly dry in the hidden clearing where I had my first kiss.

But as I felt the rain on my skin suddenly, I looked up to an open grey sky and the nostril hairs of a man, his breath brushing my bangs. "Dad?"

"Shh," he whispered into my head. "It's okay, honey. I'm taking you home."

"What happened?"

"You fainted."

"I what?" I rolled my head to the side and looked around the church parking lot. "I fainted?"

"I should have known better. It was just too soon," Dad said to himself.

"You're going to be okay, Ara," Vicki said from beside Dad, holding an umbrella over me while she dripped with rain.

I touched my hand to the back of my neck and pulled out a piece of grass. "Did I hit my head?"

Dad nodded. "David caught you, but he was a fraction of a second too late."

"He only stepped away from you for two seconds to place a rose into the, er… and you fell," Vicki added.

"I must admit, though"—Dad chortled—"he made it to your side quicker than I've ever seen anyone move. I almost didn't see it myself."

"So he didn't even get a chance to say goodbye to Nathan?"

Dad whispered something softly to Vicki—something ending in the word *David*. My ears pricked.

"Is he"—I hesitated—"is David mad with me?"

Dad's head turned slowly to look at Vicki again.

"Ara, why would he be mad with you? You didn't mean to pass out," Vicki said.

No, but David was right. I should have let him take me home.

Dad placed me in the backseat of the car and the door swung open on the other side.

"I'm fine, Vicki, you can sit in the front with—" I started, but my eyes fell on perfection personified as David slid in beside me. And that was it. That was the final straw. I buried the ugly crumple of my face in my hands. I wanted to tell David he shouldn't be here, making it harder to let him go, but as his arms fell around my body and he pulled me close, holding me so tight I couldn't shake, none of that mattered. Even the soaking rain, making his suit icy cold against my cheek, didn't bother me. I just needed him so badly.

"Shh, sweetheart." He stroked my hair, whispering into the top of my head. "It's okay. It's going to be okay."

"No, it's not." I sobbed uncontrollably. "Nothing ever is."

"Don't say that." He slid down in the seat a little. "You mustn't say things like that."

"Dad?" I lifted my head, speaking louder to project my voice over the heavy pounding of rain. "I'm so sorry. Did she see? Did Mrs. Rossi see?"

"Ara, honey. Mrs. Rossi's more worried about you, okay?"

"Oh no." My head shook against my hands.

"Ara, please stop crying," David asked softly, brushing my hair from my face.

He smelled so good and he was just so sweet. And that rich orange-chocolate scent matched his gorgeously gentle personality so well.

My sobbing stopped short for a second then when the ogre within my belly roared loudly, hungered by the thought of chocolate.

"Ara? Did you eat breakfast?" Vicki asked in a high-pitched tone.

David's chest sunk as he exhaled deeply, pressing his cheek against my forehead. "No, she didn't. Silly girl."

"Ara?" Dad sighed. "You know better than that. What were you—" He stopped, almost visibly biting his own tongue. "It doesn't matter. When we get home, you need to go straight upstairs. Vicki and I will fix you some food and bring it up. Okay?"

I nodded, letting David fold me against his saturated jacket again.

15

Dad let David *carry* me upstairs. I protested loudly, but David was stronger than me and rendered my pathetic attempt to wriggle myself free useless. When we stepped into the warm light of my room, a wave of calm washed away the tight feeling in my chest. David stood me on the ground, pulled the quilt back on my bed, and then lowered me onto the mattress, running his hands down my legs to smooth the rain away before sliding my shoes off my feet.

"Thanks." I smiled down at him.

"My pleasure." He smiled back, stepping away to place my shoes neatly by my bedroom door. And something clicked then.

The air stopped flowing to my lungs for a second, as pieces of my life over the last few weeks started to fit together. My window—that night I fell asleep crying at my dresser—I'd *closed* it. But it was open in the morning. And my shoes… I would *never* put them neatly by the door like he just did. Neither would my dad.

"Lie back," he said, and I did, all the while moving pieces of the puzzle around in my head.

"David?"

"Yes, Ar—" He stopped as he pulled the quilt up to my chin and met my eyes. I saw his throat move then as he looked over at the shoes.

I looked at them, too. And that was all the confirmation I needed.

"I can explain," he said.

"You snuck… into my *room*?" I said, disgusted and a little bit freaked out. "Why? I mean… how did you even *get* in here?"

"I—" He stopped speaking and straightened up suddenly, keeping his eyes on me as he called, "Come in."

"Hey, honey." Dad popped his head in, smiling widely at a plate in his hand. "Made you a sandwich."

"Thanks, Dad." I sat up. Though I was hungry and felt pretty sick because of it, all I wanted was for him to go away so I could figure out what the hell David was doing in my room that night and, more embarrassingly, how long he'd been watching me. If he saw me crying that way—ugly crying, with loud sobs and so much sniffling I gave up using a tissue and wiped it on my arm—I would be mortified!

"Mrs. Rossi called," Dad said, sitting on my bed as he handed me the plate. "She asked me to tell you that she was overwhelmed with happiness to see you today, and she said not to worry about fainting, because if you hadn't done it first, she would have." He laughed softly. "And then she added that she wouldn't have had a handsome young man there to catch her."

David's shoulders lifted once with a chuckle.

"I told her I'd have caught her, but *apparently*"—Dad looked a little solemn—"I'm not a handsome young man."

I smiled softly. "It was nice of her to call."

"She was worried about you."

"We all were," David said, then moved away and leaned on the wall beside my door, his arms over his chest, a thousand thoughts dancing across his face. And all I read there in his eyes and on his brow was fear.

"Ara?" Dad waved a hand in front of my stare.

"I'm okay, Dad." I snapped back to the present, taking in my father's worried expression. "Really. I guess I just need to eat."

He exhaled, nodding. "Okay. Do you need some time *alone*?"

"Just give me a second to talk to David?"

"Sure thing, honey." Dad stood up, and patted David on the shoulder as he passed, shutting my door behind him.

The silence in the room hovered over the howling winds outside. David closed his eyes for a second, rolling his chin toward his chest. I wondered who should speak first: the prosecutor or the defendant.

"Eat," he said out of the blue.

My eyes narrowed and I bit my teeth together. "I think you have a few confessions to make before you go telling me to do anything."

David sighed, exasperated. "I'm not talking until you've fed the ogre."

"Fine." I picked up the sandwich and tore a corner away with my teeth. "Happy?" I muttered with my mouth full, slamming the sandwich back down on the plate.

David nodded once, a frown erasing the usual smile from his eyes. Everything about him seemed odd without that smile. Empty, almost.

"Okay," I said after I swallowed, "I've eaten now. 'Fess up."

He walked slowly over and knelt by my bed, taking both my wrists and setting them gently beside my legs. "I love you. I would never do anything to hurt or dishonor you, and I would never intrude on you in a corrupt manner. But I *did* come to your window that night and I *did* come in to your room."

"Why?"

"I've been worried about you. Your dad said you were suicidal, and I thought he might be correct. After we"—he rocked his jaw, blinking a few times—"after I kissed you and then took you home, I knew what you were thinking, Ara. I knew you just wanted to stop the pain. I was really worried you might. So I"—he shrugged and jerked his head to my window—"I came to check on you."

"So it was you who put me into bed?"

David swallowed. "I'm sorry. I shouldn't have interfered. But when I found you at your dresser, I nearly fell to pieces. You looked so alone, so *destroyed* and, Ara, I did that to you. I made you sad because I never told you the truth about me leaving. If I had, you would never have let yourself fall so in love with me, and the worst part is, that's exactly why I didn't tell you."

"How could you be so mean?"

"It wasn't my intention to be mean. I just wanted to love you. I really *honestly* thought things would be different—that when it came time for me to leave, you either wouldn't care as much as you did, or you might—" He exhaled, rubbing his brow.

"Might?"

"Might come with me."

I sat up and moved the plate off my lap. "Would you want that —really?"

He frowned. "Ara. That's *all* I want."

"Well—"

"But if you come with me, my love, you couldn't live a normal life. You wouldn't be able to see your family anymore."

"Why?"

"Because… because of my dark secrets."

"Well, what are they, then?"

"Are you ready to hear them? Are you ready to hate me?"

"Yes!"

He laughed, shaking his head, and sat on the bed beside me. "I shouldn't be doing this today. Not while you're in a poor emotional state."

"No way!" I wagged my finger. "Don't you dare make excuses, Mr. Knight. It's time to let me in."

"Fine." He laughed shyly. "But…"

"But?"

"But." David turned and grabbed both my arms, squeezing firmly. "By hearing this, you're… well, you're making a verbal agreement, Ara, as am I."

"What do you mean?"

"I mean I have obligations to fulfill, should this go bad."

"Which are?"

His fingers tightened around my arms again.

"David, what?"

"I might have to kill you."

"What?"

"If…" His jaw went tight. "Look, in the past, people have reacted poorly to this news and there have been instances where *some* in my position have had to kill those they've told."

My mouth hung open. I rolled my quilt away and slowly rose to my feet.

David shuffled back, letting me walk to the other side of my room.

"Would you really be capable of doing that to me?" I said.

He looked down. "I don't *want* to. Which is one of the many reasons I haven't wanted to tell you thus far."

"You're serious! You'd kill me?"

"No, Ara. But if you"—he lowered his voice, looking over his shoulder at my door for a moment—"if you told anyone, if you freaked out, it would be out of my hands."

I nodded. "Okay, so I won't freak out."

"I hope you don't." He patted the mattress. "Sit with me."

I shook my head.

"Ara, please?"

I shook it again. If this secret was so bad he might have to kill me, there was no way I was sitting next to him. No way!

He looked down at his hands, readying himself with a breath before he said, "Ara, I'm a vampire."

"A what?"

"A vampire." He flashed his sharp fangs. "You know, guys who drink blood—fangs, all that stuff."

A loud snort of laughter grumbled in my throat.

"It's not funny, Ara."

"No, it's cool. Hey, can you turn me?" I elongated my neck. "I think I'd suit fangs."

He rubbed the bridge of his nose. "This isn't a joke."

I folded my arms. "Prove it."

"P—" He shook his head, wiping the incredulity from his lips. "Prove it?"

"Yeah. If you're really the un-dead, prove it."

"Ara, we're not un-dead." He stood up. "And what do you want me to do to prove it, eat you?"

I shrugged.

He groaned. "Fine."

I had time only to smile before he rushed in and wrapped his arms around my waist, burrowing his face into my neck. The tickly sensation of his cool breath made me laugh, but the feel of his lips on my skin made me shiver in a new way.

"You are a very silly girl," he said calmly, kissing my shoulder. "What if I'd bitten you? What then?"

"If you really were a vampire, you could do a lot worse than bite me, if you wanted to."

"Right. If I *wanted* to." He stood behind me and gently swept my hair over my shoulder, clearing way for his lips. "Remember that when you freak out in a minute, okay?"

I laughed. "Sure thing."

"Okay. Now, see that rise of hills over there?" His finger aimed to the eastern hills where the first rays of sunlight touched the earth each morning.

"Yes."

"There's a garden on the other side. Blue roses grow there. Have you seen it?" He went back to kissing the curve of my shoulder.

"The Applebury Reserve?" My eyes rolled to a close, lost in pleasure. "Yeah, I've seen it."

"It's twenty miles away. How long do you think it would take to run there?"

"I don't know? Depends how fast you run. And then, calculating that would involve math, so…"

David's irritation blew out in cold air through his nose. "What if…?"

"What if?" I said back.

His arms tightened on my waist and he pressed his cheek to mine. "What if I told you I could do it—run there and be back before you had a chance to blink?"

"I would say that you are very talented"—my voice trailed up with humor—"and I would be jealous."

"But it would prove I'm a vampire? You'd believe me then?"

"Yeah." I spun around in his arms. "Let's see what you got."

He looked out over the hills, then back at me. "So, you know the Applebury Reserve is the only place that grows blue roses, right?"

"Um, yeah… I guess?"

"Okay. Don't be scared." He inched away, holding up his index finger like a warning not to move. "Please don't scream when you see this."

My eyes locked to his. He smiled, standing so tall and so sure of himself it was hard to doubt him. I almost hoped he *could* do what he claimed. I'd hate to think he was actually insane.

He scratched his temple, nervous and a bit twitchy, then held his palms out. "Nothing in my hands, right?"

"Right."

He turned them over a few times. I nodded to confirm—again. "Now, don't move?"

"Okay," I started to say as a cold rush of air blew into my eyes. I closed them, feeling a tickle down my cheek, and the sweet, vibrant perfume of roses filled the air around me, flavoring my breath with a walk in the garden.

"Look."

When I opened my eyes and they met with his, he watched expectantly, my quick gasp making him smile.

"How did you get that?"

"I told you. I run very fast." He smoothed the petals of a blue rose over my cheek again.

"Yes. That is fast. I am jealous." My eyes narrowed with skepticism. "Now, tell me how you really did it."

David groaned in the back of his throat and took a step away. "I can see this is going to be a little more of a challenge than I anticipated."

"What is?"

"You know, if this was the early nineteen hundreds, you'd already be screaming."

"Oh, and you speak from personal experience, do you?"

Without even a smile at my joke, he placed the thornless rose in my hand and pulled me along. "Come. Sit down."

I slumped onto my feather quilt and dug my toes into the carpet. David stood before me.

"You ready for this?"

"For what?" I said. "A fashion show?"

He flashed a cheeky, lopsided grin, and vanished into thin air, appearing a second later by my wardrobe door.

"How did…?"

"Do you believe me now?" He sprung up right in front of my face, and my rose-colored glasses snapped, every intelligent bone within me finally seeing the predator in him.

A quick half-breath reached my lungs as I launched for my bedroom door, but his strong hand covered my mouth before my cry for help ever reached the ears of its intended. I convulsed violently, wriggling to break free from the intensifying hold.

I screamed into his cupped hand, trying to stomp on his toes, but he moved his foot and my heel struck the ground with knee-jolting force, sending instant tears into my eyes.

"Ara! Look at me!" He shook me once, pinning the back of my skull to his chest, his forearm firmly caging my shoulders. If I didn't believe him by seeing how fast he moved, the sheer strength of his hold would have done it. "Just stop struggling. Look at me!"

Heaving lungfuls of air came through my nose, dragging strands of my hair with it, and with each passing breath I managed to calm myself enough to stop struggling, but not enough to trust him.

David's hold relaxed a little, but stayed firm. "If I let go, will you promise not to scream?"

I shook my head. He was a monster. A killer. Oh, my God. How did I not see this? The popping-up-everywhere-really-fast thing. The teeth. The cold body. The way he described the pizza to Ryan: he wasn't talking about a pizza! He'd described a kill, and that was all I could think about right now. This David I loved was a lie.

"Ara, please?" The hurt beneath the otherwise calm tone of his voice made my heart burn. I turned my head and forced my gaze upward, meeting the painful detachment behind the emerald eyes I once loved so much.

"Mm-bm-mm-nn," I muttered under his grasp.

He released me instantly and air entered my lungs in a grateful gasp. I folded over, rubbing my sore chin.

"I'm sorry," he said. "I didn't mean to hurt you."

"I'm not hurt, I—" I bolted for the door again, reaching the handle as he pressed his palm flat to it, stopping it from opening. "No!"

"Ara, don't."

"Let me go." I tugged the handle, bucking him with my hip.

"I can't."

"Why?"

"I need you to calm down first."

"Why?"

"Because if you don't calm down, I have to kill you."

"Fine." My fists tightened and I stood still, taking labored breaths. "I'm calm."

He just smiled, shaking his head. "You're not calm."

"Ergh!" I growled, shoving his chest; he didn't shift backward, not even a little bit. "Get away from me."

"Make me." He laughed, pinning my wrists against my chest.

My eyes darted over every inch of his face: his dark pink lips, his emerald eyes, so kind, so loving, and his dimple—the moon shape one above his lip that I loved. It was all David. He looked exactly like a normal human boy, but it was a lie. An act. The David I loved never even existed.

"Ara, let's talk about this."

"What's to talk about?" I moved away, pressing my spine to the door. "You—you're a… you have fangs, and I can think of only one thing they would do."

He touched a thumb to his tooth. "Say it."

"No."

"Say it. You need to admit this, Ara."

My mouth filled with saliva, fighting to avoid the truth. He'd told Ryan his pizza slid off the table and spilled all over the floor. He'd told him it was a mess, and that he was cleaning up red sauce for weeks. How could I possibly hear that and not understand what it meant?

"You kill," I confirmed.

"Yes."

"Oh, God!" I folded over, hiding my brow in my hands. "Why?"

"For… to survive."

"Isn't that a little selfish?"

He laughed once. "You're serious?"

"Yes, I'm serious!"

"Ara, I don't have a choice but to kill."

"Everyone has a choice."

"Not in this instance, sweetheart." He wandered over and sat on my bed. I wanted to tell him not to call me sweetheart, but didn't have the guts to say that to a vampire.

He smiled—his secret smile. "Do you really hate it when I call you *sweetheart*?"

My mouth hung open. "Did I say that out loud?"

"No." He grinned, rubbing the tops of his knees. "I can read minds, Ara."

As so many instances came to mind that made me believe that *instantly*, I slid down the door and sat on the floor with my head in my palms. "How is that possible?"

"I'm sorry," David said, suddenly kneeling beside me.

"Get away from me."

He evaporated, appearing by my window. I dusted my arm off, scraping away any vampire germs that might've been left behind, then cast my eyes across the room quickly to make sure the vampire hadn't moved. He looked so conflicted yet so comfortable, as he looked out the window, considering the world below. The muscles in his arms—with the way he folded them across his chest—looked bigger, more defined than I ever noticed. And I had once wanted them around me, wanted to feel him naked against me. Now, I only felt anger at myself for that—for ever loving him when he was such a vile, disgusting monster.

"Despite what you may believe, my girl," he said to the world below, "I am still human inside. And everything you're thinking right now *does* hurt."

I blinked, trying to make my mind go blank, but it wouldn't. I just kept seeing the faces of people as they screamed and begged for their lives, while David towered over them and took it. Kept thinking about the blood that had spilled on his apartment floor when he dropped his dinner—a nuisance to him; something he had to clean.

"Have you always been able to read my mind?"

He nodded, not looking at me. I wanted to be mad, but if I compartmentalized, dividing the human David I'd loved and the vampire I never would, then the heat that rushed through me was more like boiling mortification than anger. I buried my face in my hand and groaned. Oh, so many thoughts I wouldn't have wanted him to hear.

David chuckled. "That's pretty much what everyone says."

"God, I feel so *violated*."

"I'm sorry, my love. I know it's awful, but if it's any consolation, I'm not usually listening. And I can only hear your immediate thoughts. For anything in the past, I actually have to go inside your head."

I looked up at him. "But you *can* get in there—you can find things?"

He nodded.

"That's so freakin' creepy."

"Please don't say things like that, Ara."

"Well, what do you expect me to say?"

"'Ah, it's a vampire!'" He waved his hands about like a girl, looking way too human as he did.

"I kind of did say that." I smiled. "But you muzzled me."

"I'm so sorry about that, Ara." David winced. "I just couldn't have you running down to tell your dad."

I bit my lip, knowing that's exactly what I was going to do. "So, I'm calm now. Am I free to go, or are you going to kill me?"

He turned back to face me. "Will you keep quiet—for ever?"

I nodded.

"Then you're free to go."

I felt better after a sigh of relief. Slowly, I got to my feet and opened my bedroom door. Dad's voice lilted up the stairs, comforting and warm, tinted with laughter. I listened for a second, reminding myself that normality was still out there where I could reach it, then I looked over at David.

"Was that all—is this your only dark secret?"

He nodded.

"So you…" I lowered my voice. "You kill—murder people?"

He nodded.

I stepped back into my room and shut my door, resting my head on it for a second. "Do you *like* killing them? Because you made it sound that way when you told Ryan about your pizza."

David laughed, stifling it quickly to answer in a calm, serious tone. "Yes. I enjoy the kill."

"Do you… do you ever regret it?"

"I didn't, no. Not until I fell in love with you."

I turned around then. "And what difference does that make?"

"Compassion. Vampires are nothing if not compassionate, but only for our own kind. When we fall for a human, that compassion, for some reason, extends out to their race as well."

"Except, instead of loving thy neighbor, you eat him."

"It isn't like that. We don't just walk around with a constant desire to munch on random humans. And never those in our local community. We eat only when we get hungry, like you do."

"No, not like I do," I demanded. "I go to the shop and buy a packet of chips. Not walk into a dark alley and end the local milk man."

David laughed. "Neither do I."

"How do you do it, then? Do you have a vampire supermarket—"

"Ara, don't be ridiculous."

"What? That's a pretty fair question."

David just sighed.

"So what about when you *are* hungry?" I threw my hands up in question. "Is it hard to live among us then? I mean, there's no way I could live in a chocolate factory."

"I just don't let myself get that hungry."

"How thoughtful of you."

He cleared his throat, obviously hurt by that.

"Does…" I looked past him to the grey day. "So how did you fall in love with me if I'd look better on your plate?"

"I didn't choose to fall for you, Ara. It just happened."

"How, I mean, what's a vampire even doing at our school?"

He laughed. "I'm on leave."

"Leave?"

"Yes. I work for two years in the vampire community, then take two years to be human."

"Human? There is *nothing* human about what *you* are," I said with a mouthful of spite.

"We fall in love," he offered, stuffing his hands in his pockets. "We can eat, sleep, walk in the day, as if we were still human. But—"

"But you're not."

"Actually, I was going to say *but*"—he tried to keep it light, but the hurt of my repulsion revealed itself within his eyes—"everything is stronger: our bodies, our minds, all of our senses. We feel everything with an intensity I cannot describe. Happiness, pain, heartache, and… *love* are so much stronger than you can possibly imagine."

I softened a little. It was the way he said *love*. There was something so… vulnerable about it. "I don't know." I bumped one shoulder up timidly. "I think I might be able to relate to the feeling-things-more-strongly aspect."

The sharp crescent-moon dimple returned as he nodded. "You have a lot of heart, Ara. Perhaps that's why I'm so drawn to you." His smile dropped away and he looked down at his shoes. "I am sorry that I've hurt you with my secrecy. More than you know."

The apology was *not* accepted… yet. I squared my shoulders. "Okay. So you said you eat normal food, and sleep, and everything else? Why be a vampire at all?"

"It's not by choice," he said calmly, like I was an infant. "You see, it's like an alien, I guess. I thought about it once—how I could describe it to a human." He folded one arm in and touched his chin. "It's like an alien comes down and plants itself in you. You're everything you were before, except that, now, you have these incredible abilities, and your human side is driven by the desires of the alien's first nature: blood.

"I'm still David, but I'm also this alien. I drink because I'm compelled to. If I don't drink, I become weak and desperate, then I'd eventually turn into a monster." He laughed lightly and added, "Much like you if you don't have breakfast. Only, there'd be no stopping me. I would kill uncontrollably until satiated."

Great, so I fell in love with an alien-operated mosquito.

"So, why humans? Why not squirrels? Or cats?" I subconsciously nodded toward my window, imagining Skittles on a plate.

David laughed. "It is vital to consume the blood of your own kind. I am human, in part. Without human blood, human energy, and human life force, I'm nothing. Animal blood, and I speak from experience, not only tastes like rotten flesh, but can't satiate the thirst and it won't nourish."

"What if you just didn't eat blood at all?"

"I'd end up back at square one: killing uncontrollably until my hunger was quenched. It's more humane to take a few lives than many."

"Oh, God!" I nearly threw up. "How can there be any humanity in killing?"

"Live a few hundred years, and you'll find out."

I looked at him with new eyes, a pang of excitement making mine wide. "Are you immortal?"

"Yes."

"You don't die?"

He shook his head.

"At all?" I double-checked.

He shook his head again and stood taller. "No. We're virtually indestructible."

"Virtually?"

"We can't die, but we can get hurt. Our bones are like cement—iron-coated cement. They do *not* break. Ever. And our flesh is extremely difficult to penetrate, not that it would do any good to cut a vampire, because we heal incredibly fast. But we can be hurt."

"Well, so, like, there're no stakes or holy water or silver or decapitation?"

"No. Immortal means immortal, Ara. There is no death. No peace. Only an endless eternity of mourning and solitude, watching everyone you love grow old and wither away, leaving nothing but an exhausting prospect of finding happiness again."

"Sounds"—I studied his face—"unbearable."

"You have no idea," he said through a breathy laugh, as the tension in the room eased.

"I know you, David. I know you have a good heart, but… I mean…" I thought about his soft touch, and how sweet he was with me, especially when he talked about grief. Measuring that up against the guy who whined about the mess left on his floor after his "pizza" fell… they didn't seem like the same person. "I'm struggling to understand how you can be so loving yet so... cruel."

"It takes practice," he said simply. "*You* make the loving part easy though."

"But how do you live with yourself?" I asked, thinking about how guilt-ridden I'd been for killing my mom and Harry.

"I hate myself for some of the things I've done. You just find a way to do it without leaving too many scars on the world—or your own heart. But there aren't too many vampires with empathy for humans. It gets lost when we change. Mostly, you're just food to us." As he shrugged, he flashed an easy smile, and I shuddered.

"Food?" I balked. "Don't *ever* use that term around me again, David. *I* still care for humans, you know, since I'm one of them."

"I'm sorry, Ara. We're just from different worlds, you and I. I'll be careful what I say around you, I promise." He looked into my eyes, his gaze guarded. "Assuming you still want to see me."

Honestly, the human version… I still loved him. But the vampire… "I don't know."

He looked down at his feet. "Would you like me to leave?"

I bit my lip, tapping my fingertips on my leg. "Not yet."

"May I sit?" he asked, motioning to the bed.

I nodded, letting a few minutes pass before asking, "Are all vampires totally hot and sexy?"

"Depends on your tastes, I'd say." He sat back a little, smirking. "Get to the point."

"I—" I shook my head. "I didn't have a point."

"Yes, you did."

"Did not."

"You forget," he said, pushing my quilt away from his leg. "I can read your mind. What was your point?"

My shoulders sunk. "Why me? Why a plain, ordinary, scarred human, when you could be with a hot vampire chick?"

He moved his words around inside his mouth for a second, obviously finding the best way to put this. "You do things to me that no other girl, human *or* vampire, has done. It's not optional for me to love you, Ara. When I'm with you"—he looked at me, exhaling slowly before continuing—"I'm more human than monster. More heart-and-soul than vacant-shadowy-night." He blinked softly and added, "Plus," with a smile.

"Plus what?"

"Plus, human or not, scarred, skinny, fat, ugly, you are exactly my type, and I have been crazy in love with you since the first moment I laid eyes on you."

I looked down to bite my goofy grin.

"It's not enough for me just to love you though," he said. "I don't know if maybe it's the vampire in me, but I need to be around you—to see you, to touch you. And I want that every waking moment of my day, like you're air to me. Of all the girls I've…" He cleared his throat. "I've just never been this way with anyone."

I buried my face in my hands as his words sent a rush of love through my chest. I couldn't believe I'd managed to fall in love with someone so dangerous. My parents were afraid I'd start hanging with kids on drugs. This was way, way worse.

"Ara? Are you crying, ma jolie fille?" David's hesitant embrace fell around me, and the fear I felt before edged upward from the center of my stomach, but I closed my eyes and focused on the truth. This was David. Not some cold, hard murderer.

My David.

The vampire ran a cool fingertip under my eye, a kind of affection, kind of touch, that was becoming so normal to me now. "Are you okay?" he asked, suddenly more concerned when he realized I was laughing, not crying.

"Relax, David. I haven't lost it… yet."

"Sorry." His face cracked with a breathy smile. "It's just that… when a guy tells a girl he's a vampire, he doesn't expect to be laughed at."

"In my defense, I screamed as well."

He stiffened.

"Well, would you expect anything *less* than fear, David? You're a dangerous creature… not a *Cullen*," I added, with a wry smile.

He laughed, loud and full. The sound warmed the room with its grace. "I wish." He rolled his head backward as the laugh dissipated to a smile. "Good story though."

"You read that book?"

"Of course." He breathed out, still smiling as he added, "Wouldn't life be so much easier if it were really that way?"

"No, because then you'd be icy-cold… and pale. But I *like* your golden skin."

"I know you do."

My ears and cheeks flushed with heat as I remembered how lovely he looked in the sun; how he seemed to glow, his skin so soft and smooth, hairless, as far as I could see. It made me want to take his shirt off right now just to be sure it was all real.

A tiny smile tugged the corners of David's lips, changing his whole expression.

"Stop it!" I scolded, holding my finger up to warn him against his invasive mind-reading behavior. Would there ever be any way to get used to him being constantly in my head?

"Probably not," he said, answering my thought.

I groaned to myself, rolling my eyes. In a list of things I didn't like about his true self, the mind-reading wasn't necessarily at the top. And I realized, as I wandered over and sat on my floor, that I was warming a little toward him. At least enough to hear him out before I cast him out.

"Okay. So those myths aside—"

"Just to save you time, Ara, technically everything you think you know is a myth."

"Like what?"

"For one, despite what ancient stories tell you, vampires are not actually dead." He slid to the edge of my bed and leaned forward, resting his elbows on his knees. "And we're not un-dead, either; we're actually alive."

"Really?"

"Yeah. And we're also not evil demons or weirdoes with anemia, but," he said with an upward gesture of his index finger, "we are, in fact, colder, which is where some of the stories come from, I guess."

"But... why are you cold if you're alive?"

"Why are *you* cold?" He grinned. I shrugged. "We're all different. Although, for most vampires, if we go for long periods without nourishment, we get colder and a little pale."

"So, you're not so very different from me then?"

"Ha! Maybe you're a vampire and you just don't know it." He grinned, his very cute dimple making me laugh.

It was nice to laugh with him again. "There's just one thing I'm curious about, though. You said you're not dead?"

He nodded.

Everything David and I ever did together, every moment I touched him since we met, I ran over in my mind. "I can't remember ever hearing a heartbeat. Do you have a heart?"

His gaze fell on his clasped hands. "I don't have a heartbeat, because I don't *need* my heart to beat. You see, the energy—the life force I draw from a human—moves the blood through my arteries. It's very powerful."

"Like magic?"

"Kind of. And I don't need my heart to pump blood to my lungs for oxygenation either, because I don't *make* the blood. I convert it. It comes to me with oxygen in it, but it doesn't run through the veins. It uses the deeper arteries. See?" He held out his forearm and rolled up his sleeve to reveal clear veins, slightly protruding from his skin as if he were flexing his muscles. "They carry the remaining life force of the blood I drink—the energy that makes me immortal. That's why my veins look skin-tone."

"So... really? You don't make your own blood?"

"Not really. When the blood I drink runs out of oxygen and nutrients, I simply drink more."

"So, if you get cut, do you bleed?"

"Yes."

"But... it's not your blood seeping out?"

"It technically is. Like I said, my body converts the blood I drink to use as its own."

"Wow." I stared at his arm.

"But," he added, rolling his sleeve back down, "I do still have a heart."

My head bounced and my lips pressed together into a thin smile, thinking of the many times he'd shown me that heart. "I know."

"Then you know I love you?" His hand flinched a little, like he was going to reach for me but thought better of it.

"I know you do. The trouble is… I still love you."

"Why should that be a problem?"

"Because you're a vampire, David. You… you kill people!"

He sat back again, rubbing his thumb over his chin. "I was human once, you know. And I do understand how you feel about the killing."

"Do you?"

"Yes."

But his empathy wasn't good enough. As I sat here, listening and learning, I hoped it would all sway me—make me think that none of it mattered when measured up against how much I loved him. But, so far, it wasn't working. "So, how long have you been a vampire?"

"Since nineteen thirteen."

"I knew it! I knew you weren't an eighteen-year-old boy." I shook my head in amazement. "It all makes so much sense now, especially how you keep appearing at my side all the time." After that thought came another, but a more carefully considered question this time. "Are you… alone?"

He shook his head. "I live in a large community of vampires. Plus, I have my uncle and my brother, which is more than most vampires have."

I nodded casually then stopped when I realized… "Wait, they're vampires, too?"

"Yes."

"What about girlfriends? Have you ever had one?" I probably didn't really want to know, especially if she went out to dinner with him and ended up *becoming* the main course.

David laughed again. "I'm not that careless, but yes, I have had girlfriends."

"Was anyone special? I mean, you're pretty old, right, so have you ever, like, loved anyone?"

"Loved?"

"Yeah—like you love me."

"Like I love you?" He shook his head. "Never. But there were two other girls I've loved in my existence. Neither of them worked out."

"Why?"

His eyes narrowed slightly. "Why do you want to know this?"

I shrugged.

"Fine. Well, let's just say that, for one of the girls… it turned out that we were really too different, and…" He took a breath, scratching his lip. "And the other was just not meant to be."

"Well, what happened to her?" I moved an inch closer, sensing his obvious distress.

"Perhaps this story is for another time."

"Is that what happened two years ago?" I asked after dropping it for a whole three seconds. "Is she the reason you came to live here?"

"Ara, I don't want to talk about it."

"So, you can tell me that you kill people, but you won't talk about ex-girlfriends?"

"Stop it."

"Why? Why won't you tell me?" Agitation wandered into my tone. "Was she human, like me? Did—"

"She's gone!" David yelled. "Okay? Just drop it!"

I sunk back into myself, and David buried his hands in his hair.

"I'm sorry, David."

"No, Ara, *I'm* sorry." His fingers wrapped around mine then before I even realized he was squatting beside me. "I shouldn't have yelled at you like that," he added. "It's just that… she was a vampire, and she committed a crime, so… they took her away."

"What crime?"

"Ara, please, I don't want to talk about it." He studied the ground as if he couldn't look at me.

"You really did love her?" I asked quietly.

"Yes. But nothing like the way I love you. That has no measure, but I loved her enough to..."

"To what?"

"To die inside a little because of what happened to her."

I so badly wanted to ask what happened, especially since I knew vampires couldn't die. At all. So what ever happened must have been bad. Instead, I asked a question that made me wonder if maybe I could still love him as a vampire. A question that was stained with possible future jealousy. "Will she ever come back?"

"No."

"Do you want her to?"

"No," he raised his voice a little, and then softened it, combing his fingers through his hair. "Look. It doesn't matter. I just… I don't want to talk about it yet, okay?"

"Okay. I'm sorry. I won't ask again."

"No," he moaned, rolling his head back. "You can ask. Just… not today."

"That's what you always say." In his eyes, he looked ready for a challenge, but too much was going on in my head. I wasn't up to arguing with him. Instead, my mind wandered through the past few weeks, analyzing and going over everything we said or did together, then stopped on the best memory I had: the butterflies; the look of concentration on his face as they fluttered around us; the seemingly perfect timing.

A very sexy smile spread across David's lips.

"It wasn't a timing thing at all, was it?" I asked, full of wonder. "You did that—with the butterflies?"

"It's one of my many talents," he said, still grinning.

"But how? Are you magic?"

"No." He shook his head, almost laughing. "I'm a creature of nature, Ara. Hard as that is to believe—"

"A creature of nature! But you *kill* people?"

"I'm no different to the lion killing the antelope."

"Except that the lion doesn't look like the antelope, or live among its kind."

"True, but like the lion, I blend into my natural surroundings; he has the advantage of a certain coloring, and I have the ability to emulate the human form."

"Yeah, but if you're so natural, how come your species isn't born; you're, I don't know, like, *created*, aren't you?"

"You're unbelievable, girl." He shook his head, looking ever like a predator squatting there in front of me. "Is it so hard to believe I might be one of God's creatures, just because I kill?"

I thrust my shoulders back and sat up straight. "Yes."

"Look..." He exhaled his frustration. "I wasn't created by witchcraft or magic. And yes, some do say it started as a curse, but vampirism was apparently passed on by those of an ancient bloodline; ergo, I am just another species of humankind."

"So, are *you* a descendant of this ancient bloodline?"

"No. I was human once."

"So you were... turned, not born?"

"Yes."

"Then you're not one of God's creatures."

"I am, because not everyone can be turned."

"What do you mean?"

"Well, it takes a genetic polarity in the human which, when activated by vampire venom, triggers the change in their genetic makeup."

"A genetic polarity?" I frowned, thinking over his words. I took genetic sciences in school but I wasn't any good at it, so none of that really made sense to me. "So, are you saying you have to have the right *gene* to become a vampire?"

"Yup, so even though I'm a supernatural being, I'm actually mostly natural—just also very *super*." He grinned warmly, sitting down hard on the floor and straightening one leg out in front of him.

"Then, if you're not magic, how did you do that thing with the butterflies?"

"They're just affected by humidity. And vampires? We can manipulate the elements—water and temperature for example." He scratched the back of his neck. "I can get really scientific about it if you like, but most people fall asleep after about ten minutes."

He had an explanation for everything. Always. I *hated* that. "Well, it was the most beautiful moment of my life so far." I'd dreamed about that mystical bubble of magic nearly every night since that day. Pity he had to ruin it by combining it with my first kiss—with a guy who kills people using his *teeth*.

"You know..." David hesitated. "There's a reason I did that, Ara, and it's not what you think."

"Did what?"

"Kissed you."

I hugged my knees, not bothering to tuck my dress under my legs. "I'm listening."

"I never imagined you would one day find me repulsive, and I knew then that I would be leaving you." He leaned a little closer and lowered his voice. "But I did it because I love you, and I just wanted to be your first kiss."

"That's a little selfish, don't you think? You should have asked me if I wanted my first kiss to be with a murderer."

"You were never supposed to find out." He shook his head, pressing his lips into a flat smile. "And I don't care if you're mad at me. It was worth it."

I smiled, because he was right. I could try to be mad at him for that kiss but, in truth, it wouldn't have mattered if he'd just eaten, I'd still have wanted my first kiss to be with him. I just wouldn't tell him that.

I turned my nose up with a flick of my chin. "You'd be more interesting if you were magic."

He smiled so lovingly at me that I wondered if this whole murderer thing was just a huge lie. "Well, there is an *element* of magic to my kind, by human definition."

"Guess there'd have to be with all that speed and healing fast stuff." I stopped and turned the pages of myth in my mind. "Hang on. You did say you heal fast, right?"

"Yup." He grinned, hugging his knee.

My mind was getting lost in information. "How?"

"Rapid cell regeneration. It's responsible for immortality as well," he answered with a hint of humor in his voice.

"Okay, Mr. I-Have-An-Answer-For-Everything. And what about the whole *vampires are demons* thing?" I looked at him, my tone light, quizzical. "Where does that myth come from?"

He shook his head. "There are a few different stories. But we're not demons."

"Good thing you're not, I suppose. I would've had a hard time explaining to Nathan's mom why you suddenly just burst into flames today at church."

David laughed. "Yes, I imagine you would."

"So is that why you smiled when we walked into the church?"

"It was. The whole demon thing's kind of a private joke among my kind."

"Why? And why do people think holy water can burn vampires?"

"Rumors."

"Rumors?"

"Yes. Grapevines. Very powerful." He grinned mischievously. "The whole holy water story started out, originally, when a vampire was found sleeping in his bed. The townspeople believed the man to be dead." David tapped his chest. "No heartbeat, you see. So, they buried him—alive. And when he finally woke, and dug his way out of the grave, starving and angry, he retaliated by eating most of the townspeople."

"Retaliated? But they didn't know he was alive, did they? It wasn't deliberate, right?"

"No."

"Then why did he want revenge?"

"Same reason any claustrophobic, which woke to find themselves buried alive, would."

"*Claustrophobic*?" I touched my neck. "How can a vampire be claustrophobic?"

David laughed. "We carry over many human traits when we change. We can be moody, thoughtful, arachnophobic, afraid of heights—many things. We're still mostly human."

"And this guy was afraid of enclosed spaces?"

"Right. And even if he wasn't, imagine for a second being trapped in darkness, compounded by a force you cannot see, not knowing which way is up or down." He studied me thoughtfully. "I told you a vampire's emotions are stronger?"

"Yeah."

"This claustrophobic vampire woke in darkness, terrified. As he clawed at the soil for three days, his fear became anger and his anger became fury. When he finally took a breath, he vowed revenge on all who ever laid eyes on him. Then, he stumbled into town and obliterated every soul."

"What a bastard!"

David laughed again. "Well, he did leave one alive—a small boy. Does that make him more likeable?"

"Depends," I said. "Why did he leave him alive?"

"The boy had always reminded him of his own dead son. So when he attacked the vampire with the jagged edge of a broken branch, he was amused by the fearless bravery and took pity on him. He ended his vengeful rampage there, faking his death to satisfy the boy's hunger for revenge."

"How noble of him."

"Anyway, from then on," he continued with a smirk, "the human race decided, since the wood the child used originated from a tree on consecrated ground, that these *Creatures of the Night* could be taken down by all things holy. Word spread and, like a disease, the rumors grew into the myths you still hear today."

"Hm." I considered his tale.

"And can you guess that small boy's name?"

"I'm sure you're going to tell me."

He nodded, smiling. "Van Helsing."

"And that's a true story?" I asked.

"True story, which soon became legend."

I thought about how my dad talked about facts in myths during a lecture one day. "Well… if that's true, why wouldn't you just correct them—the humans, I mean—tell them the truth about the whole demon rumor thing?"

"Because the lies assist with our cover." He shrugged. "Those who can walk in the day, go to church or wear a cross, can't possibly be one of these demonic creatures, and so we can remain secret—live in peace."

"Wow."

"Yeah. You'll find most of the myths about my kind were started in much the same manner."

"Hm." I folded my arms. "So why didn't he wake up?"

"Who?"

"The vampire. When they buried him, why didn't he wake up?"

"He was drunk."

"You can get drunk?" My words burst out in a gust.

"Of course we can." He laughed. "We can use drugs, too."

"Really? Do you get addicted, like humans do?"

He shrugged dismissively. "Don't know. Never met a vampire who used drugs. But I'll be sure to ask if ever I do."

"Thanks. Appreciate it."

"Any time." His playful smile spread the corners of his lips widely.

"Okay, so... vamp myth one-oh-one: a crucifix won't burn you?"

"I hope not." David reached into the collar of his shirt and pulled out a heavy gold chain with a cross on the end of it. "I wear it whenever I go to church."

I was taken aback. "So you *are* religious?"

"A little." He smiled and dropped the cross to his chest.

"But you're also... deadly?" I concluded.

"Very." He smiled malevolently.

A shudder crept up my spine. I didn't want to think of those who'd come to learn that as their *last* lesson. "How can you believe in God and then go out and murder?"

"It's not murder."

"Yes, it is."

"No, it's not. It's nourishment—necessary for survival. Does a farmer murder a cow?"

"That's different."

"Why?"

"Because a cow..." I bit my lip. "Because they... well..." I threw my hands up. "I don't know. What do I look like, a philosophy student?"

David laughed. "I love it when you know I'm right."

"You're not right!" The rise of anger made my cheeks burn. "You believe in the Ten Commandments, pray at church, read the Bible, but you can kill the man sitting next to you without so much as—"

"Uh-uh, hold it right there, missy." He held up a finger. I snapped my gob closed. "I said I believe in *God,* not the Bible, not the ways of the church. They are not the same thing."

"How are they not the same thing?"

"Live as long as I, and you will see. Now"—he folded his arms—"we're not having a religious debate. There are more important things to discuss at this moment."

"Fine." But I had nothing left to say. I knew enough to know I would never sleep with my window open again, and that I might actually be happy to say goodbye to David after all. I would miss the human I fell in love with—miss him for the rest of my life—but I wasn't sure how I felt about the vampire sitting before me. He'd said, at the very beginning of this entire conversation, that he wanted me to go with him. That I could never see my family again. Yet there was no way I'd give up life for the dark hell he had to offer.

"You don't need to sleep with your window closed," he said, his eyes heavy with worry. By looking at him, I could tell he'd heard everything I just thought. "There aren't many of us, you know. If that makes you feel better."

"Why aren't there many of you?"

"As it stands, fewer and fewer humans over the years have been known to have this gene. It seems to be breeding out. We've not had a successful turning in decades. Consequently, my kind has been forbidden to create vampires without approval."

"Forbidden? By who?"

"We have a normal societal structure. Just like you," he said. "We live in peace, mostly, but there are laws we must follow, and consequences. We can't just walk around doing whatever we please, or killing whomever we please."

"Really? So the killing's controlled?"

"To a degree."

"Oh..." I unfolded my arms. "What other laws do you have?"

"Well—" He looked over at the window for a second then took a short breath. "We're not allowed to occupy positions of power or fame, in order to maintain cover. And if we're in a situation or accident which would be fatal to a human, we absolutely *must* be reborn."

"Reborn?"

"Yes. Start a new human life with a new name, etcetera."

"Oh, is that why you can't be famous or anything, 'cause it would be hard to hide after you 'die'?"

"Precisely. Especially these days, with things like television and photographs. It makes disappearing really problematic."

"So what else? I mean… can you fly, do you still grow hair, do you sleep upside-down in a cave?"

David scoffed lightly, pressing the back of his wrist to his upper lip. "You really love your myths, don't you?"

I shrugged.

"Uh, well, we do still grow hair, so… sorry, if you became a vampire you'd still have to shave your legs. As for sleeping in a cave… upside-down?" He merely raised a brow to answer.

"What about fly?"

He hesitated. "Like I said earlier, we can manipulate the elements. Some of us have mastered the ability to become completely weightless and move through the atmosphere suspended above the earth. But not all can, and it's only for short distances. It takes decades of practice."

"But can *you*?" I prompted.

Hesitation controlled his smile. "Yes."

"That is *so* cool." It was the only cool thing. Everything else was disgusting and infuriating, but flying was cool. "So what else can you do?"

"Well, at this point, I can officially inform you that we are a secret society. So, much of the information about our laws and abilities, I cannot divulge." He smiled, his eyes shrinking. "Even though I already have."

"But you can reveal yourself? People can know what you are?"

"Only on one condition." He paused and leaned forward to take my hand. I let him, even though my mind raced over all the times these hands may have hurt people. "And I suppose, even though I wasn't conscious of it at the time, when I told you that my uncle wanted me to leave with him, I was hoping you'd fight me—that it might lead to you finding out what I am."

"Really?"

"Yes. Otherwise, I would've just left that day before you arrived at school."

"Like you did to all the others?"

"I never said that."

"You're over a hundred years old, David. You must've made friends. Am I the only one you ever told?"

"Yes."

And for some stupid reason that made me feel special, closer to him. But I didn't want to feel like that anymore. It felt wrong. I drew my hand from his. "So, now that you've told me what you are… do you have to kill me if I don't come with you?"

"No." He reached for my hand but I refused to give it to him. "Silly girl. No. I can tell whomever I please—"

"But you said you needed approval—"

"I only needed approval to offer you a place at my side—as a vampire—something they will only allow if I'm sure that you're…"

"I'm what?"

"I guess… my *significant other*." David read over his own words in the air. Then, seeming happy with the terminology, looked at me and smiled, pressing his finger under my chin until my teeth fit back together.

Significant other? "But… you're a vampire. I can't be your significant other, David. We can't even be together."

He swallowed hard. "We can, if you loved me enough."

"David, you *kill* people in order to live." A hint of hysteria touched my tone. "I don't know if I can be a part of that. Not as your friend, not as your girlfriend, and *certainly* not as a vampire."

David froze in place like a stone carving, as if he'd given up breathing, the hurt eternally placed within his eyes. "Believe it or not, Ara, it's a kindness to kill a human after biting them."

"Ew!" My lip twisted up in disgust. "I don't want to hear anymore, David. Kindness? I… I just..."

"Perhaps you have heard enough then." A slight nod moved his head, the smile I loved completely blanketed by pain. "I shall leave you now."

"When will you be back?"

My bedroom door swung open and he stood between here and gone. "Do you *want* me to come back?"

"I don't know. I think maybe I just need some time to—"

"Ara, you just told me you can't love me because I'm a vampire, I—"

"I know, but… I…" But what? Was that a lie? Did I still love him? Or was I just afraid to lose the happiness I'd found knowing the human version of him these past few weeks? "I don't know what to say, what to think. I…"

"I understand."

"Do you? Because I don't think you do."

"I repulse you. What more do I need to understand?"

"It's not you that needs to understand a damn thing; it's *me*! I need time to process all of this."

"Take all the time you need, Ara," he said coldly, and disappeared into thin air, leaving my door swinging in the breeze he left behind.

I sat there in the middle of my room hugging my knees to my chest until the afternoon turned to evening. When Vicki flicked the hall light on and came up the stairs, I ducked in the darkness, waiting until she passed. And I noticed then, crumpled at the foot of my bed, the damaged remains of the blue rose David stole, like a representation of the moment that changed everything.

With my butt numb and legs stiff, I jumped up and grabbed the flower, pressing it to my nose. Despite all the damage done, despite the petals weeping or falling away, it still smelled just as sweet as before. Which was comforting to me because, for all the things that seemed irredeemable, some things were still okay.

I grabbed my diary and pressed the flower between the last pages, then snapped the book shut and sat on my bed in the dull light shining in from the world outside my room.

16

After an agonizing dinner with my parents, fighting with myself not to tell Dad about the vampire, I sat at my desk and agonized a little more over everything. How had it gone from me wishing David would stay here to wishing he were an ordinary human, with ordinary problems taking him away from me?

It was impossible to comprehend what he was. That he was a killer. And that he wanted me to be a killer, too. My whole head was clouded with the options, but I knew only two things for sure: I didn't want to be a vampire. And it felt like a sin against mankind to be in love with one, as if it tainted me by association.

The fact that my love for him didn't outweigh that spoke volumes to me about what I should do.

Outside, twinkles of silver dotted the night sky. Once, they were glimmers of hope for me—wishes waiting to be made—but tonight they stared back down into my insignificant little life, offering no solace or resolution at all. Matters of the heart were never solved rationally though. Love is irrational. Love is unfair.

There would be no going back. No lazy afternoons by the lake, warm and safe in David's arms. We'd never get married or have babies, never grow old together and get arthritis, or if he ever talked me into becoming a vampire, I'd never die. I'd never get to see my mom and Harry again at the Pearly Gates. And what if I became a vampire and, after a few thousand years he got bored with me?

"*That*"—a voice broke through the silence—"could never happen."

"David?" I shot up out of my chair and pinned my back to the wall beside my dresser. "How long have you been there?"

He sat comfortably in the nook of my window like Peter Pan; his back against the frame on one side, his foot propped up on the other. "Long enough."

"Long enough for what?"

"To know that your battle of heart is not winning against your conscience."

"One will have to win eventually."

He jumped off the ledge, weightless, landing silently in my room. "I know."

"Just, please." I put my hand out. He stopped advancing. "Just stay back, okay?"

"I won't hurt you."

"I know."

He looked up from his feet, smiling mischievously. "Do you?"

"Yes. I'm not afraid of that right now. I... I'm just at odds with how I feel about you because I..."

"You loathe me?"

"Yes," I said, my whisper breaking. "I can't see you the way I did before, and yet it hasn't made me hate you. So until it does, even a little bit, I won't trust myself to be near you."

"So you *want* to accept me, but you won't allow yourself to?"

"I don't know. I mean... Maybe. Which means I'm not thinking clearly."

"Or maybe our love is just stronger than your principles."

I shook my head, reinforcing my warding hand when he took another step closer.

He sighed, letting his arms fall loosely to his sides. "If I could perform a memory charm on you—make you forget—would you want me to?"

"You could do that?"

"Just answer the question."

"I..." I wasn't sure. The human version of David made me happy, safe. All of this reality was just too unusual. I felt insecure, like I was walking on a glass cliff top, certain I might fall through at any minute.

But would I want to love him if I didn't know he was a killer? Could I go back?

"Yes," I said very quietly, looking down.

"Then why can't you accept me knowing what you know?"

"It's complicated."

"Ara, look at me," he said, his squared green eyes searching mine. "You would refuse my love, watch me walk away, for what? To make a stand against a natural predator? That's all I am, sweetheart." He slowly came closer, laughing softly. "Would you give up your firstborn to protest against lions killing a zebra?"

"That's the problem, David. I *will* be giving up my firstborn. I'll be giving up *everything*." I pushed away from him and darted across to my desk. "How can you say you love me if you would want me to do that?"

"I don't want you to give anything up, Ara. I simply want to be with you, and you once wanted to be with me. That's why we're here right now—that's what all of this is about, remember? You didn't want me to leave. You *wanted* me to tell you why I had to."

"I know." I folded my arms and rolled my chin to my chest. "But I just don't know if I can love you now. And, even if I decide that I can, what then? I have to choose between love or life, and... David? I want a family one day; I want a little Harry. I want to be a soccer mom and do carpooling and argue with my daughter over the boys I think aren't good enough for her. And then, one day, when I've had a good life with the man I love, I want to know what it's like to be old, and die." I looked up, my eyes narrowed. "Can you understand any of this?"

"More than you know," he said sadly, then evaporated. A breathless second passed before he appeared on the edge of my bed, his face buried in his hands.

For the first time since his confession this afternoon, I really let myself look at him—to see him for what he was. I pictured the vampire, the monster, but beneath it, with his shoulders stiff, his grey shirt hugging the knuckles of his curved spine, all I saw was the boy—the one with a heart, which was probably very broken right now. It surprised me that I still cared.

"Why did your uncle want you to leave with him the other day?" I asked, sitting down beside him.

He straightened up, brushing his hands over his jeans nervously. "I told him I was in love—that I couldn't leave you when the time came. And he told me that was exactly why I had to leave immediately."

"Because you were in love?"

"No. Because I love you enough to ask if I could give up everything."

Wow. That made me feel heavy and a little numb. "Maybe your uncle was right. If you'd just gone, I would be so broken right now, but it would be normal. I like normal. I don't want to feel like this—like my whole world has been pulled out from under me again."

"Oh, Ara, please don't say things like that." The anguish in his eyes forced me to close mine. "Have you truly *considered* how good life could be if you come with me—as a vampire?"

I couldn't answer him, because I couldn't give him the answer he wanted. I'd thought about it, done the pros and cons, but the cons were outweighing the pros. There was nothing appealing about living my life, my eternity, as an amoral killer.

"Amoral?" He floated slowly up to stand, casting a dark shadow across my face that reeked of rage and insult. "You think me *amoral*?"

"I'm sorry, David, but… I do." I kept my head down, my eyes on his clenched fist.

"If you could *only* see what you are doing, what it will do to me to be without you." The energy surrounding him that was normally warm and soft turned cold, chilling the air with a sudden tearing sensation. "I care about a lot of things in this world, Ara, and I do have a heart—*feelings* to be exact."

When our gazes met, my stomach tightened at the liquid agony in his very human eyes. "David—"

"No. Can't you see me for what I am? Do you truly only see the killer?"

"I'm sorry." I lowered my head. "But right now, yeah. I do."

He sighed angrily, stepping back. "You have no idea what you're giving up."

"If you knew my heart, you'd know that *being a vampire* would be giving up," I whispered, looking away from the broken pieces of the boy I once loved.

"I *do* know your heart, Ara. And I knew I should *never* have shared myself with you." He cut the air with his hand.

"You're right," I said irresolutely. "You should never've told me. Or you should have lied because, now, I have to lose you still, but it's worse because I know you're out there every day taking life. And I kissed you. I let myself love you. And I wish I hadn't."

"So that's it then?" He nearly choked on his words. "You want nothing to do with me?"

It seemed so final when he said it aloud, but I wasn't sure about that bit yet. I wasn't sure about any of it.

He took two slow steps away from me, touching his chest as the distance became greater. "Well, have no fear, my love. I do not suffer the torments of error twice. I should not have let myself love you, and I will not make that mistake again."

David sounded a hundred years old to me then, the weight of his heartbreak tearing down my walls as I watched him back away. And somewhere inside me a little voice screamed out—echoing from the depths of my soul—warning me that if I let him leave now I would *never* see him again. That wasn't what I wanted. Not truly.

"Wait!" I called in a breath of desperation, reaching for him as I jumped to my feet. "David, wait."

He stopped, crouched small on the ledge of my window, keeping his eyes on the night below.

"Please don't leave forever. I just need time to think about how I feel now—knowing what you are. You shouldn't have come back yet."

David turned his head and looked into my eyes.

A tear moved from within my lashes and down my cheek, and when the vampire jumped back in to my room and stood right before me, I didn't even flinch. Not one uneven breath escaped me. He leaned in and pressed his cold fingertips to my face, rolling it firmly upward to meet his. "Follow your heart, mon amour," he said.

"When nothing in this world makes sense anymore, just follow your heart."

I drew a shaky breath and closed my eyes as an intense exchange of hope and fear consumed the air and, in a flash, as I opened them again, he was gone.

SQUINTING IN THE BRIGHT MORNING SUN AS MY SNEAKERS clapped over the pavement, I started down the street—in the opposite direction of the school. I wanted to be as far away from that building as I could get.

I drew a deep throat-grazing breath of the near-autumn chill, blowing it out in a slow, controlled one. I'd almost forgotten how to breathe while running. I'd let myself get so unfit that, instead of feeling free and fast now, I felt like I was trying to jump under water. It sucked. And the fact that David killed people *really* sucked. No pun intended. The only trouble was, when I concluded not to love him, it hurt inside—a physical ache in my gut, like the one that made me throw up on the first day of school. I could be resolved one moment, knowing I loved the human version of him but that I would never love the vampire, and in the very next breath I would swing like a pendulum, imagining our lives if I became what he is.

It was all very—

"Hello stranger," a soft, soprano voice cut off my thoughts.

I stopped dead and turned around. "Hey, Emily. Do you live around here?"

She shook her head and motioned behind her. "Spencer lives here. I stayed over last night."

"What?" My eyes bulged. "Stayed over?"

"Yeah." She nodded. "Oh, I mean, not like that. I was just babysitting his little sister."

"Oh, okay." I folded over a little, trying to catch my breath. "Didn't you go to the wake at Betty's?"

"Yeah, but Spencer's mom's a nurse. She got called in on nightshift after."

"So, can't Spence babysit?"

Emily scoffed, obviously humored. "He's just not that kind of guy."

"Oh." I wandered over and leaned next to her on the brown picket fence. "Give his mom my number then. I love babysitting."

"Okay, I will. So"—she looked down at my running shorts, then my sweat-covered forehead—"I'm gonna go out on a limb here and guess you were... going to a ball?"

We both laughed.

"Uh, yeah." I looked down at my shoes. "I thought I better start getting fit."

"Hm." She folded her arms. "Fit. Is everything okay?"

"Of course it is," my tone rose upward.

"Is it David?"

"A little." I sighed and sat down on the curb.

"Let me guess"—she sat beside me—"he's got you all confused?"

"It's a talent of his, isn't it?" I said.

"Yeah. So what is it? What's he done?"

He's a vampire and he kills people. "He said he loves me."

Her mouth fell open a little, but nothing came out.

"Yeah." I laughed. "I know, hey."

"Hm, well he's never said *that* before to anyone I know. Are you happy?"

I nodded and sort of shook my head too.

"Have you said you love him?"

"Yeah. Why?"

"Just wondering."

I tensed. "Is it... a bad thing if I did?"

She laughed. "Why would it be bad?"

"I just... I don't know. I'm not really too good at this boyfriend thing. Normally, when I have this kind of crisis, I ring Mike, but—" But I couldn't tell him about this one.

"But?"

"I think he'd laugh at me."

"For being in love?"

"Maybe. He never really takes that stuff seriously, you know. I don't think he'd get it."

"You could always talk to me," she suggested.

"Thanks, Em. But I think I just need some time to sort my head out."

"And running helps with that?" She tried not to laugh.

"Uh, well, it used to." I sat back, leaning on my hands. "I used to run with Mike every day. It was like, even running with him, even talking while we did, I always came back feeling like I'd left my problems behind."

"How's that working out on this run?"

"Not so good." I laughed, then stopped. I knew Emily was trying to get me to open up. She was using the exact same tactics as Vicki, without even realizing it. "We had this band of seagulls on the corner of my street," I said to divert the conversation. "Whenever we'd run that course, the damn things'd barely scatter a few feet in the air to get out of the way. It was really annoying, because we'd have to slow our pace. I always promised myself I was gonna put my foot right up their butts if they didn't move." I rested my elbows on my knees, my chin on my palm. "Mike called them *gullsters…* instead of gangsters."

"You didn't, though? Did you? Kick them?" Emily looked horrified.

"No! No way. Mike would chase them off like he was planning to kick them though." I stared ahead then. "He never had any problems kicking butt. I guess that's why he's so suited to the Force."

"The police?"

"Yeah. He's joining the… kind of like SWAT unit."

"Really?" Emily grinned. "That is super sexy."

"I guess." I breathed out slowly. "It's dangerous though."

"You worry about him?" she asked.

I casually shrugged when, in truth, I actually worried a lot. "I just miss him."

"So why'd you decide to move away from your real mom?"

I shifted awkwardly. "Uh, to be with my dad."

Emily nodded, satisfied with that. "Do you like it here?"

After a deep breath, I nodded. "It's not like home. It's not hot and dry, and there's no ocean in the distance, no black cockatoos on the lampposts, but…"

"But you still like it?"

"Yeah. I think I actually love it."

"Well, good,"—she nudged me with her elbow—"because you're starting to grow on us, Ara. Everyone was really disappointed you weren't there last night at Betty's."

"Yeah." I smiled sheepishly and looked down at my untied shoelace dangling, wet and muddy, from my sneaker. "I wasn't feeling well."

"I know. I saw the whole *save me, David, save me* thing." She held her forearm to her brow as she fell backward a little, then dropped her hand, smiling. "He was really worried about you, you know?"

"I know."

"We all were."

"I know. I'm sorry. It's just because I didn't eat."

"Yeah, Mr. Thompson told me."

"I know. He said you called last night."

"Yeah." She looked up then as a car pulled into Spencer's driveway. "I gotta go. My mom's here."

I stood up and dusted the loose pebbles of asphalt from my shorts. "Okay, Em. I'll see ya later."

I waved and turned toward home, then walked the rest of the street and landed in a huffing mess on the porch step near Vicki's grey cat. "Hey, Skitz."

He ducked low, growling at me.

"What?" I leaned forward, the creaky step dipping under my weight as I reached for the cat. But I drew my hand back when his growl intensified, moving deeper to the back of his throat, his tail lashing about. Then I noticed something grey and wriggly between his paws, and it wasn't his fat belly coming to life, either. It was a field mouse.

"Hey, way to go, Skitz. Good little hunter, aren't ya?"

He scoured the scene—probably making sure it was safe to unveil his prey—then tossed the mouse into the air and caught it in his teeth, pausing to scrutinize me.

"Gross." Time to go inside. I stood up quickly but my heel sunk down hard and shattered the step under my foot, dragging my shin through before my knee smashed into the edge and sent me tumbling onto my hands. Without thinking, I rolled over and pulled my leg free from the wooden cage, scraping the flesh back the other way, making it sting as a mix of blood and sweat smeared into the shredded skin.

"Ow! Ow! Ow!"

Not bothering to see if I was okay, Skittles bolted off with his catch of the day.

"Traitor!" I yelled, blinking back tears.

"Ara! Are you okay, dear?" I jumped a little as the front door swung open, disturbing the quiet. "What happened?"

"Had a fight with the porch step." I took a breath through my teeth, rocking back and forth. "Step won."

Vicki tilted her head and sighed. "I told Greg to fix that *weeks* ago. I'll go get the first aid kit." She ran inside, leaving the front door open, and quickly came back to sit beside me on the remains of the once-creaky bottom step. "What were you doing out here anyway, Ara? It's very early."

I cringed as she smoothed some sterile solution down the minced skin on my shin. "I went jogging."

She stopped for a second. "I didn't know you were jogging again. That's really good to hear." She sounded pleased—with *herself*.

"Yeah. Guess it is." Except, it wasn't a sign of my recovery, but more of my isolation and desperate need to figure my own head out.

"Did you see Skittles out here by any chance? I thought I heard his bell. He has a vet appointment this morning and I want to bathe him before we go." She grinned.

"Yeah, well, he'll need a bath now," I said.

"Why?" She covered the cut with some gauze and tape.

"He caught himself a nice *juicy* mouse," I probed, watching her face for disgust. It licked her expression without any further prompting. Sam would definitely be bathing Skittles now. Victory move. I one-upped him and he wouldn't even know it was me.

"Why would you let him do that, Ara? You know how I feel about that."

"Why?" I scoffed. "Vicki, he's a cat—they kill mice. It's what they're supposed to do." And as soon as I said it, everything slowed down around me.

The cat killed.

I *praised* him for it. I all but patted his head not more than two minutes ago.

I'd never hated him for it. And yet, for some reason, I'd been trying to hate David. But David wouldn't kill if it weren't necessary for survival.

I understood then what he'd said to me about newborns and lions: he wasn't a serial killer. He was a natural predator. A good, kind person, but *also* a vampire. It wasn't the same thing, and it cleared the way inside my head for another truth: I loved David. I loved the human boy *and* the vampire that he was. I didn't want to be immortal, or a killer, but there was no way I wanted to let him go either.

Vicki waved her hand in front of my face. "Ara, are you all right, dear?"

Blinking, I snapped out of my trance. "Uh, yeah. I'm fine."

"Well, come on, we'll go inside and yell at Dad for not fixing that step." She took my hand and helped me to stand.

"Actually, Vicki, I think I'll just go sit on the swing for a bit."

"Okay." She frowned, forcing a smile after. "Well, I'll be inside if you need to talk."

"Oh, um"—I almost laughed—"thanks, Vicki."

She nodded and walked back up the stairs. When the front door closed, my smile dropped. I hobbled away and then stumbled clumsily over the hedge fence at the side of the house and into the backyard. Then, as I righted myself and looked up, met with the eyes of a vampire. "David?"

Perfect as always, he leaned casually against the oak tree with one hand in his pocket and a very sexy smile across his lips. "Hello, Ara."

"What're you doing here?"

"It's not easy to give you space—not when I know you're making such a hard decision right now. I feel like I should be here fighting for *us*." David looked down at his feet as he shuffled up, very human-like, from his lean against the trunk. I loved it when he looked human. "Can we talk?"

"I, uh—" I looked at his offered hand. "I don't think that's a good idea."

"Right." He dropped it to his side.

"No. I—" I stepped forward, smiling sheepishly down at my bleeding leg. "I don't want you to leave. It's just—"

His eyes followed mine, his brow pinching when he saw the gauze. "What happened?"

I flopped down on the ground in an exhausted heap, my legs and arms sprawled out to the sides. "Apparently I'm heavier than I used to be."

He laughed, gently bending my sore leg at the knee as he squatted down. I tensed a little, rolling up at the waist to watch him rest a sweet kiss to the purple bruise. "You will never have to be afraid of me, Ara."

"But you're a vamp—"

"Yes." He extended his hand and helped me to sit up. "And it would take a lot more than a line of blood across your skin to make me hurt you."

"So it doesn't bother you—the blood?"

"Not when it's yours." He sat down across from me.

"Then, it doesn't make you want to bi—"

"Shh." He placed his finger to my lip and nodded toward the house.

I stiffened. "What is it?"

"Vicki." He looked back at me. "She's watching us from the laundry."

"Well... what's she doing in there—just *watching* us?"

"No." David's intense stare softened to a smile. "She's bathing a cat, I believe."

"What?" I spun around to see her struggling with something in the sink—something slimy and dark-grey with claw-ending tendrils thrashing out of the tub every few seconds. "Why is *she* bathing the cat?"

"I assure you, I have no idea."

I turned back, folding my arms. "It was a rhetorical question. Sam was supposed to be doing it—as payback for… well… never mind." I didn't want to tell him I mucked around with my little brother like a seven-year-old the other night and ended up getting yelled at by my dad. "Those deep scratches were meant to be for *him*."

David laughed. "Revenge will not bring satisfaction, Ara."

"Says you," I scoffed, biting my teeth together.

"If you want to get back at Sam for hitting you with a towel—"

"How do you know about that?"

David only smiled, ignoring that question. "You might try stashing dirty cups in his room for Vicki to find. Then, perhaps, she will punish him with dish duty for the next month."

I grinned—a wicked grin. "You *are* evil, aren't you?"

"When it comes to little brothers, yes, I have a few tricks up my sleeve."

"So, um…" I checked behind me, then whispered, "can we go somewhere to talk?"

"That depends which direction the conversation will go," he said. "I came here to convince you to love me, so if you're planning to say anything that deviates from that, then I'm not ready to let you talk."

"Look, we have a lot to sort out, you know. I don't think we can resolve this in one conversation, and I still have a lot of questions to ask before I can even come close to making any decisions about what I want. But I do have something I need to say. In private."

"Very well. We can talk, but I will not promise to keep my lips sealed. If I see an opportunity to coax you into coming with me, I will take it."

"Well, you're only human after all, right?" I joked.

"I wish. It would make all of this a lot easier."

"Yes, it would."

"Now, would you like to change first, or are you planning to torture me with that skimpy outfit?" David grinned, nodding toward my shorts and zip-up jacket, but stared just a little too long at the space right below my navel.

If only I knew what he was thinking when he looked at me that way.

"Inappropriate things, Ara," said the annoying mind reader.

"Like what?"

His lips twitched, while his smiling eyes changed shape several times. "Go get changed. I'll meet you in the car."

"But—" I said, stopping when my words struck an empty yard. "Damn it, David." I stood up, dusted myself off and went to get changed.

17

The warm air of the fading summer skimmed across the glassy surface of the lake, filling my lungs with the scent of grass and clay. "I never thought I'd see this place again."

"Why would you think that?" David smiled, already laid out on the picnic rug.

"Well, because, *obviously* this place has no hold for me without you in it."

"I wasn't going to give up on you that easily." He paused then, thoughtful. "Does it make you afraid—to be here alone with a vampire?"

"It's no different to before, really." I slumped down on the rug across from David, tucking my dress under my legs. "I've always been out here alone with a vampire."

"Yes, but"—sadness stole his smile—"now, you're repulsed by me."

I twiddled my fingers in my lap. "I was wrong to react that way, David. I'm not repulsed by you. Not really. I just… I have to separate it in my mind; this boy I'm in love with from this vampire who kills."

"Why do you separate it? Why not just accept it—accept me for what I am?"

"I guess I accept it in my own way. It's like, I mean, if you were lost in the wild after a plane crash and had to eat the pilot to survive, no one would think anything of it. Humans are the element of your survival, and… I don't think that changes who you are inside."

"Of course it does, my love. You said it yourself: you couldn't see me being a guy who liked blood and gore. If I kill, if I enjoy killing, that has to change who I am to you."

After thinking about that, I shook my head. "No. You're a good guy. I know you are."

"I am now. I wasn't before I met you."

"Are you trying to convince me to hate you?"

"No. Only to make you realize that you can't just *say* you accept me for who I am. I am a vampire. I kill people. Some of them you may have met. If you accept me, you have to accept me for everything. Not just the lie you tell yourself."

"Well, I guess that'll take more time. Baby steps."

"Baby steps," he agreed. "Fine. But we don't have much time."

"It's okay. Making the decision to accept that I still love you was the hard part. I should move along from repulsion quite quickly after that."

"Onto what?"

"Extreme bliss, hilarity—the mind's way of dealing with what it doesn't understand."

"And then what?"

I shrugged. "Maybe true acceptance."

"But you're not about to come hunting with me or anything, are you?" He smirked.

I tried not to be offended, but I actually really just wanted to slap him. "That's not funny."

"Sorry." He looked down by his leg and brushed a few leaves away that fell from a tree. "So, you don't want me to leave with my uncle? You'll give me you—until the end of the summer?"

I nodded. "Yes."

One corner of his mouth turned up ever so slightly. "But, you won't give me forever with you?"

"Forever," I laughed the word out. "That used to have such a different meaning to me."

"Me too."

I smiled and looked away. "I can't even comprehend eternity, David. It's too much for my puny human brain to take."

"Yes, you can. Try this: think of the longest day you've ever spent," he said, sitting up.

I thought of Wednesday—the day before the funeral—a whole day not knowing if I'd ever see him again.

"Now, spend the rest of your life like that," he said, his voice dropping on the end.

"Is it really that miserable?"

"Not all of it." He tried to smile, shifting his fingers from the tangled hold in his hair to the ground beside him. "There are good things. But you get tired sometimes, you know? And then, once in a while, if you're lucky, you come across something that makes your life worth living."

I held the smile on my lips, but it went stale in my soul. "And what about when I'm gone? Will you find another person to love?"

"See, you just don't get it." He shook his head, leaning back on his hands. "There was a time where I was just existing, and I never knew any better. I liked my life. I was… for all intents and purposes, *happy*. But then I saw you, and when I held you, you burrowed right into my soul, Ara. You reached a part of me that has never been touched before and I…" He looked away. "I'll never be the same again. Wherever I go, whatever I do in this world, I will never not love you."

"If you love me that deeply, can't you just stay with me then—be human?"

"I'm not human, Ara."

"I know."

"I never will be human. I'm a vampire. Even if I could get approval to stay with you for the next eighty years, what then? I'd have one measly lifetime with you, pretending all the while to be human, watching you age just a little bit more each day until every ounce of youth withers away from your eyes and I lose you for good."

"But at least we would have lived—been a family, had a life together."

"One life. One. When we could have an eternity."

"So, that's it? No negotiation? Your way or the highway?" I scoffed.

"It's not my way, girl. Do you think I want this?" He pointed to his chest. "God, even if I *was* willing to stick around to watch you die, it's not up to me."

"Well, who decides?"

"The World Council."

"Can't we reason with them?"

"No. Discussion closed."

"Why?"

"Ara, please—just stop pushing."

"No, why can't we reason with them?"

"Because they do *not* negotiate the laws. Vampires in my position stick to their Sets no matter what."

"Sets?"

"It's what we call the communities we belong to—clubs, sort of."

"Vampire clubs?" My brow arched.

"I said *sort of* like clubs. They're there to protect vampires from *your* society."

"So *we're* the dangerous ones?"

"Yes. Do you know what could happen if vampires were discovered? It could start a war."

"Would that not be a good thing? You guys would win, then you could live in peace."

"That's not the point, Ara. And we would never be in peace. Fear can turn good people into idiots. And then… what if we lost? We'd end up locked away or in a science lab being tested on so humans could wield or recreate our powers."

"Oh."

"Yes, oh." He smiled. "Without a Set, you are exposed, out in the open—no one to help cover up a kill or collect bodies, no one to assist with identity change. And I know better than anyone that vampires must be kept under a tight rein. If not, they can become unruly. The law applies to all. Not just those who feel special because they're in love."

"But it would only be for eighty years, then you could go back."

"It doesn't work like that. They don't grant long leave to people in my political position."

"Political position?"

"Yes. I'm a Set leader on the minor council."

"Can't you quit?"

"Would you really ask me to give it up for you, Ara?" One of his eyes narrowed. "Because I could. But I would have to leave without permission and I'd be hunted like a dog—face imprisonment."

"Prison?"

He nodded. "And why would I want to quit? I've worked hard, spent decades doing unspeakable things to obtain my position. I *enjoy* my job, Ara. And it comes with a generous salary and many privileges not afforded to the general public."

"Well, can't I just come with you but stay human?" I asked carefully.

He shook his head softly. "It's against the law."

"Really?"

"Yes, either you become a vampire or I have to leave you behind for good."

"Okay." I nodded. "But, to be fair to myself, I think that decision is something I should take my time on."

"I understand."

"Just… if you can just bear with me for a bit of back-and-forth until the end of summer, I can give you my answer then."

"I can handle that." He smiled. "And you can ask me anything you like in the meantime. Full disclosure."

"Okay, since we're being open: does it hurt… to be changed?"

"Yes."

"If I… say I decided to be like you, what then?"

"Well, it wouldn't happen overnight. There are processes to go through. But we'd take our time, prepare you—get you used to the idea first. I wouldn't rush you."

"Who would I kill?"

"Who?"

"Yeah, I mean, is it random or do you choose them?"

"Uh..." He grinned and picked an ant off the rug, then tossed it onto the grass. "Well, I usually avoid eating comedians."

"Why?"

"Because they taste funny."

A small tumbleweed rolled past and crickets chirruped loudly.

"Sorry. That was a terrible attempt at humor." He shook his head and then painted on his serious face again. "Every vampire is different, and the hunt or the kill, it's very intimate. Asking a vampire how he kills is almost as personal as asking what color underwear he's wearing."

"Oh, sorry. I didn't realize."

"No, it's fine. We're in an intimate relationship, Ara, so it's okay for you to ask."

I liked that. It made me feel special. "So how do *you* choose them?"

"It used to be random, usually women. Now, it's men. I stalk them for a bit, see if they're worthy of existing, and if not—" He shrugged to finish.

"And you enjoy it? The part where they die?"

"Yes."

My body shuddered involuntarily. "And you *feel* for them after?"

"*Now*, I do. But only as bad as you'd feel for knocking an old lady over in the street."

I pictured that and, yeah, I'd feel pretty bad. "How often do you eat?"

"Every couple of days. I can go for as long as five days, but it gets very uncomfortable." He readjusted his position.

That wasn't so bad. At least it wasn't three square meals a day.

David chuckled lightly.

"So… are you hungry now?" I asked.

"No. I would never be that irresponsible again. To be here alone with you would be dangerous if I were deprived."

"But you said… just before, in my backyard, that I never have to be afraid of you."

"Only because I will never *again* take risks with you. If I were to be here whilst hungry, that would be taking a risk, and you *would* be in danger."

"So, have you ever wanted to kill me?"

"Yes." He nodded to the center of the rug. "That day when I didn't kiss you."

My breath caught in my throat, seeing that moment happen all over again, while an uneasy silence hovered around us. David's lip twitched, one eye narrowing ever so slightly, making my heart warm as I read the uncertainty behind his gaze. Then, I burst out laughing.

"You should see the look on your face." I pointed at him. "You're not sure if you should've said that, are you?"

The sweet, familiar smile tugged at the corner of his lip for a second, breaking into a broad, honest grin as he laughed along with me. "I just don't want to frighten or repulse you. I'm never sure what to say."

I let my bottom lip slip forward into a pout for a second. "I'm sorry. It must be hard for you."

"Hard?" He breathed out, leaning forward a little more. "That doesn't even begin to describe it."

"Do you find it hard keeping yourself a secret, you know, your abilities?"

"Ha! Yes. Especially in emotional situations."

"Which is why you always take off?"

"Yes, like that day at school." He smiled, scratching his brow. "In the hallway."

I looked up at him. "Do you mean when I…" I realized with a drop in my gut that he would've seen everything I was thinking that day. I covered my cheeks. "Oh my God."

He chuckled. "It was worse for me. I wasn't sure what to do, you know. That hallway was full of people, and I just wanted to stand there and watch your thoughts unfold. Then, at the point I couldn't take anymore, I wanted to…"

"Float away or something?"

"No." He looked up from the ground and laughed once. "You actually gave me cause to place books over my groin as I walked away, Ara."

"Ha!" I laughed so loud I shocked myself.

"I had to try to hide it," he added, still laughing. "Either that, or lift you in my arms and run at vampire-speed to the storage room under the auditorium stage."

"You would not," I said, my tone ringing in question.

"Ara." He raised one brow. "I'm a guy. Not a saint."

"Well, what..." I crossed my legs under me, shifting nervously. "What would you have done with me in there?"

He left the long silence hanging, smiling down at the grass. "I would've demonstrated my affections for you."

"And"—I played with the hem of my dress—"how exactly would you have done that?"

David cleared his throat and sat back up from his lean, dusting the grass and soil off his hands. "This is getting off subject."

"Right." I bit my lip. "So when you left school that day, it wasn't because of my strawberry shampoo?"

"No."

"But why leave? Why not just take me to the auditorium closet?"

"Because..." He frowned, curiosity making his eyes smaller. "Would you have wanted me to?"

Uh, yes. Hell yes! "Maybe." I shrugged.

He laughed. "And what about now? Would you still want the same things with a killer?"

"Maybe."

"So you trust me?"

"I... guess so."

"What if I were to kiss your neck?"

My heart picked up. "Um—"

The vampire moved closer, taking my hand as he knelt before me. "Is *this* okay?"

I nodded.

"And, what if I did... this?" He tilted my chin up to expose my throat, and slowly lowered his face to mine, stopping right in front of my lips. "You still okay?"

I nodded again, exhaling deeply.

"How 'bout now?" His warm breath brushed over my throat, slipping around to my spine as his lips gently made a line of kisses from my ear to my collarbone. After a moment, David slowly drew away, keeping his hand against my face, running his thumb over my lashes. "Look at me."

I opened my eyes.

"Was that okay?" he asked.

I nodded.

"You weren't scared?"

"You're just the same." I shook my head, relieved. "And I love you just like before."

A smile broke across his lips, showing his fangs. "You cannot fathom the relief I feel, Ara, to have you know what I am and still let me touch you that way."

"You're not that scary." I smirked, rubbing the moisture from my neck.

"My human self might not be. But you haven't met the vampire yet."

"When do I get to meet him?"

"I'm not sure you will."

"Why?"

"Because it might frighten you, Ara. And I. Never. Want you. To be afraid of me again."

"But I'm okay now. If you scared me, David, you could always talk me around."

He shook his head. "No. After what happened in your room that day, I will never risk scaring you again."

"Why?"

"Because I felt dead inside," he snapped. "I couldn't touch you. I couldn't be the one to comfort you. I felt powerless, like you were screaming for me, standing behind a glass partition and I couldn't reach you."

"I think you came across as rather in control."

"God, no. Do you know what it feels like when you can't touch someone? To be the one who placed fear in their eyes and be powerless to take it away? I was terrified I'd lost you"—his voice dropped—"and all I wanted was to hold you; just make you see *me* again."

"It's okay now."

"I know. And that is why I will never show you the vampire."

"You've seen my ogre."

He laughed aloud. "Yes, and let me tell you, mon amour, after meeting the ogre at the funeral on Thursday morning, I will personally see to it that you never skip another meal again."

"No, you won't." I looked down as I spoke. "You'll be gone by winter."

"It doesn't have to be that way." He reached for my hand.

"I know. But your world doesn't sound too appealing—blood and death aside. You have a lot of rules. It'd be like living with your parents for eternity. Or like a cult!"

"It's to keep everyone in line. If vampires had free rein, the world would be overrun with them."

"So, is that what you do—maintain the law? Is that what the council is?"

"Yes. You might say I'm the judge and jury. I see to it that the law gets followed, and I punish those who choose not to."

"And you said you get paid for that?"

"Handsomely."

"Who pays you?"

"All vampires pay a percentage of their wages to the World Council. Might call it vampire tax. And that's how we fund the Set, the research facilities, and the lavish lifestyle of the council leaders."

"Wow. That really does sound like a cult."

"Ha!" he laughed. "I suppose it is a bit like that."

"Hm, now *that's* the organization *I* want to belong to for eternity."

"There are good things about it, Ara. We have a lot of fun. We're like a family."

"And… if I came with you, even though you have to return to duty, we'd still get to be together?"

"Yes. Like normal people."

"Normal?" I laughed.

"We could wake up beside each other every day."

And those few words almost sold me instantly. I drew a deep breath, biting my tongue before I could tell him to take me away and turn me. "And what about school? And my dreams of being a famous pianist?"

"School, you can still attend. But… as for fame…"

My stomach sunk. "Could I be famous without a face? You know, just sell my music?"

"No."

"Oh." I looked into my lap.

David moved closer and pulled both my hands toward his chest. "Tell me something, my love."

"Anything," I whispered, feeling my heart cry with the gravity in his tone.

"If I were to leave today and promise never to come back, and you knew you would die an old woman—that you would meet your mom and Harry at the Pearly Gates, but you would've missed a lifetime with me—is that something you could live with?" His hand tightened on mine. "Could you watch me leave, knowing you'll *never* see me again?"

The thought filled my mind like a roll of film from a sad movie or a Kleenex commercial. And it hurt. But while love could blot out all my morals, it didn't quell my desire to live, to die—to see Mom and Harry again at the end.

"Ara?" He slid his fingers along my chin and turned my face toward his. "You've got to stop making your life about Harry and Eleanor's deaths."

My heart jumped with the mention of my mother's name. It had been a long time since anyone said *that* name.

"Sweetheart, you don't have to live in my world, but if you decide to stay human, you do have to *live*. I care so much for you. And this sadness you keep inside will stop you from finding happiness," he said softly. "Your every thought, every path you take, is influenced by their death. It *has* to stop."

"I'm trying. But it still hurts so much sometimes that I just want to die. If you're gone, I'm not really sure what I actually have to live for."

"You will find something one day—when the grief is not so raw." He touched the back of his finger to my trembling lip. "I'm sorry, my love. When I decided to be a part of your life, I never meant for you to hurt like this."

"I'm okay." I sniffed, wiping my tears away. "It's just been a big couple of days and I have a lot to think about. And… who knows? Maybe I'll change my mind about becoming a vampire once I've had some time to think about it all."

He released a very long, very slow and shaky breath. "Do you really think you could change your mind?"

When I thought about it, no. I was certain I'd never go with him. But my heart never did agree with my mind, and if I asked it quietly, without my head hearing, it responded with a big fat and very loud 'Yes!'.

"God." He breathed the word out. "I know you won't say that aloud, but hearing you think it… I… You can't possibly know what I've been through these past few days, Ara. There is no way to describe the agony I've suffered worrying, even driving out here today, that you were going to tell me goodbye." He propped his elbow on his knee, burying his fingers absently in his hair. "If I had lost you… if you had told me that you could never love me for what I am, I would've died inside—enough that I would've spent eternity searching for a way to end my life."

"Please don't think like that?" I got to my knees in front of him. "Suicide isn't the only way to make things better, David. I don't ever want to hear you say that again."

"Oh, look who's talking." He laughed sardonically. "Do you really think I don't hear *your* thoughts, girl?"

My mouth fell open. He'd obviously been listening to me a lot more than I thought. "Those thoughts are private."

"Not anymore."

"How dare you!"

"How dare *you*." He rose to his knees as well, becoming taller than me again. "You are my soul mate, Ara. Your life belongs to me, and I will not let you have thoughts like that. Not ever. Clear?"

"No. Not clear. Those thoughts were…" I looked around for the right words. "Were images conjured up in a moment of extreme heartache and loneliness, David—fleeting thoughts—never intentions."

"So you will never act on them?" he asked, looking down at me.

"God, no. Never. But *you* would. That's the worst part about this.

You lecture me, but you"—I stabbed my fingertip into his chest —"you'd take the first express to Purgatory if it meant easing your own heartache."

"If I didn't have you, and it were possible for me to die,"—he held back a smile—"yes."

"No!" I panicked, seeing a future in my head for him that was bleak and sad if I didn't go with him. It wasn't fair. It put too much pressure on me to give up my human life just to save him from one lonely night of crying alone. "You don't get to say that. No matter what happens, no matter what life throws at you, you always have to keep going. *I* did." I pressed my palm to my chest. "It hurt me to keep going when Mom died, but what would *you* be doing if I just gave up when the pain got too much?"

"Well, it won't matter what happens to me in our case, because if you stay human, you will never know, will you?"

"No. You can get through it. You can live and find happiness again."

He shook his head decisively. "I won't be the same man if I lose you."

"No one stays the same, David. Everything you are is as a direct result of something that's affected you in your past, whether it was horrible *or* wonderful, and no one has the right to destroy themselves because they can't deal with the pain," I said. "You have to *learn* from it. It's not over—the good in your life—it's not over until you're dead."

A pompous smirk occupied his face. "Pretty passionate about this, aren't ya?"

"Don't mock me for feeling strongly on this, David. It's because I've been there. I almost crossed that bridge a few times."

He swallowed hard, becoming very still. And I realised then that he suddenly understood the depth of my earlier mention of suicide on a new level. "Be honest, Ara… will you come to that bridge again when I leave?"

"No," I lied. "And you won't, either. Look, I know you can't die, but you have to promise me that, if I decide to stay human, you'll keep going and that you'll try to make your life good again."

David wrapped his wrists around my lower back and drew me to his waist. "I am *nothing* without you. I won't promise to go on, because it would be a lie. When you die one day, when you no longer exist, I will give myself to the monster inside me, Ara. I won't survive," he said, then smiled. "You will just have to promise me forever."

"I want to. But today, I can only promise *my* forever—not yours."

He exhaled heavily, a mischievous grin igniting his eyes as he looked into mine. "I'll make you see reason. I can be very persuasive."

"And I can be very stubborn."

"And that, mon amour, is one of the things I love about you," he said with a husky laugh. "But please just don't be too stubborn. I only have until the end of fall—winter, at most. Then, I must go."

There was nothing more to say. A choice had to be made. We could have the summer together—it was our only promise. Everything else would just take more consideration, but it felt good to at least be resolved on one issue. I wasn't half as confused as I was this morning, and I was actually looking forward to learning more about David and his kind.

I got the sense then that this would be a fun summer, no matter how it ended.

18

Leaning my shoulder against the window frame, I watched the sun rise over the hills to the east—the same hills David ran to when he stole the blue rose. It'd been only four days since I was thrust into the world of the supernatural, but no clarity had come with time passing. No decision had come waking me in the middle of the night, telling me if I should go with him or remain human. I was starting to wonder if it would.

I looked down at my delicate white hands and the little blue veins running under the skin, rising slightly over the bones. *These* were the hands of a mythological vampire. Not David's. His were warmer than mine, and pink and strong, and they shook a little when he held them out in front of him for too long. I wondered how much of that was well-rehearsed human behavior, or really just the way his hands were, which made me wonder what he would have been like when he was human.

"Morning, beautiful." He sprung up on my windowsill.

I stumbled back, trying to keep my leaping heart in my chest. "David. You have a habit of popping up when I'm thinking about you."

"Do I?"

"Mm, but I think you already know that."

He grinned and placed a paper bag in my hand, kissing my cheek as he stepped into my room. "For the ogre."

"Ooh. Yum." The warm scent of vanilla and cinnamon wafted out in a moist puff from the bag. "Afraid I'll bite you if the ogre gets *tempestuous* again?"

"Don't joke, fangless wonder." He pointed at me as he flopped down on my bed. "Your bark is sharper than your bite, and it's a hell of a lot scarier than *me*."

I laughed, walking over to sit next to him. "You want some?"

He shook his head. "I've eaten already."

"Food or…"

"I missed you last night," he said softly, pushing the curtain of hair away from my face, totally ignoring my question.

"Oh, what? You mean you *didn't* sneak into my room?"

"Well, I came by to check on you, but I never stay if your dreams are peaceful."

"How would you know they're peaceful?"

"I can see them." He grinned and laid back on my pillow. "Last night, you were dreaming about Mike."

Dread spread through me, stiffening my arms.

"Ha! So you remember your dream?" He laughed.

I rolled my eyes. "It wasn't like that."

David scoffed, tucking his hands behind his head. "Looked pretty intense to me."

"You're reading into it wrong," I said, trying my hand at dream analysis. "I wasn't dreaming about *Mike* specifically—just the friendship I had with him that I now have with you. Only that, with *you,* I have so much more. His face was a representation of our *relationship*, but the body," I scoffed, motioning to David's fine chest, "was clearly you."

David nodded, with an edge of mockery in his smile. "Should I be worried? Do you have feelings for Mike that extend beyond friendship?"

"No," I said with a mouthful of pastry. "Don't be silly."

He sat up, dropping his elbows onto his thighs, his hands clasped between them. "You sure?"

I sighed. "Look, I do love Mike, but it's a different kind of love. Here." I took his hand and placed it against my cheek. "You told me you can see the past if I let you. See for yourself. Read my mind." I wasn't sure what he'd see when he looked, but Mike had rejected me; hurt me deeply when he did. I might love him, but that love could never be a threat to my relationship with David.

"Really?" His emerald-green eyes darted over my face. "You'll *let* me read your mind?"

"Mm-hm."

The energy in the room seemed to change then, and David exhaled. "Thank you, Ara."

"Did you see?"

"No." He pulled his hand down from my face. "If you say you don't love him that way then I believe you. I don't need to see it in your memories. Just don't break my heart, okay?"

"Okay. I promise. Now, can you stop hassling me and let me get ready for school? We're gonna be late." I popped the last bite of pastry into my mouth and kissed David on the lips. "Thanks for brekky, by the way. It was delicious."

"I imagine it must've tasted the way you would," he said thoughtfully.

"Well, *you'll* never know." I winked at him then practically skipped into my wardrobe. After I pulled my shirt off and snapped the clasp of my bra behind me, a warm, honest chuckle filled my room. I peeked around the corner.

"How old were you in this photo?" David asked without looking up from the small square sheet.

"Two or three, I think."

"The boy next to you is Mike?"

"Yup, and he'd just tipped a bucket of bathwater over my head."

"Yeah, I kinda gathered that." David nodded, smiling tenderly at the picture. "He picked on you a lot, didn't he?"

"Yup. Not much has changed, really."

David slipped the photo back into my nightstand where he'd been snooping. "You were a very cute baby."

"I know. So what about you?" I headed back to my wardrobe and shimmied into my jeans. "Do you have any baby pictures?"

"I..."

His pause of consideration turned into a long silence, so I stepped back into my room. "David?"

"There were some." He nodded, his gaze distant. "My father was never one for portraits. As Jason and I grew older and would sit for long enough, my uncle had a few done. There may still be one in existence."

"Didn't your mother ever have one done?" I asked, and David's eyes darkened instantly. I covered my mouth with both hands. "I'm sorry—that just slipped out. I forgot she passed away."

"No, Ara, it's fine. Please"—he offered his hand—"don't be sorry."

"But I am. I feel really bad. I should've remembered that." I slumped down on the bed beside him, sucking my gut in a little since I had no shirt to cover it.

"Make you a deal?" He ran his fingertip over my bra strap. "You can say whatever you want to me if you do it dressed like this."

I laughed. "Should I go put on a shirt?"

"Please don't." He smiled.

"Will you tell me about her—your mother?"

His gaze drifted to distant places. "I mentioned once that she died when I was a baby?"

"Yes. Childbirth?"

"Yes."

I clicked my tongue. "Aw, David."

He shook his head. "It was common for those times, especially with Jason and I being a multiple birth. She simply gave birth then fell asleep—never woke up again."

"Did she ever get to see you?"

"She named me before she died, since I was the firstborn. Jason came shortly after, but she simply had nothing left to fight with. Before the midwife even cut the cord, she was gone."

"So, did your father ever talk about her?"

He shook his head. "I'm told she was beautiful and loved by many. But my aunt was the only woman I ever considered my mother."

"Well… what happened to her?"

David's smile tightened. "Another time, my love."

"Okay." I stood up. "Another time then."

He stood too, taking my hand. "Thank you."

"What for?"

"For dropping the subject without the usual fight."

"Well, thank you for letting me into your past."

"Anytime." He nodded, but his tone suggested this might be the last.

School could not have been more boring this week. With David in only three of my classes per day, it made the rest of them drag on. But I did find one positive to his vampirism: we'd definitely spent more time together. We were inseparable at school, and he spent every night in my room until, kissing me sweetly, he'd say "Goodnight, my love," then leave through my window before I could convince him to go further than kissing.

The downside to all the extra time together was that I really *felt* it when we were apart. I really missed him.

In History class, I at least had Emily to keep me distracted. Well, when she wasn't turning around to giggle at her new crush, that is.

"So… you and David seem to be okay now?" she whispered.

I nodded. "Yeah. We're happy." He's a vampire, but we're happy.

"Oh, and hey, I never got to thank you for hooking me up with Spence." She smiled, tilting her head into her shoulder.

"Yeah, no worries. Did he ask you out on a real date yet?"

"Yep. And guess what?"

"What?" I said, grinning in exaggeration of her expression.

"He asked me to the Fall Masquerade."

And there was the squeak. One of the things I loved about Emily was the way she could display excitement so easily. She was just so…

normal. "Awesome. Got a dress yet?" My enthusiasm needed some practice, though.

"I'm going shopping with my mom tonight."

"Cool. Yeah, I'm not looking forward to being dragged from shop to shop with Vicki and forced to try on everything with fluff." I laughed, but Emily frowned at me.

"Who's Vicki?"

"Um, she's my stepmom."

"Oh, right. Duh." She slapped her brow. "So, you don't like her? I mean, 'cause you call her Vicki not Mom?"

"Yeah, um—old habit, I guess." I shrugged and turned around to talk to Spencer. "So, Spence, you gonna save me a dance at the ball?"

His cheeks turned bright pink. "Ah, yeah. If that's okay with Emily."

"Of course it is. As long as Ara doesn't mind if I dance with David."

"Cool with me," I lied, practically digging my nails through my own palm.

"You three!" Dad barked from the front of the class.

Everyone turned and looked at us. I shrunk to about the size of a quarter. Conversation: over.

When the bell rang at the end of class, everyone broke formation and dispersed quickly.

"Ara, come up and see me before you leave, please," Dad said, not looking at me.

"Yikes. That sounded like an order," I said to Em.

"Sorry, Ara." Her shoulders lifted a little. "Will you be in trouble?"

"Em, don't worry about it. He's my dad. What's the worst he can do? Ground me?"

"Yes. That's worse than he can do to me."

I laughed, slinging my bag over my shoulder as I walked away and stepped up in front of Dad's desk. "Sorry for talking in class, Mr. Thompson. It won't happen again."

"Ara." He exhaled, leaning back in his chair. "I appreciate that you've had a hard time adjusting to a new school and, don't get me wrong, I'm very happy you've made new friends, but there's a time for work and a time for play. I don't want to catch you gossiping in class again or I will move you to Mr. Adams' class. Do I make myself clear?"

I forced back a grin. David was in Mr. Adams' class. I'd *love* it if he moved me. "Sorry, Dad. It won't happen again." Or maybe it would—just a bit.

"Good. Now, how's that mythology paper coming along?"

"Uh. Great. I'm doing mine on vampires." I just decided.

Dad raised one brow. "Is that inspired by last week's intriguing lecture on Lilith?"

"Actually, it is." And the fact that my boyfriend just happened to know *that* history firsthand. "But, if my essay concludes that vampires are real, are you and Vicki gonna have me committed?"

Dad laughed once. "Aw, honey. We'd never do that. Even if you decide *I'm* a vampire and try to stake me through the heart." His grin softened as he shook his head. "I love you, okay. I know we've been a little watchful of you lately, but it's because we care about you."

"We?"

"Ara, you know Vicki cares for you."

I scoffed unintentionally loud.

"She's just trying to give you space," he said. "She's afraid you'll accuse her of trying to replace your mom."

I softened a little. I guess that would be pretty scary for her. "Okay, Dad. I'll try—with Vicki. It's hard, you know. I'm just afraid to let her in, that's all."

His stern expression melted and he stood up. Then, even with his next class filling the room behind us, he walked all the way around his desk and wrapped his arms around me—really tightly. I patted his back, dreading the thought of everyone watching.

"Um, Dad. Sorta need to breathe here."

The old man pulled back and held me at arm's length. "I love ya, honey. Now get to class, you're late."

I waved and threaded my other arm through my backpack, making haste for the exit—with thirty pairs of eyes burning into my spine.

WARM WATER SPLASHED OVER MY WRISTS, SPRAYING UP IN MY face a little. I readjusted the faucet and rubbed my hands together under the soft flow of water, studying my face in the mirror. The last time I looked at myself in this mirror, I felt completely alone, isolated, unsure of anything. But so much had changed since my first day of school, and even my reflection somehow looked different.

I smiled, drawing my hands away from the basin and dried them on my jeans as the door opened and two cackling girls came in with the steady breeze.

"Oh, hey new girl," said Gypsy aka The Short Girl Summer Hangs Around.

"Hi." I shouldered my schoolbag. "Did you guys come in here to bitch about somebody else today, or am I on the hotlist?"

"Actually, you are on the hotlist." She leaned on the counter, folding her arms. "Rumor has it you and *David Knight* are an item."

"Rumor would be correct—this time." I folded my arms and leaned beside her.

"You know there's only one reason that boy dates girls, and it's *not* love," Summer said, propping her hand on her hip.

I shrugged. "He loves me."

"Sure he does." Summer's eyes flicked to Gypsy. "He says that to every girl."

"I'm sure he does." I stood up from my lean. "But I bet he's never said it to you."

Her head bopped from side-to-side in the hollow of her shoulders. "What if he has?"

"Nah, I doubt that." I shook my head, gazing down my nose at her as I passed. "You're a little out of his league. He only likes us ugly girls."

Her mouth fell open, allowing for a high-pitched huff. "You bitch."

"Uh, Summer. I think that was a compliment," Gypsy said, looking a little confused. "I think she just said you're pretty."

"Have a nice lunch," I called over my shoulder as I stepped out of the stinky toilet block, leaving them and their gossip where it belonged.

"Ara?"

The white glare of the open corridor framed the vampire's silhouette, making him look menacing. "David, I thought we were meeting in the auditorium for lunch."

He unhitched himself from the railing. "We are, but I..."

"You?" I prompted.

"You were late, so I went looking for you. Then I saw Summer and Gypsy, and..."

"Aw." I slid my hands inside his denim jacket and snuggled against his chest. "You were worried about me."

"I'm sorry." He kissed the crown of my head. "I know you can take care of yourself, but I just didn't want them to make you cry again."

"Aw, David." I hugged him tighter, breathing deep his vibrant, heart-tingling scent—all sugary and mouth-watering. "You're so sweet."

"Mr. Knight!" A booming voice shocked my thoughts from inappropriate paths. "Not on school grounds."

"Certainly, Mr. Rogers. Won't happen again." David held me out from his chest.

I kept my face down until Mr. Rogers left. "Didn't you see him coming?"

"Yes, but what was I supposed to do?"

"Warn me."

He smiled his secret smile. "Getting sprung showing affection on school campus is not a good enough reason to step away when you've got your arms around me like that."

"Maybe not for you, but he might tell my dad."

"He won't." David started walking—without touching me. "He was a boy once himself. He understands."

"So does my dad. Except when it comes to me."

"Okay, we won't touch at school then. Will that make you happy?"

"No. Just keep watch next time. What good is a vampire boyfriend if he can't use his abilities to keep you outta trouble?"

"Oh, I don't know, I must be good for something." He grinned widely, opening the door for me.

"Well, you're a good kisser, but that's the human in you, not the vampire."

"That's because the vampire me hasn't kissed you yet."

"Ooh, scary," I joked, but was suddenly intrigued and a bit tingly. "Well, maybe you should let him out for a while then."

David leaned closer as we passed a group of students. "Meet me under the stage, and I'll show him to you."

"Don't tempt me." Again, I played it like I was joking, but I actually wanted to see what the big deal was about this so-called scary side of his.

The second toll of the lunch bell rang loudly as David went to speak. He swallowed his sentence, remaining quiet then until we reached the auditorium.

"After you," he said, opening the door.

"Thank you, kind sir." I curtsied, making him laugh. I loved making him laugh.

"Hey, guys." Ryan stood up and waved from the front of the room.

"Ryan. Emily." David nodded.

"How's rehearsal going?" I asked, stashing my schoolbag next to the group of desks.

"Eh." Ryan shrugged. "Haven't started. We've mostly been making paper airplanes and seeing who can hit the lighting rig."

"Sounds productive." I looked at Emily, who rolled her eyes and leaned on her hand.

"This might be a little cold," David said, sliding a tray of food in front of me, then flashed a wildly mischievous grin. "I made it to the cafeteria line first."

"Well"—I sat down between him and Emily, dipping my fingertip into the lukewarm nachos—"you do run really fast."

"So, Ara, did you get totally busted by your dad?" Alana asked.

"Uh, not really. Why do you ask?"

"I was in the next class when you were talking to him at his desk," she said. "Em said it was 'cause you were all talking during a lecture."

My brows rose. That had to be the most I'd ever heard that girl say. "Um. No, he just wanted to find out how my mythology paper was coming along."

"I'm doing mine on fairies," Alana said in a dreamy tone. "I love fairies."

"Yeah, I'm doing mine on trolls," Ryan added. "What about you, Dave?"

David looked up from thumbing his phone, and the words he was holding back washed across his face: he hated being called "Dave", but he'd never say it. I smiled sympathetically at him.

"I'm uh… I'm actually in Mr. Adams' class. We're doing a different topic this semester," he said.

"Yeah, me too," another kid added from the other end of our little rectangle of friends.

While the conversation continued, I excluded myself, watching David focus intently on his phone, wondering what he was doing.

He grinned without looking up, then inched his body closer so our shoulders touched and his screen sat between us. "I'm tweeting."

"Really?" I whispered, reading the reply he'd sent to an EricDelaR. "I didn't know *your kind* used social media."

He laughed once and slipped the phone into his pocket. "How narrow-minded of you."

It amazed me how much more human he was around everyone from school and how, now I knew what he was, I could see right through his poorly executed disguise.

"What about you, Ara?"

I looked up like I'd been sprung talking in class.

"What're you doing yours on?" Emily finished.

"My what?"

"Honestly, Ara." Emily shook her head. "Do you *ever* pay attention?" I stared blankly at her; she smiled and said, "Your mythology paper. What are you doing yours on?"

"Oh, um… vampires."

David coughed beside me and shot up out of his chair, wiping soda off his jeans. "Damn it!"

"You all right, man?" Ryan frowned.

"Uh—" He stood up straight, holding a now oddly shaped cup out from his body, glancing over the wide stares of all the other kids at our table. "Yeah. Swallowed the wrong way."

Emily's cheek tightened on one side, and the others, not thinking anything of David's strange reaction, went back to their food and conversation.

"David?" I whispered, mostly talking through my teeth. "What's wrong?"

"Can we talk?" he asked, his eyes widening for a second. "Alone."

"Sure." I stood up. "Where?"

He jerked his head in the direction of the stage. "We'll be back," he said to everyone else.

"Okay, don't be too long," Emily said, "I'm gonna kick everyone's butts soon and get this rehearsal into swing."

"Of course." David nodded, though it looked more like a bow. Then he took my hand and led me away.

Is this just an elaborate escape plan to get me in private? I asked.

"No," David said.

Hmph!

19

The heavy black door creaked as I pushed it open. David ducked under the low frame, closing us into the musty darkness, thick with the smell of latex and old books.

"Ara, you can't do your paper on vam—"

I cut his words off with my lips, flinging my arms around his neck. He tried to protest, laughing within the kiss, but after a yielding breath, slid his long fingers up the sides of my face, finally letting me have my own way.

"Show me the vampire," I whispered into the hollow of his mouth.

He pulled away softly. "Not here."

"Yes." I grinned. "Here."

"What if I scare you?"

"Then we're in a perfect place for me to try really hard not to scream."

He clicked his tongue, shaking his head. "Do you even understand what the vampire is?"

"A less-guarded side of you?"

"Yes. Very much so. And he may be inclined to bite you or, in the very *least*, be rough with you. Perhaps even do things I might regret after."

That only made me want it more. I knew deep down inside that David would never actually hurt me. So the idea of him as a primal being, with all his emotional guards down—just David: raw, instinctual, completely exposed David—made me hot in places I'd never been hot before.

I jumped up and wrapped my legs around his waist, forcing his lips open with mine.

"Ara, please," he groaned loudly, but it only took a second for him to give in to my will. He tucked his hands beneath my butt to hold me up, and finally took control of the kiss. "You know, you really shouldn't wear dresses to school."

"Take it off me then."

"Ha!" His breath burst from his lips in a cool gust. "Don't say things like that. I haven't eaten enough for this kind of misbehavior, my love."

"When did you last eat?"

"Monday morning—right before I brought you the pastry."

"That's two days. You should be fine."

"Ara." He set me down on the ground. "This isn't a game."

"Who says I'm playing?"

"Ara, be sensible."

I chewed the tip of my finger for a second, attempting control, but it was just too much—his skin, his warmth, my breath coming back off his chest. I slid my fingers into the neckline of his jacket and pushed it away from his shoulders.

"You don't know how to take no for an answer, do you?" he said, casting the jacket across the room.

"You never said no," I teased, moving closer. "So, you gonna show me this vampire, or what?"

"Why, Ara?" He took a small step back. "What's with the sudden change of heart?"

"It's not sudden—not for me. I just… I like you." I walked forward and closed my fingers together behind his neck. "And now that I've come to terms with this vampire thing, I wanna take things to next level."

"Next level?" he said through a smile.

"Yeah. I guess I'm ready to know *all* of you now."

"No matter what, even if it scares you again?"

"I don't know if it would, David. I… can't you tell?" I traced a loving gaze over his jaw and along his stubbly chin, meeting his eyes again. "I trust you."

He took a breath and cast a long glance to the darkest corner of the closet. "That's a pretty convincing argument, I must admit."

I grinned at him. "So you'll do it? You'll bite me?"

"Even if I show you the vampire, Ara, I can't actually bite you."

"Why?"

"Because if my fangs break your skin, you'll be injected with venom."

"So?"

"So, if you're injected with venom, you'll… it's just a bad idea."

"Oh." We stared into each other, both of us clearly thinking it all through, and in the dim light of the room, his eyes almost looked completely black, like dark desires overshadowing sensibility.

He unlatched my hands from around his neck. "We should get back out to rehearsal."

"Wait." I grabbed his sleeve. "What if… I mean, when humans bite playfully, we don't actually break the skin." I looked at his neck. "Can't you do it like that?"

He frowned, thoughtful. "I don't know. I've never done anything like this with a human before."

"Well… here." I leaned closer. "Let me show you how it's done."

Before he could stop me, I pushed his jaw to one side, rising onto my toes as my teeth glided over his flesh, coming closed again with a mouthful of David between them. Under the moisture of my tongue, his sweet scent became his flavor, the lovely orange-chocolate replacing the gritty, salty taste I'd expected. I bit down harder then, catching the tendon in his neck, feeling his jaw stiffen, his arms tense, his ear move away from my cheek as he opened himself up to me. And I loved it.

"Ara, you have the sweetest little bite." He cupped his hands loosely around my face, but they went tight suddenly and he pushed me away. "Ouch!"

"What's wrong?" I wiped my mouth dry with the back of my arm. "Did I hurt you?"

"Yes, you little leech." He cupped his hand over the bite then looked at it. "I may not have a heartbeat, but I still feel pain."

"You're bruising." I squinted through the dull light to see his neck.

"I know. I can feel that."

"I'm sorry."

"Are you kidding me?" He laughed, bending to scoop me up and wrap my legs around him. "That felt amazing. It hurt, but *damn* it was hard to control myself."

"Control yourself?"

"Yes." He looked down to where the apex of my thighs met his stomach. "I wanted to do… *things* to you."

"What kinds of… things?"

My hopes ignited when he reached up slowly and slipped the shoestring strap of my dress down my shoulder. "Very bad things."

"Show me, then?" I closed my eyes and tilted my chin up—exposing my throat. "I'm not scared."

"I know," he said. "Which is a very big turn-on."

I giggled.

"Urgh." He rolled his head back. "Don't do that adorable giggle. You've no idea how crazy it makes me."

I did it again, laughing louder when his upper lip and nose pressed into the sensitive hollow of skin between my collarbones, the stubble on his chin scratching my chest. "That tickles."

He grazed his teeth playfully along my flesh. They felt sharp, like the edge of a blade. I knew the control he would've used to stop them cutting, but for some reason a deep part of me, a part that rose too close to the surface, really didn't care if he cut me. I wanted to be cut by him.

"David?"

"Yes."

"Is it normal for me to think this way?"

He laughed into my skin, kissing but not biting. "Yes. It's my predatory lure making you think that way."

"Oh." Well that was a relief. "But you won't, right—you won't cut me?"

"No. I won't. But I am going to feel your flesh against my teeth." He turned us to the side and placed me on the table, stepping in closer until his hips once again rested between my thighs. "Do not scream," he warned. "It will only excite the monster."

"Is that not a good idea?"

His hands flew up and tangled in my hair, his thumbs on my cheeks, holding my face in front of his. "If you do… you will die."

I held my breath, lost in the intensity of his penetrating gaze. But something inside told me not to worry. Maybe it was the way he held me, his hands so tight around my face, or maybe it was the concern in his own eyes that made me sure he would never let himself destroy me.

My jaw jutted forward a little, my bottom lip catching his in a delicate kiss—a wordless reassurance. He kissed back, his lips moist, cold like the lips of a person who just ate ice. And as it intensified—as his hands slipped beneath my dress again, finding my hips—I grinned playfully, resting back on my hands.

Undress me, I thought.

"Jesus Christ, Ara." He folded over a little, resting his breathless lips against my shoulder. "You don't know how close you are to losing your innocence right now."

"Maybe I'm ready for it." I lifted my dress a little.

David leaned back, looking down at my floral-print undies. "To lose your virginity in a closet space?"

I parted my legs a little more, inviting his touch to where his eyes and thoughts lingered. "Yes."

His heavy breath stopped, his hand slowly reaching toward my upper thigh. Then he grabbed it in a firm palm, letting his thumb fall against my delicates. "You shouldn't play games like this with a dangerous predator."

"A dangerous predator shouldn't bring young girls into dark spaces —alone."

"It wouldn't be a problem if that girl would stop showing the vampire parts that he's wanted to see for the longest time." He lowered my dress and smoothed it over my legs.

"Did you ever think maybe she's wanted to *show* him for the longest time?"

"What is wrong with you?" he said with a smile. "Why do you say things like that? I want to do any number of unsavory things to you right now, including kill you. Can you comprehend that?"

"That's what makes this so romantic. I know you won't, even though you want to."

He shook his head, trying to wipe off a smile with a frown. "Only *you* could think something like that is romantic."

"David." I ran my fingers through his soft hair and rested them behind his neck. "You're a vampire. Don't even pretend you don't think it's romantic."

A breathy laugh parted his lips. "I really love you, Ara. You are just so perfect for me."

I rolled my head to the other side, lengthening my neck. "Good. Then show me what it feels like to be under the spell of the vampire."

"I—" His eyes met mine with hesitation. "I'm afraid I'll enjoy it."

"Isn't that a good thing?"

"No. I mean…" He looked at my neck, pressing his thumb to the pulse. "You know my teeth are sharper than yours. Even if I don't use my fangs, chances are I'll cut you."

"You won't." I smiled. "I know you can control yourself when it comes to me."

"Perhaps, but… I've wanted this for too long."

"Wanted what? To cut me?"

"Yes. Eat you, feel your blood pulse under my teeth, see the life leave your eyes, breath leave your lips."

I let out an indignant huff. "How rude."

"I know." He laughed timidly. "It's a vampire thing, and… I'm afraid I might enjoy hurting you, Ara. If we do this and the vampire in me takes control, there will be no going back."

"As in… you'll kill me?"

"Perhaps. Or I will not be able to stop thinking about killing you—hurting you—even after the day is done and we've parted ways."

I thought about that for a second, feeling a mischievous smile creep its way into the corners of my eyes. "Then it'll be a true test of our love, won't it?"

"No," he said, sweeping my hair away from my shoulder. "It will be a test of my willpower." And before I could respond, his teeth started my heart, coming closed tightly around my flesh. I squirmed, a cold shiver running down my spine while hot blood rushed up under the grip of his bite. Everything in me from my toes to my shoulders tensed, the tendon in my neck going rigid like wet rope, and all the nerves under it screamed out in agony while my heart pleaded for more. He kept his fangs away, but every now and then they brushed against me like the pointed tip of a blade.

"Bite me harder, David." I grabbed his arms, digging my nails in, half pushing him away, half pulling him closer. I felt his body go colder, like the heat of desire pushed his hunger deeper, making him icy between my legs. He became more ferocious as he lost himself to the bite, his hands searching wildly, travelling under my dress and commanding my craving skin to crawl into his touch.

"David?" I squeaked as he bit down harder, pressing me against the chairs stacked on the table. "David, it's hurting a bit."

"Shh." He shoved the chairs off with a quick push and rolled me onto my back as they crashed noisily to the floor. The people outside laughed raucously, their familiar, human sounds setting my heart on fire.

"David. Stop."

My neck burned where he pulled away for a moment, but he didn't stop; he moved to the other side and wrapped his lips hard around my skin as I pushed against him. I felt the scrape of his fangs, sharp, as if he'd cut through, stinging like a thousand hot little needles under my skin.

"David. It's hurting."

His cold hands went up my dress again, slipping my underwear past my hip on one side as he dragged me closer, thrusting his pelvis into mine. And though I wanted him to—wanted him to make love to me right here on the table—I also wanted him to kill me. I could see it all, as if his intentions became my thoughts. But I didn't want to die. And I wasn't truly ready for sex.

"David!" I burst into tears. "Please don't."

"Don't what?" He looked down at me, confused.

I shoved him away and rolled up to stand, darting across the room to the safety of the wall. "Why did you do that?"

"Do what?" He appeared in front of me, his eyes wide and black. "Do what, Ara?"

"Why didn't you stop?"

"Ara, I'm sorry." He reached for me but I jerked away. "I didn't realize you were frightened."

"I asked you to stop," I cried. "That's a pretty clear indication, don't you think?"

"Yes. But, I—" He rubbed his brow. "I didn't hear you. I only stopped because I tasted your tears."

"What?"

"I was drawn in completely. Compelled by the scent of adrenaline —the fear—it makes the hunger *unbearable*."

"But…" I cupped my hand to the swelling on my neck. He hadn't broken through. "You didn't bite me?"

"Ara?" He frowned as if the suggestion insulted him. "I would never do that. I always had control over that. I just"—he stuffed his hands in his pockets—"I couldn't control the vampire."

"Isn't it the same? I mean, the bite *is* the vampire?"

"No. The bite is the hunger. The lust *before* is the vampire—it's what made you want me to bite you in the first place."

"Oh." I touched my collarbone. "So, you wouldn't have bitten me?"

In one long stride he closed the gap and cradled my face in his hands. "Not in a million years."

"Then, why couldn't you hear me?"

He closed his eyes. "I can hear the resonance of your voice in my head *now*, but I was so lost in your touch I could think of nothing but…"

"But what?"

He shook his head. "It doesn't matter. I wouldn't have done it, anyway. Not with you."

"Not with *me*? What do you mean?" I folded my arms as he walked away. "What wouldn't you have done with me?"

Ignoring my question, he leaned against the table and reached out his hand.

I hesitantly took it.

"I'm sorry I scared you, my love. But have no doubt that my lips, my teeth, or my touch would not have done anything you didn't want me to." He held back a cheeky grin. "Except maybe tear your clothes off."

I smiled, relenting.

He pulled me into his chest, and the cool of his skin through the thin fabric of his shirt surprised me. "From now on, if I'm in that state, use your thoughts to reach me. It's clearer."

I nodded against him.

"I'm so, *so* sorry I scared you." He exhaled, smoothing his hand over my hair.

"I'm okay." I rolled my face upward to look at him. "Well, now I know for certain you wouldn't have bitten me, I'm okay."

"Aw…" David touched my neck. "Look what I've done to you."

"It stings."

"You're bruising badly."

"You were pretty rough." I smiled, pressing my palm to the mark.

"I won't do that to you again. Ever." He looked up from the bruising, the promise of his words filling out the green in his eyes again.

"What if I want you to?"

His jaw tightened, but his smile remained soft. "No. Not ever again."

"But, I liked it." I pulled my hand down from my neck and gasped, seeing a red smear of blood.

"I know." He caught my wrist, holding it away from him. "I was hoping you wouldn't notice that."

"What… I mean… how…? Did you *cut* me?"

"No. It's just from the sucking." One corner of his lip quirked upward. "I drew your skin a little too… eagerly."

"Can't you smell it—the blood?" I held my hand up to him.

"Yes."

"Didn't you taste it?"

He shook his head. "It broke through as I pulled away. I was trying to ignore it."

"Does it make you want to bite me?"

"It makes me want to *taste* you—to see if you taste the way you smell."

Holding my hand near my nose, I sniffed. "I can't smell anything."

"That's because you're not a vampire."

"Here." I held my hand up in front of his lips. "Taste it."

"Ara, don't!"

"David?" I frowned at the empty space in front of me, then spun around a few times until my eyes found him leaning against a stack of chairs across the room. "What's wrong?"

He inched away from me as I approached. "I can't do that. One taste could be enough to make me lose control right now."

My nose crinkled, and I looked down at the bloody smudge on my hand then pressed my tongue to it. *Erk!* "Gross. How can you drink this stuff? I taste like a coin."

David laughed softly. "You silly girl, of course you won't like it."

"Well, how do you know you would?"

With a deep, heavy sigh, he reached across and wiped his thumb over the bruise.

"David, what are you doing?"

"Tasting you." His shoulders lifted once, dropping as he popped his thumb in his mouth and closed his eyes.

"David?" I said in a shaky voice, taking one step back.

His eyes shot open and I jumped inside. "Just like I thought," he said sweetly. "Vanilla and honey. Kinda like a cupcake."

"Are you…" I took another step away. "Are you okay?"

"Actually?" His lips turned down as thought washed across his face. "I'm fine. No sudden urge to kill you."

"Really?"

"Strangely, the vampire is screaming for me to suck the life out of you"—he rolled his head to one side and studied me quizzically—"but the human me wants to kiss you and tell you how much I love you."

"Well, I always have liked the human you." I wrapped myself in his arms.

"Then the human me you shall have."

"But, David?"

"Yes," he said distractedly, kissing my hairline.

"You were scary as a vampire, but only because I didn't know what you were capable of. But now I've seen it,"—I smiled at the memory of him losing control—"I *liked* it."

"You're not serious, are you?" He held me out from him by my shoulders. "Ara, are you joking? Please, because I can't take that kind of a joke."

I frowned, shaking my head. "Why would I joke about that?"

David's eyes closed tightly. "You don't know what that means to me."

"Is that... a good thing?"

"It's amazing, that's what it is. You"—he dropped a quick kiss on my lips—"are amazing. Do you have any idea how precious you are to me? I never knew such a creature could exist, and now I've found you..." A wave of sorrow softened his eyes. "I have *no* idea how I'm going to let you go."

"Same way you stopped yourself from biting me, I guess," I said, pulling his hand away from my face.

He nodded once. "This is a first for me, you know. I've never had to do that before—to control myself. It took everything in me not to rip your throat open and drink your blood, and even more to stop enticing you."

"Enticing?" I pouted in thought. "Is that what made me want to... you know, die?"

"Yes." He laughed. "It's how we kill. We seduce you into trusting us."

I wondered if that was what I felt that day by the lake—the gravitational pull. "So, you seduce men too?"

"No. I've never seduced a man. I use an attack kill for them. It's more brutal, more painful for the human, but I can't bear the thought of seducing and killing girls since I found you."

"Why?"

"Because I see your face and think how I would feel if that was you." He looked up as, above us, the loud thunder of footsteps sent vibrations through the walls. "We better get back out there. Lunch will be over soon."

"Okay." I exhaled. "But what will we tell everyone? They all saw us walk in here. I don't even wanna imagine what they'll think."

"Ara, what do you *think* they will think? We're teenagers. Let them think what they want. They'll never guess the truth."

"Well, at least that part's true." No one would guess that I led a vampire under the stage and let him bite me. Or that I bit *him*. It didn't matter what they thought, anyway. I was so damn hungry that if I didn't go eat, *David* would become the next victim of the ogre. Then, he wouldn't need to worry about me becoming a people-eater, because he'd be in my stomach.

David shook his head, laughing softly. "I can think of a few ways I could be in your stomach, Ara, without being eaten. Of course, you'd still have to put a part of me in your mouth."

My lips gaped, a giant huff expelling between them.

His eyes widened. "I didn't mean it that way. I meant blood—drinking my blood." He held his wrist up.

I giggled into my hand.

"I'm so sorry, Ara. That came out sounding… incredibly wrong."

"Yes, but it was also funny to watch you react that way."

He lowered his head and shook it, a sharp intake of air whistling through his teeth.

"I love you, David," I said, still laughing.

"Come on." He reached for my hand. "Shall we head back out and face the music?"

"Yes." The reality simmered over me then and I shook my head at myself. "I can't believe I just provoked a vampire into biting me." Therapy, anyone?

David cleared his throat. "You said it first."

"Hey!" I propped my hands on my hips. "I'll give *you* therapy in a minute, if you don't stop reading my mind."

He chuckled, wandering across the room to grab his jacket. I loved it when he laughed. It made him seem so normal—so human.

"Except there is *nothing* human about what we just did," he joked.

"Stay out of my mind!" I headed for the door in a stormy huff.

"Wait." He grabbed my arm and held up his jacket. "You might want to put this on."

I frowned at him. He pointed to my neck. If that bite looked as bad as it burned, people would think David did something really horrible to me.

"I did." He held his jacket out, pulled it closed around my chest once my arms were in, and kissed my brow.

"What about you? I bit you."

"I'll be healed by the time I cross the room. But you"—he laughed, running his finger over my bruise again—"you may take a little longer."

"How long?"

"If you heal fast, a week. Maybe. If not… a month."

Crud! "If Dad sees it, he'll freak."

"Ara, he'll freak if word gets back to him that we were even in this closet—alone."

Damn. Didn't think of that. I wrapped my hand over the bite. The rough denim of David's jacket rubbed against it, making it sting more, but since he'd been wearing the coat all day, the strong smell of him was all over me like a warm breath, so I didn't mind one bit.

"Oh, and one more thing." He grabbed my arm again. "The history paper?"

"What about it?"

He kissed my temple quickly. "Don't do vampires."

"Why?"

"Just don't."

"You never give me a reason."

"I don't have to. You should just trust me."

"No way. What do you think this is, the eighteen hundreds?"

"No. I think you are a human, and I'm a vampire, and I have my reasons." He turned away with a sly smile, and the room filled with light as he opened the door, severing any further discussion.

Hmph! I'm still doing vampires. You can't stop me.

He leaned closer and muttered, "Try me."

A group of David's friends—only at rehearsal for their stupid comedy skit—burst into a Mexican wave as we walked out, sending me spinning back toward the closet.

David grabbed me by the coat. "Keep walking, Ara."

"Hey, Dave? Man, did you miss?" One of the gorillas pointed to the soda spill on David's jeans.

"Funny. Real funny." David nodded and took my hand.

"Now I wish you *had* eaten me in there," I said.

He laughed as we wandered back to our table. "Don't worry about it. No one will pass any further comment on it. I'll *personally* see to that."

"Okay."

"Okay." He squeezed my hand.

"Oh, hey, you're back." Emily smiled casually.

"Do I need to ask what *you two* were up to in there?" Ryan's brows rose and fell a few times.

"We were just talking," David said casually, and pushed my chair in for me as I sat down.

"Right, 'cause everyone goes to the make-out room to 'talk'," Spencer said.

"As a matter of fact, that's exactly why we were in there," David said, then winked at me. "I would never be so inappropriate as to display my affections for the girl I love in a closet space."

Everyone looked into their laps. Conversation: over.

"So… subject change anyone?" Emily chimed in, motioning around the table. "The memorial concert? The whole reason we're here?"

"Let's start the rehearsal then." I grinned, biting into my nachos, but they tasted boring in comparison to David.

From the corner of my eye, I saw him grin, and while conversations went on around us, David reached into my lap and took my hand, winding his leg under my ankle. And it felt nice—like the way things should be; sitting at lunch with friends, talking about normal things, concealing the burning desire to run away with the guy you love and never let him go.

THURSDAY PASSED WITH A RHYTHMIC PACE: NOTE-PASSING WITH David when we were in the same classes—only I didn't need to pass them to him, since he just read my mind; talking with Emily in History, trying to get kicked into Mr. Adams' class, and lunch times with my group of friends in the auditorium. When the day ended, I said my goodbyes and wandered across the field toward my dad's house, stealing the quiet for my own *private* thoughts—for once.

The sun warmed my upturned face and the wind caressed the crevices around my nose and under my chin. I closed my eyes, entrusting my blind steps to the safety of the widespread field of grass as I bounced along, smiling to myself for no other reason than that I was happy.

"Haven't you learned not to walk with your eyes closed?"

So much for private thoughts. "Well, I'm happy. If you want me to get across the road safely, you'll just have to walk me home." I opened my eyes to look at David. He looked so normal with a schoolbag on his back—just a boy, just as everyone else saw him. His dark side was a secret. No one could ever imagine he was a vampire, and no one would ever know. Except me.

"So, I was thinking?" He glided along at my pace, with his hands behind his back and that cheeky grin slipping into place.

"Mm. I'm listening."

"I want to buy you a dress for the Masquerade."

"A dress? Why?"

We stopped for a second, and David took my hands. "This will be your first real ball. I want you to feel like a queen. And"—he turned and started walking again, smiling—"I won't take no for an answer."

"But… Vicki?" I ran after him. "She wants to take me shopping."

"And she can." He spun around and walked backward. "But when you find the right dress, I want to pay for it."

"David, I can't—"

"Ara." He pressed a finger to my lips, and it might have been insulting if it weren't so obvious he was being playful. "I'll have no more of this. Just accept it as a token of my affection for you."

David was sweet, but he didn't know the old me—the girl before the accident—because if he did, he would never have offered to spend money on me. And labeling it a 'token of his affection' made it *really* hard to decline. I wasn't sure how to tell him now that I hated people buying me things, so I didn't say anything at all.

SAM'S SCHOOLBOOKS ENGULFED THE DINING TABLE, LEAVING ONE space for me to do my homework: the kitchen counter. I wilted over my books, munching an apple, spinning my hips from side-to-side on the swishy stool. I'd deliberately moved my schoolbag off the seat beside me, hoping David would sit there to either help me with my homework or just plain old be close to me, but he went and sat next to my pesky brother instead, and helped *him*. Except, he wasn't helping him with his math, he was doing it for him.

"David, will you stay for dinner tonight?" Vicki asked, casually chopping away at vegetables.

David looked up from the page. "That'd be great, Mrs. Thompson. If Ara doesn't mind."

A giant invisible question mark formed above my head. *Why would I mind, dummy? Unless you plan to eat* us *for dinner.*

He smirked.

"Great," Vicki beamed, without needing my answer. "It's nothing special. Although, I am making apple pie for dessert."

My vampire flashed the most incredibly charming smile and said, "Apple pie just happens to be my favorite."

"Oh, really?" Vicki's whole face lit up. "That's great then."

I groaned quietly, rolling my eyes. *I think my stepmother has a crush on you, David.*

He nodded to himself, his eyes small with humor, aiming the pen tip to the top of the page. He went on then to explain some number jargon to Sam, and I turned back to my books, a breath away from asking for his help. I really just didn't get this Pythagoras' Theorem crap. I never had.

Out of the corner of my eye, I saw David look over at me for a second, but as the numbers on the page started to shift magically into place in my brain, I phased him, Sam, and Vicki out, and concentrated on my homework—taking a sideways glance every now and then to see David look up at the same time. All I really wanted though was to go upstairs to my room so David and I could do our 'homework' in private.

A roll of paper hit my forearm then and bounced up, landing between my wrists.

David winked at me, rolling his hand in the air as if to say 'Open it.'

As I unfolded the paper, perfect Victorian cursive handwriting stared back up at me in the words: 'What, exactly, would we be doing in your room—other than homework?'

Stay out of my head!

He laughed and took a sip from his coffee cup. I threw the paper back at him, but he caught it without even looking.

Smart-ass, I thought. *But if you were any decent sort of mind reader, you wouldn't need to ask what I wanted to do with you in there.*

He looked over at me, his face tight with a curious frown, cup poised at his lips. I waited until he dared to take another sip then showed him where I'd put my mouth if Vicki trusted me alone upstairs with a boy in my room.

Brown liquid burst all over Sam's homework, spraying from David's lips as he jerked up out of his chair, wiping his chin on his sleeve. "Ara!"

That'll teach you. I giggled, covering my mouth.

Vicki stared between David and I while Sam, oblivious to all other life forms aside from himself, simply shook his head and sighed like *we* were immature, then went back to his homework.

"Ara," Vicki said, handing David a dishcloth. "What did you do to the poor boy?"

"Nothing," I said innocently.

"I'm sure."

David placed the cloth and his cup in the sink, shaking his head the whole time, then popped up beside me and whispered quietly in my ear. "You need a filter on your thoughts, Ara-Rose."

I brushed the side of my face affectionately down his chin, closing my eyes when his soft lips left a kiss behind. Then he wandered away and sat beside Sam again, still shaking his head.

"So, Ara," Vicki said casually, "you have the girls coming for a sleepover this Saturday, right?"

"Mm-hm." I nodded.

"When are we going dress hunting then? I assume you'll want to do it soon, before Mike arrives?"

"Did Ara tell you, Mom?" Sam interjected, winking at David. "David's gonna buy her a dress."

My head whipped around to look at my vampire; he smiled behind a book, keeping his eyes on the text and nowhere near my infuriated glare.

Vicki looked at me, then at David. "That's a very kind offer, David. Are you sure?"

"I'm positive, Mrs. Thompson. If you take her shopping, I'll cover the costs."

"Dresses can be expensive," she said in a remarkably condescending tone.

David leaned back in his chair and flopped his arm over the backrest. I knew he was probably thinking, *I'm about eighty years older than you, lady. I think I know what things cost.*

"There is no price too high. I want Ara to have the prettiest, most extravagant dress money can buy," he said instead.

Vicki looked hopeful. "How much do you want her to spend?"

Don't, David, please don't. Vicki would definitely make me accept his 'sweet' offer. There'd be no arguing with her.

He grinned, completely ignoring me as he ripped a corner of his notepad, scribbled something down on it, showed it to Sam, who nodded, then passed it to Vicki. "No less than this."

Vicki gasped.

"What? Vicki, how much? Tell me?" I whined.

She folded the paper and slipped it into her pocket, spinning back to the stove with a bounce in her step. "So we'll go shopping on Saturday morning then, before your friends arrive?"

I folded my arms and looked at David.

"What?" He shrugged, holding both hands out, looking so cute and human that my heart melted, once again rendering me unable to defend myself and my beliefs.

You're cheeky, David, but I love you. Doesn't mean I'm accepting your money though.

He just cleared his throat as if to say, 'We shall see.'

WHILE DAVID HAD MASTERED THE STYLES AND BEHAVIORS OF THE twenty-first century, when it came to automatically switching to 'good boy' mode around a girl's parents, old habits died hard. He ate with the perfection of his inner English Lord, talking topics over dinner that had my dad more than a little impressed, and even complimented Vicki's cooking. I kept watching his fork go from his plate to his mouth like a graceful bird flying, wondering how it affected him to eat human food. But when it came to the apple pie, I don't think he was lying about it being his favorite, because he ate mine too. Then, he scored extra points with the parental units by helping me with the dishes, forever winning Sam over by giving him the night off. Didn't earn enough trust for my dad to leave the kitchen, though. Instead, he decided to 'read his paper' while David and I stood by the sink, trying to talk about 'human' stuff.

David finished wiping the counter, and re-rolled his sleeves before sticking his hands back into the water and pulling out a soapy plate.

"Is it awful?" I asked, taking the plate in my towel-covered hand.

"Is what awful?"

I inched closer, keeping one eye on Dad. "Eating?"

David let out a short breath of laughter. "No. It's very normal for me. I mean"—he bent his knees so his lips came in line with my ear —"it's not totally necessary, but I still enjoy it."

"Really? So, it tastes okay?"

"Yeah." He laughed. "I guess it's like chocolate; you don't need it, and you can't survive on it, but you can enjoy it now and then."

"Oh." I nodded. "I thought it'd be like vamp—I mean, like your kind in the movies, you know, how it tastes like ash."

"Nope. Things actually taste better," he added, handing me another plate. "My senses are very finely tuned, so taste is enhanced, touch is enhanced. *Everything* is." His smile was oh-so incredibly suggestive.

"So?" I said slowly, running one finger at a snail's pace down his spine, feeling the soft silk of his shirt bunch up as I glided along. "*This* feels better when you're a vampire?"

"Shh." He nodded toward my dad, his shoulders lifting with the slow breath he took after. "And, yes. That feels incredible."

Dad stood up suddenly and walked out of the room then.

I held my breath. "Did he hear me?"

David tuned his 'ear' to Dad's thoughts for a second. "No. He's gone to talk to Vicki about Mike coming to stay."

"What about it?"

"He just realized he might need some help getting that giant sofa out of the spare room. He's going to ask me."

"So he trusts you to help move furniture and do dishes, but not to be alone in the kitchen with his daughter?"

"Sounds pretty standard for dads, Ara."

"Yeah, well maybe we should tell him you're a vampire. At least then he'd stop worrying about me getting pregnant."

"Why wouldn't he worry?"

"Because you're a vampire. Vampires can't have babies."

"That's… not entirely true."

"What!" I nearly dropped the plate I was holding.

He laughed and looked at the pile of dishes still ahead of us. "You know, I can think of at least three better ways to be spending our evening. You want me to get this done in record time?" A hint of mischief shimmered behind his eyes.

"Okay," I said slowly, unsure what he meant.

He grabbed both of my shoulders and gently directed me to stand center to the room. "Count to twenty," he said, and then disappeared into a blur of grey and black, like watching the road out the window when driving down the highway. The faucet ran, cupboard doors shut and opened, and I stood, mouth open, towel and plate still in hand, until David grabbed it and placed it on the shelf, closing the cupboard door after. "All done."

"I never even started counting!" I said.

"Told you." He jerked one shoulder up and dropped it. "I'm fast."

"Hm." I wrapped my arms along the sides of his waist and pressed my cheek to his shirt buttons. "I knew there was a reason I should keep you around."

"Shall we go upstairs? I'll give you a few more."

"Tease." I smiled, squeezing him tighter. We both knew he wouldn't come upstairs with me. It was past ten o'clock, and he had his rules.

"It's out of respect for you, Ara."

"I know, but it's annoying." I pulled my scarf away from my neck a little, allowing the bruises to breathe.

"Look at you." David ran his thumb over the skin just beside the mark. "We shouldn't have done that. You're going to have bruises for weeks."

"I'm fine."

"No, you're not." He covered the welt again. "I watched you fidget with that all night. I know it's bothering you."

"It was worth it."

"No. I was way too rough with you."

"I *liked* it." I looked up, my voice and my eyes filling with all the guilt of a child who just stole the last cookie.

"You're not the shy, meek little thing I thought you were, are you?"

"No, I'm really not and, you know, when you did that to me, it made me feel… I don't know." I shook my head, lost for the right word.

David smiled warmly. "I do. I believe the words you're looking for are excited, awakened"—his voice lowered before he said—"aroused."

That one struck a chord, making my cheeks hot. "What does that mean, though? Is that just because you're a vampire, or am I messed up? Like, would I want you to do it if you were human?"

"Yes, it's likely you would still enjoy it if I was human, but that does not, by any standards, make you messed up, Ara."

My breath shuddered as I recalled the way his mouth felt on my neck. "Surely that's not right—for me to be *turned on* by you doing dangerous things to me?"

"Of course it is. It's called human nature. What's not right is taking pleasure in taunting me when I'm about to kill you."

"Is it..." I bit my lip, fighting back a smile. "Is it wrong for me to want you to... Nup. I can't say it aloud."

"Ara?" David stepped closer. "S'il te plaît, mon amour? What is it?"

"I want you to—"

"Ara," Vicki called from the den. "It's late, time you were getting to bed."

I huffed the awkwardness out in one gust. "Sure, Vicki."

"Ara, please?" David said quietly. "What were you going to say?"

Come back? I looked up at him. *When she's gone to bed?*

"You know how I feel about that," he said firmly.

I grinned. "Well, then I guess you'll just have to wait until tomorrow to hear what I had to say."

Vicki waltzed in then to see that we were obeying her command. "Goodnight, David."

"Goodnight, Mrs. Thompson, and thank you for a lovely meal." He smiled at Vicki with all the charm and sincerity of an eighteenth-century prince. She totally fell for it.

"Well, you're welcome. Any time. Maybe next time I'll cook something a little more interesting."

"To be perfectly honest"—the prince bowed his head—"I've not had a meal that delicious in a long time."

Vicki's chest puffed up, and the smile on her face spread so wide I pictured her as a big feathery chicken that just laid an egg.

"I'll see you *soon*?" I linked arms with him and led him to the door.

"You will. Until then"—he backed out the door, kissing my hand —"tu es dans toutes mes pensées."

I heard Vicki gush behind me. Sucker.

But as the door closed, my own heart fluttered and a pathetic girlie giggle escaped. I didn't even know what he said, but I bet it was romantic. All I knew, from growing up with Mike saying stuff like that all the time, was that *S'il vous plaît* was please, respectfully, and *S'il te plaît* was for addressing a close friend, while *mon amour* was my love. Not that Mike ever said that to me, but I heard him groaning it to other girls when I slept over his house. He really used his French heritage to his advantage when it came to girls. I wondered if David was doing that—trying to woo me—or if it was just a habit for him to speak it.

"Ara?" Vicki stood beside me.

"Hm?" I looked away from the front door, shaking off that pleasant little shiver David left in me.

"Stop staring at nothing. Go to bed."

"Oh. Right." I rubbed my head. "Sorry."

As I took the first step, Vicki gently grabbed my hand and smiled at me. "And by the way, David is a very lovely boy."

"Thank you." I smiled, gripping her hand for a second.

"And he's more than welcome here anytime."

"Cool." I grinned and ran upstairs. I just wanted to be in his arms again. Having him in my room past bedtime was a real treat. I wasn't going to waste even one second more talking to Vicki, even if she was actually being nice.

I flung my door open to a dark room, pushing it shut with my heel. "David?"

"Ara." Dad pushed my door open then without even knocking and flicked on the light.

"Dad? What's up?" I quickly checked around my room.

"Just wanted to say goodnight." He smiled warmly, resting his shoulder on the doorframe.

"Oh. Well, you should've knocked, Dad. I was just about to get changed."

He looked at my clothes, his eyes going wider. "Oh, I'm sorry, honey. I forget you're all grown up now."

"It's okay." I walked over and gave him a quick hug.

He kissed the top of my head, patting my hair, then stood back. "I'll see you in the morning."

"Night, Dad."

"Night," he said again and closed the door.

I spun around a few times, but the quiet emptiness of my room remained the same. I figured maybe David was waiting until my parents actually went to sleep before coming back. So, I took a shower, washed my hair, and slipped into my nice pajamas—the ones that actually matched—then jumped into bed to keep warm in the cooling air.

But the cold turned to frost and my tired eyes felt sandy by the time Dad and Vicki finally shut their door. Then, with a stealthy silence that even the cat on the end of my bed didn't pay attention to, David slipped through my window, lifted the covers and snuggled down beside me, pulling me onto his chest. His jeans were cold against my legs and he smelled like grass and fresh air.

"Hello," I whispered.

"Hello."

"Mmm." I breathed him in deep, finding a sweeter, more concentrated version of his scent underneath the smell of night, kind of like a Terry's Orange Chocolate treat. "What've you been doing?" I asked. "Your arms are warmer than normal and you smell so nice."

"Do you really want to know?"

"Were you hunting?"

"Would it bother you if I was?"

A minute's silence passed in a second. "I'm not sure."

"Just don't think about it, sweetheart." His long fingers swept my hair back over my forehead, leaving behind a chill.

"So that smell, it's the blood you just had?"

He laughed a little. "Kind of. It's how my body *interprets* the blood, which is unique for every vampire."

"I like it."

"That's because you like me."

"So it's also why you're so warm all of a sudden, then?"

"Yes."

"Then why are your hands cold when the rest of you is so warm?" I traced a line over his index finger.

"Because it's cold outside. I've been waiting for your dad to go to bed."

"Why? He wouldn't have known you were in here."

"I wouldn't be so certain about that, my love."

"Mm. I like it when you call me that." I smiled and slipped my fingertips under David's shirt, resting them on his belly. "I like it even more in French."

"I know," he said.

"How do you know?" *I've never let myself think that around you.*

"Your body temperature changes when I speak French."

"Hm." My eyes narrowed with a disapproving grin. "I'm not sure I like that."

"Don't fall in love with a vampire then." He kissed the top of my head.

"Okay. I'll remember that next time."

"You had better," he said, sounding a bit British. "Staying human to be with a human is one thing, but if I ever find you in the arms of another vampire, I'll turn you myself."

"Duly noted." I kissed his chest, smiling to myself. "What did you say when you were leaving tonight—when you said 'Until then,' and added a whole string of words I doubt were in English?"

He laughed once, combing his fingertips gently through the front of my hair. "Until then, you are in *all* my thoughts."

"And then you went hunting?"

"Yes."

"Do you think of me when you hunt?"

"Sometimes." He let the word hang for a minute then added, "But not in the way you might think."

"In what way?"

"I imagine you with me, enjoying the uh… the life of a vampire." He paused and lifted his head off the pillow a little to look at me. "Does that bother you?"

"Not in the way you might think."

"In what way then?"

"I'm not sure." Maybe it bothered me that I couldn't really picture him when he was gone. I mean, if he were human, I could picture him at home watching TV or eating dinner with his uncle. But no, my boyfriend had to go into dark alleyways and stalk my species. I didn't *want* to picture myself beside him, enjoying the kill. I had tried a few times before, but it never felt right. My mind would always stand on the sidelines, seeing his victim; focusing on his lips as they parted, noting the way he'd hold her or pin her down like he did to me when I tried to scream that day. My blood would run hot watching, but not because I wanted her to die; it was because I wanted...

"Ara. Stop it!"

"What?"

"I can see that. I can see what you're thinking."

The blankets rustled under me as I sat up to look at David, blinking to focus in the dim moonlight. "Does it bother you? I mean, is it because I can picture it, or is it because I picture it wrong?"

"Neither of the above."

"Well, what then?"

He grinned slowly. "It's because you want to be the *victim*."

I meshed my lips together. "Is that sick?"

"That's it, isn't it?" David sat up and grabbed my arm, squeezing it gently. "That's what you were trying to tell me in the kitchen tonight—you want me to drink your blood?"

"Yeah. Kinda."

"You've seen what my monster is capable of now, Ara, are you really that stupid?"

I held his gaze, letting my drumbeat heart fill the tense silence that surrounded us.

"I'll never do it." He dropped my arm and sat back.

"I'm sorry." The awkward silence grew fatter and shrunk in around me. "It's just that there's this strange pull urging me to want it. I feel like I *need* your teeth against my flesh, I—"

"Ara, stop talking."

"But I just need you to understand what I'm feeling." I had to take a deep breath as I pictured it again. "It's like sex and blood are—"

"Ara. I said stop talking!" he yelled, and disappeared.

My mouth hung open on the words I never finished. "What's wrong?"

"You can't think like that around me. It's dangerous." He leaned against my dresser with his arms folded. "I will never do that with you, so get the idea out of your head."

Like a drop in my stomach, guilt, humiliation and rejection spread heat through my limbs until it formed a layer of tears in my eyes.

"Ara, don't cry." David appeared on the bed again, smoothing my hair from my face. "Please don't think that I don't want to drink your blood, mon amour. There are just so many reasons not to."

"Like?"

"Well, I'd have to cut you, for one. I can't bite you, and I can't use my venom to numb the flesh first."

I looked up from his shoulder. "We could cut where no one would see?"

"How will that be any different? I still have to cut you."

"I don't care. Something's happened inside me, David. I feel confused about it all. Like, it's really gross when I think about it—the idea of drinking blood—but when I *feel* it..." I placed my hand in the center of my chest. "It just feels so right."

"I know. And like I said to you in the closet at school, it's only human to feel that way," he said. "You're instinctually drawn to me—to my bite."

"But why?"

He shrugged. "Surely you've watched documentaries on animals and insects that kill by luring their prey?"

"Yeah."

"Well, I give off a sort of chemical that affects the way you would otherwise respond to me—"

"Like the spell of lust you were talking about?"

"Precisely. I'm technically luring you, you might say. So it isn't really what you want, Ara, which is another reason I will never share blood with you."

"But you're not on the hunt, so you're not luring me right now, are you?"

"No. Of course not."

"Then why do I still want you to drink my blood?"

Beneath his smile, his white teeth gleamed. My eyes traced the sharp edges of his fangs and the straight lines of the front teeth, going a step too far in my thoughts for his liking.

"Maybe you're more like my species than you care to admit." After a long pause, David took a deep breath through his nose and let it out. "I'm sorry, Ara. Okay. I just don't want to taint you any more than I already have. Sharing blood is one of *the most* intimate exchanges of passion. Lust and desire mean nothing in comparison to blood sharing. God knows I want to do that with you. I just..."

"Just?"

"Just... I won't. Okay?"

My mouth filled with saliva as I looked at his neck. "I wish I knew what you tasted like."

"I've been told it's a little like milk with too much sugar."

"What do you mean by *told*?"

"I'm pretty old, Ara. I have been with other—"

"Wait!" I held my hand up. "Don't go there."

"Okay." He laughed. "I won't. If you promise to drop this blood-sharing thing."

I looked down at my hands. "Are you afraid you might kill me if we did it?"

"I don't know."

"Are you picturing it?"

"I'm trying not to."

I watched his eyes, so lost to thoughts I wished I could be a part of. "Why don't we just try it? Like, maybe just a small cut at first—"

"I said stop it, okay?" He firmly planted his hand to my shoulder. "I'm not going to hurt you like that."

"Then I'll do it myself." I jumped off the bed and ran to my desk.

"What are you doing?" David seized my arm as I grabbed the scissors.

"I'm gonna do it myself. Then you don't have to hurt me."

"Ara, you've lost it. You've actually gone crazy. Give me those." He snatched the scissors from my hand and threw them back in the drawer, slamming it shut.

"You're right." I sat down in my desk chair. Maybe all this had been too much for me. Maybe finding out about vampires was the last straw. Vicki warned me that the side effects of trauma and grief could manifest themselves in unusual ways—ways you might not recognize. But she was talking about things like promiscuity and drug use, right?

"This isn't manifested grief, Ara. It's a collection of thoughts and cravings over a period of time that have grown into desire," said the voice of reason from beside me. "There's nothing wrong with you aside from wanting to cut yourself open with scissors. But you have to drop this. All right?"

I nodded.

David ran his fingers through his hair and down the back of his neck, giving it a firm rub, then he grabbed his jacket off my desk and slipped it on. "Come on," he said.

"Where're we going?"

"We both need some fresh air."

"Fresh air?"

"Yes."

"And, where *exactly* are we going to get that from?" I asked, a little concerned when he scooped me up into his arms. "And how are you planning to get there?"

He smiled secretly, saying only, "You may want to cover your eyes."

"Holy shi—" I rolled my face into his chest as we jolted forward and the cool of night wrapped us up, the wind moving beneath us like we were flying. We landed with a jolt, and though we weren't moving anymore, I couldn't bear to look at where we were.

"You okay?" he asked.

I think so.

"I'm going to put you down now, okay?"

"Okay." I clung to his shirt as he set my bare feet to a cold, slanted surface, and a dewy breeze circled my ankles, howling a warning. "Are we up high?"

The kidnapper wrapped his arm around my waist and whispered in my ear, "Open your eyes. See for yourself."

"Do I have to?" I shut them tighter.

"You're not afraid of heights, are you, Ara?" He chuckled lightly.

"I'm going to kill you for this, David Knight." But a breath of awe numbed my fears as I opened my eyes and saw the endless skyline trailing off to a dark blue horizon, where the hills that were grey in the day looked invisible under the scattered stars. "Wow, it's so beautiful up here."

He shrugged. "I come here all the time."

"Is this where you spent the summer? Spying on me?"

"Yes," he said with a cheeky grin, taking my hand to help me sit with my legs dangling over the slant of my dad's roof. "But you know that was only while I was worried about you."

"So you don't do it anymore?"

"Ha! Ara, if I was going to be at your house, I'd be in your room *with* you, or I'd be at home leaving you to rest."

I rested my head on his shoulder. "So, if I was depressed again, you'd stay with me more often?"

"No," he laughed the word out. "You're a little suicidal for me right now."

I slapped his chest with the back of my hand. "Wanting to share blood with you is not suicidal."

"Oh boy." He shook his head, still laughing. "If you only knew the truth of what you do to me with your thoughts, my girl. You have no idea how close you've come to death, do you?"

A cold shiver raced down my spine and sent my heart back into my chest with a jump. But even after the eerie feeling subsided, the shaking remained and my teeth chattered together.

"You're so human," David remarked lightly, wrapping his jacket over my shoulders.

"And you're so warm, *like* a human." The heat within the leather felt like that warm spot in someone else's bed after they get up, layered pleasantly with the scent of citrus and that woodsy smell his car had. I slipped my arms through the sleeves, and then moved to sit between his legs, lacing his arms tightly around my ribs.

"Are you frightened up here?" he whispered against the back of my ear.

"Not with you holding on to me."

"You know I'd never let you fall, right?"

"Even if I do fall"—I yawned as I spoke—"I know you'll be there to catch me." I smiled, and as I looked at the eastern horizon, a flicker of silver glittered across the night sky. "Did you see that?"

"A shooting star." David nodded. "Make a wish."

With my eyes closed, I crossed my heart and wished that David would get the happy ending he longs for, no matter what happened from here.

"Why did you wish only for *my* happy ending?"

"Because then I know that even if our happy ending isn't together, you'll still be happy."

He swallowed hard and looked away. "I thought you said you were a selfish girl."

"I am." I shrugged. "I didn't wish for world peace."

"My darling," he scoffed, "there are more than enough people in the world to wish for that. But it requires sacrifice and tolerance, not hopes and prayers."

"Like us," I said.

"What do you mean?"

"I mean, happiness is a possibility for us—we *can* be together. It just means a sacrifice on one side."

"No, just tolerance on yours."

"You can't ask a human to tolerate the death of another human. That isn't fair."

"But your species kill each other all the time."

"I don't. Not personally."

"Okay, well you tolerate the death of animals for *your* nutrition."

"Spoken like a vampire." I smiled ruefully.

"Well, my love, I am a vampire. Get used to it." He kissed my temple.

"Bite me," I scoffed.

"Don't tempt me, young lady," he said with a laugh, "your death wish may just become a reality."

I rolled my eyes. "So… if you drank my blood and we made love after, I could get pregnant?"

He coughed out loudly. "What?"

"You said, when you were washing the dishes tonight, that it isn't entirely true about not being able to have children with a vampire?"

"Oh." He wiped his hand across his jaw, shaking his head. "Well, it's rare. You would've heard of it in your much-loved mythology: the incubus and the succubus."

"Is that real?"

"In a way. It's not like the horror stories, though. Supposedly, the babies are mostly human—not immortal. They can survive on less blood than vampires, but still require food. I'm not sure how it works for female vampires. None of the girls I've ever known have fallen pregnant, but for males, we can still, you know"—he shrugged—"we can still create life. There's a rumor among my Set that my uncle has a half-blood son."

"Why wouldn't you tell me about this, David?" I asked softly. "You know my plans to have kids is one of the reasons I can't promise you eternity."

"Yes, but it's not the only reason." He moved his stubbly cheek down mine. "I didn't think it necessary to tell you."

"Like so many things."

"Yes. But, if you don't ever want immortal life, then what good would it be to have a child, and have maybe five years together before you grow too old to be with a teenager?"

"It would still be better than having only a few weeks."

"True, but after those five years, I would lose you *and* my children—not to mention, they would one day out-age their father."

David? The father of *my* children? I really liked the way that sounded.

"Besides, even if I was selfish enough to take those five years from you, I'd be away for the first two. I *have* to return to duty, and what then? You'll be a single teenage mother. No." He shook his head, tightening his hold around me. "I want you to have a good life, Ara-Rose. I want you to be mine for all time, but if having a family means that much to you, then perhaps it is kinder for me to just leave."

"Don't get so decisive yet. We still have time to balance the pros and cons."

"I can't help it. I *want* to be decisive. I want to sleep soundly at night knowing that you'll be happy—either way."

"I'm not likely to be, David. No matter what I end up doing, I'm either living a life I don't want, or living without you." I rested my hand in my lap. "It's all just unfair."

"Life's not fair. Haven't you learned that by now?"

I shook my head, turning around to face him. "Yes. And I refuse to believe that. Life is what you make it. Sometimes things happen that suck, but it doesn't mean your whole life is unfair." I shrugged and looked at the stars. "Life is just life, and sometimes you just get dealt a different hand to what you wanted."

"And you don't think that's unfair?"

"*Situations* can seem unfair, but all things considering, David, we're still alive, still breathing—not ill or starving or dying of disease. In that sense, I think we're kinda lucky, right?"

"I suppose." He reached out and brushed my chin with his thumb. "After all, we did find each other against all odds."

"Right. And I wouldn't be here—alive—if you hadn't come along."

He went quiet for a moment. "So you think you really would've acted on those… what did you call them, *fleeting thoughts*?"

I shrugged. "I don't know."

"You scare me, Ara-Rose." He cupped my cold ankle, rubbing it affectionately. "What's going to happen to you if I leave?"

I didn't answer; I didn't feel it needed an answer. And I wasn't sure I had one to give anyway.

As if most of world died then and changed the chemistry of those left behind, I felt a major physical shift in David's spirit. "Are you okay?"

"Every day I wake," he started hesitantly, "and I tell myself that I'll let you go; that it's the right thing to do. And then you say things like that to me—tell me that you're not sure about living—and I wonder if I should just make you come with me. But then I look at you and I see this young human girl who has never really *lived*, and I just can't do it. I have to bite my tongue every time I'm about to say something that would convince you." He pressed his brow firmly against mine for a second, breathing me in. "I'm just a guy, Ara. I'm not perfect. In fact, I'm more perfectly imperfect than a human, and I have this evil side in me that is *screaming* for me to kidnap and turn you."

"I know, and sometimes I wish you'd just force me to do it, too. But I'd hate you for it. It's just so dumb." I shook my head, frustrated. "I wish it were different."

"Well, you know what they say?"

"Yes. *They* say a lot of things that don't really make sense. But which 'They' quote were you referring to specifically?"

"Wishing is good time wasted."

"Wow, you are *so* negative." I reached across to give his arm a little slap. "You know, you might not, but *I* still believe wishes come true."

"That's because you're still a child."

"Then what does that make you?"

"Ha! A twisted hundred-year-old man with a fetish for teenagers."

I laughed too, turning in his arms again to rest my spine against his front. "There is still magic in the world, you know. You don't have to be a child to find it. Even my dad believes in it, and *he* wasn't a child when he taught me how to make wishes."

"How can you *teach* someone to make wishes?"

"There's a special way to do it."

"There is?"

"Yes."

"Will you teach me?"

I smiled and cleared my throat as I turned my face to look at David, noticing the tiny silver reflections of stars in his eyes. "Well, when you see the first star of the evening or the last star in the early morning, close your eyes, cross your heart and make a wish. If you keep it secret, then it'll come true one day."

"And you still believe that?"

"Yes. I do. And no one is going to take that away from me with borrowed philosophy about life. When you find that one of your seconds has been wasted on a wish, and you think you could've really used that second—really need it back—then I'll agree it's wasted time wishing. But not yet." I looked back to the sky. "Not while I still have hope."

"My only hope is that you see sense, realize that being a vampire isn't so bad, and let me change you." David sighed, closing his eyes and crossing his heart.

"And there's that evil side," I noted with a smile.

"Yes. But I will never stop wishing for it, Ara. I know that's wrong, but I can't control my heart's desires."

"As long as you control your venom, then I'm fine with that."

"But you asked me to drink your blood. What if I lose control?" he said playfully.

"I'm not having this argument with you."

"Okay. No more talking about it." He kissed the top of my head and held me to his chest. "When you've decided you can't live without me anymore, *then* we'll talk about it."

"But I already decided that."

"Well, when you decide you don't want to be a frail old lady and *die*, then we can talk about it."

"Frailty and death doesn't scare me—not as much as eternally thirsting blood."

David exhaled softly. "You know, I've never met a girl so eager to die in all my life."

I shook my head and folded my arms across my chest. "I'm not eager to die, David. I'm eager to *live*." And for the first time since I lost Mom and Harry, that was finally true. Love had given me a reason to exist, and now, even if I was going to lose that love—for the first time since I lost them—I really just wanted a life.

20

"Wake up. Wake up." Vicki slapped my bedcovers. "Time to go."

I groaned, shielding my eyes as she threw my curtains apart, blinding me with the white glow of morning. "Vicki. It's Saturday."

"Yes. I know." She opened my window, and the fresh scent of cut grass and rain blew in with the light breeze. "Good to see you've finally started sleeping with this closed."

"I didn't. Dad must have closed it." Or David. I tried to remember last night, but could only half-remember falling asleep against my vampire's chest.

"Ara?" Vicki said, staring at my face. "Are you awake?"

"Yes." I flopped back on my pillow. "I don't wanna go to school today."

"You know full well where we're going today, young lady," Vicki said in an insistent tone.

"Yes, which is why I'm staying in bed."

"That's enough. Now, just humor me *and* your boyfriend, and let him spend some money on you."

I pulled the covers over my head. I never agreed to this and I didn't see why I should have to let *anyone* spend money on me if I didn't want them to.

"Be nice." She ripped my blanket away and dumped it on my chair, leaving me cold in the nakedness of my bed. "Is it really so bad that David wants to buy you a dress?"

"Yes." I pushed up on my elbow. "I have savings, Vicki. I can buy my own dress."

"Ara-Rose!" She folded her arms. "Where are your manners?"

"In my drawer, where I left them."

She shook her head, sighing, and wandered over to find them, pulling out some jeans and a T-shirt instead. "Get dressed. We leave in ten minutes."

"Argh. Fine."

"Thank you."

I flipped my legs over the side of the bed and stumbled to the window. I wanted to grunt at her but held it in, folding my arms and resting my head on the glass pane instead.

Outside, the dull grey clouds hid the sun, making everything under its suppressed glare seem vividly white—lighting up the entire yard and all the garden debris. "Did it storm last night?"

"Yes. You didn't hear it?" Vicki folded her arms, looking out at the clouds as they spilled over and the soft pattering of rain filled the desolate street below.

"Nope. Slept like a baby." I shrugged. "Maybe I'm just getting over my fear of storms."

"Well, lucky Dad closed your window then."

A knowing smile tugged at my lips. "Yeah. Really lucky." Thanks, David.

"And tidy this room," Vicki added as she closed my door.

With a certain amount of dread, I studied the chaos around me; clothes on every piece of furniture, covering every scrap of carpet, looking remarkably like a storm broke loose in *here* last night.

I got dressed then shook my quilt out over my bed and hid my clothes, clean and dirty, in the laundry basket so Alana and Emily wouldn't think I was a total pig when they came to stay tonight.

"Ara. I'm going to the car. Hurry up," Vicki called.

"Just a sec." I ran to the bathroom, locking both doors, then smeared another layer of concealer over the bruises David left when he ate me in the auditorium closet. The leftover proof of my insanity looked mean and ugly—like a swollen, purple infection, leaking some kind of clear fluid. But, thanks to Vicki's shopping obsession, another layer of this two-hundred-dollar bottle of concealer made it disappear.

I stood back and observed my handiwork. I'd actually healed pretty well for such a short time really, but a part of me wished it would leave a little scar—a permanent mark to remind me that I was David's and he was mine. And as that thought entered my head, a giant hand came down across my brow.

"Sick, Ara-Rose. You're sick," I said to the girl in the mirror.

All the common sense I once had evaporated when it came to David—even making me delusional enough to offer him my blood. And in the clarity of daylight, I was glad he didn't drink it. I could see the insanity in it now. But deep down inside, that lust-driven human in me was screaming for him to do it.

Outside, a horn beeped twice. I patted my pocket, slipped my shoes on, and stuffed the last of my savings into my purse as I left my bedroom. But as I reached the front door, a hand grabbed mine.

"You won't be needing *this*."

"Hey!" I screeched, watching my purse leave my grip by force of David's. "It's for lunch, or if I need anything else, you know, for the sleepover or, like, girlie stuff."

"Nice try. If you need anything else, *I'll* take you shopping later." He tucked my purse into his pocket and kissed my cheek, then, as the front door swung open and Vicki called out again, he disappeared.

A victory grin spread across my face, though, as I slid into the car, patting the roll of bills I'd stuffed in my pocket earlier. He clearly didn't see that thought, and since he didn't check my purse to see the grand amount of ten dollars I really put in there, he'd never know about it.

Human: one. Vampire: zero.

VICKI PARKED AT THE CENTER OF THE LONG, OUTDOOR STRIP OF shops. I jumped out of the car and looked up at the sky. Even though the sun wasn't shining, as it had been last time I was here, everything just felt so much brighter. The shopping strip was quiet for a Saturday, not that it was usually very busy anyway. It reminded me of my hometown; how there were people out and about, but scattered and far between. I checked my watch, hoping we'd be out of here by the time Emily and Alana came over.

By eleven o'clock, Vicki insisted on getting an early lunch and talking about all the dresses I'd tried on. But after thirty dresses, the only one I remotely liked was an emerald-green one—like David's eyes. But it wasn't really grand enough, so Vicki said. I thought it was fine.

"I still have to find some pretty new underwear and a mask." I laid my shopping list down on the table beside my plate.

"Well, you can't get a mask until you have a dress," Vicki said with a mouthful of salad. "And the underwear you get will depend on the fabric of the dress too."

"Why?"

"Because if you get a fitted satin dress, you won't want lace underwear. The pattern will show through."

"Oh," I said, swallowing a chunk of salt-coated steak. "I think I'll just get that green dress then—the satin one. I'm kinda done with shopping for today."

Vicki stopped chewing, making her glare seem more severe. "Ara. David has given you a *lot* more than *that* to spend. The green one's pretty, but you can do better."

"I know. But I'm not gonna let him buy the dress, Vicki."

She took a deep breath. "I had a feeling you'd protest at some point."

I smirked.

"Well, I guess it's up to you, Ara-Rose. But before we go home, can you please just humor me and try a dress in *that* store?"

I looked behind me to the front of a very expensive-looking store, with fairy-tale-perfect dresses beyond the windows. "Fine," I rescinded with a small huff.

"Thank you," she said kindly.

WE STEPPED CAREFULLY AROUND THE SILKS AND TULLES FALLING over the wooden floor as we entered the realm of couture, and a thin girl smiled from behind the counter before turning her attention back to her magazine.

"This is beautiful," I said, spinning slowly to take it all in.

"Told you," Vicki beamed.

"Okay." I held my arms out. "Dress me up."

Turns out, you should never say that to a woman who never had a daughter, in a room with a commission-based sales clerk. I unwillingly tried on every dress in the store, all the while lost in some mind-blank brought on by constant movement and the repeated inhalation of the manufacturer's fabric preservatives and dyes.

But when they threw a shimmering sky-blue dress at me, I woke suddenly. It slid onto my body like silk to satin, the carefully tailored lines fitting the contours of my hips like a glove.

I stepped onto the box in front of the four-walled mirror and smiled as Vicki and the clerk gasped.

"You look like a princess." Vicki almost started crying.

Spinning around slowly, running my fingers over my hips, I marveled at the soft organza bunched together at the waist on one side and shrouded with little diamantes. The strapless corset bustle hugged my body until the full flowing drop of the skirt glided out from my hips and over the ground, like a wedding dress, but blue. And even better, the clerk had pulled the corset so tight my waist became a half-size smaller and I totally looked like I was wearing a push-up bra.

Vicki was right. The dress was amazing.

"We'll take it," Vicki all but squeaked.

I shook my head. "No, it's a thousand dollars, Vicki. I can't. I'll just get the green one in the other store."

"But why, Ara?"

"I told you. I'm not comfortable letting my boyfriend buy a dress for me. I didn't have fine things like this growing up, and it just seems insane to waste so much money on something I'll only wear once."

"But it's not your money."

"Which is even worse. You just don't get it because you've never had to scrape up change to buy milk." I jumped off the podium and moved away quickly, hiding myself in the change room.

The girl in the mirror looked up at me. She was thinking the same thing: the dress was beautiful. I wished I could afford it, because it definitely was *the one*. But I wouldn't take advantage of my boyfriend just because he happened to earn a great income arresting and imprisoning bad vampires. It felt like blood money. Dirty money.

"Stop pouting," I said to myself decisively. "We're getting the green dress with our own money."

VICKI WALKED QUIETLY BEHIND ME AROUND SUMMER MAGIC Masks and Hats Boutique.

"This one would've been perfect with the blue dress," she teased, holding up an almost transparent blue mask. The little stones around the eyes were patterned out like a butterfly, and as she angled it just so, it caught the light, shimmering like a diamond-powdered oil painting.

"Yes." I swallowed, switching to 'indifferent mode' with a noncommittal shrug. "It's great. But I have the green dress."

"Oh, well the only mask here that goes with green is this gold one." Vicki's lips spread into a sinister grin. "I know how much you *love* gold."

I tried to swallow the vomit in the back of my throat. "I do love gold. And you're right, it'll look great with the green."

Begrudgingly, I took the mask, purchased it and left the store, gagging on the bitter taste of regret. After the first five minutes into the drive back home—in complete silence—the pig-headed me softened a little more. Sam was her only child. He would forever be her only child. I felt kind of guilty for ruining her only chance to do the mother/daughter 'going-to-a-ball' thing. Maybe I should've just let David buy me the damn dress.

"Vicki?"

"Mm?"

"I, um… I had fun today."

She gave a small smile as we pulled up to the garage door, and my heart sunk into the pit of my stomach when I saw David's car.

"What's David doing here? He was supposed to be here at two." I was supposed to have this dress hidden by then.

Vicki shut the engine off. "We thought it might be better if they started earlier."

"But—"

"What's the matter, Ara? I thought you'd be happy to see David." Her tone had all the malice of a person who knew that I knew that she knew I was totally getting busted, and she was relishing in the idea.

"Of course I'm happy to see him." I closed the car door with my hip and folded the dress over my arm. "I can't wait to show him my dress."

"Me too." She walked ahead and opened the front door for me, all the while grinning like an evil stepmother.

The skin on my neck tightened.

"Greg? We're home."

"We're upstairs," Dad called. "How was shopping?"

"Great," I said.

"So you got a dress?" David, with his fingers wedged into his pockets, looked down at me from the top of the stairs, anticipation lighting his eyes.

"I did, and I think you'll love it."

He kissed my cheek as I passed him and, as Vicki followed, my shoulders subconsciously hunched around my ears.

"Did you have fun?" Dad asked, standing behind the big red sofa that was wedged in the doorway of the spare room. Vicki shrugged and sat on it. "That good, huh?" Dad wiped his brow, winking at me.

"She hasn't changed a bit when it comes to shopping, Greg," Vicki whined.

My vampire folded his arms, his eyes narrowing as he stared at Vicki for a second. Then his head whipped up and he looked at me with an open-mouthed frown: my cue to leave.

"I'll just hang this up." I darted into my room quickly.

When I headed back out to help get the spare room ready for Mike, I half expected David to jump out and berate me. But he didn't. Worse, he continued to help Dad, all the while saying nothing at all. Well, nothing at all to me. He was mad. I knew it. I could tell.

The two boys struggled with the offending sofa while Vicki, who must've climbed in past it, vacuumed the imprints off the carpet where furniture had been. At last, the bulky lounge shifted, and David pretended to struggle with its weight as he and my dad carried it out of the room and angled it up the stairwell to the attic.

"Ara?"

I looked at Vicki, then the stairs and the front door, and considered running.

"Come help with the dusting please," she said.

Against my better judgment, I sauntered into the spare room and took the feather duster from her.

"Make sure you dust the cornices too. I hate cobwebs."

"Don't go to a vampire's house then." I grinned, imagining coffins, cobwebs and bats. If David invited Vicki and Dad over for dinner, she'd sneak off to the bathroom every five minutes to secretly remove all of his eight-legged pets. Then again, the only reason a vampire would invite Vicki and Dad to dinner is if they were the main course.

"I suppose you think you're pretty funny?"

I looked up at David, snapping out of my reverie in a suddenly Vicki-less room. "Actually, I do. I think you'd look rather fetching in a coffin."

"Coffin?" His eyes narrowed in obvious confusion. "Ara, what are you talking about?"

"The cobwebs." I pointed to the ceiling, then dropped my hand slowly, realizing that wasn't what he was referring to. "Oh. The dress?"

"Yes. The dress."

"I… you know what?" I sunk my hip down on one side, propping my hand on it. "Bite me!"

"Don't tempt me, young lady."

"It's just a dress. Get over it."

He shook his head and backed away as Dad and Vicki waltzed in, carrying the bedhead. "Vicki, let me take that." The human David took over for the angry vampire, and I secluded myself in my task while the three of them continued furnishing the room around me.

As time ticked on and my mediocre chores came to completion, I leaned on the tall chest of drawers across from the foot of the bed and watched David, suddenly aware that he probably wasn't *angry* that I hadn't accepted his gift, but perhaps hurt. In his day, it was common for a man to send his date a pretty dress. And my declining it was probably seen as very rude. But these were modern times. Things had changed. Women had rights now.

David dusted off his hands after he placed a small set of drawers next to the bed, then smiled at me—the conceited I-know-what-you're-thinking-and-I'm-finding-it-funny smile. Well, I wasn't finding it funny that he was listening in on my one-sided argument.

"That's *so* rude, David!" I stomped my foot, balling my fists up beside me. "You're so annoying."

"Ara!" Vicki looked up from making the bed, then looked at David as I stormed out of the room and slumped on the settee in the hall.

Dad walked out after me and stopped by the door with a look of intense thought, then snickered and walked away. Vicki, with her arms folded around a spare blanket, followed him—after casting an accusatory glare my way.

"Another one of Ara's infamous tantrums." David stood in front of me.

"I'm not throwing a tantrum." I slid down in the chair, biting my teeth together.

"Hm." He turned and headed back into the spare room. "Coulda fooled me."

"Coulda? You mean… did!"

"Yes." He stopped and leaned on the doorframe. "I must admit, that was very clever of you—stuffing your purse with a lesser amount. But you can't read minds, mon amour"—he tapped his temple—"so your plan was flawed from the start."

"Well, you assumed I was submissive, so yours was too."

"Submissive?" He lowered his arms, moving over to me. "Ara, is that what you think?"

"I don't know. You seem to know all my thoughts, so you tell me."

"Don't be like that." He knelt in front of me. "Look at me. Please."

With my movements as rigid as a frozen elastic band, I rolled my head upward, but kept my bottom lip in a completely tight pout.

"My love, I'm sorry. I never meant to offend you. I—" He took my hand; I let him, with only a little bit of a fight. "I was being playful, mostly. I truly did not think that my spending money on you would be considered controlling."

"It's not that, David." My tone sung with reason. "It's that when I tried to decline, you got mad at me."

"Mad?" He pulled back a little. "You think I'm mad?"

"You've been ignoring me," I said quietly.

"Ara," he laughed my name out. "I'm not mad. Not at all."

Tears coated my eyes. "I thought you'd yell at me."

"Yell?" His brow pulled low on one side, thought washing across his face. "Ara, what kind of man do you think I am?"

"One that likes to get his own way."

As if a rope had just pulled his soul out onto the carpet, his face went slack, his eyes draining of the smile. "I'm so sorry if I've given you that impression. I… I truly never meant for you to feel that way."

"Aw, David, now I just feel guilty."

He smiled reassuringly. "Don't. Look, I'm sorry I was pushy, but if it means that much to you, I'm glad you bought your own dress, and I will be happy to see you wear it."

"Really?" A half smile crept onto my lips.

"Oui, jolie fille." He touched his hand to the hollow between his collarbones. "I am your eternal servant. You should never feel pressured to do something because I want you to. And you should never be afraid of me—*or* my reaction."

"I wasn't really afraid, per se. Just anxious." My shoulders dropped. "I just don't like disappointing you."

"My love, nothing you want with your heart will ever be a disappointment to me. You must know that."

"I do. *Now.*" I shook my head, laughing softly.

He looked down then, his eyes focusing on something far away while his lips turned up, and my heart skipped at the sight of his dimples.

"What are you smiling at?" I asked.

"Uh… I hope you like scary movies."

An eerie feeling swept over me as my gaze followed his to the front door at the base of the stairs. "Why?"

"Come in, Emily," Sam said as he passed.

"Hello," Emily chimed in her high but elegant voice, opening the door.

"Hey, Em." I stood up.

"Hey," she said, then turned and waved to someone outside. "Bye, David."

Not surprisingly, when I looked back, my eyes fell upon the plain colors of the corridor walls and the rosewood floorboards below the rug David *had* been kneeling on.

"Right on time, Em." I checked the clock on the wall as I reached the base of the stairs.

"Yep, and I hope you like scary movies." She held up a USB stick. "It's based in Australia—some place called Wolf Creek?"

I shivered. *That's* what David meant. "Uh, wow. That'll be great," I lied, not really sure why I did that.

I could almost hear David laughing down the street.

Well, I hoped he enjoyed his little joke, because he'd be paying for it when I called *him* at two in the morning, scared of the boogeyman in the corner, instead of calling Mike, like always.

My arms folded in smug gratification. Well, there you go, that was *one* thing I'd let him pay for.

21

"I don't know." Emily grinned at Dad as he stood up. "I think Sam has a point."

"See, old man?" Sam said. "If a senior agrees with me, I must be right."

Dad, with a humored grunt, stacked a pile of plates in the sink and leaned against the counter. "Well, I happen to know that this particular senior is an A grade student because she *doesn't* play video games." He motioned a hand to Emily, who sat taller, bristling with pride.

"Dad." Sam smirked. "Emily's only an A grade student because she has a cru—"

"Good work ethic," I cut in, sure Sam was about to say "crush on her teacher."

Sam bit his lip, offering Emily an apologetic look. She just shook her head, picking the pineapple off her pizza.

"If only a good work ethic was addictive, like those video games you play, Samuel." Dad sat back down at the table. "The fact is, my boy, you have an example to set for the other students, being that you're a—"

"Teacher's kid. I know, I know." Sam rolled his eyes. "We've all heard the speech, Dad. But you can't debate my argument with your uneducated reasoning. I learned more about physics by playing Halo than I did from Mr. Ester, and unless you've also played video games, then you can't, beyond all reasonable doubt, say that it doesn't teach physics."

Dad let out a long breath, pinching the bridge of his nose.

"It's okay, Mr. Thompson," Emily said in an encouraging tone. "Alana and I still believe in the importance of homework, isn't that right, Lani?"

Alana looked up from her plate and nodded.

"I'm sorry." I folded my arms. "I'm with Sam on this one. Burnout taught *me* the logistics of driving a car."

Dad jostled with a little chuckle. "Exactly."

"Hey. What's that supposed to mean?"

"I mean"—he sat back, folding his arms—"that there's a reason you don't have your license yet."

"You don't have your license?" Emily practically spat the words out.

"Um… no." I sank into myself. "Not yet."

"Why?"

"I uh, I'm not very good at driving," I lied. Truthfully, I just didn't see the need to be behind the wheel.

"Maybe Alana and I could teach you," Em offered.

"I think we'll leave the driving lessons to the experts," Dad chimed in.

"But if your methods aren't working, Mr. Thompson, maybe she could learn from those of us closer to her age," Emily said.

Dad raised a brow. "When did I become the old guy?"

"Uh, about forty years ago, Dad." I laughed.

"Hm. Should've seen it coming. So," he said with a change in tone, "what are you girls up to tonight?"

"Scary movie," Emily said.

"Yay." I waved an invisible flag with mock enthusiasm.

"Yeah? Which one?" Sam sat up, suddenly more eager to be a part of the conversation again.

"No way, pest. Girls' night," I said.

"Aw. No fair."

"Life's not fair, son. Get used to it," Dad said distractedly, the common disease of resorting to philosophical one-liners taking the intelligence out of any point he may have been trying to make.

"Well, Sam, if you want to paint your nails and look at pictures of Ara's hunky BFF, then you can have a girls' night with us," Emily offered.

"Yeah, I'll pass." He slumped back in his chair.

"All right, well"—Dad stood up and took the last of the plates—"Sam and I will get the dishes, and you girls can go talk about boys."

Awkward. "Yeah, um, that's our cue to go." I stood and motioned the girls to follow.

THREE PAIRS OF FEET DANGLED OFF ONE SIDE OF MY BED, THREE ponytails off the other, while the sun slipped behind the house, bringing darkness down the walls.

"So, whose idea was it to hang the crystals over the window?" Alana asked. "It was so magic in here with all those rainbows as the sun went down."

"Oh, um, Pollyanna."

"Pollyanna?" She rolled onto her belly.

"Yeah. It's from an old movie my mom used to love."

"Hm. Never seen it." Alana looked at Emily, who shrugged, shaking her head.

"So Ara, are you gonna show us these pics of Mike, or what?"

"Sure, but you're with Spence now, Em. Do you really need to be checking out other guys?"

"Who says I'm checking him out?" She sat up beside Alana. "I'm just curious as to why *your* eyes light up when you mention him."

"They so do not light up," I demanded, feeling them light up.

"Um actually, Ara, they kind of do," Alana said carefully.

"Yeah, you sparkle." Emily waved her fingers around. "So"—she shuffled to the edge of the bed—"let's see them."

"Fine." I rolled up with a huff and wandered over to my desk. "I don't have many, though. I only grabbed one box when I moved, and it was the wrong one."

"That sucks. So what got left behind?" Em asked.

"Just some old family ones." I shrugged, as if it didn't matter. "I'd switched the boxes about a week before and just didn't realize until I was already here."

"Why not ask your mom to send them over for you?" Alana suggested.

"Yeah. Guess I could." I bumped the drawer closed with my hip and plonked down on the ground with the box in front of me. Alana sat beside me, waiting anxiously while I fingered the lid, trying not to peel back the rainbow and kitten stickers Mike had randomly stuck on when he was bored one day.

"Oh, my God!" Alana reached past my wrist and grabbed the first picture the light touched, then jumped up and handed it to Emily, who smiled.

"Oh. Yeah. He *is* cute."

"You think?" My lip curled in false disgust, when secretly, Mike had always been just my type.

Emily lay back on my pillow, her silky blonde hair spilling out around her like liquid. "Hell yeah. He's kinda rustic, isn't he?"

Alana, with another picture in hand, nodded. "Is he a surfer?" She flipped the image around of Mike in his board shorts on the beach, golden and tanned. His scruffy yellow hair had blown over his eyes, the wet sand sticking it together on the ends, like dreadlocks.

"Yeah, I suppose." I shrugged. "He does surf."

"I can't believe how cute he is."

"Even by my standards," Alana said. "He reminds me of that Australian actor."

"Which one? We spew out quite a few good ones," I said.

"The one who plays Thor in that movie—"

"Oh, yeah." I nodded. "I thought that too when I saw it."

"And you two never uh…" Emily let her suggestive tone end the question.

I shook my head. "It's really not like that."

She grinned, seeing the pathetic liar in me. "Oh, my God. You so had a fling!"

"We didn't."

"You did," Emily insisted.

"Did not."

Alana studied my smirk. "Ara, you're a terrible liar."

"Drat." My shoulders sunk. "Okay, maybe I did *kind of* throw myself at him. Once."

"Really?" Emily sat up and crossed her legs under her. "Well? Come on, girl, fill us in!"

My head dropped to one side with a groan. "Okay. Um, so it was my friend's eighteenth…"

"Ooh, wait, wait, wait." Em waved her hands about, coming to sit down in our little circle around my box of Mike. "Okay. Go."

"Um." I laughed at her. "So… I had a drink at her party. Well, maybe three." I laughed. "Or more."

The girls gasped, wide-eyed.

"What?" I shrugged.

"You rebel." Alana breathed the words out.

"I know, I know. It's not one of my proudest moments. But it was her eighteenth birthday and the legal age for drinking in Australia *is* eighteen," I added. "So I'm not that far off, not like here."

"Huh! So lucky," Emily scoffed.

"Anyway," I continued, "I walked to Mike's house to stay the night so my mom wouldn't find out I was drinking and—"

"Did *his* mom know you were drunk?" Emily sat forward.

"Let me finish." I held a hand up. Alana laughed. "It was actually Mike who picked up on it, like, before I even got in the door."

"How did he know?" Alana asked.

"He's been a cop since he was eighteen," I said. "He knows the signs, and he knows me, and *I* don't act like that."

"Wait. I thought he was just getting into the police," Alana asked.

My head moved in a 'no' as I popped a candy in my mouth. "He's just getting in to the Tactical Response Group. That's where he really wanted to be. But he's been a beat cop for a bit now."

"So…" Emily led, "what happened then?"

"Um, well, so he took me upstairs to his room and sat me down for a severe talking to. But I just thought he was hilarious. I couldn't stop laughing at him."

"My mom does that to my dad all the time. He hates it," Em said.

"Yeah, but Mike's feathers aren't easily ruffled. Like, basically, I can do no wrong. And he was trying not to laugh too, but... then I kind of threw my arms around him and kissed him." And told him I've always loved him. It was the first time I realized there was a limit to what he'd put up with from me; that I could, in fact, do wrong.

"Mm. I don't blame you," Emily said. "*I'd* like to kiss him."

"Did he kiss you back?" Alana asked, completely arrested by my tale.

"Yeah"—I lowered my head—"for a moment. But then he pushed me away."

"Like, a small push or a big mean push?" Alana asked.

I hadn't really thought about it. The force of his rejection felt like he'd flung me across the room, but now I looked back on it for the first time since that night, it was more of a gentle shift. More like he *pulled away* from me. "I'm not sure," I said. "It was rejection, and that's kind of all I really noticed."

"Ouch." Emily winced.

"It hurt more that he yelled at me, I think. I mean, he had *never* yelled at me before—for anything." I laughed it off, but I'd pushed that memory so far down that remembering it came as a shock. I'd almost convinced myself the kiss never happened. I'd almost convinced myself that all those feelings were a mistake, or at least that meeting David had eradicated them. But they were still there, and it made me feel unsteady, like the feeling you get when you've left your assignment at home on its due date.

"Why'd he yell at you?" Alana asked.

"Was it because you kissed him?"

"It was because..." My eyes narrowed to better hear the memory of his words that night. "You know, it's funny. I *thought* he yelled at me for kissing him, but he actually said he was just really disappointed in me for drinking. He was worried, I guess."

"So what did he say about the kiss then?" Emily asked.

"Nothing really." I shrugged casually. "But it was a mistake. I don't really feel that way about him. It was just the alcohol."

"Or did you just tell him it was liquor-lust to save face?" Emily smirked.

"I didn't tell him anything." I shook my head. "I kind of ran home after that—never talked about it again."

"Like, never?" Em asked.

"Nope. I moved here after, and I've barely spoken to him since."

"Oh. So… how will things be when you see him on Tuesday?" I could see the word *awkward* appear in bold all over Emily's face.

"It'll be fine." I hoped. "So, have you guys got a dress for the Masquerade yet?"

Alana, detecting my need to divert, knelt up and placed the picture she was holding into the box. "I'm wearing the same dress my mother wore, and her mother, and so on."

"Wow, that's so cool." I started gathering the pictures into a pile.

"Mm-hm. It was actually first worn by my great-great-grandmother at the very first town Masquerade."

"That is totally cool." Emily handed me a stack of pictures. "I haven't found one yet. I'm still looking. Just… nothing seems to suit me."

"I find that really hard to believe, Em." I rolled my eyes.

"Well, what about you, Ara? Have you got a dress yet?" Alana asked.

I grinned, placing the lid on the box. "I thought you'd never ask."

"Ooh, you do." Emily squeaked. "Let's see it, let's see it!"

"Okay." I bounced to my feet. "I'll just be a sec."

They both positioned themselves on my bed, anticipation alight in their eyes, and I bounded into my wardrobe, stopping dead as I closed the door behind me and saw a giant white bag hanging on the hook.

My breath quickened, my throat constricting to the size of a straw, when I slowly tugged the zipper down the length of the bag and saw blue. "Damn vampires!"

"What?" Emily called.

"Oh, ah, nothing. Just got bitten by a mozzie." I sucked my finger, drawing away the mock-irritation of a mosquito bite.

Alana and Emily laughed. "You sound so Australian when you say that."

"Well, I *am* Australian."

"Yeah, I know," Emily called, "you just never sound it."

"Well, they say practice makes perfect." I looked back at the blue dress inside the bag, wondering where those conspiring renegades had stuffed my pretty green dress. And when my eyes brushed past my old purple sweater and faded blue jeans, I saw it there—shoved away like some ratty old coat. "Huh!" I scoffed, reaching for it. But at the last second, stopped.

The blue dress and I stared at each other across the silent battleground of conscience.

It was a pretty dress, and I did love it.

It couldn't hurt just to try it on again—see if it really was as perfect as I'd been dreaming it was all afternoon.

Without allowing a second for my conscience to overreact, I unbuttoned my jeans, tore off my top and bra, and crawled into the dress, leaving it on the hanger until I had my arms through. Then, I unhitched it from the hook and let it slide into place around the shape of my body. It was hard to think I'd be telling him to return this when it felt so amazing on my skin.

As I reached around to tighten the satin ribbons at the back, I felt a cool touch on my wrist. I spun around mid-gasp, and a tall, handsome vampire placed an elegant finger to his lips. "Shh."

"David, I—"

"Shh." He smiled and nodded in the direction of the girls.

"You're lucky you're so cute."

By the turn of his hand, I faced the wall again, closing my eyes when his deft fingers took my ribbons and twisted each one through the loops of the corset, tying them up. It tickled so softly that it made my knees weak. I rested a hand to the wall for support.

"All done," he said, but as I tried to turn around, he held me in place by my shoulders.

"What're you doing?"

"Shh." Using the tip of his very cold finger, the vampire traced a line ever so slowly from the base of my neck all the way down my spine and across my shoulder blades, resting just under where my bra would sit. "I've never seen this part of your body before."

Despite the urge to dissolve under his touch, I held tight to good sense, jerking around to protest the unwelcome gift. But all my anger dissipated as liquid adoration melted the green in his eyes.

"You look so beautiful in this dress, Ara."

"I do?"

David placed both hands in his back pockets and lowered his shoulders, shaking his head. He just had this way of looking at me, like the human, the cheeky boy from school stared out from one eye, while the truth of his devious thoughts hid within the other. And every time he did that, I was lost. All I wanted now was to take this dress off and tell the girls to go home.

"I love you." David laughed and kissed my cheek. "I have to go."

"Hurry up, Ara. What are you doing in there? Sewing the seams?" Emily joked.

"It's a corset, Em. Good things take time." I turned back to look at David but, as usual, he left without saying goodbye, leaving only an empty space behind.

I drew a breath to calm the cells he excited in me, and then stepped out to show the girls my dress.

"Oh my God!" Emily jumped up and ran over. "Ara, you look like a princess."

Alana shook her head, walking slowly over. "No way, she looks like an angel."

"Look at the way it sets off her eyes. They're bluer than the sky against that dress, Ara." Emily ruffled the layers of my skirt, then sighed. "I wish I could find a dress like this."

"You will. Hey, why don't we all go shopping next week? We'll find something just as perfect for you," I said.

Emily nodded eagerly. "I'm in."

Alana cringed. "I'd rather not. I hate shopping."

"Really?" I asked.

"Yeah, I mean, not hate it, but I'd rather do other things," she said.

"I'm sure you and I are kindred spirits, Lani."

"Perhaps." She shrugged. "Except I have better taste in boys."

As I turned away, chuckling softly, I caught my reflection in the window. The sky was dark, and though the howling wind and the pattering rain outside made my stomach sink for fear there might be a storm on the way, I saw only a smile on the face of the dark-haired beauty in the glass. She looked happy. And I felt happy.

"Oh my God, Ara!" Emily grabbed the price tag from under my arm. "Was this dress really a thousand dollars?"

"Um. Yeah. David bought it for me."

"What?" Alana picked up the tag and flipped it over, searching for a sale price, I guess.

"He wanted me to feel special. I tried to stop him, but he did it anyway." And without that cheeky grin distracting me, I found it so much easier to be mad at him.

Emily sat rigidly down on my bed and folded her hands into her lap. "I can't believe it, Ara. I never thought I'd see the day when David Knight fell in love."

"Did you not think he was capable?" I asked.

"No. I'm sorry. I didn't. I was sure that, ten years from now when we met for our high school reunion, he'd be America's most eligible bachelor."

She had no idea how right she was. Ten years from now, I might be so much older than him, and our high-school-sweetheart-romance could be a memory I only thought about when I was alone.

"He might still be," I added with a light giggle. "Just because we're in love now, doesn't mean we're gonna get married or anything." Only, I knew we would—if things were different. We loved each other enough to commit to a lifetime together, but I just couldn't commit to eternity, and David couldn't commit to a life.

"Are you serious?" Emily stood up. "He spends a thousand dollars on a dress, because he wants you to feel *special*, and you're not sure if you're going to marry him?"

"It's a dress, Em. Not an engagement ring." I sighed, feeling utterly defeated. I wanted to tell her the truth. I knew she'd understand—be able to give me advice and take some of the burden of life and death decisions off my shoulders—but I was forbidden to speak of it. Although… if it just slipped out; if I just said it, right here, right now, maybe David wouldn't be that mad with me; maybe he'd understand that I needed *someone* to talk to. And if Emily helped steer my decision toward becoming immortal, then David would only be grateful, right?

I opened my mouth and, as Alana sat down in my desk chair, the squeaky hinge woke me to the reality of what I was just about to do. I snapped my stupid gob shut.

Emily squinted, studying my face. "There's more to it, isn't there?"

"More to what?" I shrugged casually and started untying my dress.

"Is it… are you still in love with Mike?"

"What? I never said I was in love with him."

"Then, I don't understand!"

Of course she couldn't. How could anyone? David was perfect. Why would I not want to marry him?

"What's to understand, Em? David and I… we're in love, but we want different things in life." I grabbed a shirt off the end of my bed. "Eventually, we'll have to go our separate ways. We both know that."

"Who are you trying to convince, Ara? Us, or yourself?" Emily asked.

I held my dress in front of my chest, pulled the shirt over my head and, once covered, stepped out of the dress and threw it on the bed. "What does it matter? It's not like *you're* losing him, Emily."

She shook her head. "It matters because I care about him. We've been friends for years, Ara, and I've never seen him like this. He's happy. And it was like he knew you were coming; like he predicted it, or something, because about a month before we even met you, he *changed*—became the David everyone else can tolerate."

Which was about the time I arrived at Dad's. "So?"

"So, he smiles. He laughs," Emily continued. "And the only time that hasn't been true, since the moment he finally asked you out, was the day of Nathan's funeral. What's going to happen to him if you don't love him like he loves you?"

Her ignorance just made me insanely mad. "Who says I don't?"

"You just said you had no plans to marry him. Ara,"—she pointed to my door—"that boy is practically picking out goddamn rings. You have no idea how lucky you are."

"I do, actually." I sighed, dropping my arms to my sides as I sat on the bed, wishing I could fall against her shoulder and cry hysterically. "I hate that we can't be together. More than you know. But it isn't my decision to make. Not really. There are outside factors involved."

"Why should it matter? When you love someone, you give up everything for that," she said.

I kind of laughed. I didn't know Emily went so deep.

Everything she said was true, though, and it hurt. I just wasn't brave enough to risk everything for love. And my mother would be disappointed in me if I traded my soul for immortal life. So I just wanted to forget about decision-making and enjoy the time I had with David and maybe, somewhere in time passing, the answer would just come to me.

"That's the worst advice I've ever heard, Emily."

She opened her mouth and drew a long breath. "You're just too blind to see the logic."

"Or maybe too sensible."

"Guys!" Alana ditched a pillow between us. "Stop fighting."

Emily sat on my bed, shaking her head. "Sensible people die alone, Ara—like my gran and my Aunt Betty. My dad says *if you don't fight for love, you have nothing to fight for.*"

Despite numerous arguments I could squash that statement with, I decided to sever the conversation instead. "I'll keep that in mind. Shall we watch that movie now?"

THE QUIET HUM OF RESTFUL BREATHING FILLED MY ROOM UNDER the howling of the wind outside. I lay awake, sending waves of anger to the mattress on the floor—cursing Emily's film choice—wishing I could put my bedside light on to illuminate the scary corners of my room. I should've told Emily I hate scary movies.

My phone lit the roof green for a second then. I flipped over and reached across the gap between my bed and nightstand cautiously, in case the Bogeyman reached up to grab my hand, then tucked my arms back in quickly with my phone in hand. The message on the screen read: *Call me if you need me.*

I smiled and texted back: *Thanks, David.*

But it wasn't him I wanted to speak to. Recalling the last night I had with Mike again had reopened old wounds, old feelings, and I needed to poke them to see what they meant. Maybe they could help me finally make a decision about whether or not I'd go with David.

Emily stirred when the keypad bleeped as I pinned in a familiar number, settling again when I put the phone to my ear. All I wanted was to hear the familiarity of Mike's voice. And with the mere buzzing of the ringtone down the line, the eerie feeling of isolation slipped away a little.

Pick up. Come on, Mike. Please, pick up.

"Hey, beautiful. What's up?" he asked, bringing me home with the sound of his voice.

"Hey, Mike," I whispered.

"What happened?" he asked quickly. "Are you okay?"

"Sleepover," I said. "Watched a horror movie."

"Oh, baby girl. Why do you do it?"

"I know. It was stupid."

"What movie was it?"

"It doesn't matter. I'm never sleeping again."

"You will—you always do eventually."

"Not for a few weeks, though."

Mike laughed. "It'll be all right. I'll be there in a few days, then I'll sleep by your wardrobe and keep the monsters from coming out to get you."

I chuckled. "It wouldn't be the first time."

"Ha, yeah. How old were you the last time I did that?"

"Um, thirteen, I think."

"Well, I'm sending a hug through the phone for ya, 'kay?"

"Okay," I whispered, actually feeling a little better with that thought.

"Hey, so I was thinking about you before you called. You must've read my mind."

"What were you thinking about this time—me in a blender or something?"

"Ara, I don't only reflect on memories of you in pain."

"Seems like you do."

"It was one memory. Once."

"Two."

"No. It was only the ice-cream truck one."

"And the other one."

"Which one?"

I couldn't think of one, realizing then that I was wrong. "So now you expect me to document every conversation we have?"

"Ara, what is wrong with you tonight?"

"What do you mean *what's wrong with me*?"

"You're doing your thing."

"My thing?"

"Yeah, when you twist my words around until we get in a fight. Don't do that. I'm not trying to fight with you, baby. I was just… I wanted to call you. I was thinking about you, then you called. It surprised me, that's all."

"You should be used to it."

He paused. "It's been a long time since we've been that in tune with each other, Ar."

"What's that supposed to mean?"

He paused again.

"Mike?"

Emily rolled over and stirred with the disruption of my voice through the perfect silence.

"I'm still here, Ara. I just… I need a few seconds, okay?"

"Okay. I'm just moving into the spare room." I walked into the hall, my toes balancing over the quiet spots in the floorboards that I'd memorized, and closed the door behind me.

"Is that the room I'll be staying in?"

"Yep." I grinned and leaped through the dark, landing with a bounce on the mattress. "I'm sitting on your bed."

"Maybe you can keep it warm 'til I get there."

"Yeah, sure, I'm gonna stay in bed for the next few days," I said sarcastically.

He paused again, then after a long breath through what sounded like his nose, asked, "So, how are things with the boyfriend?"

"Not so good." I winced, not meaning to say that. How was the truth so automatic with Mike? "We've kind of decided to break up after summer." I think.

"What? Why? I mean, why would you do that? I thought you guys were a sure thing?" Mike's sympathetic tone brought my pain to the surface.

"I don't want to, Mike. But he. He has a. Kind. Of. Problem." I sniffled before the tears came breaking through.

"What is it, baby? You can tell me."

"I know, Mike, but—" I could feel Mike in the room with me, the way he'd normally hang up the phone right about now, and no more than two minutes later be knocking on my window. But that wasn't possible anymore, and I missed it. "I… he has a secret and I have to keep it," I said, sniffling. "I want to tell you. But I can't."

"Ara, baby, you know damn well if there's a secret someone says you shouldn't tell, you absolutely shou—"

"It's not like that, Mike. Okay?" I took a moment to compose myself. "Anyway, none of it matters. He has to leave, and after the last leaf of autumn falls, he'll be gone."

"What?" Mike scoffed. "What the hell is that? Some fairy-tale timeline bull crap? Leaves falling? Ara! Did he hurt you?"

"No, Mike. He didn't hurt me. I mean, not physically. I'm hurting inside, like I always do, but it isn't his fault. It's my decision that caused it."

"Wait. *Your* decision? Ara. If he hurt you, I swear to God, I'll—"

"Mike, he never hurt me, okay? He asked me to come with him. To go away with him."

A moment of silence passed. "Where?"

"Far away. I'd never be able to come back."

I actually heard a dense cloud wander into his breath—the kind that makes everything silent before the imminent explosion occurs.

"Don't worry, Mike. I told him no," I added quickly, before he could freak out, even though it was a lie.

The explosion came across the miles in a loud whoosh of air, the phone line interpreting it as static. "So, you… what, you're breaking up *when*?"

"When winter comes—maybe before. He said I could count on him staying until at least the end of autumn."

"And how..." I heard him sniff once. "How are you coping with that?"

The sadness of the idea felt so final, so eternal now that I'd said it aloud. "Not sure."

"Well, you still have me."

I laughed out in one short burst of air. "I know. I've always had you."

"It's just not really a consolation, is it?"

"Don't be like that, Mike."

"I'm sorry. I just..." He paused for a few ticks of the clock on the wall. "Do you hate me, Ar? Is that why you didn't take my calls?"

"Hate you? Why would I hate you?"

"Because of... because of what happened that night."

It crushed me to realize he thought I hated him. Not one bone in my body could ever hate him. "It would be easier if I hated you."

"Don't say things like that," he said softly.

"Why?"

"It hurts me to think of you wanting to hate me."

"Why?"

"You know how I feel about you, Ar."

"Yeah. I know."

"I don't think you do. I don't think you get it."

"What do you mean?"

"You can't... you can do no wrong. All that stuff—everything—it doesn't change the fact that I will always need you in my life. You know that, right?"

"I know, Mike. I just..." I wasn't sure I'd ever recover from the fact that I wanted more, and he didn't. "Can we just forget it ever happened, please?"

"Already forgotten."

I sighed and stood up, looking out at the twinkling stars in the sky to the west. They reminded me of David—after our blissful night on the rooftop—and for the rest of my life now, they always would. Which was funny, really, because while thoughts of my dark knight remained with the midnight sky, thoughts of my Mike—my warmth—would always be with the beaches and sand and the blue skies. Two separate parts that made my days whole; made my world whole. It reminded me of my earlier analogy of that song, "Unintended", how I'd said it was like the sad story of the night sky in love with the sun. Except, I was the earth in love with both the night and the day. I couldn't really see how a happy ending could resolve from that.

"You okay, Ara?" Mike asked.

"Just thinking how much I'll miss you."

"I'll be there soon," he said.

"I know, but you'll be gone soon too."

Mike sighed, and the sound came through so perfectly down the line that it strengthened the memory of his face: his jaw, with an almost arrogant set to it that was completely softened by his charming smile—the kind of smile that made you a part of his world. I could see his shaggy sandy-colored hair, the blond tones lighter in the summer, and his autumn-brown eyes—deep, like leaf-covered pools. It made me miss him so much more.

"Where are you, Ara? What world of thought have you slipped away to this time?" he asked in a soft, almost whisper.

"A world where there's no up or down. No right or wrong." Where I could have Mike, and keep David.

"Just hold tight a few more days, kid. I'll be there to pull you out soon."

I smiled to myself. "I miss you."

"I miss you too, kiddo."

22

"I'll be back before dark," I called to Dad, closing the lid on Vicki's sewing box.

"It's going to rain. You'll need a coat," he replied from upstairs.

I stuffed the stolen pin into my pocket, taking a quick look at my bare arms, then tiptoed out the front door, pulling it quietly closed behind me.

"Take a coat," David said sternly.

"God!" I jumped back from the vampire. "You gotta stop popping up like that."

"Coat."

"Ergh, fine." I went to obey but stopped, folding my arms. "Actually, no. If you want me to bring one, *you* can go get it."

His eyes slowly narrowed above a tight jaw, an invisible rope bringing his shoulders back and straight. I swallowed, stirred by the authoritative stance, about to shift my hand and place it on the doorknob. But a breath of wind swept my hair back and David grabbed my hand, leading me to the car—with my jacket over his forearm.

"I love how you do that."

"Hm," is all he said.

We sat quietly on the first half of the drive out to the lake. Not a peaceful silence, either; a deliberate one. I had nothing good to say to him today after he bought me that dress last night. I loved it, still loved him, but there's no way I could let this go without at least yelling at him first.

"Vicki seems happy about your new dress," David chimed, a flash of pure white teeth gleaming through his dark pink lips.

"Hmpf." I folded my arms.

"Oh, come on, Ara. You're not really mad, are you? It's a dress, let it go."

"It's not the dress I have a problem with." And all of a sudden, we were arguing again. "It's the fact that you went behind my back. You picked through mine or Vicki's brain until you found what *you* wanted, then took it upon yourself to force me in a direction I told you I didn't want to go."

He was quiet for a moment before saying, "But you love the dress."

Even though I refused to look at his charming smile, I could still feel its warmth. "I do love the dress. But I'm just afraid it'll always be like this, David. That you won't respect my decisions." Like the one to stay human.

"I never thought of it that way." He looked down at the steering wheel. "I'm sorry, Ara. I must have misinterpreted your thoughts yesterday when we talked. I'll take the dress back."

"No. Don't do that." I choked on my own words. "Just… in future, even if my thoughts indicate the opposite, listen to me when I *say* no."

He nodded. "So you'll wear the dress?"

"David, of course I'll wear the dress. I love the dress."

"I know you do."

"I know you know I do." And all the irritation over the dress evaporated with one flash of his irresistibly cute dimples, making the sun rise again in my world. "Thank you, by the way."

"For what?"

"The other night when you closed my window. It stormed, and everything would've been drenched if you—Ah!" I projected forward, nearly striking the dash when the car screeched to a halt in the middle of the empty road. "David! What the hell!" Prying my fingers from their grip of fear on the seat, I slapped him hard. But he didn't even flinch.

"When was this, Ara? Which night are you talking about?"

"Friday. Why?" I rubbed at my now throbbing hand.

"Tell me exactly what you think I did." He grabbed my face, turning it from one side to the other.

"Umm, you closed my window." I pushed his hand off my cheek. "Why the sudden freak-out?"

After a moment of stillness, he looked over his shoulder, then back at the dash. "Because, Ara, I *never* close your window. And neither does your father. We know you hate that. I'd more likely have moved your books aside if it was going to rain."

My blood ran cold. "Then, who did close it?"

"I'm pretty sure my brother came to visit you."

"What? How do you know that, and what makes you so sure it wasn't my dad that closed it?"

David reluctantly turned his gaze to me. "The scent."

"The scent?"

"Yes. It's nearly exactly the same as mine, only… I should've followed my gut when I realized it was on things I never touch—things I've never been near."

"Are you saying there was some strange vampire in my room? While I was sleeping? Oh my God." I shook my hands around, taking short breaths. "I think I'm gonna be sick."

"It's okay, Ara. Really. He would never hurt you. You have nothing to worry about." He placed a calming hand to my shoulder.

I didn't feel convinced.

"He's like me, my love—in so many ways," he said, rubbing my back. "Just… not quite as dark. He was just curious about you."

"Then why did he sneak into my room? What is it with you Knight boys?"

"It's my fault. I wouldn't let him meet you."

"Why?"

"Because my personal life is not his business."

"How is it not? He's your *brother*."

He looked forward, almost pouting. "You're starting to sound like my uncle."

I reached across and touched his arm. "David?"

He looked at me again.

"Tell me why you won't just let him meet me. It would've saved all this"—I motioned to us, stopped dead in the middle of the desolate road—"drama."

"He doesn't fit into your world as well as I do—anymore." David wrapped his fingers over his thumb, cracking it absentmindedly. "I was afraid he might scare you."

"Scare me?"

"Yes." He smiled into his lap, tossing a sideways glance at me after. "He can come across as a little… malevolent."

"And you tell me not to worry that he was in my room? With me? Alone?"

"Yes."

"David!"

"I'm sorry."

"How do you know he didn't do anything unsavory? I mean, like… touch me, breathe on me? Look at me?"

"I know my brother. He's… for all his faults, violence and depravity are not among them. He wouldn't do anything dishonorable to you."

"Then why did you study me like that?" I asked, referring to the way he checked my neck when he pulled up.

"Involuntary reaction." He shrugged, looking so human when he did that. "It was silly of me, though. If he'd bitten you, you'd already…"

"Do you really think he'd have done that?"

He rubbed his chin. "I don't know. I guess I was just worried he might."

"But you said he's not the kind of guy who'd do that."

"I… I know. But…"

"But what? Is he or isn't he? Should I be worried, or not?"

"No, but—" His gaze drifted, coming back a second later with a trace of alarm. "If you ever see me or speak to me, and you feel something is slightly off, just… just ask me something only *I'd* know, and don't think about the answer."

"Why? Can he read minds, too?"

"Yes. And not just human minds, either."

"What, like, dogs and cats?"

"And vampires."

"Really?"

"Yes."

I held back the urge to laugh. "So he's more powerful than you. I bet that sucks."

He brushed my hair from my face and stared at me intently, a hint of a smile returning to one corner of his mouth. "What would suck is having your fourteen-year-old brother inherit the height in the family, while you were left… short."

"Hey! I am not short."

He laughed and put both hands back on the steering wheel. "Yes, you are."

"Well, you make up in annoyance what I lack in height." I folded my arms. "So? Can I meet him?"

"Who, Jason?"

"Yeah."

"No," he answered swiftly.

"Why?"

"There's no need. He was obviously satisfied."

"Ew! That's so creepy." I dusted myself off as if I'd walked through an empty web.

"I'm sorry, Ara. I'll talk to him, okay?"

I swiped my hair from my face, looking out the window. "You'd better."

David put the car in gear and we pulled away again, gaining speed a little faster than usual. I sat watching the world go by for a minute, sorting out my inner fears by imagining everything: that vampire slipping through my window and standing over me, his face and his smile just like David's, while his eyes told a different story. And that damn cat. He was on my bed that night. How could he call himself a guard cat if he couldn't even alert me to strange predators sneaking into my room? I bet he would've slept through my death, had it been a murderous vampire.

"So, you said I'd already be changed if he'd bitten me. How long does it take?"

"I didn't say you'd be changed. It doesn't work like that."

"What do you mean?"

"Nothing. It's not important."

I folded my arms. "You always say that."

"I know."

"Well, I'm still curious. If I was turned, how long would it take to become a vampire?"

"A day or so. For some it can take only hours."

"Why?"

"It's based on the strength of your immune system. The venom kills it slowly, and when it finally gives out, you change permanently into a vampire—assuming you have the gene."

"What if I don't?"

"Well, it won't matter, because you refuse to become what I am. So—"

"David! Tell me. What if he'd bitten me, and I didn't have the gene?"

"Then"—he went quiet again until he looked at me—"you die."

"Whoa! Hold on." I turned in my seat. "So if you feed off a human and you don't kill them, they become a vampire?"

"It's not that simple. Like I said, they have to have that recessive gene," he said, scratching the back of his neck. "I've never turned someone. Of all the people I left alive in my years, not one has survived. My uncle is the only person I know who's done it successfully." He picked at the crumbling leather where his fingers had gripped the steering wheel during our abrupt halt. "It's more complicated than just biting, I believe. In fact, the exact method's a closely guarded secret—to prevent unauthorized transformations. All I do know is if Jason and I hadn't been compatible for the change when my uncle turned us, we would have grown ill."

"Grown ill?" I said the words to myself as they sunk in. "So… it's *kinder* to kill them?"

"Yes." He looked back at me. "Our venom numbs the skin and induces euphoria; they desire the bite, the kill. Then we drain them and… they die from blood loss," his voice softened. "It's peaceful, serene. But if we leave them alive, the venom becomes parasitic; they get a fever, their immune system deteriorates, as do the cognitive functions, then they fall into a coma. It's a degrading and painful death."

"*Can* someone survive if they don't have the gene?"

"I've heard of a few cases. But it's rare, and they're never quite the same again."

"So… I could choose to give up my life—to be with you—and it might not work?"

"It's a possibility."

"Oh my God!"

"It's okay, Ara. Do you remember that feeling you had at the lake? The uh"—he smiled, rubbing his chin—"*gravitational pull*?"

"Yes?"

"That's how I know you're my soul mate, and—"

"Really?" I pulled the seatbelt away from my neck a little so I could turn more in my seat. "I just put that down to the spell of lust, you know? The vampire thing—"

"It wasn't." He answered too quickly.

"Okay, so that… *pull* means I can be changed?"

"Kind of. It is my belief that soul mates are designed for each other perfectly. If you couldn't be changed, it would be incredibly unjust."

I wasn't sure I understood what he meant. Was he saying there was a science to this, or was he saying it was some unfounded belief that I must have the gene simply because he loved me?

"Did you feel that gravitational pull with the person who changed you—with your uncle?"

He laughed. "No. You only feel it with your soul mate, and it's especially rare for humans to feel it. My uncle took a risk changing Jason and I on the hope we would be more like him genetically. And there was nothing to lose anyway. We'd just signed up to join the army. He wanted us protected if we ever went to war."

"Really? *That's* how you became a vampire?"

"Yeah."

"Why would he do that? He could've killed you."

"He swore an oath to protect our bloodline. It was either death by Arthur or by something possibly a lot worse."

"So, he risked killing you to save you?"

"Love works in mysterious ways, Ara."

"Love? Love is not plunging two *barely* nineteen-year-old boys into a world of murder."

His knee sunk as he pressed his foot to the clutch and changed to a lower gear, bringing the car smoothly onto the gravelly roadside. When we stopped, he sat staring at the dash for a second in silence.

"Being a vampire's not all bad, you know."

"I know. I'm sorry." I reached across and grabbed his hand. "I didn't mean to imply your uncle didn't care for you or anything, I just —" Was just implying that if he loved the boys, why would he possibly think a life of vampirism was better than death?

"I've lived a good life, Ara. I have no regrets about immortality." He smiled at our hands then, opening my palm to trace a line down the middle. "And you wouldn't either, you know—once you got used to it."

"Used to the killing, you mean?"

"There is a bright side." He followed the Fate Line along my palm. "You never age."

"I'm seventeen. I think I have a few years before ageing is going to bother me."

"I don't know," he teased. "You're already changing. Look." He pointed to the line. "This is shorter than it was a week ago."

I snatched my hand back. "Are you saying my days are numbered?"

"No." He smiled to himself. "Just that things are… changing."

"Nothing stays the same forever."

"*I* do," he said. "Well, physically, anyway."

"I don't know. I think your maturity levels stayed the same as your eighteen-year-old human self."

"Is that so?" His emerald eyes met mine. "This coming from a girl who thinks throwing a tantrum is an acceptable method of getting her own way."

"I don't *think* it gets me my own way. It *actually* does."

He laughed. "Only because your dad's treading on eggshells around you until he's sure you won't run away or commit suicide."

"Then why do my tantrums work on *you*?"

"Because," he said, kissing my hand, "I am completely whipped."

I laughed and then sat back in the chair, letting my hand fall into my lap. "I wish we could be like two characters in a book; that some miracle could keep us together."

"I know, my love, but this is life," David said. "And our reality is that fiction doesn't mix with fact."

"Yet I'm sitting beside a vampire right now," I said sarcastically.

"The only thing fictional about vampires is the possibility of one falling for a human."

I smiled to myself.

He stole my hand again and sat quietly, tracing his fingertip down the middle of my palm.

"It really bothers you, doesn't it?" I asked.

"What?"

"The lines—the changes."

"It's representative of many things, I believe."

"Like what?"

"Perhaps not just the future, but maybe…"

"Maybe?"

"Nothing." He laughed and folded my fingers around his, but the smile faded from his eyes and a flicker of something foreign flashed for only a second before it disappeared. "I'm just being melodramatic."

"David." I squeezed his hand a little tighter. "Is something wrong?"

"I—No." He patted my hand and released it, smiling. "It's nothing. Let's just enjoy this day."

"Okay, but you'd tell me, right? If there was something wrong?"

"Probably not."

I cleared my throat, unbuckling my seatbelt as the vampire appeared at my open door.

"Would you like to go back to the island today?"

"Yeah." I took his hand. "Sounds great."

Raindrops broke the glassy stillness of the water, distorting the deep red reflection of autumn foliage. Ripple upon ripple stretched closer to the shore, pushing the clusters of orange and brown leaves in laps up onto the clay banks. David and I stood at the cusp of the lake, hand in hand, considering the watery road out to the island.

"It's magnificent this time of year, isn't it?"

"It's always magnificent," I said. "But I wish I'd worn a skirt instead of jeans."

"Hm," he hummed, giving an automated smile.

I stood between him and his distracted glare. "David?"

"Hm?" He managed to look at me this time.

"I know there's something wrong. What is it?"

"Nothing."

"That's not nothing."

"Well, it's nothing that needs discussing right now."

Above us, the dark grey clouds closed in, swallowing the last smudge of blue left in the sky. A storm was on the way. I hugged myself, shivering a little as dots of rain fell over my bare shoulders.

"Are you cold?" David asked, rubbing my arm.

I nodded. "I can feel the autumn coming on."

"And so follows the winter," he said absently, his shoulders sinking. "Come on then."

My hand linked with his. "Should we go home?"

"No. We'll go to the island. Never know when it might be our last chance to go back there."

"I'll always go back there, even if… you know."

His nose and chin stayed pointed at the island, while his eyes slowly drifted onto me, narrowing, as the obvious questions on his mind rested a breath away from his lips. When I opened my mouth to probe him further, a squeal escaped me. My arms flailed out like an octopus's as he bent down and scooped me up.

"What are you doing?"

"Getting us to the island faster."

"Oh. Crap!" I buried my face in his neck, my teeth caging as gravity tried to hold me down under the vampire's need for speed. It felt kind of like going upside-down on a roller coaster, with invisible forces pushing at my head, compressing my arms and legs, possibly trying to cube me.

We stopped abruptly and my gut kept going as my feet touched the ground. I folded over, feeling heat rush into my cheeks and ears.

"You gonna be sick?" David laughed.

"I'm okay." I reached up and grabbed his arm, using it to steady myself. "I'm okay."

"Just take slow breaths. It'll ease off."

I nodded, rolling to a stand under the majesty of our secret little island. Even if I was about to puke, the cool cave of foliage stole my thoughts enough to make me forget how fast I'd just travelled, while the fruity tingle of wild flowers filled my senses, making it easier to breathe.

"Better now?" David asked.

"Yeah. Better."

"Good."

In my periphery, a vibrant purple petal caught my eye. I turned to David and smiled.

"For you," he said, tucking my hair back with the flower.

"You know, I still have the one you gave me here last time."

"I know," he said, sliding his hand down my arm to take my hand. "Ara?"

"Mm?" I tore my eyes away from the canopy.

"I need to tell you something." As our eyes met, a flash of sadness tinted his pale green. "Something which, I'm afraid to say, is not good news."

"Okay."

"I told you I'd warn you when it was time for me to leave?"

My stomach sunk, and I bit my bottom lip.

"I…" His deep voice steadied with a chest-lifting breath, gaze fixing on my lips before rising up to my eyes. "The time has come."

"What? When?"

"Two weeks."

"Two weeks? But, that's not enough time. How can I… how can you expect me to…" I fought several arguments with him in my head, not winning any of them. "No, you can't do this. You have to tell them no."

"That's not the worst part, Ara." He took another deep breath. "In that two weeks, I am expected to operate the Set from the New York offices. I will only be able to see you at night."

"Night? Two weeks? And that's it? For forever?"

"Unless you become a vampire," he said in a low, dry tone.

"David. I can't make a decision like that in two weeks. How can you possibly expect me to—"

"Because you have to, Ara!" He stared at my face just long enough to see his harsh tone hurt me. "The time is now. Like it or not. You have to choose. When the full moon rises in a fortnight, I will be boarding a train and leaving for Le Château de la Mort—with or without you beside me."

"You can't do this to me. Mike's here for the next two weeks. How am I going to choose between life and immortality while he's distracting me?" I wiped fat raindrops off my shoulder, moving out from under the giant leaf collecting them. "Can't you reason with them? Can't you do something?"

"Ara. You don't understand the ways of the Set. I've been ordered to return by the head of the World Council—the *King*, for God's sake. One does not refuse an order from the King."

"But—"

"Look." He dropped his head with a dejected breath. "Two weeks to get my affairs in order was a generous courtesy. He needn't have offered that at all."

"Why? Are you in trouble?"

"In ways." He looked up at the leaf above us and then took my hand, leading me to the shelter of a larger tree. "The man I entrusted to run things in my absence has proven less than reliable. I must return and pull things into line."

"But you have a life here. What about school and—"

"The Set do not care! It's a part of being on the Council. I knew this when I joined; I accepted that with all of its glory and all of its responsibility. I *must* leave. That is all there is to it."

The pattering of rain filled the silence around us while it all sunk in, and a part of me wondered if this was a lie—his way of pushing me to make a decision.

"I'm not pushing you to make a decision, Ara," he said coldly. "It's pretty clear already that you have, and when your so-called best friend arrives, I'm pretty sure he'll help cement it."

"What's *that* supposed to mean?"

"Nothing."

"David?" I demanded.

He stared at the ground, his caged teeth making his jaw tight.

"David, I don't understand where this is coming from." I went for his hand but he jerked it back. "Please?"

"I was listening," he confessed, "when you spoke to Emily and Alana about Mike."

My lips parted for some kind of explanation, but only air came out.

"I didn't hear all of it, but I heard enough to make a few connections." He looked at me, his eyes void of love. "That's what happened, isn't it? The reason you were crying the night you asked your mother to pick you up? The night she—"

"Yes," I whispered.

David softened immediately, cupping the back of my head and squishing my cheek against his warm, soggy cotton shirt. "He was a fool to turn you down."

"No, he was probably smart."

"I suppose that explains your over-analyzing when *I* wouldn't kiss you. I'm sorry. If I had known—"

"It's not your fault. You did the right thing. Better to feel undesirable for a few days than to be dead, right?" I laughed a short release of tension.

"Do you love him?"

"Who?"

"Mike."

"I—" My thumbnail came up slowly and wedged itself between my teeth.

"S'il te plaît, mon amour, tell me the truth. It will hurt more if you lie."

I closed my eyes and a tight cramp twisted my heart. If Mike had loved me that night, I wouldn't be here. But he didn't, and now I had David. Yet a big part of me still wanted Mike, just not a big enough part to want him over David.

"I love you more than I love him," I offered, but it wasn't enough. He stiffened, straightening away from me. "Please don't be upset with me, David."

"I'm not upset, Ara. It's just clear to me what this means."

"What does it mean?" I asked accusingly.

"He's better for you. You can live with him; die with him; have a family—have the life you *want* with him."

"But he doesn't love me."

"I gave you a chance to be upfront with me," he said coldly. "When I asked you if you loved him—in your room that day—you had every opportunity to tell me the truth then."

"I know." My eyes closed involuntarily. "I'm sorry. It's just that… I'm really confused. When Mike rejected me, I locked all the feelings I have for him deep inside. I felt so damn stupid. I didn't even want to admit them to myself." I searched for compassion in David's eyes, but only a hard man glared down at me, his jaw stiff. Everything around me felt colder then: the air, my arms, my face, even my heart. "I just… nothing I ever do will change how he feels about me, so there wasn't a point in hurting you with the truth."

"And what is the truth? That you would never have been with me if he had loved you?"

"Maybe," I said, looking at my feet. "But only because I would never have come here in the first place, never even met you, but now—"

"Perhaps, with this information coming to light, I should just leave today."

"David. No," I said, grabbing his arm, but my next words disappeared under a roll of thunder. "It doesn't have to be this way—"

"It already is. You love Mike, and you don't want to kill for me."

"I never said that. Please, we can make our own future. I still believe there's hope for us, for our lives tog—"

"Shh." He placed a finger over my lips and brought his face down to align our eyes. "You need to stop, Ara. It is all too clear to me now that I have to be the strong one, for both of us"—he dropped his finger—"and you have to be the one that goes on. You *must* go on, have babies, beautiful babies, and be happy."

"Don't you get it, David?" I shook my head, my eyes watering. "You're the only thing that makes me happy now."

"That won't always be true, Ara. Look, you've been waiting for me to tell you I'll stay; that all of this is some nightmare. But, my love"—his eyes softened, a hundred years of sadness flaming within them—"it's not."

I managed one syllable before the smoke of his words stung my eyes, forcing the volcanic eruption of tears.

"Don't cry, sweetheart. I love you, and you will always belong to me. But I can't keep lying to myself, believing you'll change your mind."

"But, maybe I will."

He shook his head again. "Even then, it would only be to save me from eternal solitude. It would not be because you wanted it. And for that reason, I just can't take your dreams away. Your human life is your greatest gift, and leaving you to live it will be my greatest sacrifice."

I sniffled, wiping my hand over my nose. "It doesn't have to be that way."

"It does, my love." He pointed to a blue and black butterfly dancing in the shelter of a silky leaf. "You see that: it's a sign."

"How so?"

"Ever since that day we first kissed, those butterflies have been everywhere I go. And I think, symbolically, they represent you."

"How?"

He wrapped both arms around my waist from behind, tucking his chin against my shoulder. "She started her life in the shadows, close to the ground—lived and existed only as others saw her: a caterpillar, nothing more. Then one day she bloomed into a beautiful, brightly winged creature—something she could never have been had someone ended her before she had time to change.

"And though that life is short in comparison to most, she will *live* each moment, spreading her beauty and her life through this place so that when her existence comes to an end, as the sun goes down on her final day, her beauty will go on, and there will always be another to carry on her name."

David kissed the top of my ear, smoothing his hands against the skin on my belly just under my top.

"I love you," he said, "and your spirit will go on. As long as you have happiness, I have everything I will ever desire."

"But what will you do without me?"

"At the risk of sounding overly philosophical, I am the rain." He looked up at the sky; I looked too. "I exist each clouded day whether the butterfly flies or falls. A human life is but a blink in the eye of eternity. I will go on when you are gone, I will have no choice."

"Go on, or *move* on?"

His arms tightened around me. "I will never move on. The pain I will feel for eternity without you is a sacrifice I am willing to make to save you from forever longing, wishing you'd been given the chance to live. I owe that to you." He nodded once. "For the love I feel, I owe that to you."

"So that's it? You're making the decision for me?" I turned to face him.

"I have to, Ara. I've been watching, waiting, scanning your thoughts to find some hint of promise for us. But you don't, *anywhere* in your thoughts, want to be a vampire. And yet you keep making me wait for your answer. And stupidly, I keep waiting."

I had nothing to say. He was right. Life was just too important. I'd seen it in action: the beauty, the magic it had to offer. And I feared, if I gave that up for immortality, I'd never forgive myself, or worse, never forgive David.

"Just give me two weeks more. Before you're gone forever, please? Just let me have the last two weeks with you."

"Two more weeks?" He stepped back. "While I work the days in New York and you spend them with another man—one you happen to love?"

My head hung in shame. "Please don't hate me for loving him, David. I loved him for such a long time before I ever even knew you existed. I can't just shut my heart off like that."

"I do know that." He exhaled, stepping into me. "I just… I suspected it. I'm actually angrier with myself, Ara, for not listening to my own gut. *Again.*"

"What would you have done if I'd told you I loved him in that way?" I rolled my face up to look at him. "Or if you had've looked into my thoughts that day and seen it? Would you have left?"

"That's the stupid thing about all of this." He sighed, casting his gaze to the heavens. "Even if you *had* admitted your feelings for Mike, there's no way I'd have left you. I love you, and that love has made me stupid and irrational and way too forgiving."

We both laughed softly.

"To be honest," he added, "I knew a large part of your heart so obviously belonged to him, and it was my hope that I could somehow overshadow that, but we were just never given enough time."

"Then don't leave yet." Hope filled me. "I love you, David, and I know for a fact that the messed-up last few months of my life are clouding all of my thoughts right now. I have so much I need to work out—stuff I need to work out with Mike, too. Don't run away just because I'm too messed-up right now to think clearly."

He softened, shaking his head. "You know I won't. How can I not savor those last precious moments?"

I melted against him again, relieved. "Thank you, David."

After a breath, he turned my face so our eyes met. "I'm not usually this pathetic. If you were any other girl, I'd have drained you and left you for dead by now."

"You'd kill me just because I'm in love with someone I grew up with—someone I spent every day of my life with?"

"And because I know you're about to break my heart in the worst, most final way."

"How so?"

"When he arrives, and all those feelings you have come to the surface, what do you think will happen?"

"Nothing. We're… are you worried about me cheating on you?"

"Perhaps. But it's not the only thing I worry about."

"Well, I *can* have feelings for him and still make choices based on my feelings for you."

"But you will not ever make the choice to come with me, even when grief no longer clouds your mind." He sighed. "And here we are, going around in circles again. We know how this ends, and it's stupid for me to hang around here waiting for you to end up with Mike."

"That won't happen. Especially not while you're still in the picture."

"I need you to promise me that, Ara." He held my gaze firmly. "I just need to hear you say it."

"I promise," I said, my eyes flicking to each of his. "And I just need you to understand that I might still decide to go with you. Nothing is final until you're gone for good."

He groaned and turned away.

"Come on, you know I'm not myself right now," I insisted. "I could change my mind at the drop of a hat."

"Stop it." He grabbed my shoulders firmly. "Ara, just admit it. Just tell me you're not coming with me once and for all, like ripping off a plaster."

"No. Because that's not what I've decided on." I folded my arms. "My head wants one thing but my heart wants another."

David turned away from me again, extending his arm to grasp a tree branch. "You will eventually have to say it. Either way, a decision has to be made. Wholeheartedly or not."

"Okay, then… ask me on the last day of our two weeks. That way I can be sure you'll stick around."

"That's the night of the Masquerade?"

"Yeah. It's perfect." I carefully touched his elbow until he turned his face to me. "You can ask me on the last dance."

"The last dance?" He dropped his hand from the branch, his brow staying up in an arch of mockery. "On the last stroke of midnight?"

I nodded, smiling. "Perfectly corny."

He gently grabbed my arm and pulled me into his chest. "I'm sorry I yelled at you."

"That wasn't really yelling, David."

"No matter. I shouldn't speak to you that way, despite how I feel."

"I yell at you all the time."

He laughed. "But you're harmless. When you yell, it's merely amusing."

"Thanks. Glad to know you take me so seriously."

"Only as seriously as you take me."

"Hey." I slapped his chest softly.

He laughed. "So, I guess that means you don't take me very seriously."

"Not really." I smirked, then remembered the gift I had in my pocket.

"Gift?"

"Stay out of my head, vampire!"

"Make me."

I ignored that and reached into my pocket, keeping my hand there, unsure if I should do this. "It's a little corny, but—"

"I like corny."

"I know." I smiled warmly. "I figured the old guy in you might like it."

David's lips quirked up on one side, his eyes lighting with curiosity. "You're getting good at keeping your mind clear when you want to hide something from me."

"I know." I grinned and pulled out a small white square of cloth. "You know in movies how the fair maiden would sometimes give her knight a handkerchief?"

"Well"—David swept the beads of water through his hair—"it wasn't a custom that began in movies, but… yes?"

"Um… well, since you have this strong set of beliefs about not sleeping over, I figured you could at least take a part of me home with you after you leave my room each night." I pressed the cloth into David's palm. "It has my scent on it."

He sniffed it. "So that's why you were sleeping with this under your pillow the last few nights?"

"Yeah. You saw that?"

"Yes. I thought you might have had a cold or that you were… crying."

I pouted, reaching back into my pocket. "No, I've actually had this diabolical plan going all week."

"Plan?"

"I… it isn't just my scent I want you to have."

"Okay." His brows pinched with confusion. My shoulders lifted as I clamped my index finger onto the pin in my pocket then drew my hand out. "Ara!"

"This is my perfume," I said, before he could get mad, then dropped a dollop of blood onto the hanky. David's fingers tightened around it for a moment. "It's the best way I could think of to give you a part of myself."

"You silly, sweet girl." He shook his head then kissed mine. "Thank you."

"Eeesh! It hurts. I must've pricked it pretty deep." I squeezed the base of my finger. "It's still bleeding."

"Don't squeeze it, you'll make it worse." David pocketed the hanky and took my hand, pausing for only a moment of hesitation before he slid my fingertip into his mouth, closing his lips firmly around it.

I wasn't afraid. I wasn't worried he might lose control. There was no urgency to his touch. Just a deep longing within it.

When he was done, he slid my finger past his lips, dropping a kiss to the cut. "Sweet and yet so powerfully intoxicating."

"So it…" I watched him standing there, lost in his own bliss. "You liked it?"

"Liked it?" His eyes changed color as they opened, just like in the storage closet at school, the growing pupil almost entirely consuming the whites of his eyes. "I can't keep doing this."

"Doing what?"

"Telling myself not to touch you, not to want you. Not to drink from you."

"Then stop denying yourself. Don't you know how badly I want that too?"

"Yes. And that's what makes it so much harder for me to refuse you."

I smiled. "I don't want you to refuse me."

He tried an accusatory glare, but the look washed away quickly as he ran his tongue over his lips one last time and the history of my blood clearly fell against it. "Fine."

"Fine what?"

The vampire surfaced within his touch, a firm hand holding me in place at the side of my neck, his body inches from mine. "I'm going to drink from you. But not with your clothes on."

I looked down at my jeans, then back up at the vampire. "Huh?"

"Vampires like skin; we *need* skin. If we do this with clothes on"—he looked away for a second—"when I get carried away, I might rip them off you. I don't wish to explain to your father why I'm bringing you home naked."

"Oh." I laughed, but a sudden sinking feeling shot through my arms, like a hot blast of toxic adrenaline-inducing drugs.

"It's okay." He placed a steadying hand over my heart. "I won't do anything to hurt you. You have my word."

"It's not that." I released my fingers from their ball-grip. "It's just that no one's ever seen me… *naked* before."

"Are you uncomfortable?"

I nodded.

"Why?"

"I'm… I guess I'm afraid that you might be… disappointed." I tensed, waiting for him to laugh, but he slid the backs of his fingertips along my cheekbone and stared deeply into my eyes.

"What if I were to undress, and suddenly you decided I was not as *hot* as you thought?"

"Point taken," I said, because I wouldn't care. I loved him. Fat, skinny, hot or not. "Naked then?"

"Yes." He fingered the base of my tank top suggestively. "Naked."

My shoulders rounded slightly as he lifted it, unveiling my belly and then my ribs. And I stiffened all over, realizing I hadn't planned my undergarments to suit this kind of misbehavior.

"Don't worry," he said with a laugh. "You won't be wearing them for much longer anyway."

And so many pictures of all the things we would do ran through my mind. I knew David could see every one of them.

I lifted my arms above my head, and a breath of a smile swept across my lips as David dropped my top to the wet grass and stepped back, shaking his head.

"My love." That look warmed his entire face. "You are more than perfect."

I quickly covered my purple-and-pink candy-striped bra. "Even in a bra I bought from the same boutique as Bozo the Clown?"

David's burst of laughter caught me off guard, making me laugh too. He reached out, took each of my hands, and pulled them away from my ribs. "This"—he nodded to my bra—"is just another thing that I love about you. I didn't expect black lace."

"But, I look like a flamboyant zebra."

"You look beautiful."

"I feel naked."

"Well, you're not—yet." His eyes slowly drifted to my jeans. "May I?"

"Mm-hm." I nodded, holding my breath.

In one yank of my button-fly jeans, the denim parted, revealing my pink underwear. I wedged my thumbs into the waist and shimmied them down my hips, feeling the air cool my skin where the rain made it soggy. David watched, his eyes falling past my underwear to the apex of my thighs, down my skinny white legs and to my knees.

His lips split into a grin when I carelessly stumbled and tripped, kicking my ankles free of my jeans with about as much finesse as a drunkard.

As I stood expectantly in front of him, more naked than I'd ever been with anyone, the whirling winds circled the clearing and brushed my hips, my arms, my belly—all the places I knew David was thinking about touching. And for the first time in my life, I felt beautiful before his eyes.

The patters of rain stopped completely then, and the beads of water glistening in David's hair and over his lashes looked almost out of place. His wet T-shirt hugged the curves of his chest and arms, showing his golden skin through the fabric. He spread the collar and slipped it past his head, then dropped it to the grass beside my clothes. When the sun wandered in for a peek at this innocent step toward danger, it made the water on David's skin sparkle, as though he was starring in the wrong storybook.

"What's funny?" he asked.

"I like the sun on your skin."

He angled his arm outward and studied it, running a hand down the droplets, his eyes flashing to another thought for a second.

"What?" I asked.

"What's what?"

"What were you just thinking? You looked worried."

"Oh. Uh—just that…" He laughed. "I hope the rain didn't soak through my jeans."

"Why?" I asked, watching him unbutton them.

"Because," he said, slipping them down his hips, "my briefs are white."

"So?" I said, but as soon as I heard my own words, the white of his shirt, all see-through with the water, registered in my mind. "Oh."

He winked and tossed his jeans aside, allowing me a moment to scrutinize. My gaze drifted over his broad shoulders and the tight skin across his chest, down his cagey ribs, stopping above the thick band of his underwear. He didn't have the obvious six-pack I kind of expected, just that nicely contoured 'V' leading up smoothly to his hips from below his briefs.

"I always wondered if you were a boxers or briefs guy."

David looked down then shrugged. "These are kind of in between."

"They're kind of sexy and"—I pouted—"they didn't get wet."

He threw his head back, laughing. "Quite frankly, I'm relieved."

"Well, they won't be dry for long." I nodded to the sky as the heavens opened up again.

"No." He caught a few raindrops in his hand. "I should be taking you home."

"I don't want to go home."

"I know." His words landed all hot and moist on my face, his brow coming to rest on mine as he suddenly appeared with his body pressed against me. I looked up into the anguish that his closed eyes tried to hide. "Lie down," he whispered.

The grassy bed beneath my feet felt sticky, the summer's dying heat making the rain rise off it in a warm cloud. David stayed standing, stiff and tall as a tower, while I pressed my palms to the grass, my elbows shaking, and edged jaggedly onto my back.

"Close your eyes," he demanded sweetly, still not opening his.

"Okay," I said, but after six long breaths and two fistfuls of grass pulled from the soil, only an empty breeze had caressed my half-naked body. I opened my eyes. "David?" I watched him expectantly, waiting for him to look at me. He didn't. He was fighting that battle within—the war between the vampire and the human—and as he dropped to one knee, then the other, my main concern was not the possibility of my own death, but that he might deny himself the pleasure of my blood.

"You remember not to scream, right?"

I nodded, biting my lower lip.

Without a second thought, both his hands cupped my face then slid down my jaw and over the curve of my neck, slipping my bra strap off my shoulder. "Just stay still, Ara."

"Are you… are you going to take my bra off?"

"Not if you don't want me to."

My thoughts moved to his breath on my chin, his lips within reach, his body immensely close but not touching; wanting but not taking, practically floating down the length of mine like he was just a layer of heat in the atmosphere. Every nerve in my brain called out to him; every part of my body, tingling hot, begged him to press himself against me.

But he didn't move. He just smiled to himself, leaning on his elbow beside me. "Well, do you want me to take it off you or not?"

I could feel my pulse racing like a twitch in my neck; felt my body succumb to the lust—scream out its own instinct-driven desire to die at his hands.

But I wasn't ready to undress completely.

"Not yet," I whispered.

His eyes stayed on the bare patch of skin under the bra strap, lips softly landing there as he smoothed it back in place. "You okay?"

"Yeah," I said, then quickly reached down to scratch my leg. "The grass is just really itchy."

"Shall I run to the rock and get the picnic rug?"

"No," I said, eyes wide. That would just give him too much time to think about what he didn't want to do to me.

He smiled to himself—his secret smile—and cupped my neck, his thumb sliding down over my chin easily with the rain's assistance, coming to rest just under my jaw as he tipped it up to expose my throat. "Your life is in my hands right now," he whispered against my pulse. "And the most beautiful thing about that, Ara, is that all I can read in your mind is desire."

"You don't scare me, Mr. Knight."

"I wish I did."

"No you don't."

"You're right," he said, keeping his eyes on mine as he reached down and took my hand, folding it open to press a firm kiss on the softer, more delicate side. "I like you this way."

I looked at his nail, sitting ready at my wrist, one firm indent away from releasing my blood. "Then what are you waiting for?"

"Someone to stop me."

I gave him a reassuring smile. "I trust you, David."

"You shouldn't." He made a shallow, horizontal cut, drawing slivers of red out over my milk-white skin. But I didn't feel the cut—just the pressure of his fingers gripping my bone.

Only a beat passed after that before the black in his eyes washed the human away again, the vampire taking control, pressing his teeth down on the outer edges of the wound to open it.

Thousands of tiny bubbles raced up my veins, making my fingers want so badly to flex out and either shove him away or run along his jaw to feel his throat move as he drank me. My blood was finally deep inside him, touching his heart, coursing through his veins, warming everything I could never physically touch. I wanted it to stay there forever. I wanted the sun to go down around us, and rise again tomorrow, leaving us here like this, always.

I rolled my face to the leaves above and watched them swirl around, my lungs filling with humid air, as the rain moistened the back of my throat with each shallow breath. And the feel of David's thumb in the cup of my palm, holding my hand in place against the stubble on his chin, made me feel so close to him—to the human that loved me; the human that was buried deep beneath desire right now.

The trust was magic—almost euphoric—as if I could fall asleep and leave my body open to anything he might want from it. The world around me faded to a soft echo, like being lost in the perfectly tuned note of a song I'd never heard. I could float away, were it not for David grounding me, keeping me here.

It sickened me to think it, but I was excited to finally know what it felt like to be his victim: a human that could nourish him, but loved enough to be left alive. I could feel the lick of death, feel the peace others must do when they finally give over to it—how nothing in the world really mattered anymore. In a funny way, it all just seemed kind of silly to worry about the things we did.

Slowly, David drew away, leaving a cool moist patch on my wrist, and smiled down at me. A stain of crimson bled from his lips in rivulets, seeping out over his perfect smile. "Are you okay, my love?"

My chest and shoulders lifted with deep breaths, guiding my soul back to the present. "I might actually have found Heaven on Earth."

David studied my face for a second then cupped the back of my head and rolled me up, slipping in behind me, his arms looping my shoulders like the wings of a swan. "I think you're delusional."

I giggled quietly, resting my feet beside his, our knees bent, committing the feel of his bare chest on my slippery, rain-soaked spine to memory. If I ignored the breeze making my wet bra cold, I could actually pretend we really were naked together. "Thank you, David."

"For what?"

For letting me have my own way; for wanting it and not denying that he did; for being more than just an ordinary boy—for… "For being real." I tucked my brow against his ear and slowly tickled the back of his wrist, imagining his blood in my mouth.

"You don't have to imagine it, Ara," he said, kissing just above my eye. "If you want it, you can have it."

"Really?" I turned slightly to look back at him.

He lifted his wrist and shut his eyes tight as he bit into the skin, turning me straight in his arms again as he brought his bloody wrist around to my mouth, balancing the liquid there carefully.

Without hesitation, I scooped up the runaway drops with my tongue, wrapping my lips around the warmth of sweet orange-chocolate.

"Describe it to me," he whispered into my hair. "In your thoughts."

I swirled it around on my tongue and let it slide down my throat and into my stomach, like the first hot cocoa of winter: smooth and rich, warm. Like liquid made of satin ribbons. *You taste like… like…*

"Okay." He slid his index finger into my mouth, gently forcing it away from his wrist. "That's enough, my love. I'm not sure what it'll do to you."

Through the whir of the world spinning around me, I turned my head and looked up into David's eyes, filling with that amazing, almost transparent shade of green. But it was brighter than *ever* before, like Dorothy's Emerald City exploding in the gaze of a vampire.

"David, I think I can see your soul."

He closed his eyes around a smile, laughing softly to himself. "I'd say you've lost your mind, but that was just so damn sweet I have to let myself believe it."

I licked my teeth, tasting his blood again. "Mm. No, *you're* the only thing that's sweet around here."

"I am, huh?" He looked at my lips, moving slowly onto his knees in front of me. "Let me taste it."

I opened my mouth for David's tongue, holding my breath as it skimmed across mine to push it away from the sharp edges of his fangs. Warm sweet butter and salty copper mixed in our kiss, and it almost felt like David and I were thinking the same thing. Thinking how amazing it was to taste the essence of him and me, of everything that made us exist, broken down to two flavors between our lips; tangible, real.

My body sung with ideas and desires that had been too long refused.

"I know," David whispered into my mouth.

"Know what?" I angled my face to the sky, lying back on my elbows as his soft kisses travelled down my neck, over each and every one of the tiny scars there.

"I know how you feel."

I moaned, the sound ending in a half gasp as his lips circled my navel. "Mm. I don't think you do."

He laughed, my wet skin making the path of his breath obvious. I parted my knees and let him kiss my inner thigh, feeling his face brush against my undies.

"What are you doing down there, David?"

"I want to know every inch of your body by only the memory of my lips."

My eyes flung open as he kissed fabric, folding it down over my hipbone a little.

"Don't worry. I won't go there—today," David said, bringing my ankle over his hip as he slid up my body and drank the rain from the curve of my waist to my neck.

I buried my fingers in his wet hair. "David?"

"Yes, my love?"

"I want to feel you pressed against me."

"I know you do," he said, and when I hooked my fingers just under his elbows and tugged him upward, feeling his bare chest and the weight of him on top of my body for the first time, it was like a hunger finally fed; a wave finally meeting a rock, dissolving into spray. For everything else in the world that hurt, in this moment I finally found the reason why we live. I wanted to tear away the wet remains of fabric between us and feel him inside of me.

He laughed breathily into the flesh just below my ear. "Ara, I can't think straight when you think that way."

"Don't then. When you think straight, you deny me what I want."

He stopped and pushed up slowly, lifting his chest away from mine.

I stared him down, beads of water blinding me, the rain pouring into our quiet little world as if it had no care for the fact that our forever was limited.

"I know what you're doing," I said. "I know you're about to tell me we have to stop."

"I have good reason for that." He rose onto his knees, keeping his hands beside my shoulders, his body forming a shelter over mine.

"What reason?"

David nodded to the now dark sky. "That rain's gonna get heavier any minute."

"No. This sucks! You never give me my own way."

"That, my love, is because your own way involves me taking something from you I'm not willing to take."

"My virginity?"

A cheeky grin spread across his face, golden under the grey sky. "Yes."

"Oh, my holy freakin' God. You have got to be kidding me!"

"Sorry. I'm not."

With the cold conclusiveness of reason, the small split in my wrist started stinging. "Why? Is my virginity like kryptonite or something?"

"No. Even better." He dropped a quick kiss on my mouth. "It's sacred."

"Sacred?" My arched brow thickened the sarcasm.

He closed his lips into a thin smile. "Yes, my love. You will always remember your first. If you choose not to come with me, one day you *will* belong to someone else, and you'll want to be pure—untainted—for him. If I take you now, you can never go back. I would hate for you to regret any of our interactions one day."

"David. This is the new world. It doesn't work like that now."

"That may be so, but it still works that way for me." His wide, sincere eyes looked right into mine, his voice intense with conviction. "In my society, virginity is a virtue to be praised and cherished, not something girls give away without reflection or care."

"But—"

"Ara, please? It's what I want for you." His sudden harsh tone forced me into silence. "Sometimes you can think too much with your heart and not enough with your head. I have to be the adult here. I have to protect you from yourself; from your human nature."

"I can take care of—"

"It's my job to protect you," he scolded, softening when I reacted. "Even if it means I'm falling apart."

"Fine."

"I'm sorry, Ara."

"I said it's fine." I looked at the trees so he wouldn't see the tears of rejection coating my eyes.

"Come on then." He jumped back and helped me to my feet, making the world spin with the speed he lifted me. "You okay?"

I nodded.

"Then let's get you home before you catch a cold."

"No." I threw my arms around his ribs and cupped my wrist, forming a chain of unyielding force. "We're staying a little longer today."

"Is that so? And…"—he tried to lift my chin; I held fast, refusing to even look at him—"what, exactly, are you going to do if I decide to force you?"

"You won't."

"Hm, you're so sure of yourself," he said, but I heard the smile in his tone, and the fact that he did nothing else except for tangle his fingertips in my hair proved I was right.

My bones turned to rubber inside my flesh then, and though the summer rain continued, I felt only warmth. His blood had awakened me like a powerful drug, and mine had filled his veins, giving him life, fuelling his movements. There was no fear, no weight to the truth right now.

One day, he'd be gone, and my arms would fall empty to my sides; the need for his embrace just a gaping hole, his smile just a memory fading, and his lips never more a kiss that belonged to me. But I could exist eternally right now, living forever in this one moment with my everlasting knight because, for today, there was no tomorrow.

23

"Ara-Rose?" Vicki called from downstairs.

"Yeah?" I answered quickly so she wouldn't come up and spot my vampire pillow.

"Emily's on the phone," she said.

"Ergh! Why'd she call the home line?" I said to myself. "I have a mobile."

"She was probably hoping your dad would answer," David said, his voice a gentle hum against my ear through his bare chest.

"If that's the case, she needs therapy."

"Good, then you could go together."

I slapped his arm; he pretended to be hurt.

"Ara-Rose! Now!"

"Coming," I called.

David grabbed my hand as I fell away from his arms, making me want to lie against his skin again. "Be quick. It's cold here without you."

"I will," I said, closing my door. Since David shut my curtains when he came through my window earlier, I didn't notice the grey day until I stepped into the cool air of the hallway. As usual, the windows all around the house were open and the soft lemon scent of Vicki's bathroom cleaner mixed with the moist weight of freshly cut grass, drying the back of my throat as I drew a deep breath. I tucked my hands under my arms, wishing I'd put on a sweater to come down.

"Morning, Dad."

He smiled over his newspaper. "Morning, honey."

"Any good news?" I hurried past him to the phone on the wall.

"No news is good news," he moaned, lowering his nose into the paper again.

I took the phone from Vicki, shaking my head affectionately at Dad. "Hey, Em."

"Hey, Ara. What are you two doing today?"

By 'you two' I assumed she was adding David to me. "Lazing around. Why?"

"Everyone's going bowling tonight. You guys wanna come?"

"Um—" Bowling versus bed with David. I leaned against the wall. "Maybe. What time?"

"About six."

"Oh okay, well, yeah. I'd say we will, but I'll have to check with David."

"When will you see him?"

"When I hang up the phone." I grinned, watching Vicki. She had no clue what I was talking about, thank God.

"Oh my gosh, Ara. You rebel. Did he stay last night?"

"No, no. Nothing like that. Just… early," I hinted, hoping she'd catch my drift.

"Oh. Okay. So, like, sneak-through-the-window sort of thing?"

"You got it." I grinned. Vicki looked at me with a raised brow. "So, six then?"

"Yep."

"Okay, see you then."

"See ya."

The phone clinked, and suddenly I was back in the kitchen with my parents.

"What did Emily want?" Vicki asked.

"They're going bowling tonight."

"Are you and David going?"

"Yeah, probably. I'll have to check if he wants to, but I'd say he will." I shrugged.

"What time is David coming over today?"

"Don't know. But I'm going to get some more sleep before he does."

"Sleep? It's nine in the morning, Ara," Vicki stated.

"I'm a teenager," I offered. "Aren't we supposed to hibernate on weekends?"

She issued a smile that said she was pleased with *herself.* I guess she wanted this for so long now that she'd let me do anything, as long as it was deemed 'normal' by the greater population. Sleeping beside a vampire might sit outside that realm, though.

As I headed back up to my room, the soft strumming of a guitar filled the air, but when I pushed my door open, expecting to see the outline of a vampire, my smile dropped within the bright yellow light of morning shining through my open curtains onto my empty bed. My eyes darted quickly to the iPod in its dock with a song playing at a volume my dad would approve of, and as I watched the rain spatter on the glass of my window, blurring the outside world, I listened to the words, gathering that my vampire meant them as a musical sticky-note saying, *My love, I shall return soon.*

Not that that's what the words were, but that's how David would say it.

With the absence of an all-hearing vampire in my room, I took a moment to be human, then jumped into the enveloping heat of the shower and washed my hair quickly, wrapping the towel around my chest as I hopped out. But when I stepped back into my room, a sudden breeze swept through my window and knocked all the papers off my desk.

"Damn it, David," I said to myself, squatting down to pick them up. I was sure that window was closed a second ago.

"It was. I opened it."

"Agh! David!" My heart jumped to its feet and punched my chest. I looked up from my precarious squat on the ground to the vampire perched on the windowsill, like a pterodactyl. "You scared the living bejeezus out of me."

"Sorry."

"What are you doing just sitting there with the window open?" I stood up, tapping the pages to force them into a neat stack. "You ruined my homework pile. Now I have to reorder these before I hand them in to Dad tomorrow."

"I'll do it for you." He shrugged, obviously in no hurry to remove himself from the path of the whipping breeze.

I looked at him suspiciously. "Are you hiding something?"

He shook his head, one eye narrowing slightly as he looked over my wet, towel-covered body. "I'm just admiring the view."

"You better mean the stunning panoramic view of the hills and my backyard, David Knight." I dumped my disordered papers on my desk and took a step back.

"Nope. I meant my beautiful, almost-naked girlfriend." He jumped down from the ledge, slowly pushing the window closed behind him. "So, bowling?"

"That's the plan," I said, inhaling the fresh cologne wafting off this suave guy as he stepped in front of me, hair all wet and brushed back, for once, showing his forehead. He looked more like a man today in that black hoodie and grey V-neck shirt than he ever had before. It almost made me sad that he'd never grow older than nineteen.

"Do you actually *want* to go bowling?" I added.

"As long as I'm with you, I will do anything." He smiled down at me, his eyes shrinking with warmth. "But you shouldn't stand in front of me like this, my love. You make me think inappropriate things."

"Oh. Sorry. So"—I took a wide step back—"are you any good at bowling?"

"You forget"—he used a louder voice to call out as I disappeared into my wardrobe—"I lived through the fifties. Bowling was huge then."

"Doesn't mean you're any good at it," I stated, slipping my emerald-green sweater over my head.

"True. It's more like I have to *try* to be bad. I'm a little too precise. I've also been known to break a pin or two."

I turned around, buttoning my jeans, and met cheek-to-chest with the rain-dotted fabric of David's hoodie. "Hey! How did you even know I was finished getting dressed in here? I could've been naked."

He tapped his temple, grinning.

Hmpf! "Is there any point in me even dressing in a different room, with you and your mind-reading invading my privacy?"

"Etiquette?" He shrugged. Then, as his eyes traced over the rounded neckline of my sweater, his finger copied. "I like this."

I closed my eyes. "I like you touching me like that."

"So." His touch came away, his somewhat urgent tone forcing my eyes open. "Are you up for a little outing today?"

"I can't. I have a few notes and references to finish on my paper."

"Which paper?" He followed me out of the wardrobe.

"The mythology one—on *vampires*," I teased.

"The subject I told you not to do?"

"Yup."

David smiled, nodding toward my now neatly reordered pile of papers. "Or do you mean the report I just finished for you? The one on *angels*."

"Angels?" I ran over to my desk and flicked through the pages. "No! I spent *hours* working on that, David!"

"I know. And it was a great report. But I told you not to do vampires." He shrugged. "You didn't listen."

"But, why?" I spun around and leaned on the desk. "What does it matter?"

"Because you know things you shouldn't, and if you happen to publish any minor detail or fact, and my Set were to somehow find out, I could be punished, and you…" His words trailed off.

"I what?"

"You could be killed. It's not worth the risk."

"Killed?"

"Shh." He rested a finger to his lip. "Your dad doesn't know I'm here, remember? Look, I didn't want to tell you that because I didn't want you to worry. I just hoped you'd listen to me—for once."

"That was naïve." I smiled.

David smiled too. "I know that *now*."

"So, that's what you were doing when I came out of the bathroom?"

"Yes." He laughed, wiping a hand across his jaw. "*You* actually snuck up on *me*—for once. The evidence was still in my hands. I had to leave it on the windowsill and hope it didn't blow away while you were standing there."

"You could've just told me the truth." I stepped into him, tucking my arms along his ribs. "That would've made me change my mind."

"I'll remember that for the future." He kissed the crown of my head.

"So, what punishment?"

"Huh?"

"You said they'd punish you if I published any facts. What would they do?"

"Oh, I don't know, maybe a seven-day-burial, a month being tortured by the First Order, or a personal favorite of my Set: a complete draining," he said casually.

"Draining?"

"Mm." He nodded. "They drain every ounce of blood from your arteries and leave you parched and partially insane in a dark room for a few weeks."

"How do they drain you? You heal like superglue—how do they get the blood out fast enough?"

"They place metal retractors right here." He pinched his fingers then spread them outward a few inches above his wrist. "It holds the arteries open. Prevents closing and healing of the wound."

"That's horrible."

"That's why I didn't want to tell you. I knew you'd ask these questions and not let up until you had all the gory facts. Well"—he stopped with a noncommittal shrug—"either that or not speak to me for the day."

"Okay, well, with that in mind, a paper on angels will be great." I pointed into his face. "And I better get an A."

David laughed. "Don't worry, you will. So"—he scratched his nose—"an outing then?"

"Where to?"

He walked away and opened my bedroom door, then turned back with a grin. "I thought I might teach you a little about history."

"You know, I live with a History professor." Our hands linked back together. "There's not much *you* can teach me."

"Oh, I don't know about that," he mused. "Come on, meet me at the front door in twenty seconds."

"Twenty?"

He kissed my cheek and, with less than a sweeping breeze, disappeared out the window—closing it behind him.

"Ara?" Sam called a moment later. "Prince Charming just pulled up."

"I told you not to call him that, Sam."

"You're not the boss of me."

"Argh. You're such a pain!"

"Better than being a troll." The front door opened. "Hi, David."

"Sam," David said.

Do me a favor, David, I thought, *tie his shoelaces together when he's not looking.*

"I see you two still haven't managed to find common ground." David walked in and looked up expectantly at me.

"Hard to find a way to relate to a serpent," Sam said, keeping his nose in his book. "Maybe I'll just have to dumb myself down a little so we can hold a decent conversation."

"See what I have to put up with?" I said to David, grabbing my coat as I shut my door.

"Good morning, Ara."

"Morning." I stomped down the stairs.

"Sleep well?" he asked, pecking me on the cheek.

"Better than ever before." I grinned, because I always slept well when he slipped into my bed at unholy hours.

Sam groaned, rolling his eyes. "Get a room."

"Grow up, Sam," I said, shutting the front door behind us, but an almighty crash on the other side of it stopped me in my tracks.

"Hey!" Sam's high-pitched screech echoed across the street. "Who tied my laces together?"

I looked up at David.

He shrugged and smiled.

THE CAR DOOR OPENED AND A COOL BREEZE EASED THE DREAD that the cemetery across the road brought. Slanting trees with wiry branches guarded its iron gates, warding visitors away from the dwelling of the dead or, perhaps, imprisoning them. And the worst part was, something told me that *that* was our destination.

"David?" I grabbed his sleeve, folding myself against his arm. "What are we doing here?"

"Come on—it's okay. I wanna show you something." He took my hand and led me through a gap in the creaking gates, lifting the heavy chain so I could duck under. The air smelled murky with rotting leaves, mingling with the diluted scent of dead roses, their brown petals blowing away in the wind and littering the cobblestone path like confetti.

"I don't like it here."

"You will. I'm taking you to an older part of the cemetery. There are trees there and it's not so"—he looked around the yard; I looked too, at the way the low cloud in the sky made everything dark grey and… "—eerie," he finished.

"Yeah, eerie is exactly what I was thinking."

He laughed softly and held me close as we strolled past rows and rows of headstones. In the distance, a murder of crows blackened the grass, gathering at the feet of a caretaker tending a grave. They cawed loudly, their sinister fables setting me on edge.

"See that grave there?" David pointed to a cracked plaque, barely able to stand within the stone grasp of its template.

"Mm-hm. Marcus Worthington—died eighteen forty?"

He nodded. "He's a friend of mine. Goes by the name of Philippe now."

"So… he's not actually buried there?"

"Nope. In fact, some of the graves in any ancient cemetery are actually empty. The bodies either still living, or removed for scientific research hundreds of years ago."

"Freaky."

"Mm. I suppose it is."

"Well, I'm glad you're not in one of these graves." I snuggled against his shoulder.

"That's just the thing." He pointed to a towering oak tree at the top of a small hill, sheltering five headstones from the threatening storm. "See that line of graves up there?"

"Yeah."

"That's my family's plot."

I stopped walking. David grinned and walked ahead.

Oh boy, when he said history, I had no idea he meant *this* kind of history. I caught up and stood beside him, watching his nostalgic smile fall on the first headstone.

"See this?" He pointed down.

"Here lies Thomas Arthur Knight. Beloved father and husband. Died nineteen-oh-four," I read aloud. "Who was he?"

"My father."

My head whipped back up to look at David. He stuffed his hands in his pockets, a cheeky grin spreading over his face.

"You were nine when he died?"

"Turning ten."

"Well, who was this?" I stepped around the base of the grave, so as not to walk on the dead, and dusted some dried orange leaves off the next stone. "Mary Elizabeth Knight?"

"My mother." His tone softened on the word.

I looked back at the grave with wide eyes, kneeling down to dust a few more leaves from the base. "Died in childbirth, eighteen-ninety-four."

The inscription on her headstone made me sad. She never made it to motherhood; they couldn't even give her the dignity of citing that she'd been *a beloved wife and mother*. Only *died in childbirth*. It seemed so cold.

"It wasn't cold, sweetheart. Not intentionally."

"Even still," I said, dusting off my jeans as I stood back up, "it *sounds* cold."

"I know." He nodded, considering the grave. "My father was

destroyed when she died. He was expected to put up a strong front, but his grief went so deep that he became a recluse—couldn't even make arrangements for her burial. In the end, Father John had to step in and take charge."

"That's so sad."

"Yeah. The worst part is"—he pointed to the word *Mary*—"no one ever called my mother by her real name. She was known as Elizabeth. *That* name should have marked her final resting place, but the priest didn't know."

"Why didn't you change it?"

"Uncle Arthur wanted to. He and my mother were... close, but my father forbade it. Even when Father passed, Arthur would not go against the right of a husband."

"How noble of him."

"Well"—David took my hand and led me away—"he's been around a while. He's old-fashioned." When we stopped in front of the next two headstones, David smiled, rocking back on his heels. "These two are the best."

"Jason Gabriel Knight. Nineteen sixteen," I read aloud, but it was the second one that grabbed my attention straight away. My heart jumped into my chest when I saw his name written there, even though I was standing right beside him: David Thomas Knight—beloved son and hero. 1894-1918.

"Why did you die?"

"There was an explosion. A bomb." His tight smile caged a memory. "There was no way anyone could've survived it. Pertinent to our laws, I had no choice but to move on and become somebody else."

"Were you the only one killed?"

"Thankfully, yes. But I had established quite a good life for myself; had plenty of money in the bank, a house, friends, but no last will and testament. So, with my brother and only kin supposedly dead, my estate went to the government, and I had to start all over again." He laughed. I covered my mouth. "Talk about learning from your mistakes."

"Well, what good would mistakes be if you didn't get to learn from them?" I shrugged then looked down at the next headstone in the plot. The name didn't match the others though. Hers was Deveraux.

"She was my mother." David answered my thought. "Aunt by blood, but mother by choice." He stepped away and drew the dried brown vine hugging the stone top away, revealing a name and an inscription on the bronze plate:

Arietta Mary Deveraux
Beloved Mother and Aunt.
Sent to the earth with child in arms.
Safe for eternity in the embrace of the Lord. 1908.

My skin tightened with little bumps. "Child?"

"Yes," David whispered. "She died the second the child was born." He focused on his toe as he scuffed up a chunk of grass. "We buried them together."

"Nineteen-oh-eight? So you were only..." I counted in my head for a second.

"I turned fourteen a few months after she died," David said.

I watched the grief trickle across his brow before he contained it. "After all these years, you still feel it? You still feel her loss so strongly?"

He bit his lip. "There are some things you can never move on from, Ara."

"So, she died in childbirth—like your mother?"

"No." The way he said that, his voice laden with detest, made my blood run cold.

"Will you tell me what happened?" I asked cautiously.

David looked up at me quickly. Then, leaving my words alone behind him, walked over and sunk down on the grass with his back against her stone, as if he'd sat there a thousand times before. "You look like her," he said.

"I do?"

He nodded. "Her hair was long like yours, but as gold as the sun. And her eyes"—he closed his, dropping his head with a soft smile—"as blue as the ocean. She would have loved you." He patted the spot next to him.

I sat down with my legs crossed, my back against the stone.

"She would have been proud of me to have found such a sweet girl," he added.

"I'm sure she knows—somehow." I wanted to take his hand, but there was an air of tension around him that was threatening, like he'd explode if I touched him.

"So you believe in the afterlife?" he asked. "Believe they're watching over us?"

I shrugged. "I guess I have to. Otherwise it all just feels too final."

"It *is* final," he said coldly, obviously not realizing how deeply that hurt.

I nodded, looking down at my hands in my lap, hoping to God that I never believed that.

"Ever since the day she came to retrieve us from the orphanage, after my father passed away, she treated Jason and I as if we were her own sons," he said coldly. He wasn't being cold to me, I could tell—just cold to the memory.

"Why were you in an orphanage?"

"It was temporary, while they waited for her to arrive from England." He seemed to watch the memory on the grass between his feet. "But we were treated kindly there."

"So no Oliver Twist scenario?"

David laughed once. "No. Nothing like that."

"What about your uncle? Why didn't he take you?"

"Set rules," he stated.

"Oh." Of course, silly me.

"Well, in Arthur's defense, when Arietta passed, he managed to have many rules bent in order to have us in his charge. It's never been done before, or again."

"Whose butt did he kiss?" I joked.

"The King's."

"Oh," I said, and something in the brevity of his words made my curiosity on *that* subject expire. "So, how did Arietta die?"

He picked up a dead star-shaped leaf, scratching the veins with his thumbnail. "I knew you couldn't resist asking me that again."

"Sorry. You don't have to tell me." I folded my hands into my lap and looked up at the tree above us. The leaves rustled lightly in the breeze, sounding a bit like rain on paper, and despite this being a place where the dead rotted, I felt comfortable here, like it was just some pleasant picnic spot—somewhere to sit and think about the past.

"She always wanted children," he said out of the blue. I sat still, holding my breath in case he should change his mind. "She loved my brother and me, but she used to play hopscotch with the little girls on the sidewalk outside our house, and I knew how badly she wanted a daughter."

"I love hopscotch."

David smiled at me. "The summer after my father's passing, Arietta was walking to the market when a sailor stopped her on the roadside. He asked if she was okay, and she asked why he would inquire such an odd question to a stranger who showed no signs of distress. When he said he was concerned for her pain, since it must have hurt when she fell from Heaven, she fell completely and unconditionally in love with him."

"Well, he sounds charming." I grinned woefully. "In a corny kind of way."

"He *was* charming. And kind. He treated Jason and me as if we were his own sons. Victor Stronghold was his name, and soon became Arietta's. And we were happy." He nodded. "Victor took us fishing and camping, taught us how to play baseball and showed us maps of the world. But happiness was short-lived. They had tried for so long to have a child, and when the days of waiting for the stork to arrive became years, we all lost hope.

"I was nearly thirteen when Uncle Arthur came to visit. Within the two years of his leave, he and my aunt became close. Victor was called away to duty in the Navy for six months and"—David scratched his brow—"when he returned, Arietta was pregnant."

"So it was your uncle's baby?" I asked, my eyes wide.

"Yes. Victor was devastated and humiliated. He left town for a few months, but returned later and begged her to stay with him, despite her indiscretions."

"He must have really loved her."

"Apparently. But she refused. Repeatedly. I remember them

fighting about it… at night… while we cowered in our beds, frightened Victor would hurt our aunt. Until one night she announced to him that she'd be marrying Arthur. So he left, and life went on."

"Wait. So, just to be clear: Arthur was a vampire then?"

He nodded. "He was. He planned to change Arietta after the child was born."

"Wow."

David plucked the dry edges of the leaf in hand and flicked the debris onto the wind. "The doctor predicted the child would arrive in spring, but the snow had started to melt and the days turn warm, and still, nothing happened. I stayed home from school for more than a fortnight to watch over her until, one day, she packed my lunch and sent me out the door—told me she would be fine." He rested the back of his head against the stone. "I remember it all like it was yesterday. So many things aligned to allow tragedy to upturn our lives that day."

"Like what?"

"Uncle Arthur was running errands on the other side of the Port, a day's travel by foot,"—he straightened his leg—"and Jason and I would not be home until sunset at the earliest."

"So…" I waited, but he'd obviously continued living the story inside his mind, forgetting to share. "What happened then?"

"I—" He rolled his head sideways to look at me. "I just don't know if I can talk about this, Ara. It's too…" I watched his flat palm smooth circles over the left side of his chest. "It's too painful."

I nodded. "That's fine."

"But…" He sat up more and reached for my face. "I could show you, if you would let me."

"Show me?"

"I can share memories," he said, his voice trickling with hope. "It's… it won't be very clear, since I haven't mastered this technique yet, but it will save me the lengthy monologue." His lip quirked on one side.

"Okay." I grabbed his hand, rolling my cheek against it. "Show me."

"Close your eyes." He shuffled closer and rested his other hand on my cheek. "Try not to fight it when you see memories that don't belong to you. Just watch, like a film."

"Okay," I whispered.

A faint image—like a photo taken on a sunny day then placed in a dark room at a perpendicular angle—appeared on the backs of my eyelids. I drew a deep breath and watched the slanted image, kind of squinting a little, even with my eyes closed.

"Sorry. I'm unpracticed at this." David's breath brushed softly against my ear. "Does it hurt?"

"No. Is it supposed to?"

"No. But it can."

"I'm fine," I said, and settled back internally to watch the movie.

The evening sky hugged the ground in the distance, red bleeding into night. For as far as the eye could see, the undisturbed horizon ran off into hills, tan roads snaking inward and disappearing among them. The last dregs of light turned the grass orange where it lined the dirt road under a boy's feet. He whistled and waved to his neighbors as he passed, but in his heart, the depths of his worries flared. He walked with an edge to his step, half hurrying, half skipping, as if to pretend he felt no concern. But when he looked up to a house at the end of the street, the open front door seemed to stop his heart.

Silence seized the sound of children laughing, dogs barking, and his own quiet thoughts. I couldn't understand why, but I could sense something was off. So could the boy.

Two breaths passed before the thump of his knapsack hitting the ground brought all life, all sound back.

The movie played in slow motion, making the distance between the picket gate and the porch steps seem like a hundred yards as he ran, his heels kicking up clouds of dust behind him. But everything stopped, the color draining from the day, shadowing out the warmth as only absence greeted the boy's call. He stood in the frame of the door, his eyes tracing the raw pine staircase, the archway to the left, and finally falling over a table knocked to its side. Shattered blue pottery lay among twelve rose stems, the red petals crumpled and torn, smudged into the hardwood floors all around his feet.

"Arietta?" he called again, expecting to hear her reply. He held his breath, this boy with gold-brown hair and fair skin, and bravely entered, though he could feel the grip of tragedy climbing the walls.

When he toed the edge of the table to shift it away, four curled fingers, tipped red with blood, revealed themselves.

"Aunty?" He rushed to her side, falling to his knees at the sight of her fragile, slender body, twisted awkwardly as if she'd fallen from something impossibly high and landed without bones in her body. Stringy red tendrils mocked what was once hair of gold, and as the boy reached forward and stroked it from her cheek, he turned her face toward him and let out a shallow, empty cry, falling back on his heels.

An unrecognizable face stared back at him, eyes swollen shut, a deep void where the other half of her skull should be. Her lip had been torn up to her nose, revealing several teeth missing, and my heart suddenly beat faster.

The boy got to his knees again, swiping tears from his cheeks, and lifted the bodice of her dress. With another panicked cry, he felt helplessly around the blackened dome of skin, searching for the feel of life within.

As the seconds passed, staining his shaking hands with truth, he turned his head to read something inscribed on the wall beside him. The memory blanked out the words, leaving only the feeling that followed, and I knew they were a passage from the Bible, condemning infidelity.

David covered the belly of his aunt and sat up suddenly, his ears pricked, eyes wide. Then he launched to his feet and extended his hand toward the door. "Jason. Don't come in!"

A boy, an exact copy of David, stopped dead in the doorway—his boisterous smile slipping away at the sight of his blood-covered brother.

"Get Uncle," he said shakily.

The hesitant boy tried to look past David, so he stepped into the path of his gaze.

"Jason, run. Get Uncle!" David yelled his command, and Jason moved. Swift and graceful, he tore down the street, his lanky limbs blurring with speed until he disappeared from sight.

David turned back to his aunt and fell to his knees again, his body submitting to grief. But he stopped suddenly as the deathly figure beneath him groaned.

"Aunty!" He held his breath, not sure if he should touch her. "Aunty!"

"Da-v-id…" She moved her hand to reach for him, her soft gaze suddenly slipping past him to a white look of terror. Like a tidal wave preparing itself for slaughter, the silence drew in around them then cracked apart like a shattering vial of terror. The woman clutched her belly and rolled upward, screeching for all the pain Hell had summoned.

"Aunty? What can I do?" His voice trembled with helplessness. "Tell me what to do, and I'll do it."

"Save him! Save my baby!" She rolled away, covering her stomach in a tight, protective embrace.

The memory faded out to white dots around the edges of the film, and the birds in the tree above us sang a melody I had no mind for a moment ago, but was completely aware of.

I lifted my eyelids, blinking against the grey day, and turned my head to look at David—the grown-up David. "You found her?"

"I delivered her baby."

I covered my mouth. "But you were just a child. How did you do that?"

He swallowed a hard lump. "I was simply there to hold her as she was born. I did little else, and there was nothing I could do to help my aunt." His fists clenched. "No one came to the sound of her screaming. No one called for a doctor. She was a woman scorned for her sins, and they let her die like a dog." His lip stiffened and anger flooded his voice, a kind of anger I'd never ever seen in him. "I wrapped the child in my coat and laid in my aunt's arms until nightfall.

"By the time I heard footsteps on the porch outside, I was numb —*completely* numb. I simply stood, held the baby out to my uncle as he burst through the door, and told him I lost her."

"What did he say?"

"Nothing. He took her from my arms and, though I knew nothing of the world back then, I saw a piece of his soul die as he closed her eyelids and covered her face delicately with my jacket." He sniffed, his jaw set hard. "I will never truly understand what my uncle lost that night and, at the time, I thought nothing of the fact that he fell to the floor beside Arietta, with his child crushed against his chest, and laid there until they came to take her. Only now do I see it for the madness it stirred within him."

"Did he ever recover?"

"*Can* someone recover from that?" David asked rhetorically. "He went on with his life, like any wise vampire on the World Council would, but he never spoke of her. Even now, the mention of children sends his eyes soulless." David reached over and wiped a warm tear from my cheek, then smiled softly. "The police came; they took Victor and charged him with aggravated assault. He was jailed for a month, then released with a warning, since the evidence was inconclusive."

"That's it? He killed her and he got a month?"

David nodded and clapped his hands together once, as if closing the door on the past. He rearranged his facial features then and laid his elbows loosely over his knees. "And life went on. Uncle Arthur left town for a while, promising to return when he had made arrangements for us." He brushed his palm across the headstone behind him and nodded toward it. "We buried her on a warm spring day with her baby in her arms, where she will lay evermore."

"David, that's so sad," I whispered, feeling the rise of little bumps over my cold skin.

"Hers has been a loss I have never moved past." He inclined his head to his position on her grave. "And this is where I'll sit one day, feeling the grief for another, with no hope of ever holding her again. Only the name will read a different story: it will be one of true love lost tragically to poor timing." He looked down at the ground. "For me, Ara, your death will be only but a breath away; a second in time, and you will be gone. You have your whole life ahead of you, but for a vampire it's nothing but a heartbeat."

"I'm sorry, David. I wish with all of my heart that it were different."

"I know. But you will never feel the pain of it as I will." He rocked his jaw, nodding as if to make himself stronger. "When you die, I will *never* see you again. Can you comprehend what that feels like for me?"

His words were almost enough to make me change my mind in that breath—to save him from this horrible reality. But his sadness would never make me want his life. It all just seemed so hopeless.

"I'm not telling you this to make you change your mind," he said.

"Then why did you bring me here?"

"It was supposed to be… I just wanted to let you into my past. I never meant to make it about our future."

I laughed softly. "I get it. I find myself doing the same thing—turning the simplest situation into an argument with myself about what I should do."

"Come on then." He stood in front of me, his hand outstretched. "I heard the ogre complaining about ten minutes ago. Let's get some food and stop dwelling on our problems."

"Okay." Gravity pulled on me as I rose to my feet and followed David, still pushing as I stole a glance back to the hill where Arietta would stay. Once, she had been promised a future, and now she was in the ground—never to know her child's name. I could see myself sitting up there beside her, and though my feet led me away, my heart remained where my body would one day return to meet it. And that idea scared me to the point of shaking: the idea of death. It never used to, but seeing those graves painted the truth on a canvas of reality, textured in rough strokes of dark grey, blue, and black. It was real. Death was real, and it was coming for me—getting a little closer every day.

Bowling had never been my forte, and even though David rolled a perfect strike every time—with the exception of one, because I shot him an inappropriate thought which put him off his game—we still lost. Ryan and Alana took home the win: a giant stuffed bowling pin purchased by all the losers. It was nice to spend an evening being normal, not thinking about the bleak future I had to face.

"I'll see you guys at school." Emily waved as we headed out the door.

"Actually, I won't be attending tomorrow," David said.

"Why not?" Emily stopped beside Spencer.

"I'm going away." His matter-of-fact tone disguised all the agony he was in, knowing he would never see any of them again. "My uncle is taking me on holiday, so tomorrow is my last day here."

"So you're skipping school too, Ara?" Ryan asked, raising his brows a few times.

"Probably."

"Ara's going to be so lost without you, David," Emily said.

"One can only hope," he beamed, "then I can be sure she won't give her heart away to someone else while I'm gone."

"Not a chance of that. I think you might be stuck with this one." Emily winked at me.

David's strong arms wrapped my waist and pulled me close. "I hope so."

"What about the concert and the ball?" Alana stepped around the giant toy, and her wide jet-black eyes reflected the neon lights behind me.

"I can come back for the concert, but as for the ball—well, I may make the last dance," he said.

"Well, good luck, David," Emily said, her tone holding way too much gravity.

David tightened his grip around me.

"O…kay. See ya, guys." I waved again and dragged David toward the car.

He opened the door and grabbed my wrist as I bent to climb in. "What is it, Ara? What are you thinking?"

"Didn't you hear me?"

"Not clearly. You had about four different thoughts at once."

"Oh, um… well, I was wondering why you didn't tell them you're *never* coming back."

David smiled. "We never do that. That's why telling you about leaving in the first place was such a big deal."

"Really? So you just disappear in all aspects?"

"Yes. Mostly. We send letters to people in positions of authority, like schools or employers, once we're safely away, but if there had been any suspicions surrounding our stay, announcing plans to leave could spark a sudden need to investigate before it's too late."

"Oh." I traced the rubber seal along the base of the window. "But there's no suspicion this time, so why not just tell them?"

"There's no way of knowing that. People mostly keep their suspicions to themselves, and besides"—he pulled my finger away as I peeled the rubber back—"it's the way we do things. We're consistent in our behaviors."

"But you told *me* you were leaving." I smiled sheepishly, forcing down a rising yawn.

"Which is rare, mon amour, like I said. Now, come on"—he offered the seat—"let's get you home before you fall asleep where you stand."

I sat down and the door closed behind me, giving my head support as I drifted away. I felt my seatbelt clip around me a second later, followed by a cool kiss on my hand, then nothing more until the quiet thud of his door woke my mind a little.

"Shh," David whispered into my brow, lifting me from the car.

Quietly conscious of his embrace, I rolled my head into the hollow of his shoulder and fixated on the gentle, soapy smell of his shirt with each restful breath.

"Oh, she's exhausted," Dad's voice hummed as a pale ring of light broke the darkness under my eyelids.

"Shall I carry her upstairs?" David asked, holding me a little closer.

"Uh, yeah, sure. No need to disturb her further."

The front door closed behind us. I stayed in the blissful elation of dream world, in David's arms, until the cold touch of my pillow fell along my cheek and I sunk into the softness of my mattress. My shoes came off and a still silence filled the room; it sounded like no one was there, but I could feel David's presence.

"Goodnight, my love." He pressed a cold kiss to my brow.

I lifted my mind out of sleep just long enough to whisper, "David?"

"Yes, sweetheart."

"Stay with me tonight?"

"I planned to," he whispered, and the bedroom door closed, leaving me in darkness.

Outside, I heard Dad saying goodbye to David as his car pulled away from our house. And the only other sound, after Dad's footsteps trailed away behind his bedroom door, was the rhythmic tick of the clock on the wall by the front door, timing my dreams while I slipped away.

Just before the grasp of sleep possessed me, two cool arms fell around my shoulders, and I let myself wander into the peaceful harmony of the night, against David's chest.

THE SWEET CHOCOLATY SMELL OF DAVID STIRRED MY SENSES through the night, waking me with surprise when I looked up and saw the morning sun on his cheek. "You stayed!"

"Of course." He stretched his arms out above us. "You asked me to."

"Hasn't mattered in the past."

"Yes, well," he said, his arm landing back down around my shoulders. "In the past, I didn't only have two days left with you."

That put a dampener on the day.

"Sorry," he said.

"It's okay."

"No, it's not." He rolled me onto my back, his long body against the length of mine. "Just don't think about it. In fact"—he couldn't help but smile, his eyes drifting to a thought—"why not go back to thinking about that dream you were just having?"

My mouth popped open. "You saw that?"

"My love." He kissed my nose. "I saw everything."

"Goddamn mind readers!" With a feisty huff, I threw the covers back and headed for the shower—and maybe a few minutes of unheard thoughts.

"Your thought patterns are not muted by short distances, Ara. I can still hear you," he called out as I shut the bathroom door.

"Argh! Stop it." I covered my ears, as if that would help. But I couldn't stop seeing those images: David and me naked, tucked in a loving embrace. And the worst part was, all of it was my own desires—like writing a porn entry in a diary and having someone read it out loud. It was just too personal to share.

I took off the jeans and green sweater I slept in last night and stuffed them in the laundry basket, burying my undies and bra in case David needed to use the bathroom.

"I've already seen your underwear, my darling girl," he called out. "You don't have to hide them now."

My shoulders dropped with a vocalized breath. At least there was one good thing about having a mind-reading vampire boyfriend: I'd had plenty of practice at emptying my thoughts and focusing on nothing. I was sure, in some odd way, that that could be a good skill to have.

"Speaking of skills," David said from just outside the bathroom door, "we need to rehearse for the benefit concert. I'm not even sure which song we're supposed to be playing now."

I reached into the shower and twisted the faucet, then stood back and waited for the water to get hot. "Um, we're doing that one from that movie—the one Nathan liked."

David chuckled softly. "He liked a lot of movies, Ara."

"Well, you know which one I mean," I said. "I can never remember the title."

"Are you still doing a solo performance?" His voice echoed slightly too loud through the door, making me cringe a little in case Dad should hear.

"Yeah, and we're also doing *Somewhere Over the Rainbow.*" I waited in case he replied, looking over my thin body in the reflection of the shower glass. But when the silence lasted a few seconds, I stepped into the welcoming steam whorls and ran my hands over my hair. The running water and locked doors offered me a kind of privacy I wasn't used to anymore—one where I could imagine my thoughts were unheard... just like my shower singing.

"Ara!"

I jumped out of my skin at the sudden thud on the door.

"Save some water for future generations, please."

Jeeze. "Yes, Dad—just rinsing my hair."

"It doesn't take your mother that long."

By *mother*, he meant Vicki. "She has short hair, Dad."

He groaned loud enough that I heard it through the door.

"Hmph. You'd do a lot more than just groan if you knew I had my boyfriend in my room right now," I said under my breath. Thing was, Dad would freak if there was a boy in my room, but I bet he'd take it really well if I told him David was a vampire. I think he'd see it as a rare opportunity to hear tales of History firsthand.

I finished washing my hair and hopped out, just slipping my blue cotton dress over my head when the phone on my desk rang.

"Hang on!" I yelled as though the caller would hear me. But, quick as I tried to be, my dress bunched up on my not-quite-dry skin and got stuck halfway down my waist. I tugged harder, a rise of frustration nearly turning to tears. I didn't want to miss that call if it was Mike ringing before he got on the plane. What if it crashed and I never got to hear his voice again? What if it—

"Hello." David's melodious voice filled the room.

I froze, listening.

"Yes, she's getting dressed."

Oh, God, don't tell him that! He'll freak out, thinking you're watching me, or something.

I pulled my dress down and tripped all over myself to get out of the wardrobe. "I'm here. Gimme the phone."

David grinned, holding his index finger up. "No, nothing like that."

"David," I huffed impatiently, opening my hand for the phone.

"Yes. It's all she's talked about for the last couple of weeks," he said, then laughed.

"Okay, okay. That's enough." I snatched the phone from him and, assuming I knew who he was talking to, said, "Hi, Mike."

"Hey, baby girl. How's things?"

"Great. You at the airport?"

"Yeah, just thought I'd make sure you hadn't forgotten me."

"Yeah right. It's all I've talked about, isn't it?" I poked my tongue out at David.

Mike laughed. "Well, I've been looking forward to it, too. And I expect the biggest hug you've got tucked into those skinny little arms tomorrow, Ara."

"Oh, trust me, I've been practicing my squeezing," I said.

"With David?" he teased.

"Uh-huh, but *you* get a different kind of squeezing."

"Oh, fine then, I know where I stand." I could hear the amusement behind his feigned insult, and I heard David scoff.

"Still in exactly the same place as always," I said, trying to ignore the hidden meaning behind David's throaty noise.

"Okay, well, have fun today and... I'll see ya tomorrow."

"Yep, bye." I had to dig my heels into the carpet to stop from bouncing around like a little girl. And as the phone line went dead, severing the connection to my best friend, an empty feeling swallowed my soul for a second, until I looked at David. But he looked troubled —leaning back in my chair, drumming his fingers on the desk, his thoughts a million miles away. "David?"

He looked up at me, snapping out of his stare.

"What is it?" I asked.

"You're right." A very cheeky grin lit his eyes. "He did not approve of my being here while you were getting dressed."

"So?"

"So, he's overprotective. I know the sort, Ara. He *will* ask questions about me."

"Can you read his thoughts over the phone?" I said as I walked over and leaned my butt on the desk.

David shook his head. "No. I can only read certain electrical wavelengths, which don't travel through phone lines. But I've been around humans and been subjected to their thought-patterns long enough to make conclusions from very little detail."

"Like one of those cool detectives on those crime shows?"

David laughed, resting his chin on his hand. "Yeah, something like that."

"And you think you've summed Mike up, huh?"

He scratched the corner of his brow, taking a deep breath. "All I know is it's a good thing I won't be here during the day. I can't be around you if he is."

"Why?"

"I might be tempted to kill him," he muttered with a certain amount of animosity.

"Wow. Hostile much?"

"You don't get it," he said, folding his arms. "Your history together has afforded him some unspoken claim to you that no new relationship stands a chance to sever."

My cheek tightened on one side with a half-smile. "You know, you're cute when you're jealous."

"Ara, be serious." David inclined forward, elbows over his knees. "He's obviously a smart man. If he gets wind there's a guy in your room every night, you know what he'll do."

"Look." I sat on the desk, letting my bare feet dangle. "You might think he's got some weird Spidey sense that can track the scent of another male like a teacher to cigarettes in a schoolbag, but I'm not sure I really care if he finds out I have a guy in my room at night."

He looked up at me. "Ara, if he finds me in your room and we're forced to meet in person, it will only be a matter of time before he starts asking all the wrong questions."

"And I'll give all the wrong answers. I won't tell him the truth about what you are."

"It's not the questions he asks you that I worry about; it's the ones he asks himself."

"Well, is it that bad if he figures out what you are?"

"You mean aside from the fact that he'd steal you away from me, take you across the country and lock you in a closet, then fly back here and start a pitchfork rally against me?"

I laughed, rubbing my hand over my neck, where droplets of cold water dripped down from my hair. "You know, the chances are he'll figure something's not right anyway. I mean, especially when I refuse to laze around and watch movies with him at night."

"I know. But…" He sighed. "This is just hard for me, Ara. I don't even want to think about you lazing around with another man."

"Well, just don't think about it that way. It's like I said: I might still have feelings for him, but I also have feelings for you. And I would never do anything inappropriate with him, David. You can trust me."

"I do trust you."

"But you don't trust him?"

"No, I don't trust the fact that you're human."

"What does that mean?"

"It means... you're barely clutching on to life right now. Your whole world has been turned upside-down, and you need stability. He *is* that stability—has always been—and your subconscious mind is going to force you to reach out for *him*. Not for me."

"Wow, you should be a psychologist," I laughed, and he nodded. "If only you weren't so full of shit."

"You don't have to believe me," he said. "I'm old, Ara. I've seen it all; I know how these things go."

"Well, I don't. I'm young and I have no idea what's going to happen in our future, but I know for a fact that I won't betray you with Mike. Besides, he doesn't even love me like that, David."

"He does."

"Does not."

"He does, and you're going to realize that when you see him. And as soon as you do, it'll rehash all your old feelings and you'll fly lovingly into his arms."

"Then you don't know me very well at all."

He stood in front of me, lifting his hand to cup the side of my neck. "I know you won't betray me, but your human instincts will drive your heart toward him in order to protect you from me. You won't have much control over that. It's purely self-preservation."

"Wow. It's worse than I thought: you *really* don't know me." I smiled, laying my hand over his. "Besides," I added, my entire heart melted by those loving green eyes, "when you're gone, missing you will be way more damaging than anything else life could throw at me, so maybe my heart will do everything in its power to protect me from *that*. Maybe I'll decide to become a vampire."

David shook his head. "You won't. And you *will* one day get over me. Personally, I will exist as if I were a rose without the grace of rain. There will be no peace for me—ever. But you will eventually be fine."

"What makes you think it'll be so easy for *me* to move on?"

"The human heart," he said simply, "it does not love as deeply as a vampire's."

That's where he was wrong. Again. I knew a love more perfect and more devastating than any other feeling I'd ever had in my life; a love made tragic only by unfortunate timing. I would forever be David's girl. After he was gone, I'd look for him in the face of every man I passed for the rest of my life, and though my physical existence on Earth would end one day, I knew in my heart that I would love him for eternity.

The school bell ringing in the distance broke the silence in my room then. I watched David as he turned and stared out the window, the morning light shadowing and highlighting the contours of his body. All his thoughts seemed to fall away from the hold of his gaze and onto the world below my room, while my thoughts consumed the empty space around us. I didn't care that he could hear them, and I didn't care that if Vicki came home early from shopping she'd find David and I ditching school. Nothing mattered to me in the same way it used to. It all just seemed inconsequential with the idea that these were the last touches of light I would ever see on his skin. I would never see the summer sun making marbles of his emerald eyes again, never see it kiss his hair with tones of gold, and never again feel it warm his fingers as he touched me. All we had was one last day, and two weeks of nights. And even the nights would disappear in a countdown around us until he was gone. In this moment, I felt like an idiot for giving him up in exchange for a human life.

"Come on." He turned suddenly and smiled, offering his hand. "Let's not waste this day on solemn thoughts."

"What do you want to do then?" I took his hand.

"I wanna teach you a song."

"What song?" I asked, grabbing the guitar when he pointed to it.

"One I wrote."

I stopped for a second and watched him sink down on my bed. "You write songs?"

"Course I do." He patted the space of mattress between his legs. "Sit here."

"O...kay." I sat with my back against his chest, and David took the guitar, positioning it across my lap in front of us. "What's the song called?"

"The Knight of the Rose."

"What's it about?" I asked, letting David take my fingers and place them on the strings.

He paused. "You."

"About leaving me?"

"No. It's not a goodbye song; it's a love song." His tone softened away to near silence. "It was just written with the tears of farewell."

Somehow, that made it hurt more.

David smiled against the side of my face, then took my hand again. "After the first chord, place your fingers here."

"What's that chord? I've never seen it before."

"I think I invented it." He laughed shyly, then strummed it once.

My eyes widened. "Wow. That's really... intense."

"Yes." He arranged my fingers on different strings and pressed them down firmly, as if to ask if I had it. I nodded. "Okay. I'll whisper the chords as we go along. I want you to know this song by heart, Ara."

"Why?"

He moved my fingers back to A minor—the first chord. "So you can play it when you miss me."

I didn't want to think about that right now. "Don't be silly. I won't miss you," I said playfully instead.

"My love"—he reached his right hand around to touch the strings—"if you never, not for even one second, miss me once I'm gone, then I will be happy eternally." He pecked my cheek, drawing a smile to my lips, and gave the song life in the same breath, his fingers dancing in an elaborate pattern over the strings. We changed chords then, and the flow of my favorite notes, nearly each and every one I loved, filled every corner of the darkness in my heart. I could've sworn the room illuminated with bright white light. It was as if he'd taken every song that ever made me feel something and combined them, crafting the notes with an ethereal life force.

David whispered the next chord in my ear, moving his fingers with mine. I wanted to separate myself from this world, try not to feel all the pain in this song, the loss, the dying hope of the future climbing to the surface and making me want to cry. He said it wasn't a goodbye song, but it had all the sadness of parting in the flow of its notes. How could I not cry; how could I not fall to my knees right now and beg the universe for one chance? Just one little piece of hope that there'd be a happy ending for us. I'd give anything. *Anything* for that.

The song floated softly to a haunting end, leaving the room silent for a heartbeat. I tried to take a breath but it came out of my lungs instead of going in, making the grief shriek from my lips.

David pried the guitar from my tight grip and placed it on the ground, pulling me against him on my pillows. "Shh. It's all okay, my love. Everything will be okay."

But he didn't believe that. He couldn't even convince himself.

He stroked my hair back, tucking me up like he'd never let go, and the last of my strength dissolved. I closed my eyes and drifted away in his arms, allowing myself to dream for a moment that things were different—that David and I could be together for the rest of my life.

Our future danced around in my head like a short black-and-white film. I walked toward that boy at the end of the aisle, whose green eyes reflected the awe in his heart as they fell over my white dress, his joy dissolving my nerves and making the people in the pews disappear. It was just us, alone on the edge of fulfilling one of our hearts' greatest desires.

As I finally came to stand beside him, he took my hand and smiled down at my bouquet: a soft, simple piece of completely white roses, with one immaculately blossomed red one set center.

"What's that one for?" David's soft, warm breath brushed the top of my head, waking my mind a little as he spoke.

"The part of my heart that will never belong to anyone else; the part of me that will always be only yours."

"How appropriate," he said, and shifted under me as he reached into his pocket. "I have something—a gift for you—which comes bearing the exact same sentiment."

I looked up to the golden light of the morning sun on my walls, my eyes drifting from David's lips, down the curve of his arm around my waist, and to his closed fist. "What is it?"

He unfolded his fingers, revealing a pool of delicate silver chain, slightly covering a heart-shaped locket. "So you may never forget that you"—he pointed to the engraved rose on it—"are in my heart."

"David, it's beautiful." I turned the locket over and ran my finger along the fine inscription on the back. Though I wasn't sure, it looked like it was written in French. "What does it say?"

"Tu m'appartiens." He kissed my cheek and smoothed my hair back, leaving a cool tingle behind where he linked the chain around my neck.

As it fell onto my chest just below my collarbones, my hand rose up instantly to hold it tight. "What does that mean?"

He slowly pressed his lips to my ear. "You belong to me."

"For as long as I live."

"No, mon amour. For all time."

"I like that," I said, sitting back against him, and he wrapped his arms across my waist, holding me that way until the sun went down, stealing away the last day of our forever.

Part Two

MIKE

24

Orange shadows stretched across the highway in the early morning sun, and my thoughts seemed lost far beyond the car window too. I leaned my weary head on the glass, trying to hold on to that last moment before everything changed. Even though Mike was arriving today, excitement was not the first feeling I had as my alarm startled me from peaceful slumber: it was devastation, weighed down with a tight ache in my throat called sorrow. I really thought Mike's coming to stay would ease the pain of losing David, or at least make me more decisive on the whole human or vampire thing. But I was wrong.

Dad moved his gaze from the road and smiled at me. I knitted some semblance of a grin across my face, but nothing could make me smile for real. Thing was, with the days of losing David coming closer and closer, the idea of killing for love seemed less horrific. Not enough that I was ready to tell him that, or think it around him. I just… I needed guidance, I guess—a friend to advise me. Or maybe a sign from Above.

Oddly, at the exact moment I thought that, we turned onto the interstate and a giant black billboard with a white circle of light caught my attention. I spun in my seat and read the words on the perfume ad as we whizzed past: *Let Fate Decide.*

Dad turned the radio off then, leaving my thoughts exposed in the silence as an idea took shape. I sat back in my chair, smiling. Maybe if I couldn't decide what to do, I could ask a higher power to grant me an epiphany—or at least an answer. Mike loved me, but he in no way loved me like I loved him. It would take some miracle for his heart to change, just like the kind of miracle it would take to convince me to go with David and be a murderer. So maybe that was it; maybe that was my answer: if David was right, and Mike did magically have feelings for me—feelings he'd kept hidden—then I'd stay human, live my life, have babies, and one day die.

But if I was right: if Mike really only loved me as a friend, then it'd be a sign that I should go with David and become a vampire. A killer.

It was perfect. Like rolling the dice and saying 'seven'. It removed any real responsibility from the decision-making for me, but it was what I needed right now.

Dad looked sideways at me and changed gears as we slowed, coming into the airport. "You excited?" he asked.

"Kinda nervous, actually."

"Nervous?" he said. "Why?"

Part of me wanted to tell Dad about the 'Tragic Rejection Moment' between Mike and me, but the sensible part said to him, "It's just been a while, is all. I'm not sure if we'll be friends like we used to."

"Honey." Dad pulled over in the pick-up zone and placed his hand on mine. "I'm sure you'll be fine. You may have been apart for a while, but Mike's been there the whole time. I've been talking to him every couple of days, giving him updates on you."

"Dad?" I groaned. "Really? I mean, I knew you were talking, but… updates? Come on—"

Dad shrugged. "He asked. I told."

"I don't know how you thought telling me that would make things better." I folded my arms and looked out the window.

"Because I don't want you to feel like he abandoned you by not pushing you to talk to him. He's just been giving you some space."

I unfolded my arms and looked beyond the glass entrance of the terminal to the people flooding the airport, gathering around the baggage collection for flight 728. Mike's flight.

"He's here." I unlatched the seatbelt, my heart picking up about ten paces. I wished I could see him—just make him out among the crowd so I could sneak up on him, see how different he looked—before he saw me.

"Go on." Dad grinned, watching me edge forward in my seat. "I'll wait here; give you two a minute."

"I'll be back soon," I beamed as I sprung from the car.

While people gathered their bags from the conveyor belt and hugged their families, I pushed against the tightly-packed bodies, using my elbows to almost swim through the crowd. My gaze shifted, scrutinizing every man with his physical features, until I spotted a guy on his phone by the Coke machine: sandy-colored hair, broad shoulders. I squinted, jutting my neck forward as I took baby steps in his direction, seeing only flashes as the crowd of people stole my view several times. It looked like Mike, but if it was, then he'd changed. A *lot.*

A wave of certainty flooded me when he threw his bag over his shoulder and flipped his phone in the air before stuffing it in his back pocket. That was him! He was so much taller than I remembered, though, and bigger, too. His blue shirt fit snuggly around the bulges of his arms, as if he hadn't realized how big they were and that his shirt no longer fit, but there was still that something in the way he held himself. It was sort of a tall stance, with the kind of confidence that came from being an officer of authority. He looked good. He looked… *sexy.*

Mike spun around suddenly, eyes lighting up when he saw me. "Ara?"

I couldn't move. I'd imagined this moment so many times in my mind—how I'd run into his arms and he'd lift me off the ground and kiss me like he loved me—but that was always only a dream, and I left that behind. I found another reason to exist. Yet still, as I looked upon my old crush for the first time in so long, my new reason to exist seemed to fade for that one moment. And whether it was by habit or longing, for that single moment, I still wanted Mike just as bad as before.

"Ara." He ushered me to him. "What ya waitin' for? Come here."

With no mind for the family walking in my path, I darted forward, forcing them to part as I launched toward Mike, barely giving him a chance to drop his bag before I jumped into his arms. We stumbled back a few steps with the force of my eager embrace, a physical reaction my steady-legged vampire could never have, unless he was pretending to be human. I just loved how human Mike was right then.

"Whoa, baby. That's happiness to see me." His widespread fingers pressed firmly against the back of my ribs.

I squeezed his neck, wrapping my legs around his hips, probably showing my undies to every dirty old man who cared to look. He just felt so good to hold, though; a little piece of the past, with a warmth that could only be human, as if he'd carried some of the Perth sun all the way to the U.S. with him.

I rested my cheek in his neck. "I missed you so much."

Mike's arms stopped the air from coming into my lungs. "I missed you too, kid."

When he went to lower me, I held on tighter. "Not yet. Just... not yet."

"It's okay, Ara. Let go. I'm not going anywhere." He unwound my arms from his neck and placed me on the ground. I pulled my dress down to cover my undies. "Let me get a look at you." He shook his head, smiling. "You've gotten thinner. Are you eating?"

"You sound like my mom." I clutched the edges of my dress in fists of nerves. "And, yes, I do eat."

"What's this?" He reached for my locket.

"Oh, um. A friend gave it to me." I took it from his hand and dropped it back into place.

"You belong to me?" His eyes narrowed under a rutted brow.

"Ah, yeah. It's um... a good friend?" I offered.

"David?" he asked accusingly.

"Maybe."

Mike just blinked a few times, then drew a deep breath through his nose and placed his arm around my shoulder. "Should I be worried?"

"Mike? You've been here for a whole two seconds. Don't start."

"I don't like it, Ara. You *belong* to me? It sounds possessive."

"You're just jealous," I said, smiling.

"Jealous, huh?" His face lit up and his eyes warmed with so much familiarity that all the pain of the separation over these last few months melted away. He grabbed my hand. "So what if I am? You've always been *my* best friend. Then, out of nowhere, you meet some random guy, fall in love with him, and he brands you with his mark. Now, all of a sudden, you belong to *him*?"

Brands me? A quick breath came cold into my lungs as I reached for the yellowing bruises on my neck, but when Mike's eyes narrowed as he looked at my hand, I tensed from toes to shoulders, realizing that wasn't the *mark* he was referring to.

He grabbed my wrist and pulled it away from my neck, gasping loudly when he saw what was hiding beneath my carefully styled, bruise-covering hair. "Who did this to you?"

I shrank into myself, looking around. "Mike, stop it. Please. People are staring."

"I don't care. Look at you. What kind of a guy would bruise a young girl like this?"

"It wasn't like that."

"Oh, really. Then what's the story, Ara?"

"Look, he wasn't *trying* to hurt me, okay? Just stop worrying about me all the time."

Mike grabbed my chin and studied the marks on both sides of my neck. "Stop worrying, huh? Well, it certainly *looks* like I should be concerned. Have you seen this? Have you looked at yourself? Jesus, girl." He released my face gently. "What the hell is that? A hickey? Because it sure as hell doesn't look like any hickey I've ever seen."

"It was an accident," I said bashfully. "We were just playing around. I bit him and then when he… well, we got a little carried away."

Mike's arms dropped to his sides and disappointment filled his watery eyes. "Did you sleep with him?"

"No."

He looked around the busy terminal, rubbing at the frown on his face. "I'm sorry, Ara. I just… I've been missing you for *so* long; worried because I can't be here to look after you, and I find *this*." He held his hand out, presenting the bruise. "It looks like a severe case of abuse."

"Stop it." I lowered my head to hide behind my hair. "I know it looks bad. I don't need *you* making it worse."

He clicked his tongue and wrapped both arms around my shoulders, muffling my breath against his chest. I hated the fact that our dramatic reunion in the middle of the airport was on display to hundreds of people—all watching.

"I'm sorry, Ar." He rubbed my back. "Okay? I'm not mad at you. I'm just"—with a sigh, he pulled back, carefully studying every inch of my face—"I'm mad at *myself*. I never should've let your dad take you away. I should've come after you, or kept you with me."

I shook my head. "He'd never have let me stay, Mike."

"He would've let you stay with *me*."

I shook my head again. I was glad I came here; glad I met David—even though I was going to lose him. "He didn't hurt me, Mike. I wanted him to do it. I liked it."

"Ara? You're just a girl. You shouldn't be playing games like that with boys. *He* should've known better," Mike said in a singing tone. "Look, I'm sorry. I just lost it, is all. I just never expected to see you with bruises."

"I know. I said I was sorry."

"You don't need to be sorry, Ar. I've done the biting thing with girls, so I get it, okay? I really do. And I'll let it go. Just, please don't let him do it to you again. Promise?"

I nodded, crossing my fingers behind my back. I wondered then if explaining to Mike that David's actually a vampire might ease his disdain for the whole biting situation, since it could've been worse.

When Mike laughed, I thought he'd read my mind, but he simply shook his head and said, "It's really damn good to see you, kid."

"Yeah. It's kinda weird. I feel like I'm imagining this."

Mike reached across and pinched me. "Feels pretty real to me."

"Ouch." I rubbed my forearm. "That hurt, you know."

"At least I didn't bite you," he said with a grin.

I smirked.

"Shall we go home?" he asked.

"Sure."

Mike bent and grabbed his suitcase, then shouldered his backpack swiftly, wrapped his arm around my neck, and we wandered slowly out to the parking bay where I left Dad.

"Mr. Thompson. Good to see you again." Mike shook Dad's hand firmly.

"Yes, yes, it's good to have you here." Dad cupped his other hand over Mike's in the 'double' handshake. "We've been hearing a lot about you these past few months."

"Really?" Mike asked in a leading tone. "*Ara* talks about me?"

"Yes." Dad grinned. "I started to wonder if you were my daughter's only friend."

"Ha!" Mike looked at me with that cheeky, cocky grin. "I am."

"Are not." I punched him in the arm.

He leaned away, rubbing off my pathetic effort at violence.

THE WARM SMELL OF BACON AND TOAST WAFTED INTO THE entranceway, with the sweet aroma of sugared coffee lingering in a pleasant layer over the top. I stepped in and closed the door, smiling at Sam as he ran upstairs carrying—or dragging—Mike's suitcase.

"Sure you don't want me to take that, Sam?" Mike asked.

"He's got it," Dad said, leading Mike into the dining area. "I think I smell breakfast."

"I think I smell Heaven," Mike added.

I rolled my eyes and pushed past him and Dad to sit at the table. Mike was such a suck-up. He knew exactly how to get into the oldies' good books, and he was holding no bars back. It was also one of the things I really loved about him.

"Mike, good to finally meet you." Vicki left her practically permanent kitchen position to hug him. "How have you been?"

"Good, Vicki. Really good," Mike said softly. "It's nice to finally put a face to the voice."

Great, so Vicki had been talking to him on the phone too. Just bury me now.

Vicki smiled. "I've made you some breakfast. I figured you'd be hungry after all that travelling."

"Yeah, great," Mike said and sat at the table next to me. "The airport food was pretty average."

"So, Ara tells us you've been accepted into the ah… what was that called again?" Vicki asked, fussing over the plates.

"Vicki," I moaned. "Dad already interrogated him on the drive home. Do you have to do it too?"

"I don't mind an interrogation, Ara." Mike elbowed me gently. "It's uh—it's called the Tactical Response Group. We get to use cool guns, basically." He grinned at Sam as he sat down.

"Do you get to shoot people?" Sam asked, leaning right across the table to be in Mike's bubble.

"Well," Mike's voice softened, "the only place I like to shoot people is in the digital world. Other than that, we try to avoid it as much as possible. But I have a taser?" he offered.

"Awesome. Hey, do you play online—" Sam's voice became background noise while the boys talked video games and Vicki served breakfast around all the commotion, sitting quietly down after. Without touching my food, I leaned on my hand and listened to the sound of normal; how the laughter, forks clinking on plates, and cups resting with a clunk on wood could echo familiarity and contentment. Once upon a time, being normal meant having a life with two parents, no grief, and no scars. Now, normal meant I could sit in my kitchen, eat food with my family, and at the end of my life, die.

A few months ago, I didn't know how much I had to be grateful for, but the hourglass of Fate could rock and tip everything out of balance at any time—take the people you love and leave you with nothing but a broken heart. So I knew now that I had to take each breath with a kind of appreciation I never understood before, because imagining my life with David's interpretation of eternity—imagining it without any of *this*—I would miss it all terribly. I'd even miss Vicki.

"Well, Vicki,"—Mike wiped his mouth with a napkin and rested his arm on the table—"that was the most amazing breakfast I've had in a long time. Ara's right, you are a good cook."

"*Ara* said that?" Vicki's wide eyes landed on me. I wanted to brush them off. "Well, thank you, Ara, and thank you, Mike. I really enjoy cooking, especially for people who eat it without *salt*." She glared at Dad.

"What?" Dad shrugged, holding his hands out.

Mike laughed and placed his napkin on the table. "Well, my mother raised me with the strong belief that it's considered an insult to the chef when one puts salt on his food."

Vicki's smile pushed her brows up. "See, Greg? You could stand to learn a few table manners yourself."

Sam laughed.

"Hm. Ara?" Dad cleared his throat, ignoring Vicki and Sam. "Why don't you give Mike the grand tour?"

"I'm sure he's seen a house before, Dad."

"Not yours, though," Mike said, encouraging my new role as Tour Guide.

"Okay. Come on." I stood up, but when I reached for his hand he quickly drew it away. Even Dad and Vicki saw it, disguising their shock with a swift glance at their plates, while I ate the swell of mortification.

"Thanks again, Vicki." Mike grabbed his plate and mine.

"You're welcome, Mike."

He dumped the plates in the sink as we passed the kitchen and headed through the arch to the forbidden formal room.

"So, this is the dining room…" I explained.

"Two dining rooms?"

"Yeah, for all those dinner guests Vicki entertains." I laughed.

"Right." Mike nodded, crossing his arms. I don't think he realized I was joking.

"And out there is the backyard." I pointed beyond the windows.

"Is that the swing? Where you sit when you're sad?"

"No, it's a slide."

"Ha-ha." He flicked his hand out and knocked my ponytail.

"Uh!" I held up a finger. "No mucking about in here. You'll hit the chandelier."

Mike looked up. "Hm. Look at that. A real chandelier."

"It's plastic," I remarked and walked on, leading him to the room that met back up with the front entrance. "We watch TV in here."

Mike stood by the suede sofa and considered the giant LCD sitting neatly on the white cabinet. "No drinks in the lounge," he read the 'house rules' painted on a wooden wall-plaque. "No name-calling. No…"

"Okay." I grabbed his shoulders and spun him toward the door. "We all know the rules."

"I don't." He tried to walk back to the TV room. "I wasn't done."

"You can read them later. I wanna show you your room."

"Okay. But only because I stink." He lifted his arm and sniffed his own odor. "I need a change of shirt."

"No kidding." I pushed his arm down.

"Now, Sam!" Dad's voice echoed into the entrance.

"Why does *she* get to stay home?" Sam said, and I imagined him pointing off in some random direction as if pointing at me: the '*she*'.

"Because she has a friend who just arrived."

"There's always some excuse. It's like she never goes to school."

Mike rested his forearm on the balustrade, half laughing, and looked at me. "You never go to school, huh?"

"Not a lot." I toed the carpet at the base of the stair.

"How's it been"—he nodded toward the dining room—"having a little brother?"

"Not much different to putting up with you."

He laughed and looked around, his eyes taking in the stairs, then the window above the front door, before landing back on me. "I like this. It's a nice house. It's good to see the places you've been talking about all your life."

"Well, later I'll show you where I landed when I broke my arm that time."

"Sounds good." He tugged on a strand of my hair, making me lower my foot from the first step to look up at him. "I really missed ya, Ara."

"I know." My eyes moved slowly from his camel-skin boots, over the light denim jeans, and traced swerves along the ripples under his shirt, stopping in a hold on his warm eyes. The caramel brown had always reminded me of autumn—once my favorite season—but there would have to be a different comparison for his eyes now that my autumn would forever be a reminder of losing David. Maybe…

"Ara?"

"Hm?" His face blurred and sharpened into focus.

"Did you hear anything I just said?"

"Um—"

"Seriously? You heard *nothing*?" His voice cracked.

"Um…" I flashed him a cheeky grin. "Sorry?"

Mike's shoulders dropped and he nodded to himself. "Come on, why don't you just show me upstairs?"

I knew he was upset that I'd zoned out. And I didn't want him to be upset, so I tried to make light of it by saying, "Race you?"

It worked. His mask cracked, bringing warmth back to his eyes. "Nah, forget that," he said, taking a quick step toward me. "This is more fun."

"No!" I squealed, rapping my fists on his leg as he swept me up like a football under his arm, my legs kicking behind us, and bolted up the stairs. "Put me down!"

"Make me." He laughed, so I angled my head just so, and bit his thigh. "Ow!"

A jolt went through me as I landed hard on my hands and knees.

"I can't believe you just bit me."

"I can't believe you just dropped me."

"Sorry. Defensive reaction." He rubbed his leg.

I stood up, dusting myself off, and we both held eye contact for only a second before laughing.

"Truce?" I offered my pinkie.

"Truce." He linked his with mine then pulled it close to his body, wrapping his other hand behind my head to force my face against his chest. "Come here, you."

"Yeah. I missed you, too." I patted his back a few times then stepped away.

"So"—he looked from one door to another—"which one's my room?"

I pointed to the spare room.

"Which one's yours?"

I nodded to the one behind him. He took a look, then hobbled over to his door, his hand firmly on his thigh like a wounded soldier.

"Oh, grow up, Mike. I didn't even draw blood."

"How do you know?" He dropped the act. "I might need a tetanus shot."

I wanted to whack him, but knew it would start the war all over again. So I took the moral high road instead, and opened his door for him, ruffling his hair as the light from his room swept the carpet by my feet. "Does poor baby need a cuddle?"

"Quiet, you," he said playfully, and then his eyes widened as he looked into his room. "Ooh. Nice."

"Yep. And you can thank David for putting the bed up," I said, crossing the room to close the window. "Dad was trying to put the foot at the head."

"David, huh?"

"Yes." I pushed the curtains further apart to allow for more light, then turned around and opened the door adjacent to the window. "So, there's a bathroom here."

"Wow, my own bathroom. Nice." Mike leaned his head around the bathroom door, then smiled back at me.

"And you have a TV." I walked to the wardrobe—the door on the left of his bed—and rolled out one corner of the LCD. "We usually roll it away to make more space."

"Great." He grinned. "I've got a stack of our favorite movies on my hard drive."

"Awesome." I nodded, pressing my lips into a thin line.

Mike stared down at me with a half-lit smile, his hands on his hips like he was questioning a suspect, and a narrowed look in his eyes that made me clear my throat.

"Why do you keep staring at me funny, Mike?"

"I'm sorry. There's just… Never mind." He went to walk away, but stopped and gave that same look again. "Did you dye your hair or something?"

"Why?" I toyed with the ends. "Does it look different?"

"Not sure."

"Okay." I laughed. "That makes perfect sense."

"Sorry." He hooked his fingers under the handle of his suitcase. "I just haven't seen you in so long. I think I forgot how you looked."

"Oh. Well, didn't you have a picture?"

He shrugged dismissively, placing his suitcase on the end of the bed. "Probably somewhere. Why?"

"You could've referred back to that."

"I s'pose I could. Guess I just didn't think of it."

"Oh." I nodded solemnly.

"What?" he said, looking up from the padlock on his bag. "What's with the long face?"

"Um… well, it's just David," I said, instead of blubbering that he clearly didn't miss me like I missed him. I'd looked at his picture a million times since I left, and he hadn't even thought of looking at mine. "I told you he has to go away for a few weeks before he leaves indefinitely, and—"

"You'll miss him?"

"Mm-hm." I nodded.

Mike softened then and grabbed my wrist, pulling me into his chest for another way-too-tight hug. "It's all right, kid, you got me. I'll keep ya company."

"I know." I pushed out from his arms. "But I've relied on him so much to get me through. I just don't know how I'll cope now."

"Well, what was I, if not the one who helped you get through things before you came here?" he said. "You'll be fine, Ara. It's not the end of the world. And he'll be back for the whole long goodbye thing, right?"

I nodded. It was all I could do for fear of crying hysterically.

"Good." He patted my arm. "So just… cheer up and enjoy this time with me. Okay?"

"Okay."

"And sit down. You're making me nervous just standing there hovering by the door." He motioned to his bed.

I looked at it for a long moment. It didn't seem right to sit on his bed—now that I had a boyfriend.

Mike looked at the bed too, then smiled. "What? Did you booby-trap it?"

"No," I said swiftly, then wandered over and slumped down in the center with my feet dangling off the side. "I just… I don't know if I'm comfortable being in your room now, is all."

"Right." Mike nodded, letting his gaze slip past me to the window.

I rolled onto my side and propped my head up with the heel of my palm. "So, what's the plan today?"

"Well, a change of shirt's first on the list." He unzipped his suitcase. "Then I wanna hear all about this boyfriend of yours."

I grinned at the sound of his accent; how, alone in a quiet space, the Aussie in him became more prominent, more noticeable. Not a strong accent, just enough to surprise me.

"What?" He frowned.

"Oh, um. It's the accent," I said. "It sounds so foreign."

"Have you heard *yourself*? You're all *American*." He put on a mock American accent, but it sounded more Canadian.

"Hey, don't knock the accent." I rolled onto my back and looked up at the ceiling. "Took me weeks to get it right."

"Well, it sounds very authentic," he said warmly.

"Thank you."

"Don't mention it."

He chatted away then, zipping and unzipping pockets in his suitcase, laying things in the drawers across from the bed then closing them gently, while I watched in a sort of dream-like state. He still didn't seem real. I half-wondered when I was going to wake up.

When the suitcase scuffed along the floor, I looked at Mike as he kicked it under the bed and laid a clean shirt on the blanket. "Hey, wanna see what I've been doing lately?"

"What?" I pushed up on my elbows.

He yanked his shirt from the back of the neck and pulled it over his head, and my mouth dropped.

"You like?" he asked, spreading his arms to show off his body.

"Looks like you've been working hard for your new job." I smiled at him one last time before a shiver ran down my spine, forcing me to look at the roof again. "There's no way *not* to appreciate that kind of workmanship."

"They expect a certain level of fitness," he said, ruffling about at the foot of the bed. "It's my duty to exceed that."

"Well, you certainly didn't look like that the last time you took your shirt off, so… duty fulfilled," I scoffed, and everything went dark with the strong scent of Mike. "Ew. Wash this thing. It stinks," I joked, peeling his shirt off my face then tossing it back at him.

He caught it, held it to his nose, then shrugged and threw it behind him. "Come on, move over."

"Make me."

"Fine." The giant jumped onto the queen-sized bed and sunk his elbows heavily into the softness beside me, making me roll slightly into him.

I shoved my palm against his arm and rolled onto my back. "God, you take up so much space."

"If you don't like it, you could just get off my bed."

I smiled as he shoved me gently. "Like I said, *make me*."

"If anyone could *make* you do anything, Ara-Rose, my life would've been much easier."

"Ha-ha." I flicked his earlobe.

"Ouch." He laughed, cupping it. "That actually hurt."

"Sorry."

"Yeah, right." He pretended to flick mine, pressing the tip of my nose when I shied away. "Pain."

"Wide load."

"Meany."

"You know I'm joking," I said softly.

"I know." He inhaled slowly through his nose, his gaze tracing circles over my features.

I smiled back up at him, seeing the fine lines I'd memorized and the little pupil-sized scar on the bridge of his nose that he got when I threw a rock at him one day. I felt at home in the comfortable silence —the kind we were used to.

"Know what?" he said in that husky whisper.

"What?"

When his face came closer to mine, I held my breath, thinking he was going to kiss my head, but he rolled onto his back with a rather large huff and linked his fingers behind his head. "I'm tired."

"Yeah. Long trip, isn't it?"

"Especially changing over at LAX. I was stuck at customs for an hour."

"An hour?" I blew my fringe off my face. "They must've had lots of extra staff on."

Mike laughed softly and grabbed a pillow from the top of the bed, stuffing it under his head. And as his breathing slowed and the noise in the house died down after Dad and Sam went off to school, and Vicki started the car up then drove down the street, I looked out at the clouds through the top of the window, just happy to be by Mike's side again. Mostly, I could only see the eaves of the roof jutting out above the glass, but beyond that, the summer sky went on forever, leading to the place, to the world David was living in today. Even though I knew he was a fast runner, part of me wondered how he was going to get all the way back here from New York every night and still be back there in the morning to start work. Then I wondered what he actually did while 'operating the Set'.

As the shadows and the yellow glow of the sun moved across the floor and to the wall, I rolled onto my side and watched Mike's chest rise and fall with his quiet breath, the vein on his neck pulsing lightly on each heartbeat. It was something so small—seeing someone's body live, function—but until I'd spent so long with a vampire, who didn't need a heart, I'd never really appreciated the miracle in our design. I wanted to reach inside his chest and feel the blood pulse through his heart, feel it full and fat and living, feel the life in his veins—the life David took from others. And looking at my best friend sleeping so peacefully, so trusting, a small occurrence crept up: how could I ever take that? How could I reach into a person's life and take them from the world, destroy their family? Destroy their future, their hopes and dreams. What if it were Mike? Or my dad?

It was all very easy to brush it off and think, "Well, I don't know this person," but at the end of the day, how would I feel if a vampire killed Mike?

"What you thinkin' 'bout?" Mike's voice startled me.

"Oh, hi, I thought you were asleep." I tried to smile; it was a pathetic effort.

"*Clearly.*" He sat up and shuffled to the edge of the bed. "What was on your mind?"

"I don't want to talk about it," I stated.

He sighed and dragged me by the hand to sit beside him. As the weight of his heavy arm fell around my shoulder, I nestled my brow under his jaw, the deep, almost candy-musk scent of his cologne taking me back home to his bedroom for a moment.

"You smell good," I noted, then *It* growled.

"Ha!" Mike poked my belly. "The ogre! I see some things haven't changed at all."

"Nothing's changed, Mike—not really," I hinted, wishing I hadn't done that.

His eyes narrowed, boring into mine. "What do you mean by that, Ar?"

"Um…" A novelty-sized baseball bat of the imaginary kind came down and struck me across the head. "Nothing. Why would I have meant anything by that?"

Mike stopped halfway between getting up and sitting back down, then shook his head and pulled me off the bed. "Come on, let's just feed the beast."

"Okay. Then I'll take you across to the school so you can meet my friends."

"Friends, hey?"

"Yup. I've made this whole new life for myself, Mike. I'm almost totally normal now."

"You'll never be normal, Ara. You've always been… special."

I waited for the head-tilt-eye-wink combo that usually followed those kinds of comments, but instead his gaze held onto mine, like he wanted me to understand something deeper than what he said.

"I hope you don't mean that in a derogatory sense," I said.

He rolled his eyes, groaning. "Come on, I need food—it's past lunchtime already."

"Don't have to tell me twice." I ran down the stairs ahead of him.

And everything was just the same as before—before all the tragedy and the awkward I-don't-love-you-the-way-you-love-me stuff. Mike stood chopping onions and coriander at the counter, his sleeves rolled up, looking so tall and so grown up that I tried not to look at him. Tried not to feel anything. But the strange thing was that, no matter how much I loved David, I'd loved Mike first, and that feeling was still there. Still just as strong. I wasn't and probably never would be wholeheartedly decided about staying here or going with David, but I knew now that if I could feel love for Mike still, then maybe I *could* love someone else again after David. It wasn't my final decision, but it gave me something deeper to reflect on.

When the plates no longer contained food and the last of the enthusiastic catch-up wore down to more planned questions, Mike shook his head and smiled. "Know what I found the other day?"

"What?"

"Remember that picture we took at the golf course?"

"Oh, when you tried to teach me how to swing?" I started laughing, already replaying the tragic ending to that day in my mind—tragic for the window of a golf cart, that is.

"Yeah." Mike laughed. "I couldn't believe how small you were then, and you still had that gap." He pointed to his front teeth.

I ran my tongue over my gums. "I thought you said you didn't look at any pictures of me over the last few months?"

Mike looked down at his hands, smiling under reddening cheeks. "Well, maybe a few."

I shook my head. "Then how did you forget what I looked like?"

"I guess I didn't, really. You've just… you know? You've grown up so much while we were apart."

"Of course I have. Did you think I'd stay a little girl forever?" Although, that was a likely possibility if I became immortal.

"I just never expected time would change you so much while I wasn't around to see it. You're"—he considered me carefully—"I guess… you're a woman now."

"A woman? Mike, I'm seventeen. No older than when I left." I laughed.

He shook his head. "It's not your age, it's something else. I don't know, maybe it's just that you've been through a lot. Guess it's bound to leave its mark."

"You mean *scar*."

He reached across the table for my hand. I reluctantly placed it in his.

"I'm here now, baby. I didn't know how much I was missing you until I saw you. Now it feels almost like my heart might quit on me if I have to leave you again."

"I'm sure you'll change your mind after two weeks with me. Then you can go back and get on with your life," I said, laughing to change the energy in the room, since it suddenly got very intense.

He nodded as he said, "I'm beginning to rethink that."

"Rethink it? Rethink what?"

"I miss you, Ara. You belong in my life, you always have. I… look… I have to tell you something." His shoulders lifted a little. "Please don't get mad, okay?"

"Okay?" The lack of air in here made my lungs weak.

He looked down at our hands for a second, those caramel eyes coming back all warmed with a smile but infused with anxiety. "The truth is, I came here to say goodbye—one final goodbye before I let you go for good. You seemed to be getting on with your life. But now I'm here, I can't do it." He shrugged and one corner of his lip turned up. "So, I'm going with plan B."

"What's plan B? Hire a time-machine for the week and change the past?"

"Ara." He groaned, giving an intense stare that pleaded with me to take this seriously. "I… on the plane over here, I was sitting next to two old ladies, and I was so stuck in this *cage* of uncertainty that I actually talked *their* ears off."

"Oh dear."

"I don't know the best way to say this, and I don't know when's the right time, so I'm just gonna come out with it."

"Wait." I pushed my chair out a bit so I could run if I needed to, terrified that he'd say exactly what I'd wanted to hear.

He shook his head, already decided. "Baby, I love you."

My heart imploded, but I pulled myself together quickly, opting for ignorance, hoping he'd do the same. "I know you do, Mike, and I know you'll always be my bestie."

"Yeah, but that's not what I meant, and you know it."

I felt instantly sick. One half of me wanted to kiss him and tell him I love him too, while the other just burst into tears. It was exactly what I wanted to hear and yet it was the last thing I needed to hear. I needed more time. Why couldn't he have told me this in two weeks? Why couldn't he have waited until David left for good? He'd never stay now that Mike's feelings were out in the open, and I couldn't keep it from him. It was fine while it was just a suspicion, a fear, but not as a cold hard fact. David would read my mind and he'd know instantly, and then he'd leave.

And that was worst part: it was for my own good. Because it would be better for me to stay human and live out my life with Mike. Fate agreed. Fate gave me the sign I asked for. But I needed to hold onto the hope that I might change my mind before the ball because, without that hope, I felt like I had no control over anything; like I was hanging upside-down in a car wreck with no one to hear me scream.

"You know, you're not supposed to cry when a guy says he loves you," Mike said.

I sobbed into my hand. "Tell me you don't mean it."

His upturned palm appeared under my cave of asylum. I ignored it, looking away. "I do mean it, baby. And I want you to come home with me when I go."

"No!" I shot up out of my seat. "Don't say *that. Don't* say that."

"Are you serious?" He stood up.

I pointed a stern finger toward him. "Take it back."

"What! Why?"

"Take it back! Now!" I tried to rub it away from my mind. He'd see that. He'd see it and it would be exactly what he'd want for me.

"Baby, I can't take it back." He touched his chest. "It's how I feel."

"No, no, uh-uh." I waved my hands around, blinded by tears. "Nope. Nup. You don't. That's not right."

"Ara?" He walked toward me, primed to steady the crazy beast.

"Don't come near me." I shoved him really hard and took a few steps back when he didn't even shift an inch.

"Okay. I can see you're a little upset, so I'm gonna just"—he motioned to the table—"I'm just gonna sit. Okay?"

I stood there hugging myself tightly, my cheeks wet with tears.

As soon as Mike sunk into the seat, he breathed out profanity and dropped his head against his hand.

"Please tell me you don't mean it?" I could feel my world falling apart—all the indecision about David coming to rest before the mirror of Fate—telling me now in clear bold print what I was 'meant' to do. "Please tell me you just feel bad for me because my mom died."

"That's what you think this is?" He stood up again. "A pity party?"

I nodded.

He went to reach for me but stopped and swiped a hand across his nose. "Is that what you *want* it to be?"

"I..." I folded over a little, feeling myself die. "Please just take it back, Mike. You can tell me again later but I need more time."

"Why?" His voice broke.

"It's... you just don't know what you're doing right now."

He took a quick stride toward me and wrapped me in his arms. "Baby."

I sobbed a snotty mess of heartache into his shirt, making it wet as he just held me with an almost delicate touch.

"I'm so sorry. I know it's a bit—"

"No." I shook my head. "Just stop talking. Don't make this any worse."

"It's okay, baby. It's really okay." He laughed.

"No, it's not. Nothing is, and it's never going to be okay again."

"Why do you say that?" he asked in a gentle tone.

"Mom's dead, Mike, okay? And you can't make it better by telling me you love me. It doesn't work like that."

He laughed. "Even if it could change the past, that isn't something I'd lie about. Come on, you know me better than that."

"No." I wiped the tears from my face with the back of my hand. "You're confused."

"Ara?" Mike started again.

"No!" I took short, quick breaths, holding my hands over my ears.

"Will you just listen?" he said.

"No." I could feel Fate taking a step closer to me every time he opened his mouth, swathing me in the cloth of mortality. David was once the glue that held me together, but when he saw this—saw this memory—he would bind me to Mike with unyielding force. I'd be given no choice. I would have no way to find him again, no way to reverse his decision. I'd never see him again.

"Amara, calm down." He pulled my hands away from my ears. "Please listen. You never—that night—you never let me explain it to you. We were trying to make the transition from childhood friends to something so much more; something I was afraid *you* weren't ready for. God!" His arms tightened around my body, almost completely consuming my shape in a snug cloud of safety. "I have *never* been able to forgive myself for that."

"Forgive *yourself*? Mike! It was me—"

"No, it was *my* fault. I wanted you. I wanted you so *damn* bad, but..." He rolled my face upward, his eyes so wide I could almost crawl inside them. "You ran away; you thought I was mad at you for kissing me, but I wasn't. I was mad at you for waiting until you were *drunk* to do it. Ara, you know I don't mess around with intoxicated girls; it's wrong. And when I told you no, you got so upset, I just didn't know what to do and I let the ball drop."

"Why are you telling me this now?" It came out as a whisper, perhaps less. "Why not then?"

"I chased after you. I searched the streets for an *hour*. I called your house, no one answered. Then… I got the call from a mate at the station."

And we both knew the ending to that story.

He wiped the tears from my face and kissed my brow.

I could feel my hands shaking again as blood came back into my limbs and, slowly, I let myself accept what he was telling me, because I had always wanted him to love me and I needed him so badly right now. If David was going to be gone anyway, I just needed Mike to keep me sane through that.

But I knew what accepting this meant: David was supposed to sneak into my room every night for two more weeks, but this would be our last. "Why didn't you tell me before I left Perth then?"

"I tried. You wouldn't see me, remember?"

"Then why not on the phone—after I left?"

"Why? So you could feel worse, or so I could feel worse? I couldn't come to you, Ara. It's been killing me, I"—he dropped his head into his palm and closed his eyes—"I don't sleep anymore. I play it over in my mind all the time—the things we should've done that night."

"Things *you* said no to."

"You know why I said I no." He gently clutched the base of my jaw in his hand. "I just didn't want *you* to have regrets in the morning. I knew I wouldn't. I knew how I felt about you, but I had *no* idea you felt the same."

I wanted to look away from his penetrating stare, the way his eyes seemed to read mine, but he held my chin and forced me to keep looking at him.

"I'd been watching you for months," he continued, "just waiting for you to realize this wasn't just a friendship for me and then, that night, you took me by surprise. I didn't know how to tell you what I really felt, and I was so afraid if I did, and you were just confused because you'd been drinking, that it'd ruin our friendship forever. It was just one stupid misunderstanding, and I lost you. Lost *everything*." Mike smoothed my tear-soaked hair from my temples and along my chin. "Ara, I don't know why you're so upset, baby. It's not the end of the world if I love you."

"But it is!" I pushed his arms off me. "It is for me. You don't get it. You don't know what this means."

"I do, baby. I get it. Your mom and Harry died becau—"

"No! It's not that. You're not even close. God, you don't know anything about my life." I turned away, seeing him take a step toward me as I fled the room, but he stayed where I left him.

I burst through my door and slammed it shut with my foot before collapsing into a pair of strong, cool arms. Salty pools distorted the face of my vampire, spilling past my lashes as I blinked away my disbelief.

"What are you doing here? You're supposed to be at work." I needed more time to bury this argument from his view before I saw him—somewhere deep in the darkest corner of my mind.

"I felt…" He touched his chest. "I felt something shift."

"Shift?" I wiped my face.

"I think it was you." He wrapped me up safely in his arms. "What is it, my love? What happened?"

"I'm not ready to lose you," I blubbered. "I can't go with you. I just can't, and I wish I could, but I'm never going to be happy if I become a vampire."

"Ara, what are you talking about?"

"I needed this time. I needed our last two weeks."

"Don't cry." His voice was liquid with worry. "It's okay. Everything will be okay."

I shook my head, sniffling. "No… it's over… it… I—"

"What are you talking about, Ara?"

I tried to speak, but even my thoughts wouldn't form the truth for him to see; the truth that Fate itself—a higher power, maybe even the lingering spirit of my mother—wanted me to be human. I was 'meant' to be human. I knew what I had to do and, worse, it's what I wanted to do. I just wanted human David—for ever and always—but if I couldn't have that then I wanted to be with Mike, and I just didn't know how to tell him that. I didn't know how to make him see that it didn't change the way I loved him.

He looked at me for a long moment, obviously trying to find a thought among the mess of confusion in my mind. "Just cry, sweetheart." He kissed the crown of my head then swept me up in his arms and carried me to the bed. "I'll be here. I'll hold you until you fall asleep."

I settled against his chest and even though he had no heartbeat to show his emotions, I could feel the pain my every thought inflicted on him; feel his body stiffen every time I saw Mike's face in my mind; feel the thorn through his soul with every beat of my heart that wasn't for him.

But he stayed with me, loved me a while longer as my heart tore itself apart and shattered in two: one piece for David, and one for Mike—who really owned that part of me all along.

And as the sky turned dark, I drifted toward a deep, exhausted sleep. Images I had no control over flashed in downward scrolls like an old film before my eyes—the movie jagged, cut and crudely stuck together in an incomprehensible storyline. The color was gone, leaving only greyed hues through an unfocused lens. I couldn't change them or shape them; it was like a dream, but I wasn't sure I was sleeping.

Faceless strangers stared as I passed each row of seats. I held my bouquet closer to my heart, protecting what was within, because they could all see the red rose sitting in contrast to the white flowers surrounding it—the only color in this grey little world. I could feel their curiosity, hear their whispers, but no one would understand. So I held my head high and walked on, each step taking a lifetime, as if I was being slowed by a force unseen.

At the end of the aisle, where the light touched the lip of the steps, a tall man stood waiting; hands behind his back, eyes watching, face shadowed by the darkness of this never-ending walk. The light around him faded more each step I took, the dull, lifeless toll of church bells ringing somewhere out there in the world beyond my future. As I finally reached his side, my red blossom wilted, tar seeping up its veins and soaking away the color around the shrinking petals until, finally, they fell like black snow toward my ruby slippers.

David and I held our breath in the real world, watching the petals leave their life behind, decaying into ash.

"See, you don't need it anymore," the man said.

"Don't need what?"

He nodded toward the ash. "Life."

I looked up into his proud eyes and held my breath. It was time. It had to be now or never. "You're wrong," I said, placing the remains of the pale bouquet in his hand. "That's not what it means."

"What does it mean, then?"

"It means"—I slowly drew a breath, hesitating on the preface of his destruction—"that I don't need *you* anymore."

His eyes brimmed with liquid, the green appearing as a vibrant color among the greys of this world.

"I have to go," I said in a whisper.

"Where are you going?"

I reached behind me and took the firm, strong hand that grabbed mine. "To live."

He seemed to own no comprehension at first, but as my mind woke a little with the feel of cool arms coming away from my body, I saw his eyes move through realization to deep sadness. He nodded, taking slow steps backward; his elbows, his arms, his waist tapering into the darkness until, finally, the shadows consumed him.

"I'm sorry, David," I said, knowing what would come next.

A lifetime seemed to pass before the ground quivered beneath my feet, the ashes around my ruby slippers rising into the air, floating like dust particles in a smoky cloud. And inch-by-inch the ground crumbled toward me, narrowing in my little world. I felt for Mike's hand, turning to look back at the emptiness of my own faults. But he was gone. The only thing out there was Fate; I could hear Her laughing, could feel Her eyes on me, watching on as the ground came away completely and empty air wrapped my form, dragging me down in an eternal fall toward the darkness of mortality.

Gasping, I jolted awake, grabbing the edges of my blanket. I looked behind me, under me, beside me. But David was gone. He'd seen the dream—the entire thing.

"What have I done?"

The clock in the hall ticked loudly, each second timing the beat of my heart and bringing the rise of realization a little closer to the surface:

Mortality.

Death.

Life.

Mike.

I was meant to be human with Mike, and David finally got his answer in the worst, most heartbreaking way possible.

Exhaustion made me flop back down on my pillow, and as my hand fell beside my face, something cool and smooth touched my fingertips, filling my senses with the floral perfume of roses.

"Morning, sleeping beauty." Mike leaned against the doorframe with a tray in his hands.

Sound suddenly came rushing back to my ears. "Morning? How long was I out for?"

"All night." He shrugged and walked into my room. "You cried for a long time at first, then you went quiet. I came to check on you, but you were asleep." He set the tray down on the bed beside my legs, bringing the smell of toast in behind him. "Still your favorite flower?" He nodded toward the rose.

"*You* left this?" I picked it up, being careful of the thorns on the stem.

"Who else?"

"I don't know." I sniffed its sweet, soft scent, fading as the autumn destroyed everything that was once beautiful in the summer. He had no idea how symbolic this was right now—of many things.

Mike sat beside me, moving the tray onto my lap. "Are you okay, Ara?"

"Not really. I just can't believe it, Mike. All this time I thought I was wrong. I thought I misread everything between us." I put the rose down. "I need to know: is this how you really feel, or is it guilt?"

Mike grinned and looked down, rubbing the back of his neck. "Will it matter? You love *David*."

I frowned at him.

"I heard you talking in your sleep," he said sheepishly.

"Really?" Was there no privacy in this world?

"Okay. I'm just gonna throw it out there, and you can do with it what you want." He turned his body to face me, then took both of my hands. "I am in love with you, Ara-Rose. You were never wrong about that. You never misread anything, okay? I love you." He squeezed my hands on each of his end words. "I'm a complete moron, and I'm so *bloody* sorry for that. But I loved you before your mom died, so I'm pretty damn sure it's not guilt, baby."

"I..." His words soaked through me. "I can't respond yet, Mike. I need to think."

"I know." He nodded. "So, for now, your dad has arranged for you to have a few days off school if you want. He said he should've given you more time before sending you back in the first place. You weren't ready."

I nodded in agreement. Back home, I never took a day off. Not for anything. And now, I'd had more time off since I moved here than I had in my entire life. "I'd like that. Some time to think would be nice."

"Good." He winked at me and smiled, but it faded quickly, leaving the serious Mike behind again. "Your dad loves you, you know. He was worried about you last night."

"What did you tell him—about why I was crying?"

"Everything."

"*Everything*?"

"Yeah, I told him everything."

"You what!" I jolted forward, nearly sending the breakfast tray flying. "Mike, how could you?"

"Ara." He pulled my hand away from my mouth. "I know you didn't want him to know what happened the night your mom died, but he's your dad and he loves you—no matter what."

I shook my head. "Not now that he knows she died because of me, I—"

"Ara. Don't say that." He grabbed my arms firmly and pulled me over the tray on my lap for a short hug. "*I'm* the loser that turned you down. *I'm* the one to blame. Not you."

I gently shook my head, calling on the strength I'd grown since meeting David, trying to believe my next words. It was one thing to blame myself, but I couldn't let Mike live with that blame.

"It was no one's fault, Mike. I guess it's natural to look for someone to blame, but neither of us intended that to happen. We should *both* stop blaming ourselves."

He smiled, and tucked a strand of hair behind my ear. "Your dad was heartbroken when I told him you were carrying the blame. He hadn't even guessed it, you know. He's been so worried about you, and when I told him you felt responsible for what happened to your mom, he was actually relieved that *that's* all it was. He doesn't hate you, baby, he can't hate you. He loves you too much. That's why he let you have a few days off—to be with me."

"He likes you," I noted begrudgingly.

"He's an excellent judge of character." Mike grinned. I smiled back. I couldn't resist it. He just had this presence about him that sometimes excluded people from his inner circle of love, but when he smiled like that, it meant you belonged.

"I can't believe you told him about us," I said. "I yelled at him, you know—when he accused me of loving you."

"Is that such a bad accusation?" Mike asked, a little insulted.

"It's not true." I smiled.

"Ouch." He laughed, and then leaned over with his face right up close to mine. "So? What do you want to do today?"

"Honestly?" I unfolded my arms. "I think I'd like to just sit around and watch movies."

"I thought you'd say that. But I get to hold the popcorn."

"No way! You always do."

"I'll fight you for it." He tickled my ribs.

"Stop it!" I giggled, wriggling about, trying to pull his hand away without knocking the tray.

"Make me."

"Mike!" I squealed. "Stop it or I'll wet myself."

"Stopping." He raised his hands above his head and sat back.

"Ha!" I said. "Works every time."

My thoughts tuned back in to the conversation at dinner and my food art sighed at me, wishing I could eat it. I hadn't spoken much, or eaten much since the little conversation with Mike this morning, and strangely, I wasn't even hungry. At all.

"Yeah? That's a great business to get into," Mike said, but I wasn't sure who he was talking to. "Especially now with all the developments in graphics and, not to mention, you can actually make more money in the gaming industry than the film industry."

"Dad doesn't agree." Sam's eyes dropped their hopeful glimmer. "He says I need to be serious. That designing games isn't gonna get me a stable income."

Mike just laughed. "It won't—if you don't have a good education. How many companies do you think will hire a kid who can't even commit to homework?"

Sam looked puzzled. "What difference will that make?"

"Well, it's not just about what you learn at school. It's also about proving you have the ability to put your head down and do the work, especially if you care nothing for it. If you can't do that, Sam, you don't have the right to a job you love doing, and I can tell you"—Mike scoffed—"even in a job you love, there'll be moments you hate."

Sam became smaller in his chair.

"Point is, mate, you work hard through the crap so you can enjoy the other eighty per cent that's good. Not to mention, if you want to design games, you *will* need English—and math." Mike winked at me. "Creativity, passion, and some mad computer skills won't be enough if you want a stable income. You need that piece of paper they call a degree, and the only way to get that is to do this 'pointless' work they give you at school. That's all there is to it. So, in that way, your dad's right. But"—he held a finger up while he shoveled a spoonful of potato in and swallowed—"if you just do all the hard work while you have nothing else to worry about except being a kid, when you grow up and you want the job stability you care nothing for now, you won't have to fight for it, it'll be yours."

Sam's eyes changed, narrowed with thought, then he stood up and dumped his napkin on his beef and gravy.

"Sam, where are you going?" Vicki asked.

"I just realized I didn't do my essay," he called from the stairway, before we all heard his bedroom door close.

Dad grinned and patted Mike on the shoulder. Then the conversation went on without me again, while I pushed the food around on my plate a little more. I just wanted to go upstairs and be alone. Despite enjoying watching movies with Mike, I found myself checking the length of the shadows outside his window for most of the day, just waiting for night to fall.

"You okay, baby?" Mike asked quietly, leaning closer.

"Mm-hm." I nodded, forcing a smile. "I'm just tired."

"Maybe you should get an early night." He pushed my bangs off my face.

Vicki held back a smile, watching us.

"You do look a little tired," Mike added after a lengthy silence. "Why don't you head up now and take a shower? Doesn't look like you're getting any closer to consuming your dinner by transforming it into a plate."

I looked down at my canvas of mash and gravy. "Can't yet. Gotta do the dishes first."

"Ara." Mike's brows lifted, sarcasm hovering in his tone. "*I'll* do the dishes for you. Just go get some rest."

I shook my head. "No way. You're a guest. Guests don't do dishes, right, Dad?"

Dad looked at Mike, then shrugged. "I don't see why not—if he's offering."

"Dad! You never side with me!"

"I'm sorry, Ara, but Mike's not really a *guest*, is he?"

"Then what is he?"

"He's practically family."

My mouth hung open, allowing only a breathy scoff to show my disapproval.

"Besides, Ar, you always made me do the dishes at your old house," Mike added with a cheeky grin.

"That's different."

"Why?"

"I don't know. It just is."

"Ara?" Mike scratched his eyelid and sighed. "Go to bed."

"Make me," I said playfully, folding my arms.

He merely glared at me with one brow arched and a look of intent behind his half-smile, and I knew that if he did 'make me', it would have slightly humiliating consequences.

"Okay, going." I stood up quickly, darting up the stairs before he could begin the chase.

My room greeted me with the crisp scent of fresh linen and a diluted waft of strawberry shampoo, but no orange chocolate. No vampire. I didn't really expect that he'd come back after getting his answer the way he did. It was only a hope.

But he did say he would never leave without saying goodbye. And I wasn't sure I'd ever move on with my life if he broke that promise. So why wasn't he here?

Surely my dream, or even Mike's confession, wouldn't be enough to make him leave without at least saying goodbye. Not forever. It just seemed too final.

In one sweep, I sent my orderly homework into a spread of disarray across my floor then climbed over the desk and tucked myself into a ball against the cold glass of the window. Pale blue light filtered in from the world outside and lit the edges of my knees, while the streetlight below seemed to sing loneliness down onto the vacant sidewalk. There was nothing out there that resembled life tonight, and strangely, though my heart was beating, there was nothing here that much resembled it either.

With a long, dejected sigh, I lowered my head onto my knees and closed my eyes, but a loud chime set my heart ablaze with a start a moment later. I looked up from my knees, instantly regretting having moved my stiff neck, and I scanned my empty room, then the street, counting the chimes I heard in my head: one, tw—

There were only two! There should've been more than that. I came to my room at seven. It couldn't be two in the morning.

My window was still shut fast into place, no sign of any vampire having entered, and as I rubbed the tingle of pins away from my toes, realization sunk right into my heart. It really was two in the morning.

David never came.

He just left me without giving me a chance to memorize his skin, his hug, his green eyes. It felt too sudden, and I panicked for a moment as I tried to remember his face, a tear rolling down past the tip of my nose and onto my thigh. But the gentle sobs of my heart breaking stopped abruptly when the door handle twisted and light spilled into my room, creeping in a yellow line along my floor, up my desk and over my toes. I rubbed my nose and eyes into my knees to dry the tears, feigning sleep.

The deep, husky voice of my best friend reached me with a breath of concern. "Baby girl, what're you doing asleep here?" he whispered to no one in particular.

His wide, broad arms fixed a hold under my knees and around my back, then swept me off the windowsill, over the desk and into his body like he was some kind of ultra-hot fireman rescuing me. I stayed floppy in his arms, breathing long and deep as if I were asleep, until the softness of my bed—much warmer than the cold glass my elbow was leaning on—cocooned my body safely. Mike tucked my feet under my quilt and brought it up around my shoulders as I rolled away.

"Night, baby." He pressed a quick kiss to my temple and left the room, closing the door behind him.

"Thanks, Mike," I whispered quietly, allowing a smile to appear for one second before it melted away in the darkness.

"IT'S ALIVE!" MIKE WAVED HIS HANDS DRAMATICALLY AS I zombie-walked into the kitchen and sat on the stool.

"Barely." I laid my head on my arms, watching him by the stove.

"Hungry?" He held up a spatula.

"Not for plastic kitchen utensils, if that's what you're offering."

"Oh, a comedian today, huh?" He turned back to the stove, grinning. "So, are you hungry or not?"

"A little." I grabbed an apple and took a bite. "Where is everybody?"

"Sam's at school, Vicki's gone to the movies with her friend, and your dad's at work." Mike turned back and winked at me. "It's just us."

"Okay, so is that why you think it's acceptable to wear a pink apron?"

He laughed, untying it. "Thought that might cheer you up a little."

"What makes you think I need cheering up?" I turned my wrist over in question, the apple still in hand.

"Ara, I know you better than you know yourself. You need cheer. So,"—he grabbed the fry pan and tipped the contents onto two plates in front of me—"I made your favorite. Pancakes!"

I glared at him skeptically. "Is there maple syrup?"

Mike grinned, placing his hand on a bottle of brown liquid right by my elbow, and slid it over. "Would I forget the syrup?"

"It wouldn't be the first time." I snatched the bottle.

He walked around the counter and sat on the stool next to me, dumping a fork by my plate. My moodiness fizzled away completely when the first bite of his light, fluffy pancakes touched my tongue. Like sugar-coated puffs of heaven, the golden exterior of the pan-fried breakfast melted with the syrup at the perfect ratio of sweet and savory, sending trickles of warm delight down my spine.

I stopped eating and studied him: the chef, the wonder-cook, the man who knew no failure. The man who made it incredibly easy to be in love with him.

"Something wrong, baby?" Mike asked, mid-shovel.

"I uh—I just remembered I have rehearsals today."

"Rehearsals?"

"Mm. For a benefit concert we're doing to raise money for this kid who died."

"Oh. Okay. What time?" he asked.

"Dunno." I shrugged. "I don't think I'll go." David wouldn't be there, and that meant I'd have to perform my duet with someone else. I couldn't face that today.

Mike sat taller, eagerness replacing his grin. "Wanna go for a run with me instead?"

"Yeah. Actually, I'd love that."

"Great. Maybe we can make a picnic out of it. What d'ya think?"

I nodded and filled my gob again. "Yeah. I'd like that."

We finished up, cleaned up, and then dressed up in our running gear and headed out. And it felt good to be out in the sun again, hearing the sounds of people and cars, as if there were still a world existing outside of my head. But, for the most part, I had gone back to pretending to be happy—putting on the mask; the facade that kept me safe from a padded cell in the past.

When we pulled up in the driveway at home, and all my problems piled on top of me again, I promised myself I wouldn't think about it until after I'd gone to bed. The last thing I needed was for Mike to catch on to how I was feeling. If I let one long sigh slip or got caught in an absent stare at a wall, he'd push and push until I told him the truth and, in my emotional state right now, I was sure the words 'vampire' and 'eternity' would slip out. And it wouldn't be my fault. What had David called it? Self-preservation. I needed to release the pressure of my grief, and if it didn't come out in words to a confidant, it was going to come out in hysterics. I could feel it.

A finger appeared in my periphery then, and Mike nodded at my foot. "Might wanna tie that up so you don't trip."

"Uh, crud." I bent over my legs and twisted my lace into a bow, then looked up as the car door popped open.

"Thanks," I said, unbuckling my seatbelt and jumping out, only noticing the odd look on Mike's face as the door closed. "What?"

"Ever since you became friends with that man-hater in the eighth grade, I get in trouble for opening doors or paying for your movie ticket." He stepped away from the car like it was diseased and making him see things. "What just happened here?"

I laughed. "Sorry. Would you like me to yell at you for opening my door? I—"

"Please don't." He placed his hand firmly on my shoulder. "I like this new you better."

With my arms folded, I made an obvious point of scanning his broad shoulders and the rest of his very impressive body, giving the nod of approval. "And I like this new hot-guy you."

"You think I'm hot?"

"Don't flatter yourself. I was joking."

He faked a pout and we walked up the newly fixed porch step.

"After you, my lady." He bowed, opening the door for me.

"Thank you, kind sir." I ducked through, my voice lilting upward playfully.

"You are more than welcome, my pretty friend."

"Hey there," Dad said as he came down the stairs.

"Hi, Dad."

"Did you have a good day?"

I looked at Mike, then back at Dad. "Actually, yeah."

"Good. That's good," Dad said, smiling softly.

"Anyways, I'll go unpack the picnic basket," Mike said. "I'll see you upstairs for a movie?"

"Yeah, sure."

He walked away, and Dad's gaze seeped into my skin.

"What, Dad?"

He leaned in, kissed my cheek and said, "I'm just happy to see you happy again." Then he followed Mike into the kitchen, leaving me alone in the wake of his mistaken belief.

I was glad he'd fallen for the illusion that I was happy; he needed it—needed to relax a little and not worry so much about me. And even though I could feel a small sliver of happiness right now, when I looked up to the coming night through the small window above the front door, I knew that feeling was fleeting. I knew that if David didn't come last night, he wasn't coming back tonight. Or ever. And I would never be truly happy again.

25

It might've been a dream, but it was as close as I'd been to him in two days. I rolled over in bed and flipped my pillow to the dry side, wiping the moist layer of ageing tears from my cheeks.

Outside, the thunder rolled again. It'd been that way all night. Bad weather was brewing, but it hadn't the strength to burst out and become a storm.

I didn't mind the thunder tonight though, because I understood its pain—how it beat at its cumulus confines but just couldn't get free to be where it was supposed to be. It was trapped, caged in by the wrong conditions.

"Hey, you're up," Mike whispered softly, pushing my door open a crack. "You ready to leave?"

"What, you wanna go *now*?"

"Yeah, it's a long drive."

"You never mentioned leaving *this* early."

"I know." He grinned, opening my door fully. "I planned to wake you—figured I'd save my ears from all the whining last night about getting up early."

"What makes you think I'd have whined?"

Mike just raised his brows, rolling his head down a little.

"Okay, fine." I jumped out of bed. "I'll get my bag."

"Might wanna put some clothes on, too." He nodded to my pajamas, and closed the door.

I threw on my bikini, shorts and a shirt, then slipped into my flip-flops and met Mike at the car, dragging my feet the whole way. We stopped off to grab an egg muffin from Macca's, then took to the highway, leaving this sleepy little town behind for the day.

As the sun peeked out from the eastern hills, I rested my head on the window and tried not to fall asleep. "So, why are we going to a beach so far away?"

"Because." Mike shrugged, tossing his coffee cup into the empty brown paper bag our food came in. "There's better surfing conditions there."

"Fair enough, I suppose," I said, then reached for the dial on the stereo. "I wanna play that one again."

"You liked that?" Mike put his window up as he spoke, and my cheeks tingled where my hair had been whipping my face.

"Yeah. I mean, it's a little morbid for my tastes, but—"

"Hey. There's nothing morbid about Metallica."

"There is about that one."

"It's one song out of how many?"

I shrugged.

"Fine. I'll play it again. But no more knocking the music," he warned with a joking air to his tone.

We arrived at the beach just as the Sunday sun woke the rest of the world. Mike parked Dad's car in the only empty space left near the boardwalk and wandered casually around to open my door.

"Your Majesty." He bowed, offering his hand.

"Merci," I replied politely, returning the bow.

"Ah, so the neck-sucker finally got you speaking French, huh?"

"How'd you know he spoke French?"

He frowned at me for a second, his eyes falling on my silver locket. "I just assumed, because of the—" He pointed to his own neck.

"Oh." I touched the locket. "Yeah. He did—*does*—speak French. But I don't."

"Well," Mike said, sounding awfully cheery, "it suits you. You should speak it."

"Nah. I don't wanna learn it then wake up one day and realize all the disgusting things you'd been saying to those girls all these years."

"Ha!" His whole upper body jerked toward the heavens with his laugh. "Yeah. On second thoughts, don't learn French."

I smiled, folding my arms across my body as Mike walked to the trunk, flipping the keys around on his index finger.

"Nice beach, isn't it?" he said.

"Yeah." I turned and faced the coast, the gentle breeze greeting me to the day. Down by the water, families built sandcastles and couples walked hand-in-hand, stopping to kiss and marvel at the horizon.

"Well, what're you waiting for?" Mike offered his hand to the view before us. "Go ahead. I'll catch up."

"Really? You don't want help carrying all that?" I nodded to the picnic basket, the surfboard and a dozen other things.

He closed the trunk and shook his head. "Just go, baby."

Without further encouragement, I pulled off my shorts and shirt, threw them to Mike, and flew to the call of the ocean, my feet barely touching the sand before I hit the whitewash with the grace of an elephant. The waves enveloped my ankles, cooling the balls of my feet and leaving behind a tingle as they receded, like sherbet mixed with cola.

Standing here, I could almost believe I was back home in Perth. And even with my eyes closed, unable to see the origins of the noise around me, I could *feel* the brightness of the day filling me with the hope that some things in life were still good. I placed my hands to my knees and bent closer to the water to catch the light breeze coming off it, feeling my toes sink into the soft, grainy sand as the waves swam back out to sea.

"You still look like a little girl—standing there in that rainbow bikini."

I opened my eyes to the portrait of ocean, and Mike's arm around my waist. "Well, I'm not a little girl anymore, Mike." I pushed his hand off my skin.

"I know. I just thought you looked cute, that's all."

"I don't do cute," I said sarcastically, but a band of 'gullsters' beside us drowned out my retort with their hideous squawking. I jumped a little, clutching my locket. "God, I'm not used to that sound anymore."

"Scat!" Mike said, waving his hand at the gulls. "Get outta here."

"Don't you dare kick that bird!" I grabbed his arm as he stalked toward them.

"I never actually hit them, Ara. I wouldn't do that."

"Doesn't matter, what if you did? By accident?"

"Then I would apologize… profusely." He bowed his head. "But you know what I wouldn't apologize for?" The corners of his eyes sharpened as he smiled and leaned slowly closer, then the world came out from under me. I flew through the air, landing on my back in a massive cool splash, with Mike's hand catching the base of my neck before my head went under water.

I opened my mouth to yell, gurgling the salty burn of a wave down my nose and throat instead. "You asshole!" I coughed, sitting up as he jumped back. "I'm so gonna get you."

"You have to catch me first." He started running.

I hesitated only for a moment; we both knew I'd never catch him, but it was damn well worth a try. Each time I reached for him, he darted out of the way like we were both south poles on a magnet, but at last I managed to grasp the rim of his shirt. I closed my fingers in a tight grip, wearing a victory grin for only the breath it took him to roll out of it and leave me, and the shirt, face down in the sand.

"You'll have to do better than that, baby." He laughed boisterously.

I pushed up on my hands and sat hugging my knees, the sand sticking to the water all over my body, making me feel like a crumbed steak. Well, it was time this steak got a little revenge!

"Ara, you okay? Did I hurt you?" Mike asked, leaning over me.

Wrong move. He didn't even see it coming. I grabbed the back of his neck and pushed the entire force of my shoulder into his chest, rolling his head under my arm as I flipped him into the water. His weight came as a shock; he never used to be that heavy. But he went down hard, wetting my legs, arms, shoulders, and the kid a meter down from us, as the water exploded out from under him.

"Well," he said, clasping his hands over his belly, taking a breath after a wave rolled him. "Girl: one. Guy: nothing."

I stared at him, an impish grin making my eyes small, wondering if I should point out that we both knew he *let* me flip him. "Well, you taught me that move, oh-wise-Master." I sat down on the edge of the ocean. "You should be wary of your students; they can supersede you."

He rolled onto his stomach and smiled at me, the magic of the ocean lighting him like a happy feeling. He seemed more alive, more spirited, sort of… free here. He belonged on the beach, with the sand and the blue skies.

"What ya thinkin'?" He jumped up, ruffling his hair into a mess as he landed beside me.

"I was just remembering home." I shrugged. "Thinking how easy all this is. Like, sometimes when I'm with you, I forget they're gone." I wrapped my arms around my legs and linked my fingers together. "The sunlight, the beach, all of this stayed with you when I left, and now you're here… it's like you've brought it all back with you."

"You say that like it's a bad thing."

I shrugged again. "I don't wanna lose that when you go."

He gave a gentle smile and let his elbows hang loosely over his knees. "You know it doesn't have to be that way."

"Mike?" I dragged out the vowel.

"I'm sorry." His smile dissolved. "I just miss you too, you know. I went to the beach a few weeks ago—watched the storm come in across the bay—and it didn't feel the same without you."

I half smiled, allowing memories in. "Did you sit on the fishing jetty while it was raining?"

"Yeah." He nodded, dusting a line of yellow sand off his shin. "But I just didn't get it anymore. It was just cold and I felt silly."

I drew a really long breath. The salt in the ocean was so strong I could almost taste it, as if the air were made of sand, brushing the back of my tongue each time I swallowed. Even though this beach wasn't nearly as pretty as the one back home, it was good to feel the crisp water and the weight of my body sink into the sand again. I ran some of the cool ocean water over my cheek, over the menacing scars the accident had left me, and the heat dissipated with a soft tingle.

"This looks better," Mike said.

"Don't!" I spun my face away from his cold touch.

"Whoa. Ara. I'm not going to hurt you." He leaned around and looked at me.

"I'm sorry." I frowned, touching my jaw. "You just... I'm not used to people touching me there."

"Are you defensive about those scars?"

I lifted one shoulder and dropped it again.

"You know, you shouldn't be."

"They're hideous." I blinked, fighting back tears.

"Hideous?" Mike's voice trailed up. "Ara, you can barely see them."

"Then why did you touch them?"

"It's just… the sun was reflecting off the water beads on your skin and I noticed that the scars were fading. I didn't mean to offend you."

"You didn't offend me," I stated. Just made me want to run away. I had mastered the art of ignoring them now to the point where I'd convinced myself they were gone. But Mike noticing them made me feel uncovered and monstrous, like they were as pink and raw as the day of the funeral.

"Ara. I'm serious. They're barely visible." He shuffled closer and turned my face. "You're still just the same beautiful girl you've always been."

"You're wrong, Mike," I said, my eyes burning with salt as they teared up, blinding me. "I'm not the same. I changed. I tried *hard* to change—"

"Ara, what are you talking about? Ara!" Mike called as I stood and walked down the beach, dusting sand off my butt.

No one understood. No one could possibly understand. He didn't see how hideous the scars were because he didn't want to see it. But they were there. They would forever be there as a reminder of who I used to be—who I had tried so hard not to be anymore. Maybe my selfishness ran so deep I would never be able to change, but I had tried hard. I had. And Mike saying I was the same girl I was back then—when I killed my mom and my brother—it hurt. It cut as deep as the glass that scarred my face because I knew, as deep as I knew pain, that losing David was the penance, the Karma, the price I had been waiting to pay.

"Ara." Mike's hand clasped my arm. I stopped walking with a jolt. "Don't walk away from me like that. Talk to me."

"I'm *not* the same, Mike," I said, my voice sounding funny under the emotion. "I changed. You don't know what I've been through. You—"

"Ara, baby." He wrapped me up in his arms. "I wasn't saying that. I just meant that you're still beautiful—"

"But I'm not. Can't you see?" I stepped back, angling my chin up so he could see my face in the light. "Everyone can see them—"

"No they can't, baby," he insisted in a gentle tone. "They'd have to know they were there to notice them."

"Why do you lie to me? What good does it do? I can see in the mirror, Mike—"

"Baby. I'm not." He stepped into me and his eyes narrowed as he studied my face, tracing the curve of my jaw where only David's eyes had previously been allowed. "Do you still see them there?" he asked, his tone thick with worry. "Honestly?"

I nodded, turning my face away.

"Shit. I… I don't know what to tell you. I think it might be some kind of psychological side effect of the accident or something."

"Another side effect?"

He tried to smile but I could see how sad he was for me. "Look, I don't know what you see when you look in the mirror, but all I see is perfect skin on the face of the prettiest girl in the world."

I touched my scars with my fingertips.

"Ara." He gently took my wrist and moved my hand down from my face. "I promise, on my own future grave, you have completely healed."

"Really?" I whimpered in a breaking voice, looking down at my sandy toes.

"Yes."

That singular word came through with so much compassion and so much love that, even with the warm sun, the salty air, and all the families around us, I felt the pain I'd held in all these months—the pain I never got to share with Mike—bubble up in my chest, then my throat, like an aching blockage of air. I wanted him to hold me. I needed his arms to make everything okay.

"I've missed you so so badly, Mike." My lashes burned on the edges as hot tears filled my eyes again and the beach disappeared behind them.

"I know." He caught me against his chest, the rough sand scratching my jaw. "It's okay. I'm here now."

"I needed you, Mike. I *needed* you," I sobbed almost inaudibly. "All this time, and you haven't been here."

"I wanted to be here. I just… I thought you hated me."

"I did." I sobbed harder. "I'm so sorry, Mike. I did."

He clicked his tongue. "Aw, baby, what has life done to you?"

Safe in his arms once more, I sobbed my heart out loudly, letting all the pain I stored up free itself into his skin.

Only he knew, only he understood how much I missed Mom and how deeply I'd regret Harry's death for the rest of my days. He was there when I bought Harry his first train. He was there when my mom grounded me and when we invented our silly joke game. He was there for everything, and only crying with him seemed to make my pain feel like it was understood. Only he could see how raw and how black it was, and only he could fully comprehend the reason I blamed myself for their deaths.

I didn't care that people on the beach could hear and see me. The funny thing about breaking down is that you can't choose when to do it—it just hits you like a storm; a flash of heat, an overpowering surge of anger, and then the pouring rain.

But Mike was my umbrella, and I knew he'd hide me from accusing glares until the pain died inside me.

"Yeah, she's okay," he spoke softly to someone behind me. "She lost her mom recently."

"Oh, poor dear," an elderly-sounding lady said. She said something else, but I didn't hear. Mike pressed my face so tightly against his bare chest that he caused a sort of unintentional vacuum seal over my ears.

The sobs slowed after a while, and I scratched the salt away from my cheek as I looked up at him. "You really can't tell my face is horrifically scarred?" Strangely, I realized, his opinion mattered to me more than almost anyone else's—even more than David's.

"No." He held both my arms and leaned back a little. "You can't tell at all. Okay? So stop feeling so bad about yourself, baby." He bent his knees so his eyes came in line with mine. "You are beautiful."

I nodded and ran my fingers over my jaw. It was hard to even feel the slight bumps anymore. They used to feel like little pins rising up from under my skin. But maybe he was right: maybe they were gone now and what I saw in the mirror was just a psychological scar.

"I hate looking at myself, you know. I don't look like me anymore."

"You look the same to me. Maybe a little older—wiser, even."

I smiled. "I really missed you, Mike."

"I know you did."

"I really miss Mom and Harry, too." I looked at the water, trying to stop the memory of their faces. "I keep thinking I'm just gonna go home and they'll be there, you know, like always."

"Is that why you don't want to move back with me?"

"I never said that, Mike." I moved out from his arms. "Don't you get it? You just came in, and on the first day you get here, you tell me you love me, with no mind for the fact that I have a boyfriend—"

"Boyfriend?" Mike said. "Ara, you knew him for a day before you decided you were in love with him."

"I did not. It took me ages to decide that."

He scoffed. "A week then."

"Are you kidding me?" My head jerked forward. "You're the one who told me I was being silly for not following my heart."

"What was I supposed to say? Should I tell you to stay away from the only thing that'd made you happy in months? I'm your friend. I care about you. I wanted you to be okay." He dropped one hand to his side. "I just never thought you'd actually *believe* you were in love with him."

"*Believe* I'm in love with him?" My lip lifted in disgust. "What would *you* know about it? You don't even know your own heart. It took my mom's death for you to admit it—"

"Ara—"

"No." I shrugged away as he grabbed my arm. "You think you love me, but you don't—"

"Ara. Stop it." Mike reached out again, reminding me of the staring people around us with a look in his eye.

"I don't care if they look. Let them look. I'm not going to stand here while you tell me what's in *my* heart."

"Okay, I'll stop. I—"

"Stop trying to touch me." I jerked away from him again. "I do love David, Mike. I do. You have no idea how much, and you never will," I added coldly, folding my arms as I turned away.

"Oh, never, huh?" He followed, raising his voice. "So this freaky possessive thing you have with David, that's true love, is it? Is that how it works?" he asked in a conceited tone. "You're telling me that when you love someone more than anyone in the world has ever loved *anyone else* before, you let them hurt you and leave bruises on you?"

I huffed.

"And don't think I didn't see that cut on your wrist, Ara!"

My steps came to an abrupt halt. I unfolded my arms and looked down at my left wrist—the place David had drank from me.

"Yes. I saw it!" His voice broke with a husky crack, as if it killed him that he'd had no power to protect me. "I know *you* didn't do that. I know you better than that."

"I—"

"David did it. Didn't he?" He came up out of nowhere, spinning me around sharply and held my wrist up. "Is this what love is, Ara? Because I love you more than this. I would never hurt you like this."

"You're hurting me now." I twisted my wrist in his grip and yanked it out through his fingers. "Just leave me alone, okay? I've had enough."

"Ara?" he called as I walked away again.

"I can't do this, Mike," I called back. "I just can't fight with you. I need to be alone."

I didn't need to stand there and have him tell me I knew nothing about love. I'd felt its spiny sting. I knew exactly what it was.

Mike was just worried because he thought David… well, I actually couldn't even imagine what he thought David had done to me. But it didn't matter. I couldn't tell him the truth, and I just didn't feel strong enough to make him understand without it.

"Ara. Stop."

"I said leave me alone, Mike."

"No," he said, following me. "Ara, I love you. And I'm sorry, okay? I'm a dick. I shouldn't have said anything about David."

I stopped walking.

"You're right," he added. "I don't know anything about what you had to go through just to want to *live* over the last few months, and if David is the rock that held you down, so be it."

I slowly turned around to face him.

"I'll drop it." He held both hands out by his sides: his white flag. "But please don't be mad at me for being worried about you. You have cuts and bruises that a guy inflicted on you"—he laughed nervously—"what kind of a man would I be if I wasn't worried?"

Across the carpet of sunburned backs and multi-colored towels, the salty plastic smell of sunscreen wafted between us, and even in the brightness of the day, the compassion in his eyes shone out like a beacon among the darkest sea. I dropped my hands to my sides, cursing his kind eyes.

"Mike, I—"

"Don't." He shook his head and launched into a half-run, sweeping me into him. "You don't need to say a word, baby. Okay?"

The hot sun beat down on us as he held me close, making sweat trickle down my temples. But I closed my eyes and held my breath in the intense squeeze of his arms, knowing from his touch that he never wanted to let go—that he *did* love me deeply—not like he loved the ocean or the sunset, but like the way I loved David. True, honest, and intense love.

"I'm sorry, Ara. For everything. It's just"—he brushed my hair from my face, then lifted my locket for a second—"I love you. I really do. I love the way your eyes turn deep blue when you're sad; the way you bite your lip when you play piano; I love your smile and the way you view the world, Ara. I absolutely love *everything* about you." He paused and his eyes darted over my face. "I just wish you could understand that; wish you'd forgive me for making the biggest mistake I ever made, and love me back."

I folded my face against his chest again. The sand had dried in the heat, soothing the itch along my jaw, and the sound of his heart through the thick of his skin had an oddly comforting hum to it. I could tell from the way he took shallower breaths that he was waiting for me to say something, but I couldn't grace him with a response, because I had nothing to say. Not yet.

26

No one even looked up as I stepped into the auditorium and dumped my bag by a chair. "Hi, guys," I said, unwinding my scarf from my neck.

"Hey, stranger," Spencer called from the stage.

"Hi," Emily said as I sat beside her in the front row.

"Where've you been, girl?" Ryan landed in the next seat and gave me a skinny-armed hug.

"Just hanging out at home." I sat back in the chair. "Good turnout for a rehearsal."

Emily nodded, her eyes on a notepad. "Most of them are just here to watch—or distract those who are *trying* to practice."

"Yeah," Ryan said. "We have to be out by ten, but no one's taking things seriously."

"Oh." I slid down in the seat and put my feet on the crate in front of me. "Well, do you mind if I take the stage now? I gotta get back early tonight."

"Yeah, sure," Emily said to her page. "Everything okay?"

"Mm-hm." Except, I didn't really want to be around this place any longer than absolutely necessary.

"Where's David? Is he coming tonight?" Ryan asked.

Emily looked up from her book. I shrugged, reaching for my locket.

"Oh, I thought he said he'd make it for dress rehearsals." Ryan looked a little confused.

"He did." I tipped the crate with my foot, trying to look disinterested. "But I guess the plan changed." Or the heart.

"Where's your new pal… Mike?" Ryan asked.

"Uh, he's taking my brother to a movie tonight."

"Sweet." Ryan nodded. "Well, I'll fill in on guitar for David, if you like?"

"Okay. Let's just get this over with then." I gave a reassuring smile to Emily's frown as I stomped up the stairs, then stopped dead. "Hey, where'd the piano come from?"

"Oh, it's on loan from Musicology," Emily called out.

"What's Musicology?" I sat down on the stool in front of the baby grand, flipping out imaginary coat tails first.

"Music store," Ryan said, walking past me to grab his guitar.

"Oh, cool. The keys feel nice."

"Wait 'til you hear her." Ryan sat on a stool near Alana, who turned the pages on her music stand. "We're calling her Betty."

"Calling who Betty?" I said.

"The piano," Alana said.

"Oh." I looked at it. "Why Betty?"

"The song…" Alana said, rolling her eyes in Ryan's direction. "Black Betty."

"Hm." I looked down at my fingers as they positioned themselves on the keys. "Okay, we'll start with 'Somewhere Over the Rainbow'."

Ryan nodded and found the page in his sheet music, then repositioned the capo on the neck of his guitar. "Hip, bubbly, Ukulele-style or…"

"Longing misery," I said.

Ryan nodded. "Nice. Let's do it."

They played, all of them, including the version of me who took over when the real one could no longer bear to feel. In those moments, sometimes I felt like I was watching from outside myself, while another version of me lived inside my own mind. I tried so hard to imagine David sitting in place of Ryan, smiling over at me. But no matter how hard I tried, the image wouldn't alter, and wishing with all my heart wouldn't change things either. It would be a waste of time.

Ryan gave a nod of approval, and I smiled back because, in truth, our song did sound amazing. The three instruments harmonized so well with each other, even though my fingers were a little stiff and the flow of emotion through them was rigid, if not absent.

When I opened my mouth to sing the words, my voice cracked and we all burst out laughing. All the sea-salt I swallowed the other day made my throat dry and hoarse. But I was glad Mike took me to the beach, because, despite our argument, the rest of that day went really well: just two old friends hanging out, eating salty fish and chips, talking about nothing, as the sun went down.

While my mind wandered into the other days we'd spent together, the performance moved to the next song on our list: an instrumental piece from one of Nathan's favorite gangster movies.

"Ryan?" I stopped playing for a second.

"Yeah?" He looked at me over the music stand, and Alana lowered her violin.

"On that last bar, can you give me a B flat instead?"

"Uh, yeah, okay," he said slowly and frowned, but did it anyway, and then his face lit up when I came in with the piano.

"Okay. Cool, so just remember: B flat on the second verse, okay?" I said, flexing my fingers. "Em? You got the time?"

"Uh, yep," she said from the base of the stage. "Eight-thirty."

I closed the cover on the keys. "I'm gonna call it quits, guys. I need to get home."

"Okay, but… Ara?" Emily's light footsteps made a dull thud as she came up the stairs and stood beside me. "Um, I hope you don't mind, but… being that your act has the most heart, I thought I might place you last in the set. You know, kind of thought if people leave on a sad note—"

"Yeah, all cool." I held my hand up. Em obviously didn't realize that closing a show was actually a great honor.

"And, um, that sounded amazing, by the way." She ran her

fingertip over the glossy top of the piano, her reflection appearing upside-down.

"Thanks. Looks like I still have enough soul left in me to play music." I smiled, trying to sound light.

"You miss David?"

"Yeah. Kinda."

"He'll be back." She shrugged, then smiled and walked off to bark orders at the next act.

It really was such a shame David never fell for Emily. She would've been a perfect match for him; she wasn't complicated or moody, like me, and she would've given him eternity.

A jaded smile grasped my lips while I watched her falling into Spencer's embrace, tilting her face up so he could kiss the tip of her nose; they were so in love, like normal teenagers—so innocent and so easy. They'd never know the complexities of my life, and could never even imagine them. Somehow, that made me angry, or maybe it was jealous. Or maybe it just made me feel more… alone.

"It's not all bad." Ryan sat beside me on the piano stool.

"What's not?" I switched on my happy face.

He elbowed me softly. "David? I know you were missing him just now."

I looked down at my thumbnails, clicking them over each other. "Yeah. I kinda was."

"Well, he'll be back before you know it. So, chin up, m'kay?"

"Yeah, okay." I smiled at him. "Thanks Ryan." But he was wrong. We were just another town David was moving through, and I was just another ending to a tragic love story. None of us would ever see him again.

When I arrived home to see Mike's smiling face, it instantly lifted some of the gloom. I even managed a smile.

"So, how was rehearsal?" He closed the DVD drive and grabbed the remote as I shut his bedroom door.

"Crowded." But lonely.

"I'm looking forward to seeing you play."

I bounced onto his bed and propped my back against his pillows. "I wish *you* were doing a duet with me."

"Well, maybe we'll have to sneak over to the school during lunch and use the piano one day." His face lit with a cheeky grin as he slumped down next to me, right on top of the popcorn bowl.

"Ah, crap!" We both cursed, catching the popped kernels as they scattered.

"Here, I'll get that." Mike knelt by the bed, took the bowl from me, and started scraping the salty snack off the edge with his broad, square palms. He'd always had such big hands. So strong and protective. Like somehow, if he was holding me and the world was burning around me, I wouldn't be afraid.

"Something wrong, kid?" He looked up.

I grabbed his salt-covered hand and placed my palm against his, comparing them. Mine were thinner and more petite, the top of my oval-shaped nail only just falling in line with the first fold of his fingertips, but there was so much familiarity in his hand that it was like looking at my own.

"I missed your hands."

He laced his fingers through mine, then flipped them over and traced circles over my knuckles, seeming distant, almost sad.

"Are you okay, Mike?"

He moved the popcorn bowl to the nightstand and shuffled up to lie beside me. "You have her hands, you know? Your mom's."

I tucked my arm under my rib and snuggled against his chest. "I know."

I had a lot of my mother in me: her hair, her heart-shaped face. But I got my dad's eyes. Harry had her eyes. Harry had her smile. But they were gone. The only thing left from that life now was Mike, and I was so glad I at least had him.

It made me wonder how things might be if I went home with him. How those hands had always made me feel so safe, and how every thought behind his eyes placed me first. If I went with him to Perth, would it always be like this? Would we be happy, get married and have little dark-haired babies with caramel-colored eyes and strong hands? I liked the idea—liked the idea of always feeling this loved.

Mike looked down at me, watching my eyes expectantly, like he was waiting for me to say what he knew was in my heart. But, after a quiet moment, he pulled me back to his chest and pressed play on the remote.

As the opening credits rolled across the base of the screen, I closed my eyes and listened to the hum of human normality. I loved it—loved Mike—and I wished I could tell him that. Wished he knew.

We'd laid like this so many times as friends, but in his arms tonight I felt the difference. I felt how real it was. And it drove a strong urge within me to look up at him and say, "I'll come with you. Let's go home to Perth."

But I knew that my current desires were at odds with my heart, and the war raged inside me, unresolvable still.

"Ara?" Mike swept his hands through the front of my hair, his low voice coming from above my brow.

"Mm," I muttered sleepily, keeping my eyes closed.

"You still with me, baby?"

"Hm?"

"Shh." He kissed my head and the volume on the TV decreased. "Just sleep."

THE SMELL OF MORNING AND THE CRASS SOUND OF A CROW somewhere outside brought my mind back from sleep. I rolled up on my elbows and looked around the room—my room. It was dark still, the curtains closed—obviously by Mike; unopened by David—and the house sounded quieter than usual. Even the gentle hum of cars and the distant chatter of school kids outside were absent from the day. It almost sounded like a Saturday, but without the lawnmower.

Last night, while I fell asleep in my best friend's arms, a few things became so clear to me, and I was afraid clarity would be gone come morning. But the feeling I had as sleep arrested me remained the same.

I jumped out of bed, dashed my curtains across and looked to the eastern hills. Somewhere over that rise, somewhere further than I cared to imagine, my David went away. I could feel him; feel his soul aching beyond the rising sun. He never told me where he lived, or even which direction he ran to each night, but I could feel him over there —somewhere.

Down below, nestled into the long yellow-tipped grass in the backyard, the oak tree sat staring back up at me. As many times as I'd looked at that tree since David left, I had also let my heart believe he would be there beneath its leafy boughs. But for some reason, as I watched the gentle motion of the rope swing absently batting the trunk, I felt none of the surprise that he wasn't there. The only thing present in my heart was that warm feeling I had in Mike's arms last night, which suddenly burned into a flaming heat.

With a tight fist, I rubbed my chest and grabbed the edge of my desk. Was it possible that Mike managed to crawl his way a little bit deeper into my heart while I was sleeping; that my brain finally understood the fact that David was gone—that even tomorrow, when I looked for him on the stage where he should be performing our duet, I wouldn't see him? Did I finally get the message?

I backed away from the window, clutching my locket, and turned to face the girl staring back at me from my mirror. She understood. I could see it in her eyes: she knew David wouldn't return for anything. Not for the concert, not for all the tears in the world, not if Skittles got stuck in the tree, and not even if I threw myself from the window and splattered all over the ground.

David Knight was gone. For good.

But I didn't feel anything. Nothing. The admission should've changed something in me. *Anything*. But it didn't.

I needed to think. I needed to let it all sink in. I felt catatonic, empty, hollow. Afraid, because the feeling in me—of not feeling anything—felt like suddenly waking up deaf.

"Run," the girl in the mirror said.

"Run?" I looked back at her.

She smiled and nodded. "Run."

In my running gear, my feet moved me over time, over distance, and it wasn't until I felt my limbs shaking from hunger that I realized how far I'd run. Or where I'd needed to run to—going far away from home before circling back. When I found myself at the school, I knew why. I could feel the deep burn to play the piano tightening my fingers.

No one noticed me sneak into the school; no one even passed me as I reached the darkness of the auditorium. Everyone was at lunch, thankfully, and the stage was set for the concert tomorrow night.

I kicked the door ajar a little, placed the doorstop in the crack, and hugged myself as I headed down the aisle, walking the path of the thin blue line of light from outside.

The warmth of the day remained behind, making me shiver as I reached the stage. Across the room, I could make out only a faint silhouette of the seats—enough to see that there was no one here—and despite that, I stopped dead, certain I'd heard my name in a whisper.

"H-hello?" I waited, motionless at the edge of the stage. "Hello? Is anyone there?"

All around me, the shadows carried eerie secrets and the unmistakable feeling of being watched. I knew I shouldn't be in here. Knew I should be at lunch, be attending school today like everyone else. But, like a beacon of salvation, the piano in all its majestic glory told me to forget about everything right now and just play. So I took a seat and obeyed.

For a moment I just needed to sit; just to exist in the space where music was the center of my world; where the only thing that mattered was the notes, the keys, and me.

My heart was trying to make sense of the fact that David didn't say goodbye to me, all because I had that stupid dream, even though I had no control over it. And I guess that was the problem, wasn't it? What we dream *does* have meaning. Consequence. What we think, feel, desire, it matters. And it hurts.

And it sucks.

But life taught me that prayers are just words, and there's no one to answer them. We are the authors of our own stories, and what we suffer is our own fault. How we endure is determined by our will to survive in a world we're forced to accept. You can either fly or fall.

But I would survive this. I had to stop asking, had to stop wondering if there was some point to it all—some lesson to be learned—because, in doing that, I was holding myself back from moving on.

I closed my eyes tight, trying to imagine a world where David was human, the sultry notes of that impossibility ringing loud through the auditorium while I played.

"Ara!" Mike's angry voice broke my thoughts apart. "Where have you been?"

The room fell silent instantly as I pulled my hands from the keys and placed them in my lap. "What do you mean?"

"Do you have any idea what I've gone through this morning?" The stage thudded under his feet. "I was about to call the police."

"Police? I was at school—"

"Don't give me that rubbish. I knew you didn't attend school today because your dad's been out there searching for you since we realized you weren't in roll call!"

My mouth hung open in shock. "I… shit. I didn't… I'm sorry."

"You should be! Your father is irate, Ara. He was so mad he couldn't even come in here to talk to you. He called *me* when he found you." He pointed to his chest. "How could you just run off like that? Not tell anyone where you were going—"

"I didn't even think—"

"No, you didn't, and that is exactly what got you into the last mess!"

My blood ran cold. He was right.

"I've been driving all over town looking for you. We had no idea what time you left or how long you'd been gone." He looked at his watch. "It's twelve-thirty, for God's sake."

I looked down at my lap, running my thumb over my locket. "Please stop yelling at me."

"No. I'm mad, Ara! I thought you might've thrown yourself off a bridge and—"

"Why would you think that?"

"Because you've been deeply depressed! So much that I don't trust you to be alone right now. I was so worried that I nearly shook Emily when I asked her if she'd seen you."

"What! You talked to my friends?" I smacked the stool with both hands. "Mike, how could you? Now you've gone and made a huge drama out of thi—"

"No. Ara. *You* did that. You took off without leaving a note to say you hadn't gone to school. You've been gone all bloody day!"

"I lost track of time. I—"

"That may be the case, but you've caused a lot of worry. People care about you, Ara. You can't do things like that."

"I had a lot on my mind, Mike." My voice broke as I stood up.

"I know you do, baby, but after what you've been through, you can't just disappear like that and not expect everyone to freak out."

I nodded, hugging myself.

"Where have you been all day?"

"I went for a run." I shrugged. "I lost track of time."

"Why didn't you ask me to come with you?"

"I needed to be alone—to clear my head."

His eyes narrowed at me as if he was trying to see inside my head. "What's going on with you lately, Ara? You're… something isn't right."

My lungs deflated with a heavy sigh as I walked over and sat down on the edge of the stage. "To be honest, Mike, this is all because of *you*."

"What have *I* done?" He followed me, the stage thundering as he sat down beside me like a heavy sack.

"You said you love me."

"You're still sore about that?" he said, sounding hurt. "Because if you don't love me back, Ara, just say it and—"

"That's just it, Mike. It's not about whether I love you or not. This is so much bigger than what's in my heart."

"What do you mean?"

The build-up of sadness and worry and fear shook my ribs. I rolled my face into my hands and let myself cry for a moment.

"Baby, talk to me." He rubbed my back firmly. "Please don't be so closed off. I just want you to be happy."

"If you wanted me to be happy then you should never have told me you love me, Mike." I looked up at him. "Now I'm just confused and empty."

Mike jerked back, dropping his hand to his lap as the blade of my words hit his heart. "You don't mean that," he whispered.

"I do." I nodded, sobbing harder because I also knew how much that killed him. "I'm sorry. I do. I've never been happier or clearer about anything as I was when I was with David—"

"So that's what this is all about?" He motioned around the room. "All your depression and angst—the running off this morning—it's all because of that freak show you think you're in love with?"

"He's not a freak show, Mike!" I yelled, jumping down off the stage, the ground sending a jolt through my heels. "You don't know anything about him!"

"I know he hurt you. I know he changed you; made you sad and quiet and secretive, Ara." He followed me up the aisle. "Don't you know how that looks from my perspective—from your dad's? We're worried about you!"

"Well you can stop worrying," I called back. "David's gone, and I just have to get over it."

"But you're not getting over it." He grabbed my arm and spun me around to face him. "You're *dangerously* depressed, Ara."

"I'm not depressed. I'm just sad. And lonely."

"Well you're not alone. You have *me*," he said softly.

"I don't think it's enough," I said in a weak voice, holding his gaze.

When he dropped his head, even the shadowed darkness did nothing to hide his pain. "So that's it then? You don't want me now because of some boy you just met; some boy who doesn't even want you?"

"He does want me!"

"Does he?" he asked conceitedly. "Because I don't see him around here, Ara. I—"

"He's not. But I can go with him—"

"Go *with* him?"

"Yes. Like I told you on the phone that night, remember? I can be with him, but I have to..." I hesitated, not sure how he'd react. "I have to leave everything, everyone behind."

"Is that what you want? Do you *want* to move away?"

"No."

"But he won't stay here to be with you?"

"He *can't*," I said to the ground.

"Can't or won't?"

"Can't!"

"But *I* can," he stated. "I love you, Ara—"

"And I will always love *him*!" I looked at him for a moment, watching the damage bleed deeper into his soul before I sunk to the ground, hugging my knees. "I can't do it. I can't do it anymore, Mike."

He dropped to his knees and gingerly touched my shoulder. "What, baby?"

"I'm so tired. I'm so goddamn tired. I just can't do it anymore."

"Ara. Please. Why are you shaking? What did this guy do to you?"

"He didn't! Do! Anything!" I screamed, shoving him onto his ass as I got to my feet. "He loved me, Mike. That's all he ever did!"

"Okay," he said in a cautious tone. "I've heard you. I understand. But now I'm worried. Really worried."

"About what?"

He slowly got up, taking small, hesitant steps toward me. "I know you don't want to hear this, but I'm gonna say it anyway, okay?"

"No. Just leave me alone," I said, turning away.

"I can't. You"—he caught my wrist and made me stop—"you're not okay. You need someone to guide you right now, and I know you better than anyone. This isn't normal—the way you feel about David. This is *grossly* magnified by grief…"

"You're wrong, Mike."

"I wish I was." His eyes rounded with deep sympathy, like I was a stupid young girl that just didn't understand the world. "I'm not devaluing what you feel for him, but I'm saying that you need to take a step back; that maybe you need time to process it all and see if it's real, or if it's just a coping mechanism—"

"David is not a coping mechanism!"

"Can you just…" He edged closer, moving to grab me with both hands. "Can you just stop for a moment, and realize that there might be a grain of truth to what I'm saying, Ar? Please?"

His last word sounded desperate, as if he'd tacked on in his mind that if I couldn't be reasoned with, he'd be forced to take action. And by action, I knew he'd tell my dad it was time to lock me away—for my own good. So I closed my eyes, taking a deep breath as I thought about everything he said. I wanted him to be right. I wanted David to be a 'situation' I could medicate and talk away on a leather couch. But he wasn't. No matter how badly I wanted that.

"I love him, Mike."

"I know." He moved in then and put his hand firmly on my lower back, kind of holding me there without actually restraining me. "I know you do, baby. But he's gone, right?"

I nodded, my face crumpling with sadness.

"Okay, then you need to let me help you accept that, okay?" He braved another inch closer, wrapping both arms around me. "You need me to hold you and love you until you feel okay that he's gone."

"Or I could go with him."

He shook his head. "No, baby. You can't."

"Why?"

"Because we love you. Your dad, me, Sam, even Vicki. You can't go away."

"It's my life—"

"Yes, it is. But we'd miss you."

"And I'd miss you, but—"

"It's not right, baby. It isn't right for a man to ask you to do that. No one should have to leave their family for love."

"You just don't understand."

"Then let's leave it there for now, okay? You're shaking and I can tell you haven't eaten. You don't think clearly when you're hungry, you know that."

I nodded.

"Come home with me. Eat, and process things, okay? Get a clear head, and then we can talk about David."

"I don't want to talk about him, Mike."

"Okay." He nodded against the top of my head. "Then we won't. But you know I'm here if you do want to, right?"

"And you won't tell my dad that David asked me to go with him?"

"No, baby. I won't." He kissed my brow, leaving his lips there. I could feel the concern in his breath, though, and I knew I must have sounded incredibly insane to him, which is why I knew damn well that if I had any desire in my heart still to go with David, I needed to make a decision either way and I had to do it quickly.

"Can you ask dad not to be mad with me—about running off?" I looked up at him. "I honestly just didn't realize the time."

Mike smiled softly, wiping a drying tear off my cheekbone. "Of course."

The last chimes of the principal's speech resonated in my thoughts. Even with my eyes closed, I could feel the pale glow of the spotlight over me as my fingers scaled across the keys, breaking the hearts of those in the crowd tonight.

Of all the worlds my mind created, this one, where I lived each day, was the most painful one: the world that hovered on the wrong side of truth; the one I could not escape from, even if I closed my eyes or woke myself up. In this world, everyone I loved was gone, and the boy the crowd mourned, Nathan, was gone too. No matter how much we played for him, he would never hear our songs, but I would play for them anyway—for all those who lived only in my memories. Including David.

I sang the words of the song from memory, not from my heart. All the joy, all the passion I once felt when singing was non-existent. But my music teachers taught me well how to perform when everything around me was falling away. No one in the crowd would have known how much I was suffering.

We finished the song to a standing ovation, and Mike wiped a mock tear from his cheek as I smiled at him. I took a bow then and sat back down at the piano for my solo.

No one made a sound. Not a murmur was heard from within the crowd as they waited.

After a deep breath, I closed my eyes, and in the moment it took to open them again, the room went dark and ultimately quiet. A wispy cool encircled me, the absence of life filtering emptiness into my world. I sat taller and looked around the vacant auditorium.

I was alone; everyone was gone.

How long had I been sitting here?

The whisper of a memory salted my thoughts, making me look

down at my bone-white fingers. I remembered playing. I remembered the faces of the audience; how they greeted me and shook my hand afterward. I'd smiled and accepted their praise while, inside, I was dying. I could see it all as it happened, but couldn't remember living it.

I just wanted to rain my heart into a song until it no longer felt like it was bleeding. So I did, each note pouring through my hands like rainbow-colored grief—strings of light that, with every pull on my heart, tore away another part of my soul; brought to the surface another emotion, another painful memory I thought I'd locked away for good.

Through all of this that I'd suffered, I knew I was destroyed. I would never be the same again. I tried once to move on, to be normal, but with the loss of David, I knew that moving on was never in the cards for me. Whatever my existence here was fated to be, happiness was not it. David was not it.

Like a strong link to a powerful memory, the faint hint of a familiar scent touched my lungs. I drew a deep breath of orange-chocolate, and my body rejoiced at the sensation of oxygen, as if I'd not taken a breath since I last held David.

My head whipped up then toward a feeling. I looked back to the chairs that only hours ago had been filled with friends and family, and all of a sudden, in the middle seat, softly lit by the light from the corridor outside, I saw a face.

David.

He stood up slowly, like a ghost weighed down by the anguish in the world.

How long had he been there? What had he heard in my thoughts while he was watching me?

"I know this is hard." He appeared behind me, his gloriously real form pressing against my back, so cold I knew it wasn't just an apparition. "But breaking up was never going to be easy."

"So that's what this is?" I asked in a quiet voice, looking down. "We're broken up, now?"

"I wish it wasn't so."

"It doesn't have to be."

"It does."

"But, maybe it wouldn't be so bad to be…" I stopped then as I spun around on the seat, hit hard by the reality that he was here after I was sure I'd never lay eyes on him again.

"What wouldn't be so bad?"

"Being like you."

He shook his head. "You can't be like me. I've spent so much time thinking about it—desperate to find some way this could work. But, Ara? There's no saying you even carry the gene. What if we tried, and you…" He shook his head again. "No. You have to take a chance at life. You have to live it to its fullest before I could even *dream* of changing you."

"But—"

"No." He cupped my jaw firmly, coming so close I thought he might kiss me. "If you die, Ara, without ever knowing life, I could not live with myself. It is better to have lived your life in heartache than never to have lived at all."

"But the heartache is worse than I thought."

David's eyes moved to my hand over my heart, and he nodded. "I know."

We looked into each other for a long moment then, leaving our future resting on the pause of a few simple words. After a while, I sighed, turning my face away when the words refused to come.

"He's right for you, you know." David broke the silence, though the tension stayed as thick as blood.

My quiet breath sunk.

"I want you to go back to Perth with him."

I looked up quickly.

"I see in his thoughts, Ara. I watch him with you. He loves you—deeply." He lost his voice on the last word, closing his eyes as he said it.

"I know." I had to whisper, afraid my words would wound him forever. "But I can't go with him. I can't. I just can't leave you here al—"

"Ara. Be smart." David dropped to his knees in front of me. "I can't have you here, lingering in a place I may one day return. That's not living. You have to go. You have to be far away so I can never find you."

"But—"

"No. I won't do it. I won't return and ruin your life and, knowing how close you are—that I could just drive to you—would be more agony than I could bear."

The tears in my eyes turned to thick droplets as they spilled onto my cheeks and over my lips. He was right. It would be selfish of me to wait around here for him; to hope he might change his mind and become a fake human. If he left his Set, he'd have nothing, and one day, I'd be gone anyway. At least, for now, we suffered the absence in union—desolate union.

"Please, just don't make me say goodbye, David. Go, leave me, but let me believe that we'll see each other again one day. For one last goodbye."

He smiled and sat beside me on the piano stool. I tried to steady my pulse, pushing away the memory of the first time I saw that dimple; how I wanted nothing in the world except him—just him. Life or death or murder meant nothing. I just wanted him.

"This is not goodbye, Ara. Not yet. I still have a few more days."

"I know." I cleared my throat. "Until the last red leaf falls, right?"

"Until the last red leaf falls," he said with a grin.

"Where will you go—what will you do when I'm gone?" I asked.

He looked down and then smiled as our eyes met again. "See the pyramids." He shrugged. "Maybe head to a tropic isle and watch a sunset."

I managed a soft smile, thinking about the song he was referring to.

"Don't you ever forget, Ara, how much I love you." He placed both hands on my face, then turned my head slowly. "You still, and always will, belong to me."

I nodded, rolling my cheek into his thumb as he wiped a tear away. Then, he slowly lowered his lips to mine, and like so many times before, they fit to perfection, as if we were made for each other, but so cruelly unsuited to each other. We'd kissed for love, kissed for lust, for happiness and thankfulness. But this was a kiss of sorrow, of loss and despair, yet so full of love—so soft and so gentle, like a beast handling priceless porcelain.

But even with the warmth his touch brought my soul, the small silver locket around my neck felt heavy under the pain of imminent separation. It had felt that way for so long now, but only in his arms, with his lips once again belonging to mine, could I finally see that it always would. And I wasn't sure I could bear it.

I yanked the chain loose as I pulled away from the kiss. "I'm sorry. I just can't do this."

"Ara?" His voice overflowed with confusion as I laid the locket in his open palm.

"It's too painful for me. I can't keep this as a memory of you. I need to forget. I need to try to move on, and every time I do, *this* is a constant reminder that you're no longer a part of my life." My voice broke, *shattered,* as I tore out his heart.

His rounded eyes burned deep into my soul; he wanted me to feel what he felt right then, but I already knew. I could feel it myself, in my bones, breaking my resolve.

I looked away. It hurt too much to see that on his face. It would only destroy me over and over again.

The locket sat in David's outstretched palm, shimmering like moonlight on sand in the cold, dull light of our eternal darkness. I closed his fingertips around the locket and held my grip there for a second.

"This is not goodbye, remember?"

"Not yet, anyway." He nodded solemnly as he placed my heart into his pocket, and then, like so many times before, without a word, without a sound, the darkness was the only thing I saw in his place.

27

With my back against the wall outside Mr. Benson's class, I hugged my books—the books David usually carried—and watched everyone pass. They didn't talk to me. They hardly even gawked at me anymore, and the horrid yellow linoleum just seemed to be a part of the scenery, ironically, like me. Didn't mean it fit, though.

"Hey, did you hear?" Emily came bounding over.

"Depends. What was I supposed to hear?"

"The benefit? We raised enough to cover Nathan's funeral." Her lips practically touched her ears. "And due to an anonymous donation, Mrs. Rossi won't have to pay the hospital bill, either."

"Wow, that's really great." We moved aside for Mr. B to get into class. "So, who's the donor?"

Emily glared at me. "Ara, the point of being *anonymous* is that no one knows who you are."

"Oh, right." I closed my eyes for a second. "Sorry. I'm just—I'm not really with it today."

"Are you ever?" she asked. I shrugged. "So, what happened to you anyway, after the show? You just… disappeared." She fluttered her fingers as if throwing a handful of butterflies into the air.

"I uh—"

"Oh, by the way." She gave me a little slap on the arm with the back of her hand. "Mike. Gorgeous! You were definitely right about his cuteness."

"I know." I tried to smile. "And he feels really bad for practically shaking you the other day."

"It's okay. Really. I get it. He was worried." Her smile subsided to a frown. "Really worried, actually."

I nodded, feeling pretty awkward.

"So, how's David?" she asked. "Have you two run up a huge phone bill yet?"

"I uh… I actually haven't spoken to him since he left."

"Why's that? Has he lost his phone again?" She grinned, poised for a laugh.

"Um, no." My jaw tightened to hold back the quivering lip. "We broke up, actually."

"What?" she screeched, and a few kids nearby turned to look at us. "What do you mean? Why?"

"He… he wasn't really going on holiday when he left, Em. He… was moving away. Permanently."

Her face contorted into an illustration of her thoughts. "But… he didn't even say goodbye."

"I know. He hates goodbyes," I lied.

"But, he was my friend!"

Mr. B glanced up from his desk inside the classroom.

Emily cleared her throat, blinking back tears. "He wouldn't just leave without saying goodbye."

"I'm sorry, Em. He did."

Her lip trembled, her gaze shifting sideways to make sure no one could see her tears. "But… I knew him longer than you. Why would he just… that's so *mean*."

"And you're surprised? You know what he's like."

"Yes." She scowled at me, like this was *my* fault. "But he was never mean to *me*, Ara—never intentionally, anyway."

"Well, I don't think he left to be mean, Emily."

"Why did he leave? Did he tell you?"

I bit my teeth together and shook my head, angry with him for doing this. He said he avoided goodbyes to avoid questions being posed, but he was happy to leave everyone else to pick up his pieces. "His uncle got a call to move, and David had to go with him."

"His uncle?" She frowned. "David doesn't live with his uncle anymore."

I was taken aback by that. "How do *you* know? Did you ever even go over to his house?"

"House? Ara, he lives in an *apartment*."

My stomach dropped through my legs and onto the floor. "So you went there?"

"Of course I did."

"Oh. Um." *Ouch.* "Well, I'm sorry he didn't say goodbye, Em. Maybe he'll call you or something."

She looked down at her books, folding her bottom lip over her top one, her eyes awash with thought. "How are *you* coping then?"

"Me? Fine."

She smiled, her eyes glassy. "Liar."

I laughed once. "No, really, I knew this was coming, so I'm okay."

"How long have you known?"

I shrugged.

"Did you know at the sleepover?"

"Mm-hm."

"Oh." Em nodded. "So, that's what you meant when you said you weren't planning to marry him?"

I nodded.

"I'm sorry, Ara."

"I'm okay."

"Ara, I'm your *best* friend. You don't have to be strong around me."

Funny thing was, she had become my best friend, and I knew I could tell her about David—and she'd understand. "Thanks, Emily. But I really am okay."

"Did he say where he was even going?"

"No. Only that he won't be back. That's why we broke up."

I could see the thoughts flickering across her brow, in her eyes and over her lip, changing, forming into questions. "Why didn't you go with him? I mean, if I loved someone as much as you loved David, I would've just jumped in his suitcase."

I laughed. "Um, I didn't really want to, I guess."

"Why?"

"He… he wants a kind of life that I… I dunno"—I shrugged—"we want different things."

"Like?"

I swallowed. "Well, I want a family one day, and he—"

"He?"

"He wants a career in…" Punishing naughty vampires. "Politics. He can't have distractions, like a family." Or food he's in love with.

"Kids?" Emily practically spat. "You let David go because you want *kids*?"

I nodded, knowing it wasn't as strong an argument as vampire versus human.

"I don't get you, Ara." She dabbed her teary eyes with her fingertips.

"Not much to get, Em. It is what it is."

"So…" A bunch of kids moved past us and into the classroom, where I should be. "Is Mike taking you to the ball then, or are you abandoning me like you did with our shopping trip?"

"Shopping trip?"

"Ara, you have the *worst* memory." Emily sighed, shaking her head. "Remember we were supposed to go shopping for my ball dress?"

"Oh, my God. Emily. I'm so sorry. I totally forgot."

"I don't blame you, not with a hunk like that hanging around." She elbowed me softly, hugging her books to her chest. "Why don't we go tonight? Maybe have some dinner out?"

"Yeah, you know"—I grinned—"that may be just what I need. What time?"

"Six fine with you?"

"Sounds… great." Really great, actually.

We parted ways then and I suffered the trials of obligation for the next seven hours in silence. When I finally got home, Mike sprawled out across my bed and sorted through the playlists on my iPod, while I fussed about in my wardrobe, choosing a dress to wear out.

"So, what's this shopping trip for again?" he called.

"Um. Emily needs a dress for the ball. I was supposed to go with her last week, but..." I shrugged to myself.

"Ball?" The words came from directly behind me.

I spun around, cupping my hands over my bra. "Mike? Get out of here!"

"Relax, kid, I've seen it all before."

"No," I scoffed, shoving him. "Get out. You can talk to me when I'm decent."

"You look pretty decent now." His smug grin made me smile, but common sense took over and I shoved him again.

"Out. Now!"

"Okay, okay." He laughed as he backed away, palms raised. "So, are *you* going to the ball?"

"Well, I—" I looked at the dress, hanging in all its glory on the hook beside me.

"Was David supposed to take you?" Mike asked from right behind me again.

"Hey. I said out!"

"Just answer me and I'll go."

"Don't give me that cheeky grin, Michael Christopher White. I said out. Now, out."

He grabbed the finger I pointed in his face. "Make me."

"I shouldn't have to. You should give a girl some respect."

"I do respect you." He pulled me close, cupping his warm hands on my bare waist. "I'm also just very attracted to you. So"—he grinned, running his thumb from my rib to my hip—"can *I* escort you to the ball, since the flesh eater isn't here?"

Flesh eater? Oh, right, he was referring to the bruises on my neck. "Don't talk about him like that, Mike," I said. "Besides, I thought you hated getting all dressed up?"

"Who me?" His eyes flashed with mischief. "Ara, I would like nothing more than to dress like a penguin and dance with the most beautiful girl in the room. Besides, we both know I look hot in a suit."

I glared up at him, making my eyes small. His hands clasped together so tightly behind me then that I couldn't really move. I wanted to tell him to get out, but I also wanted him to stay. I just wanted it to feel right. But it wasn't right. Not yet.

"So, what d'ya say? Will you let this lowly Aussie hunk escort you to the ball?"

"No, but I'll let my best friend do it."

"Great. I'll go buy a suit tomorrow then."

"Okay, thanks, Mike."

"No worries, baby." He rested his head on mine, continuing his welcomed intrusion.

"Um, Mike," I said into his chest, my lips practically eating his shirt with each word. "Kinda need to breathe."

"Oh, sorry." He let me loose. "I always forget how fragile you are."

I rolled my eyes. "Okay, now out. I need to get dressed."

"Ara?" Vicki called. "Emily's here."

"Send her up," I called back and glared at Mike.

"Okay." He laughed at my 'nose in the air' stance, then turned around, but didn't leave. "Maybe I'll take Sam to another movie."

"You two are getting pretty close."

"Yeah. He's a good kid," he said, leaning on the wall, forgetting he was supposed to be looking away.

"He'll be sad when you go."

"Maybe I just won't go then?" I could hear the question in his suggestion. He wanted me to ask him to stay.

I shrugged instead, buttoning my jeans. "I'm not having this conversation with you right now, Mike. I have too much on my mind."

"Okay." He nodded, then wedged both hands into his pockets, took one last long look at me, and left with a cheeky grin on his face.

A LOUD CRACK OUTSIDE STARTLED ME, AND A BRIGHT FLASH turned my legs white for a second. I froze, afraid to close my window in case the menacing storm noticed me here.

It grew in the sky above the house, howling like the battle that had been raging in my heart since Mike arrived, stirring my emotions again with the force of a hurricane that threatened to reopen the overly traversed door of Mike versus David.

Then, in a second attempt to demonstrate its power, the thunder ricocheted off the distant horizon with a sharp snap, receding to a dense growl. And I believed it. Like prey believes the hunter will kill, I jumped off my chair and ran from my room, my heart skipping with a beat of relief when I looked across the dark corridor to see Mike's door open.

I leaped toward his bed without touching his floor, and fell into him.

"Hey. There you are." He wrapped his arm around me as I snuggled up as close as physically possible to his bare chest. "I was wondering how long it'd take you to come in here." His voice sounded so light. I could tell he was laughing at me, but I didn't care.

"I'm sorry, Mike. I—"

"Shh, don't be sorry, baby. I was actually hoping you'd come in."

"You were?"

"Why do you think I left my door open?"

I smiled, listening to each beat of that heart come as reliably as the next, letting my shoulders drop as he stroked my head, easing away the knot in my stomach. "Thanks, Mike."

"Any time."

And I knew that was the truth, more than an automated statement. Just like every moment in the past, Mike had and would always be there to comfort me through the storm. "Hey, Mike?"

"Yeah, baby?"

"Do you remember the year I told my mom I was too old to be afraid of storms?"

"Yeah." He laughed. "I'm not sure if she actually believed you or just *wanted* to believe you."

I snuggled my face into his bare chest. "I think she knew the truth."

"*I* knew the truth."

"I know you did," I said.

"Yet you always freaked out when I tapped on your window during a storm," he mused.

"Of course I did. How scary do you think it is to completely believe The Bogeyman comes out to get you in the thunder, and then see a face outside your window?"

He laughed loudly. "But you knew it'd just be me."

"Yeah. Still scary, though." I closed my eyes and let myself remember lying with him, safe and happy in his arms all those nights. "Mike?" I whispered.

"Yeah?"

"I… I."

He laughed and kissed the top of my head. "I know, baby. I know you're scared."

"No—"

"Ara, baby, we'll talk in the morning. It's after midnight. Go to sleep."

I swallowed my courage and stuffed the words *I love you* back down where I'd stored them all these years, then closed my eyes and let Mike's heartbeat take me away to the peace and silence of dreamland.

A SONGBIRD ANNOUNCED THE ARRIVAL OF MORNING, WAKING MY mind from the best sleep it'd found in ages. I inched one eye open, blinded by the glare of sunlight streaming in, its soft yellow glow making me smile because, finally, the rain had passed.

If I could sleep like that every night, I'd make it my occupation to go to bed. But the bed moved under me, rising softly before warm, moist lips touched my brow.

I pushed up onto my hands and knees. "Mike!"

"Hey, princess. You slept well," he noted.

"Yeah." I rubbed my face, checking to see if his door was shut. It was. "I did, actually."

"You okay?"

I blinked a few extra times to focus properly on the way the morning seemed to make his skin look like honey and his eyes as warm as hot cocoa. He was very beautiful in the morning. "Um, yeah. I'm sorry. I didn't mean to fall asleep in your bed."

He laughed, shaking his head. "And I'm sorry it doesn't storm like that *every* night."

My cheeks lifted first, forcing my lips to follow.

"Come here." He placed a hand on my shoulder and tugged.

My muscles were so stiff that I slumped down heavily on his bare chest, and every inch of skin that wasn't covered by my tank top touched his, making me shiver inside—a good shiver. "Why did you keep me last night, Mike?"

"Are you kidding?" His arms tightened around me for a second. "You snuggled up so close to me, Ara, with your face and your soft breath over my chest. Why on *earth* would I put you back in your room?"

"Because my dad would kill me if he found me in here." I moved my hand from his chest down to his firm stomach, gently thumbing the fine hairs around his navel. "What time is it?"

"Um..." He stretched his arm out around my back and looked at his watch, forcing me closer. "Midday."

"Midday!"

"Wait a sec." He grabbed my arm as I leaped for the side of the bed. "It's the weekend, baby. Just chill."

"Oh. Right."

"Here. Lie down. I'll get breakfast. Well, brunch now, I suppose." He grinned, and his unshaven, sandy-brown stubble did nothing to hide the sexy indent in his cheek—not even a little bit.

As he gently pushed me back onto the pillows, everything from my heart down went numb. His kiss-me lips came toward me so slowly that I closed my eyes and held my breath, waiting for them to touch mine. But, he pecked my forehead instead and walked out the door, leaving me breathless.

I rubbed at my face, as if maybe I could chafe off some of my awkwardness. Then I checked to make sure I didn't have bad breath. I was certain he'd been about to kiss me—properly. So why did he pull away? My breath didn't smell and I couldn't think of any other reason.

Except maybe that I hadn't told him I loved him yet. And now I thought about it, I think maybe I wanted him to ask me again—to open the door to that conversation, since I was struggling to do it. But he wasn't a mind reader, and having to speak my mind would take some getting used to.

"What ya thinkin' 'bout?" Mike asked, leaning against the door with a tray in hand.

I hadn't realized how much time had passed. "You."

He placed the tray on the foot of the bed. "Good thoughts?"

"Mm-hm." I nodded, warming my smile a few degrees.

"Good. Then eat." He patted my leg through the covers, sitting down beside them. "And if you're still thinking those same thoughts that I just saw across your face, then we need to talk."

I bit my lip. He knew too well what I'd been thinking; he didn't need to be like David to be in my head, which was as comforting as it was awkward.

"Here." He passed me a plate, and I swapped my lip for toast, closing my eyes as the peanut butter swirled around with the jelly on my tongue at the prefect ratio. It didn't even stick to the roof of my mouth.

"Mmm. You've always been the best at making toast."

"Must be the chef in me," he joked.

"So, if the chef in you makes good toast, what can the cop in you do?"

"I could arrest you? For dangerously good looks."

I choked on the toast for a second, nearly losing it out my nose. "That's the worst joke I've heard in ages."

Mike chuckled. "So, I'm still King then—of bad jokes?"

"Right? I forgot about that," I mused. "No one here gets it. They think you're just trying to be funny and not succeeding."

"Don't worry. I get ya." His teeth showed with his gentle smile.

"You always did," I said sweetly, moving on quickly after. "So if you're King, I'm Queen, right?"

"To be my Queen you have to be in love with me."

"Who says I'm not?" I said with a shrug.

"Ara?" Mike put his toast down. "Don't joke about that, okay?"

"I wasn't." I shook my head at him, my lips tight with amusement. "Come on, Mike. You know I do, otherwise I would've told you already that I don't."

"Shit." He wedged a hand into his messy hair, studying my face. "You're serious?"

"You thought otherwise?"

"I..." His hand moved down to rub his brow. "I wasn't sure anymore. I thought maybe you'd subconsciously rejected any feelings you have for me because they led to your mom and Harry dying."

I pouted at him. Poor Mike. "Did Vicki put that idea in your head?"

Mike pressed his lips into a line, smiling. "Maybe."

"Well, it's a good thing she doesn't work in that field anymore, because she's so full of it I would hate to think how badly she might mess up her already messed-up patients."

He let out a singular laugh. "I just... you have no idea how long I've waited to hear you say that."

"Don't get too excited." I bit my toast again, adding, with a full mouth, "It's not like it can go anywhere now. You live in Australia and I live here, and—"

"Come home with me, Ara."

"I can't. I—"

"Yes you can. If you *wanted* to." He looked at me for a long moment. "You know I'd look after you, right?"

He would. He'd take very good care of me; love me, protect me, and I'd never want for anything. "I know," I said softly.

"Then come with me." He took my hand, his gentle touch littered with hope. "You could finish school, go to uni and become a teacher like you always planned?"

"Mike?"

"Please. Don't say anything now. Not if you're going to say no. Just..." He paused, blowing out a really deep breath. "Whatever you choose, I already decided I can't go back—not without you."

"What?"

One shoulder lifted toward his chin in a very timid shrug. "If you stay, I stay."

"Really?"

"Yeah."

The little fold between my brows tightened. "But what about your career?"

"Ara, you are the *love of my life*." Mike took both my hands, knocking the toast out of them. "What would my career mean to me if I didn't have you? God, I only accepted that interview because I thought I'd lost you."

"Lost me?"

"When you moved away—when you refused to even speak to me —I figured you hated me. And… I don't know, I guess I decided that if I didn't have you to look after, I'd be a perfect candidate to risk my own life, because it'd be worth nothing."

"Mike? What a horrid thing to say."

"I know. I'm sorry. It wasn't like a suicide mission or anything. But, I could've joined Tactical six months ago. I chose not to because I didn't want to leave you alone if anything ever happened to me." Mike's eyes softened as they scanned my cheeks and my lips. "When you told me you fell in love with David, I *died* inside, Ara. I thought everything was lost. So if I have to give up Tactical to stay here and be with you for the rest of my life, it doesn't even need a second thought. All I ever wanted was you."

"So you'd move here? Throw it all away? What would you do for a job?" my voice of reason challenged.

"I'll be fine. I used to be a part-time chef, remember? I can get work anywhere."

"But you'd need a working visa."

"Or"—he bit his bottom lip and looked into me with those charming, caramel-colored eyes, melting my heart like maple syrup on pancakes—"we could get married. You're an American citizen now, right?" His tone softened on the end into a shrug of his shoulder.

"So that's all I am to you? A ticket to work in the US."

"Oh, come on, Ara." Open fingertips feathered his hair back in an awkward but sexy gesture. "I was using it as a line to open that door. I've bloody been trying to cough out a proposal since the first day I got here."

My tonsils dropped down into my neck. "What!"

"What did you expect? I've loved you my whole life."

"But… we're so young still."

"I know. But you're also amazing, Ara. And if I don't put a ring on you, reserve the right to have you forever, someone else will. We don't have to get married right away, but it was always my intention to at least let my intentions be known," he said, giving an awkward grin.

"I… I… Why didn't you just ask me that day you told me how you feel?"

"Because you would've said no."

"You don't know that."

"Ara, you *cried* when I told how you how I feel. I was devastated and humiliated. If I'd told you I want to marry you one day, you'd probably have imploded on me."

"You were humiliated?"

"You know me, Ar. I uh… I don't take rejection as well as I'd like to think I do." We both laughed softly. Then, he shuffled closer, and the serious Mike I'd come to know more recently slipped into place. "All I've been waiting on is you: for you to realize you love me. And then, that night back home, when I ruined everything…"

I looked away, feeling the pain of loss etching into my heart.

Mike hooked a finger under my chin and pulled my face toward his. His lips were so close I could smell the peanut butter on his breath. It smelled nice. Comforting.

"You took me by surprise, Ara. It was all I'd ever wanted, you know. I'd imagined it so many times, and when it finally happened, I acted like a damn fool. And I lost you. I had to accept that you were being dragged away from me; had to accept that you wouldn't even speak to me and then, worse, had to break apart hearing you speak about loving another guy. Do you know how hard it was for me to play the supporting friend, when all I wanted to do was coax you into believing he didn't want you?"

"Why didn't you?"

"Because I love you." He squeezed my hands. "I wanted you to be happy, and you sounded happy with him. But… now… I'm glad he's gone, because all I've seen so far is the damage he's done to you."

I rubbed my hand over my neck. "It wasn't like that, you know. He loved me."

Mike nodded. "I know."

"Do you?" I asked conceitedly.

"Yes, I do. And I guess, now is probably a good time to tell you something." He scratched his brow.

"Mike, what did you do?"

His shoulders dropped. "I stole David's number from your phone and I called him."

"What? Why?"

"Come on, Ara. Why do you think? I'm not stupid. I've watched you pretending to be happy, but I knew there was something up with you. I've known you all your life. I knew he was hurting you. And I was afraid he might be one of those controlling types, you know? The kind that makes you feel like you need him to feel good about yourself."

"Mike? He's so not like—"

"I know." He smiled and flattened my frown with his thumb. "He's a decent guy, Ara—physical damage aside."

"So, when you talked to him," I asked delicately, "like, what… what did he say?"

"He told me he's leaving and that you couldn't be together. He told me you wanted a family one day and a normal life, but he couldn't give you that."

"So"—his words echoed in my mind—"he… what, he told you to *have* me?"

"It wasn't like that, Ar." Mike cocked his head. "He just said he knows I'll make you happy, and that's all he ever wanted for you."

David gave me away?

"Please don't be mad, Ara."

Mad? I wasn't mad that he called David. I felt hurt that he knew everything, and embarrassed, but it wasn't Mike's fault. It was so like him to do this. He was my protector, he always had been. My best friend. My Zorro.

"I'm not mad at you, Mike."

"Well, don't be mad at David, either. He just wants you to have a… a normal life."

"And you think *you* can give me that?"

"Ara, I'll give you everything. I'll be whatever you want me to be. I'll be a husband, a father to our children, a provider, a protector, but most of all, if you say you'll marry me, I will love you—more than anyone has ever been loved in the history of mankind, and I will devote every breath I take to being the best husband you could ever have."

"But what about what *you* want, Mike? I don't want you to be what I want. I want you to be happy, too. I mean, do you even want children?" We'd never discussed that. Mike was good with kids, he always adored Harry, but never spoke of wanting a family.

He took a breath, lifting his shoulders as he did. "All I ever wanted was you—a thousand times over and every day for the rest of my existence. I've never really thought about kids before."

I nodded, looking down at my fingers.

"But..." His gaze settled on my belly, lost in a smile.

"But?" I said.

"If I could place a piece of myself inside of you and"—he lifted my top and traced little circles around my navel—"that would grow and become a life that's a part of you and me combined, I can't *imagine* something more magical. So, yes." He broke eye contact for a second and reached into his nightstand, closing the drawer with his pinkie after. "I want to have babies with you. I want a hundred little dark-haired, blue-eyed babies running around. And you and me? We'll be together. Always. *That's* what I want."

The breath I finally released quivered its way out.

"Please?" Mike slipped off the bed and knelt in front of me, lifting the lid just a fraction on a small purple box. "Make me the happiest man on the planet, Ara. Marry me."

Every flower that once was dead bloomed within my heart, and the ashes of my soul circled in on the breeze, showing me how to breathe again. I looked into the small box and a red blossom shimmered back: a ruby rose, with two emeralds on either side. A promise in the shape of life, bright as the color of blood; a color so exquisite in the shadowed parts of my broken past that it cast a spotlight on the door to a future I thought was gone—a door that opened by the key of one word.

"Yes," I whispered so quietly that Mike's eyes focused on my lips.

"Did you just say yes?"

"Yes. I… yeah, I did." I could feel the light sparkling off my tears.

"Seriously?"

"Yeah, seriously."

Mike laughed, his shaky fingers removing the ring from the box and holding it to the tip of my nail. "I… I have a speech."

"A speech?"

His cheeks and forehead went pink. "Yeah, I uh… I kinda planned this for a while."

I shrugged, smiling widely, and rolled my legs over the side of the bed to sit up. "Let's hear it then."

He cleared the awkwardness from the back of his throat, holding my fingers firmly, almost unintentionally too tight. "I designed this for you, because any other stone, any other ring would never have been perfect enough to tell you how much I love you; how you're a part of everything I am, and how no matter what I see in the world, I will never see anything that is quite as bright and perfect and sparkling as you. You're my girl." He pointed to the ruby stone. "My beautiful rose."

The ring slid perfectly into place on my finger, fitting like the way Mike fit me; like we were made to go together. I smoothed my fingertip around the gold, shaking my head. "It's perfect, Mike."

"I know." The corners of his eyes softened and he grinned, running his fingers along my forearms, bringing them to rest just on the backs of my elbows. As I parted my legs and let him kneel between them, my confident, womanizing best friend became a little rigid; jittery, I suppose, with a kind of schoolboy awkwardness I'd never seen in him before.

"What're you thinking, Mike?"

"Nothing," he said, but his eyes held the smile of poorly concealed desires.

"Liar."

He looked away. "Sorry. It's just… I've never felt this way before. About anyone. Not like this. I just don't know what to do with you."

I pulled his face toward me and closed my eyes tight. He smelled so fresh and sexy, with a vibrant, musky cologne—mixed with the peanut butter. I just wanted to press my face into his neck and breathe him in. "You could start by kissing me."

"I can't. Not right now."

"Why?"

"My knees are shaking, baby." He laughed and looked down. "I've wanted this for too long. It's taking everything in me right now not to throw you on the bed and tear off your clothes. If I kiss you, that's exactly what'll happen."

"Then just shut up and kiss me."

"No." He shook his head, moving out from between my legs to sit beside me. "I'm twenty-one, you're seventeen. It just doesn't feel right."

My mouth wouldn't close. He just asked me to marry him, but I was too young for him to have sex with.

"Look, let's at least wait until we're married."

"Oh, God." I rolled my face into my hand. "Not you too."

"What?"

"David forbid you to have sex with me, didn't he?"

"What, no. Why would you think that?"

"This no sex before marriage rule—it seems to be a thing between you two?"

Mike grinned. "He… he refused you? You're still a virgin?"

"Virgin?" My neck jutted forward with incredulity. "Yes, Mike. I already told you that—at the airport."

"I'm sorry, baby, I didn't believe you." He rolled his hands out as he shrugged, looking ultimately innocent and sweet.

By the time my infuriation simmered and I looked over at him, he was shaking his head, smiling down at his lap.

"What?" I said.

"I always wanted to be your first."

His glittering grin infected my scowl, making me smile. "Then let's…"

"No way," he cut in, knowing exactly what I was about to say. "You are the only girl left on this planet that still has her innocence. There is no way I'm taking that from you until we have officially tied the knot. We're gonna do this the right way."

"And what if I disagree?"

He sighed. "It'll be your first time, Ara. Why not wait—just a bit. Wait 'til we're back home in a place we both feel comfortable, so I can take my time with you." His imagination spilled ideas across his face. "I want to enjoy the first time we get to be naked together; touch you slowly, kiss you in places I only ever dreamed of."

I took a quivering breath and moved his hand closer to the apex of my thighs, keeping my fingers twined in his so it seemed like an innocent gesture. He caught on though, and pulled our hands back toward my knees.

"You're really going to hold firm to this, aren't you?" I said.

He nodded. "It's not easy. But you'll thank me one day."

"Always the upstanding citizen."

"I've done the bad boy thing, Ara, with a lot of girls," he said, and we both laughed. "I never respected or loved any one of them, okay? But I love you, and out of respect for you, and for your father, I am not going to take your innocence when you're seventeen, while I'm a guest in your dad's house."

I bit my teeth together and pulled my hand from his so I could fold my arms. "It's not the end of the world if we make love, Mike. It's not like you're going to eat me alive."

"You mean like the last guy who put his mouth on you?" Mike laughed.

I cupped my faded bruise. "That's not funny."

"Sorry." He touched my face and turned it toward him. "That was in poor taste."

I gave him a half smile. "Well, it was *kind* of funny."

"It was kind of true, too. But my point still stands. No sex. Yet." He winked at me. "But I am going to kiss you."

"Okay," I breathed.

Inch by inch, his face came closer to mine, his hot breath sweeping my chin. I swallowed, and moistened my lips, not daring to breathe in case my peanut butter breakfast was still on my breath. And the smile I gave when Mike tilted his head made him laugh just as our lips touched. *Finally* touched.

He was so warm, so solid, so real.

His stubble scratched against my chin while the air from his nose brushed over my upper lip, and it was perfect: gentle, loving—not wet or sloppy, like Emily described Spencer's kiss.

He closed his lips around my tender pout, held there for just a second, then pulled slowly away, both of us breaking into a smile.

"Perfect," he whispered.

I had to agree, but my body refused to move so I could tell him that.

He picked up my rigid hand and brushed his thumb over my ring. "Are you happy, Ara?"

"Mm-hm." I reached for my locket, dropping my hand when I realized it wasn't there. "I guess… I guess it just sunk in, you know? I've kind of been waiting for that kiss since before…"

He cupped my face, his sympathetic gaze easing my soul. "It's all okay now, Ara. We're gonna be fine. We'll go home, we'll get married, and everything will be okay again."

I nodded, but my heart sunk, and I knew he felt the shift.

"What is it, baby?"

"I…" I looked at my ring. "Marrying you, I'm sure about—one day—but I don't know if I'm ready to leave Dad, you know. He's—"

"He's your dad." Mike nodded. "I get it. We don't have to think about that part yet, okay? We'll figure all that out later."

I nodded.

"Okay," he said, then kissed my forehead. "Hey, I gotta go call my dad. He's gonna be so happy I finally asked you."

"Okay." I smiled, sweeping a lingering tear from my eye as Mike leaped off the bed and headed for the door.

"Baby?" He barely got a step away before turning back and kneeling down in front of me again, taking my hand. "You. Have made me. The happiest man alive."

I looked up from our hands and into his smile.

"I was sure I'd come here to say goodbye," he confessed. "I was prepared to leave with a broken heart, but instead, I'll be bringing yours home with me."

I smiled, even though one part of that story was wrong: I didn't want to go back to Perth. I wanted to stay here.

As Mike stood up again and walked away, I twisted the ring around on my finger. It was so delicate that if I knocked it the wrong way I was sure it'd break.

Mike popped his head around the corner then, phone in hand. "Dad says it's about time."

I grinned at him.

"Yes, Dad. I did." He turned away again. "No. Well, I need to be home next week, but we haven't told Ara's dad yet."

My smile dropped when Mike disappeared down the hall, leaving me alone with my thoughts.

What would my dad say? He'd make me wait until I turned eighteen—or twenty-one. I knew what my mom would've said: she'd be happy. Even though I was young. She would've been able to see that I loved him; she would've taken me shopping for a dress, and....

I let that thought slip away with the agony it brought.

What would David say? After all, he wanted this. He *gave me away*. He must've known when he told Mike to have me that this would happen.

I wondered where he was. If he was far away, working in New York, or maybe watching to see if I'd moved on. But though that was a sad thought, the next one was a happy one, because Mike's deep, husky voice travelled down the hall and into my ears. I could lie all day and listen to him talking, especially knowing he'd come back in here after to see me, because I was his world.

I looked down at my left hand then and traced my fingertip over the ruby. It really was such a pretty ring, and I couldn't help but to smile at the odd significance of the single red rose.

28

A pale blue light filtered between a crack in my curtains, casting shadows of raindrops across my carpet, while memories of David paraded in my mind.

The celebration dinner Vicki made for Mike and I tonight kept me distracted until I was tired. But all it did to be distracted was make me realize how hard it was going to get to find things every day that made time pass until I grew old and died. Accepting life, accepting a future without David brought me more clarity than I expected, but sadly, no less pain.

"I dream about you, you know?" I whispered, imagining David sitting beside me on the bed. "When I go to sleep at night, I imagine I'm still with you. Will I ever stop?"

The apparition shook his head and reached out to touch me, then, like a cloud of steam brushed away by a hand, he vanished. Only a streak of yellow light remained in his place, filtering in from the hallway. I looked up and smiled at Mike, who leaned against the wall with two steaming mugs in his hands.

"You awake?" he whispered.

The clock beside me said midnight. "I am now," I lied.

"Sorry, baby. I'll leave you to sleep."

"No. Wait. I'm awake. Please come in." My feather quilt ruffled as I sat up.

He closed the door with his foot and walked through the darkness to my bedside. The cups clinked together on the nightstand, and as my eyes adjusted to the dim light, I noticed his look of concern.

"You okay, Mike?"

"You were quiet tonight—at dinner," he said. "Is something up?"

"What makes you think there's something wrong? Maybe I'm just tired."

"Ara, come on. I'm the one person in the world you can say anything to—without consequence." He placed the warm mug in my hand, securing my fingers around it before letting go. "Don't shut me out."

I sighed and looked down at the creamy layer of warmed milk, forming a white coating of froth in the mug. "It's David."

He nodded after a deep breath, sitting down. "It's going to take a long time to let him go, Ara."

"And you're okay with that?" I asked slowly, like he was crazy.

"Why wouldn't I be?"

"Because it's… I mean, how can you want to be with me, knowing I'll always have another man in my heart?"

He exhaled, his expression changing with thought. "Ara, I love everything about you: past, present, future. He was obviously a big part of your life the last few months, and he kept you safe while I wasn't here," he said simply. "So if you always have a place for him in your heart, baby, that's something I can live with."

My eyes filled with liquid. I smiled down at my hot chocolate and then took a sip through my teeth, swallowing down the rocks his words put in my throat.

"You don't know how happy I am to see this on you." Mike unfolded my ring hand from the cup, pressing his thumb firmly to the stone. "I dug it out so many times, practiced my speech, then put it away again."

"How long have you had it?"

"I, uh… I *designed* it when I was seventeen." He scratched the back of his head. "Ara, I've been in love with you for forever. Even when I was ten and we'd play that game where we get married, I knew that one day you'd be the girl I asked. I was just too stupid to do anything about it. It wasn't until about a year ago that I took the design to a jeweler and had it made, in case I ever got the guts up."

"A year? God, you *are* stupid," I scoffed.

He sighed a few times, opening his mouth to speak then stopping, until finally he quietly said, "Your mom said the same thing."

"Do you mean Vicki?"

"No." He smiled. "I mean, yes, Vicki knew about the ring—"

"Since when?"

"Uh, I told them about a month ago." And suddenly, her strange behavior toward Mike made so much sense. "But, I was talking about your real mom."

I looked at the ring. "She knew about it?"

He nodded. "She cried."

"So, she approved?"

He laughed. "Of course. She practically had us betrothed from the day you were born, Ara. She did make it very clear that we'd have to wait until you were eighteen, but she approved."

The soft smile I gave felt nice across my mouth. I liked smiling, especially for my mom. "Well, it's easily the most immaculate ring I've ever seen, Mike. I can't believe *you* designed this. For *me*."

"Well, you are and always have been my beautiful rose." He laughed then—at himself, I think. "Look at me, Mike the poet."

"I like poetry. I've always been a sucker for a romantic." I placed my cup on the nightstand next to Mike's.

He smiled. "Squidge over."

I moved to the cold side of the bed, letting him slip beneath my covers, coming to rest my cheek against his ultra-warm chest. He felt so different from David; he was bulkier, warmer, and the sound of his heart beating in his chest brought a kind of fear to my own, knowing it could break or stop beating by the smallest, stupidest mistakes. But the humanness of Mike made me feel oddly safe in a way I hadn't always felt with David. I was comfortable with him; we matched. Mike was my human match.

His arms fell heavily around me then, like wearing a bead-filled doorstop as a hug. This would be my life from now on, and I had to admit, after all the pain, after all the loss and loneliness, it finally felt like I could breathe.

A semi-conscious dream stole my eyes to the images in the back of my mind. Walking down a long aisle toward my destiny—toward Mike—I tried so hard to picture David there, but I couldn't. It was Mike.

It had always been Mike.

Stopping at his side, I pulled the red rose from my bouquet and gave it to him, but when our hands touched, I jumped back with the cold shock of electricity, waking to the feel of icy skin—something real, tangible—and a familiar sweet scent hiding under the shadows of dawn: orange and chocolate.

"David?" I whispered.

No one replied. But I could feel him. I knew he'd been here just moments ago!

I jumped out from the warmth of Mike's arms and ran for the window, stopping dead when I spotted a yellow rose on the windowsill.

My ruby ring suddenly felt heavy then, as if I was wearing the pain in my soul, knowing David would have shattered to see me sleeping in Mike's arms. I picked up the cold, thornless blossom and pressed it to my nose, spotting my iPod underneath it.

Our lives, every inch of our journey, had been mapped out in song on that device—from the first time I saw him, through the days of wondering if he loved me, to the heartache of knowing he only loved me enough to leave me and, finally, to losing him. It would do me no good to listen to that playlist again, even though I knew that's what David wanted. But I just couldn't live my life in the past anymore. I had to find a way to move forward.

The street below was desolate, no sign of David having been or gone. The dawn sky looked cold and grey, like the world was readying itself for rain, while a soft red glow outlined the mountains to the east. I looked over at Mike, sleeping peacefully, and drew in the sweet pear scent of the rose once more. Then, as I went to press the Home button on my iPod, noticed a new playlist there titled

"Ara". It only had one song, so I popped my earphones in and pressed play.

A delicate piano told a sad story, making my heart ache in the first bar. I pushed open my window, leaning on the frame as the words began. I'd never heard this song before. I knew David liked John Mayer, but he'd never even said which song was his favorite. I wondered why he put this one on my iPod and no other song. And then I listened more carefully to the words, relating instantly to the feeling of falling asleep thinking about the one you love; your heart so broken because they're gone. You dream for a moment that they're right beside you, that everything in the world is finally all right. But the warmth of their hand, the clear memory of their smile dissipates suddenly, destroyed by waking. It almost makes you want to sleep for the rest of your life so you can be together.

I checked the title of the song again, smiling: "Dreaming With a Broken Heart."

Tiny bumps of chill dotted my belly with the kiss of a cool breeze, and the sun touched the earth just over the horizon, warming everything around me; the treetops became pink and gold, and orange leaves floated softly down to the ground like autumn snow. I pinched three of the yellow petals from the stem of the rose and held them out over the lip of the window frame: one for my heart; one for my soul; one for eternity. They all belonged to David. Each and every bit of me would always be his—no matter what my dreams may tell me. No matter what Fate made me do.

When the wind swept past my window again, I flicked the petals into the day. They floated downward on the breeze, following the autumn leaves to the old oak tree in the garden and coming to rest, with one last kiss from the wind, right on the seat of the swing.

"I love you, David. Forever," I whispered into the nothing, reluctantly shutting my window as I spotted the last morning star.

"Make a wish." Broad arms wrapped my waist from behind, startling me.

"I don't believe in wishes anymore, Mike."

"Well, I'll make one for you, then." He closed his eyes and crossed his heart.

"What did you wish?" I asked.

"Can't tell you. It won't come true."

"That's so lame," I said, rolling my eyes.

"I know." He pressed his hands to my waist and turned me around, slowly plucking my earphones from my ears. "Why are you crying?"

"So much has happened." I sniffed back the runny liquid in my nose. "Everything's changing for me now, Mike. Sometimes I feel like I'm losing control of it all; like it just goes too fast."

"It does go fast, princess," he said. "But that's why you've got to make the most of every day." He kissed my forehead. "You gotta laugh at stupid jokes and eat bad food"—he kissed my nose—"and try to find the good in every moment; happy or sad or difficult." He pulled back for a second as he moved in to kiss my lips, and added one more thing, "And I'm going to be here to do it all with you. For the rest of our lives."

As his lips touched mine, I closed my eyes, teaching myself to accept my new reality.

My phone forced me to get up off my back, leave my comfy pillow behind and wander across to my desk. "Hello?"

"Hey, Ara."

"Hi, Em. What's up?"

"Um. I need you to do me a favor."

"Sure. Anything," I said, peeling the curtain back with my fingertip, looking down over the evening.

"I… I kind of need you to tell Spencer I can't go to the ball."

"What!" I screeched. "Why can't you go, and why can't you tell Spence yourself?"

"He… well… I was kind of going to get you to tell him I have laryngitis."

"Why?"

"I didn't want to tell him I can't go. I just… I think I might cry."

"Em, I don't get it. Why aren't you going?"

"I haven't got a dress." She started crying.

"But, after we failed at shopping the other day, I thought you said you were just gonna wear an old one from your closet."

"I was. But my mom cleaned everything out a few months ago and donated it all to charity."

"Oh, Em."

"I only have this ugly red thing that I wore when I was twelve. And I can't go to the ball in a dress that short. I'll look like a hussy."

"Ara?" Sam said, popping his head around the wall.

"Hang on, Em." I looked over at Sam, covering the mouthpiece of the phone. "What are you doing in my wardrobe?"

"Can I borrow your hair gel?"

I raised a brow at him. "Why?"

He stepped into my room, grinning. "I got a date tonight."

"A date?" I smirked.

"Yeah. Can I use it or not?"

"Fine. But shut that bathroom door. I'm talking girl stuff."

He walked off, starting up the hairdryer in the bathroom, but didn't shut the door. I hated sharing a bathroom; I hated it even more that it had two doors.

"Argh. Sorry, Em. Pest control."

She laughed.

I walked into my wardrobe and glared at Sam through the bathroom mirror. "I told you to shut this."

He shrugged. "So shut it."

"Argh!" I slammed it behind me and stormed out of my wardrobe, but a flash of blue fabric on the hook caught my eye, and as I thought back to the night David forced me to accept that dress, an epiphany hit me like a rock in the head. "Oh my God. Em!"

"Still here."

"Come over. Right now. I have a dress for you."

She didn't even get to say anything. I hung up the phone and ran downstairs to wait for her, opening the door seven minutes later to a solemn-looking Emily.

"Hi," she said.

I gave her a hug, and she smiled as she pulled away, but not at me.

"Hey, girls," Mike said, sitting on the stairs behind me.

"Hi, Mike," Em said.

"You back for another shaking?" he joked.

"I'll pass," she said sheepishly. "You know, you look kind of different when you're not mad with worry."

Mike laughed. "Yeah, guess it's easier to see my face when I'm not towering over you, harassing you for information on missing girls." He cast a raised brow my way.

Emily giggled. "It's okay. You didn't actually shake me."

"Okay, enough small talk." I grabbed Em's hand. "Come see your dress."

Mike laughed as we rushed past and then shut my bedroom door on him.

"Now, close your eyes. And stay here." I held out a warning finger.

"Can't go far with my eyes closed," she said.

I left her by my bed while I ran to the wardrobe to get the green dress, and came back holding it against my body. "Okay. You can look."

Emily's eyes lit up and her mouth popped open as she ran toward me, well, to the dress. "Oh, my God, Ara. This is perfect. Where did you get this?"

"Had it for ages." I shrugged.

"Can I try it on?"

"Of course, dummy, that's why I asked you over. Here." I handed her the dress and directed her to my wardrobe. "I hope it fits."

"It looks like it will," she said, her voice muffled under a shirt or something.

"Yeah, we're the same size, so it should be fine."

"I can't thank you enough for this, Ara. I just haven't found anything I love enough to wear, but I think this"—she stepped out and her beauty struck me—"might do?"

"Emily?" I couldn't help but to rush over. "How perfect is this on you? Oh my God!"

She readjusted the shoestring strap on her shoulder and spun slowly to reveal the low back, the shimmering emerald green hugging her curves and making her skin look luminous.

"I hate you, you know." I sighed enviously, folding my arms. "It never looked that good on me."

She laughed. "Sorry."

"Don't be sorry. I was just playing."

"I know. But I do *love* this dress."

"Well, then it's yours."

"Mine? Ara, I can't—"

"Yes, you can. I want you to have it. It was"—I shook my head, looking for the right words—"meant for you."

"Thank you." She reached out, so I hugged her again. "I'm so glad we're friends."

"Me too. Come on." I took her hand, leading her to the door. "We have to show Mike."

"Wait." She pulled back a little. "Are… are you sure it looks good? I mean—"

"Em. It's great. Stop worrying." I stuck my head around the corner. "Mike?"

"Yeah?" He flashed a really sexy grin, stopping just as he was headed down the stairs.

"What do you think?"

When I pulled Emily out of my room, Mike tilted his head to one side. "Wow. Yeah, that's a great dress. Do a spin," he said, twirling his finger in the air. Emily spun around. "I don't know, Ara. Perhaps I'm marrying the wrong girl."

Emily's head whipped up and her mouth fell open. "Marrying? Did he say *marrying*?"

I shot a death glare at Mike. "Um, yeah. We're… Mike asked me to marry him," I said, showing my ring.

"Oh my God," Emily squealed, grabbing my hand. Mike rubbed his ear with his finger. "When did this happen?"

"Yesterday."

"Wow." She pressed both thumbs to my ruby, becoming seemingly smaller from the shoulders down. "And… what about David?"

"Um—"

"He's out of the picture," Mike said swiftly, but very politely.

Emily's eyes screamed her true thoughts. "Well, that's just, like, so great, Ara. I'm so happy for you two."

"I'm just gonna…" Mike jerked his thumb toward the stairs and walked a few steps backward before fleeing with the speed of a man in trouble.

"Emily?" I closed my bedroom door, then spun around to look at her. "What's wrong?"

"What have you done?"

"I already told you, Em." I sat on the bed, shifting her jacket out of the way. "David and I broke up. Why are you so surprised?"

"Because, you were supposed to meet again one day on a windy autumn morning and fall in love all over again. Not go and marry another man!" She pointed to my door.

"Em?" I chuckled. "This isn't a fairy tale."

She looked at me for a long moment, and then threw her hands up in the air. "I don't know what to say to you, Ara. He *loved* you. Why should kids or careers or anything stop you from being together?"

"It's not just the kid thing."

"Then what else is there?" She sat beside me.

"He… he has things in his life that he doesn't want me a part of—that I don't *want* to be a part of."

"Like what?"

I raised a brow at her. "Em, come on, you know David's got secrets."

Her eyes narrowed. "So you can't love him if he has secrets?"

"No, it's not that." I stood up. "It's that I can't be with him now I know those secrets."

"Are you kidding me?" She stood too. "His *inner demons* are stopping you from being together?"

"Yes." In a roundabout way.

"That's not love then, Ara. It never was."

"Shut up, Emily. You don't anything about what I felt for him."

She recoiled a little.

"Argh, I'm sorry." I dropped my arms to my sides and slumped back down on the bed. "I'm just tired of people thinking they know my heart."

"I wasn't saying I did. I just don't get it. You wanted him so bad. I remember you telling me you'd give anything if he'd just ask you out. What changed?"

"The heart." I shrugged.

She shook her head. "I gotta know."

"What?" I asked, confused as she reached into her bag and pulled out her phone.

"I gotta ask him."

"Ask who what?"

"Ask David what he did that's so terrible it's destroyed this magic love I thought you two had."

I smiled. "He'll never answer his phone, Emily. He's probably got a new number."

Em shrugged, holding her phone to her ear. "It's ringing."

I tensed. What if he answered? What then?

I felt my toes edge out, turning in preparation to run and snatch the phone.

"Jason!" She screeched, almost projecting forward. "Hi, um, I… uh… where's David?"

I had to force my brow into a dismissive position to hide my obvious confusion at the way she spoke to Jason: like she'd known him for years, or had at least met him before.

"Just tell me where he is," she said, then went quiet. "Well, does he know what Ara's gone and done?"

"Hey!" I scoffed.

She bit her lip, ignoring me. "She's marrying him, Jason."

I gathered, from the look on her face, that Jason didn't really have a lot to say about it. And why would he?

"Okay." She shrugged. "He's *your* brother."

Emily hung up the phone and looked at me. I felt like a school kid in big trouble from the principal.

"You are the stupidest girl I've ever met, Ara."

"Hey! I am not. I'm just trying to be happy."

She shook her head, conceit littering her smile. "By living without David?"

"Yes."

"Then that just makes you even dumber than I thought."

"Look. Stay out of it, Em. It's *my* life."

"And I'm your friend. That means I get to tell you when you're being a dumb cow!"

"No, Emily, I'm being *sensible.* I'm doing what any sane teenager should do."

"That's the point! Don't you get it? You're a *teenager*. You don't have to make smart choices."

"That's the stupidest thing I've ever heard."

"Well, exactly. And I have the freedom to say and do stupid things, because I'm young, Ara. And so are you. And if you let love go now for reasons only an adult would care about, you'll regret it for the rest of your life."

"What would you know about regret? You're the same age as me."

She looked down at her feet. "I have my regrets."

"Yeah well, for me, David won't be one of them. It'd be worse if I stayed with him."

"What is wrong with you?" She tossed her phone onto my bed. "Do you need a brain scan or something? It's David *freaking* Knight, Ara! Not just some random guy."

"Just stop it, Em. Okay!" I stood up, thrusting my body forward a little, tightly holding back tears. "He's gone! He's not coming back, and I don't want to talk about it!"

"That's because you know you should have gone with him."

"What the hell does it matter to you?"

"He was my friend, Ara. I cared about him. And I care about you. God only knows why I bother, because you obviously don't care about yourself."

I shook my head, looking away.

"I'm sorry, okay," she said. "I just… I've never really had close friends before and, I mean, David was my first one. He was the first person that ever understood me."

Yeah, or read your mind.

"And you," she continued, "you became my friend because you actually *liked* me. Not because I was popular or knew all the guys. You actually liked *me*, Ara, and I don't have any other friends like you and"—her lip quivered—"he's gonna take you back to Australia, isn't he?"

"Who?"

"Mike."

"He wants to," I said, unable to look at her.

"And what then? Then I'll have no one."

"You have Alana."

She swiped her tears and sat on my bed.

I sat down beside her. "I'm sorry, Emily."

"I'm sorry, too." She picked up my hand. "I don't mean to interfere, I just—"

"You care?"

She nodded. "I don't like him."

"Who?"

"Mike."

"What? Why?"

"I don't like how he calls you *baby* and *girl* all the time." Her nose crinkled. "Don't you find it degrading?"

"Why would I?" I shrugged. "It's just a pet name."

"But you're not his pet. That's just the point."

"And he doesn't treat me like a pet, either. It's a term of endearment. I, unlike you, have an appreciation for verbal affection."

She laughed through her nose. "Gosh, you sounded just like David."

"I did?"

"Yeah."

I shrugged. "Guess he was starting to rub off on me."

"Guess so."

"It started out as a way to tease me, you know." I smiled at a distant memory.

"What was?"

"*Baby*. The way Mike always calls me *baby*. It started because he was always faster, stronger and smarter than me. No matter how hard I tried, I could never beat him at any game or race or anything. So I'd sulk." I shrugged again. "He'd always call me a baby, then after a while, he just started saying it after pretty much everything he said, until one day it changed—there was a warmth behind the word that hadn't been there before, and"—I smiled—"I kinda liked that. It made me feel special."

"I guess I know what you mean. We kind of let almost anything go when they make us feel special, don't we?" Em twiddled her fingers in her lap, then exhaled as she stood up. "But let the record show: I don't like Mike. I don't think he's good enough for you."

"But he is good for me."

"They're not the same."

"Are in my world," I scoffed. "So, anyway, how do you know Jason?"

Emily stiffened, paling.

"Oh, now you *have* to tell me," I said, pointing at her.

Turning away, like gravity had turned her legs into iron, Emily leaned on my window frame and hugged herself.

"Em, are you okay?"

"It's nothing, Ara. Really. It was just a summer fling. It ended." She braved a teary glance at me as I stood beside her.

"Doesn't mean it didn't happen," I said.

The corners of her lips twitched, turning downward. "I was in love with him."

"Love?"

"Mm-hm." She grabbed a tissue from my desk and wiped her nose, nodding. "We dated for a while and then, when summer ended, he just left."

"Left? As in he moved, or he just didn't come back?"

"Just gone." She stood back, wiping her face again.

"Really? Without a goodbye?"

"Can you hear how fast my heart is beating?" She touched her chest. "That was the first time I've heard his voice in nearly a year."

"So, what, he never even left a note to say where he'd gone?"

"No, that was the worst part. He just didn't show for our date and stopped answering his phone. I asked David if he knew what was going on, but he said his brother was a player; that I'd just been one of his victims."

"Victims? That's a pretty cruel way to put it."

She nodded. "David had a way with words."

"Yeah, he did," I said with a laugh. "Actually, he told me his brother was a bit… *malevolent.* Why would you be with a guy like that, Em? You're gorgeous, you can do better."

"That's just it." She sniffled. "He wasn't like that at all. I don't know what David was talking about, but Jason was really sweet."

I smiled. Brotherly love. I guess it was the same as me telling everyone Sam was a troll. He wasn't actually a troll. And I was glad that Jason wasn't malevolent. I could never picture David's twin being a creepy, stalking vampire. I tried so many times, but putting the face of David on anything cruel just never fit.

"So, is it true that they're identical?"

"Yep." She nodded, eyes wide. "Like, *perfectly* identical."

"That must've been hard for you after Jason left, you know, being friends with David—always seeing his face."

"Not really. They are *very* different people. David's cute, but he has boundaries you can't cross. You can never be, like, *relaxed* with him."

I shrugged. "*I* could."

"I get that." Her sadness faded with a soft, distant smile. "I really do. It was the same with Jason and me. People always seemed to avoid him, you know, and I just didn't see what they saw."

The predator.

"He was gentle and loving and…" Em looked at my bed then. "He jumped through my window on the morning of our six-week anniversary and filled my room with frangipanis, waking me up by running one over my face." Her fingers traced the memory over her skin. "I loved him."

"Really?"

"Mm-hm. Enough that we talked about growing old together and what we'd name our kids."

"And then winter came."

She nodded. "Literally."

I wished I could tell her about the Set laws and bi-annual sabbaticals. She probably blamed herself deep down inside for making him leave. "Guys do that," I said instead. "Summer flings."

"I know." Emily lifted her hand from the fold of her arms and wiped another tear, nodding. "It just hurt to think we had something special, only to find out it was just a game."

"Is that what you really believe? That he was using you?"

"I never used to believe it—never wanted to. But it has to be the case. You don't just walk out on those you love."

I shrugged. "Maybe he was like David. Maybe he had secrets."

"No. I think they're both just assholes. I mean, how could David just go and leave like that? He *saw* how broken I was when Jason left. *He* was the one who picked up the pieces. Surely he must know what he's done. Why couldn't he have just said goodbye, at least to *me*?"

"Maybe he just thinks it's better this way."

"Better for who?"

I clicked my tongue. "I wish I could fix this, Em. I really do."

She shook her head, looking out the window. "There is no fixing it. There's not even any point. They're gone and we just have to move on."

"Exactly," I said, waving my ring hand in front of her.

Her smile wore a white flag. "I guess I see your point now. But… David still wants you, Ara. I'm sure of it. If I had that choice with Jason, I would've taken it. No matter what."

"I know." I rubbed her back gently. "Do you think he still thinks about you—Jason?"

Emily inhaled slowly, her eyes on the dreary day. "I hope so. I think about him from time to time. You never genuinely get over your first love, Ara. This"—she lifted my ring hand—"this will be a long journey for you."

"I know." I nodded. "Trust me, I know."

"Just… if Mike steals you away and takes you back to Oz, will we still be friends?"

"Of course," I said, dragging the word out. "I think we'll always be friends."

"I hope so," Em said sadly. "So, what does Mike think—about David? Does he know how you feel?"

I nodded. "He's okay with it."

Her eyes rolled as she looked out the window again. "I really don't like him."

"You don't have to like him, Em. I do."

"I know, but I think that…" she hesitated, "if he weren't here, you would've gone with David."

"Nup." I shook my head with certainty. "I wouldn't have."

With a shrewd smile suppressed, Em shrugged one shoulder. "I think you would."

As I said goodbye to Emily, Mike stood behind me with one hand in the small of my back and the other waving.

"She hates me," he said as her car disappeared.

"No. She just doesn't understand." I turned and closed the front door. "She thought David and I were a sure thing. So all of this"—I held up my ring hand—"is a little sudden for her."

"I get it. No offence taken. So?" He stood taller and grinned. "'Terminator' or 'The Mummy'?"

"You choose. I'll get popcorn." I grinned.

Mike walked up the stairs and when the door to his room closed, I headed into the kitchen.

"Hey, Dad."

"Hey, honey." He looked up from his newspaper for a second.

"Any good news?" I asked, opening the pantry.

"No news is the only good news," he scoffed.

I shook my head. "You know, Mom always said that, too."

"Did she?" he said absently, staring up blankly at the wall. And in that moment of unguarded expression, I could actually see his regrets.

With a soft sigh, I walked over to sit on the chair beside him. "How long, Dad? Before you stopped missing her when she left?"

He sniffed once and folded his paper, smoothing it out on the table. "Never."

"Never?"

He looked into my eyes then. "I *never* stopped missing your mother. Sure, after about ten years or so it got easier to bear, but I still miss her even now."

"Oh." I looked out the front window.

"I did wrong by her, Ara. I made one stupid mistake and I lost her.

But when you love someone like I loved her, you will always miss them. I try not to think of her if I can."

"But you love Vicki, right? Doesn't that make it easier?"

He nodded thoughtfully. "That's the only reason I didn't go back and beg your mom to forgive me. I did love Vicki—*do* love Vicki, I mean," he said with a laugh. "But I loved your mom, too."

It hurt to hear him speak of her in the past tense like that.

"I don't think you ever truly get over losing someone you love, but after time passes, you can get through the days without missing them so much," he added, probably in response to my horrified expression. He couldn't know how much I was relating his story to my own experiences with boys. He was the only person I could think of that suffered a loss as great as mine. I needed to know if there was a life after love—after true love. "Is this about David?" he asked.

"A little." I smiled at the table.

"Ara, Mike loves you. He's been trying to ask you to marry him for the last year." Dad cupped his hand warmly over mine. "He was so worried you'd turn him down that he almost asked me to ask you *for* him."

"Really?"

"Yes, honey. Look, I know you love David, but you loved Mike first. And if you thought you could move on from love once, then there's a good chance you can do it again, right?"

He was right. It was just going to take some time. But of course I'd move on eventually. Nothing ever lasted forever, right?

"See? That's why you're a teacher, Dad. The all-knowing." I waved my hands around in the air, then stood up and kissed him on the cheek. "Love you, Dad."

"Ara?"

I turned back to his insistent tone. "Yeah?"

"I uh… I need to talk to you."

"Okay…" I sat back down.

"I received a call today… from Ray Bougerstern."

"Dad!" I slammed my palms on the table and stood up.

"Ara. Sit back down. We need to discuss this."

"Why now?" I felt the blanket of fury wrap my shoulders. "Mike's waiting for me to watch a mo—"

"And he'll wait. You can't keep avoiding this. The insurance policy has cleared the account. I need to know what you want me to do with the money."

My lip quivered as I looked down at my feet. Blood money. The money a company paid out because my mother no longer existed. A consolation. Condolences in the form of green notes.

"Keep it. Give it to Sam."

"Ara. Your mother took that policy out so that you could take care of yourself if she were no longer around."

"I can do that without money, Dad!"

"No, you can't," his voice grumbled as it peaked above calm. "She's gone, Ara-Rose. She's not coming back, no matter what tortures you inflict upon yourself. No amount of your own suffering will change what happened." He reached for my hand. I kept it tight in the fold of my arms, biting my lip. "Honey, just take the money. Use it to start your life. Use it to—"

"You're not going to let this go, are you?"

"I'm sorry. I haven't wanted to bring it up again. I know it's hard for you, but—"

"Just put it in a trust fund," I said finally. "Put it in a high interest account until I turn eighteen or something."

"Thank you," Dad said with a nod. "I know what this means for you, Ara. I—"

"It means she's gone, Dad," I said, holding his gaze. "It means she's never coming back."

"I know, honey."

I nodded, upper lip stiff, then walked away so he wouldn't see me cry.

29

Dad and Mike played chess in the formal dining room, Vicki hung laundry on the clothesline, and Sam stood talking to Mr. Warner over the fence, but something about the lazy tone of the day made me edgy.

My old rope and wood companion rocked gently under me while I strummed my way through months of painful and also happy memories, trying to make some sense of it all. My life had changed so quickly from being a normal teenager going to school, practicing for my big ballet recital, to losing my family and then my first true love, all while discovering the existence of monsters. And perhaps that was it. Perhaps it wasn't the calm of the day that had my gut churning, but the monster called Truth: the knowing in my heart that, tonight, on the last stroke of midnight, the part of me that wouldn't believe David was gone would turn and look up at the clock tower on the chamber building, hoping he'd tap me on the shoulder. But both *me* and *myself* knew he wouldn't show.

For my own sanity, I blocked out the thoughts of David, strumming random chords on my guitar, while the representation of my confused brain paced around in my head, calling himself Holmes.

Nothing really made sense anymore. When bad things happened

to me in the past, I could usually always see some reason, some lesson I needed to learn from it after time passed. But everything over the last few months just seemed pointless.

I dropped my fingers from their position on the strings, letting the song die without a name.

The whole world seemed pointless.

I couldn't let my mind wander that path though: the trying-to-find-meanings-or-reasons path. Every time I walked that road, I came to the same conclusions, leaving that train of thought with nothing more than a large suitcase of frustration. Perhaps we were here to love, or to experience and overcome trials, or maybe even to *feel.* Who knew? Pain was the only constant thing in life. So maybe the meaning of life was to cram as much pain and heartache as we could into the puny timeline of our miserable existence.

Satisfied with that dismal conclusion, I started playing again, watching through the window as Dad and Mike mused over their chess game. It was like looking across the waters of reflection, reading the story of my life: two elements of my past—from different worlds—coming together in battle. And it occurred to me then, as I watched their hands meet in the offer of peace, that this was it: that was my Dad and my *fiancé.* There would be no more boys for me. Mike would be my first and my last. A chapter of my life had ended before it even began.

Maybe that's why my dad liked Mike so much; he'd never have to worry about me ending up with a loser—or alone. But that didn't save me from eternal loneliness.

By my foot, a grey fluff-ball meowed, rubbing his spine against my ankle.

"Feel like flying up into a tree, Skitz?" I joked, with a weak smile, as I placed the guitar on the ground and let my heart sink down with it.

The cat looked up at me, his big yellow eyes soft and round.

"Okay." I chuckled lightly. "Maybe I like you a little."

"I should hope you like me a lot, since you're marrying me."

"Hey, Mike? Did you win?"

"Nah." He placed his hand down on the grass, the rest of his body sinking into it. Skittles leaped onto his front paws, ready to run if Mike was a threat, but then he just closed his eyes without re-adjusting his position and started purring. Mike laughed at him. "Your dad's too quick. He beat me twice."

"He never beat my mom, you know? Not once," I said.

"Yeah? I didn't know that. I don't really remember much from the time when he lived with you."

I shrugged.

Mike jerked his head toward my bedroom window then. "You're not upstairs putting on your war paint?"

"It won't take long once I start."

"Hm." He picked a strand of grass and curled it around his finger.

"What's *hm*?"

"Are you sure you want to do this, baby? It's not too late to change your mind."

"About going to the ball?"

"No." Mike pushed up off the ground, shuffling over to kneel in front of me. "About marrying me. I'll be okay if you changed your mind."

"Why would you think I don't want to marry you?"

A watery glaze glimmered under the light of the sun in his eyes. "Since I asked you, you haven't been happy. Not really."

"I'm trying, Mike."

"I know. But is trying enough, Ara? Am *I* enough?" The pain in his words came through with the firm clasp of his fingers around my hips. Mike was scared, I could feel it. He had as much to lose here as I did. I mean, was love enough for this relationship to work when it wasn't enough for David and I?

"I just need to get away from here, I think, Mike." My voice trembled. "I think I wanna go home."

"Ara. Baby." He pulled the swing into him, wrapping me up in his arms. "That's fine. We'll go. We'll leave tomorrow, if you like?"

"I would, but I think we better plan it properly first." I flashed him a grin, which he returned.

"Aw, baby girl. You're gonna be so happy. I promise. I'll buy you a house and give you everything you want." He squeezed me way too tight, forcing me to hold my breath against the base of his jaw. "I love you so much."

"I love you too, Mike."

And that was the truth. It felt good. Normal. Like everything would once again be right again in the world, even if it wouldn't ever be right in my soul.

THE QUIET WHISPERS OF MY FAMILY LILTED UP THE STAIRS, carrying my mind back from the hold of a masked stranger's gaze. Her blue eyes stared out at me from a place and time I no longer belonged. She was the lie after the truth, hiding behind this beauty in a blue dress. And I couldn't stand the sight of her.

Somewhere, at some point, I'd split in two, and the innocent, dream-believing girl that tragedy left behind disappeared when David ran away with my heart. I was *his* picture of beauty, created *by* him, *for* him, but I'd never feel his cool fingers under the ribbon of my corset. The only thing left was the other half of me: the shell. And I'd dusted enough shimmer powder over my skin that I could almost disguise myself as a sparkly vampire. No one could see the depths of my darkness underneath.

Except Mike. He knew there was something different—that something had changed. But I bet he never even conceived of the idea that my depression went so deep that fleeting thoughts of suicide were slowly creeping into possibility. I'd overheard him tell my dad he was worried that I might be depressed. My dad just said it wasn't a chance but a fact, and all we could do was be here for me. But the ever-watchful eye of my fiancé was getting overbearing.

While I'd been lost in my own thoughts, the night had fallen into a complete and eerie silence; the crickets hushed, even the voices downstairs. Nothing I'd ever known could make the night go that still, except for a vampire lingering in the shadows.

I spun around and darted to my window with my heart in my throat, hope filling me as I held back the call of a name on my lips. But as I searched the darkness frantically, the quiet street below revealed nothing but a flickering streetlamp and that same emptiness I'd come to hate. The only thing out there was the beginning of another night. And for the rest of my life now, that's all there'd ever be.

Sadly, I closed my bedroom door and left it all behind, stopping when Dad looked up at me from the base of the stairs, his eyes brimming with tears.

"You okay, Dad?"

"You look so pretty, honey. Just like your first ballet concert."

"Uh, yeah, well, just don't lift me onto your shoulders this time."

"Why not? You're still my little girl."

I stopped on the last step. "I'm not a little girl, Dad."

"Honey, you'll *always* be my little girl."

"I wonder what's taking Ara so lo—" Mike stopped dead as he walked in, his lips splitting into a pearly grin, eyes sparkling behind a black mask. "Wow!"

"Hey, Mike."

He leaped up onto the step. "Look at you."

"You like it?" I brushed my hands down my hips.

He shook his head slowly, considering my dress. "More than the outfit I saw you in when I re-pierced your ear."

Dad's eyes narrowed at us.

I looked away, clearing my throat. I'd asked Mike to help me with my earring earlier while I was getting dressed, not really thinking about the fact that I was only in my underwear when he knocked on the door. But at least I got to show them off to *someone*. They were the prettiest, laciest and newest things I owned, and they deserved to be seen.

"Come on then." Vicki held a camera up and waved us off the stairs. "Time for pictures."

"Really?" I groaned, taking Mike's arm.

"Ara, this might be the last ball you ever go to," Vicki reasoned. "I want memories."

"Okay." I sighed, and Mike grinned at me with a kind of enthusiasm that wasn't there when he was forced to escort me to the high school dance last year.

Vicki posed us in awkward and weird places to snap her memories.

I stood in the warm embrace of my fiancé, smiling for reasons I could only pretend I felt, watching everything move as if it were a film with no volume. The voices, the wind, the laughter, it was all gone. Everything in my world was kind of silent, empty. Wrong. This should have been David; it was always supposed to be David.

But once upon a time, I'd have said the same about Mike.

Everything was back where it was before—before the universe flipped the hourglass, before I lost everything in my world that grounded my soul, and before I ever knew anything about David Knight.

It was an odd learning curve, and a painful one, but I just had to accept it. When I got home, when I landed in Perth and went home to Mike's house, *she* wouldn't be there. Mom was gone. Harry was gone. And I had to move on.

This was moving on.

I closed my eyes and let the world pass by for a moment, feeling it whirl like the snow in a musical glass dome. When I opened them again, fairy lights twinkled from the tall white trunks of bare trees, and soft music eased my soul as sound suddenly enhanced my world again.

An almost magical glow seemed to surround the old council chambers, standing majestically as the backdrop to the candle-lit space, where masked dancers twirled with hypnotic cadence, sweeping and bowing to the harmonics of a string quartet.

Mike and I stood at the cusp of the wooden dance floor, surrounded by the beautiful gowns, but my eyes delighted only in the canopy of stars observing the Masquerade from a kingdom above.

"Do you recognize anyone?" Mike asked.

I shook my head, feeling a little lost, like I was alone in the crowded space. The dance floor, the stairs, and even the balcony off the council chamber were filled with people—all masked, just like me—but for all I felt in my soul, the court could've been completely empty.

"Would you like some refreshments before we dance?" Mike gestured toward the balcony.

"I'm fine."

"Would you like to dance?" He bowed, offering his hand.

"Not really."

"Aw, come on, Ara. First rule of a dance is never to refuse a dance," he said with a grin, stealing my hand.

I gave in with a warm smile and sunk into a curtsy. Then, with one step over the threshold of the dance floor, he swept me into his safe, strong arms, and we joined the flow of dancers like a rose petal on the breeze, never missing a beat. I followed each step of Mike's wide stride elegantly, closing the movement with a short, gliding turn.

"When did you learn to dance like this?" I asked, impressed.

"Well, a guy's gotta know a few tricks if he's gonna get the girl." He flashed his cheeky grin, and a small flutter started my heart.

"I like this new you," I said, turning my head to rest it on his shoulder.

"Good, because this is the me you'll be marrying."

The music faded out then, and the room came to a standstill. Mike kissed my hand and bowed, while the rest of the crowd softly applauded the musicians.

"Can we go find Em and the others now?" I asked.

"Of course. This is your night. We can do whatever you want." He looked over his shoulder. "Come on, we'll go to the balcony. It'll be easier to see from up there."

As we passed through the crowd, I leaned closer to Mike, feeling too many eyes on me. "What are they staring at?"

"You," he stated.

"Why? Is my bra showing?" I quickly tucked my thumb around the rim of my dress.

"No, baby." He laughed, pushing my hand down. "It's just because you're the brightest thing in the room."

Shrinking into myself, I glanced at the other costumes: pale grey, coffee, burgundy, black. No blue. I was the only girl in a color this bright.

"Great. I feel like a wasp at a bumblebee convention."

Mike laughed. "Well, you look like the flower."

"Erg." I rolled my eyes, but secretly gushed.

We stopped by the marble balcony railing and looked down onto the room of dancers, swirling under a blanket of stars, and I felt like a god between worlds.

"Wow, it's so much prettier from up here."

"Yeah. These Yanks really know how to throw a shindig."

"Yanks?" I raised a brow at him.

He just grinned, inching away from the slap he expected. But as he went to lean on the railing again, he stopped, watching a young couple giggle their way into the darkness on the other side of the chamber court.

"What's down there?"

I looked, too. The gardens were dark tonight. The lights that usually lit the paths winding through the endless trees and wide plains of grass were switched off; an obvious attempt to deter hot-blooded teens. Little did the planning committee realize, dark spaces made it so much easier to be… 'romantic'.

"Do you think your friends might be down there?"

"Nah," I said with a sigh. Above, the clock on the tower chimed nine, its hollow, long tolls haunting and dreary, like warning bells down the streets of death and plague.

Mike nodded a few times, his eyes narrowing. "You're missing *him*, aren't you?"

I drew a breath and nodded. There was no point in lying.

"I'm sorry," he said, looking down at his clasped hands.

"Mike," I started, "it's—"

"Hey, there you are." Before I even spun around, Emily wrapped her arms over my shoulders and squeezed. I gave Spencer, who stood awkwardly in the dust cloud of Emily's enthusiasm, a short wave. "We've been looking everywhere for you guys."

"Yeah, sorry." I stood back from her, swiping my hair from my face. "But we're here now. And look at you!"

Emily twirled around to show her long blonde ponytail in a spiral down her back, and the perfect fit of the dress.

"I can't believe how grown-up you look," I finished.

"Yeah, my mom says—" She stopped and looked beside us when Mike and Spencer shook hands. "Oh yeah, sorry guys. Um, Mike, Spence; Spence, Mike."

"G'day." Mike grinned.

"So you're Ara's fiancé?" Spence looked at me for confirmation.

"The one and only," I said. Mike grinned as I linked my arm with his. He liked that. I could tell. And I liked that he liked it. "So, Spencer? You scrub up nice," I added.

"Yeah, thanks. You're not so bad yourself, Ara." He appraised my gown.

"Where's Alana?" I asked.

"Haven't seen her." Emily shrugged.

We looked over the crowd of dancers for a moment. Each one was hidden beneath a mask of feathers or sequins, their hair drawn up in dazzling ringlets or left down to flow over their shoulders. It seemed futile to find a friend among them. Then I spotted a girl at the center of the dance floor with a tall, sandy-blond-haired boy. Her cream-and-black dress with pink accents of lace took my breath away, fitting Alana's description of her hand-me-down perfectly.

Mike looked over my shoulder, following my gaze. "Wow. That's quite a dress."

"Oh, wow." Emily sighed, leaning against the railing beside me.

"And Ryan looks so... vintage," I added.

"They make a good couple," Mike noted.

"Yeah. I'm a good matchmaker." Emily grinned, hiding her piercing, Mike-directed gaze of abhorrence under her mask.

I got the sense then that maybe she really did hate him.

"Well, Miss Ara." Spencer bowed to me. "I believe you owe me a dance."

Emily gave me a smile of approval.

"Very well, Mr. Griffin. It would be my pleasure," I said in a formal English accent, then hooked my arm over Spencer's.

Mike walked behind us with Emily on his arm. I felt a little sorry for him, knowing Emily would probably step on his toes deliberately.

We danced, the flow and magic of the masquerade concealing my pain and emptiness for just a while. Passed from arm to arm, I danced with about six different guys, and when I finally fell back into Mike's embrace as the first stroke of midnight chimed through the air, my head was swirling like a room full of butterflies.

The enchanting tone of the evening burst into a spectrum of color above us then, with blue and pink electrifying the skies before dissipating into yellows and whites as they dissolved among the stars. Everyone stood still, tilting their faces upward, while the clock chimed each agonizing toll of realization.

Midnight.

The music played on, saddening my heart with its desultory notes. All the beauties around us smiled in awe at the colors of the end, while my heart fought to ignore the somber melody of loss and separation.

He wasn't coming. David really wasn't coming.

Mike pulled me close, pressing his fingers firmly between my shoulder blades. "I love you, Ar. You know that, don't ya?" he whispered.

Wiping the tears from my lips and cheeks, I looked up at his face, hearing the last chime of midnight pass and take all my hopes with it. "Mm-hm."

"Then don't cry," he said sweetly, and the fireworks cracked over his words, echoing off the horizon. But the noise faded into the background when his lips touched mine, flooding back as he broke away with a cool wash of air and looked over his shoulder.

"May I?" a gentle voice asked, and a tall stranger stepped into view. His soft brown hair caught the light as it fell over his eyes, and though his face was hidden behind a black mask, he was instantly recognizable.

David?

Police Dept.
Suspect List:

~~Jason Knight~~
Unknown

Description:

Hair: Dark brown

Eyes: green

Height: Unknown

30

Mike kissed my cheek and took a step backward, giving the last dance of the evening away to this guy he'd never met. He didn't even ask if I knew him.

My heart raced, breath quickening. But it all stopped. All the hope, all the excitement just trickled away when his cold touch met mine with no familiarity.

It wasn't him. It wasn't David.

The stranger swept my hips toward him, his green eyes locked to mine. "Moonlight Sonata," he said in a smooth, gentle voice, gesturing toward the piano. "Your favorite piece."

"One of." I squinted against the dark, trying to see him better beneath the mask. "Do I know you?"

He shook his head once and said nothing more.

The song's harmonies set the pace to his stride, while the elegance in his stance seemed to be adopted from another era: one hand gently resting under my shoulder blade, the other extending our arms out widely. He seemed ill-placed, not of this time, which was unnerving.

Immediately, the curiosity and fear subsided for a sweeping wave of romance, my mind slipping in to a dream-like state. A state I'd only felt once before, when I first tried to kiss David.

I looked up at the guy, his smile showing only by the dimple beside the curve of his lip, and a strange sensation saturated the air: a feeling like energy closing me in, making this dance a secret from the rest of the world.

From the sideline, Mike stood watching with his arms folded, whispering to Alana and Ryan every few seconds. I wondered if he could see us; if he could see the way this stranger held me; if he found it odd that he pulled me so close, like he'd held me there a thousand times before. All the laws of nature said he could, but I *felt* invisible.

"Can you feel that?" I asked.

He turned his head an inch and looked down at me, his mysterious eyes dark and foreboding. "I'm the one doing it."

I looked at Mike again—having a thumb war with Spencer—and my heart hurried a little. I wanted him to come over here, tap this guy on the shoulder and ask for me back.

"Our dance is not yet complete, my lady." He squeezed my hand gently, tightening his hold on my back. "It would be incredibly rude to leave a man in the middle of the dance floor. You wouldn't want to be rude, would you?"

"I'm sorry. I didn't mean to be," I said softly, and something inside me screamed, wriggling about, warning me to move away. But I stayed in his arms, smiling his smile as we passed each dancer, softly nodding my head in greeting. It felt unnatural.

When the music ended, he stopped and clapped gently. "Thank you, my lady."

"You're welcome," I said, but made no haste to move away from him. I stood, staring up at him like a stuffed animal, and with clarity returning outside the circle of his arms, a name suddenly came to mind. "Jason?"

"Très bien, mademoiselle." He stood taller, his lip creasing in one corner, leaving the smile to come only from behind his eyes, the way David's did when he read my mind.

"You look so much like him."

Jason exhaled and offered his arm. "Walk with me?"

"Where to?"

"Just to the balcony," he said, curling my hand into the crook of his elbow.

We passed right by Mike and my friends, who didn't even look up as this stranger led me away from the dance floor.

"It's a beautiful night, wouldn't you agree?"

"A perfect night." I leaned on the marble railing, watching the other dancers in the final act.

"Perfect for one's last," he said softly.

"Last?"

Self-amusement slathered Jason's expression. "I meant that if this were your last night, it would be a grand way to spend it."

"Yeah." I looked down at the dance floor again. "I guess so."

"Do you know why I've come?"

I shook my head. "Are you here because of David?"

"In ways." His eyes focused on something distant, while the same malignant smile as before settled onto his dark-pink lips, sending shivers down my spine. Bad shivers.

"Where is he?" I asked.

"In pain, I suspect."

"What do you mean by that?"

Jason turned and leaned on the ledge, his back to the crowd below. "I mean you hurt him. Badly. I would imagine he's wallowing in self-pity, at this time."

"What would *you* know about it?"

"I know you gave him your heart, then denied him your future."

"That's none of your business," I snapped, turning to walk away.

His hand lashed out and caught my arm, spinning me into his chest with a breathtaking jolt. "On the contrary, my dear, it is."

"And what makes it your business?" I wedged the heel of my palm into his chest. "Let go of me."

When a few curious glances flicked our way, Jason placed his hand firmly on my lower back and forced my arms into position. "Dance with me."

"No."

"Then I'll make you." He held me tighter, spinning us around like we were just two masked teens in love. I tried to fight him, but he was strong. He didn't look that strong, but his hold was unyielding.

As each person passed us, my eyes searched theirs, pleading for help. But it was like they didn't notice me here at all. When it became clear that help was not coming, I moved my attention back to the eerie vampire, trying to figure out what he wanted from me.

"Let's just say," he answered my thought, his simpering eyes shrinking behind that black mask, "I'm not here for pleasure."

"Well," I said, sounding amazingly calm, while the pulse between my collarbones seemed to shoot out through my spine, filling me with a sudden urge to run. I cast my eyes to the dance floor, but Mike was gone. "If it's not pleasure, it must be business. What business do you have here?"

"The concluding of an age-old quarrel among brothers. One you so, unfortunately, have found yourself a part of."

"What quarrel? And what do you mean that I'm a part of it?"

Jason's head moved a fraction of an inch, the green in his eyes occupying the corners. "Someone is looking for you."

I followed his sideways gaze to see Mike running through the crowd—panicked, touching the shoulders of various individuals—obviously desperate to find me.

Look up, Mike, look up.

"I'll kill him, Ara. If he comes for you, he will die."

"Why?" I gasped.

"It's nothing personal, really." He cocked his head, taking me in with a creepy leer. "Then again, perhaps it is."

I stared at him in confusion as he laughed. "What have I ever done to you?"

"Nothing. I'm just going to hurt you to hurt my brother."

My mouth fell open with a huff. "Don't you dare touch me!"

"Oh, I'm going to do worse than *touch* you."

"No!" I sunk my knees down and slipped free from his hold, but he grabbed my arm before I found my feet to run, and forcibly walked us toward the dark chamber gardens. "Let me go, Jason," I ordered, "I'll scream."

He just smiled wickedly, keeping his eyes on our destination. "You won't scream. Because I'll kill them. All of them. I will drink down every last life in this miserable gathering, and I will save *you* until the end, make you watch as I tear apart your friends and eviscerate your replacement lover."

"You can't do that." I tugged hard against him. "Your society has laws!"

"And I have planned this meticulously, so that I act within the limits of those laws," he advised, revealing the true depths of his cunning. "So come quietly, or I will honor my threat."

"No." I drove my thumb between his hand and my arm, trying to unwind his fingers, but they tightened, his nails digging in. "Let me go!"

He just smiled malignantly to himself, lip curving up on one side.

As we neared the step, my darting gaze of desperation flicked around the balcony, passing over the smiles of distracted couples. But no one was familiar. No one knew me. No one knew I was being kidnapped. And not one of the faces was David. He was supposed to be here. He was supposed to come. The last dance on the hour of midnight. That was the deal.

The haunting piano ceased below us, and the gentle clicking of applause filled the air as Jason pulled me along, attempting discretion and, to my amazement, achieving it.

We stopped by the stairs, waiting as a few flushed couples emerged from the darkness, straightening their clothes. Jason smiled at them knowingly, drawing me in to conceal his tight grip within the closeness of our bodies. It made my skin crawl to feel the fabric of his suit against my arm, but when I tried to push my hips away from his, he hooked his foot around my ankle.

"If you bring attention to yourself, young lady, I will dig my fingertip into your flesh and cut your bone in half."

"And then I'll scream, and everyone will know there's something wrong."

"Go ahead," he said. "I'll just kill them all. But you will still have a severed bone."

I stopped struggling, taking shallow breaths to suppress the deep urge to fight, and when I looked at my hand against the lapels of

Jason's jacket, my ruby ring standing out like midnight blood, Mike's face—the way he smiled when I accepted his proposal—came to mind. All those things that seemed lost right now filled my heart with regret. I wanted Mike to come, wanted him to save me. And a part of me didn't care about anyone else in the room; a part of me just wanted to scream out while I still had the chance. But if I even indulged in the idea, I'd be risking Mike's life too.

"Mike can't help you now, anyway. He's only human."

David could help me. I…

"David will not help you, either. He's not coming back for you." Jason's eyes flooded with amusement as he looked down at the cold liquid running from my nose and eyes, trickling past my quivering lip. "But you already knew that, didn't you?"

I shut my eyes tight, flooding with regret.

"It's quite the poetic ending, really: you despised him, shunned him because you could not become the beast he is. Yet, in dying, your beautiful face and body will be marred beyond recognition, crafting you, essentially, into an *eternal* beast."

"What are you…?" A rush of panic became a steel band around my lungs. "What are you going to do to me?"

"Just have a little fun with your body before I kill you."

"No!" The fright left my lips in an uncontrolled wail, but several other cries came from nearby and drowned out my own. Couples parted, nearly toppling over the railing as a bulk figure burst through them on the stairs.

Jason slowly turned his head, gaze meeting Mike's for a split second, as a lifetime of comprehension passed the invisible barrier between them.

Mike's face paled with realization. Then, he started running.

I wriggled in Jason's arms, torn between reality and the paranormal. I couldn't let my world touch Mike's—couldn't let him die for me, no matter how badly I wanted to be saved. If I broke free and landed safely in his arms, it would only be for his last breath.

"Jason!" I gasped in a low voice. "Run!"

"As you wish."

In that moment, as he reached down and swept me off the

ground, Mike knew. I closed my eyes and prayed as the darkness closed me in, seeing Mike's face, seeing all hope slip for that one heartbeat when he knew, to his core, that he would never see me again.

An icy chill and the rush of speed beneath my feet ended suddenly, making the blood hurt my head. I opened my eyes again to kaleidoscope shadows of leaves on my hands and dress, as the last dregs of light from the clock tower filtered down through them. Jason spun me at the shoulders and pointed past the border of the forest to the top of the stairs.

"Look at him," he whispered, his lips to my ear. "I want you to suffer as you witness his suffering."

Mike grasped the railing and leaned into the night, searching the darkness as my name echoed, his voice breaking beneath the panic.

"He won't give up, you know," I said.

"Then he'll die."

I looked back at Jason and, seeing the seriousness in his eyes, slowly looked upon my Zorro one last time. Mike's hands flew into his hair, gripping tightly as he sunk down onto the step.

"That's quite a warrior you have there," Jason said. "Perhaps I should oblige him to a duel?"

"You came here for me. You leave him out of this," I warned, clenching my fists.

Jason watched again for a second as Emily landed beside Mike, her head whipping up a moment later to search the gardens before she took off up the stairs, running.

Mike looked up at the sky and then reached into his pocket, his phone lighting his face a second later.

"My dad. He's calling my dad."

"No," Jason said. "He's calling the police."

The severity of the situation hit me then. I drew a shaky breath, the frosty pine-scented wind grazing my throat. "You won't get away with this."

"That was never the plan."

And that made this so much scarier. My shoulders slowly inched toward my jaw. "I don't want you to hurt me."

"Of course you don't," he said, amused. "It wouldn't be any fun if you did."

"Fun? This is fun for you?"

He turned to me, slowly spreading his fingers over his mask to draw it away, revealing a face that made me want to cry. "To a degree."

"You're sick, Jason." I looked away from the eyes of my David, offensive on this vile man.

"I'm not the sick one. Your *beloved* vampire ex is."

"David?" I scoffed. "At least *he* would never take an innocent life for revenge."

Jason's sudden burst of laughter was revoltingly boyish and sincere; a different kind of laugh to his brother's. "Oh, that's right. You think he's kind and compassionate."

"I don't *think*. I *know*."

He spun around about a foot away and bowed with humor, crossing his hands over his stomach theatrically. "My dear, young lady, you *have* been kept in the dark, haven't you?"

"Not as far as I'm concerned." I wedged my hands onto my hips.

"As far as you're concerned?" He stood tall again, walking toward me. "As far as *you* are concerned, my sweet girl, he is a vile, disgusting vampire who kills people with his teeth; not good enough for you to love eternally. Is it any wonder he might have done something terrible in his past that, perhaps, hurt another?"

"Like what?"

"Like killing the girl I was in love with!" Jason's cold breath infected the side of my face as he sprung up suddenly in front of me, whispering his next words into my skin. "And I intend to repay him the favor."

I jerked away, shoving him. "Go ahead, Jason. If you're going to kill me, just get it over with."

"Excuse me?"

"You heard me." I wiped my stiff upper lip, rolling my shoulders back. "I'm tired of this. In fact, since you obviously want to taint his honor with your little story about how *evil* David is, why not break into a bad-guy monologue?" I challenged. "Maybe you can get stuck in it just long enough for me to escape."

Jason's hand moved swiftly, and every muscle in my throat seized up, the blood filling my head above the cage of his fingers. "Do not speak to me with such contempt, you haughty little bitch." He thrust his arm downward, slamming me to the floor.

I coughed out, clenching the grass in a small fist as I tried to catch my breath, half-suffocating under the rattling of my heart.

The predator towered over me, ready for his next move.

"Just leave me alone." I sniffled, rolling onto my knees and tearing the mask from my face.

"Leave you alone?" He knelt beside me and snatched the mask. "Why would I go and do a thing like that? Especially now you're crying again."

"What's that got to do with it?" I asked, dabbing a finger under my lashes.

"She cried. She begged him to stop." He turned my jaw until it faced him. I wouldn't look into his eyes, though. "You, my dear, have only reached phase one of your torture."

"Then what's phase two?" I asked through my teeth, scrunching the grass tightly. "If you're going to kill me, I'd rather not drag this out playing guessing games."

"Oh, but my lovely girl, games are half the fun. They're what will climax the ending when I show him the way I hurt you," he said in a kind voice, like he was talking to a child. "Finally, he will get to see how it feels to watch someone *he* loves die at the hands of someone he's trusted his whole life."

"You *saw* him kill the girl you loved?" My whisper came out ragged, my throat raw.

"I did—in his memories." He seemed to choke, visibly struck by the recollection. "You cannot fathom the disgusting things he did to her, Ara. You cannot comprehend what she suffered in those last moments."

"So *you're* going to be the one to *make* me understand?" I said sarcastically.

"I don't need you to understand. I need *him* to understand." Jason thumbed a tear away from my chin. "But first, let me make you see."

When his hand came up fast I cowered, shielding my cheek, but he shoved my wrist away, gripping both sides of my face to pull me closer.

"What're you doing?" I screeched, nose to nose with this man who meant to hurt me.

"Blessing you with the gift of insight." He squeezed my face tighter as I fought him. "Sit still."

"No. I don't want you to touch me."

"You need to see this," he said, breathless. "You need to know what you're dying for."

"Why?"

"Why?" His voice broke, weighted with raw grief. "Because it matters."

And a small part of me actually felt a pang of pity for him then. I held my breath, listening for the voices in the distance calling my name. All I wanted was to run to them, to get away, but he pressed his thumbs under my eyes to hold me in place.

"Take a deep breath, Ara."

"Please—don't." As his icy touch sent a sharp jolt through my cheek, I jerked back, wriggling like a fish on a hook. Pushing my wrists down on his forearms only made him grip tighter, the indentation a warning that he'd crack my skull. "Get off me, it hurts."

"I know."

"Please." I tugged at his thumbs. "Please stop."

"Close your eyes," he ordered. "It will hurt less."

A whimpering cry shook the back of my throat. I swallowed hard, scrunching my eyes tightly over the hot, stinging tears, and drew a quick breath when I saw a girl. She looked like a memory, one that didn't belong to me, but she was as clear as a reflection.

"Rochelle, Rochelle, Rochelle," a man sung her name, standing over her where she cowered in the corner, her head in her arms. I looked down at her bare toes, her golden legs, and the honey blonde hair falling over her shoulder. She looked just like Emily.

"Yes." Jason's grip eased and the stinging in my face turned numb and cold. "She did. Will you sit still now?"

As I nodded, the film became clearer. The girl looked up, her eyes round with fright, her whole body convulsing uncontrollably.

David knelt beside her and softly ran his fingers down her arm, taking her hand to kiss it. "Such a pretty little thing. It's a pity you had to cry, Rochelle—you really are repulsive when you snivel."

She buried her face again, her delicate, feminine voice so high with fear. "Please. Please let me go."

He smiled softly. "I will. I just have to do something first."

"W-what?" Even in a quiet voice, her French accent was so thick.

His hand slid along her ankle and up her leg, coming to rest on her knee. "If you promise to lie still, I will be gentle."

"No. Please!"

"Don't beg, Rochelle." He unfastened the top button on her dress, parting the collar. "It won't hurt for long."

"Va te faire foutre, trouduc." She spat on him.

"You dirty little whore!" He thrashed the back of his hand across her chin with lip-splitting force.

I squealed, covering my mouth as she did.

"Shh." Jason squeezed my face. "You'll expose our position to your little hunting party."

"I'm sorry," I said.

"Just watch." He pushed my mind closer to the memory: David lowered his face to the girl's and whispered something in her ear, turning her cheek to lick the blood from it after.

My chest squeezed.

"Your taste does not really appeal to me," he said.

"Then let me go."

"I would, if you were merely my next meal, but I'm here for another reason."

"What reason?"

"My brother does not have the courage to do what must be done." He ran his finger down the opening in her dress, pushing it off her shoulder. "This is not personal, Rochelle. It's just business."

"What must be done?" I said. "What?"

"Please?" she shrieked. "Please don't, David, I'm p—"

"Shh." He covered her mouth, slipping behind her and cradling her spine to his chest. "It will be over soon."

She hummed her aversion in the back of her throat, tugging at his hand, but like Jason, he was too strong for her.

"It hurts more if you fight, Rochelle," he whispered into her hair, meticulously rolling her head to expose the vein on her neck. "I'll try not to enjoy this."

"David, no!" My squeal broke off as he sank his teeth in, yanking the girl's head back until a bone broke through her collar. I covered my face, trying to hide from the reality.

"Look at it. You need to see."

"Please, Jason. Please don't make me watch."

He ripped my hands from my face. "You *will* watch."

As I looked back into the memory, David's eyes met mine, disturbing my soul with the ferocity behind them, and tearing out my every ill-conceived notion that he was human, anywhere inside. I hated him then. I saw the monster he'd warned me about so many times, and I *hated* him.

Sobbing loudly, I watched his victim go limp in his arms, her last breath releasing in a whisper, "David?"

He moved closer.

"I'm pregnant."

I drew back as the realization flooded my angry soul, bringing a cascade of tears down my cheeks.

Rochelle faded.

David dropped her lifeless corpse to the floor, letting her head hit the ground, her neck twisting awkwardly as she fell. Then, he stood up and walked away. His heavy black boots were the last thing I saw in the memory before reality washed in like cold water on my face, making me jump involuntarily.

"Jason," I cried. "I'm so sorry."

All I could see was her face as she tried to beg David—heartless, merciless, and unrelenting David—for her life.

Jason wrapped his arms around his knees and crossed his ankles where he sat on the grass beside me, looking like something so far from a vile predator that it was hard to be afraid of him. "This is the pain I've lived with for so long. Do you see now?"

"I don't want to see it." I rolled forward, rooting my trembling hands to the grass, my soft curls sticking to the tears around my lips. "Please get it out of my head."

"I can't. You own it now."

I couldn't breathe. I couldn't believe what I'd just seen. "Why? Why did he kill her?"

"The child."

"He killed her because she was pregnant?"

He nodded once. "At the preliminary hearing, he claimed he was keeping the peace—ridding the world of an unauthorized half-blood."

"Did he… was he ordered to do that?"

"No. He took it upon himself."

"Then how do you know that's why he killed her? How do you know it wasn't an attempt to change her so you could keep her?"

Jason stiffened. "He tried that one. Outside the council chamber, alone, he told me he meant it as a surprise—that he lied to the King about his reasons in order to avoid punishment."

"Then why didn't she change?"

"Even if he was speaking the truth, even if he meant to change her, only one soul can be immortalized, or they will both die."

"So, then, maybe he didn't know she was pregnant?"

"My brother is not ignorant, Ara, you know this."

I exhaled. He was right. David always had the upper hand. Always. Nothing got past him. "You loved her—like he loves me?"

The grip around his knees tightened. "She was *everything* to me. Fifty years has passed, and that has not changed."

"But… now you're planning to do the same thing to David. Don't you know what I am to him?"

He studied my face with repugnance. "Yes, and I will take that from him."

My head rocked from side to side in astonished, intensely maddening disbelief. How could my David be capable of such horror?

"I know it means nothing to you, Jason," I whispered, "but… I am so *so* sorry."

"You're right. It means nothing to me. And it changes nothing," he said resolutely. "Now you know why you must die."

"Ara!"

I looked up to the sound of Mike's voice. He was close. So close that if I dared to scream, he'd find me.

Without warning, Jason swept me from the wet grass and threw me over his shoulder. All the blood rushed into a tight pulse in my lips and cheeks, making it hard to see, leaving only the whipping breeze as evidence of the ground moving beneath us. I didn't care if he took me away, though. I hung limply over his shoulder, unable to feel anything anymore. All I could think about were Rochelle's eyes in her last moments—the fear, the desperation for her life and that of her unborn child—while a soft whisper repeated itself on my breath, "David. How could you?"

31

We broke through the trees into a clearing, and a dense shadowy darkness overtook. The only lights around were a thousand twinkling stars in the sky and the distant flash of police lights at the council chamber.

Jason set me down in the long grass, my bare toes sinking into the dewy soil. I hadn't even noticed my shoes fell off until now.

The voices of the hunters were as faint now behind the height of the towering trees around us as the soft, magical music of the ball, still playing, perhaps to keep the patrons calm. But I knew they could search all night, put posters up on every tree, phone every television station in the world, and they would never find me.

"They *will* find you," Jason said, his voice revealing his position in the darkness. "Once I'm finished with you, that is."

"What!"

"It's an element of the theatrics, Ara. They have to find you. I have to share my craftsmanship."

"Please, Jason. Don't," I begged, reaching for the place my silver locket used to rest. "Just think about it for a second."

"Ara-Rose, I *have* thought about it—for a very long time." He appeared in front of me, laughing to himself. "I know exactly what I'm going to do to you, and how deeply it will wound those that find you."

I swallowed, trying to be strong. "Then why haven't you done it yet? Are you waiting for some perfect moment?"

As he stepped forward, the darkness lifted, leaving shadows around his eyes like hollow, yawning caves. "I'm a vampire; we like to *play* with our food."

"I'm not your food. You came here to kill me. That makes me a murder victim. Not dinner."

"Yes, I suppose it does." His sudden grip sent a rush of blood shooting from my arm to my heart. He jerked me closer, his orange-chocolate scent tainting every beautiful memory David had connected it to. "But still, I have a few games—things I want you to suffer before I kill you."

"Don't do that," I said, pushing his chest but unable to get my arm free. "Don't keep saying things like that."

"You really are such a stupid little thing, aren't you?" he said with a laugh. "Or perhaps brave—making demands of your reaper."

"I'm not afraid of you."

"You should be."

Something exchanged between us then, a kind of knowing that came from experience; it was as if I could see every thought beyond the darkness of his eyes. He wanted to do something to me then. What it was, I didn't know, but it made me suddenly not so sure of myself.

"Do you know what his favorite film genre is? Did he tell you?"

"Horror." I nodded, eyes on the ground.

"With that in mind, I thought I might make this little tragedy as gruesome an end as I could dream up." He walked slowly around me, the feel of his eyes gliding over every bare inch of my skin, stopping in front of me with his cold breath moist on my brow. "But that won't be easy. His mind is already twisted, already desensitized from the horrors he both enjoys watching and inflicting. I had to get creative in what I came up with for you."

I closed my eyes, crossing my forearms over my chest. I wanted to retort, but his cold, calculating voice made me feel sick and dirty.

"I've touched your hair before," Jason whispered, grasping a handful of my curls and pressing them to his nose. "I watched you while you slept, and I never intended to touch you, but your hair…" He breathed in deeply, closing his eyes. "You smell so pretty. Did he ever tell you that?"

I nodded.

"And it's not just your blood; it's you, your human cosmetics, your hair, your clothes. All of you." He considered the chocolate-brown curls against his palm for a moment, running his thumb over them. "This is easier than I thought."

"What is?" I asked, my shaky breath brushing warmly across my tear-stained lips.

"I was sure your beautiful face would force compassion within me, but"—he shook his head, dropping my hair—"I feel nothing for you, as if you were merely a dog who had bitten a child. I just want to see you dead in the worst way possible."

My crossed arms tightened.

"And don't get me wrong: I do see this as a waste of life—beautiful life. I will not deny the fact that you are undeserving of this, Ara, but I cannot let you live. You understand this, I hope?" He lifted my chin. "However, I would like to dance with you one last time before I begin."

My body moved with his, close, circling like two birds falling mid-flight. The feel of his cool fingers at the ribbon of my corset and the softness of his palm against mine made me wish only that I were his; *his* girl, for *him* to touch, to love, to hold. I wanted to be a part of him, as I once was with David.

He spun me out from his body gracefully, and I twirled back into his chest, completely intoxicated by his spell, and entirely aware of it too. We swayed together under the cool breeze, surrounded by the trees, where no one could see us and no one would ever find us—not until he was finished with me.

"Beg me not to kill you," he whispered against my hair. "Beg me, and I will show you mercy."

"I—" My throat tightened, eyes spilling with tears as I looked into his. He was just like David. But he was going to kill me no matter how much I begged. And the worst part was, it didn't matter to me because, as if a thread of finely woven silk had bound us, I was unable to resist. I *wanted* him to kill me; I *wanted* him to hurt me first.

"That's not a very convincing plea for your life, Ara," he said.

The faint blue sparkle surrounding my thoughts persisted like delirium consuming an otherwise rational mind. I smiled up at him, wishing we would dance this way together forever. "What are you doing to me, Jason? Why doesn't anything make sense?"

"Hush now, sweet girl. I am making this easier by allowing you to feel safe with me. It is one of *my* many talents."

"But I—"

"Shh. This is a time-limited extension of kindness."

My throat fought hard for its own vocabulary. But he smelled just like David, and I missed him so much I just wanted to believe he was David; to imagine for one last moment that I was in his arms, that I still mattered to him.

"Close your eyes and you shall believe it."

"You can never be him. And you'll just be closer to becoming the monster he is by killing me." My gaze delved deep into his hollow, shadowed eyes. "But you will never have a heart like his, and I will never give you mine."

His hands slipped from my waist, and an icy rush tore away the cloud of my confusion, leaving behind a sudden explosion of terror.

"I don't *want* your heart, you stupid girl." He peeled me from the closeness of his body, tossing me off to the side by my arm. The long ball gown caught under my toes and I tipped backward, a sharp sting ripping through my hand as it caught me against the ground. Before I could even find the source of the sudden pain, blood gushed out over my fingertip. I screamed, pinching the edge of a partially detached nail, my arm shaking like glass in an earthquake.

"Ooh." Jason stood over me, wincing. "Nasty. You'll need to fold that back or it'll come right off."

"I know!" I yelled at him, trying to use my thumb to roll the nail back in place, but every time I touched it, it shifted and the pain intensified, closing in around me as if I were in a red box.

"Settle down." Jason took my hand and straightened my arm out to the side, away from my line of sight, and...

"Ah!" I screamed, the sound reducing to a tiny whimper as the agony receded. When Jason released me, I doubled over and wept breathlessly into my skirt, the blood staining the blue. I just wanted to go home. I didn't want to die like this. Not like this.

"Ara, look at me."

I struggled to push myself up to my knees, falling on my elbows each time.

The killer just watched. I couldn't even look at his face to see if he was enjoying it. I felt pathetic and helpless, humiliated by my own whimpering. But I couldn't stop it. It just kept coming out.

"Why are you crying like that?" He grabbed my arm to help me.

I tried to speak, but the words had no shape. They were just distraught sobs, like an hysterical child. All the anger had trickled away with realization: he wasn't playing games. He really was going to kill me. This was real. I was going to die here. Tonight. Even the distant sound of voices searching, having grown in number, couldn't be sounds of salvation for me; they were merely a cruel, cold reminder that there was life beyond this. And I would never know it again.

"Please just let me go, Jason."

"I can't."

I wiped the tears and dribble from my chin. "Please. I had nothing to do with her death. I—"

"But your lover did."

"No." I covered my ears, shaking my head. "David's not to blame, either. It's *you*. You loved her. You brought her into your world. *You* didn't protect her!"

"You know nothing!" I felt only a brash jolt, nerves burning in the base of my skull as he grasped a handful of my hair, his shaky breath coming through his teeth in three short words. "You. Know. Nothing."

"I know what you are," I said, arching my neck to stop my hair from coming out. "I know the things you're capable of."

"Then you can imagine what I'm about to do to you."

I tried to shake my head. "You won't hurt me. Emily told me that you're swee—"

"You shut your mouth, you horrible little human." His fingers knotted tighter, dragging my scalp upward.

"Jason, please." I slowly reached for his arm. "Please, look at me. I'm not the enemy. I'm not the—"

"One does not have to deserve the misfortune they suffer." His anger landed in my face in dots of saliva. "You were to die by torture for his crimes, but now you will endure it more slowly for your own mouthy impudence, you stupid, *stupid* girl."

"Ara-Rose!" Voices echoed off the shallow valley, getting closer then. Jason's grip eased until he untangled his fingers gently from the loose remains of hair and removed his hand.

I looked up at him, my scalp burning like the rage rising within me. "Go ahead. Do what you want. It will never change the fact that Rochelle's dead, and all it will achieve is your own pain when David takes revenge on you."

"Actually, my dear, the laws of our kind prevent him from seeking retribution for the death of a human." He squatted down beside me, seemingly pleased with himself. "The unlawful changing of one to a vampire, yes—but not death."

"What?"

"I have the right to mutilate my kill in any way I see fit, as long as I eat you. The law will not side with David this time," Jason explained. "There is nothing he can do, since he did not see fit to mark you as his own. And he will have an eternity to reflect on the horrific way in which I hurt you. Oh, Ara"—he rolled his head back, sucking down the bliss of his own deranged ideas—"it will kill him inside. The images I will savor for him shall be etched into the iris of his mind's eye for all time."

"That isn't fair."

"Life is not fair. But you refuse to believe that, don't you?"

I shook my head, the anger becoming a physical form of hatred inside me. "I won't let you destroy my faith in—"

"I don't need to destroy it," he yelled. "I will destroy *you* instead; then David's hope, his faith in life, in *love*, will be lost forever."

"No. You *will* let me go. I will not be the victim in your family feuds," I demanded with an unsteady cry, trying to sound strong.

"You know"—he stopped and listened as the hunters came closer —"you only make this more of a game for me—to see how long I have to hurt you until you finally realize that no one is coming to save you."

"And all that will do is prolong my life, because I will *never* lose faith. Love will prevail. David will come for me, and I will go home and live my life, and you"—I spat the words out—"will suffer for eternity without Rochelle."

He reached sideways and knocked his forearm across my chest. I yelped out an odd sounding whimper as I fell to the ground with my hands across my ribs, winded. "Keep up this attitude, and I will see to it that death and torture is not the worst you suffer."

I snickered miserably to myself, pressing my hands to the ground to sit up. "What could be worse than that?"

"Many things," he scoffed. "How 'bout if I ensure your replacement lover is the one who finds you: his precious *baby girl*? No one will have a chance to cover your naked, defiled body before he sees it. He will be privy to every sordid thing I did to you."

"Please! No!" I jumped to my knees and grabbed his sleeve. "Kill me, do what you want, but don't let Mike find me. I'm begging you."

"Begging?" he asked, cold amusement oozing through his voice. "I gave you the chance to beg, but you were too proud. Curious though…" He rubbed his chin. "You care not for what I show David, but for Mike… you wish him to be free of this detest. Why?"

"He's good, Jason." Hysteria turned my words to hiccups. "He doesn't deserve this. It has nothing to do with him. Please just don't hurt him like this."

"Shh, hush now, sweet girl. It will all be okay—for you. You'll be dead in a few hours, and all of this—the cold, the dark, the fear of what his last vision of you will be—will all be over." Jason softened then and stroked my face gently, making my stomach turn.

"No it won't. Not if you plan to let him find me like that."

"I know how much Mike means to you," he said softly, rising to a squat beside me. "I know that finding you brutally eviscerated and spread-eagled, your breasts and vagina exposed, will haunt him every time he closes his eyes. But that's really half of the fun, Ara," he added, speaking softly, as if he were trying to cheer me up. "You cannot deny me the satisfaction of seeing the look on his face."

As his laughter filled the silence, images flashed in my mind of so many horrible possibilities. I shook my head, trying to find words in the back of my closing throat. I didn't want Mike to see. I didn't want his last memory of me to be something horrible. Already, my mere death would destroy him more than anything in this world ever could. Especially because he was just inches away from me when I was taken. He'd blame himself, and nothing that anyone could say would fix it.

I had to escape. I couldn't let him do this to Mike.

"Now, let me start by undressing you," he said, tracing a fingernail from my chin to the front of my dress, relishing in his own sickness. I gauged the distance between his parted knees, leaving open the one place *no* man was immune to pain. Then, with every ounce of force I could muster from my weakened body, I lifted my foot and slammed it down into Jason's groin.

A bawl of anguish rang out into the night. The vampire folded in, clutching his weak spot. As I spun quickly onto my hands and knees and jumped to my feet, his fingers caged my ankle. I screamed and managed to kick them off, but I jerked away too fast, losing the grip on gravity.

A wicked jolt sent me down to kiss the grass a few feet away from him, and as the blow wore off, I pushed up on my hands again, spitting lawn clippings from my mouth.

"Get. Back. Here," Jason grumbled, so strained with agony I knew there was still time.

I got back up, stumbling onto my fingertips for a second before finding my feet, and ran. Just ran, ignoring the sear of pain in my nail as I hoisted my skirt above my knees, fighting for each step I took. I wanted to look back. Wanted to see if he got up—see if he was behind me—but I'd watched enough movies to know that would be my final mistake. So I charged on, my legs hot and shaky with adrenaline, making them move faster than I knew possible. But not fast enough. I pictured the face on the vampire behind me, feeling the crawl of my skin as I imagined him rising to his knees and watching me run—giving me a moment to believe I'd escaped.

But hope filled my chest as I reached the border of the trees, my feet slipping for a second on the skinny dregs of pine needles. I searched the darkness for a shadow—a figure, a person that might have wandered away from the hunting party. The beat of my heart was so ferocious I could hardly breathe, but I took a gulp of the icy night air, shaping it to scream, "Hel—"

"Nice try."

My body shot backward like a lasso snagged my neck. The iron grip of the vampire cut off any hope of rescue, muffling my scream. Only a whimper escaped, lost to the empty silence of the dark night, where no one would hear it.

"You cannot outrun a vampire. It is pointless to even try."

A series of consonants rolled from the back of my tongue, trapped by his stranglehold, my nose and cheeks pulsing like they were about to pop open.

"I want to kill you right here, right now," he said through his teeth, his voice quivering with rage. "But I will not show you such mercy."

Nearby, the hunters finally came so close that I could hear their private chatter and the instructions being called out to each one from the voice of my fiancé. If they'd only been there two seconds ago, they might have heard me.

Jason squeezed my throat tighter as I wormed my fingers under his, kicking at the ground to break free.

Please, Jason, I thought, *You're hurting me.*

"Do you think I care? If I had any compassion for your adversity before, you just destroyed it," he muttered, his grip easing. "It's time to begin."

He moved quickly, folding my chest across his arm while the other hand tore the back of my dress open, the grass pinching my bare skin as he threw me down hard onto my back.

I coughed the air from my lungs, nudging my elbows into his chest as he landed on top of me, but he separated my hands and forced them onto either side of my head.

"I didn't want to do this to you, Ara, but I need him to see you suffer, and this is the only way."

"Please! Please don't!"

"Keep begging, human. It turns me on." He slipped my dress quickly down my waist, jolting my hips upward as he tore it past my legs and tossed it away.

I pressed my knees tightly together, fighting him. "This is rape, Jason. This is worse than murder."

"I thought you said death was the worst one could suffer," he said cynically, winning the battle to subdue me.

I shook my head, panting heavily beneath his weight, my teeth so tightly knitted I felt a chip come loose and fall under my tongue. Digging deep for the training Mike gave me—for the times he laid on me just like this and wouldn't back down until I broke free—I tried to find a way to get him off me. But it was gone. All of it. I couldn't side-step the paralysis of fear enough to think straight.

But I wasn't about to let him have me, either.

I kicked my heels into the ground, rocking my whole body from side to side.

"Stop struggling." Jason jammed the full force of his elbow onto my shoulder. I cried out, my upper body locked into submission beneath his arm. "Shut up or they'll hear you."

"I don't care," I cried. "I don't want you to do this to me."

"I know." His palm cupped my mouth completely, only a weak sign of terror surviving in the back of my throat. "But I promise, if you lie still I will only hurt you enough to make you cry. After all"—he pushed his knee between my thighs, forcing my legs up and open—"you are a virgin. There are bound to be a few… rips."

My soul drew away inside me, wide eyes closing as I tried to escape to someplace else in my mind.

"I'm going to enjoy this a lot more than you will." He repositioned himself, freezing then. "Ah shit."

"Over here!" called a stranger, and my eyes flew open to see an army of yellow torchlights. "I thought I saw something."

"Ara?" Mike called, his deep voice almost touching me.

My heart skipped so fast. I looked up just as Jason looked down at me. *Please don't kill him, Jason. Please don't.*

Oh God. I wished he'd just taken me far away. I couldn't die knowing Mike would too.

"If he finds us, he has to die. All of them do." Jason released me.

"Please. Please, don't kill them! Do what you want with me, but *please* just let them live?" I begged, staring into his softening eyes.

His brow pulled tightly together, forming two lines in the center. He gently took my wrist, tugging it to roll my shoulders off the ground, and then cradled my face to his chest. "Shh. Okay, just hold tight."

Before I had a chance to react, we flung like a rocket into the trees outlining the field. My stomach hit my hips, and I wrapped my fingers firmly around his jacket, letting go once we landed on the long, scratchy limb of the tallest tree—what seemed like miles off the ground.

Peering back down, the men who circled the clearing looked like figurines, so small from up here. But most of them branched off then and disappeared through the trees when someone called out "Blue dress!"

I shivered all over, looking away. The air up here was cooler, thinner, making the cloud in my head fizzle a little. My heart was so confused by the combination of terrors that, if I was afraid of being this high up—of looking out across the city and the steep valley of trees—I didn't notice it. All that stopped me from falling right now was the splintery shelf of a branch as wide as my hips, and the secure grip of the predator's fingers around my arm. But, somehow, that made me feel safe.

Jason watched as Mike appeared in the clearing below, following his instincts and not the clue that had been thrown to the other field.

"You know, I'm in the mood for a little game."

"What? Flesh-bombing hunters?"

He turned and smiled at me. "You're funny when you're frightened."

"It's a common emotional reaction," I said. "I'm kind of embarrassed by it."

Jason just laughed through his nose, his eyes filling with fondness before he looked back down at Mike, standing a few hundred feet away, talking on his phone. "He's good. If I were a human attacker, he'd have found you by now."

"I know."

"Let's have some fun with him, shall we?" he said in an unsettlingly smooth tone, then reached around my body. "And since you won't be needing this."

My hands shot up to cover my chest as my bra came away, leaving a loose feeling around my ribs.

"Just think of the things he'll imagine when he finds it." Jason laughed, and we both watched as blue lace floated like a ribbon on a breeze to the earth below—a part of me finally to touch the hands of the man I loved again.

"I'm sorry, Mike," I whispered.

Jason smiled down at my crossed arms and then pried them open, drawing me into his lap with my legs around his hips, my chest against the silky fabric of his suit. Perfect position to scratch his eyes out.

"Be nice, Ara, and you shall live longer."

"Stop trying to kill me, and I'll be nice," I retorted.

"Right now," he whispered into my cheek, making my skin crawl with the gentle caress of his fingers down my spine, "I am not trying to kill you."

"No, but you shouldn't hold me this way. I don't belong to you."

"But you want to belong to me." His words came out with a smile.

"You're just confusing my mind. It's not real."

"It's as real as you want it to be."

I went to speak, but the truth was ugly and terrifying. I did want him. I wanted him to touch me. I wanted him to move his lips from their gentle whispers over my shoulder to the purlieu of my mouth, and kiss me. I had no control over my hand. I felt myself slowly move it and cup the side of his neck, my breath falling heavily against his jaw with soft little kisses. And even when I felt him expand between my legs, not one part of me wanted to move away. I saw what my brain craved, saw myself reaching down to unzip him—slip him inside of me—and dared not move in case I obeyed that desire.

"Mmm," he hummed, running his hands down my thighs. "You're

getting hotter. This will make a nice memory to show my brother; the way you hold me, as if I were him."

"In my mind, it is him," I whispered.

"And yet"—he grabbed my wrists and yanked me away from his chest, my breasts exposed to him—"when you scream for mercy, it will be *my* name on your lips."

I pulled my elbows in to cover myself. "And in that, you will become everything you despise about him."

"I am *nothing* like him."

"An eye for an eye says otherwise."

Like a flash going off in my face, everything blanked for a second. I woke to a branch against my spine, my fingers clutching it tightly to stop from falling to the depths of the empty space behind me. And as the shock of his slap wore down to the pain, I wanted so badly to cry out to the hunters below—to David. To yell out and beg him to save me. I couldn't understand why he never came. Surely my dad called him—told him what happened. He would have known right away that it was a vampire. He would have come… if he still cared.

"I'm sorry." Jason gently laid my arm across my bare chest to cover me. "It is horrible that he made you believe you meant something to him."

I looked up, livid with spite. "I meant *everything* to him."

"And yet you refer to yourself in the past tense. So, you understand then, that he's moved on?"

"I…" I wiped my cheek on my shoulder, trying to blot away the last of his slap. "I don't know."

Jason smiled sympathetically. "Yes, you do."

Below, the voices of the hunters became louder over the savage barking of dogs, headed quickly in our direction.

"Oh, look." Jason jerked a nod at the ground. "Your replacement has unearthed a clue."

32

I turned my head to see a bulky figure drop to its knees at the base of the tree, his anguished, incomprehensible sobs rising up as audibly as if I were standing right beside him. The lacy bra in his hands screamed every sordid tale to him that he'd feared as he hiked these gardens, searching for me all night.

"Oh, baby." His voice carried on the trunk of the tree, all the way to my heart. "What has he done to you?"

"Mike!" Emily ran up behind him, barely able to catch her breath. But her steps slowed when she saw it, and a crowd gathered around them, dogs tugging at their master's leads, eager to catch the scent in Mike's hands.

"I'll take that, Mike," a man said, scooping up the lacy delicate and passing it to a woman in uniform.

I looked away, my limbs running hot with shame. All I could control in my world were my own tears, so I held them back, refusing to even breathe. "You're a monster, Jason," I whispered.

"Let's see if you can't come up with a new name for me once I finish with you. Now…" He pressed a flat palm to my chest and slowly pushed me backward. "Shall we continue?"

The scratch of bark on each bone in my spine meant nothing to me. I held onto the branch with both hands, letting tears trickle down my temples and over my ears as I watched my Zorro walk away, stumbling through his own deep agony. Emily wrapped her arm around him, and as each person finally melted into the shadows behind the eager dogs, the emptiness that their silence left behind took the last promise of survival. I closed my eyes, whispering goodbye.

"Are you done feeling sorry for yourself now?" Jason asked, looking down at me with a smug grin.

"Should I be?"

"I suppose not." He pried my hand away from the branch and held it up, leaning closer. "Do me a favor. Don't scream."

Would there be any point?

"No." He moved in with his mouth open, then stopped. "Do you always answer a question with a question?"

"Only when I'm being murdered and have no other means of defense."

The vampire smiled warmly. "Don't worry. This isn't the *murder* part yet."

"Oh, good. I can relax then." I pulled tightly against his touch as he drew my wrist toward his mouth, the point of his fangs showing in his smile, reminding me of what David said about the effects of venom on the human condition.

As the cold of Jason's lips mopped my flesh, I shut my eyes tight, waiting for the sear of his razor teeth. They popped through the surface like the first cut in the flesh of a peach, and the scream I promised not to release etched its way up my throat. I jammed my tongue against the roof of my mouth, twisting my lips, fighting against all human urges.

His bite eased after the first break, blood drawing past his teeth like string up a straw, the spicy venom rush along my veins pulsing and twisting them like worms under sand.

All sound blotted out around me, leaving only him and me in a world standing excruciatingly still, until the subdued cry in the back of my throat turned to a high shriek. Jason's fangs tore from my flesh without loosening their hold. The skin came away with a long peeling sensation, each nerve disconnecting with one last shudder.

I couldn't scream then, couldn't make my voice find my lips; they quivered, fighting to feel the air come past them. But there was none —no air, no hope. The muscles in my wrist had detached from the bone, I was sure, leaving the edges of my skin floating on a wild, hot wind, freezing then burning as the venom raced back through in the opposite direction.

Please stop! Please.

"I'll stop when you're dead."

I tried to roll my body—to send myself to the ground—but he held me fiercely, slowly smearing his tongue across the wound. I kicked both legs, hooking my heels into the bark to push my hips out from under his, but couldn't get free.

And all the lies David told me... *The venom numbs the flesh... You know I'd never let you fall... I will always protect you...* thrashed about on the trails of my agony, rising in waves of hatred for all—all man, all vampires, for everything that ever was or ever would be. I wanted it to stop. Life to stop. The world to stop. I wanted to scream, to cry with all my heart and beg him to tell me why. Why? Why aren't you here? Why did you leave me to die like this?

This pain didn't belong to me. I shouldn't be here.

I cried, letting the sound be whatever the agony in my soul needed it to be, and as I imagined my Mike finding me, cradling me in arms of safety, saying, *Baby, I'm here. I'm here, you're safe now*, the cry came from a place so much deeper than I'd ever cried before. He'd make it all okay. He'd make it stop.

But so would David.

David? I turned my head to look at the empty expanse beside me. *David. Please come for me. Please don't leave me here to die.*

Jason drew his lips away and moved them up my arm, over my shoulder, stopping just below my breast. His silky hair smelled like apple, making me relax a little.

"Is that it?" I asked softly, my legs gently falling on either side of the branch, feet dangling into oblivion. "Will I die now?"

Jason laughed against my ribcage. "No. I'm going to bite you again."

Before I could think to react, the sear of venom barred my tears and the weight of his body against mine forced the branch into my spine, as if it would rip me in half. I opened my mouth to scream, but Jason pinched the base of my throat, gagging me with my own tongue.

I dug my thumb into his wrist, merely making him hold tighter—trapping my anguish inside of me. Then, like holding a breath for a second too long before finally exhaling, he released my throat, leaning back to look down at me.

Tiny, rasping gulps of air lifted my chest in quick jolts. I ran my swollen tongue over the roof of my mouth, trying to open the passage again. "I can't—" I stammered. *I can't breathe.*

"Okay, just calm down. I'll fix it." He rubbed his thumb across the lump in my throat, and the tension eased, oozing past my dry lips, as if the venom in my limbs had finally seeped into my muscles. I could actually *feel* it assimilate, like a drop of food dye in a glass of water, making the burn in my arm sting like hot sauce on raw lips.

The predator wiped his sleeve along his mouth, breathing heavily as if he'd just enjoyed a swig of cola on a really hot day. "I knew you'd taste lovely, Ara-Rose. After all, my brother always did like them… sweet."

I really didn't care if he enjoyed my blood; all I could focus on was the violent quiver in my jaw, making my teeth clatter in my mouth, and the deepest, most binding cold I'd ever suffered.

"K… K…"

"What?" He brought his ear to my lips.

"Kill. Me."

He leaned back, a cruel smile shining out under the blood. "Only if you beg me nicely."

"P—" I shut my eyes, moistening my throat. "Please."

"As you wish."

Nothing but a breath of perfect silence passed me then, a cool breeze parting my lips and lifting my hair from my face, as the ground rushed up to meet me.

SHARP VIBRATIONS RATTLED THROUGH MY CORE, RESONATING

with the sound of dry pasta snapping between teeth. The impact struck me only as a memory when my body came to rest in a disheveled lump at the base of the tree.

Jason appeared beside me then, crouching into a soft landing. Though I was weary and suffocating under pain, I could see his face perfectly in the darkness now. His tight lips broke into a malicious spread as our eyes met, and he reached down to shift my body, curving my rag doll limbs to the correct position. I could feel them move, but they felt lank and hollow, like the empty sleeve of a coat.

"Shh," he said, brushing my cheek. "Don't cry."

I tried not to, tried to just breathe, but every time my lungs expanded, a sharp jab made me stop. I just wanted to be dead.

"You will be soon, sweet girl. And it's better this way—if you can't move." He sat taller, indulgently eyeing my half-naked form. "It won't take me as long if I don't have to pin you down."

My lips arched tightly, trembling. I lay perfectly still, wiping an imaginary cloth over my body to rid the creeping, icky feeling tingling up my spine, branching out from where his hand rested against my leg. I didn't want this to be my end. I didn't want to lose my virginity like this. I just wanted to be loved; to feel the touch of a person that wanted me like I wanted them.

Please not this, Jason, please. Kill me, but don't do this to me.

He studied my face for a long moment, as the crease in his brow slowly deepened, his eyes narrowing. Warm tears ran in streams over the sides of my face, and the burning in my limbs ceased, giving way to a dull, hammer-like pulse. But my mind focused only on Jason towering over me; my legs apart beneath him, his body free to enter mine, as I had no way to stop him. I just wanted to bend my knee and kick him in the groin again, send his balls into his throat.

"Now, now, sweet Ara. Be nice." He rose up over my body to wipe the tears from my cheeks, but stopped, his head cocked. "Look at you: so broken, so sad, but still just so pretty."

And he was just so much like David. If I watched his face, ignoring the deeper, almost timid tones of his voice, I could imagine he was David—needed to imagine he was, so my heart could survive the fear.

They say that fear paralyses, but that was the wrong word. It felt more like running full speed then stopping at a dead end with no air.

Each breath I took responded to my panic, rising inch for inch with Jason's lips moving down my body. He kissed me sweetly on my ribs, running his thumb over the bite, then moved down along my flesh to the very top of my inner thigh.

"He wanted to bite you here… that day he drank your blood." He kissed me there. "He was afraid you'd die if he bit you. But luckily"—he looked over his shoulder for a second—"I don't have to worry about that."

No, please stop. Please don't, Jason.

The familiarity of pine and grass made my heart ache for normality. Even the stars, once so mysterious, seemed only so recognizable to my weary eyes as I watched them, wishing on each one for something, *anything* to come along and save me from this.

"I've already bitten you, Ara. Only death can save you now," he advised, and like a serrated clamp breaking the flesh, he sank his teeth into my leg. A surge of agony stole a squeal from my lips and it split the air like a thousand knives through an eternity of silence, ringing out off the emptiness all around me.

My thigh bone seemed to lengthen with the ferocious burning, making the scream move deeper into my soul—resounding from the back of my throat in the highest save-me-God-save-me pitch I'd ever heard until, finally, all life, all sound faded, my cry becoming only a distant shriek, like a whistle blowing.

But even when I closed my mouth, panting as the pain blast through my hip, the whistle continued.

Then, I heard a holler. "She's over here! Over here!"

The whistle blew once more, ringing in my mind as if I were spinning in a giant plastic bin, while others shouted the same sentence out across the park, the words reaching each group like stones falling down a quarry.

Jason sighed. "Why did you have to go and scream? Now you've ruined all my fun."

The cold night air burned my throat as it scraped into my lungs, dragging vestiges of Jason's sweet scent with it—a scent that once reminded me of love, but now, only reeked of cold fear.

He landed on the grass, his body stretched out alongside mine, a cheeky grin putting the vampire to rest. "They're coming for you."

I tried to nod. I knew this much, but I knew he wasn't finished with me yet. Vampires were fast; he had plenty of time.

Just promise me you won't hurt any of them.

His immaculately green eyes softened, turning bright as his body absorbed the life-force of my blood. "I want you to know, Ara"—he leaned down, his deep voice vibrating warmly against my brow—"I've enjoyed our time together, although it's been cut short. And I will watch when they come for you. I want to see what your replacement thinks when he finds you all broken and demoralized; this worthless, unwanted little girl that nobody cared to fight for."

I swallowed back the lump in my throat. The venom had burned in my limbs for so long now that they were numb to all he could think of to hurt me—except the truth. Jason was right. David never came for me. Even until I hit the ground, I still stupidly believed he would. And now I would die alone, disgraced, and all hope for an eternity of blood would only ever be a promise I *wished* I'd made. When I still had the chance.

I ruined my own life by loving a vampire. But I destroyed my future when I denied him an eternity. And now nothing would alter the outcome.

A sharp, tight grip capped my throat, and Jason's cheek touched my jaw as he sank his teeth into the curve of my shoulder. My body twitched, convulsing without the knowledge of my brain. I felt calm inside, unable to process what I was suffering.

"Your blood is running thin," he said, his wet red mouth right in front of mine.

I studied it carefully, seeing my David in the way he smiled, the way he closed his lips for a second like he was considering kissing me.

"I *was* considering it," he said, and he looked up from my mouth, his eyes cold again. "I know how much it'll hurt my brother to see our lips touch." He came down slowly and opened my mouth with his tongue, sinking it inside with a mix of blood and venom or spit or something that burned the back of my throat. I tried not to swallow, holding my breath, but as I coughed from the sting, spitting back in his mouth, I had no choice.

"Don't drown in it," he said, drawing back to turn my head so the blood dribbled out the corner of my mouth.

It was nearly over now. The nightmare was fading away with the stars in the sky, the fear easing with the serenity of near-death, and I was sure I smiled as I looked up at Jason.

"Tell David... I love... him," I muttered weakly—not a message for Jason to deliver, but a part of the story before the end. David would hear it when Jason showed him the memory, and he'd know that even in death, it was *his* name on my lips.

I exhaled and looked up at the sky. The stars blurred into a thin silver line and the night surrounded me. For a second, I saw them—Mom and Harry—nothing more than a flash, or maybe just a flicker of a memory standing there behind Jason. I wanted to run to them, call to them, ask them to help me. But I knew they weren't really there, and that even if they were, they couldn't help.

There was no help. People died every day. People suffered every day. No one came to save them, and no one was coming for me.

I'm sorry, Mom, I thought, *I know you wanted better for me.*

"It's okay now." She nodded, reaching out. "Come on, it's time to go."

But I need to see David again. I need to tell him that I changed my mind.

"About what?" she said.

Dying. I don't want to die. I want to live—forever. With him.

"I know." A sympathetic smile warmed her face, like everything was okay. But it wasn't. Not at all. She wasn't going to help me. She wanted me to come with her—to end it all right now. Right here.

"Death is only the beginning, Ara." She smiled. "There is so much more for you now."

No! I want to go home!

"Please?" Cold air brushed out past my lips, colder than it should be. I thought I felt my hands shaking, but wasn't sure. The only thing I knew I felt was the warm, mucky feeling of something sticky under my head and all over the side of my neck. I struggled to open my eyes then, feeling myself being pulled down, like I was swimming against a strong current and losing the fight. I tried to kick my legs, to clutch at my throat and tear away the belt of restraint, but my hands were gone; there was nothing to move, nothing to free me from the sweltering wrap of my own death.

And then, from deep in the darkness, a warm hand pulled me back to the night. I held onto it with my mind, focused on it with all of my strength until I heard a voice.

"Ara? Baby, oh baby." It echoed like an old memory. "God, what has he done to you—?"

"Mike?" I think I whispered.

"Ara." His golden voice hit the walls of my subconscious and bounced off the empty space around me. "You stay with me… with me… with me," it echoed again. "Ara, please—don't let go… let go… let go—"

I felt a hand around the back of my head, and a heavy cold settled on my limbs, making me wish I could sleep. Just fall asleep and everything would be okay.

"Oh, God!" His distraught voice cut out under grief. "Get help—please, she's losing too much blood. Get help!"

33

Nothing. No stars. No sound. I tried to open my eyes to see against the black, but as I truly noticed the emptiness for the first time, I felt my heart stop; my eyes were already open.

"Mike?" I called, but my own voice fell flat in front of me, as if I'd spoken into cupped hands. I waited. Waited past that moment you expect everything to be okay, past the breath you held when you thought you heard something, and finally realized what happened.

I'd let go.

Perfect silence. Complete weightlessness; it made me breathless, like I needed sound or a horizon to remind me how to breathe. I couldn't breathe, couldn't even suffocate because there was only emptiness where my lungs should be. All I could actually feel were tingles, shivering across every part of my body that had turned into air. I wanted to break free, but there was nothing to break free from.

I was gone.

Mike was gone.

The world was gone.

Everything was gone…

Floating through space and time, I waited for morning to come and light the corners of this dark room, but the sun never rose. I wasn't sure how many days or years had passed, but this couldn't be sleep; it couldn't just be a dream. In fact, I was pretty sure this was Hell.

No fire, no pain, just eternal blackness slowly, second-by-quiet-second, driving me mad.

It reminded me of the time I went swimming as a little girl. I'd closed my eyes and floated in the water for a while. With my ears under the lapping of waves, aware only of my own body, I had thought it was peaceful then, but here in this unimaginable expanse of nothing, floating, unable to find the shore, it was just agonizingly confining.

The only thing I ever found down here was the memories, hidden behind shadows in the darkness. And when the darkness got too much, those memories became nightmares—unhappy endings I'd keep examining in my mind over and over again, never able to find the conclusion, because there'd never be a conclusion. Not for me. In death, we have no resolution.

My last breath would have been taken in the arms of my best friend; my naked, twisted body would have stirred thoughts in him I couldn't control; he'd think Jason raped me, did other unspeakable things to me, and I couldn't tell him the truth.

Tears of frustration and anger wanted release, but with no face and no eyes to cry from they were trapped, lodged like a rolled-up sock in my chest—quivering and growing into a feeling I had never known before. I wanted to rattle the bars of my cage, to scream at those responsible.

But the rage always wore down to misery, and when misery was unreleased, trapped in by nothingness, it turned to fear, then to rage again. It was an endless cycle. And even that made me mad, because there was just nothing… *nothing* I could do to make it stop.

"Let me out of here!" my mind called into the darkness. I imagined myself circling around, gripping my hair with both hands and falling to the floor with my head in my knees.

It did no good to picture it, though. I still felt just the same.

"Mike." I imagined myself looking up to wherever up was. "Mike.

He didn't rape me." I needed him to know that. I needed him to know how sorry I was for leaving the dance and for not remembering how he taught me to survive, how to fight. "Mike? Please, please be there. Please."

But nothing ever answered back.

The rage subsided again and I watched my imagination fall to her knees. She looked so fragile and human, so broken and alone. But she wasn't fragile or human anymore. She was dead.

DREAMS HAD HAPPENED IN THE BLACKNESS. ONCE OR TWICE I'D seen myself somewhere else, only to wake in the nothing again. As I wandered forward, of full body, I knew this was just another dream.

Blue plumes of smoke colored the emptiness around me, rising up to grip my ankles and hips like creeping fingers. The message I'd been trying to get to my fiancé was still trembling on my lips, stuck, like a ghost that couldn't cross over.

"Mike?" I said weakly into the darkness. "Mike, please listen."

With each step I took, I could feel the tickly tips of the grass between my toes. I walked through the smoke, reaching out to touch anything at my fingertips. I'd take a tree in the head right now, just to feel.

When the sound of soft, ragged breaths came from somewhere ahead, I looked deeper into the darkness, past the blur, past the shadows.

Then, I saw him.

"Mike?"

He didn't look up. As he became completely visible for the first time, so too did the world around him, but not me. Storm clouds overhead raged and swirled, lapping the horizon with the promise of a wild night. But my hair, my dress, and my existence stayed frozen in time.

Mike stood hunched and shaking, one hand spread out on something stone, while his lungs fought to find the breath that would make it all okay.

"Ara, baby. I'm so unimaginably sorry. I should've protected you. I should've been there to stop him from hurting you."

I watched on, my lip trembling, tears edging tightly on the brink of hysterics.

"You would have called for me," he said. "Every time he touched you, you would have looked for me, waiting for me to save you. And I let you down."

Mike lost his words to grief then, sobbing heavily into his fingertips. When he finally composed himself, he reached into his pocket and drew out a closed fist. My thumb landed on my ring finger when the gentle tink of glass drew my eyes to what he placed atop the stone.

"This is where it belongs now," he said and backed away, wiping a weary hand across his lips. As his shadow receded, allowing light against the words on the headstone, the core of my being imploded:

'Ara-Rose: Loved Eternally.'

All life drew from my soul, like my existence happened in reverse for that split second, and the remains of the ring I once wore for love bled out over the stone, weeping crimson tears across my name.

I stumbled on my heels, reaching for something to ground me, but the dream slipped away, becoming smaller until the blackness swallowed it whole.

He was gone, but I knew he still existed out there, somewhere I could never go, just like everything I loved: lost in a world I would not see again; their smiles, their voices, their warm arms. All gone. They would grow old and pass, time would pass, and I would remain here.

Ghosts were supposed to watch, to see who was at their funeral, who mourned them. I was supposed to see David again, to know if he came to my grave. I was supposed to sit beside him, comfort him, though he'd never know I was there. Everything just turned out so wrong. How had it all gone so wrong?

The imaginary me appeared in full light again: a soft, golden glow in the darkness, her pale dress billowing like the fingers of a ghost. She was the storybook version I thought death would be. But I was the reality, sitting across from her. An empty vessel—dark, invisible, tortured. There were no happy reunions in the afterlife, no peace and, from what I could tell, no God, either. I had called to

Him; called to everyone I could think of, even called to Rochelle. But she wasn't here. God wasn't. Buddha. Anyone. Just me. And my regrets.

"And me," said my imagination.

I wanted to shake my head. She wasn't there either. I wasn't sure there was even a mind. I knew only an eternity of nothing; my punishment, I guess, for condemning David's heart to the same.

It was the little things I missed the most, like a smile or color or twisting my ring around on my finger—my ruby rose. Mike would be so sad that I couldn't wear it now. And I once thought David would be so sad that I did. But I guess time changes our assumptions. Or our hearts.

"I wonder what he'll do—David—when Jason shows him the memory of what he did to us," the imagination said.

We didn't need to wonder, though. "David will hate me for letting Jason hold me the way he did in the tree."

That was supposed to be *David's* right.

He told me once, so long ago, that the touch of human skin to a vampire was like a thousand kisses of ecstasy; like satiating an eternal hunger with the warmth of one breath. He'd never forgive me for giving that to his brother.

I wished I could go back and tell him I was sorry. Tell him I should have chosen immortality.

"Maybe it was never an option," the apparition said.

"What do you mean?"

"Don't you remember?" She smiled wickedly. "He told you that vampires leave and move on without saying goodbye—without telling people why."

I nodded. "Yes, because it raises more suspicions when questions are asked. They simply send a letter resigning from jobs or schools, and they're never seen again." As I finished the sentence, realization struck me worse than shock. "Is that what he did to me? Did he leave me, and I never saw it coming? Did he convince me that he'd come back so that I wouldn't try to find him?"

"I think you already know the answer to that question, Ara."

"No. That can't be right."

"But it is right. David didn't come to the ball because David *never* was coming."

The remains of my existence suddenly gave up in that one moment.

"Then he really is just as heinous as the man in the memory Jason showed me."

"Yes," the apparition snickered, "and you were just another victim of his cruelty."

34

An alarm clock set my mind on wake, its incessant bleeping stirring me before I was ready. But the sun, usually always up at this hour, was missing. I blinked a few times, thinking maybe my eyes were still closed, and as my breath came back hot against my own lips from a flat surface right above me, dread caved my chest.

My world sunk backward as I placed my hands in desperate layers over the sides, the top, the base of this space I was laying, folding my toes down and pushing against the hard surface there, making my head hit the firm one above it.

"Hello," I called, but my voice came back dead, absorbed by the wood it fell against. And the tiny box got hotter and smaller around me, my shoulders folding in, narrowing my lungs.

They thought I was dead!

I felt my heart, placed my hand right over it to see if it was beating, but I couldn't feel it; couldn't feel the wound on my neck or my wrist or anywhere. They'd healed. They were healed and I was in a box.

Panic filled me up before a chain of fierce screams burst suddenly from my lips, blocked only by the forcing drive of each blow of my elbow, my knee, my foot being cast down on the solid surrounds.

"Please don't leave me here!" I scratched the wooden roof, my fingers splintering. But I didn't care. "Please. Please, God. Please!"

A violent cough left my lungs in a vulgar bark, fine particles of earthy powder spiking the back of my throat. The box compressed my shoulders on both sides, stopping my lungs from expanding, denying me the breath of relief I fought for.

I stopped moving then. Stopped kicking, breathing, everything, and laid perfectly still, listening to the flow of dirt rain down in a heavy pile over my ponytail, cooling my head through the strands of hair.

The first rule in this situation would be to not panic. But my chest moved in quick hitches. My fingers balled up so tight my thumb cut my hand, I was sure, and I couldn't stop the thoughts entering my mind, things David told me: vampires, buried alive for seven days. They survived. They lived through that, tortured, alone, unable to breathe.

"David!" I bent my knee to the highest angle it could achieve and jammed my foot against the floor, pushing on the lid of this coffin, thrashing about like a beetle caught on its back. "Ahh!"

"Ara," a muffled voice came gloriously through the wood then, thick with grief.

"I'm in here!" I screamed. "Mike. Get me out. I'm in here." I banged on the roof, making the dirt pile grow. But I didn't care. Mike was there. He'd get me out. He'd—

"Just squeeze my hand," he said, cutting off my thought. "Please. Just once. That's all I need."

"Mike. I can't," I screamed. "I can't get out. I'm in a box."

I waited, listening, but this container seemed to be soundproofed, from the inside. I tried to sit up, to move, to struggle against the pine confines, but the dirt formed a mound under my head as I lifted it, pushing my nose closer to the lid and arching my neck at an awkward, unnatural angle. And panic returned with a layer of sweat, turning the dirt to mud around my temples and nose.

"Oh God." I looked up, shutting my eyes tight. "Please. Please get me out of here."

"No change?"

My thoughts halted at the sound of another voice.

"Hello?" I called.

"No. Doc says her heart's not coping," Mike said.

"Time will tell." The other voice sounded void of all emotion.

"Where are you going?" Mike's tone peaked with incredulity.

"She needs rest, and my being here is…" There was a long pause. "Pointless."

Only a sigh followed that, leaving me by myself again, confined in a space made for those not living.

I shut my eyes tight and took slow, deep breaths through my mouth, tasting the raw, almost freshly cut pine against my lips. I tried to imagine pretty things—butterflies, the sun—not the crawly and possibly un-dead creatures that might be buried beneath me. I'd run out of air soon if I didn't calm down.

And strangely, as my belly lifted and fell with each breath, the air trembling out of my tight lungs, so too did the panic.

I looked around the dark box for what felt like the first time, and instead of pitch black staring back at me, I could make out the ridges in the panels and the oddly-angled nail sticking out beside my eyebrow.

They'd put me in a *box*—not a coffin—just a pine box; laid me down, closed me in and nailed it shut.

But I *would* find a way out of here. Come Hell or high water. This would not be my death, and if it was already my death, I'd be damned if I'd let it be my eternity.

"HOW IS SHE?" THE VOICE ECHOED THROUGH MY ENDLESS night, resonating from somewhere behind me.

My eyes shot open and a cool and airy space greeted me. I brushed my arms, feeling as though there'd be dirt there. But I was clean. I couldn't remember where I'd been or why I thought I'd be so dirty, but I *felt* dirty, and starved for air.

"No change," said a woman suddenly.

"Pardon?" I said, looking up, searching the empty room for a crack of light to mark my position.

"Can she hear us?" a man said.

"Who?" I asked.

"Her monitor changes when I speak. See?" he said, and I got the sense then that they weren't talking to me.

"It's just static." As soon as that man spoke, I knew it was Mike. The other one sounded almost too smooth to be Mike—liquid, if that was the right word.

"It's not static. Look, she can hear me."

"You wish."

"Mike," the woman whispered. "Be nice."

"Fine," Mike said in a tone that indicated a set of folded arms to go with it. "From what I know, the doc says she can."

"Ara? My love." Mr. Smooth sounded closer than before. "I'm so sorry," he said. "Please? Please come back to me?"

"Excuse me. Are… I'm sorry, are you talking to me?" I called.

He didn't answer.

I blinked a few times, noticing only as I looked down at my feet that my feet weren't actually there. I held my arm out and ran my fingers over it, feeling the soft skin, but couldn't see it. There was nothing there to identify me: no nails, no skin color, no age spots or bracelets. Not even a bed or a surface to show what kind of room this was. Maybe it was a prison, a hospital, a bedroom, a padded cell, perhaps even a ballroom with no people. Could even be the White House for all I knew. But that word "*Ara*" rang a bell somehow.

I dropped my arms to my sides, quickly yanking my hand back when it touched something cold. It stung, like dry ice, sticking to me even as I shook my fingers.

"Did you see that?" the stranger said. "I think… I think she just squeezed my hand!"

"It was probably just a flinch. She does that from time to time." I heard the silky pages of a magazine turn.

"Maybe," the smooth voice said, dejected. "It just seemed almost like… My hands are cold. Do you think she…?"

"She what? Knows you're here? Hates you?" The pages flicked

again, and it sounded as though a metal-legged chair scraped along vinyl. "Chances are, she's shaking you off. Maybe you should stop touching her."

I frowned, looking down at where my fingers were supposed to be. And like a puppet master, I focused on them, closed them tightly and squeezed the nothing, letting go when that voice laughed.

"She did! She squeezed my hand. Look!"

"What do you mean *she squeezed your hand*?" Mike's voice came from closer than before and, though it was still dark, I felt gravity around me, felt him near me.

The echoing mist of eternity flowed out through the cracks in my subconscious then, leaving me solid, heavy. Really heavy. I didn't remember being this heavy. I didn't remember having laid down on my back, but when I tried to get up, my chest stayed stuck, glued to my spine against this flat surface.

"Ara." The smooth stranger interrupted my moment of confusion.

"What is it?" I called, irritated.

"Ara," he said again, as if I hadn't answered him.

And now I was getting cranky. It had been God knows how long since I'd eaten, felt the sun, slept, or even seen my own toes, and now this person was talking at me and not answering. I just wanted to get out of here—wherever here was. I just wanted to go home to Mike and lay in his arms. I was tired of the dark, of the black. I couldn't even remember where I'd been all this time or even *why* Mike was important to me.

"She's not in there, man," Mike said. "And if she was, she's not gonna come to the surface for *you*."

"Oh, I see, so you think she'll wake suddenly to your soft *whispering confessions* of love, do you?" Mr. Smooth said sarcastically. "Do you have any idea what she and I—"

"Stop it. Both of you," a woman said. "It's three o'clock. Take yourselves home and get some sleep."

"Fine," Mike said.

"Fine," the other man said, and I heard his breath, felt it suddenly close to my face, though there was no one in this room. I held my own breath, scrunching my eyes. "Ara?"

But before I had a chance to answer him again, the surface quaked suddenly under me, my legs tilting through the earth and angling my entire body away from existence. I reached out, grabbing at imaginary branches as my head followed my feet, sliding downward.

There was no wind and no trees for which to show my descent, but I felt it—felt the earth rising up under me. I tensed all over, ready to hit the surface, but nothing came. There was only the emptiness of my eternal, hollow Hell.

I didn't bother to cry this time as the darkness swallowed me, and hope had been lost so long ago that I'd never truly allowed it back in. I simply existed. In the dark. Alone. My body alive out there somewhere, an empty vessel in their living world, while my soul was slowly dying beneath it.

"I DON'T KNOW. SHE'S STRUGGLING TO BREATHE."

I frowned, clearly having woken to the middle of a conversation.

"I know," Mike said. "They're gonna put her on a breathing machine."

The smooth voice sighed. "I don't want that for her—she's been through enough."

"I know, mate, but it's for the best." Mike's warm energy emanated from his voice somewhere near. I wished I could feel him, like, *actually* touch him. "I can't lose her. I'd rather see her with a tube down her throat than in a coffin."

"Don't you think that's a little selfish: prolonging her life merely to save your own grief?"

"Only as selfish as to wish she'd die so you don't have to wonder where she is, what she's doing, for the rest of your life," Mike spat.

"You know nothing about what I wish for this girl." His smooth voice cracked like a volcano erupting. I could hear the rumble of anger raging too close to the threshold of release. "If I could heal her, I would, but you don't know what she may be suffering in this sleep, Mike. For all we know she's—"

"She's unconscious. She suffers nothing."

All was silent until the smooth voice said flatly, "You don't know that."

"Look," Mike said. I could imagine him rubbing his face roughly in the pause that followed. "We're getting off track. Right now, what's best for her is—"

"For us to let her go. Stop sticking needles and tubes in her, trying to make her body live a little longer. She's gone." I felt something touch my head. "Her body is the only thing left of her."

"She might still recover," Mike offered.

"Recover?" his voice pitched high. "Look at her—does she *look* like she's going to recover?"

"Stop yelling." Mike's tone of reason made my heart soar with desire to be on the receiving end of one of his lectures. "If they hear you, they'll make you leave. One at a time in here, remember?"

There was a short pause. "It's five in the morning. Technically, it's my shift."

"Don't start this again, Da—"

"Look, I'm not saying you have to go, just—"

Suddenly, my hand returned; just my hand, with a sharp, cold sensation travelling right through each bone in my fingers. I tensed. It hurt, like holding onto ice or snow a little too long.

"Just don't talk about hope, okay? I can't bear to even hope."

The silence lingered a while, and all I could focus on was the deep burn of cold in my bones. I wanted to push it away, to make it stop. It branched out from my wrist, slowly trembling up my arm and along my collarbones. I tried to hold my breath, but my lungs weren't there, a hollow void occupying my chest instead.

"Maybe you should take a walk. You look… stressed," Mike said.

"You're right. I've been here too long. I'm losing my mind, I—" The cold in my hand suddenly came away, replaced by a warm touch that melted the chill. I knew it was Mike. I remembered touching him once, but not the reason why. I wondered if we were friends or if he loved me maybe. Whatever the reason we'd touched, I liked it. I wanted him to know I could feel him; wanted him to know that, despite the fact that I couldn't talk to him, I was still here. Somehow, I was still here.

"Is she… smiling?" Mike's voice peaked on the edge of excited curiosity.

"It means nothing," said the smooth voice. "It's just a muscle reflex."

"No," Mike said. "No, she *is* smiling."

The smooth voice sighed.

"I'm here, baby girl. I'm here." Mike whispered in my ear, the warmth of his breath brushing against my hair. It was pleasant, not at all like the cold that had brought me back into reality. But even without the cold to grab onto, I stayed aware, in *this* consciousness, still surrounded by the black pit of nothing. I could even smell him now—Mike; he smelled like… a feeling. Like… home.

I wanted to go home. Wanted to be like Dorothy and find my magic slippers—wish my way back. So I shut my eyes tight and imagined them: red ones, like in the movie, not silver like the book, and clicked my heels together, repeating the words Dorothy used as a spell to get home.

"What's she saying?" asked the smooth stranger.

"Something about…?" Mike paused, then repeated my words. *My* words. They could hear me!

"Do you think she's dreaming?" Mike asked.

"Perhaps. Or trying to find her way home," Mr. Smooth suggested.

I tried harder, cupping imaginary hands tightly together, praying he'd hear me again.

"Look at her skin." A hand fell on my brow, a warm one. "She's pale. Do you think she's turni—?"

Silence.

An empty chill stole the hum of the world and a flat, dense darkness consumed my hope like a vacuum sucking a hole in my belly, leaving me alone in darkness again.

I was alive, but I was clearly never getting out of here.

An alarm clock somewhere out there woke me. I wanted to reach over and hit snooze, shut it up, but I was so tired my body wouldn't wake enough to move. I imagined doing it so many times that when the beep lifted me to the surface of my dreams again, I actually thought I'd already turned it off. It was annoying, but somewhere in the back of my mind, as I tried to drift back to sleep, my brain interpreted it as rhythm—reminding me of something I'd forgotten.

Music.

I remembered music. I remembered a song that I heard once, in a place that felt like home, with a boy I know I loved but could no longer see when I closed my eyes. His song had the same hollow, kind of sorrowful rhythm as that beep.

When I opened my eyes, foggy light flooded the room, creeping along the walls and floor like the morning sun sweeping the grass in the early hours. It touched my toes, my ankles, and flowed up over my denim jeans and tank top until, as I looked around me for the first time, saw the orange trees and foliage-covered floor of a forest.

I knew this place…

The lake! It was the lake.

David!

His face shot into my mind, bringing with it a flood of painful memories.

Eternity.

My love.

The red rose.

The silky voice.

It was like I could see him so clearly, sitting just across the way with a blue guitar, his voice so heartbreakingly beautiful. With each note he played, my heart beat double-time, the alarm clock beeping out there in the same rapid pattern.

"David." I covered my mouth with a shaky hand, feeling tears track my cheeks like unfamiliar friends in a home they once knew well. "I'm sorry."

David's song faded then, drowned out by the incessant bleeping of that damn alarm as it got louder, more powerful.

"I'm sorry, ma'am," a stiff-sounding man said.

My body became stiff too, and tight. I could feel gravity again, but couldn't use it.

"Once the tube is out, she may just slip away," he added.

"But..." Someone burst into tears. Vicki, I think. "She looks perfectly fine. How can she be brain-dead?"

What? Brain-dead? I'm not brain-dead. I struggled against my confines, trying to get up. What did they mean by brain dead?

"The tests were conclusive, ma'am. I'm sorry. In some cases, the patient can stay in a coma, on life-support, for years to come. In your daughter's case, it would be best for her if she didn't."

Wait! No, I yelled. *I'm not brain-dead. Vicki. Dad. Please?*

"Wait!" Vicki said. "Just... don't take it out yet. Please? Give her more time."

"Her father signed the forms, Mrs. Thompson. I'm sorry."

"Greg?" her voice broke. "Greg, please?"

"Vicki. Just stop," Mike said. "She's gone. Don't make her suffer any more than she already has."

Mike? No. Don't give up on me, Mike. I'm still in here. They got it wrong.

"Hand me that tray, please?" the stiff-sounding man said to someone, and in my dark world I clutched my own chin as the feel of muggy, sweaty hands touched it.

Get off. Stop touching me!

I felt my body, felt my arms, my face, but couldn't get his sticky hands off me.

Please? Don't let me go yet. Don't give up on me.

A tugging sensation snaked up my throat, grating my insides like the ribbed curve of a straw. My lungs felt tight, strained, as if air was being drawn in through a thick cloth over my mouth.

The room went silent for a breath, then, the alarm sounded in one flat pitch.

"Greg, please?" Vicki whispered. "Please don't let her go."

The anguished sobs of those around me flooded my heart, making *me* sad. I focused on the beeps—willed them to move—but they rang out in monotone.

"Fight, Ara," a smooth voice hummed, the melody dark with sorrow as a pair of cool lips brushed softly over my eyes...

Wait! Cool?

David!

He was there in that room beside me. Right there where I could touch him if I could just wake up!

Like a door slamming shut at the end of a long, empty corridor, a dead echo made the space around me grow. I felt myself become whole —felt my fingers, toes, arms, legs, everything was here in this room with me, but I couldn't see them—couldn't open my eyes.

"Tell me how to get out of here," I yelled up at the uninhabited void. "I know you're out there. I know you can hear me."

An eerie feeling lingered along my neck then. I turned slightly, noticing a thickness to the dark, like a shadow stood right there behind me. But when I tried to focus on it, it was gone.

Closing my eyes tight and crossing my fingers, I willed the beeps to move again. "God, please. If you're up there, please…?"

Then, I heard a sound.

I opened one eye and looked around, sure it wasn't possible. Until I heard it again: small, faint, and such a long, quiet pause between each one.

My heart skipped excitedly then, and the beep copied.

"Get the doctor," someone ordered.

Vicki's high voice broke into sobs, while my Dad's deep, soothing whisper rose above it with comforting words.

I missed my dad so much. Would give anything to see his smile again.

"Mike?" Dad said. "Just breathe."

"I can't." Mike's voice sounded so heavy with sadness. "I can't. Where's the goddamn doctor?" he yelled.

"It's just a glitch," the stiff man said suddenly.

"It's not a goddamn glitch," Mike screamed. "She's alive. She's—"

"She's gone," the man said, and Mike's words ended in heart-breaking cries, disappearing as suddenly as the world had entered my darkness again.

I held my breath, listening carefully, but there were no voices now, no beeps—nothing.

"Ara!" David's hand swept my brow, bringing the world back

again, desperation rising up in his controlled tone. "S'il te plaît, mon amour, lutte, bats toi pour vivre."

It was no good. I couldn't wake my mind. I couldn't reach over and press snooze. I couldn't even understand what he was saying to me.

I'm sorry, David, I whispered with weakened resolve, finally ready to let go.

And as if David felt me give up, his cold hand slipped behind my neck and lifted my head. "Ara? My love, please be in there."

"Mate," Mike said. "Don't move her. They said not to move her."

David's arms wrapped me tightly, his hands searching, touching every inch of flesh as if to caress me back to life. Then, as the panic reduced to realization, his hands slowed and a cold drop of liquid fell onto the bridge of my nose.

"Please fight. I can't lose you." He took a deep, strained breath and pressed his lips to my brow. "Je vous en prie, Dieu, sauvez-la." Another jagged gasp made his chest rise. "S'il vous plaît, ne l'enlevez pas loin de moi. Ne me l'enlevez pas."

His words hung in the back of my mind, resonating with a tone of understanding, and as I felt a touch of fabric on my cheek, they became suddenly very clear. "I'm begging you, God, save her. Don't take her from me. Don't take her away."

His devastation broke my heart.

I'm so sorry, David. I love you. If you can hear me, please know that. Please take care of Mike—tell him I love him too.

He didn't answer. I wanted him to answer just once; just so I knew he heard me, knew how much I loved him, knew he'd heard the words I wished I'd said when he asked me to change for him.

David? Please?

Nothing…

David? My throat hurt.

"Ara?" Something moved under me as he spoke. My body, I could feel my body, feel the bulky, uneven surface I was laying on. A cold grip tightened ever so slightly around my waist. "Ara?"

"David?" I tried again. I could hear the terror in my cry, but it was real—my voice—it came from somewhere different than it had before.

David laughed from behind me, his lips on the side of my face. "Yes. Yes, my love. Yes. You're talking. Open your eyes."

Gravity pulled my skin, dragging it down. I fought against the push and lifted my eyelids, blinking rapidly.

Bright.

Light.

Tears rushed to my irises to protect them from this new experience, burning my vision into a white blur. I couldn't focus on anything, but I loved it more than the breath I could suddenly feel through my lips.

"David?" I smiled. "Am I… am I out?"

"Oui, mon amour, oui, you're safe."

"You… you saved me. You pulled me out." I held his hand tight over my belly as the gift of sight was restored and I felt his arms become the cold that was restraining before. His chest quivered beneath my spine, tears dripping from his chin and falling onto my shoulder as I took in the room: a white room, a bed, a chair, a glass window looking onto the corridor of a hospital.

"What… happened?"

"I," he started, but couldn't finish.

"We lost you, baby," said Mike.

Oh, Mike! That's when I felt my heart—it was still beating, and it was strong. "Mike?"

"I'm here, Ara." He appeared by my side, his warm hand closing around mine. "I'm right here."

"I don't understand. What am I doing in a hospital?" I asked, rubbing my face.

David looked at Mike, then they both looked at me. "You lost a lot of blood. They had to put you on a life support system." Mike's eyes narrowed slightly.

"Okay, but what *happened* to me?" My memory hit the foggy wall of perplexity. I didn't even remember getting up this morning.

"It wasn't this morning." David answered my thought.

"When?"

"Ara, you've been in a coma for three months." Mike's voice

cracked and he turned away so I couldn't see his face, but I only had to see his shoulders shaking to know he was crying.

Three months? I tried to look around the room to get my bearings. *Three months?*

"Okay." I took a few deep breaths, bringing myself to terms with this new information. "So, a coma—but why? How did I *get* in a coma?"

Mike's shoulders rolled forward even more.

"Mike?"

He just shook his head, refusing to look at me.

I looked down at my hands, felt my face, my throat, checking for something, anything that would give me a clue. Then, I noticed the silky, lumpy rise of gathered skin on my neck, and as I looked down to nothing in particular, saw the horrid parallel lines of raised pink skin down the length of my forearm.

I drew a breath, tracing the scar with wide eyes, afraid to touch it —not sure if it was really there or if this was some nightmare.

"Did I do this to myself?"

Mike released the sob he'd obviously restrained, and David held his breath, pressing his cheek to mine with the same intensity as his grip around my waist.

Then, with a wash of cold trepidation, the memory hit me.

Jason did it?

David squeezed me tighter.

I rubbed my head, my eyes burning with tears. Jason. He hurt me. The cold. The dark. I remember.

"Shh, hush, my love, it's going to be okay," David said.

"What's happening?" Mike leaned over me, studying my face as I fell apart inside. "Why is she breathing like that?"

David stood up and laid me flat on my back.

"Get the nurse," Mike ordered, moving a pillow from under my head.

"No!" I held my hand out, taking deeper, more controlled breaths. "No, I'm okay. I'm okay."

"Ara, you're as white as a ghost." Mike folded himself around me, and the warm smell of home reminded me that I was safe, that I was okay now and the darkness was gone. Jason was gone. I rested my chin in the curve of his neck.

David?

He looked at me, his emerald-green eyes shining out under his low-pulled brow.

Did he find me, David? Did Mike find me? I clutched Mike's shoulder tightly, studying David's face, trying to feel my heart beating —to steady it—but after months of sensory deprivation, everything was so loud and so bright.

David closed his eyes, nodding, and looked away.

I knew what Mike would've seen. I knew what David would've seen in Mike's head, because even *he* couldn't look at me.

"I'm sorry, Mike," I cried. "Oh, God. I'm so sorry."

Mike let out a gust of air and his sad gaze drew me in as he pulled back. Tears streamed down his bearded cheeks in thick lines, his eyes falling stunned into the silence that stopped on his lips. "Ar, I…"

I turned my face away.

"No." Mike took my chin in his fingers and made me look at him. "You have *nothing* to be sorry for. You did nothing wrong. This is something that was done *to* you."

"He bit me." I touched my neck.

"Yes." Mike's eyes met mine. "Do you remember anything else?"

I looked at David, who lifted his head when he read my thought: *He bit me, does that mean I'm a…?*

He shook his head.

I'm not a vampire?

He closed his eyes and shook his head again.

My breathing slowed entirely. I lowered my head and rested my hand across my lips, not sure if I was relieved or devastated.

Why? Why aren't I dead then? He bit me. I should be dead, right?

Our gazes locked again, and David nodded.

"I wish I'd never let you out of my sight," Mike said. "Just a split second was all it took. I just… I was watching you. I was right there and…" He bit his knuckle for a second. "I tried to get to you, but he was gone."

"It's not your fault, Mike," I whispered. It was all I could do to console him. My throat hurt and the muscles under my jaw felt strained.

"I should've protected you. It was my job, Ara." Mike looked at David for a second. "They... the doctors say you have the same mark on your neck as that kid who died—Nathan?"

What? I looked at David. *Nathan died from a vampire bite?*

David nodded.

A vampire? Not you, David? You didn't do it, did you?

He closed his eyes.

Mike studied the both of us, no clue we were exchanging our own private words.

I looked past Mike, my wide eyes studying every inch of David's face. There was no way David killed Nathan. I couldn't believe that. I *wouldn't* believe it. He might have killed Rochelle, but that was fifty years ago. He'd changed. I was certain of it.

David looked up, his warm eyes softening as he muttered, "Thank you," under his breath.

"They just can't understand why—if it was the same guy—why Nathan didn't report an attack," Mike said. "Ara, you shouldn't be alive right now. Your attacker was carrying some rare tropical disease. You died!"

"I *died*?"

"Yes. They said you were brain-dead. You flat-lined when they took out the breathing tube and your heart stopped! But then"—he looked at the small screen behind me—"somehow, you found a way to keep going."

The air became thick and hard to inhale, closing me in as the dry smell of dirt choked me, reminding me of my time in the darkness. I looked down at my hand. "My ring?"

"It's here." Mike pulled it from his pocket and held it up; it looked so small and fragile in his broad, strong fingers.

"I thought it melted." My voice quivered as the reality of being alive set in.

"Melted?" Mike laughed, and David closed his eyes and looked away as Mike slipped the ring back onto my finger. I had no time to stop him; it just happened, and the hurt on David's face tore my heart as it dropped into my stomach.

"They wouldn't let you keep it on," Mike said softly. "But I kept it close to me every day."

Like a habit that had been formed over years, I twisted the ring around on my finger, regretting having asked Mike about it. "Where's Vicki? And my Dad?"

"They went for coffee," Mike said. "They stayed for a while, but your dad needed a break. He's not doing so well."

"Can you call them?" I asked Mike, but looked at David quickly. *I need him to go, David. I need to talk to you.*

"Sure." Mike nodded. "Sure, kid. I'll be right back. David, man?"

David snapped out of his stiff-lipped stare.

"Don't let her go, okay?" Mike pleaded.

He nodded and took my hand, crushing the ring against my finger as he squeezed it. "Don't worry, I'll take care of her *for you*."

Mike paused a second, ignoring the resentment we all heard in David's tone, then, with his phone in hand, closed the door as he exited. I turned to David, biting my quivering lip.

"I know," he said. "I know where you've been. I tried to bring you back, but I just couldn't reach you."

"Why did he do that to me?"

David's face crumpled, but he stiffened immediately and held straight. "He wanted to hurt me."

"But why hurt *me*? Why not someone else—*anyone* else?"

"An eye for an eye. A girl for a girl." He looked away. "He's never forgiven me. I thought we'd moved past it but he was just waiting, all these years, until I finally fell in love."

"Fifty years is a *long* time to hold a grudge."

David nodded, stroking my cheek with the back of his finger. "I'm sorry, Ara. There are no words…" He shook his head. "*No* words I can offer you to make this all right."

I grabbed his hand and held it where he rested it along my cheek. "It's okay. You're here. That's all that matters."

"No. What matters is that you're alive, and that this will never ever happen to you again."

"So he won't… I mean, he won't come back for me?"

David shook his head, seeming to swallow the words that might've accompanied the action.

"How can you be sure?"

"Because he left you alive, Ara. For what reason, I do not know, but the fact that you're still here, that he gave you the chance to survive, and that he didn't kill Mike when *he* found you—"

"What? Jason was there when Mike found me?" I pushed myself up to sit.

David nodded, pressing my chest until I lay back down.

"How do you know?"

"I saw it all." He rolled his chin toward his chest.

I looked away, going numb all over. "He told me he was going to make you watch." I hoped he wouldn't.

"It wasn't like that, Ara. He wouldn't show me." His fists clenched. "I all but *ripped* it from his mind."

"Why would you do that?"

"When I saw you here—saw the tearing on your throat, I knew it was a vampire. And there is only *one* person in this world who would dare touch a girl that everyone *knew* belonged to me." He took off across the room, stopping by the window, the daylight reminding us both that the real world still existed out there. "I went straight to him—*forced* him to show me. Only… I wish I hadn't."

"I'm sorry, David. I should never have went with—"

"No, Ara." He appeared beside me, taking my hand. "None of this is your fault. None of it. I left you. I did this. Not you. You should hate *me*."

That's not possible, David. It's not your fault. Jason did this, no one else.

He sniffed once, staying silent for a while, eyes fixed on my ruby ring. "I will never understand why he didn't finish what he started, but I am eternally grateful that he didn't."

"The darkness? He wanted me to be lost down there," I concluded.

"No." David shook his head. "No. He said something as he left you. Something that just didn't fit."

"What did he say?" My brow creased. It felt so weird to use those muscles again.

"He kissed you on the cheek and touched your hair, but he did it gently." David absentmindedly copied the action of his brother. "He touched you the way *I* would. Then he said, *You don't know how special you are. I had to break you to realize.*"

I looked up into the confusion on his face.

"It just doesn't make any sense," he added. "I *know* him. I know the dark place he was in when he hurt you. Whatever changed his mind, you don't know how lucky you are, how lucky *Mike* is. Ara, he was going to—" He closed his eyes, biting his tongue.

An involuntary shudder edged up my spine. "But he bit me. Why didn't I change?"

David drew a long breath and let it out slowly. "I'm sorry, Ara. You—"

"I don't have the gene?" Hot tears filled my eyes again. I felt myself being pulled backward, like I'd stayed put in the crowded lounge of an airport and watched myself leave.

David looked away.

"But, I..." I swallowed hard, barely able to speak. "I changed my mind."

"Changed your mind?"

"I want to come with you—"

"God!" He turned away, covering his mouth.

"Tell me it's still possible. Tell me I can still—"

"I'm sorry." David turned his sad eyes back to me, his lashes dark with tears. "You just... it's just not in your blood, Ara."

My whole body stilled, eyes closing tightly around hot tears. "I don't want to die anymore, David. I can't be without you again."

"I know. I know, my love." He stroked my hair, holding my face to his chest, but there was nothing he could say. "You can never be a vampire. The promise of eternity was never mine to give."

Something died within my soul then, as all hope fell away like a rose through eternity. David rested his forehead to mine and tucked a lock of hair behind my ear.

"How can that be?" My breath touched his lips. "How can it be over now that I've made up my mind?"

His jaw tightened. "Sometimes, Ara, life is cruel."

"I can't do this, David. I feel like I've lost a part of myself that I'll never get back. This can't be the end."

"You're marrying *him*." David's voice quivered as he nodded toward the hall—to where Mike went to call my dad. "That's as concluded as things get."

"But you *told* me to. You *wanted* me to."

David's fingers tightened around my face. "I'm no saint, Ara. I want what's best for you, but at the same time…" He let out a heavy breath. "I couldn't care less if being with me meant the end of your future."

"Then don't let me go." Hope filled my voice. "Stay with me. Run away with me, I'll—"

"Ara, I can't. You know I can't. I have things I need to deal with, things I must return and take care of, and running away"—he looked down into my eyes—"it's not the answer, my love. *Life* is the answer, even if loneliness is the outcome."

I went to protest, but David shook his head and pressed his thumbs firmly into my cheekbones, gently pressuring me to silence.

"You *will* have a good life with him. I know now that I'm leaving you in good hands."

We both looked to the hall—to Mike, to my best friend and fiancé, practically bouncing around the corridor, with more joy radiating from his face than I'd ever seen.

When I looked back at David, he was already looking at me, his lips twitching as if something rested there, maybe words I wanted to hear him say.

"I don't want to have a life anymore. I want to be with you."

"I know," he said sympathetically, but with a finality to it that discarded any hope.

"Don't do that. Don't speak to me like we can't change this."

"We can't, Ara—"

"That's not true. I had a lot of time to think in the darkness, David, and none of it matters to me now." I sniffled, wiping the liquid from my nose. "Love. True love. That's all that matters."

David shook his head. "You can never be immortal. I sat here by your side, all this time, and I *watched* you die. I was helpless, unable to save you—forced to let you fade away a little more every day." His voice broke to a whisper. "You disappeared into nothing, until every trace of what made you mine, what made you *real* was gone."

"But I'm still here. David, I—"

"It doesn't change things, because venom will not change you." A tight crease pulled his brow at the center. "Look, I know I said once that I will always hope you would one day change your mind, but that hope no longer exists. It's been ripped away by reality, Ara. I will *not* stay with you as a mortal. I *have* to leave."

"Why? Am I so repulsive that you can't love me with a heartbeat?"

David stood back and looked down at his clenched fist. "You know it has nothing to do with love—"

"Then what is it?" I almost screamed. I could feel my face burning with heat. "Why won't you just love me enough to think I'm the only thing that matters? I know I messed up. I know I'm moody and spoiled and I'm sorry. I'm sorry I didn't let you take me away, I'm sorry I went with Jason, and what you're doing to me now, David, is making me goddamn sorry I ever fell in lo—"

"Ara!" He held a finger up, tilting his head awkwardly away as if he were fighting a deep, instinctual urge within him. "Don't say what you're about to say. If you say it, it's been said, and you won't be able to take it back."

I held onto the urge to yell at him, to scream at him, but I could only hold it in so long; it burst out in a singular cry. I folded my face into my hand. "I hate you. I hate you. I hate—"

"Ara, stop." He gathered me in his arms. "Ara, please, please don't do this, my love."

"No. You stop it. Don't you call me that. You can't call me that and then leave me." I grabbed his shirt and looked deep into his eyes, my tears stopping. "You don't know what you're doing. I'll die if you leave, David. I'll never be able to cope if—"

"You *have* to cope, Ara." He unfolded my fingers from his shirt. "You've got no goddamn choice."

"No. I do. This is love. This is life. I'm alive." I tapped my chest. "I'm alive. We get a second chance, David. Don't waste that."

"I won't." He looked into me, and I could almost feel him reaching out to stroke my face, but his hands stayed by his sides. "I'm leaving you so you can live. A life with me, running, hiding, like dogs, Ara, would be a waste. I will walk out that door"—he pointed across the room—"and you have the choice to either say goodbye to me now, or *never* have the chance again."

I rolled my head back, letting my face crumple with the pain of his impassively conclusive words. "David. Please. You can't. I won't live without you. I won't, and you can't make me."

But he took another step away from me. "I'm sorry, Ara."

The fight in me turned to fear then, and I tried to move my legs—to get up and run after him—but they felt like jelly. I could barely even move my toes. "David." I reached out. "David. Don't. Please. Don't go."

He looked away from me, reaching for the door.

"David, I love you. If I could take it all back, I would. Just, please. Please stay with me—please don't leave me again. I want to be with you."

"Don't you think I want that, Ara?" He appeared beside me, stroking his thumb over the release of tears down my cheek. "But I left you with scars from my involvement in your life, and it's time to put it right again. I love you too much to run away with you, knowing what could happen if we were found. I won't let you get hurt like that." His voice trembled but he steadied it with a breath. "And I can *never* watch you die again. I swear"—he clutched a fist over his heart—"as long as I walk this Earth, as long as I continue to move, I will have to believe that you are alive; that you still exist, or I will not survive this human life."

"No." I reached for him, just managing to grasp his shirt before he could pull away. "David, please. You're making a mistake."

Behind David, the door flung open and Mike's smile dropped when he saw my face. "What have you done to her?" he growled, bounding toward me.

The tense energy tore away from the space between us as Mike pushed David aside. My outstretched hand gripped tighter, but my fingers slipped, and David backed away.

"Ara, what happened?" Mike asked, tucking my abandoned reach into my lap.

I pushed up from Mike's embrace and searched the room for David. He hesitated by the door, holding it ajar as his gaze quickly averted once it met mine.

"I know this will be hard for you, Ara. *Believe me*, I will regret this decision for the rest of eternity." His silky voice trembled. "But I cannot love you the way you are. I will only bring you pain."

"David," I whimpered. *I'll die without you. Can't you feel that?*

"Non, ma cherie. You will live."

"I don't want to," I whispered one last time.

"And yet you will, because all human hearts eventually forget. This… us…" He motioned between us. "This future I wanted, it was just a dream of mine, Ara. And *all* dreams eventually die."

My eyes closed as his words cracked my soul, breaking my heart into a million pieces. When I looked up from Mike's embrace, my David, my knight, was gone.

35

Death: those of us who outrun it can never truly escape it.

My body would heal, so they told me. It would take months of rigorous and painful physiotherapy, but it would eventually return to what it once was.

Eventually, I would be able to walk to the bathroom by myself or breathe easily when sitting up, but no one could say how long it would take to resurrect the part of me that *wasn't* rescued that night—the part that still suffered the incessant torture in my nightmares, the flashbacks, and the unending misery. They thought I was strong because I survived what he did to me. But I didn't survive anything; I *lived through it.* They weren't the same things.

"Ara?" Vicki broke my reverie, knocking on my already open door.

I looked up from pretending to read my book. "Hm?"

"Um…" She shuffled her feet, nervously trying to spit the words out. "Emily's on the phone."

"Tell her I'm sleeping," I said simply.

"But, Ara it's been *weeks*. She just wants to see you're all right."

"I'm not all right." I moved my attention back to the book, which I hadn't even been reading.

Vicki stood for a moment, as if I might suddenly change my mind, then left, closing the door behind her. I stared at the empty space for a moment, on the brink of calling out and asking her to bring me the phone. I missed Em so much. I missed school, missed normal life, but I was so goddamn ashamed. I didn't even want to look at my own father, let alone my friends.

My door swung open again as Mike passed. He knew how much I hated it being closed. But he didn't pop in and try to speak to me. Even he'd given up now, because I shut down whenever he tried to talk to me. It was just that every conversation led to him trying to find out what happened that night. I knew he just wanted to help, and that he wanted to catch the man that did this, but since he was a cop, he believed that the only way to do that was with some damn good police work. Which was impossible when the victim insisted she can't remember a thing. So now, I avoided talking and he avoided trying.

In his room across the hall, I heard the news come on the TV, and tried to tune out when I heard them mention me.

"Police are still investigating the brutal attack on a seventeen year old girl, who miraculously woke from a three month coma after…"

Mike popped his head in then. "Hey, baby."

I snapped out of my stare, wiping hot tears from my cheeks and hurriedly grabbing my book.

"Hey, are you crying?"

"Nope." I held the book to my chest as he sat beside me. "I'm good."

"So these are tears of hilarity?" He looked at the title.

"Yup. Funny scene." I forced a smile.

Mike's eyes narrowed and I could've sworn he was shaking his head, even though it didn't move. He sighed then, his eyes landing on my engagement ring.

I tensed, praying he wouldn't bring it up. We hadn't mentioned the engagement since I woke from the coma, and I wasn't sure I wanted to yet, because I wasn't sure I wanted to marry him anymore. So I hid my hand under the blanket, and he took that to mean exactly what I'd intended.

"Are you hungry?" he asked instead.

"No."

"Do you want some company for a while? We could watch a movie."

"I'm fine."

"Would you like your light out—"

"I'm fine," I insisted, wishing everyone would stop babying me, and checking in on me.

"Okay," he said sweetly, standing to move away. But he hesitated by the door, then thought better of what ever he was about to say, and walked away, heading down the stairs with his shoulders hunched.

I stared at the window above the front door for a while, trying not to embrace the past—not to look on it and remember the bad or the good. It was, and would remain, exactly as the dictionary described it: the past.

As another night rolled to a close, Sam sat at the base of my bed and sketched pictures in his journal. He was good company. It was enough for him to just sit and be silent. He rarely probed for details, and when he did, it wasn't to assess my psychological state, like everyone else. Before the attack, I was 'depressed and unsteady' but now I was 'completely messed up'. It didn't take a genius to figure that out. But Sam was happy just keeping me company.

"What do you think?" He held up his book.

"Wow, Sam, that's amazing." Not just because the grey sketch of the girl looked exactly like me, but because she was smiling—something I'd not done since coming home.

He rested the book in his lap and kept his eyes on it. "Ara?"

"Yeah, Sam?"

"Does it still keep you up at night?"

I put my headphones in my ears, making a point that I didn't want to talk about this. "Yes. It does."

His finger moved over the lines on his sketch to shadow them. "Me too."

"Just try not to think about it."

"I'm sorry," he said. "I wish it'd never happened to you."

"Me too." I rolled over and covered my head with my blankets.

No one told Sam the finer details of the attack, but gossip had a way of oozing from the mouth of one person and creeping into the ears of another. He came home late from school the other day, kept back on detention after punching a kid, who told him that my attacker really had violated me—that he'd heard it from Mr. Thompson, my dad. Which was a huge lie!

But I'd take the truth to my grave, however far away that may be. And I didn't plan to stay in New England, either. There'd be no escaping the stares if I went back to school, no escaping the news reporters that had camped outside our house for three days once I came home. I'd already planned to jump on a plane and go back home as soon as I was better. Whether that was as Mike's fiancé or not, I didn't care. I just needed to get away from here. Away from it all.

David once said that it was kinder for a vampire to kill a human than to leave them alive, suffering in agony until they finally passed. Turns out, he was right.

Death would have been kinder.

Maybe that's why Jason left me alive: so I'd walk the Earth for the rest of my days, not only ashamed and broken, reliving his cruelty in every nightmare, but also that I'd suffer it alone—without David. He must have known David would leave me if I weren't compatible for the change. He must have known I wouldn't turn, wouldn't die. His plan was executed so perfectly to punish *David*, yet *I* was the one made to suffer.

A wild winter gale rattled my windowpane, and the darkness of the night touched every corner of my room then. I couldn't remember Sam leaving, and though I heard Dad and Vicki go to bed, I couldn't remember if they came in to say goodnight, like they always did.

The music bleating through my earphones helped filter out some of the clatter from the wind, but I should've been more careful about the playlist I chose because, tonight, in the darkness, these songs reminded me too much of David.

I made myself small against the wall and hugged my pillow to my chest. The skin along my cheeks hurt from the constant wiping of tears, but as the cold turned them icy against my lips, I forced myself to blot them away.

The memory of David's scent blew in under my window then, and an apparition of him resolved itself before my heavy eyes. I could hardly breathe as I took in his face, the softness of his smile, and the dimples both above and beside his lip that I'd almost forgotten existed.

"You're not really here, are you?" I whispered.

His liquid-green eyes were intense with sorrow, as they lowered reluctantly away from mine. "If I were, my love, I shouldn't be."

Then, as swiftly as he appeared, he was gone again, the tone of his smooth voice ringing in my ears as if he'd really spoken. And though I could still smell him, I knew he hadn't actually been standing there. Even the cold I felt on my legs from when the window opened and then closed again, it wasn't real. It didn't happen. The over-tiredness, the lack of food, and the emotional damage was finally sending me mad.

But I didn't want to be crazy. I almost died, and spending my life locked up in an institution wouldn't be any different than being held prisoner in that darkness. I needed to move past this. I needed to get out of bed and start living again.

I tore my earphones out and ditched my iPod across the room, tossing my pillows and blanket on top so I wouldn't have to think about it.

David and every song on the iPod needed to be deleted tomorrow. Getting over the attack was one thing, and it was possible that I might never be free of it. But if I didn't forget David—delete all traces of him—it would be a guarantee.

I rolled over, shivering in the nakedness of my bed, wishing I'd at least kept my blanket. But regret only lasted another few sobs as the exhaustion swept me under the grasp of sleep.

As the new day peeked through my window and I opened my eyes again, almost as quickly as I'd closed them, I listened to the sound of birds singing praise to the calm sky. The unruly wind from last night had receded with the moon, and there was enough chill in the air to make snuggling warmly into my blanket immensely pleasant.

I sat bolt upright though when I slid my hand under my pillow and touched something there; something thin and metal. My eyes moved from the iPod that had been buried under my blanket across the room last night to where it now sat in its dock, and my blood ran cold. I reached under my pillow again to draw out the cool silver chain, my skin going tight with little bumps as I looked down at a heart shaped locket.

He left this.

He was here.

As if he might still be, I looked at the window, but I could no longer smell him or feel him. I grabbed my blanket in a fist and tucked it to my chin, wondering why he came. Why he would leave this here when I gave it back to him so I could move on.

But I promised him my forever.

And he promised me eternity.

I *had* to move on. He made me move on, and yet he would never let me go.

It occurred to me then that I was kidding myself to think I could delete him from my mind any more than I could my heart. I needed to stop *trying*—needed to wear this locket, keep David alive in my thoughts, because he was a part of me. I felt nothing if I didn't love him.

I could never move on, not really. I could live for the rest of my life with Mike, and I could be his wife, but as the fine inscription on the back of the locket read: I belong to him—to David. I always would.

"Forever," I told myself as I linked the chain around my neck, and let it fall against my collarbones, back where it belonged.

As day turned into night again, I listened to the familiar sound of conversations going on in the dining room without me. Mike's booming laughter flowed up the stairs and poked me in the heart. I wished I could laugh. I wished I could laugh with Mike. But he seemed to be avoiding me. I think. Or maybe he was just trying to give me some space, I wasn't sure, but he hovered by my door a lot—hardly ever knocked or came in… just hovered. Before the attack, there were never closed doors between us, but now it seemed like even the windows were shut, and I was all alone on the other side.

A screech of disapproval rose above the loud chatter downstairs. "Greg, you can't say that," Vicki said. "It's politically incorrect."

Dad didn't respond, but I pictured him laughing into a fist, his face red.

"But it's true, Vicki," Mike insisted, "It's rude, yes, but…"

I stopped listening. I didn't want to hear what they were saying. I didn't want to be a part of their conversation, nor did I want to sit here wishing I were.

I clutched my secret locket and waited for the arrival of another tear-provoked sleep.

When the conversations downstairs ended, the plates were all cleared and the lights and doors were positioned in their nightly rest stop, I snuggled down in my bed, closed my eyes, and imagined David beside me.

In these moments, we were together again as if nothing had ever happened; as if I'd decided long ago to become a vampire and be with him for eternity. These were the only moments I lived for and, sadly, they weren't even real.

My door swung open then, and I quickly tucked my locket away, pretending to be asleep but keeping one eye open to watch in the darkness. Mike stood in the doorway, waiting to see if I'd stir, then, as usual, wandered over to lock the window I'd already double-checked, drawing my curtains closed again after.

"Oh, Mike. I didn't realize you were in here," my dad whispered.

"Yeah, I like to check on her before I go to bed," he said in a deep, husky whisper.

"Is she sleeping?"

"Yeah." His solemn, almost broken tone obviously set my dad's mind wandering as it did mine.

"You okay, son?" Dad said, and the light filtering in from the hall disappeared.

"I'm worried about her, Greg."

Dad leaned against my dresser. "Me too," he said. "I don't think she's okay, you know. She plays it tough." Dad looked right at me; I closed my eye for a second. "But I never see her cry. Not once, in fact. Surely this kind of thing has got to leave a girl feeling *something*?"

"She cries," Mike stated. "I know you don't see it, but that's because she wants everyone to think she's okay."

"You've *seen* her cry?"

Mike shook his head. "But I hear her. At night, when she thinks everyone's asleep."

Dad rubbed his chin, shaking his head.

"I've hovered by her door a few times, trying to decide if I should come in, but she smiles and plays it cool when I catch her." Mike paused. "She won't talk to me, Greg, but she *needs* to talk to someone before she buries this grief too deep and we lose her for good."

"Maybe she'll talk to Emily?" Dad suggested.

No, I won't.

"I doubt it," Mike said, then sighed heavily. "I don't know. I guess we just need to give her more time."

"I think we're past that point, Mike. Vicki's worried." Dad combed the front of his hair with arched fingers. "She thinks we might need to get her some professional help."

"Don't do that," Mike warned. "She'll shut down if you do that. I'll try talking to her tomorrow."

I rolled onto my back and groaned, deliberately, to get them and their gossip out of my room so I could go back to my fantasies of David.

"Okay." Dad clapped Mike on the shoulder.

"But, don't worry," Mike said, looking at me again. "She is still capable of feeling."

"I hope so," Dad said. "Otherwise, what was the point?"

"I know," Mike said. "But she's alive, Greg."

"I'm starting to wonder if that's all that counts."

It's not, Dad, I thought. I wished I *had* died. There was a point in the darkness when I wanted to come back, but not to this. Not to the recurring nightmares I had for the way Jason hurt me, the emptiness I felt for the way David left me, and the shame that hit me when I'd stand naked in the shower—feeling the air on my skin—knowing I was safe, but feeling so exposed and so bare. No one warned me that being awake again would be worse. No one told me I'd have dreams where I fell, over and over again, from that tree, waking up just before I hit the ground.

Life *wasn't* all that mattered, and I learned that, unfortunately, a little too late.

The light from their world intruded on my David fantasy for a while longer. Dad had left the door open when he walked away, but I could feel Mike lingering at my bedside. He leaned over and stroked my hair, his hand absently moving down my cheek and onto my neck —the one place he wasn't supposed to touch me anymore.

I curled my fingers into a tight fist, on the brink of shoving his hand away, when everything around us seemed to stop, as if I could feel the air change.

"Where did this come from?" he whispered to himself, lifting the silver chain from under my shirt. He sighed my name out then, his warm, heavy breath brushing across my nose and lips. But he placed the locket gently back down on my chest after, and kissed my head, closing the bedroom door behind him as he left.

THE SUNLIGHT OUTSIDE REFLECTED OFF THE ICY ROADS AND shone through the window with its early morning glow. It felt like months since I'd seen the sun, and years since I'd looked up at the blue sky. I wondered now if I'd even love the summer anymore when it came around again.

"Hi, gorgeous." Mike glided into my room with breakfast. "You hungry?"

I shook my head.

"Okay." He lowered the plate of toast, his smile dropping with it. "I'll take it back down."

"Thanks, Mike. But…" I sat up a little. "Don't tell Vicki. She's worried I'm not getting enough nutrients."

"Right." He paused, chewing the inside of his lip as he studied my probably very blotchy nose and cheeks. "Ara?"

"Mm?"

"No more, baby." He squatted beside me, placing the plate on the ground. "You gotta talk to me."

"I do talk to you."

"No, you don't. You haven't even been able to look at me. You flinch when"—he dropped his hand away from my face as I recoiled—"when I touch you."

"Well, what do you expect, Mike?"

"I get it. I do. But I don't understand why you're pushing *me* away. I'd never hurt you, Ara."

"That's not what I'm afraid of," I said with a hint of detest.

"Well…" He dropped back on his heels a little. "What is it then?"

I stared at him through a film of tears, and as the words rose to the surface at the same time the tears spilled onto my cheeks, I spat them out, "I'm just so humiliated. I never wanted you to find me that way."

"What way? Ara, how do you *think* I found you?

"He—he," I stammered. "He said he was going to leave me naked… exposed…I—"

Mike's eyes widened and his hands shot out so fast that I squealed, ducking my head as he sat on my bed and pulled me to his chest, stroking my hair. "You never told me that. Why didn't you tell me that?"

"I didn't want *anyone* to know."

"Did you at least tell the cops?"

I shook my head. "I haven't told anyone. I only told them the basics."

"Then you remember more than you say?" His tone was soft, not angry, like I expected.

"Mm-hm."

"Oh, baby. Why? Why would you do that? How can they catch this guy if they don't know the full story?"

"They'll never catch him." That much I was sure of.

Mike ignored that comment and took a deep breath. "Do you

want to know what I saw when I found you? Can you cope with this yet?"

"I need to know, Mike. It's been eating me up."

"Ara." He exhaled my name. "You should've talked to me about this before now. I could've helped you."

"I wasn't sure I wanted to know."

Mike laid me back down on the pillow, and his hand fell gently into the curve of my neck as he studied me, swiping his thumb over my cheekbone.

"Mike!" I pushed his hand down. "Please don't touch my neck."

"Right, sorry, I forgot." But his eyes stayed there for a moment, not on the jagged, silvery bite shape, but on the place the attacker's grip left a mental scar. "You were covered when I found you."

I looked up quickly into his soulful, caramel gaze. "I was?"

He nodded. "Your hair was laying over your... over your chest, like it'd been positioned that way. No one saw anything, and I had you covered with my jacket before anyone else came."

Tears of relief overflowed and swerved down my cheeks. Mike started to wipe them away, but gave up in vain when they kept flowing.

"So... all this time? You thought I'd found you... exposed?"

"Yeah." I wiped my nose. "I thought... I mean, I didn't know what he did to me after I—when it all went black. I didn't know if maybe he'd done worse, or—"

"Oh, baby. I really wish you'd said something."

I felt pretty silly then. "So do I."

Mike laughed softly, but the smile in his eyes faded away to something darker.

"What, Mike? What is it?"

He pinched his lips, rocking his jaw. "You don't know what I went through looking for you. And when I found you..." He let a breath out through his nose, battling with the words inside his mouth. "I expected, given what I was sure he'd done to you... I was surprised when I found you still wearing your underwear."

I cringed, my mind shooting back to that night.

"But your legs..." A grave, haunted look widened his eyes. "You were just so so covered in blood. I thought the deranged prick had actually dressed you again after he…" Mike couldn't say it.

I touched his arm, wishing I could have been there to comfort him through that.

"I cried when they told me," he said, cupping his hand over mine. "When the doctors said he hadn't raped you, I just cried. Baby, it was so dark in that field. Without a torch, I might not've seen you at all. And when I found you, I noticed only one small flicker of pale skin, and I ran, faster than I've ever run before."

In my mind, I could see it all as it happened. And I let myself imagine it, because seeing it from another side helped me to blot out some of the fear—the emptiness of being alone, scared, feeling like no one would ever come for me.

"All we'd come across so far was"—he paused and lowered his voice—"was your bra. And I can't tell you what went through my mind when I found it."

I felt my cheeks flush.

"The things I imagined he was doing to you while I wasn't there to protect you. I felt so helpless. I couldn't walk properly; every step I took was like my legs were carrying the weight of a train. But I kept going. I had to find you—to hold you and make you safe again."

"I knew you'd find me eventually," I said softly, because I'd never lost faith in him. And I didn't lose faith in David, either. That faith was ripped from me, killed, illuminated by the truth that I just wasn't important enough to him.

"If you could only feel what I felt when I saw you there," Mike added, eyes lost to the memory. "I wasn't disgusted, like you seem to think, princess. I was *overjoyed*. And I promise you no one saw your body, except for Emily; she was right beside me the whole time." When he looked back unexpectedly, I nearly jumped out of my skin. "I covered you with my jacket," he continued, "and checked every square inch of your body to make sure I wouldn't break you more if I moved you. And I know you didn't want me to see you like that, but I never looked at anything in that way. I was just so happy to find you still breathing. All I saw was the girl I'm in love with, and the only memory I've taken with me from that night is the way you looked up suddenly, so scared, and then smiled when you saw *me*." He squeezed my hand, meshing his lips together as his tears entered his mouth. "You closed your eyes then, and I thought that was the last time I'd ever see the blue."

An audible sob escaped my throat.

Mike gathered me into his chest, tighter than ever before, and I felt nauseated for feeling gratitude toward Jason for not doing as he'd threatened. But the sick feeling welled up into a circle of anger within me, making my fists clench behind Mike's back. I closed my eyes tight and made a promise to myself that, one day—I didn't know when or how—but one day, I would make Jason pay for what he did to me.

Mike leaned out from our embrace and looked at my lips, then my eyes, stroking my hair off my brow. "Is this why you won't see Emily—because she was there with me?"

I nodded, looking down.

Mike took a really long breath, letting it out slowly. "You know, she *needs* to see you. She blames herself for not chasing after you when she saw you walk away with that man."

"Really?"

"Yes. She cries every time I see her, and there's nothing I can do to console her."

"I didn't know that."

"Then will you please just see her? She loves you, just the same as we all do."

"But she saw, Mike. I can't help how I feel."

"Oh, baby. Please don't be like that. Emily's your friend, and she's a girl. I'm sure she's seen it all before."

"That's not the point."

"I know. But I'm just trying to get you to understand how little any of that means when, in the greater scheme of things, we thought we'd find you dead—or much *much* worse."

I wedged the tongue of stubbornness into my cheek and shook my head.

"Ara. Emily's not to blame. You can't hide from this, and you won't make yourself feel better by punishing her."

"I'm not punishing her, Mike."

"Then stop punishing yourself. I know you miss her. I know you *want* to see her."

My shoulders dropped as I let out all the tension I was holding on to. It was time to move on, I decided. And this was the first real step. "Fine. She can come for a visit then."

Mike let out a quick huff of relief. "Really?"

"Yes. If you shut up."

"Shutting up." He kissed my lips, pinching my cheeks between his hands. "I'm gonna go call her, okay?"

I nodded and fell against my pillows as he backed away and closed the door. It only felt like ten minutes passed before Sam popped his head around the corner and said, "Emily's here."

I put my book down and pressed my hands into the mattress until I was sitting up properly, my arms and hands still very stiff from months without use. "Send her in."

"You sure, sis?" Sam asked, slightly closing himself in the room with me. "Because, I know Mike kinda pushed you into this."

I smiled at Sam. "It's okay. I'm okay."

He nodded, then signaled into the corridor.

Emily, with her hands clasped in front of her, walked very slowly into my room and smiled.

"Hi," I said.

"Hi." As soon as the word left her lips she spun around to close my door, and then she just stood there with her forehead against it.

"Em?"

"I'm okay." She nodded, exhaling.

"What's wrong?"

"I... I have rules. Things I'm not allowed to say, but—"

I waited, allowing her to pull herself together.

"I just don't know *what* to say. I'm so... so sorry." She turned to face me then, tears raining over her crossed arms, past her elbows and onto the carpet. "It's my fault. I should have—"

"Em. Don't. Okay?" I held a hand up. "Just don't. Say. Anything about it."

After a moment, she sighed. "Okay."

"Thanks." I opened my eyes.

"We'll just talk about the weather then." She smiled a weak smile, then sat beside me on the bed.

"That's what I need."

And we did talk about the weather—the past, the present, the future weather. The coming spring, the wild winter, and I know a few times Emily wondered if I was talking in code, referring to David as the rain, the sadness, or talking about the attack when I spoke of the storms. And who knows, maybe I was, maybe I wasn't. But it was nice to just talk for no other reason than to exchange words in the company of someone you'd come to love.

By the time Dad told Emily to 'let me rest', I had formed a real smile at least twice and had managed to forget about the attack for a while.

"Em?" I said as she left.

"Yeah?"

"Can you come back tomorrow?"

She pressed her lips into a tight line, nodding, then closed the door before I heard her burst into tears on the other side.

Rising from my first dreamless slumber since I woke from my nightmare, I drew a deep breath and extended my limbs into a careful stretch, waking the rest of my body. But as my toes curled and my ankles rolled, I had to stop and wait, listening carefully to what my bones were saying. Strangely, it didn't hurt. At all. I stretched my legs out again and… yep, it didn't hurt.

When I pushed my covers back, the morning cold felt as if it were only cold—no sharp pins—which allowed me a small moment of appreciation for the beautiful winter that had set in deep while I was in a coma. It had been a shock to my nerves when I felt the sting of the frost on that first day they brought me home. But I was beginning to like the way winter made everything feel closed in and off limits, as if I could hide out here forever and never be disturbed.

"Hey? Good morning. I didn't know you were awake," Mike chimed, leaning on my doorframe.

"I've been awake for the last three weeks, Mike."

"You know what I mean." He looked rested today; his hair was still wet from a shower and the smell of his fresh, powder-scented cologne filled my room, making me feel normal.

"Yeah, I know. I was joking around with you." I sat up in my bed.

"Joking?" He nodded, pursing his lips in consideration. "That's a good sign."

"So is general conversation." I waited, expecting him to chuckle. "You know, 'cause dead people don't talk."

"Oh. Ha!" He laughed once. "Sorry, I'm not used to the lame joke game anymore."

I shrunk a little. I wasn't playing the lame joke game. I was actually attempting to be funny.

"Something wrong, kid?" Mike dropped his folded arms and moved to sit beside me.

"Nah, I've just been doing some thinking."

"What about?"

"Stuff."

"David?"

I didn't mean to, but I stiffened all over. "Maybe."

"Ara..." He paused, seemingly assessing his words. "I love you. And I'm your best friend. I always will be. But I'm not stupid and I'm not blind. I know... *things*... and I know that he—"

"He's not what you think he is, Mike." I cleared my throat, sorting out a response in my head. "You might *think* you've pieced it all together, but you're wrong."

His eyes narrowed. "I know you're upset that he left you, but I don't think I'm wrong about him. I really do think he loves you and he's just trying to do the right thing by you."

Cold shock washed through me. "*That's* what you think?"

He frowned. "What did you think I thought?"

That he was a vampire. But that was crazy. How would anyone come to *that* conclusion? "Oh, um... I thought you might've thought he was a jerk, you know, for leaving again."

Mike shook his head. "No, baby. Not at all. I mean, I... in the hospital, I saw the way he loved you. It was undeniable. And I don't know what happened between you two, maybe you'll never tell me, but you need to know that although that part of your life is over now, *I'm* still here. It's unfortunate that you fell in love with another man when I dropped the ball, and that's something both of us will always have to live with now, but you still have a chance to be happy."

"I'm not sure I'm capable of that anymore, Mike."

He nodded. "What if I could promise that you are? What if I could guarantee that you will one day find a reason to smile? Would you believe me—at least start *wanting* to be happy again?"

"I..." I frowned to myself. "I do *want* to be happy."

He went to shake his head, but stopped and exhaled. "Only you know the truth of that, Ar."

He was right. I'd been pretending to want to be happy, because that's what you were supposed to be. But, deep down, I didn't want to be, because being happy meant moving on from David, and moving on meant that I didn't love him.

"But I'm not giving up on you," Mike said. "Not ever. I don't care what you say to me, or do to make me mad or hurt, I love you, and I'm not giving up on you."

My eyes watered. "What if I *asked* you to go?"

He didn't even answer. We both already knew the answer. But I wondered if he'd stay if he knew the real reason I was attacked: that I'd let a vampire into my life, then followed one to my own detriment. And I wondered how he would feel to know that the core of my sadness was not because I was attacked, but because of David; because he was gone and because time, death, and tears hadn't changed what I meant to him and wouldn't, *couldn't* make him stay.

But Mike had stayed, even though everything he worked for back in Australia had fallen apart, and he would always stay, no matter what; if I was human, if I was weak and frail, even if I asked him to go.

And that was more than I could say for David.

"You're a good man, Mike." My head rocked from side to side. "And for what it's worth, I'm glad I'm marrying you."

His frown softened and a broad smile spread across his face, like the light touching the earth at sunrise. "Then... you still wanna get married?"

"Of course I do, dummy." I slapped his arm. "Why wouldn't I?"

"I just thought… with the whole near-death experience and all, you know, people change from those things, Ara. I didn't know if you'd want the same things anymore."

"And you stayed? Even though you weren't sure?" Admiration crinkled across my nose.

His eyes narrowed in confusion. "Ara. I'm in this for *life*. Whether you marry me or not, I will always be here to love you *and* be your friend. That will never change. Never."

And it really only sunk in right then that I had missed this: all along I'd been looking across the road to the boy I thought I loved, when I should've been looking right beside me. *This* was my savior; this was my knight in shining armor. He always had and always would come to my rescue.

"Good," I said. "Because I don't want you to go *anywhere*."

He leaned down and his warm, velvet smile melted onto my lips. It was the first kiss. My first kiss in my new life. I'd been given the chance to start over—cleansed of all the mistakes of my past. The hourglass had rocked and the balance tipped in reverse, but everything was back in place and, today, I began a new journey with the man I was *supposed* to be with. We would go on—live, as living was intended—and I would love him for forever. For our forever, because they'd *always* been the same.

36

True love, by definition, means "someone that is truly loved."

By the Dictionary of Ara, true love means you could not live without that person. That the love you feel for them is as honest and deep as the love they feel for you; a soul mate; a perfect match.

David was my soul mate, but Mike is my perfect match. They were like two parts that completed one whole: me. But since I could only have one in my life, I was going to make damn sure it didn't leave. Which is why I agreed to marry Mike today.

With my hand over my belly, I tried to settle the feeling there—like a swarm of black bats had assembled in my gut and bludgeoned the ogre to death—but I couldn't make myself calm because, in truth, I wasn't ready for this. Dad wouldn't let me go back to Perth with Mike unless we were married first, so I had no choice but to move the wedding up a few years. I just needed to go home, away from everything that reminded me of… everything.

Now, standing in front of the full-length oval mirror, with golden light spreading its warm beams of morning over my bedroom floor, I let time pass around me, unable to control it or make good use of it; just existing as a part of its greater plan.

After a while, I reached across and tilted the mirror's frame, changing the image to the plain white of the roof. I couldn't look at the reflection staring back at me today; she was error beautified by justification: a young girl who was doing what was expected of her, not what her heart wanted. I loved Mike, I really did, but the quiet prelude to the tempest had me wondering if I was doing the right thing; if marrying one man when I was still in love with another would, perhaps, destroy not just my life, but Mike's as well.

Behind me, in the near-empty room, my bed was gone and the spongy white carpet dominated the space. A new daybed in the corner had become a shelf for all things bridal, except the bouquets, which were lined up on the hall-stand beside the window. It might not have been my room anymore, but it still felt like my room, except that, like me, it was changed beyond recognition. My face, my hands, everything was polished and shined, shaped and fashioned to look like the bride standing by the mirror in her wedding dress. The swirling vortex of time had swept everything up, and I was next—destined to leave everyone behind.

But that was always my destiny, wasn't it? And one day soon, I was sure it would carry me away from Mike.

Just… not today.

Outside my window, the familiar chatter of a little bluebird formed the soundtrack to my faraway thoughts. I snapped from my reverie, tilted the mirror back down and watched the bird dancing happily in the reflection, as if life just went on. So simple. That's it: eat, sing, dance and play.

I wished I were a bluebird. That it could be that easy. But life was not a novel and people didn't really get happy endings. I finally understood all the negative philosophical one-liners this town loved so much. They were phrases invented by smart people, who knew life wasn't made of dreams, even though it sometimes felt like one.

David said it best, though: "All dreams eventually die."

We're not the leading ladies of our own illusory films. This is life and we are real. The time had come for me to grow up, and if I couldn't live the life I wanted, I had to at least live the lie.

I took a wispy breath and felt my heart flutter as I pushed David's face away from my mind. I couldn't have any thoughts of him today or I'd fall to pieces.

There is, and never was, a David Knight.

He died in nineteen thirteen when his uncle bit him and turned him into a vampire. He never loved me, never promised me eternity—never existed. I was moving on, as he did, leaving all hope of love and destiny to the children who read fairy tales.

I looked at myself in the mirror again, at the bride, the woman that now stood before me: this was moving on.

"Ara, are you okay?" Emily smiled at me from the doorway.

"Emily! You look beautiful." I all but squealed and hugged her as she walked over. Then, standing her at arm's length, I smiled, admiring her dress. "Yellow is definitely your color."

"Well, thank you for choosing such a tasteful bridesmaid dress." She smiled, running her fingers over the chiffon.

"I'm glad we went for the shorter dress; it says spring to me." I tapped my chin.

"It doesn't feel like spring. It's so cold today." She smiled and tilted her head to one side, pausing there for a second. "Is it David? Is that what you were thinking about just now?"

A rush of hot blood shot through my stomach and I reached for my silver locket. On my own, with the four walls of my room surrounding me—closing me in—convincing myself that I could move on was easy. But in the presence of those who proved life was still real and still hurt, pretending I no longer belonged to him made me want to fold over and cry.

"You know me too well." I sighed, forcing myself to release the locket. "I'm gonna miss you, Emily."

"Don't worry, I'll come see you real soon. And, as for David… well"—she touched my shoulder—"Mike's better for you than him, Ara."

My eyes nearly popped out of my head. "What! Did you just say what I think you just said?"

She laughed. "I know, I know. It's a bit of a turnaround, but… I'm sorry, Mike's proven himself in my books."

"Yeah, he's pretty likeable." My fingers found the locket again and held it tight. "And I am happy, you know? I do love Mike."

"I know." She nodded.

"I just miss David, is all, and..." I faced the mirror again, dropping the chain from my fingers and letting it fall against my skin. "I just needed a moment to reflect on that, I guess."

Her eyes moved to the veil hanging over the chair then, and she ran her thumb along an embroidered flower. "Is this the one Mike brought from Australia when his parents forced him to come home for Christmas?"

"Yeah." I laughed, remembering how much I'd cried when he handed me the box with this inside. "He said it was the only reason he didn't protest having to go home."

"I can't believe he thought to keep this when he and his mom cleared out your old house. What a sweetheart."

"He really is," I said, thinking of his warm smile. "And, did I tell you he even paid for the entire phone bill we ran up while he was back home?"

"Aw, that's so like him, though."

"I know. I think I did pretty well in the fiancé department," I mused. "He said it was small change in the greater scheme of things."

"He's a keeper," she said. And he was. That was true.

Emily reached over and plucked a thread from the yellow cherry blossom on my dress, the collection flowing like a swarm of butterflies over the fitted bodice. "Are you happy with your dress?"

"Still not sold on the full hoop skirt." I faced the mirror and ran my hands down it, angling myself this way and that to get a better look. "But if I didn't choose an out-there color, like yellow, Vicki would have made me accent everything with red."

No one could ever understand what the red rose once meant to me; how it represented the part of me that would always belong to David. And yes, it was a different time, but I wished it were a different life. It had caused massive debates, though, because red was a pretty common color to use in weddings, and Vicki just couldn't understand my aversion. But Mike stepped in and told her it was my choice.

She meant well, and I gave in on most things, like the dress, but I couldn't let this one slide.

"Oh!" We both looked up as Vicki walked in and burst into tears—again. "My beautiful Ara-Rose. I can't believe you're getting married."

"Been that way for a few months now, Mom," I said and hugged her, being careful of my cascading curls.

"I know. It just feels like we only got you a few weeks ago, and now look at you: all grown up and leaving us." She wiped away her tears. "Oh. Look at me, I've gone and smudged my makeup again."

Emily and I exchanged a humored smile as Vicki headed into my bathroom. The wardrobe she passed through was empty now. The rows and rows of clothes she bought me, the yellow dress, my box of pictures and everything else that made this room my own was on its way home now. On a freight plane back to Perth, which, after tonight, when I officially became Mrs. Michael Christopher White, I would be too—except… not on a freight plane.

"Come on." Emily patted my arm. "It's nearly time. Let's put this veil on."

I lifted my blanket-heavy skirt and sat down on the stool near the mirror. It felt good to sit. I'd been standing for too long.

"No looking until I get this in, okay?"

"Em, my back's to the mirror. How can I see, anyway?"

"Oh, I'm sure you'll find a way if you want to."

"You know me too well." I smirked. "So, where's Alana?"

"Finishing her hair. And still trying to practice walking in those heels."

"I hope she doesn't trip over."

"No one will notice," she muttered with a few bobby pins between her lips, "they won't be able to see past you."

With the veil in my hair, Emily took a step back. Adoration flooded her eyes, like a little girl getting her first kitten.

"Does it look nice?" I asked, touching my fingertips to the meshy fabric.

"Oh my God!" Alana squealed.

"Don't cry," Emily warned. "I'm not re-doing your makeup."

"I'm not. I'm not. Aw, Ara," Alana hummed, waving her hands near her moistening eyes. "You're so pretty."

"Thanks. You look nice too."

"I know." She curtsied. "Ryan said his heart stopped beating when he saw me."

"Aw," Emily and I said.

"I know." Alana walked over as I stood up. "He's really sweet. So, you're finally ready then?"

"Yep."

"Now, you have something old." She touched my veil. "What's your something new?"

I motioned to my dress. "This will do, won't it?"

"I guess."

"Okay, here's something borrowed." Emily clasped her silver bracelet over my wrist—over the scar David left.

"Well, that just leaves something blue." I searched the room, half expecting to see the bookshelf behind my bedroom door, where I used to keep a bluebird pin my mother gave me when I was little.

"Um, Ara?" Vicki stood nervously behind Emily. "I… I have something blue."

When Em stepped aside, Vicki reached across the pale beam of sunlight and placed something cold and kind of heavy in my hand, cupping hers there for a second. "My mother gave this to me on my wedding day—when I married your father."

I hesitated to look down at it, keeping my gaze on her teary eyes for longer than needed. But when I finally unfolded my fingers, I gasped. "Vicki! This is beautiful."

"It's a brooch," she said, turning the delicate glass blossom in my open palm.

"But"—I stole my gaze away from it to look at her—"this should be passed down to Sam, shouldn't it?"

Vicki shook her head and closed my fingers around the flower. "It's been passed down in my family from daughter to *daughter*; it belongs to you now."

"Vicki, I… how can I ever thank you for all you've done for me?" I leaned in and hugged her tight, gripping the sapphire blossom in my hand. "I love you, Mom."

"And I love you." She drew back, blinking her tears away. "Now, enough fussing. Where shall we pin this?"

We placed the brooch, after much deliberation, to the largest cherry blossom on the bodice, right where the skirt met my hips. And as everyone stepped back to take a look at me, I drew a deep breath and squared my shoulders.

"So, that's everything?"

The chatter of four girls suddenly burst into the roar of twenty screaming fans at a boy-band concert. I calmed myself to a picture of composure while they gathered their bouquets and then hurried downstairs.

"You coming, Ara?" Alana turned back to look at me.

"Um, yeah." I nodded, biting my lip. "I'll just be a sec."

She smiled knowingly and walked away.

I wanted to stay in here and reflect for one last moment before my final goodbye, but the silence seemed to be filled with all the thoughts I'd been afraid of; all the truths I couldn't own today. So before it could destroy my resolve, I wandered out quickly, looking back for only a moment before shutting the door on the warm yellow light of the past.

Dad came out of his room at the same time, and I waited in anticipation for him to turn around. His face moved from the thoughts of the day ahead to a round-mouthed, wide-eyed smile. "Oh, honey," he said, raising my hand above my head to spin me around. "Look at you."

"It's not too overdone, do you think?" I looked down at the marshmallow skirt.

"No, you look perfect. You're so grown up, so before your time." He kissed my cheek, drawing away with a sigh. "I'm proud of you, Ara-Rose. And your mother"—Dad touched my inherited veil—"I know she'd be proud of you too."

I nodded, looking down at Dad's hand in mine.

"You know you're supposed to take your engagement ring off for the day?" he advised. "It goes on in front of your wedding ring after the ceremony."

"Really? Well, here, hold on to it for me."

He placed my ruby ring in his top pocket with a little pat. "Are you ready?"

Ready? I wasn't sure if that was the right word.

I inhaled a deep, shaky-yet-excited breath, and then let it out in a blast of panic. "No! Wait. I forgot my bouquet." I spun on my heel and hitched my dress up at the front, feeling it swish around the tops of my feet as I bolted back to my room.

The warmth of my yellow walls greeted me with the sun's smile as I burst through the door and grabbed the lone bouquet sitting on the table. But as I turned to walk away, a wave of nostalgia hit me.

I took two slow steps back to where my bed used to be, and let my arms fall to my sides. It was so empty in here now. The crystals that once cast rainbows from the sun were all gone, so too were the photos on the walls and the innocence of childhood. They were all just a memory now, and it felt strange to be saying goodbye to a place that'd been such a big part of my life for such a short time. Despite the pain I suffered here, what I was leaving behind today were mostly fond memories.

As I turned to walk away again, a splash of a forbidden color caught my eye, resting in the hinge of the old mirror.

One single red rose.

Breathless, bonded to the spot, I stared it down. No one would have put that there! I was very clear. There were to be *no* red roses around today.

I marched over and plucked it from the mirror, dropping it as soon as my fingers touched the smooth stem. There was only one person who ever stripped the thorns off a rose before giving it to me…

"David?"

A silent moment passed, but he didn't present himself. The rose lay by my feet, taking my heart into the past: one red rose—the single element of color inside a completely white bouquet—a scarlet representation of my love for David, of the part of me that would always be his.

I left it out because I wanted to move on, to forget about him. But he wouldn't let me.

No. I shook my head and backed away from the rose, clutching my white bouquet tightly. I would not let his memory reside here in this life with me. The past was his dwelling now—long forgotten and hidden in a dark corner of my heart—like a favorite old book at the back of a shelf.

In the mirror now, the reflection of the bride holding a colorless bouquet was one of picturesque beauty, but not what I saw in my dream in what seemed a lifetime ago. This was a different image. I was no longer the empty shell of a girl I used to be. I had moved on, without David, *away* from David, and slowly, I was growing out of the mask I used to hide behind. Happiness was becoming a real part of my life, and it was because of Mike that I could finally be just a girl. *Just* Ara.

I loved David with all of my heart once, and when Mike came back into my life, my heart simply grew bigger. I would be okay without David. I knew that now. So, with one hand, I unclasped the silver chain from around my neck.

"I will always be yours, David," I said into the mirror. "And you will always have a special place in my heart, but…" I laid the locket over the rose and stood back. "But this is me saying goodbye. Don't hold on to me now. It's time to move on."

Outside, I could hear the chatter of the day and the excitement as the wedding cars pulled up, but if I'd expected David to respond, if he were even here, I was left disappointed. As usual.

My heart and my voice steadied then with the last of my goodbye. "I love you, David Knight. I'll love you for forever, but it just can't be with all of my heart."

Slowly and reluctantly, I walked to the door and placed my fingers over the handle. When I turned back to look around my room for the last time, the rose and the locket were gone.

With faltering resolution and a tender heart, I blinked back the pain, and closed the door behind me.

Dad winked at me when I took his arm, and we walked down the stairs to the warm spring morning; the last morning I would ever look across at the school where I once met a boy. He wasn't there anymore

—no longer waiting by the grass for me to take his hand. He was gone, and I was moving on.

The photographer placed us in position to document the occasion before we could climb into the bridal car and drive away, leaving behind all the innocence of youth and the sadness of a lost eternity.

I looked up at the blue sky, just as I did that first day I came to live here. Back then, in my heart, I wanted nothing more than to go back home while, today, the idea had me stealing glances at my dad, Sam, and even Vicki, wondering how I was going to walk away from them. I guess life has a funny way of granting the things we want when we no longer really want them.

I came here alone, and I was leaving today with a heart full of family and friends who loved me. I knew that when the night descended, and I said my final farewells I'd cry, because at some point in all my growing up, I learned that home was built with the hearts of people you love; it was a place you knew you could always return, where waiting arms would greet you and make you safe.

And I guess, in that sense, I never really needed to find my way home, because I'd truly been there all along.

A vampire can never walk away from someone he loves.

The Heart's Ashes.

The Heart's Ashes is the highly addictive second book in the Dark Secrets series, a gruesome and often twisted story about one girl's journey through self-discovery, betrayal, and a love too deep in a world too cruel.

Each book in this series is out now!

ABOUT THE AUTHOR

Self-professed work-a-holic and mother of four, Angela M Hudson, known to fans as Angie, spends most of her day just trying to find time to put words on paper and think up new ways to get out of cooking dinner. She love cats, and dogs, and birds, but her husband will only let her have one cat.

She just placed an order for two more.

You can join her on Twitter and Facebook, where she interacts with fans on a daily basis. Check out the shenanigans, and stop in to say hello.

CPSIA information can be obtained
at www.ICGtesting.com
Printed in the USA
LVHW032347220419
615089LV00007B/893

9 780648 328025